READY FOR DEATH

—

THIS MURDEROUS SHAFT

—

MURDER RINGS TWICE

READY FOR DEATH

—

THIS MURDEROUS SHAFT

—

MURDER RINGS TWICE

A Mystery Omnibus

Helen Joan Hultman

COACHWHIP PUBLICATIONS
Greenville, Ohio

Ready for Death / This Murderous Shaft / Murder Rings Twice, by Helen Joan Hultman
© 2021 Coachwhip Publications

Cover elements: Typewriter keys (CC-BY) Helen Johnson; Library of Congress Prints and Photographs: Bridgeport Bridge, West Virginia / US Route 40 roadside diner.

Ready for Death first published 1939
This Murderous Shaft first published 1946
Murder Rings Twice first published as *Murder on Route 40* in 1940. *Murder Rings Twice* was 'slightly condensed' due to wartime paper conservation.

Helen Joan Hultman, 1891-1985
CoachwhipBooks.com / Coachwhip.com

ISBN 1-61646-515-8
ISBN-13 978-1-61646-515-5

READY
FOR
DEATH

Part One
"To Make Ready!"

I

Doc Bunting was leaving the Bly's Landing post office as Ed Verriker entered. He returned Doc's "H'are you, Ed?" with his usual gesture toward the brim of his hat. He was going to forget what Doc had told him again yesterday; Forget it if he could. He'd obey orders up to a point; his intelligence was still in the saddle. But he must try to forget, if he could, that according to Doc there was a large percentage of futility in those same orders. The sane thing was to carry on. . . .

Mechanically Verriker noted the crowd lounging in the post office, waiting for Matt Trace's familiar bellow, "Mail's up!" The personal items column was nearly complete, but until they put the *Observer* to bed that evening there was still room for a stray bit of news. Lew was a good kid, but he still didn't know enough to play up the oldtimers as Verriker could.

The general delivery window was still closed, but the *Observer* box was already full. Exchanges mostly. Absently Verriker bundled them out and cradled them in one arm. With more care he ran through the half dozen letters caught between the various smalltown weeklies, that necessarily made up most of his exchange list. He knew what the letters contained without opening them, so routine can even a country editor's mail become. Lew could take care of everything, anyway, as it was the wrong time of the month for bills. Lew still got a kick out of Miss Ivy Lotter's Pleasant Ridge correspondence.

Everything except one envelope. Deliberately Ed Verriker separated it from the others and fumbled with the post office pen as a letter opener. The typewritten address said merely Mr. Edward Verriker, with no reference to the *Observer* office. Sometimes news items came in like that. He drew forth a single sheet folded once. There was only a brief message typed in caps.

READY OR NOT
YOU SHALL BE CAUGHT

His eye swept it at a glance. He refolded the sheet and slipped it back into its envelope, hesitated a moment about adding it to the office mail, and then thrust it into his coat pocket. He smiled at young Mrs. Gus Varney stretching a plump arm to open her lock-box, gave his customary salute to Sam Falter, manager of the town's most imposing chain store, and called across to Walt Berry, just back from court, about the utilities wrangle with Tri-State Gas.

"Mail's up!" boomed Matt Trace, and the general delivery window banged open. Verriker took another look at the *Observer* box, gleaned its added contents, and got the information he wanted for the paper from the young counselor who was fighting a losing battle, though Walt hadn't accepted that fact yet, with the powerful Tri-State corporation. He tucked his crop of exchanges more firmly under one arm and ripped open the Pittsburgh papers to glance over as he walked back to the *Observer* office. The headlines danced meaninglessly before his eyes, forming themselves into READY OR NOT and YOU SHALL BE CAUGHT.

He shook his *Dispatch* pettishly as if to slide the silly words off his mind and looked up before crossing Kenawha Street just in time to avoid bumping into a man and woman who had paused at the curb. Mrs. Bellifer button-holing Hawley as usual. . . . It was all part of a parson's job, of course, having to listen to women like Marta Bellifer. Verriker heard: ". . . I could do it myself, but . . ." And the Reverend Thomas Hawley's reply: "No trouble at all. I'll see that the programs are typed. . . ."

Odd, thought Verriker, no matter whether Tom Hawley was announcing a hymn or greeting his prettiest choir member or grousing in the privacy of the *Observer* office, there was always a jocular undertone not exactly clerical in his undeniably unctuous voice.

Verriker crossed Kenawha Street and strode along toward the *Observer* office, just around the next corner. READY OR NOT. . . . He shook the *Dispatch* again. Nobody was ever ready, and sooner or later the Doc Buntings caught everyone. . . . He pulled up his mind with a jerk. No whining. Absolutely no whining.

There were Miss Judith Amberlee and Lydia across the street, bound toward the post office. To attract their attention he swept off his hat and waved it. Miss Amberlee nodded stiffly and walked on without change of pace. Lydia, bless her sweet heart, smiled and waved in return. Verriker could see her aunt's shoulder twitch with displeasure. A year ago, he thought, the child wouldn't have waved. And he was about the only person in Bly's Landing that ever tried things like that with Lydia. He sighed and walked on.

In front of the stairs leading to Alec Drummond's offices the new car was parked, a loafer or two giving it a respectful inspection. No need for him to size it up; a detailed account of Drummond's latest acquisition would be Lew Mason's biggest news story this week. Alec was an old goat and so crooked he couldn't sleep in a roundhouse. Deluxe models were not all that was coming to him.

During Verriker's infinitesimal pause beside the shine and gleam of the new car, a brisk tap-tap-tap came drifting down from the open windows of Drummond's suite.

Good-looking gal, Alec's new secretary. Betty, Dottie—
what in Sam Hill was her name? Ask Lew. He'd know. So
Alec had brought in another outsider to type letters for
him. That last mess, with the Drake girl—he'd only barely
managed to sidestep that. READY OR NOT. . . . Verriker
brushed his hand impatiently before his eyes and walked
on. This new girl was no fool, though, he'd bet on that
himself. Ask Lew. . . .

Verriker turned off Main Street at Railroad. The *Observer*
office stood between the B. & O. tracks and the alley, just
behind the hardware store. He waved to Dan Finley, on his
way to the late trick at the telegraph office, and stopped for
a word with Jim Glaye, unloading rolls of barbed wire at
the back of the hardware store. Jim had promised his wife
to tell Ed Verriker about the change in time of the Jolly
Ten covered-dish luncheon. With the item on the tip of his
tongue, Verriker entered his office.

His entire force was dutifully at work. Ethel Erbaugh
was checking a list of delinquent advertisers that she already knew by heart. Ethel could have been called elderly
by anyone whose courage was equal to the word. She was so
set in her ways and so mechanically accurate in her bookkeeping that Verriker had long ceased to give orders to her.
If the *Observer* kept out of the red by the most microscopic of margins, it was Ethel's watch-dogging, not his Pungent Paragraphs nor Lew's leg work. Lew was humped over
the typewriter, pounding away with four fingers: Lew was a
brash youngster who couldn't be told how much he didn't
know about running a newspaper, even a small-town weekly.

Verriker tossed the bundle of exchanges between Lew's
war-worn typewriter and the wall, and gave him the essen-
tials of Mrs. Jim Glaye's last-minute item. He ran through
the bunch of letters again and redecided that everything was
Lew's meat. "See what's there, Lew," he directed. "Mostly
Miss Ivy Lotter, looks like, which ought to brighten up
your day."

"And how! If the leader of Pleasant Ridge's e-light has not had another six o'clock dinner at eleven-thirty a.m., I'm going to cry right out loud." Lew's voice rose above his own clatter and he spaced his words at the jerky pace of his typing fingers. "If I can't land something of hers with the *New Yorker,* it'll be because they fake their stuff. Okay, Fult, take it away."

He ripped a page of copy from the machine and nodded toward it as a short, heavy-set man appeared at the shop door. This was Fult Dodge, high boss of mechanical production. "Job Printing a Specialty," the *Observer* letterheads said. As with Ethel and Lew, Fult knew who really kept the paper going. Sometimes Verriker, owner and editor, admitted to himself that a lifetime's experience with smalltown sheets plus an undeniably individual editorial style amounted to little beside the gifts of his staff. A nondescript young cousin of Fult's was his only assistant in the shop and, so far, this kid was the only person around the place who would not have attempted to get out the *Observer* single-handed. Perhaps he owed it to the kid to begin breaking down what must be merely an inferiority complex.

"Hey, boss, your column ready? I can begin making up any time now. I'm going to run Ivy's lot as is, and, boy, is it ever a honey! Listen to this: 'Miss Lydia Amberlee of Bly's Landing would have been the house guest of the Sandiman sisters on Tuesday if inclement weather due to the heavy rain had not detained Miss Amberlee at her home in Bly's Landing. Is that or isn't that sompin', I'm interrogating you! And this—"

"Now, Lew, there's no call to forget the Sandimans and Lydia, just to take a crack at poor Miss Ivy." He was thinking, she would have been detained rain or shine. . . .

"By which you mean that Fult will remind me that old Bill Sandiman's next lot of placards ought to be turned out of this shop. Okay, I get you. How about that column?"

"I'll give it the once-over and then it's all yours. But first let's see your story on Tri-State Gas. I saw Walt just now down at the post office. . . ."

Verriker's voice trailed off as he skimmed a string of Lew's characteristic typing. He added two sentences in his own swift script, which Fult could read as easily as type, and pushed it back. "Not bad, son. No come-back from either United Utilities or Tri-State, that I can see. Walt's been working his damnedest, but so far Alec hasn't quivered an eyelash. By the way, Lew, what's that girl's name—"

"Peggy Morgan. Oh—that is, what girl?"

"That's the one I mean. Been seeing her?"

Lew grinned and then laughed outright. "Can't kid you, even if I try. Well, here's the low-down and the reason that I have this haunted, broken-hearted look." He pawed through a stack of finished copy and read with melodramatic emphasis:

"'Miss Peggy Morgan spent a pleasant week-end in Pittsburgh, the guest of Mr. and Mrs. Robert Perry. . . . Mr. and Mrs. Perry and Miss Morgan were the dinner guests of Mr. Stuart Macklin at the 'Wharf Boat Inn. . . .'

"There's a city slicker in the case and poor little Lew just can't be seen. Me and all the other village idiots. . . . Hey, you heartless oldtimer, you're not even listening, and me baring my aching heart."

Verriker was not listening. His eye had slid over his copy for Pungent Paragraphs. When he ceased to feel a faint stir of pride over the column, then he'd know that Doc had left him nothing to live for. Pungent Paragraphs had been quoted in its time in everything from *Editor and Publisher* to *Time,* and when Lew Mason had first stumbled upon that fact, Ed could scarcely pound it through the boy's head that that was nothing to make a story out of for Bly's Landing to read in the *Observer.*

The last sheet of his copy was only half filled. The column was as long as necessary, but— He fumbled in his coat

pocket for the letter he had read, so far, only once. He flattened down the sheet and read it again.

READY OR NOT
YOU SHALL BE CAUGHT

His eyes deepened with determination and his chin set
grimly. Lew was once more humped over the typewriter,
judiciously editing Miss Ivy Lotter's news from Pleasant
Ridge. A good thing Fult didn't crab about his script. An
extra typewriter for the office was quite unnecessary. He
picked up his pencil and added a swift final paragraph.

> "The ugly pen of the anonymous letter writer
> is always busy. Cowards of that sort are sel-
> dom caught, not because their anonymity is
> so clueless a safeguard, but because it is not
> necessary that they should be. Ninety-nine out
> of a hundred recipients of such abominable
> communications promptly drop them in the
> nearest scrap basket and forget the cowardly
> attack. No doubt psychologists have a word
> for it. They could explain that the hurler of
> the venomed dart has obtained an essential re-
> lease. These ready letter writers, whether they
> believe it or not, accomplish nothing with
> the sane and sober-minded. But if the object
> should be more sinister than self-gratification,
> the ignored letter could conceivably induce the
> thwarted sender to adopt other methods which
> would lead, quite surely, to his own undoing."

Without rereading what he had written, Verriker gathered up his copy and started toward the shop. Lew grunted
as he passed, to indicate that he too was on his way for
make-up, Ethel Erbaugh banged a ledger shut and sniffed

as he skirted her cubicle. This warm September afternoon had brought Ethel's hay fever to life again; Ethel was always grouchy until after the first hard frost. She was nearly always grouchy afterwards too. Poor old Ethel. . . . Life was a damned mess for almost everyone.

Who was he, after all, to try to do anything about it? Still, it might work. . . . It was the only thing left for him to do. Damn Doc Bunting . . . he'd show him!

II

The *Observer* went into Friday morning's mail. After they had picked up the pieces, say from noon on, Verriker and Lew Mason took it easy. Ethel Erbaugh never took anything easy and Fult stayed on to take care of any job work. Lew had a third interest in a power boat and the river claimed him over week-ends. He dragged up gobs of news from the river, he explained at length every Monday morning. Verriker knew how to loaf in the grand manner, though Doc Bunting had scarcely meant the smoke-thick room and the Saturday night poker session when he talked about relaxing in the fresh air.

As always, Verriker lounged in the post office while Bly's Landing dropped in to get its individual copies of the *Observer*. During the run he affected an ostentatious reading of the *New York Times,* his being the only copy subscribed for in Bly's Landing, except the English teacher's book review section, which didn't count. Even after years of it, he still enjoyed noting what the town read first in the *Observer*. Nor had he ever tired of the stock remarks, witless as they were.

They came and went. Verriker leaned against the U. S. Navy poster, half-concealed by the wide-flung pages of the *Times,* the observer in the flesh. Once again Doc Bunting strode briskly in and snapped open his box. "H'are you, Ed?" he flung over his shoulder. It sounded casual. Too

damned casual, Verriker thought. He stayed until a brisk
tap of heels and a flirt of gay color caused his eyes to peer
around the edge of his paper. A girl at Drummond's box.
Sure, getting the mail would be one of her jobs. If the
big car was parked in the street as he returned to the
office, he'd know well enough whether Alec was in town
or not, and if he was he would have read the column, very
likely, by the next time he saw him. It would be hard to
tell about Alec Drummond. Maybe he'd drop in at Cardy's
for poker. . . .

The shiny car was not in sight. Main Street was busy
enough to please even the president of the Lions' Club. It
was noisy enough too, because of the motorcycle boys and
the through trucking and out-of-state cars going to Washington, but as Verriker passed under the windows of Drummond's rooms he caught the click of a typewriter. That cute
little trick was back on the job already.

After his noon-day dinner at Mrs. Lukey's, where he
had eaten most of his meals since the death of his wife,
three years since, Verriker lounged away the afternoon in
a favored seat of his near the big windows of the Mansion
House, Bly's Landing's musty, old-fashioned hotel. No sign
of Alec Drummond or the new car. Not until after the 4:50
up from Huntington did he catch sight of the smart vigorous figure that had dominated his attention of late as
completely as the man controlled the economic fortunes of
Bly's Landing.

Two hours later, having skipped Mrs. Lukey's supper
with Kate Ralston's brown bread in mind, Verriker was
taking the long way around from his house on the lower
hill toward the rambling cottage along River Road where
Kate kept house for her brother Joe. Kate was worth two
of Joe any day. So thought Bly's Landing, and Verriker
was inclined to agree. Easy-going and gentle, as everybody
knew Joe to be, he had been made town marshal after
Mrs. Bellifer and her embattled Civic League had forced

a non-partisan administration upon Bly's Landing. That was the fall that Drummond had been in South America, but the *Observer* had allowed Mrs. Bellifer to assume that civic righteousness had at last triumphed.

River Road had been Front Street, with no consciousness of public beauty, until Marta Bellifer got the Garden Club organized. The essential dignity of the old residence street had not suffered noticeably from the Garden Club's enthusiasm, he had fulsomely admitted in an *Observer* editorial, though after the ramblers and laurel had had their best season and the white picket fences had been photographed for *Better Homes and Gardens,* there had come the prolonged scrap between the Civic League and the men's luncheon clubs about re-routing the national motor highway. If the route went through Bly's Landing along River Road, Mrs. Bellifer's civic pride in Bly's Landing, "the Picturesque Old River Town," would have been highly gratified; if the route remained on Main Street, the storekeepers and oil men would feel that they had averted a mortal blow to the town's Big Business. The luncheon clubs had won, but, as Mrs. Bellifer had learned on her next motor trip through New England that the nicest places diverted highways from their choicest spots, she still felt smugly superior to her crass fellow citizens, and so everybody was happy.

Verriker strolled slowly along under the fine trees that arched over River Road. The warm September dusk was redolent with garden fragrance and the faint damp odor of the great river rolling silently at the base of the bluffs that gave the street its famous views. This next was Marta's place. She had let herself go the limit, regardless of the landscape man whom she had imported from Pittsburgh. Too starchy, Verriker thought, but quite like Marta herself. . . .

He was aware that the lady was bearing down upon him. Or perhaps she had been deliberately waiting for him. Everybody in town could recognize his characteristic, spaced gait.

"Oh, Mr. Verriker, could you give me just a minute? I—I really need your advice. Come on up to the sun-porch. You might just as well be comfortable. And I think I can find you something to drink."

"No, please, no drinks." Verriker wasn't thinking at all of Doc's stipulations. Marta Bellifer's ideas of mixing things in a shaker were to be avoided by any oldtimer. He stretched himself gingerly in one of her gas-tubing chairs and waited. Maybe it wouldn't matter about Kate's brown, bread, tasty as it was. There was plainly something on Marta's mind; her about-to-introduce-the-speaker manner had quite vanished. She was worried, no mistake.

"I'm alone tonight," she said. "The girls have gone dancing—those lovely new people down on the island haven't left yet, and they quite adore Nancy and Elaine. And Julian's gone to his mother's for the weekend. Even my maids are at the movies." She paused and gave a little laugh, much in her usual style. "I do feel ever so foolish, but I've been thinking about something until it's on my nerves, I must confess."

Verriker gave a sympathetic grunt and waited.

"I should have shown it to Julian at once, but the dear boy is so tired these days. Federal work is so detailed, you know. . . ."

As Julian was only Mr. Marta Bellifer and had been living on his mother's money after the bank vice-presidency vanished in January, 1933, until an office job with an initialed Federal project had been wangled for him, Verriker didn't bother to emit a second sympathetic grunt.

"Then when I read your column this morning, it occurred to me—I mean, I have been wondering. . . . That is, I've known you a long time, and I shouldn't feel the least hesitancy—"

"If there's anything in the world that I can do for you, Mrs. Bellifer, you have only to say the word. And besides, I'm flattered. A competent woman like you—"

Marta Bellifer almost bowed in recognition of his tribute. "I've had them before, of course, and I've always been
sensible and laughed them off. I quite agree with you that
the scrap basket is the only place. But somehow, this time—"

Even in the darkness of the vine-screened porch Verriker could see the dim white movement that was a twisting
handkerchief.

"Suppose you tell me right out what's wrong."

"An anonymous letter. I know I'm silly to pay the slightest attention. It came yesterday. In the mail. From someone
right here in town. At least, that was the postmark, and just
a two-cent stamp. And there's no reason—no reason at all. I
mean, it's not like the time I had the old political crowd on
my neck. I knew then that it was the Cause and not myself
that was being attacked. I expected things like that then.
And when we fought to get the new high school principal,
I just considered the source and paid no attention to ugly
letters. And nothing at all happened when we had the difference with the men about River Road. They were all very
fine, and I've never been a poor loser—"

"So I take it that my little piece this morning came in
just about right. Hm-m? Well, why don't you follow my
words of wisdom and forget the filthy thing?"

"I should, I know, but this was different. Not scurri-
lous, or illiterate, or a dirty scrawl on smudgy cheap paper,
like the others. And there was something about your paragraph that made me think—well, somehow, I wanted to talk
to you about it."

"I get bushels of 'em—always have, ever since I've put
out a paper. Take 'em in my stride. Forget 'em. No doubt
it does whoever writes 'em good, more good than the ones
that get 'em are harmed, and so why worry? What did the
damned thing say?"

Mrs. Bellifer hunched her expensively corseted figure
forward and looked about cautiously in spite of her explanations of where everyone in her household was. The lazy

eyes watching her from the opposite chair could make out the strained set of her face.

"It's so pointless, Mr. Verriker. Quite insane, really. I suppose that's why I can't dismiss it. Just a few words, well typed on good paper. 'Ready or not, you shall be caught.' That's what it said, and I know I'm silly but—what do you think?"

Verriker gave a resonant guffaw. "What do you bet it's just trick advertising? There'll be an insurance follow-up, sure's the world, or else an umbrella salesman, like these brush chaps or the kids that work their way through college ringing doorbells."

Marta Bellifer laughed too, but briefly. "Oh, I can't believe—or do you mean that a lot of people got the same letter? If I've made myself ridiculous . . ." There was a slight stirring of the chairman of the meeting.

"I haven't heard a yip out of a soul, and believe me, Mrs. Bellifer, I hear everything in this town, usually before it happens. Forget the whole thing, my dear lady, or at least, if you can't do that, wait and see. These letter writers love their job. If you get another along the same line, give me the high sign and we'll take it up in a big way."

The tenseness in the opposite figure eased out a little. "I'd rather you wouldn't mention it to anyone while we're—waiting. I mean, I've quite definitely decided not to bother Julian, and the girls are so gay and care-free. The happiest time of their lives . . ."

That smacked of Marta Bellifer's P.T.A. address, and so, until she had worked her way to a period, Verriker let himself see fat, stolid Elaine and serious, high-minded Nancy. Then he rose to go and Mrs. Bellifer walked beside him towards her over-ornamental, trellised gate.

"As I say, forget it. Don't give it another thought. You, of all women, couldn't be caught at having done anything you shouldn't. Why, bless you, good works are the breath of your life. If you had any guilty secrets, why then of

course you, like everybody else, wouldn't ever be ready to
be caught. It's just some silly fool or wretched psychopath
who's blowing off a little steam, or maybe a salesman for
cemetery lots. There's a nice grisly idea for you."

"Oh, don't!" In the darkness Mrs. Bellifer shuddered
away from him and then laughed like a proper hostess. One
plump white hand brushed his coat sleeve swiftly. "But the
echo of the same words in your column was—really, so uncanny, if you know what I mean, that I felt I must tell you
all. And you've been such a dear to listen so patiently. I'll
send Elaine down with some of my asters tomorrow. Good
night!"

It wasn't too late to drop in at Kate's, but Verriker was
tired. A little of Marta Bellifer was always too much. He'd
go home and mix himself a decent drink and read himself
to sleep. It had been a long time since he had had a session
with Samuel Pepys. It was pleasanter walking along River
Road toward the lower hill, even through the end near
the wharf where Bly's Landing's best families did not live.
Much pleasanter than the blare and noise of Main Street,
for the filling stations were still open, the last crowd from
the Regent Theater had not yet deserted the Marx brothers,
and the Golden Fountain and Ernst's drugstore had still
their after-the-movie crowds to serve. Yet Verriker turned
toward Main Street and walked through town along its
length. He crossed just below the Mansion House, so that
as he passed he could look up easily at Alec Drummond's
windows. Someone was working late tonight there was one
bright light going. Not the pretty little secretary, though.
If he wasn't mistaken, that had been she and Lew Mason
in the rumble of Jip Tredway's car. Lew undoubtedly had a
way with him, no matter what boy-friends an out-of-town
girl had left in her own home town.

During most of Saturday Verriker conscientiously abode
by Doc Bunting's injunctions. When evening came he was
thoroughly bored. The gang would be warming up in the

little room behind Cardy's smoke shop. Alec Drummond was still in town; he'd seen him stopping at the post office after the last mail went up. Maybe Alec would sit in tonight.

The first few hands were dull and the play was stereotyped. Drummond was not there; no one mentioned him. No one except Verriker and George Bruce, the noisy, confident manager of the refinery, really enjoyed playing with Alec Drummond. It was plainly a case of not naming the devil for fear he should appear. Shortly after ten o'clock a telephone call ended Verriker's share in the revels.

He followed Cardy into the cluttered space behind the rear counter where the telephone hung on the scribbled wall. "That you, Ed?" It was Drummond's voice. "Wanted to see you tonight. Thought I'd make it at Cardy's for a little while, but it's not working out that way. Meet me in front in five minutes, will you? I'll run you out to the Lodge."

That was a command to most of Bly's Landing, but Verriker agreed casually. The fourth estate didn't always truckle to economic royalists, he editorialized, and then laughed at himself.

Drummond's car slid along the curb almost as soon as he emerged from Cardy's. The two men sat in silence as the car sped up the Jug Road towards Drummond's lodge, the last word in bachelor completeness, where Alec Drummond preferred to live from April to Thanksgiving. He entertained business associates from Pittsburgh and New York there sometimes, or producers from the Louisiana fields, but it was not often that even the leading citizens of Bly's Landing were summoned there. Drummond did most of his business with them in his offices on Main Street.

The autumn air was sharper on the high hilltop where Drummond had built his retreat. He had also built the three-mile length of private road that led to it from the motor highway that stretched across the state towards the mountains and Maryland.

Lights flashed on as the car made the last hairpin turn.

"Tim's there," Drummond said. "I'll have him start a fire and then pack him off to bed. Best thing about that boy is that he's not sociable."

No doubt, thought Verriker, that was Drummond's way of saying that there was no one about to interrupt their conference.

After the cigars were going and Verriker had said when, Alec Drummond wasted no more time. He pulled a folded copy of the *Observer* from his coat pocket and tapped it with his heavy, manicured forefinger.

"Any special reason that led you to write this last item, Ed?"

Verriker gave a vaguely negative grunt and sipped his highball. "Nothing you might say special, Drummond. Just a piece I speak more or less as a matter of principle, two-three times a year, as you could easily notice for yourself if you were really one of my constant readers. There's always a lousy bunch of anonymous tripe coming in, same as with every newspaper." He lifted his glass again. "Any special reason for asking?"

"Yes. Got one myself yesterday. Marked personal, and Miss Morgan didn't open it. Hasn't been with me very long, you see. The other girls always weeded 'em out. Oh, I get 'em too—always have. Small wonder, eh?"

"Then what's got your back up? And you say, you've known how to take a lot in your time."

"Give it a look, Ed." From an inner pocket he produced a letter, but went on speaking before handing it to his guest. "From the sound of that last bit in your column, I had an idea maybe you'd got one like it, that's all. Here—"

Verriker took the envelope and drew out a single sheet. One glance was enough.

READY OR NOT
YOU SHALL BE CAUGHT

"You're right, Drummond. I did get one the exact twin of this. But what of it?"

"I'd like to take a crack at the fool that sent it, that's what of it. Want to join me?"

"What's the use? Some half-cracked sore-head. That is, unless you have some special suspicion?"

"Not at all. But if you got one too— No use putting it up to Ralston."

Verriker protested with a slight, tolerant gesture. "No need to be so hard on Joe. He's a good egg."

"I know a first-class agency in Pittsburgh. One of their men—"

"Seems to have got you, Drummond."

His host frowned and hitched his chair back an inch farther into the shadows thrown by the blazing logs. "I'm vulnerable. I'm always vulnerable. I've always been." His tone was grim. "What do you suggest?"

"Nothing. I mean, do nothing. I shan't lose any sleep over any fool message like that, and I advise you to take it the same way."

"Thought maybe you'd help a little. You're in a strategic position in town and—don't laugh, Ed; it's God's truth— you're everybody's friend."

Just the same, Ed Verriker laughed. "That's no tribute. Makes me feel the way my wife used to when folks called her sweet. Bless her heart, the word fairly made her gag." He set his glass down for the last time and refused Drummond's quick gesture towards the squat bottle. "Oh, I'll keep my ear to the ground, if you say so, unless you go bringing in big-town dicks. I wouldn't be in their class, but I don't mind breaking down and telling you that I've always wondered how I'd make out as an amateur."

"Fair enough, Ed. That's what I hoped you'd say." Drummond glanced at his watch. "I'll put you up for the night, if you say the word, but I've got to be on my way myself this minute. I've got an appointment in Washington in the morning and I'm driving through tonight. That new baby of mine will eat it up, eh? Or I can run you down now. I've got to stop at the office first."

Verriker promptly chose the latter suggestion, somewhat, he thought, to Drummond's relief. Nothing much was said during the swift breathless descent to the now sleeping town, except for Verriker's one drawling comment. "You'll sure be there and back again in no time with this thing under you."

"Can't say. Don't know exactly how long I'll be tied up in Washington."

Verriker entered his quiet, untidy house and slumped upon the bed that had not been made since Addie Wait had cleaned last. As he untied his shoes he was thinking, "Trouble is, I know too damned much myself and too many people know I do. . . . Maybe I can get somewhere, though."

His eye fell on the small envelope filled with the pills that Bunting had been so explicit about. "Might try—just to offset that stuff of Doc's. Alec's pretty definitely putting his neck out. Joe Ralston and big-time detectives—and me, Ed Verriker. . . ."

He snapped off the light and fumbled at the tangled covers. He slept.

Within the next twenty-four hours the first of the crimes at Bly's Landing occurred.

Part Two
Last Act of All

I

Aside from Mrs. Bellifer's vice-chairmanship of a national committee of the Garden League of America, the only previous claim to national notice possessed by Bly's Landing was the apocryphal tale of the underground railway station and flights across the river more incredible than Eliza's. Never again, after the series of events that began on the last Sunday evening of September, did the town have to rely on such innocuous annals. News reels, radio reports, candid camera shots, even special articles by Edna Ferber and Kathleen Norris and impressions by the First Lady on her way to Homestead . . . At last the men's noon-tide clubs had to consider what could be done to overcome what they freely admitted was unfavorable publicity.

At seven-thirty-one on that Sunday evening the down train from Pittsburgh stopped with its usual cough at the station in Bly's Landing and four passengers alighted. One of them was Peggy Morgan, regretfully returning from an all too brief weekend. The latest model in fall hats, an engaging trifle—like an ear-muff with wings, Mack had said—did what it could to console her, but she felt distinctly low, just the same. Bly's Landing was the world's jumping off place, in spite of her grand new job with an authentic big-shot like Alec Drummond. Any moment he might order her to tag along to Washington or New York.

But in the meantime there were the Amberlees and what
their morgue of a house was doing to her nerves. And Lydia.
Especially Lydia.

With distinct firmness Peggy said good night to the
fourth passenger, only a high-school senior who had practically been on her neck ever since he had boarded the train
three stations up. Being a basketball idol inflated youth-
ful egos unbearably. She would not have the pimply young
idiot carrying her bag up to the Amberlee place. If Lew
Mason should be in sight, she'd give him a break. Lew
thought highly of himself, too, but Lew was fun. He had
been a Phi Gam at W.V.U. and Mack would understand if
she decided to go to the State-Marietta game with him.

There was no sign of Lew. Peggy picked up her light
traveling case, tucked the clumsy roll of a Sunday paper
more tightly under her arm, and crossed the street on her
way to River Road. The dead calm of Sunday night lay over
Bly's Landing. At first it had amused Peggy, used to the
social activity of urban Sundays, to realize that everybody,
almost everybody, went to church on Sunday night. What
they did afterwards, some of them, might have amused
her still more, but Peggy had spent nearly every Saturday
afternoon and Sunday elsewhere since she had come to
town to be Alec Drummond's private secretary, and as yet
she had not penetrated beyond her first observations of
lighted, well-filled churches.

They were singing "Work for the night is coming" as she
passed the U.P. church and "Now the day is over" at Grace.
Though she was still a bit uncertain what U.P. stood for,
she had already learned that Grace was *the* church of Bly's
Landing. Mr. Dawson Amberlee had dealt with that point
at some length. Past the light falling from its windows, of
which Bly's Landing was mistakenly proud, she was aware
that someone was coming towards her through the darkness. The trees were low and thick along the sidewalk, but
in a moment she recognized the tall figure of the owner and

editor of the town's weekly paper. She liked Mr. Verriker. She had told Mack that he was exactly like a character out of Booth Tarkington. Peggy had never read Sherwood Anderson.

"Good evening." His first words verged on the perfunctory. Then, "Ah, it's—why, yes, Miss Morgan. Back for another week with us. I'm going in a trifle late myself, I'm afraid, but may I suggest that we share the reverend brother's exhortation? It would be a great pleasure to enter the sanctum with you on my arm."

"Yes, and my bag on the other. Even if I have a new hat, my soul doesn't need exhorting tonight."

He stood aside and waved his hat with a flourish as Peggy walked on, and then he turned into the flagged walk leading to Grace Church and Tom Hawley's sermon.

The Amberlee house was the last one of distinction along River Road. It had not been noticeably affected by Mrs. Bellifer's enthusiasm for the synthetic picturesque. As Peggy neared the cross street just below the sudden steep rise upon which the late nineteenth century residence of a first family had been starkly imposed, she once more heard footsteps approaching through the darkness. Hurried, nervous footsteps.

They were coming along the cross street from the direction of the river. It was a dead-end street, though Peggy was not wholly certain of local geography, nor had she any knowledge of who lived in the two inconspicuous houses that brought the short street to an end at the very edge of the steep bank high above the river. A man was coming towards her through the darkness. There was something faintly furtive about his swift progress, and she hastened her own steps as she began the rise that led to the Amberlee gate.

Just once she turned her head, in time to see a dark figure cross the street intersection. In fact, all that she saw clearly was a shoulder and arm. The man was carrying a bag about the size of her own. Like a doctor's bag, she thought.

Her heart sank as she neared the somber bulk of the Amberlee house. It was the tangle of un-trimmed shrubbery and the funereal rusty evergreens that tended to depress her, and she was silly to let them, for living in the Amberlee house was, in spite of everything, much to be preferred to residence in the Mansion House. She had stood that relic of the oil boom only three days, and even at that she had bought rubber sheeting to spread over the unspeakable mattress. And two weeks at Mrs. Lukey's had been getting her down, when a few frank complaints to Mr. Drummond had led to his suggestion that she speak to Miss Judith Amberlee. Her niece Lydia would probably be delighted to have another young person in the house. Miss Judith had consented vaguely to consult her brother Dawson. Several days later Peggy had found a memo on her desk in Drummond's writing that there was a room for her at the Amberlee place and that Miss Judith would be glad to have her join them for breakfasts.

It was more than a week after she had installed herself in the great high-ceilinged but comfortable bedroom at the Amberlee house before she saw any sign of Lydia. Poor Lydia, thought Peggy, and shuddered. Most certainly Lydia was not delighted with her presence in the house. Lew Mason said Lydia was nuts, and Peggy was beginning to be sure his word was right. The Mansion House, Mrs. Lukey's, the Amberlee mausoleum—where was a girl to stay whose excellent job had brought her to a town like this. She couldn't give up her gorgeous salary, but if she stayed in Bly's Landing she'd have to consider keeping house in a trailer.

She stumbled up the dark, badly graveled path that led to the front door, wishing that she had bought one of those lovely trailing bunches of bittersweet that the boy had tried to sell when the train stopped at Sistersville. Miss Amberlee might have thrown it out tomorrow, but at least its brilliant color could have warmed her heart tonight. It was hard to make her room, perfectly, even luxuriously furnished as it was, appear lived in. The three Amberlees seldom left the house except for meticulous church-going, and they were undoubtedly a family of wealth or had been at the time the great house was built and furnished, but Peggy had never been in a place that seemed more unlived in. The bittersweet would have helped a little. But what had set her to thinking of it . . .

There was a lamp burning in the hall and another light in the small sitting-room to the right where the elder Amberlees usually spent their evenings, a sitting-room which Peggy had never been invited to enter since the first brief interview that had followed Mr. Drummond's suggestion. A small room, but not a cozy one. Absolutely the wrong word, thought Peggy, wishing, she dared fill it full of cigarette smoke.

The front door was locked. That indicated that everyone was out, except possibly Lydia. It was Sunday evening and that meant church. Peggy walked across the bare, unfurnished porch and down a second set of steps that gave upon the path leading to the side entrance. She had a key for that door, though Miss Judith had intimated that it was not likely that her lodger would expect to be out much at night. The Amberlees preferred to retire early, she added.

As Peggy emerged into the square central hall from the airless corridor that led to the side door, she glanced into the sitting-room. There was no-one there. The house was no more silent than usual; it was always tomb-like, but to-night there was an unmistakable emptiness about it. Clearly all three of the Amberlees had gone to church. If she had accepted Mr. Verriker's preposterous invitation, it would have been fun to see their faces as she paraded down the aisle. My new hat, thought Peggy, is going to give the old girl a pain in the neck, and I hope it does.

She mounted the stairs, a well-balanced flight with two properly spaced landings. The upper hall was unlighted,

until at the top she fumbled for the button. The bedroom
doors opening upon the hall stood slightly open, as they
always did when they were unoccupied. All except Lydia's.
It never stood ajar. It was one of her many queernesses that
she spent long silent hours behind the closed door of her
room. Tonight there was no thread of light beneath Lydia's
door. She too must be listening to the sermon at Grace.

Peggy swung into her own room, set down her bag with
as much of a thump as its weight would effect, and flooded
the room with light. Everything was in perfect and beautiful order. She patted the high smooth bed lovingly, thinking of the noisome mattress at the Mansion House, and
then she picked up a hand mirror from the top of the heavy
old-fashioned dresser and examined the set of her new hat
from all angles. Not a mistake, she decided; definitely not
a mistake. Miss Ralston would like it and that puffy Mrs.
Bellifer would know it was right out of the next issue of
Vogue.

Peggy laid the mirror down and gave her head a last toss
of satisfaction. Her eye caught a glimpse of a bead of color
on the floor. Not a bead, a berry . . . a bittersweet berry.
Frost had not yet forced its sharp prongs open and it lay
rolling on her palm, a brilliant ball of Chinese red. Lovely,
glowing color . . . Once more she regretted the flaming
branch that she had not brought back with her. She could
have enjoyed it tomorrow on her desk at the office. Mr.
Drummond had so far made no objection to the presence
of plants or flowers. The Amberlees were a queer set, yet
if they had not taken her in, she'd still be listening to the
dripping faucets in Mrs. Lukey's communal bathroom. And
fried potatoes for breakfast, she reminded herself pointedly.

Peggy peeled off her clothes and got into lounging
pajamas. First she'd skim through the paper and then she'd
write Cousin Elsa that letter that should have been written a month ago. This great empty house would be more
cheerful if she dared set Mr. Amberlee's phonograph going,

only he wouldn't have her kind of records. Thank goodness, the household went in for reading lamps, and the big chair was far more comfortable than it looked. Even when they returned from church she would be undisturbed. Rather distinctly she was not one of the family, another matter for gratitude. When she uncurled herself again, she must remember to set her little leather-boxed clock. It had run down and stopped during her absence. And she had slipped her watch from her wrist and left it lying on the dresser.

So when, later, the telephone bell rang, Peggy did not know exactly what time it was. The bell rang twice before she moved to answer it. After all, it might be a call for her. She was no longer a complete stranger in Bly's Landing. She ran lightly down to the back of the lower hall. "Yes?" she queried.

The caller must have known at once that no Amberlee was on the line. "Mr. Dawson Amberlee, if you please. . . ."

Peggy caught something familiar about the voice. "I'm sorry," she explained. "He is not at home, but I imagine he'll soon be in from church."

"Um—aw—I see. This is Hawley speaking. Neither Amberlee nor Miss Judith was out this evening. A bit unusual, you know. And a little matter of church business has come up—rather imperative, really. I'll call again a little later, Miss—er, Miss—er, but meantime if Mr. Amberlee should come in will you be so kind as to ask him to call me at once? At the parsonage . . ."

That was all. But why didn't the man remember her name? He'd said it often enough while she was patronizing Mrs. Lukey's establishment. The Reverend Mr. Thomas Hawley was another person in Bly's Landing that she liked. He was fun to talk to; he'd been places and done things that marked him off from the professional preacher. Yet if she'd stayed longer at Mrs. Lukey's, he'd have turned amorous on her. Quite the type, she catalogued him. His wife was somewhere—if he had a wife. An invalid in a sanitarium, yes, that was what Miss Ralston had told her.

By the time Peggy returned to the upper hall it occurred to her that it was odd that Mr. Hawley hadn't asked for Lydia, since he had a family message to leave. No, it wasn't odd. Very few people put Lydia in their pictures.

She'd knock at Lydia's door just in case . . . Maybe, if she were there, since the two of them were alone in the house, she'd try her out with the new hat. Lydia couldn't be much more than her own age, and yet every attempt at simple friendliness on Peggy's part had encountered only a difficult reticence which could so easily have been described as hostility.

"She's really beautiful, too," she had said in an effort to explain her to Mack, "but she doesn't seem aware of herself. Blank and withdrawn, sort of. Lew Mason says she's slightly off, and I suppose that's the answer. If only I could find a decent place to live in that God-awful town. . . ."

Peggy's brisk rap at Lydia's door brought no response. She turned the knob expecting to find that the door was locked. It usually was, she suspected. But the door opened. There was no one within. Peggy did not enter. She stood on the threshold for an instant, the light from the hall revealing the room quite plainly. It was in delicate order, as tidy as a spare bedroom that isn't used as a place to put things in.

She turned and closed the door behind her. The light from her own wide-flung door shone into the partly open door of the room opposite, Miss Judith's room. From her position near Lydia's door she could see into the aunt's room at an angle that her own opposite one had not permitted. She could see something so strangely untidy about the floor that impulsively she stepped towards its doorway and looked again. Something like a garment, discarded and lying on the floor. Not at all like the precise Amberlees. She pushed the door wider and stepped inside the room. Stopped and bit back a squeak of fright.

Miss Judith Amberlee was lying on the floor. Her eyes were open, but they were wide and blank. Instinctively Peggy fell to her knees beside her, spoke to her, touched her cheek and then one outstretched hand with her own trembling fingers. Not till then did she see the thin trickle of blood seeping from under the woman's hair. She heard herself mumbling, "She fell . . . she hurt herself—why, she's dead!"

Terrified, aghast, biting her lips to keep from screaming in horror, Peggy backed from the room and fled down the stairs towards the telephone. Help. She'd have to call for help. . . . Maybe Miss Judith wasn't really dead. A doctor. That's it, call a doctor. . . .

But the only name she could be sure of, as she fumbled with the thin pamphlet that was Bly's Landing's telephone directory, was Hawley's. Maybe that was because he had so recently rung the Amberlee number himself. He was the one—he'd know what to do. Half crying from shock, she waited for a response.

It came at once. Would he please come up to the Amberlees' at once? She had just found Miss Judith lying hurt in her room. She was afraid—afraid maybe she was dead. . . .

Within five minutes, he promised. Was it, he asked, Miss Morgan? He'd be right up to do anything he could.

Peggy crept back to the foot of the stairs and huddled on the lowest step, waiting. She was chilled and shaken, though before the house had felt stuffy. Now the thin silk of her gaudy pajamas might have been tissue paper stretched across her shoulders, but return to her own room for a flannel robe was impossible.

Someone pounded at the front door, not six feet away from where she crouched. She shuddered and clutched the newel post before reason told her that it must be Thomas Hawley. She'd have to make him understand that the front door was locked; he'd have to go around to the side where she could admit him. But when she stumbled towards the door she saw that the heavy brass key was in its proper place in the lock on the inside. That meant . . . oh, she didn't know what it meant. This was no time to think. They

must act. Maybe that poor creature lying on the floor upstairs wasn't dead. . . .

But she was. Thomas Hawley said so, after he had followed her swiftly up the stairs and into that silent room.
He was almost as helpless as she had been in the emergency,
though he explained that they ought not to touch anything
until the doctor had seen her. In fact, his only suggestion
was that she call Dr. Bunting at once. Mechanically he repeated a number to her. "Just tell him to come at once—
that it's imperative. I'll stay up here with the—you'd prefer
to go down to the telephone, I think."

Peggy's thoughts raced aimlessly as she once more ran
down the stairs. Bunting, of course . . . the only doctor
that anyone in the town ever mentioned. . . . Imperative—
he'd used that word twice. That was nothing, just a habit
that everyone had. . . . Her horrible, violent pajamas—why
hadn't she got her dark bathrobe when she was up there?
Mr. Hawley wasn't the sort to miss silk lounging pajamas.
But he was so different, so formal. No, impersonal was the
word. Words—what a fool to think words mattered in a mess
like this. . . . His hands were shaking just like hers when he
turned and said . . . What if the doctor were out. . . .

"Is this Dr. Bunting? Will you come at once? There's
been—an accident. . . . As quickly as possible, please. . . .
Oh, to the Amberlee house. . . . I said, an accident. We
think she's dead—oh-h!"

With a clash of the receiver she broke the connection,
which did more than her incoherent words to start the doctor on his way. A harsh, masculine screech from the upper
hall had caused her to spin around and cling to the lower
rail of the stairs, gripped with fresh terror.

Thomas Hawley started uncertainly down toward the
first landing and his white strained face searched for hers.

"Dawson—Dawson, too. In his room. Dead!"

II

Dr. Bunting came. It seemed hours that they waited, though it was not more than ten minutes. Peggy knew because, when she had joined Hawley in the upper hall where he had repeated his ghastly announcement with vague nervous gestures towards the door of Dawson Amberlee's room, in her fresh horror she had backed into her own room as though his words were as yet meaningless. She wrapped her shaking figure in a dressing-gown and snapped her watch upon her wrist. It was then thirteen minutes after nine. At nine-twenty Dr. Bunting came.

Peggy had emerged from her room almost at once, to find Hawley still standing exactly where she had left him and looking as stricken as herself. He made her sit down while they waited for the doctor, but all that he said was, "On the floor—in there . . . shot."

Peggy said, "Lydia—she's not here. I mean I—" She did not know what she meant unless that, if they looked, Lydia too might be found.

But they did not look, and neither of them re-entered the rooms where the bodies lay.

Even when Dr. Bunting burst through the front door and raced up the stairs in response to Hawley's signal, Peggy did not follow the men into either room. The doctor took a hurried look at first one and then the other before settling to a more professional examination, as though he too could not believe what Hawley tried to tell him. When he reappeared from Amberlee's room after his first look, he was twisting his fingers nervously.

"Where's Lydia?" he asked. "They're both dead. It looks— I don't like it."

He hesitated as he was about to again enter Miss Judith's room and then ran down to the telephone. Apparently he knew the house; he asked no questions. Peggy and the preacher both followed him to the upper railing. They heard him say, "Ed, you'll have to come up to the Amberlee house. We're going to need your help about Lydia." Then they heard him call another number and, "Kate? Let me talk to Joe. . . ."

In the few seconds that he waited, Peggy was conscious that the man beside her made a vague regretful sound, but she was still so completely distraught that she failed to recognize the significance of Joe's name. Not from her new friend, Kate Ralston, had she learned that the town marshal's qualifications for office were not held in particularly high esteem.

The doctor was speaking again. "Joe, hell's hit the Amberlee place. You'll have to take over officially. Pick up Syd Trasker on your way. I'll have to be checked. And for God's sake, hurry!"

Once more Peggy heard a murmur from Hawley. "The coroner, of course . . . Oh, dear God in heaven . . ."

When Bunting came back up the stairs he had himself well in hand. A gesture directed Hawley to follow him as he re-entered the nearer of the two dreadful rooms, Judith Amberlee's. Peggy moved nearer the doorway but did not leave the hall. She could see that the doctor was kneeling by the body, giving it a more detailed examination but not shifting its position materially. She heard Hawley ask, "Can you tell when it happened?" but she could make nothing of Bunting's mumbled reply except that it sounded impatient. Bunting and Hawley moved on then to Amberlee's room where a similar scene followed.

They were still engaged there when Peggy heard sounds of arrival below. She too felt that she had conquered her first wave of hysteria, and ran down the steps to open the door. Verriker entered, followed by a pleasant, youngish man who must be, she thought, Kate Ralston's brother Joe, town marshal of Bly's Landing. With scarcely a word from her they hurried up the stairs to join the doctor and Hawley, but Peggy was grateful for the reassuring pat that Verriker gave her tense shoulder as he passed her. She tagged miserably in their wake and sat huddled on an upper step while the grim official inspection got under way. She could not watch them at their work. Before it was half finished a third arrival brought her again down to the door. A bluff stout man came in, breathing heavily.

"I'm Trasker," he announced himself. "Joe here? Upstairs, huh? Okay."

This time Peggy remained on the lower step, wholly wretched and inclined to weep. She could hear constant movement above and occasional low, gruff speech. Apparently someone was going systematically from room to room. In sudden fear she became aware that her room too was being entered and examined. Mack, if only Mack were here. Somebody that really knows me, she thought in panic. Mr. Drummond—he could tell me what to do. I can't stay here. They—why, they won't let me stay here. Mr. Drummond will know. . . . It seemed like a million years since Saturday noon. Her memory fought back desperately. No use wishing for her powerful, influential employer. He had told her he would be in Washington, would not be back in his office until Tuesday morning.

Someone came down the stairs, passed her. It was Ralston. She raised her head to watch but did not follow him. Snapping on lights as he went, he moved from room to room, but apparently nothing that he found detained him long. On his way back upstairs he paused a bit awkwardly and addressed her.

"You're Miss Morgan, aren't you? I really ought to know—I mean, I've heard my sister speak of you. My name's Ralston. I guess I'm in charge here, much as anyone. I'll have to talk to you now—ask you some questions. If you'll come along upstairs, I'll be ready any time now."

He made no gesture for her to precede him, but hurried on to the upper hall. Peggy patted her hair aimlessly and retied the cord of her flannel robe and then sank again into a miserable heap upon the lower step. Her knees trembled

and felt rubbery. She heard Ralston call to her and she
pulled herself upward.

As she gained the top of the flight, the doctor and the
coroner came out of Judith's room and Verriker emerged
from Dawson's. Ralston had his back to her, looking down
at something ranged on a small table between Lydia's door
and her own. Hawley placed a chair for her with something of his usual manner. The men, all except Ralston,
seated themselves on a dull oak chest in the forward end of
the hall. Peggy thought, "Miss Amberlee keeps blankets in
that chest—no, she's dead!" She braced herself once more
against hysteria and looked at the three men so gravely confronting her from the oak chest. "Like a jury . . ." And then
wished she hadn't thought of that.

She heard Ralston speaking. ". . . they've both been
shot, and there's no trace of a weapon. That makes it look
like murder. Who shot 'em, that's our problem. Nobody
in the house except the young lady here, and I take it she
hadn't been here so very long, but we'll be hearing from her
in a minute. No hired help in the house on Sundays. Take
one of us, then another, I guess we know the Amberlee set-
up right well. Only other member of the household's not anywhere about. So we've got to find Lydia and talk to her too."

Ralston stopped and looked again at what was on the
table. His face was worried and unhappy. "Well, that's what
we're up against. Now, let's run over what we've got so far.
Doc, you and Syd come to anything about when it happened to 'em?"

"Maybe three hours ago, is what we make it," Trasker
replied. "Bunting saw 'em first, close on to nine-thirty.
Might have happened between six and seven, seven-thirty.
Hard to be right sure, down to the exact minute. Kinda
think myself, Joe, that Miss Judith got it first. Hard to
prove, though, wouldn't you say, Doc?"

Bunting nodded. "You could see for yourself, Joe, that
both of them were shot from behind, but not at the same

vulnerable spot. The base of the brain for Miss Amberlee, and close up. Her hair is noticeably burned. Amberlee got it through the back, straight into the heart."

"And no powder marks on his coat," Ralston finished. "Your next job is to get out the bullets. They ought to be alike, or the thing will be a nightmare—more than it is. And better do a complete p.m. I'd kinda like to know what they had for supper, if any."

The Reverend Thomas Hawley stirred nervously. "Miss Amberlee had Sunday night tea at six promptly. I— They frequently invited me to join them before the evening service. I—I was here only last Sunday evening." He drew a folded handkerchief from his pocket, shook it out, and patted his forehead.

Ralston looked gravely at the preacher and resumed. "We think—this group here—that there was no weapon of any sort in this household, though we haven't exactly established that yet." He paused briefly and glanced at Peggy and then went on.

"Now, as to Lydia Amberlee, we've found this." He picked up a small sheet of white notepaper from the table. "This we found lying on the pillow of the bed in Miss Morgan's room. I'll read it to you."

Peggy leaned forward with a start, her lips parted in protest. "No, no—how could it be there? I didn't see it. . . ."

"That's all right, Miss Morgan. Almost didn't see it myself. White paper on a white pillow—have to look twice and then some. Just listen, all of you. Doc and Syd haven't heard it yet, either.

"'Have gone to my friend's. I'll be all right. Lydia.'"

The men all talked at once. Trasker boomed, "Don't say so much at that, does it?" He gave a sudden harsh laugh.

"Lydia was with her uncle and aunt at the morning service." That, of course, was Thomas Hawley.

"The poor child must be found at once—"

With the voice of authority Dr. Bunting interrupted Ed Verriker. "Considering the poor creature's record, Joe, you haven't much of a problem at all. Lydia's condition has shown no improvement; in fact, I've been secretly quite distressed, though I must admit that my professional inspection has been only casual. I haven't been sent for for her for some time. She certainly had motive, or thought so, and opportunity, and above all, the psychological twist that would have made such an act possible—"

"And how about the means, Doc? Seems to me you've got the detective story lingo down pretty smooth. Thought your weakness was Westerns. And besides, if you're going to call Lydia Amberlee insane, then analyzing means, method, and opportunity doesn't count for so much." Ralston's words sounded quite like a rebuke. Peggy was aware that the physician sputtered into red-faced silence and that Verriker gave a quick, satisfied nod.

But the marshal's next words gave her a fresh chill of fear. "Another thing we've got, which certainly will have some bearing on our procedure, is Miss Morgan's statement. I'd like to have you all hear what she says, and any answers she may see fit to make to any questions we ask her."

Peggy waited dumbly until a question was plumped at her. "You were not in town throughout this week-end, I understand?"

"No. I went up to Pittsburgh on the noon train Saturday and returned this evening on the 7:31."

"Clear enough, and easy, too, to find plenty of witnesses to that effect."

Though Ralston's words were uttered with easy friendliness. Peggy's lips felt stiff and unnatural as she forced them to say, "If—if you think it's necessary."

"I'm a witness, for one, Joe." Verriker smiled at the girl. "Passed her coming around from the station just as I was heading for church. Might have been twenty minutes to eight. Maybe Tom noticed I was a mite late coming in."

Peggy breathed a little easier and waited for the next question.

"Bet you passed other folks too, Miss Morgan. Came straight up here to the house, did you?"

Peggy nodded. She meant to mention the man coming through the darkness from the short street just below, but she went on with an account of her movements, as Ralston evidently expected her to do. "The front door was locked, and I thought that meant that they were at church. I let myself in at the side door—Miss Judith gave me a key—and I came right up to my room. I—I didn't notice the note, the one from Lydia you read. Was it really there all the time?"

"It's up to you or Hawley or Lydia—or the murderer to say for sure. I was the first one of the rest of us to take a look in your room, and I found it."

"I tell you, Joe, there's no doubt. That's Lydia's writing. I know it very well. Lydia's always been real human with me."

"I know that, Ed. That's why I wanted you here, I want you to be thinking where she might have gone, and you'll have to be the one to tell her when—if—"

"Exactly, Joe. When and if," Bunting snapped.

At a nod from Ralston, Peggy went on. "I didn't leave the room until the telephone rang. I was reading the paper. When the bell rang I went downstairs to the phone. It was Mr. Hawley. He wanted to speak to Mr. Amberlee. I said he hadn't come in yet, that I thought he was at church, and he said—" Peggy looked up at the preacher to find his eyes intent upon her. Somewhat to her surprise she said hastily, "It was Mr. Hawley; I recognized his voice. He said the Amberlees had not been at church and would I ask Mr. Amberlee to call him as soon as he came in."

"What time was this call, Miss Morgan?"

Peggy was beginning to explain about her clock and her watch when Thomas Hawley broke in. "It couldn't have been a bit later than ten of nine when I rang the house to ask for Amberlee. I closed my service promptly at eight-thirty, and after the usual hand-shaking in the vestibule I walked directly back to the parsonage. I was in the house by a quarter of nine. I had expected to see Amberlee at church—I wanted him to verify a matter concerning the next district meeting—and I went almost at once to the telephone."

"I don't know," Peggy faltered. "I had the feeling that I had been reading for nearly an hour. But I do know it was nine-thirteen when I—but I ought to tell it the way it happened?"

"If you please, Miss Morgan," Ralston directed. "I came back upstairs and tapped at Lydia's door. She's always so quiet, I thought maybe she was there, and the house was so still and empty—" She stopped and shuddered uncontrollably. "When I turned away from her door—I had opened it, I must tell you, but I didn't go in—I saw what looked like some clothes lying on the floor just around the edge of Miss Amberlee's door. It looked—oh, a little queer, and I stepped inside and saw her—I thought she had fallen—I didn't dream . . . She didn't move or speak—and it scared me. Then I saw—blood in her hair and she felt cold and—and I ran down to the telephone. I had to call someone quick and the only one I could think of was Mr. Hawley."

"I got her call no more than five minutes after I had completed mine."

"Touch anything in the room—Miss Amberlee's room?" Ralston asked.

"Nothing. Except her cheek and her hand. I—I was scared."

"I guess we all understand that, Miss Morgan. What happened till Mr. Hawley came?"

"Nothing. I just stayed downstairs by the door."

"She let me in through the front door and we went upstairs together."

Joe Ralston raised his hand in a slight gesture. "I'd like to get the young lady's statement first, if you don't mind."

"He just looked at her, too, when we got up here, and he said for me to call Dr. Bunting, and I did, and before I'd finished really, I heard him call down to me. Something—it sounded awful, as though he were frightened too. I think I hung up the receiver. I don't know, because Mr. Hawley said that Mr. Amberlee was dead too."

Ralston cocked one eyebrow at the doctor just long enough to permit him to add a parenthesis.

"She let out a screech, Joe, and the connection went off, and I shook a leg over here."

"All right. Now, Hawley, put your piece in. You sent Miss Morgan down to the phone."

"It was the obvious and logical thing to do, Ralston." There was a faintly defensive quality to the clergyman's excellent pulpit voice. "I followed Miss Morgan out of Miss Amberlee's room and stood right here in this hall until I could tell that she was going to connect with Bunting. Naturally I was beginning to wonder about everything, for I could see for myself that she had been shot. And Dawson Amberlee never misses Sunday night service. So I opened his door and found—exactly what you saw for yourself. I was horror-stricken. I've been an army chaplain and I've served a slum parish—violent and sudden death have come my way before this, but it's always shocking. And these people are—were my friends." His large white handkerchief flapped weakly.

"Then what, Miss Morgan?" Joe Ralston turned again to her.

"I didn't go into his room at all. What Mr. Hawley said was enough. I ran into my room and shut the door, I'm afraid. Didn't I?"

Hawley nodded and slipped his handkerchief back into his pocket.

"That's when I put my watch on and saw that it was thirteen after nine. By my watch it was . . ." Peggy felt that she was babbling. "And then Dr. Bunting came."

"Might have been nine-twenty, Joe. But exact times were no longer important."

"That's true enough, Doc, but if we all calm down and think straight, it may help a little." He turned again with grave politeness to Peggy. "I guess that's about all for to-night, except for this. Have you any knowledge of anyone in the house possessing any sort of gun?"

"No, Mr. Ralston. You must remember that I know very little about this household. And I never had such a thing myself. I've never even had one in my hand."

"Let's see; how long have you been staying here with the Amberlees?"

"A little over two months. I came in the last week of July. I've been very comfortable here, but I've not been a member of the family. I didn't want to be, for that matter."

Joe Ralston grinned in spite of himself and the doctor gave a snort of what might have passed for understanding.

"Well, anyway," Joe persisted, "maybe you might have noticed something or other that fits into all this mess." He waved a hand at the two blank doors. "Lydia been getting along all right with her aunt and uncle?"

Verriker stirred restlessly and Dr. Bunting nodded his head as if in agreement with his own private opinion.

"I can't think of anything. They were all very kind, but I never talked with any of them much. Lydia stayed in her own room most of the time. I tried to be chatty with her several times, but I never got very far. She seemed—oh, very reserved. She went out with her aunt sometimes. I mean—all I know is that I've seen them together on the streets occasionally. I'd look out of my office window and recognize them as people I knew. Everybody in town was a stranger to me at first. I don't know many people yet."

"Find Lydia, Joe. She's the answer. Incipient dementia praecox, but you don't have to take my word for it." Bunting rose and nodded at Syd Trasker. "Any objection to Syd and me getting on with our job?"

"Carry on. I'll be taking Miss Morgan out of your way in a shake, at that."

So that meant that she was going to be arrested. After she got to jail surely they'd let her send one message. Mack would know what to do. . . .

Something of this new terror must have been on her face, for Joe Ralston burst into a comforting laugh. "I mean, you can't stay here tonight. Or do you want to? I thought I'd have Kate put you up. You and Kate are pals, as I understand it. But about this note that I found on your pillow. Lydia wrote it, if Ed Verriker says so. Lydia in the habit of leaving you billy doos?"

"No, never. I don't know that she wrote it, even if Mr. Verriker does."

"Take that, Ed. Kinda funny, then, that she left word with you."

"I have no idea why she did." The horrible thought that had possessed her before came again to the surface. "Are you sure she isn't here, too, somewhere, like—like the others?"

"Not in the house, Miss Morgan, not anywhere in the house. Just forget that, or Kate won't be able to get you to sleep at all. I shall have the outside thoroughly searched before I quit for the night." This last as if in answer to the question in Verriker's eyes.

"And finally—" Ralston rose slowly and Peggy was aware that he was taller than her first impression. "You folks noticed that I mentioned Sunday night supper. The Amberlees had a very light meal, more like afternoon tea. That was well known to be their custom. There's a neat pile of dishes covered over with a towel down on a kitchen table. Cups and saucers and things for two. Just two people. That might mean something. Eh, Ed?

"Now, Miss Morgan, suppose you put a few things in a bag and get ready to come with me. Doc and Syd will be busy here for a while; and Hawley, I don't think there's anything more you can do till morning. Ed, suppose you walk

around to the house with Miss Morgan and me, and if you
have any glimmer of an idea where Lydia might have gone,
I hope to God you spill it."

In less than five minutes Peggy was ready to leave the
Amberlee house. From the bottom of her heart she hoped
that never again would she have to sleep under its roof.

"Talk it all out with Kate if you want to," Ralston advised. "Best thing you can do, at that. I can't stop now to
give her the low-down, and she'll bust a button till she
hears what's up. She heard Doc Bunting's voice cracking
through the phone and almost tagged along after me."

When he had left her with Kate Ralston, not at all
the snooping spinster type and a person whom Peggy had
already made a confidante of concerning her violent first
impressions of Bly's Landing, the two could hear Ralston
and Verriker in earnest, low-toned talk.

"They're sitting on the porch step smoking," Kate reported. "Planning a campaign, I suppose. Joe's never had a
murder case before, and the poor kid's in a dither. Ed Verriker has more sense than any other man in town, and he'll
stand by Joe. Now, Peggy, tell me everything in one word,
or I'll stick a pin in this hot-water bag and put salt in the
cocoa that I'm going to get down you, and hide the aspirin
besides. . . ."

The pair on the porch step smoked silently. Then Ralston
shook himself and spoke.

"Not a whole lot of evidence, Ed. And I meant what I
said about your rounding up Lydia."

"Before you tie everything up on that poor Godforsaken
girl, here's more evidence to be considered. I suppressed
some, Joe. Just as well for you to keep a jump or so ahead
of Hawley and Bunting. I found these—" He pulled two
folded papers from his pocket, but continued to hold them
loosely in one hand, his pipe in the other. "One in each
room. This one that's folded twice was in Amberlee's watch

pocket. And by the way, it's our bad luck that his watch kept right on going when he fell. You'd know then precisely when he was shot, instead of the times of all the phone calls. And the other one, folded only once, was in Judith's writing-case, that old walnut box—belonged to her grandmother, likely."

Already Ralston, had whipped out a flashlight and had it spotted on the folded papers, though Verriker had not yet relinquished them. "I just gave 'em one look, Joe. I thought they ought to be spilled to you first. I don't know what to make of 'em, exactly, except that it looks better for Lydia. Here—take 'em."

Flash in one hand, Ralston used the thumb of the other to flip open first one sheet and then the other. "For bustin' into big tears, Ed," he breathed, "I don't get it. They're both alike." He read hoarsely:

> "READY OR NOT
> YOU SHALL BE CAUGHT"

And again, like an echo:

> "READY OR NOT
> YOU SHALL BE CAUGHT"

"Gosh, Ed, I do wish I'd found just one of them myself. This town thinks I'm plenty dumb."

Verriker's pipe made a protesting gesture, but the younger man scowled into the darkness.

"I searched her and you gave a look around the room, and before you had quite finished I hurried on into Amberlee's room and started on it. That's the way it was, see. And you started in on him. . . . Still— I get you all right about piping down on Doc and Hawley."

Ralston pored over the papers, examining them as minutely as the uncertain light permitted. "Same kind of typing on both, looks like, and same kind of paper. How come it looks better for Lydia, Ed?"

Verriker knocked out his pipe before he replied. "I know that girl as well as any person in this town, better than she knows herself, far better than her aunt and uncle did. Take it from me, Joe, she's not crazy. Her life with that disagreeable old pair has been unnatural, and it's warped her nature, but fundamentally she's gentle and sweet, and she couldn't have done what's been done in that house tonight."

"I never liked 'em myself," Ralston murmured. "But Doc ought to know—"

"I agree. If Doc Bunting had done the right thing, he'd have had the child away from that poisonous atmosphere years ago. I'm so sure I'm right, Joe, that I'm going to make it my business to find Lydia and prove it to you."

"If we don't find her before morning, Ed."

Verriker groaned. "That's possible, Joe, and no matter what pills Doc thinks I ought to take, I'm going to stick with you till we know. And then tomorrow I'll go on the trail of her note."

"Come on, then. The boys will be waiting for me at the Amberlee place. She could have typed these, though." He tucked the two warnings into his pocket.

"I won't keep it from you, Joe; she knew how to type. I turned her loose on the *Observer* machine myself. Thought it might give her a new interest."

The two men moved off into the darkness.

III

By Monday morning gossip and rumor and excitement were flooding Bly's Landing. Ralston and his force had searched every inch of the Amberlee grounds, including the steep bank that fell to the river, but the fear that had been Peggy Morgan's first, was not realized. No trace of Lydia was to be found.

Most of the town were willing to call Lydia Amberlee a murderess at once, though there were those who mentioned Drummond's uppity new secretary with zest. She'd been alone in the house with Dawson and his sister, hadn't she? She hadn't called for help until she was good and ready, had she? And who was she anyway? Someone from away . . . It was all quite clear, such technical trifles as medical evidence and *rigor mortis* and the undisputed fact that Drummond's secretary had returned to town on the 7:31 train being lightly omitted in the circulation of this theory.

Thanks to Kate Ralston, most of this seeped but slowly back to Peggy, and by that time she knew almost as much as Ralston himself about the progress of the case.

That Lydia Amberlee was responsible for the crimes was certainly a more logical idea. Everybody knew she was queer. It was surprising how many people now announced that they always knew that the reason that Miss Judith had kept her in so close was that she was half crazy. Besides, the Amberlees had never told anybody who her father was, and it was a fact that her mother, Dawson Amberlee's younger sister, had been mysteriously absent from Bly's Landing for months before her reappearance with a baby and that she had committed suicide not long afterwards. Bly's Landing hadn't needed to be told what that meant, no matter how tight-mouthed Dawson and Judith were. And now, Lydia had vanished. There was no doubt; she'd done in the old man and her aunt first. That note that Joe Ralston found didn't mean a thing. She hadn't a friend to visit anywhere, and if she had walked in on anyone in town, they would have heard about it by now. And so on and so on, up Railroad Street and down Main and all over Bly's Landing. . . .

Joe had come in at daybreak, Kate told Peggy as they breakfasted on Monday, and was getting a little sleep before digging in for the day. He appeared for a belated cup of coffee, but said little beyond reporting the negative results of the search. The first problem, he said, was to find

Lydia, but he also intended to reconstruct, if he could, what had gone on in the Amberlee house after their return from church at noon Sunday. Surely, between that time and Peggy's arrival in the early evening, someone would have seen at least one of the three Amberlees, or have noticed something.

In spite of her shocking experience, Peggy insisted that she must report for duty at Drummond's office, Mr. Drummond would not be in himself as he had gone to Washington, and someone must look after mail and telephone calls. Moreover, routine would be good for her.

"Come back here for lunch, then," Kate urged, "and if everything's going smoothly, take time enough and I'll go with you up to your room so that you can gather your things together properly. You might as well pack up and leave the place for good."

By the time Peggy made a trip to the post office and returned to Kate's at noon, she had reason to know that Bly's Landing regarded her as a principal figure in the case that was rocking the town. She felt splashed, she wailed to Kate, with innuendo and suspicion. Kate's quick sympathy and common sense rallied her, but when they were permitted to enter the Amberlee house, guarded by one of Joe's deputies, the chill fear that had gripped her the preceding night was still lying in wait for her. With Kate's help she made quick work of the packing, but as she moved from drawer to drawer and from closet hooks and hangers to the contents of her writing table, she knew without being told that her room and her possessions had been methodically searched.

She worried about that throughout the afternoon. Lew Mason breezed in, demanding an exclusive interview with the star witness. Her taut nerves flared first into sharp anger and then she wept as dolefully as a small child. Lew preferred himself in the role of comforter rather than in that of persistent reporter, and ceased to nag her. Plenty of time for his *Observer* story anyway, and Ralston and. Verriker had both furnished him enough for the first report he had filed with the Wheeling and Pittsburgh papers. This case was going to carry him far. Solacing her with a cigarette and sage but not disinterested advice about sidestepping fresh guys sent down from other papers, he eased himself out. He even snapped on the lock, so that after that no one could barge in upon her.

She was glad to get back to Kate at the close of the day. The house was a friendly haven, in spite of the fact that Kate's brother had surely been the person who had gone over her intimate belongings with a fine-tooth comb. Joe himself appeared for dinner. Kate kept at him until he told her what she wanted to know.

Peggy listened and relaxed somewhat. Of course she was vitally connected with what had occurred, but how silly for her to imagine even for a minute that anyone seriously suspected her. Joe Ralston was including her in what he was telling as though he regarded her as ally and confrere. There were no positive developments, he said. Everything so far was negative. No weapon had come to light, though the report from the p.m. had established the fact that both the Amberlees had been shot by bullets from the same gun, a .32. From the state of the food in the stomachs, it looked as though they had been killed within a half hour after their last meal. As for the time that had occurred, all there was to go on was the fixed habit of the Amberlees' six o'clock Sunday evening tea. Nothing in the house had been disturbed and nothing, apparently, was missing. The cashier at the bank, and plenty of other people, had informed him that the Amberlees never kept much money in the house, and there were no portable valuables except the family silver, which was untouched.

Verriker had given the day to making the rounds of every possible church and former school friend in the entire district with the hope that the "friend" mentioned in Lydia's note might be found.

"The girl had no friends," Kate reminded her brother. "Her very use of the word seems odd to me."

"I know, and Ed realizes that too, but just the same he's being painstakingly systematic about lists of names. The people in her high school class—it's also odd that Aunt Judith let her go to school."

"Just her senior year, Joe. They'd made a point of tutoring her themselves. That was the year I substituted for Matilda Wilcox. I remember, Lydia never took part in anything that went on. She came to school and studied her lessons and that was all. We couldn't even get her to recite, but her written work and examination papers were almost letter perfect. Well, to come back to Ed's hunt—"

"He phoned in at noon—no news, and he's back again by this time. I'm to meet him before the up train runs, so I'll have to hurry. But if he'd unearthed anything he'd have said so."

Nor had Ralston gleaned anything about the activities of the Amberlees during the course of the Sunday afternoon. The three of them had attended church in the morning, but apparently no one had laid eyes on any of them since they turned into their grounds upon their return. Several groups of the congregation had observed the three walking sedately up River Road, and old Mrs. Prescott, who lived on the short street below, had been panting along behind them. When she stopped to catch her breath before turning off River Road, the Amberlees had paused at the front door while Dawson unlocked it. Mrs. Prescott had distinctly seen the top of Judith Amberlee's hat. It was the third season for that felt with the grosgrain stick-up, and you couldn't fool Mrs. Prescott.

The Amberlees kept help, as Bly's Landing put it. There was a cook and a man who did outside work and heavy cleaning inside. But the woman had Sundays off, austerity in Sunday living being part of the Amberlee code, and Jed Combs came when he was sent for, except after the furnace was started. So the three members of the family had had the house to themselves on Sunday.

Ralston sighed as he accepted his second cup of coffee. "No one is known to have gone there during the afternoon, or to have left. The only contact with the outside world that I have come across means nothing. Mrs. Bellifer called Judith on the telephone between four and four-thirty to tell her something about a program for some church affair. She stopped me as I went by the house this afternoon to tell me. She said Judith answered the phone herself and talked in a perfectly natural manner."

"In that case, your problem is: what happened at the Amberlee house between that time and half past six?"

"Sounds simple, Katie, but wouldn't I like to know. . . . By the way, Miss Morgan, before I set out again, I wonder what you can tell me about this." Ralston drew a twist of tissue paper from an envelope and shook its contents out upon his palm.

It looked like two coral beads, but it wasn't. It was two bittersweet berries.

Peggy regarded the spheres of rich color blankly. She would remember in a minute maybe, but what could she possibly tell Ralston about bittersweet berries?

"Found one on the floor near the bed and the other in a trinket box on your bureau," he went on, "Looked kind of fresh to me. Had 'em long?"

Peggy remembered. The berry that she had picked up from the floor near the edge of her dresser. Automatically she had dropped it into something. But she had seen only one berry. She told Ralston about it, but he gave her no clue to his own interest.

So she added, "I've had no bittersweet in my room, though I love the stuff. But Miss Amberlee—"

"I know," Kate laughed. "There was not even a rubber plant or a pot of ivy in that house. Judith was a trial to Marta Bellifer."

Ralston picked up his hat and went to the door. "There's no telling when I'll be back, Kate. Listen to anything you're told, but you don't know anything yourself, see. And, Miss Morgan, Hawley seems certain that he called you no later than ten of nine last night. You still think it seemed later than that to you?"

"But it couldn't have been, could it? And the next fifteen minutes were like fifteen years as I think of it now. Nine-thirteen, my watch said, when I picked it up. . . . It was right, too. I checked it this morning with Western Union."

"Yes, your watch is correct. I checked it myself—last night." A detail which made Peggy shiver a little and feel alone in the friendly Ralston dining-room.

Ralston found Verriker waiting for him at the *Observer* office. His face looked gaunt and tired and he was stretched out in his tilted office chair with his feet on another.

"Well, Joe, looks like I'm stymied on Lydia's note. She's not anywhere in town, and no one saw her leave, by train, car, or boat. She couldn't drive a car herself—guess you know that. And I've checked every family in the county whose young folks ever knew her in school or church. But there's one more thing—one more stone to upturn—no, don't ask me. I'm not going to tell you. I'm going up the line on the next train and when I get back tomorrow, whether I succeed or fail, I'll tell you."

Ralston's nod was glum, but he did not protest. "It's too much for me, I guess, but I'm not going to like it much when they begin riding me."

"They? Who? There are no Amberlee relatives. Nor will the *Observer* view with alarm."

Whatever Ralston was thinking, he let it drop. "So you still believe Lydia had nothing to do with it."

"I do, and I still think I'm going to prove it to you. Just let me finish my job. . . . Get anywhere with the typed notes?"

Joe shook his head.

Verriker scrambled among the papers piled high on his desk and thrust a copy of the last *Observer* at Ralston. "Didn't read us with much care last week, did you, Joe?" His finger indicated the end of Pungent Paragraphs. "Anything click?"

Ralston read the brief item slowly. He looked across at Verriker with a sober face. "Sounds to me, Ed, as if you had received one of the same yourself."

"That's exactly what happened, Joe, and so did two other people, to my knowledge. Wait, I'll show you—"

Again he rummaged through piles of papers and correspondence. "Here it is. Stuck it in my personal pigeon-hole. Ethel and Lew leave that one strictly alone."

Ralston cleared a space on the desk and ranged the three sheets side by side. He studied them for a silent minute. "Um-m, they're triplets, sure enough. Better spill me the whole story, Ed."

"I was told confidentially, Joe, and whether you like it or not, I'm not going to mention names. Not yet, that is. I saw one of the other two. It looked like mine—looked like these the Amberlees got. And all five of 'em read the same way. You've got enough there to go on with, son, and my advice to you is to see where it takes you before any more hell pops."

Ralston gathered the three sheets together, found a blank envelope on the editorial desk, slipped them within, and it into his pocket. "They can be traced. I'm no detective— never had to be one before, and if I can't do it according to Hoyle, I can find out how to get the job done. It's about time for your train, Ed."

The two men walked in silence around to the station. The night express to Pittsburgh thundered in. Verriker

moved towards the steps of the day coach and raised his
arm in his familiar salute.

"I wish it was tomorrow and you were getting off
instead of leaving," was Ralston's farewell. "I'd kinda like
to hear now what you're going to tell me tomorrow."

He turned away without waiting for the train to pull
out. Verriker had not bought a ticket, so Joe did not know
where the search was taking him. Ed always used a mileage
book, though, so there was nothing to be made of that.

IV

Kate Ralston thought Peggy had gone off to sleep. They had
postponed going to bed hoping that Joe would come in,
but at last they had settled down for the night. Then came
Peggy's voice, blithe and fresh, from the twin bed opposite
her own.

"Kate! Wasn't it funny about the bittersweet berries? I'm
so curious it's getting me down. You know—something's
tickling my mind. I can't be sure, but it seems to me that
someone I saw on Sunday had a sprig of it, but where it
was, I can't think. Maybe it was someone on the train. . . ."

"Or this Mack who was so hot and bothered when he
called you long distance tonight. For all that, there was a
huge bowl of bittersweet on the altar rail at church yesterday morning."

"Mr. Hawley's church?"

"Dawson Amberlee's church would be more accurate, my
sweet. Grace Church will probably go under without the
old boy pulling all the strings."

"Honestly, Kate, that man gave me the creeps. I can
well believe he was a blight on Lydia. I tried to talk to her
occasionally, in my big-hearted way, since Mr. Drummond
thought I'd like it up there because she was pretty near my
age. He's a grand person, but he pulled a boner sending me
up there. Where was I? Oh, yes—whenever I'd so much as

look at Lydia, it seemed to me that Mr. Amberlee would appear through a doorway or come stalking through the hall, and Lydia would fairly wilt and edge away. He never said anything, though."

"No, dour and taciturn are good words for Dawson Amberlee."

"And he was always offering me something called the *Mission Field* to read." Peggy giggled. "I wanted to trade him a *New Yorker,* but I never had the nerve. Funny thing, though, he liked the newspaper man, Mr. Verriker, and Miss Amberlee didn't."

"What made you think so?" Kate yawned.

"He was at the house once or twice in the evenings when I'd come in, and the two men would talk—oh, just as anyone would, but Miss Amberlee would always be sitting close to Lydia and before long they'd come upstairs, and once, I think Lydia was crying. That's the time Miss Amberlee locked her in her room. I had just opened the bathroom door and I saw her drawing a key from the door."

"Pleasant people, those Amberlees." Kate was thinking of her brother's parting words. Maybe this was precisely what he had meant.

"She certainly had a neat, lady-like way of being nasty," Peggy went on. "After all the wild talk I've heard today, I'm beginning to understand that household a little better. All I knew when I went up there was that they were a First Family and eminently respectable. I had a quiet room and a good bed there, but that's about all."

"You have to be born and brought up in a town like Bly's Landing, my dear, to be able to stand it. But I don't see that you've backed up your remark that Judith didn't like Ed Verriker. He's always been so good to Lydia. Most of the town has had small patience with her."

"Maybe that's the reason." Peggy twisted about and propped herself up on her elbow. "With me Judith was always mild and quiet and very solicitous about my comfort,

though in a rather formal way, but with Lydia there was
always something about her attitude that was—oh, a sort of
serves-you-right air. If she thought Lydia liked to see anyone, Mr. Verriker, for instance, I think she'd have enjoyed
keeping her away from him. I don't think she liked anybody
who was inclined to like Lydia."

"The poor girl," Kate sighed. "I'm afraid she's done for,
if they do find her. She'll crack up completely."

"Maybe that's what has happened already." Peggy sat bolt
upright in fresh excitement. "Maybe she found them—both
dead, and she ran off, cracked up. . . . It nearly finished
me, Kate, and I'm normal and everything."

"You're a perfect size sixteen and you've got naturally
curly hair, and I do wish you'd go to sleep!"

V

The next day, Tuesday, at noon, just three minutes before
the 12:10 down train was due, Joe Halston appeared upon
the platform. There was a chance that Verriker might be
aboard. Ralston had made a point of noting that the editor
had not returned on the morning local. Joe did not want
to wait much longer to hear what Verriker had promised to
tell him. Ed would have to come across about the two other
fellows too. The mess was too serious for any niceties about
respecting confidences.

Joe had spent the preceding evening on the problem of
the three typed messages that Verriker had turned over to
him. The first thing Tuesday morning he had dispatched
them to Jim Temple in Cincinnati. Jim worked for a private
agency there, whose staff expert could verify his amateur
conclusions. Also, Joe had risked a cautious chat with Matt
Trace at the post office, but it had gained him nothing.
Whoever had dropped the notes into the mail on the preceding Thursday, could not be learned from that source.

At seven minutes after twelve the station agent answered the ring of his telephone and looked out across the platform at the same instant. "Yep, I see him," he said. "Wait. . . ." He stuck his head around the half-door of the baggage counter and called to Ralston. "You're wanted, Joe."

What someone's excited voice told Ralston made his spine tingle. He replied, "Out along Big Rock, huh? Hold everything. I'll be right out. Did you say you'd called the sheriff? Better be standing along the road where I can see you. . . ."

Joe ran from the agent's office across the platform, but the roar of the incoming train brought him up short. He could take one minute to see if Ed Verriker would alight. The instant he saw the editor's lank figure he made his decision.

"An emergency call, Ed, up along Big Rock Run. Come along with me and report on the way."

Verriker gave one look at Ralston's set face and allowed the younger man to hustle him into his car. As soon as they were headed out of town Joe spoke.

"Any luck, Ed?"

"Not a trace. You've heard something. What?"

"I don't know where you've been, but Lydia's up along Big Rock. Dead. Looks like drowning. Got the word just as your train pulled in. That's why I wanted you."

In spite of the rocking car Ralston looked at the man beside him as he relayed this news. A shadow of pain passed over his face and Joe felt his body slump beside him.

"Lydia! No, no—oh, the poor child. . . ."

"I guess that cuts it, Ed. She must have wandered off— afterwards, and then finished the job with herself."

"You mean—suicide? Are you sure?"

"We're on our way right now, to see."

Ralston swerved the car sharply from the main route into the narrow road that skirted the tangled edge of Big

Rock Run. Ed had stood up for the girl all along and now such an end of the matter was going to prove him wrong. Lydia had always been at her best with Verriker; the old boy had actually been proud of the fact. No wonder he looked shot. . . .

"And anyway, Ed, I guess it's all for the best. What a life this town would have led her, supposing she had been cleared of the deaths of her folks. It would have sent her clear off."

"I know, I know," Verriker murmured. "Poor child!"

"Tell me, Ed—the guy that found the body will show up before long. He said it wasn't but a couple of miles up the run—tell me where you thought you were going to find her. I take it that's what you were up to."

The older man pulled himself together. "Yes, that's what I was hoping, and I got off that train, Joe, feeling mighty disappointed and discouraged. But this—this is worse.

"What I'm going to say may surprise you, but I'm going to tell you the whole thing, just the way I thought it might work out. Maybe you won't find it necessary to let much of it go any further.

"For some time I've been trying to do something for Lydia Amberlee. I was up against Dawson and Judith, of course, and that made it hard and uncertain. They'd brought the girl up all wrong, made her queer and differ- ent from other young people. Made her feel guilty, loaded her down with the sins of her parents—you know that old story, though of course you were only a little shaver when her mother killed herself. All wrong, all unnecessary, Joe. Why, you know as well as I do that the town's lousy with bastards and most of them are sitting pretty and getting a damn good time out of being alive.

"But there was nothing at all wrong with Lydia's mind, Joe, and nothing that she may have done to herself is going to make me change my opinion, Thanks to that damned pair of hypocrites, she was neurotic and miserably unhappy, and I made up my mind I was going to snap her out of it. I wanted to get her away from the Amberlee house, away from Bly's Landing. Get her started being a regular person somewhere else. That's the reason I let her peck away at the *Observer* typewriter, though it wasn't often that she could escape from Judith. Whenever she'd come downtown with Dawson he'd park her, so to speak, with me. He dropped in fairly often, you know, because I humored him by running those dreary church pieces of his. Then sometimes he'd go around to the church or the parsonage to tell Tom Hawley what to do next.

"Well, I made hay whenever I had a chance, but it was slow work. It boiled down to this: I suggested to her that she run off—we'd find a way to manage it. Go up to Pittsburgh, say, take a room with a nice human family, and go to business school or art classes or whatever, and just let Aunt Judith and Uncle Dawson go to pot. She was just of age, you know, and they couldn't have hauled her back. I'd have seen that she had the funds to keep her going. But she was timid, afraid . . . think of the years she'd been under Judith's thumb. I'd gone over the plan with her, over and over, and ever since that little Miss What's-her-name came to stay in the house I'd been noticing that Lydia's self-confidence had been increasing a little. So Sunday night, when she couldn't be found, and that note and all—well, Joe, I hoped that was the answer."

Ralston had been listening intently without interrupting this surprising narrative, though his eye had been alert for a signal from the farmer who should be hailing them any minute now.

"So you went up to Pittsburgh last night, huh?"

Verriker nodded. "I'd given her only one address, the people my daughter stayed with before she got married; just the place for Lydia. She wasn't there. I went to the Y.W.

too, and to that girls' club near the Institute and places like that. No sign of her. And, as you know, I'd spent yesterday scouting around here."

"It's a wonder you waited a day, Ed. Seems like you'd have gone Sunday night."

"There was the chance—I couldn't down the thought— that whoever murdered Judith and Dawson, had done in Lydia too. A killer, Joe."

"A killer, yes. Lydia . . . Hey, there's our chap!"

A flapping arm and a scared-looking individual half hidden in the flaming sumac along the roadside brought Ralston's car to a sharp halt. "Down thisaway," the man said, and disappeared.

Ralston and Verriker plunged after him down the steep rough bank to a little flat of gravel at the edge of the slow, muddy water that filled Big Rock Run. A half-grown boy, plainly the son of the man who brought them down, stood looking at a slight object lying on the gravel.

Lydia's body. Ralston and Verriker stared down at the pitiful form with the dank clothing twisted about it. Aside from the grim fact that they were looking at one drowned, there was nothing unusual about her appearance. She wore a dark silk dress and a plain tweed topcoat. Even her plain little felt hat had fitted her head so snugly that it was still in place. Verriker could probably verify it, thought Joe Ralston, but he himself was willing to bet that she was wearing exactly what she had had on when she attended church on Sunday morning. Except for one thing. Through the belt of her coat drawn tightly about her slender waist and held by two wooden buttons, was thrust a trailing branch of bittersweet. Limp leaves still clung to it, but the scarlet berries caught the sun and glowed warmly against the soaked cloth of her coat.

His eyes questioning the bittersweet, Ralston spoke. "Well, what's your story? You say your name's Jarman?"

The man nodded and began a stumbling recital. His boy had come down to the run to look for muskrats. He come runnin' back, along about eleven, sun time, screechin' about a woman caught in the roots of the sycamore there. Jarman pointed at a giant tree from whose roots the stream had sucked away most of the earth. Sure enough, there she was. He and the boy had pulled her out, kinda easy-like, and laid her on the flat. The boy said he wasn't skeered to stay and watch the corp'—she was daid, sure enough, and he hiked off to git help. His woman reckoned he'd better telephone down to the Landin' and the folks where he'd phoned at had heard that they was all lookin' for the Amberlee girl down there. They told him to ask for a man named Ralston, and the first place he called said maybe he could ketch'm at the deepo. That was all he'd done, except to leave word at the sheriff's like Ralston said.

Joe nodded. "Get back up to the road. He'll be right along, likely, and maybe Syd Trasker too."

They could hear Jarman thrashing his way through the brush up to the road. Jarman's boy edged nearer, enjoying the show. Ralston began to question him. "Find her just like this, did you? Decorations and all?" He pointed at the trailing bittersweet.

The boy nodded and licked his lips.

"Anything in her hands?"

"Naw. One of 'em was under a root, like. That's how come she was stuck."

"Show me, son."

Verriker followed them to the sycamore. The boy balanced himself on the smooth trunk and pointed. "Right there," he announced with pride. "Them mud holes is where pap and me stepped, pullin' her out."

Ralston slid along the trunk and bent closely over the thick muddy water, but its murkiness revealed nothing. He cast a questing look about and Verriker promptly picked up a dried, fallen branch and handed it to him. He tried the depth of the water in the eddy under the roots. About two feet.

"It's deeper fur'er out," the boy volunteered.

Ralston peeled off his coat and rolled his shirt sleeve up as high as he could get it, eased himself flat upon the gleaming tree trunk, and thrust his bared arm down into the water. His fingers raked the bottom inch by inch, but he found nothing.

When he had righted himself again and dabbed at his muddy arm with Verriker's handkerchief, he said, "Thought maybe I'd find her pocketbook or something. She looks so sort of neat. Everything's there but her gloves and a purse. They'd likely have been in her bag."

Verriker sighed and walked back to the body. When Ralston joined him he said, and his voice sounded weary, "Maybe they're in her coat pockets, Joe, You look. . . ."

But there was nothing in the pockets of the tweed coat.

Not many minutes after that, the sheriff of the county arrived, accompanied, as Ralston had expected, by Coroner Syd Trasker. It did not take long for the officials to decide that Lydia Amberlee had met death by drowning, whether accident or suicide might be logically disputed, but there was nothing to indicate violence or foul play.

In view of the previous events in Bly's Landing, the sheriff was delighted to turn the matter over to his associate in town, but sure, he'd take a look up the run, just in case. That was his official duty, and if he found anything, why, he'd let Joe hear from him p.d.q.

"You might report about bittersweet along the upper road or the bank of the run," Ralston suggested. "Don't think I noticed any, as far as we came out." His look questioned Verriker, who shook his head helplessly.

"They ain't none." Again Jarman's boy volunteered. "I'd gether it and sell it down to the state road, if they was. Folks buy it, Sundays."

"You hush," Jarman growled. "What's weeds got to do, when they a drowned corp' on hands?"

Joe Ralston was asking himself the same desperate question. What had bittersweet to do with the tragic problem that he and Ed Verriker must solve?

VI

The news of Lydia's death raced over Bly's Landing. There were no longer two opinions. The case was settled. Lydia Amberlee had shot and killed her uncle and aunt, and then, crazy as a bedbug, had wandered off and drowned herself. A bad matter well ended, said Bly's Landing, but went on rattling the skeleton of the Amberlee scandal. Grace Church was packed to the doors for the triple funeral and the Reverend Thomas Hawley sought the aid of his fellow clergy in the conduct of the service. Mrs. Bellifer permitted nothing but somber bronze oak leaves to be used in the church, and most of the leading business places closed for the afternoon. A memorable occasion, altogether.

And one that successfully diverted the attention of the town from the activities of the chief police officer, Joe Ralston. This solution of the case appeared logical to him, so much so that he agreed that there was no need to divulge the plans that Verriker had so hopefully made for Lydia's emancipation.

On Tuesday night, when, rather late, he had found Verriker reading alone in the *Observer* office, he had assured him of his silence. "But Ed," he said, "I'm not satisfied, and as long as you think Lydia did not commit murder, you're not, either. I want to know who killed the elder Amberlees. I want to know what became of the gun. I want to know where Lydia was from the time she was last seen, Sunday noon, until she went into Big Rock some time on Monday. Trasker and Doc Bunting agree that she'd been dead a little under twenty-four hours when found. Where was she

Sunday night and Monday morning? And I want to know who wrote those *Ready or Not* warnings, who sent them to you and Dawson and Judith. And another thing I want to know, Ed—who are the two other people that got them? You going to tell me?"

Verriker creaked his chair about and fumbled among the papers on his desk.

"God help me, yes. But you're going to use your best judgment about blurting out that I put you on to it. I can see it's no time for me to take the responsibility of silence." He fingered something in his private pigeon-hole and thrust a paper towards Ralston. "Here's another of the damned things. Alec Drummond got it the same day I got mine. I saw him this afternoon and he gave it to me. I asked for it. You see, he'd practically commissioned me to see if I could run it down for him."

"Alec Drummond!" Ralston whistled. "The big boy himself. It's a wonder he would let on to anyone."

"Fact is, he talked to me last Saturday night. More steamed up than I ever saw him. Talked kinda big about private detectives."

Ralston stirred uneasily. "I'm no good, I know. This sort of thing needs an expert."

"I discouraged him, Joe. My opinion, you can get somewhere, soon as anybody."

Joe shrugged, an unusual gesture with him. "Well, who's number five?"

"Marta Bellifer. Though you'll find her ve-ry cagey. She didn't even show me hers. Maybe she's burned it up."

"Marta will run rings around me, Ed."

"No more than she'll be in my hair when she realizes I've peached on her."

"I've got to go on, Ed. There's something loose in this town, and I'm going to try to tie the ends together."

"You've asked yourself some pretty good questions, Joe. All about where Lydia went and what she did after—after . . ."

A faint change in Verriker's tone caught Ralston's attention. "I'd like to clear her, for your sake alone."

Verriker drew a sudden long breath and leaned across the desk. "The poor kid," he sighed again. "Maybe you all are right, and I'm wrong. I guess maybe I pressed her too far. She was so pitifully afraid of those damned relatives of hers. Perhaps, after all, she went off the deep end first and killed them. And then wandered off. . . . It could have been like that, though God knows I hate to let her down. Even now, when it no longer matters to her."

There was a long moment of silence in the *Observer* office. Ralston lounged against the side of the high old roll-top desk. He was thinking of berries, bittersweet berries. Verriker relaxed again and his chair creaked. His eyes were half closed and his heart pounded heavily. Doc was right, he was thinking. This wasn't avoiding strain and excitement. After all, it was too late to fight Lydia's battles now.

"No!" Joe Ralston snapped out the word suddenly, and Verriker jumped. "No, Ed. You keep helping me a little and I'll try to work it out. Sure, the easiest thing to do is to say that Lydia is the answer to everything; but tell me this, just how did she manage it?"

"Manage what?" Verriker pulled himself back to the problem.

"The attack upon her uncle and aunt. In the first place, where could she have got hold of a .32? I'm not so sure there's one in town outside of the hardware store, and if Jim Glaye had sold Lydia Amberlee a gun, or anyone else, for that matter, he'd come a-running to tell me. This town's crime-conscious, Ed. I can't believe she'd have known how to load it or use it, either. And also, what became of the gun?"

"In the Big Rock mud or at the bottom of the Ohio. They'll dredge it out some day, when nobody cares."

"Um-m. Another thing, Ed, those bodies up at the Amberlee house lay exactly where they fell. When the first shot

was fired, why wasn't the second person disturbed? Now
don't say silencer. A silencer and a .32 would be just too
thick for an innocent like Lydia to wangle."

Verriker was regarding Joe Ralston with renewed interest. "Dawson Amberlee was a little deaf. Did you know
that, Joe? Growing on him, too."

"At that, how could he have missed hearing a shot fired
only across the hall? Judith's hearing was okay—I happen
to know that. She must have been shot first; that's what
Bunting said. . . . Say-y!" He stopped short, gripped with a
new thought, and his eyes narrowed. Verriker waited.

"Listen here, Ed. Remember that big cabinet in Dawson's room? Radio or victrola or something like that. Suppose the thing was going full tilt. Deaf people always turn
music on way up. He'd never have heard any shot. And then
Lydia, or whoever it was, could have stepped to his doorway and let him have it. It could have been worked, just
like that."

Verriker nodded slowly and let fingertip meet fingertip.
"Just like that, only—Joe, it was Sunday. Unless there was
a church choir on, singing gospel hymns, Dawson Amberlee would never have switched on his radio. He had a good
taste in music, as a look at his records will indicate, but I
doubt if he ever touched them on Sundays. That's a combination contraption in his room, a radio and an orthophonic
victrola together, a fine, expensive instrument. And as for
listening to sermons over the radio, the men on the air
weren't fundamental enough for his soul. You're going to
check up, though?"

"You bet I am, and right now. . . ."

Ralston left the *Observer* office and loped rapidly up the
silent length of River Road towards the Amberlee house,
thinking as he went. As a result, when he turned in along
the shadowed path he came to an abrupt halt. There was
something even more pressing to see to first; he might already be too late. He stopped only long enough to see for

himself that one of his boys was still on duty, keeping away the curious and predatory public. Camera men from the city papers could take pictures of the outside all day long, but from the first he had carefully restricted anyone outside the small official circle who asked for admittance. Again he repeated his orders about letting no one in. No one at all, he emphasized, unless the permit bore the marshal's signature. Then he hurried back to lower Market Street, to the undertaker's establishment that served the police department as a morgue when necessary.

The undertaker was at work in his back room. Ralston was in time to learn what he wanted to know, if there was any way of telling. He asked questions, got technical answers, and went away again with nothing whatever positively proved. True, there hadn't been a mark on Lydia's body, not a scratch, not a bruise. If people were forcibly drowned, they struggled, and if they were pushed down and held under, bruises, even the faintest marks, would show up. But Lydia was such a frail wisp, she wouldn't have struggled much. . . .

Ralston decided to call it a day. He was tired. There was no use in thinking when you only thought in circles. Yet before he could dismiss the case for a night's sleep, two new rounds were to be added to the meaningless revolutions of his thoughts.

The first was contributed by Bunting. The doctor's dusty car turned into Railroad Street just as Joe reached the corner.

"That you, Joe?" the physician called. "I've been out on a slow case and I didn't have a chance to get in touch with you after I heard about the Amberlee girl—not that I was surprised. Suicide was exactly what was to be expected. But I wanted to tell you that yesterday morning, close to noon, I was on my way out to Newt Gowdy's place, way up Big Rock Road. I thought I imagined it at the time and I didn't even slow up, but seemed like I heard a woman's voice coming from somewhere off the road. A laugh, and then something like a yoo-hoo call. Today when I heard the news about Lydia, it came back to me, and I'm reporting it to you for whatever it's worth."

The doctor slipped his car into gear, but Ralston held him long enough to ask, "Whereabouts was it along the road, Doc?"

"As near as I can tell I'd just passed that old trail that cuts in below the back of Drummond's place, but I was going fast and I may have been farther along than I realized."

A woman along Big Rock Road on Monday. Calling . . . calling for help? Near a trail that led to Alec Drummond's lodge.

The second item was waiting for Joe when he entered his house. Kate had left a note propped against the telephone. It was a message from the county sheriff. He had found Lydia Amberlee's pocket-book caught in the bushes along the bank between the road and the water about half a mile above the spot where the body had been discovered. There was nothing in her purse beyond the usual truck. And if the marshal of Bly's Landing wanted bittersweet, there was a vine of it mixed up in the tangled thicket where the pocketbook had been lying. Not much left of it, though.

Joe Ralston's last conscious thought, as he plunged into sleep, was that, proof or no proof, Lydia Amberlee had been murdered.

Part Three
All But One

So, while Bly's Landing gave over everything to savor the morbid excitement of what they thought was the end of the Amberlee case, Joe Ralston plugged along. A question here, a comment there, one bit fitting into another, others contradicting themselves. . . . Yet his conviction grew that there was more involved than the suicide of a crazed girl could account for.

The triple funeral occurred on the Wednesday afternoon. Very early that morning Ralston was on his way out Big Rock Road. He raced his car as fast as the narrow way permitted until he had passed the spot where Jarman had hailed him the day before. Then he slowed, alert to find the places connected with Bunting's and the sheriff's reports. The rough indication of the trail came first. This left the road to his right and wound upward along the side of the hill. It no longer bore marks of frequent use and was thickly overhung with second growth and hazel bushes. There would be at least two miles of it, he recalled, before it came out in a dry rocky gully that formed one boundary of Drummond's land. He climbed along the stony path for several hundred yards to assure himself that there was probably no soft, damp earth in which footprints could have been left.

He climbed into his car again and went slowly on. Somewhere from here on, Dr. Bunting had heard a woman's voice about noon on Monday, and here, just two bends beyond the hidden trail was the spot where Lydia's pocketbook had been found. The sheriff had carefully given him exact directions about that. Joe parked his car as safely as he could on the winding road and turned down the bank to the left towards the waters of the run. The bank sloped gently at first, though the thick underbrush forced him to move cautiously. The ground was littered with fallen sycamore leaves, their brown-flecked gold contrasting vividly with the green of bushes still untouched by frost or the occasional scarlet of sumac. He pushed his way forward and slid down abruptly. The bank had shelved and he almost lost his footing. When he regained his balance he knew he had found the place he was looking for. There was a broken bittersweet vine twisted limply across a small area of flattened, heavy grass, and here were the bushes under which the pocketbook had been found.

Ralston knelt down and examined the small space critically. What did it prove, if anything? The grass and fallen leaves were trampled and broken and the ends of the bordering bushes were many of them bent and stripped. Easy enough to imagine that a struggle of sorts might have taken place here. He peered over the edge. The bank fell steeply to the water. Joe did not need to test it to know that the current eddied sharply in at this point and out again. Bracing himself, he leaned far over. Deep enough to drown anyone. . . .

He climbed back to the road, turned his ear with some difficulty, and set off back down the rutted way, but only as far as the trail where he had first stopped. He left the car again and, after a glance at his watch, made off up the trail. It was not easy going, but he swung steadily upward, his eyes ready for any significant detail they might find. After nearly a mile of the zigzag route which in general bore off to his left, he halted in surprise.

A narrower path turned off, scarcely a path, nothing much more than a divided look between the underbrush. The ground was everywhere hard and dry, but it looked scuffed and walked upon. As well as Joe knew the country surrounding his home town, he could not identify the reason for this faint trail. He plunged into it curiously and found that it was leading at another angle back in the direction of Big Rock Road. Within five minutes it brought him to a rough shack of weather-stained boards, one side entirely open. It looked like nothing more than a hikers' shelter, a crude picnic place. There was a rough table with a length of plank attached for a bench and a circle of blackened stones a few feet out from the unenclosed side, where campers had built fires. But the surrounding brush encroached upon the place thickly; apparently the spot was not often visited.

His first glance reported nothing of interest, but when he walked around the picnic table he saw a twisted bit of paper lying on the inner bench. It was torn as well as twisted. With careful fingers he unrolled it and straightened it out and knew that he had indeed found something.

The weekly bulletin for Grace Church . . . It bore the date of the preceding Sunday, the day that saw the last of the elder Amberlees. Nor was that all. On the ground rolled tightly against one of the supports of the table lay a brilliant red berry, a bittersweet berry.

Joe Ralston had no aspiration to be a sensational detective, but he prowled over every square inch of the cabin and the small clearing as though he were fully equipped with microscope and pocket glass. There was a blackened smudge and a faint trace of grayish dust in the roughness of the board table at one spot, as though someone might have stubbed out a cigarette there, but he could find neither burnt matches nor butts.

When he had finished his search he advanced to the edge of the minute clearing and looked off down towards the road and the run below. He could see neither, but he guessed that he was nearer than it might appear. He stood there looking and listening intently. The mass of brilliant foliage stretched away, unbroken and impenetrable. No path had been forced downward in that direction. His ears caught a familiar sound. A car was chugging along on the road far below. He heard the faint raucous note of its horn.

What comes up could come down, he thought. Bunting had heard Lydia on Monday. Heard her laugh, or call. . . . She was up here, and she was nervous. She'd torn the church bulletin almost in two, twisting it. And if cigarette ash meant anything, she had not been alone. . . . Then she was down in the bushes on the bank just above the water. And lastly she was in the water, drowned.

Ralston had plenty to think about as he drove furiously back to Bly's Landing. He stopped his car in front of Alec Drummond's office and ran up the flight that led to the old-fashioned rambling suite. Peggy Morgan was at work in the first room. She smiled upon him as at an old friend. She and Kate had seen little of him for these two days.

"Mr. Drummond? Yes, he's in. Just a minute. He likes to know who's coming."

Ralston could hear her heels tapping across the second room and into a third. He wondered idly why Drummond wanted to bother with so much space. Though the secretary's office equipment was modern to the last gadget, the room itself was bare and uncluttered, and Ralston knew the place well enough to recall that the same effect prevailed throughout the suite.

Drummond was standing at one of the tall windows that looked down upon Main Street. He pulled forward a stout hickory-splint chair for the marshal and took another himself. He was smoking a cigar, but he offered his caller a cigarette. Joe took it, and wondered whether anybody but Sherlock Holmes ever proved anything from tobacco ash.

"Well?" Drummond demanded.

Joe went right to it. One never knew with Alec Drummond; he might be out on his ear in two seconds.

"I'm working on a matter of anonymous letters, threatening letters. You got this one, I understand." He pulled a paper half out of his pocket and then thrust it back again.

Drummond's eyes flickered, but he drawled his reply. "So Verriker had to run and tell after all. I suspected as much when he asked for the thing yesterday."

"Not exactly. I got something out of him, not much. There have been others, besides yourselves, who received them. Dawson and Judith Amberlee, for instance."

"I see. . . . Think you can swing it, Ralston?" There was something contemptuous in Drummond's voice.

Joe Ralston ignored it. "It's up to me to take a try. I'd like to hear anything you can tell me."

Drummond waved the hand that held his cigar. "Not a damn thing to tell. Utter rot. Always getting tripe like that. Long ago I made it my rule to dismiss such things completely."

"Yet you talked to Verriker about this one."

"What if I did? I talk to Verriker about a lot of things. Smart chap, Verriker. Nobody's fool. Best head in Bly's Landing, not counting my own."

"You heard me say that the Amberlees received similar warnings. And the Amberlees are to be buried this afternoon."

"I don't scare that easily, young man. If threats could kill, I'd have been under the sod long ago." His laugh was quite without mirth, and he waited an instant as if expecting a reply from Ralston. Then he added, "If mine's to be the next funeral, so be it."

Ralston stirred the ash about that he had been depositing in the agate tray before him. "Mr. Drummond, you say you don't mind anonymous threats. I hope you won't mind a couple of impudent questions I'd like to ask you."

"The town policeman doing his stuff. Go ahead."

The scarcely veiled contempt in this comment made Ralston hot, but he forced himself to appear unaware of the slur. "You were in Washington when the excitement broke here in town?"

Drummond answered in sneering detail. "I drove through on Saturday night, registered at the Shoreham on Sunday morning, checked out Monday evening, and was back in Bly's Landing, in my office here, by nine on Tuesday morning. You can ask my excellent secretary to verify that. What I did during my two days in Washington I see no reason to tell you, but I could be checked on every hour of the time. I couldn't fool you, young man."

Ralston nodded gravely. Let Drummond think he was an officious nincompoop; what did it matter? But the effect of his next question was balm to his pride

"Mr. Drummond, how far do your holdings go between the through route and the road along Big Rock run?"

"All of that stretch, from my own private road at the end of the Jug, on to the main highway, and over the ridge where I put the Lodge, down across the gully through to the back road. There's an old trail there that marks the lower boundary on that side. Why do you ask?" He had laid down his cigar. His lips twitched a little.

"Then you must know that there's a kind of picnic shack down in there off the trail but still pretty high above the back road?"

"So there is, now that you speak of it. But what about it?"

"Is it open to public use?"

"I'm not that sort of Santa Claus, as you damn well know. I doubt if the place has been used at all since I built the Lodge. Not bad as a shelter house, though, in the hunting season. I—" He stopped abruptly and laughed again.

"I've just remembered something. I daresay my bark is worse than my bite after all, not that that fills me with pride. Hawley asked me if there was a place anywhere on my land that one of his pious bands could use for a camp supper or a prayer meeting or some such holy purpose, and I told him about that shack. Told him to help himself, but to lead his infant Samuels up from the Big Rock Road."

"I guess you wouldn't know then whether the Young Folks' League has gone on this big bust?"

"What the hell is it to me? Well, if that's all—if I get any more letters I'll come running to you. You have everything so well in hand."

Joe Ralston walked slowly back through the long rooms. He appeared to be checking office furniture. When he reached Peggy's desk he asked her a low-toned, casual question. "This the only typewriter in the dump?"

"Yes, it is. It's new—been here only as long as I have. The salesman carted the two old ones away. Oh—you've made me spoil the sheet. I never hand in erasures to Mr. Drummond."

She ran the sheet from the machine and cast it towards the scrap basket.

"Wasteful," Ralston chided. "If you've no objection, I'll use the blank side to make a few notes." He might as well begin collecting samples of typing; he might have to send a batch to Temple's friend in the lab. Hawley used a typewriter. This afternoon during the funeral, he'd slip into the parsonage . . . but first he ought to round up Mrs. Bellifer.

Nancy and Elaine jointly assured him that mamma was down at the church seeing to the Amberlee flowers. Wasn't the whole thing just awful? Positively too gruesome, according to the chubby one, Elaine, and Nancy said that the kids in the senior English class were going to read *Hamlet* right away, because of Ophelia. The new English teacher had so many cute ideas; Nancy sort of wished she hadn't graduated last year.

"You got a typewriter in the house?" Ralston cut their babble short. "I'd kinda like to get a memo down before I forget the details."

Yes, mamma had one. She did so much committee work, but she didn't like to have the girls use it on account of splitting their nails. The girls flourished vividly stained fingertips. It was locked anyway; mamma always kept her desk locked—she was so business-like, and she carried the keys in her bag. Gobs and bunches of keys, but wouldn't a pencil do?

Joe waved a genial farewell and went on up River Road. He'd have time for a look at Dawson Amberlee's room before lunch. He must have a word with Kate at noon and see Verriker before the time set for the funeral. Verriker would attend the funeral, naturally; maybe he ought to show up as well. Wasn't there a book about that? *Police at the Funeral*. Kate had had it around the house; she borrowed lots of murders from the Bellifers.

With its late occupants lying in state down at Grace Church, no wonder the Amberlee house stood gaunt and deserted. Never again would it be just a house in Bly's Landing. Forever it would be pointed out as the house where it happened. There were to be more places than one to be pointed out before the week was over.

The sub-policeman patrolling the grounds and entrances to the house reported that not a soul had tried to get in, except a bunch of fresh guys from some press service, and they'd got what was coming to them. The silent deadness of the airless rooms did not affect Joe Ralston. He ran up the stairs and along the hall to Dawson Amberlee's room and straight to the polished walnut cabinet that held the strangely modern mechanism for the creation of music. The upper lid was closed; the doors below were shut; there was a light film of dust on the gleaming wood. There would be, since Sunday. He had done what he could about finger-prints in the two rooms on Sunday night, though he knew his was no expert's job. Nothing significant had come to light. Maybe he'd better get someone who was on to all the latest tricks to go over the cabinet.

With great interest Joe inspected the radio dial. Nothing there. It was turned back to zero. That would be quite in keeping with Dawson's old-maidish ways. The volume dial, however, was turned on full strength. He snapped the switch and twisted the dial, and the instrument hummed at once. In a second or so a raucous stock-market report blared forth. Well, that was that. He snapped off the switch; no need to call in the guard.

With equal care he lifted the lid disclosing the space where records could be played. One was still in place. He screwed himself about until he could read its label, gold against scarlet. "The Ride of the Valkyries," a recording by an internationally famous symphonic orchestra.

"Whew, it all fits in. Now let's see. . . ." The arm holding the needle was thrown back. Ralston lowered it without shifting the position of the disc. It came upon the record about an inch from the inner edge of the fine rubber ridges. He fumbled for a button. "I'll have to find out," he thought, "if they ever run down, this kind that runs by electricity. Still, whoever threw back the arm and stopped the music before the end of the record was reached, didn't take a chance of letting the music go round and round. And if it was the radio it would have gone on and on, till all the stations went off the air. Peggy would have heard it as soon as she came in."

He found the control button, and the great music crashed forth, but only for an instant. He had learned what he wanted to know. If Dawson Amberlee had sat beside the cabinet listening to either the radio or the record, it was not likely that he would have heard the shot that killed his sister, nor the steps of the murderer approaching with his own death.

Lunch was waiting for him and Kate was full of questions, but he demanded to know where the Sunday papers
had been stacked and ran through the radio sections of the
two that they had had that day. The only scheduled program
that Dawson Amberlee would have listened to, according to
Verriker, had been on between six and seven, a Wagnerian
hour played by a full orchestra, and broadcast by KDKA.

That discovery gave Joe an extra zest for lunch. At the
table he asked two questions, one of which interested both
Kate and Peggy. The other meant nothing to a newcomer in
town and Kate could draw no inferences from it.

"Any picnics or camp suppers among the youngsters at
the church lately?" he asked, breaking open his third pop-
over.

"There was something said about one week after next,
time and place to be announced. Marta Bellifer's class of
sweet sixteens is planning it. She's always organizing something."

"Um-m. Any more of your quince jelly about, Kate? Any
sort of jelly so it's quince, that's my platform, Miss Morgan.
You looked pretty serene and steady this morning, pounding away at your shiny typewriter. Nerves all right again?"

"Being here with Kate has done wonders for me," Peggy
smiled. "And Mr. Drummond, too. He's been so kind, but
I told him I'd rather stick it out than run away scared. I'm
really crazy about my new job, you know."

"Does he ever run that typewriter himself, or does he
make you do all the heavy work?"

Kate's eyes flashed across the table at her brother's question and Peggy laughed.

"Mr. Drummond typing! I've a picture of that. I've never
seen him touch it, and he'd better not. I don't want anybody
tinkering with that grand new model. It's a joy to use."

"Find your happiness in your work," Ralston murmured
sententiously, "and you'll never bother your boss by asking
for a raise."

There was no one in the *Observer* office except Ethel Erbaugh when Joe lounged in after lunch. The funeral, Ethel explained. She was leaving herself, as soon as it was time. Her brother's wife would save her a seat.

Joe cleared a space at Lew's desk and spread out some cryptic notes that he had accumulated. Most of them concerned the *Ready or Not* warnings, but he'd have to round up Mrs. Bellifer before he would have all the known factors in that puzzle. No use hunting her until after the funeral. In the noon mail he had received a carefully detailed report from the expert whose advice he had promptly sought without letting on to anyone, even Ed Verriker. Bly's Landing could think him a dumb bunny, for all he cared. Temple had returned the originals also, and the report verified Joe's first impression.

The four warnings had all been typed upon the same unmarked paper and by the same machine, one in excellent condition, the type faces showing almost no imperfections. Whoever had done the typing was probably not a trained operator, though the touch had been fairly uniform. Lastly, Temple's expert stated that he was retaining a set of photostats for his further study.

Ralston regarded the outlay hopelessly. He pulled out the sheet he had salvaged from Peggy Morgan's scrap basket and saw for himself what was meant by differences in typewriting. Even he could tell that Peggy's work was entirely different from the four cryptic couplets ranged before him. After he had experimented with the typewriter in the parsonage and had his set-to with Mrs. Bellifer, he'd ask Ed to go over the whole mess with him.

He rummaged about the littered table, found a strip of copy paper, and ran it awkwardly in the *Observer's* ancient model. After several disastrous starts he managed to pick out a message to leave on Verriker's desk.

"Save me some time this evening/. I8ll come around heRe. I8ve got an idea that makeS me sick. JOe."

With the comfortable realization that no one could ever accuse him of typing the anonymous messages, he slipped his note under Verriker's paperweight near an unopened *Times* and followed Ethel Erbaugh around to Grace Church.

II

Ralston stood at the back of the thronged auditorium until the service was well advanced and then he disappeared. As he expected, the parsonage was deserted and, as always, unlocked. The house was nondescript; it was only in his study that traces of Thomas Hawley's personality were evident.

Kate Ralston and her brother had liked Hawley from the beginning of his pastorate in Bly's Landing. So had everyone else. He had allowed Dawson Amberlee to dominate in the conduct of church affairs, but that only showed his common sense. Grace Church was the idol of its most powerful and active member. And Hawley had got along smoothly with the Amberlees without ever appearing to truckle. Too bad about his wife. Her persistent ill health and long stays in first one sanitarium and then another, had forced a bachelor's existence upon her husband.

It had always been a matter of conjecture to the Ralstons that Hawley was content to remain these five years in Bly's Landing. Most of the time he was conventionally denominational, but there was an unmistakable air of sophistication about the man that contrasted oddly with pastoral calls and conferences with Sunday School teachers. A wily old worldling—that had long been Kate Ralston's opinion, and she chuckled to herself at the traces of pagan philosophy that echoed through the sermons that sounded so orthodox.

All this was in the back of Joe's mind as he stood at the door of the study, looking about for a typewriter. The room was well lined with books. Nor were they all theological texts or church histories. There was Wells, and Bertrand Russell and Veblen and Stendhal and Santayana. On the desk there was an opened, marked copy of *The Waste-land* and a volume of Samuel Butler, a first edition, though Joe Ralston was unaware of that. A sheet filled with what looked like an outlined sermon in Hawley's small square script stuck out from between some new magazines. One was the orthodox weekly of the denomination, but the others were quite different.

Not admiring himself particularly, Joe found a sheet of paper and hammered away at Hawley's open typewriter until he had obtained a satisfactory sample of the machine's work. He added it to his collection and slipped out of the parsonage. He took a short cut around the house next door, noted idly that the Bryants were still announcing to transient motorists that they accommodated tourists, and returned to the church just as the last of the procession moved off in the direction of Riverview Cemetery. A group of women pausing at the corner beyond caught his eye. One of them looked like Mrs. Bellifer. Yes, and she was turning up River Road. Strange that she was going home instead of to the cemetery, but now was his chance.

He turned in under her gateway trellis just as she reached the door. "May I have a few minutes, Mrs. Bellifer?" he called.

"I'm frightfully tired—such a horrible strain, this ghastly affair, but . . ."

Marta Bellifer enjoyed her role of being the busiest woman in Bly's Landing. She was at everyone's beck and call, she often said; only the discerning noticed that she did much of the calling and becking herself. Today curiosity topped annoyance as she led the way into her living-room.

Joe seated himself cautiously upon an alarming-looking modernistic chair and hoped that he wouldn't have to manage a tea cup as well. According to Kate, Mrs. Bellifer rang for tea at the slightest provocation.

"A serious business, Mrs. Bellifer, and not over yet," he began abruptly. Maybe that would head off the teapot.

"Poor darling Lydia. After all, a blessed relief. . . ." With great care she pulled off her gloves and began to smooth them.

"I don't want it to happen to anyone else, that's all. Several of you were threatened."

"Several of—us, threatened! Oh, Mr. Ralston . . ." She picked up a fan, which the season no longer demanded, dropped it, twisted her plump white fingers, and again picked up the fan.

"Yes. You got one of the notes, I understand. That's what I want to talk to you about."

"But what has that to do with the Amberlee tragedy? I—yes, I—but I begged Mr. Verriker to say nothing. There couldn't be . . ." There was no assurance about Marta Bellifer. If a woman of her poise could be said to cower, that was what the marshal of Bly's Landing was witnessing.

"Didn't you know?" Ralston's question was bland. "Both Dawson and Judith Amberlee had received warning messages. They read, 'Ready or Not, You shall be caught.' And someone caught 'em."

Hard blue eyes, filled with fear, looked at him. The lips were only a thin rouged line.

"That's why I want you to give me the one you received. I'm tracing them. There's really no occasion for you to worry. I have the matter well in hand."

"You mean, you know who—who sent it?" When she spoke Joe could see that most of the color had been sucked from her lips.

"Have you any idea yourself? To tell you the truth, I can't see any reason for anyone threatening you, of all people." He might as well lay it on thick.

"No reason in the world. I—I scarcely gave it a thought."

"Liar," Joe said to himself; but aloud, "You've still got the message?"

She fumbled with the handbag that she had had in her hands as Ralston encountered her at the door. Its taut bulging lines reminded him of the keys that her daughter had lamented over and he wondered where the sacred desk and typewriter were. Plainly not in this gaudy room. And she was carrying the letter around with her too. The hand that extended the folded sheet towards him was trembling.

"The envelope," she murmured. "I tore it up. It was just plain typing like this. Mailed right here in town, with a two-cent stamp."

Ralston merely glanced at it and tucked it away in the pocket with the others. Then she went on, jerkily. "You'll let me hear, of course—as soon as you find out— Oh, I can't believe—why should anyone torture me so?"

Suddenly she leaned forward. Her blue eyes had lost some of their fear and there was a note of resolution in her voice. "I recognize that you are doing your duty, Marshal, and I must do mine as well, no matter how distasteful. From what you tell me about warnings like this having been received by the Amberlees, I realize that you know more than you have made public. Probably what I am going to say may already be known to you as well, but I see that it would not be right to withhold anything that might be of help to you. . . ."

"Marta's beginning to sound like herself once more," thought Joe. "Will all in favor give the usual sign. . . ." But he listened with due respect.

"Perhaps the person most concerned has already spoken, but I've heard no hint that it's generally known." She pursed her lips, her eyes intent. "It's only this: has Mr. Hawley reported anything to you about Lydia? About her movements after the time it was supposed she was last seen?"

"What do you know, Mrs. Bellifer?

"Oh, it's so likely that I'm quite mistaken, but you know how little things come back to one. I've been going over everything, trying to help. . . . Sunday afternoon late—almost five-thirty, I'm sure—I was hurrying home from a call on poor old Mr. Cardew, and as I crossed the street at the parsonage corner, I saw someone at the door. I thought it was Lydia Amberlee—it reminded me of Lydia, but I paid almost no attention. I don't even know whether she was going in or coming out. There was so little light, you know. But of course Mr. Hawley would hold back nothing. . . ."

Ralston's murmur appeared to agree with that supposition, or at least he hoped it did. "You're sure of the time?" he asked and then rose to go.

"Oh, but wait—" Her peremptory tone pulled him back. "There's something else I may as well tell you—you're handling this dreadful affair so marvelously. It's the merest trifle, but it may help to fill in your picture. I took Miss Melody for a little drive on Monday afternoon—the poor little soul gets out so rarely. I went up Big Rock Road because the foliage always changes there first of all, though of course if I'd dreamed what had been happening—" She shuddered appropriately. "About half way along the road— I'm sorry but I have no more definite idea than that and it may not matter anyway—there was a parked car. It was empty, but I thought at the time it was Mr. Hawley's coupé. Not that I noticed the number or anything, and one sees those small cars everywhere."

That was what a Packard did to the Mrs. Bellifers, Joe thought, and again rose to go. He tried to pin her down about the time. Not long after three, she thought; she had called for Miss Melody at a quarter of.

So it was up to Joe to make out a time-table for Tom Hawley, but he wasn't going to give Marta Bellifer the satisfaction of knowing it. If she were throwing dirt on the preacher to divert attention from herself, that was another idea to follow up. But Kate would have to help him out with any dark secrets that the lady might be hiding.

He was so engrossed for the remainder of the afternoon, working out a time schedule, that Peggy and Kate were already at dinner when he appeared, but he felt that he had got somewhere. The result of his labors was folded away along with the anonymous warnings and the samples of typing, ready to spread before Ed Verriker a little later. Ed would laugh at him. It was a little hard to believe, but unless Mrs. Bellifer had been lying as fast as she could talk, he had certainly caught something by the tail. Good old Tom Hawley had come across like the gentleman he was when he stopped him to ask a few questions on his way to Mrs. Lukey's just now. It had been no trouble to pump him; a parson's Sunday schedule can be backed by his entire congregation.

Before Joe left the house for his evening rounds, he mentioned to Kate his curiosity concerning Mrs. Bellifer's private life. She was to review the town's scandals and unearth anything she could that Marta Bellifer might prefer to keep hidden. There must be some reason for the woman's fear-filled eyes. Kate Ralston knew that her brother would explain himself in time and did not detain him with exclamations.

His official duties properly looked after, it was later than nine before Joe appeared at the *Observer* office. Verriker was waiting for him, at ease in his creaking chair.

"Well, son, you and I are both about to be run out of town. You stepped on some mighty important toes today, Joe."

"And I'm about to come down on some others, looks like. I take it you've heard from somebody."

"I have. Both Alec and Marta Bellifer hot-footed it around to me. What in hell did I mean, giving away letters and sacred confidences to irresponsible young fools, meaning you? Drummond was reasonable on the whole, but Marta!"

"The lady's scared, and would I like to know why! What did you tell 'em?"

"Tried to calm 'em down. Assured 'em that if anyone was likely to be bumped off it would be me, seeing that my name was on the little list and everybody knew that I was working with you. Neither of 'em will admit there's any special reason why they should be caught, ready or not. To come right down to it, I can't put my finger on anything either, and I know as much about what the town sh-sh's as anyone. Know too damn much, Joe. Why I've been a kind of repository for all the stuff that's too unsavory to be printed, ever since I got the paper going."

Joe spread out his collection impressively. Verriker at once picked up the time-table, for the typed warnings had lost their first thrill. "What's this?" he asked. Ralston let him study it without comment.

Sunday, 5:30 p.m.	Hawley leaves parsonage for tea with the Ely family. OK Lydia at the parsonage door. Mrs. Bellifer says so. Not certain.
6:00	Two people (Dawson and Judith?) have tea at Amberlee house. OK—medical evidence.
6 to 7	Wagnerian program on air. No evidence that Dawson's radio was set for it. Wagnerian record in place for playing and not played through when needle thrown off. No evidence as to when played.
6:15-6:45	Judith and Dawson shot.
6:30	Young People's Hour at Grace. Hawley present. Did not open the service, but spoke briefly during course of meeting. The Ely boy drove Hawley down,

but he dropped off at the parsonage before coming on to the meeting.

7:30   Evening service starts. Hawley in pulpit throughout. OK

7:31   Miss Morgan alights from Pittsburgh train. OK

7:40   Miss Morgan chats with E.V. near Grace Church. OK

8:30   Close of church service.

8:45   Hawley back at parsonage. OK

8:50   Hawley telephones Amberlee house. Miss Morgan uncertain about exact time.

8:55   Miss M. calls Hawley after discovery of Judith's body. Couldn't have been later.

9:00   Hawley arrives at Amberlee house.

9:05   Miss M. calls Bunting. Might have been a minute or so later.

9:13   Miss M. puts on watch. OK

9:20   Bunting arrives. OK

9:30-9:40 Ralston, Verriker, and Trasker on scene. OK

Monday, time uncertain, but at some time no later than Monday noon Lydia Amberlee and some other person were together at Drummond's shack on the hill above Big Rock

Road. Evidence of bitter-
sweet berry, twisted church
bulletin, and cigarette ash.

about noon—Dr. Bunting, passing along
road below shack, hears a
woman laugh or scream.
His statement.

no later than early afternoon—Lydia
Amberlee drowned in Big
Rock Run. Pocketbook and
bittersweet vine found between road and water close
to steep slope above deep
pool.

not long after 3—Hawley's car seen
parked along road, near
this spot. Mrs. B. says so.

Tuesday, 11 a.m.   Lydia's body found about
half mile down Big Rock
Run. Branch of bittersweet
in belt of coat.

Also note—   Drummond had given Hawley permission for young
people of Grace Church to
use shack. Plans for outing
not yet completed.

Verriker went over this document more than once before
he said, "It doesn't prove a damn thing, Joe. And why are
you loading Tom Hawley with dirt?"

"I don't know. Only—well, he seemed so insistent about
the time of his call on Sunday night. It struck me he overdid it, yet he didn't hesitate to admit that for ten or fifteen
minutes around six-thirty, at the time when the shots were

fired, he was alone in the parsonage. He says he was hunting for something by a guy named Jerry Hopkins that he
wanted to use in his evening service. The Ely kid went on
without him. The parsonage is only one long block away
from the Amberlee house. Hawley shoots too. There's a cup
from a gun club, target hitting or something, on top of one
of the bookshelves in his study."

"He'd have no motive, Joe."

"We know of none. Still, he'd put up with the Amberlees
ever since he came here."

"Any oldtimer in town has done as much and more, long
before Tom Hawley took Grace Church."

"Good lord, Ed, I'm only trying to be objective and
impersonal. I like Hawley. He's a swell guy. I can't see it,
really. But who knows anything about anybody? A man of
Hawley's type must have suppressed a lot to turn himself
into a preacher in a one-horse town like this."

Verriker picked up the time schedule again. "The OK's
mark the items you're sure of, I take it. Did Hawley verify
Marta's story?"

"He knows nothing of any visit Lydia might have made
to the parsonage. He'd gone out the back way and left by
the alley. The Elys say he was right on time for tea and he'd
been invited for half past five. Mrs. Bellifer appeared to be
guessing about the time, if she were telling the truth."

"Which I doubt, Joe."

"Lydia had to be somewhere Sunday night, Ed. And
the parsonage is never locked. Say, she could have—" He
stopped short.

The older man gave him a steady look and then an
almost imperceptible nod. "And Monday, Joe?"

"Hawley's car on Monday along Big Rock . . . He was
there, he says, trying to find the cabin Drummond had told
him of. He wanted to see what it was like before he announced the picnic. But he says he couldn't find it."

"It was early this morning, you say, that you found—er, your three pieces of evidence there." Verriker again consulted the time-table.

"Take a look at the sheet I typed on Hawley's typewriter, too. I'm afraid the type looks something like the anonymous warnings."

Verriker fumbled with Joe's display without comment. The younger man moved restlessly about the small room, even penetrating into Ethel Erbaugh's prim corner, the only neat spot in the place. His worried murmur developed into, "The evidence doesn't amount to a hill of beans. I can see that. It's only suspicious. And I don't think anyone would get far trying to trap him into a confession. I'll have to dig into a motive."

Verriker shuffled the papers together and looked up. "See here, Joe. You ought to consider the rest of us. Marta Bellifer and Drummond and me, though I thank you for your kind OK's after my name. Even Bunting, just between us two. He's in and out over town all the time and everybody takes him for granted. He made himself indecently clear about Lydia. And he was out Big Rock way on Monday."

"Doc Bunting! Horsefeathers! Might as well suspect you. And Drummond's out completely. He was in Washington Sunday and Monday."

"That's a fast car he drives."

"All right. Where were you at six-thirty Sunday? And Monday noon?"

"Lord, I don't know. Guess you could find out if you tried."

"Mrs. B's another one who is always flitting about. Somehow I don't mind cracking down on that dame. I've a sneaking feeling she lied about Hawley."

"Her husband was out of town over the week-end and the girls are always partying around. If only someone had seen a mysterious stranger snooping about. . . ." Verriker sighed. "These people are our old friends."

Ralston slumped into a chair again. He looked unhappy.

Verriker went on. "You mentioned a trap a minute ago. Let me be one. I think there's something to what I told Alec and Marta. Whoever's behind this knows that I'm working with you, and I received one of the pesky notes. If this unknown person gets the idea that we've tumbled to anything, I shouldn't be surprised that I'd be the next target. I suppose I know too much for my own good about a whole lot of folks in this town, though Lord knows I try to forget what I can't print."

The lounger man regarded him gloomily. "Maybe that's an idea, but just what will I know when you're found drilled through by a bullet? Ed, that .32 would help a lot if it would obligingly come to light. But we've got a nice, deep river here and it would be a life work to fish for a gun."

"Here's another thing I'd like to do, if you'll let me. You've done some good work here, Joe." Verriker tapped the pile of papers before him. "Maybe this typing will tell us more than we think. I know how to spot imperfections in type faces, of course, and I'd like to study these samples."

Joe Ralston hesitated, but only for an instant. "Help yourself. There's Hawley's and Drummond's and even yours there—you asked for it, Ed." Ralston grinned at Verriker in apology. "But nothing from Mrs. Bellifer's typewriter nor from the hundred other machines that could be rounded up in town. Better check on the business class up at the high school."

"Doc has one too. Ever see him pounding out a case record on that old double-decker of his?"

"Go as far as you like collecting samples. You won't need my fancy time-table, though. I'll keep that. I didn't make a copy, and that interval before Hawley slipped into the young people's meeting sort of worries me."

Joe separated the schedule from the typed papers and rose to go. Verriker followed, snapped out the light swinging from the ceiling, and slammed the door behind them.

As they parted at the corner Verriker said, "Drop around tomorrow, and I'll report like an expert."

"Don't let anyone pop you off first, Ed."

Neither noticed that it was Dr. Bunting's car that pulled away from the opposite curb just after they separated.

III

On Thursday Lew Mason had the thrill of tearing out the front page of the *Observer,* full as it was with what had been its biggest story to date, the deaths of the three Amberlees. The events of Sunday, of Tuesday, the pompous funeral on Wednesday, the activities of Marshal Ralston, interviews with the Jarmans, father and son, even one with Peggy Morgan—Lew knew the big papers would by-line that, for Peggy had scrupulously kept her promise not to talk with any other representatives, of the press. Everything had been covered. Words of encomium from leading citizens concerning Dawson Amberlee. Resolutions from the Garden Club and the Woman's Society of Grace lamenting the loss of Judith Amberlee. A sober, neighborly editorial which Verriker had composed and titled "Death by Violence"; another expressing quiet confidence and pride in the labors of the police official in charge, which both Kate and Joe clipped without mentioning the fact to one another. A guarded account of the conclusions so naturally drawn from the suicide of Lydia—no other word was used except suicide. That had been the decision reached by Verriker and Ralston. Nothing at all about the *Ready or Not* messages, partly a sop to Drummond and Mrs. Bellifer, but mainly the desire of the two men to continue their investigations without public interest or interference.

Every item to be published was well in hand by Wednesday night. Lew and Fult Dodge made up the paper Thursday morning, except for Verriker's Pungent Paragraphs. The column would be finished by the time Lew came in from lunch, Verriker promised. Too many damn phone calls. It wasn't easy being pungent this week. Maybe he'd run the piece everybody tried to quote and always got wrong. "Glory of October," he'd called it. After all, tomorrow was the first of the month.

Ethel Erbaugh and Fult went to dinner. Lew breezed out to the drugstore for sandwiches and coffee. Peggy Morgan always went to Ernst's for orange juice until this week when Kate Ralston had taken her under her wing. Lew felt that he was coming along with Peggy. Verriker was alone in the *Observer* office, staring at a half-filled sheet of copy paper. He ought to telephone Mrs. Lukey. She didn't like to keep food back for boarders who skipped meals. But he had no interest in eating. Poor Lydia. . . .

Two hours later when Lew came galloping in, eyes popping and too excited to write, Verriker naturally was not there—he'd been called by Joe Ralston at once, as soon as he'd got the message about what had happened up in Alec Drummond's office. However, the copy for Pungent Paragraphs was neatly weighted down on Lew's desk.

"Fult! Fult!" Lew shouted. "Tear it all out. Deader number four will take over everything. Up in Drummond's office. Hawley!"

Peggy Morgan preferred a late lunch hour. This had not pleased Mrs. Lukey, and therefore Peggy had taken to slipping out at one for a double order of orange juice at Ernst's Drugstore. On this Thursday Mr. Drummond had come in before ten and had kept her busy with dictation until twelve, when he had left. He would not be in again, he said. He was driving up to Wheeling to keep an appointment with the man from Tri-State. After he left, Peggy had various routine work to take care of before she could settle down to getting out Drummond's letters. It was perhaps three minutes of one when she left the office. Just as she picked up the book that was ready for the bank, there had been a telephone call, but that delayed her only a minute or two.

"I'm sorry," she explained. "Mr. Drummond is not in the office. He has left town for the rest of the day. . . . No, I'm sure he will not return today. If there's no message . . ."

Peggy stopped at the bank before turning in at Ernst's. She had been firm with Kate that morning. Hot biscuits and honey, the whole toothsome gamut of Kate's cooking three times a day, and she'd not be a size sixteen much longer. At the bottom of the steep wooden flight leading to Drummond's suite she had met Mrs. Bellifer, nervously pulling off her gloves. She hadn't blinked an eye at Peggy's new hat. On her way up to see the dentist, she murmured; she'd just lost a filling.

Ten minutes over the orange juice at Ernst's, listening to Lew Mason's line, and then she had agreed to run off with him for a twenty-minute breather. Lew could take Jip's car, parked right behind the store. They had a nice run out the Blue Lick Road and she promised to try the speed-boat next week when it would be full moon. She told him she was still thinking about the Marietta-State game.

It was only a quarter of two when they got back and parked Jip's car exactly where they had found it. Peggy said good-by to Lew and ran up the steps to get back to her letters. Lew stood looking after her and thinking it was funny how some girls managed never to let the seams of their stockings twist around their legs, and then he crossed the street. He was buying cigarettes in at Cardy's when his reportorial eye caught sight of Joe Ralston's lunge up the well of the stairway he had so nearly climbed himself. But Peggy had discouraged his further attendance upon her.

Peggy had glanced across the hall as she thrust the key into the lock that guarded the outer door of Drummond's rooms. The dentist's sign said OUT and the door of his office was closed. That made her think of Mrs. Bellifer. Snotty way she had, always asking if she knew the So-and-So's in Sewickley.

She opened the door, hung up her hat, and walked through the second room into Mr. Drummond's private office. There was some correspondence in a folder on his desk that would have the addresses she needed.

A man was lying slumped forward across the wide conference table, one out-flung hand still clutching a revolver.

Peggy screamed and flattened herself against the door. Not again. . . . God, not again. . . .

It wasn't Alec Drummond. She inched forward a little and tried to see, conscious of broad heavy shoulders and dull black oxfords.

It was—it couldn't be! The preacher. Mr. Hawley.

She fled back to her own familiar, unhaunted quarters and picked up the telephone. "I'm keeping my head," she thought. "I'm doing the right thing this time. Joe Ralston. . . ." She even remembered his office number. Kate had relayed it so many times during this harried week.

Ralston was with her before the end of the next five minutes. She kept at his heels as he crossed the long rooms and stood looking down at the body for an instant before he raised it slightly. "Don't look," he said.

Thomas Hawley had been shot through the chest. "Right to the heart, shouldn't be surprised. Looks like he did for himself. Good old Tom. . . ." Suddenly Ralston bent over the gun, but he did not remove it from the lifeless hand. If Peggy Morgan had not been so near hysterics, she might have found his expression somewhat chagrined.

Next he picked up the telephone. The doctor was out; his wife was vague. The coroner, however, he got at once, and then, after an instant's hesitation, he called the *Observer* office. By the time Verriker and Syd Trasker pounded up the stairway, Lew Mason was at their heels.

Well pleased to function without sharing authority with Bunting, Trasker went briskly to work. Ralston turned back to the outer room where Peggy had remained, a heap of misery. "Snap out of it, girl, and tell me your side of it."

She managed a brief and surprisingly coherent statement. Joe listened with a blank face.

"Um-m. Drummond left for Wheeling at noon. In his
car. You went to lunch an hour later and were back within fifty minutes. And you say it was Hawley himself who
called just as you were leaving?"

Peggy nodded. "He seemed disappointed—and kind of
anxious when I said Mr. Drummond would not be back, but
he left no message."

"You mention you were leaving for lunch?"

"No."

"Lock up when you go out, do you?"

"This door, yes." She indicated the main entrance from
the strip of corridor at the head of the stairs. "It's the
only key I have. Mr. Drummond always has the other doors
locked from the inside."

Joe Ralston looked worried. Each of the other rooms
had its own exit. "Carried the keys himself, I suppose. Any
extras?"

Peggy knew of none.

"See anybody around as you left or came back?"

"Not a soul just now when I came in. Lew Mason was
with me as far as the bottom of the steps. And only Mrs.
Bellifer on her way up to the dentist's when I left."

"Joe! Trasker wants you." That was Lew, quite delighted
at his small part in the scene.

In Drummond's office the coroner had just withdrawn
the gun from the dead man's hand and he and Verriker were
leaning over it. The editor gave a long whistle of surprise.

"Looks like a .32 to me," Trasker said.

Ralston made no comment. Verriker caught his eye and
pointed. "Make anything of this, Joe?" From his tone it was
evident that he did.

Across the dark butt of the weapon there was an unmistakable dull reddish smudge. Not blood. Paint. A smear of
long standing.

Trasker was reporting pompously. "Not dead an hour. . . . But it's suicide. No question of that. Glad to have Bunting's opinion, of course, or that new chap's. Lord knows why Tom Hawley would want to shoot himself, but that's what he's done. Gun right in his hand—"

"Don't touch that gun, Syd!"

The coroner began a speech about knowing his business, he guessed, but neither Ralston nor Verriker was listening. With his opinion of himself at a new low, Joe was hastily assembling some scattered memories. No wonder Ed had recognized the revolver. Wrapping it carefully in his handkerchief, he signaled Verriker to follow him from the room. "Try to locate Doc Bunting," he called back to Trasker and Lew.

"Right after Decoration Day, wasn't it, Ed?" he masked in a low tone when the two had halted in the center of the middle room. "That drummer who reported that a revolver had been stolen from his car?"

"Looks like it to me."

"Neither of us ever saw it, Ed, but this is a .32 and it's not likely that one out of a million would have the paint mark on it. You ran a piece about it in the paper, remember? Dig it out of the files for me, and I'll check the dope I got from the chap at the time. I did what I could when he came to me with the story, but I didn't get anywhere with it."

"Joe, who stole that gun?"

"That sure might be the answer to everything."

"But not Tom Hawley. Suicide. . . ."

"Wait till I see what this gun has to tell, and the files on that traveling man."

"And Drummond, Joe?"

The marshal nodded soberly. "Yes, and how Hawley could have got in here when the place was locked, and who heard the shot—"

He came to an abrupt stop. Peggy had told him that Mrs. Bellifer was on her way up to the dentist's as she left. In any case he'd have to step across and talk to Dr. Hotchkiss, the only other tenant on the upper floor. The storeroom below Drummond's suite, had been unoccupied since the depth of the depression. The Niftie Giftie Shop was under Hotchkiss's office. Miss Towner seldom missed anything.

Ralston might have sketched his plans to Verriker had not the editor pointed out another possible factor in the situation. "The sound of the shot, Joe. What about the one-twenty freight?" He gave his head a backward jerk, but Ralston did not need to be told that the railway tracks ran at an angle behind the Drummond Block. "Freight's been picking up right along since early spring. When a long heavy train runs through I can't even hear the presses. If I wasn't such an old die-hard I'd have moved the *Observer* office long ago."

"I've got to check everything, and I'm starting right now. I'll drop around in a little while to pick up that story you had in the paper." Ralston moved briskly on toward Peggy's office and Verriker called to Lew Mason. There would have to be a quick writeup for tomorrow's *Observer*. SUICIDE OF GRACE PASTOR . . . Ghastly, but he'd tell Lew to take care of it.

Ralston worked fast. Peggy Morgan looked so much herself again that he changed his mind about sending her home to Kate. She could handle the telephone calls, she assured him, and besides, Mr. Drummond would expect her to stand by.

"If he should come in, give me a ring at once," he instructed her. "I'll be—somewhere."

Dr. Hotchkiss was just entering his door as Ralston stepped into the hall. He'd been gone since twelve-thirty, he stuttered, and looked sickish as he comprehended the marshal's curt statement of what had happened across the hall. There was, of course, no one in his waiting room when he left, and as he had no appointments until three, he'd used the extra time at home, cutting his front lawn.

"No one o'clock appointment?" Joe queried sharply. "Okay. Suppose you look to see if anyone was here while you were out."

The dentist peered about his waiting room as though he expected the worst. "Just—just as I left it." He trotted into the operating room and bleated with dismay. "Someone—look!"

Ralston leaped at the note propped conspicuously against a row of small bottles on the swinging tray beside the dental chair. Together they read:

"Dr. Hotchkiss: Call me for your first free time. I have lost a filling. M. Bellifer."

"Guess that's your business, after all, and not mine," Joe said evenly. All officials of Bly's Landing were familiar with Mrs. Bellifer's bold, mannered signature. Peggy's report checked all right; now for the Niftie Giftie.

He had no luck there. Grace Towner had closed the shop between eleven-thirty and a quarter or twenty after twelve, while she ran home for dinner, and right after she got back the loveliest woman had stopped in—someone touring through who had seen her sign, and she'd stayed for a long time, maybe an hour and a half, looking at knitting books. Miss Towner helped her select a design for a sports outfit and she'd even bought the yarn and everything. The nicest order, Grace beamed. She'd put it on the needles for her. They'd been at the back of the shop the whole time and not a soul had come in to bother them. Yes, she remembered hearing the freight run. You couldn't hardly hear yourself think.

Ralston hurried on. His next job would be in his own office, looking up the complaint a traveling salesman had made concerning his missing revolver. That ought to take him places. But first, how about the parsonage? This was Thursday. Would there be anyone there? Joe knew nothing about Hawley's domestic arrangements, but surely someone came in now and then to keep the house going. And there was Marta Bellifer. It might be interesting to break the news to her of Hawley's death.

In brisk decision he chose the shortest route to River Road and the Bellifer establishment. It led him along the short street where the parsonage stood, serene under the autumn sun. In beautiful Christian trust, the door was seldom locked. Ralston stepped inside, first giving the bell a long ring. If anyone was working in the service end of the house, he'd soon know it. But the house was unoccupied. Swiftly Ralston looked through the rooms. He could see nothing, even in the study where he had browsed the afternoon before, that appeared at all out of the way. Nothing to indicate what had taken Thomas Hawley to Drummond's office after learning from his secretary that the man he wanted to see would not be in. And not the slightest trace anywhere in the house to back up the wild possibility that Lydia Amberlee might have been hidden in the parsonage on Sunday night. . . . He returned again to the study. Well, if Hawley's private papers and letters that choked his desk had information to yield, there would be time for that later. Cautiously he snapped the lock as he closed the door behind him. Just as well that no one else walked in and out, as he had.

At the Bellifer house a properly attired maid appeared at the door. She smiled at him amiably; he had known Bessie Peters all his life. Mis' Bellifer was layin' down, she informed him. She wouldn't like it if she was to call her.

"I'm afraid you'll have to, Bessie. It's mighty important—serious. But don't scare her. It's nothing about her family."

That turned the trick with both Bessie and her mistress. "You're to come up here," Bessie called from the landing. Ralston followed her into the room where the wide-spread civic and social activities of Mrs. Bellifer were undoubtedly organized. Before he had a chance for any shenanigans with typewriter and paper, the lady appeared, wrapped in a vast

Chinese silk kimono. She might have described herself as looking pale and interesting; Joe Ralston labeled her scared as hell.

"I thought you should be informed at once, Mrs. Bellifer. Mr. Hawley committed suicide early this afternoon."

She gazed at him blankly. "Oh! I thought— You mean our preacher! I thought—maybe you had I found out something about—my letter." Relief flickered in the blue eyes, but only for an instant. Then came suitable shock and horror. "How—how dreadful! Suicide! Our dear pastor—why, I can't believe you!"

"Yes, Mrs. Bellifer. He was found in Drummond's office, just a short while ago, with the gun in his hand."

"In Alec Drummond's office! No . . . Why, I saw him myself, this morning."

"You saw Drummond?"

She shook her head, but her face had gone blank. "No, I meant Mr. Hawley. He was perfectly all right. In the study, at the parsonage. It was about the programs for the Women's Society. Mr. Hawley has always cooperated wonderfully. This has been a frightful shock. . . . If you will—"

But Ralston had no intention of excusing her yet. "I want a few facts from you, Mrs. Bellifer. You went up to Dr. Hotchkiss's office at one o'clock. You will remember that you met Miss Morgan at the foot of the stairway."

She nodded. One hand began to caress her cheek. "A filling. . . ." she murmured.

"Yes. I know. How long did you wait in the dentist's office?"

"Not very long—I don't remember. I left a note. I am going to be out of town for the week-end, and I don't like to let dental work go. But it is impossible for me to sit around and wait— I'm such a busy person, and the doctor's sign said OUT."

"Why didn't you give him a ring at home? You knew where he'd be at noon."

"I never thought of that. How stupid of me. With the telephone right there—"

Joe waved his hand, indicating that it was only a trifle. "Notice anyone around while you were there? Anyone coming up the stairs, or about Drummond's side of the hall?"

She gave him a sharp look and ceased to act the role of a distraught lady. "Not a soul, Mr. Marshal."

"Had you closed the dentist's door behind you when you went in?"

"I daresay, but I'm not positive. I can't remember such things."

"Of course you were in the inner office, too, leaving that note and all. . . ."

"Yes," she agreed brightly, though again her eyes glinted warily. "And in there I couldn't have heard or seen a thing."

"Except the down freight, I'll bet." Joe laughed. "Everybody in town hears it tearing through."

"I recall hearing it— When the League takes up its anti-noise campaign, I promise you . . ."

"Well, that's all, Mrs. Bellifer. Sorry to have to disturb you while you were taking a nap, but you people at Grace will have plenty to see to now. I figured you'd like to be told at once."

"Yes, indeed. I shall call Mr. Ely myself, and we must wire the Bishop—"

Joe interrupted. "And you'll be in town over the week-end, of course. You'll be needed."

That brought another glint from the ice-blue eyes. "My duty is here, unquestionably. But, Mr. Ralston—" She had risen and now laid her hand upon his arm. "Surely you can understand how shocked and disturbed I am at this dreadful news. There isn't—there couldn't be—I mean, that letter?"

"Don't give it a thought, Mrs. Bellifer. I have that matter well in hand. If Hawley had been hounded in the same way, I should have uncovered the fact by this time."

But, he thought as he raced back to his office, that was just one other little thing that he'd have to be sure about. The papers in Hawley's desk. Tonight would be a good time, unless the traveling salesman's .32 took him elsewhere.

IV

Ralston did not search Hawley's desk that evening. It got done in time, as a minor routine job, but the clergyman's private papers had nothing to do with the solution of his problem. Before the close of Thursday, the day of Thomas Hawley's death, it was far more necessary to act on the statement made by Alec Drummond.

On his way to his own quarters, Ralston looked in at Drummond's. A curious crowd was milling about on the street below and pushing up the stairs, until the marshal stationed a man to clear the way of all except those with authorized business with Drummond, his secretary, or the police. Within the rooms, he found that Trasker had seen to the removal of the body. Peggy Morgan was doggedly working at her letters. Dr. Bunting had not been located; she had heard nothing from Drummond. She gave him promptly the name of the Tri-State man in Wheeling whom he had gone to see.

"I'll be in my office for the next half-hour," he stated, "in case you want to reach me," and left.

Peggy could have grown hysterical again. Since Sunday night, hurry calls to the police had left their indelible mark upon her. If there should be another . . .

Back in his official headquarters Joe Ralston ripped into his files. There it all was, under the date of the second of June. A man named Leland B. White, wholesale electrical supplies, Cincinnati, had stopped overnight in Bly's Landing. Possibly because he had known the Mansion House of old, he had lodged with Mrs. Bryant, who had been taking tourists ever since the beginning of the depression.

There was something there, maybe. Grace parsonage was next door to Mrs. Bryant's.

Joe went on with the notes. The next morning, after breakfast furnished by Mrs. Bryant, White had driven away. Parkersburg was his next business stop. He pulled in at a filling station at the lower edge of Bly's Landing and while his car was being checked he had rummaged idly through the pockets of his roadster. He had at once discovered that his revolver was missing. The boy at the pumps had told him where to find the town police and within ten minutes he was reporting his loss to the marshal.

White's permit to carry a weapon, his driving license, all his papers were in proper order, and Ralston had promised his immediate action. A promise which, so far, he had been unable to keep. He had searched the Bryant garage with the fascinated attendance of a visiting small boy—it was really silly to suspect Mrs. Bryant—and had raked the town, but no trace of the missing .32 had come to light. He had even passed word up and down the river, together with the number of the gun and the one distinctive item of description that its irate owner had provided. There was a smear of dull red paint along one side of the handle.

No wonder Ed Verriker had given a long whistle of surprise when he saw the gun still clutched in Hawley's hand. It was the identical weapon that had been stolen from Leland B. White. Paint or no paint, the numbers corresponded. And its owner had insisted that the revolver was in the car when he locked it after running it into place in the Bryant garage on the night of June first.

Who had stolen it? Or was the vital question, after all, who had used it? He was the wise guy, all right, so largely announcing to Ed that he didn't believe there was a .32 in town. The two of 'em had sure slipped up not remembering about White's stolen gun.

With great care Joe packed the .32 together with the bullets that had killed Dawson and Judith Amberlee. As soon as Trasker sent over the one that had ended the life of Thomas Hawley the package would be dispatched to the ballistics expert in Wheeling. The rush report that he would ask for might answer a lot of questions. If all three had come from the same .32, his time-table and the black marks against Tom Hawley might have to make more sense than they did at the moment.

He pulled the sheet from his pocket and looked at it, frowning. If the people who knew what had happened were all dead—Dawson, Judith, Lydia, Hawley—how could guess-work ever settle anything? Marta Bellifer's stories—a scared woman will lie, and there was fright gnawing at Marta Bellifer's smug soul. Still, Hawley could have been somewhere besides in the parsonage study during the twelve or fifteen minutes at the beginning of the young people's service on Sunday night. But why . . . . why? There were the papers in his desk and there was the chance also that some of the boys and girls at the meeting might have something to tell him. Surely somebody had noticed the entrance of the preacher.

Ralston reached for his telephone and called Peggy Morgan. No news. Okay, he assured her and said she could reach him around at the *Observer* office next.

The *Observer* office was roaring with excitement. Even Ethel Erbaugh's hair was beginning to string. Lew and Fult Dodge were yelling back and forth over the new make-up. Verriker was trying to handle a long-distance call from the *Times-Star*. He was gray with fatigue. When he saw Ralston his eyebrow indicated a paper tucked under the desk lamp. It was the *Observer* for June 4.

Lew Mason had probably written the story about the traveling salesman and his stolen revolver. There were no facts in it that Ralston had not known. There could scarcely be; he had provided the data. However, as faithfully as Bly's Landing read the town's weekly, everybody in the place had been fully informed that a .32 was missing. Whoever had stolen it or whoever had found it had certainly not been interested in the reward that Leland B. White had offered.

Ralston's eye wandered down Ed's Pungent Paragraphs. Joe thought Ed's stuff ought to be put into a book, like Eddie Guest's. With sincere admiration he reread a brief paragraph.

"'. . . and no questions asked.' Very comfortable words, those, when you have something that isn't yours and don't want to do much explaining about it. There was once a nice young fellow who tried to steal a car. He didn't quite make it, but no questions were asked. And there was the girl who didn't come home one night. I never asked her any questions either. If your paragrapher asked too many questions, he'd be reduced to making up the valuable information he puts into this column, a mental strain that would soon wreck his health. Vacations at the Greenbrier are too expensive."

After all, it didn't make what you might call sense, Joe thought, but that was the way Ed wrote.

He stuffed the paper into his pocket. "Be seein' you, Ed. Later, when you're not so rushed."

"Tomorrow, Joe, about that typing. I haven't forgotten. There's been too damned much to take care of today."

"Anybody wants me, I'm around at Trasker's," he called back. The third bullet should be ready by this time and the package be put into the up mail.

Peggy Morgan still had nothing to report from Drummond. Joe had not explained to her or to anyone that he had already called the Tri-State office in Wheeling only to be told that Drummond had been there and left. He had arranged that the instant the big car should be sighted on the streets of Bly's Landing that he be informed. Also, a man was still stationed in the building, who had been ordered to tell Drummond what had happened in his office that afternoon and to inform him that the marshal wanted to talk to him at once. Joe had even remembered Tim out at the Lodge and had left a call there.

He was at dinner and had not properly finished Kate's peach cobbler, when a telephone call came. It was Drummond himself, speaking from his office. He had just got in. If Joe Ralston wanted to talk to him, he could get the hell down there. He wanted to get out to the Lodge for dinner.

Ten minutes later Ralston was facing Alec Drummond across the very table upon which Hawley's body had sprawled. Drummond took the interview in hand at once. The half-wit at the door, he said, could tell him nothing more than that. Hawley had committed suicide in his private office that afternoon. And just what did the town marshal of Bly's Landing expect him to do about it?

"First, I expect you to listen while I state a few facts, and then I expect you to answer a couple of questions and give me what assistance I ask for." Joe would not soon forget the slurs he had taken the day before.

Drummond took an appraising glance at the younger man's sober face and steady brown eyes. "It's your lead, Joe. Go ahead."

Briefly he related what was known concerning the finding of Hawley's body. "You left at twelve; Miss Morgan an hour later. The doors were locked. Hawley called asking to see you just before Miss Morgan went out. Within the next forty minutes he had got in here, somehow, and was found with a gun in his hand that I have already succeeded in identifying."

Ralston's last words created the first sign of personal interest on the part of Drummond, but he asked no questions.

"Those are the facts," Ralston continued. "Here's the first question. Do you know what Hawley might have wanted to see you about?"

"Church finances, at a guess. He always has his little tin cup out."

Joe chanced a shot in the dark. "Maybe he wanted to talk about that little shack above Big Rock."

"Your guess is as good as mine." Drummond was imperturbable.

"My second question. How could he have got into this suite?"

Drummond waved his cigar lazily. "My charming secretary can probably answer that."

"She cannot. Her key is accounted for and her story is straight. Besides, I'm asking you." For some reason Joe felt anger stirring.

Drummond drew a key-case from his pocket. "These were with me. This one is the mate of the one I gave Miss Morgan. These fit the door that leads from this room to the back exit and the door from the middle room to the hall. You say you found them both locked, at that."

"Duplicates?"

"Naturally. Right here in this drawer." He swung around to his desk and pulled open a small compartment. The keys were there.

"You use the other outside doors much?"

"Oh, I frequently ease myself out from this office, and an occasional caller, too, if anyone else is waiting in front. I can't remember when I last unlocked the middle door."

"Um-m. Good locks, too, nothing you'd collect at the five and dime. . . . Well, looks like that's a tough one to crack. Another question. Keep any sort of gun up here? I've issued you a permit or so, seems like."

Drummond could not deny that but he declared there was nothing of the sort in the rooms. His arsenal, such as it was, was housed at the Lodge. He never carried a weapon. "Search me and the place here and my car," he offered generously.

"You forget I've got the gun that killed Hawley."

Again Drummond asked no question.

"Now for the touchy part, Mr. Drummond. You'll understand I'm just doing my duty and all that." Ralston let his voice drawl, but his eyes meant business. "Where were you between twelve and two this afternoon?"

"So it's not suicide. . . . Of course, with your limited experience you may not know that such questions are out of order for suicides. But I'll tell you, Joe, and then you can have the fun of checking up on me."

Joe kept his temper. Drummond cast aside his cigar and settled back in his chair, his eyes meeting Ralston's.

"Not five miles out of town I developed a short in the car. I pulled into a wayside garage, that place just the other side of Cherry Island. The chap there said he could fix me up, but I'd have to wait until he finished the job he was working on. It was a dirty hole to loaf around in, so I started off to find a phone. The delay meant that I had to call the man I was going to see in Wheeling. I made the call from a lunch counter joint at the Cherry Island landing, and then, Joe, I took a nice solitary ramble through the beautiful autumn countryside. Flaming hillsides, hazy skies, scarlet maples—we tough-skinned tycoons soften surprisingly when we let ourselves draw near to Mother Nature's heart."

But he dropped that mocking tone at once. "I got back to the garage just as the mechanic had the car ready and I drove away at two-thirty. There, I've presented you with an extra half hour."

"You left your office at twelve. Drive out of town at once? How about lunch?"

"Buttermilk and a sandwich at Ernst's first. It was scarcely twelve-thirty when I noticed the trouble with the car."

Ralston got to his feet. "That's all for now, Mr. Drummond, and I'm much obliged for your cooperation. If you'll just let me out this door, I can save a little time with your short-cut myself."

Drummond had not called it a short-cut, but once more he made no comment. He fished for the proper key and stood aside as Ralston stepped out. Joe heard the lock click behind him.

This door did not give upon the main upper corridor of the building. It had been several years since Joe Ralston had poked about at this end of the Drummond Block, but in an instant or two his memory had recalled the general arrangement. Maybe it was too late for fingerprints now—he'd been a fool not to think that far when he had first come on the scene. Now he had to go on with what he had just started. He was standing in a small square landing. There was a door opposite. Guarding its knob with belated care, he tried it; it was locked. It presented no particular mystery, for it was the back entrance to that part of the building occupied by a moribund fraternal group.

Before him was a steep, narrow flight of stairs. He ran silently down their length, quite certain that he had recalled correctly where he would find himself at the foot. Not an alley exactly. It was the B&O right of way that cut at an angle from the station and Railway Street toward the road-bed along the river through the lower end of Bly's Landing where the drifters lived. The back wall of the Drummond Block hemmed in one side of this stretch of tracks, the lower windows boarded up, those of the lodge rooms above dustily curtained. Across was the totally blank side of the hardware store and the high-fenced corner of the Mountain State Lumber Company's yard. Just now the cindery space lay quiet and deserted. It was so still that Joe could hear the presses over at the *Observer* shop beyond the hardware store.

He slipped around the corner of the Drummond Block into an authentic alley and so back to Main Street. He'd check Drummond's glib story at once. It wouldn't take long to run up the road toward Cherry Island. He'd have to wait till morning to talk to the Tri-State people again. He already knew that Drummond had kept his appointment, but he might as well verify the call from the hot-dog stand and the time of his arrival in the Wheeling office.

He'd been plenty dumb about fingerprints that afternoon. He'd been careful enough about the gun, and a clear case of suicide doesn't call for a general dusting of powder over everything. He'd tried the two locked doors himself and now all he'd find would be his own marks. Ed should have stood by him better than that.

A brief delay in his Cherry Island expedition wouldn't matter. He raced back to his office, got out some rarely used equipment, and took himself back again to the rear entrance he had just left. He tiptoed up the stairs; no use to advertise his return. As rapt as a small boy with a mail order detective outfit, he proceeded to dust the entry door-knob and the adjacent jamb and panels with the powder. Nothing whatever showed up. In rueful distrust of himself and his outfit he went through the same procedure with the opposite door, the back way into the fraternal shrine. Again he drew a blank. He experimented with a fresh print of his own on the baseboard. Every ridge and whorl returned to him.

As he drove out of town, five minutes later, on his way to find a garage mechanic and a hamburger chef in the neighborhood of Cherry Island, he was thinking that there were two ways of looking at his recent activities. Either the doors in the back entry had been untouched for so long a time that no traces of prints remained, or someone had carefully wiped them clean very recently indeed.

He thought backward again. Hawley commits suicide in a room to which he could scarcely have admitted himself. If the story told by the man who possessed the keys held up, then that man was out of the picture. If the .32 in Hawley's hand had been used on the Amberlees, then it was pretty clear why Hawley had committed suicide. If somebody had deliberately cleaned off the door-knobs, then Hawley had not committed suicide. . . . . .

Round and round, and none of it made sense.

V

A couple of wayfaring cars had just pulled in to claim the
attention of the Jack Sprattish individual who ran the
lunch-shack opposite the Cherry Island wharf boat. Joe
Ralston paused only long enough to ask him how late he
stayed open. "I'll be stopping on my way back before long,"
he promised, and drove on. Not more than a half mile farther he came upon the garage. It was closed, but there was
a light burning in an unpainted house on the other side of
a bone-yard of derelict cars.

A voice hailed him from the narrow porch as soon as
he had brought the roadster to a stop. "Shop's shut for tonight. A body's got to have some time to hisself."

"Okay by me, buddy, so long as you're the guy that runs
the joint." Joe's voice was cheerful.

"Well, say, if it ain't Joe Ralston from Bly! And still
drivin' the same old crate. Them 33's were darn good cars,
at that. Sit down, Joe. Plenty room on the top step. The
middle one's busted."

"Little matter of business, Red. Thought I'd get right
after it before it got cold." He looked around. The lighted
room of the small house appeared deserted.

"After a stole' car again, I'll bet. Seems like I'd ought to
git me a police badge myself."

"You had Alec Drummond's new Lincoln in the shop
this afternoon?"

"I sure did. Right after dinner he pulled in. Nothin' so
much wrong, but it took a pesky while to find the bit of
wirin' that made the short. I never did work on that model
before."

Ralston went on to inquire what Drummond had done
while the job held him up, and Red Gaynor verified the
statement Drummond had made. He'd walked back toward
Cherry Island in search of the nearest telephone and he
reappeared at the garage almost two hours later, just as
the big car was ready to roll out of the shop. He'd come

in lookin' kinda hot and with his shoes all dusty, like he'd been walkin', and he had picked hisself a nice bo-kay of bittersweet.

"Lots of that growing all along here." Ralston's comment sounded idle.

"Not unless you climb back up the hills a piece. The kids keep it cleaned off along the road. They do a big business, sellin' it."

"So that's the last you saw of Drummond and his new car?"

"Yep, he headed straight up the river, and, boy, can that baby ever burn up the road!"

"So long, Red. I've got to beat it back to town, but I just wanted to check up a story."

"Any time, Joe, any time. . . . Look out—that's the kid turnin' in."

The incoming and outgoing cars avoided each other adroitly, and just in time Joe recognized that the kid was Red Gaynor's younger brother and helper at the garage. He hailed him. It wouldn't hurt to hear what he might say. The kid said, yes, he'd watched the big-shot walk off down the road just like anybody. He'd even used his thumb a little. At least he was pretty near sure he'd thumbed hisself a ride before he got to the bend. Anyways, he'd seen a car with a outa state license, a '35 Plymouth, slow down and pick up someone.

Turning that over in his already puzzled brain, Ralston went on to the lunch-shack, now deserted of custom. The proprietor, a man from beyond Woodsfield on the Ohio side, whom Ralston knew nothing of, listened to his questions and replied curtly but intelligently. Yes, he remembered the man who came in to phone, but he didn't know who the guy was. Plenty of jack, judging by his clothes and the bill he left to cover the phone call. Toll call up to Wheeling, but he hadn't paid no attention about who to or what he said. And then he'd walked away, down towards

the wharf, though he wasn't just so sure about that. No, he
hadn't got out of no car when he come—he was just walking
down the road, and he hadn't really noticed what become of
him after he left.

Ralston inquired about the ferry. Ves had just made
his last trip over to the Point—wouldn't be over again till
morning.

The out-of-state Plymouth and Ves and the ferry, if they
were to be used at all, would have to wait, until morning,
along with what the Tri-State office in Wheeling could tell
him. Joe made the short run back to Bly's Landing debating the further wisdom of theorizing so wildly. The next
day would surely present him with certain necessary facts
that he could only guess at tonight. Besides, he was dog-
tired and it was after ten o'clock. When he had completely
checked Alec Drummond's alibi, when he had heard from
the ballistics expert, when he had conferred again with Verriker about the typed warnings, then he would know more
certainly which set of contradictions to discard. After he'd
checked with the boys on duty, he'd hunt up the remains of
Kate's peach cobbler and send himself to bed.

Kate and Peggy had convinced themselves that it was
chilly enough for a fire and were installed in comfort before its valiant crackling, "In here, Joe," Kate called as he
came through the hall. "Peggy's remembered something that
sounds deliciously creepy. No, there have been no messages
to worry you. Only a call from Rena Bunting a while ago.
The doctor had just come home and hoped you could wait
till morning. I suppose she meant about Mr. Hawley."

Joe dropped into a chair and stretched his legs. "Yes,
that can wait. Syd Trasker'd just as lief Doc would stay out
altogether, and there's no possible reason to doubt Syd's
report. I must say, girls, if it's warm enough to have the
windows open, it's too hot for a fire."

"Just a matter of morale, Joe. Peggy has had more than
her share this week."

"Then why remember creepy things?" The marshal's brown eyes smiled across at the girl tucked snugly at one end of the deep davenport.

"I do try not to dwell on all the horrors of this awful week, and I suppose I did almost forget about this man I saw on Sunday night. I know I thought of it when you first questioned me up at the Amberlee house, but what had happened there was so much more important. I mean, I didn't want to ramble all over the map."

"Don't ramble now, Peggy. Tell him."

And so Peggy told Ralston about the man who had hurried out of the short dead-end street just below the Amberlee house.

"He crossed River Road, as though he might be going towards a car. I didn't actually see him, only his shoulder and arm. He was carrying a bag. Like a doctor's bag. I mean, not a traveling bag."

"Hm-m. Nothing creepy about that. Probably was Doc Bunting himself."

"Anyway," Kate concluded, "the Amberlees had been dead an hour by that time."

"There you go, Kate, and I am trying to forget," Peggy wailed. "I'm going to bed and if I have a nightmare, it's going to be your fault."

Kate vanished with Peggy but reappeared later, just as her brother dragged himself out of the depths of his chair where he had been gazing trance-like at the dying fire. He began to snap out lights. "I've assigned you to Mrs. Bellifer, Kate, and you might add this one, too. Talk to Rena Bunting about Doc's calls Sunday."

VI

By Friday afternoon Joe Ralston knew much more than he had tried to speculate about the night before. The Tri-State people in Wheeling verified the time of Drummond's arrival.

He had telephoned ahead that a little car trouble was delay-
ing him. He had been in their office between four and five
on Thursday afternoon. The secretary who talked to Joe
had such a pleasant voice and was so clear and exact in her
replies that he decided her common sense would not snap
under a more pointless sounding question.

"Did Mr. Drummond have any sort of posy in his
buttonhole when he came in? A piece of bittersweet, for
instance?"

The pleasant voice never faltered. "No, he didn't, but
he brought me some. A very beautiful spray, dripping with
gorgeous berries. I have it on my desk this minute."

Also, Ralston had a report from Leland B. White, who
wired that he had never laid eyes on his revolver since the
night of June first last, that for the past two weeks he himself had been in California on vacation, and that he would
make a point of stopping off at Bly's Landing on his next
trip up the river to identify and claim his stolen property.

Furthermore, a quick run up to the Cherry Island ferry
had led only to negative results. Ves, the ferryman, had
seen nothing of Drummond the day before. Sure, he knew
Drummond. He'd once been a rigger on one of his productions. When an accident had carried away most of his right
hand, he'd got damned little out of Alec Drummond. He
knew him—the bastard. Ves spat.

Before turning back to Bly's Landing Ralston again had
a few words with Red Gaynor's kid brother. The boy was
no more certain about his story than he had been the night
before, except that the car that had slowed in response to
someone's signal must have carried a state license that he
didn't see often. He'd have known for sure if it was Ohio or
Pennsylvania. Whoever it was that got the lift might have
been Drummond and again it might have been someone
else. He just couldn't be real sure. . . .

Grimly Ralston admitted that Drummond's alibi, if that
word should be necessary, was not being knocked out.

Since the afternoon before, Bly's Landing had done nothing but dissect the suicide of the pastor of Grace Church. From the flux of gossip, rumor, and obscene speculation with which the town was washed, Ralston had counted on picking out a few minor facts. He knew that Mrs. Bellifer had been at the parsonage. Mrs. Bryant next door had seen her go in. The Weldons across the street had seen her leave at a quarter of twelve. No one reported noticing any other callers. No one had seen Hawley leave. All that Joe could be certain of was that the preacher had telephoned to Drummond's office just as Peggy Morgan was leaving at one o'clock.

Consequently Ralston climbed the stairs to the telephone office for an official interview with the chief operator, a thin-faced widow who had a significant way of twitching her lips when gossip was being dished, but who had long since proved that she could keep her mouth shut.

She answered Joe's questions without hesitation, as one official to another, but her information was of little value. She had been on duty throughout the preceding morning and had taken Mr. Hawley's calls herself. There had been three or four rather early around nine o'clock. She hadn't listened in. Joe knew she'd outgrown that long ago, but she was pretty sure they were just routine pastoral inquiries, like asking about old Sam Huey, who had his second stroke, and about the little Carter girl's broken arm. After that, she didn't think he'd used his phone again until after twelve, when he'd called the *Observer* office. She remembered the Drummond call, though she wasn't just real sure now what time that had come in. What calls had been put in for Hawley she did not know. Joe could talk to Esther Briggs about that. Esther would be back on the other board at noon.

Esther Briggs was thrilled to cooperate with Marshal Ralston, but her mind was more or less blank about yesterday morning's calls. Joe was afraid it was more his suggestion than her own memory that assured him that she did

kinda recall Mrs. Bellifer's ringing the preacher. Yes, she
had. . . . Esther repeated after a period of intense concen-
tration. Just after she'd asked for the number of Mr. Drummond's place up on the hill. That was a private number, not
in the book and they always noticed it, for the excellent
reason that it was the only unlisted one in Bly's Landing.

Had Mrs. Bellifer got the Lodge when she called, Joe
asked, thinking of fixing the time. Peggy had said that
Drummond had been in his office at ten. Yes, she had, but,
Esther added virtuously, she had trained herself to pay no
attention to what people said.

If this information was reliable, and Joe felt that it was
reasonably so, then Mrs. Bellifer had called the Lodge before
ten and the parsonage after that hour. She had gone to the
parsonage at eleven. She would say that her call to Hawley
had been to advise him that she was dropping in for a conference about programs. It was her word for it either way.

But the odd thing was that no one, in spite of the high
exchange of talk, reported having seen Hawley on his
way to Drummond's suite. Marta Bellifer might be lying
her head off, but Main Street between one and two of an
afternoon was not unpeopled. Yet no one had seen Thomas
Hawley on his way from the parsonage to the Drummond
Block.

Persistently Joe Ralston's mind swung back to the rear
stairway leading to Alec Drummond's private office. A
locked door bare of fingermarks. . . .

Either Hawley would have had a key to admit himself or
someone had been waiting to admit him. The only one who
rightfully possessed a key was Alec Drummond. If Drummond had been there, instead of communing with Nature
five miles up the Wheeling road waiting for Red to repair
his car, then had Thomas Hawley committed suicide?

At this point, with his self-opinion at a new low, Ralston
hurried around to the undertaker's. He'd made a routine
examination the afternoon before, but early last evening

he'd been shown something that might click a little more plainly now. Once more he looked at the contents of Hawley's pockets. He picked out a bunch of keys and loped back to Drummond's rooms.

Brusquely, without explanation, he asked to see the duplicate keys he had been shown the evening before. With a slight shrug, Drummond pulled open the drawer and produced them. Joe stalked to the exit door, but the key he inserted was not the one Drummond had just handed him. It was one from Hawley's bunch. It turned the lock and opened the door.

"I'll have to take these keys for a little while, Mr. Drummond. Don't worry; they won't get away from me." He left by the back stairway, so that if Drummond had anything to say to that, he didn't hear it.

Back in his office Joe compared the two keys. Both had opened the lock of the back door, yet there was an obvious difference between them. Drummond's was beyond question the official duplicate that had come with the lock. The one on Hawley's ring looked as though it had been recently cut, and not by an expert, and it was bare of stamped number or trade name. A hole had been punched through the finger end so that it could be strung on a ring and from that opening toward the edge there ran a distinct scratch. A fresh, sharp scratch.

Joe was about to set out on a run for the only locksmith in Bly's Landing, when an incoming telephone call presented him with decisive news. The ballistics man from the Wheeling police department had found that all three bullets submitted had been fired from the same weapon, the .32 that had accompanied them. Photographs were being dispatched forthwith, and of the fingerprints also, as Marshal Ralston had requested. Their man had found but one set of prints, thus verifying the marshal's first examination.

Joe banged the receiver into place. Hawley's prints. The Wheeling pictures would tally with his own amateur record taken at the morgue. He slumped back in his chair and let his mind race round in circles again. If Lydia Amberlee hadn't killed her aunt and uncle, then who had killed Lydia? If Hawley had committed suicide with the same gun that had killed the Amberlees, then he must have shot those twin pillars of his church. If Hawley possessed a key to Drummond's office, then Alec Drummond's alibi for Thursday was as good as it looked in spite of the out-of-state car that might have given him a lift in the direction of Bly's Landing. And anyway, Drummond could have had nothing to do with the crimes of Sunday night. . . .

Joe ran his fingers through his hair and sighed. It was high time to dump some of the puzzle on Ed Verriker. He'd talk to him before he went around to the parsonage and began looking through the preacher's papers. Leaving word where he expected to be he made off to the *Observer* office.

Fult and the boy were alone in the shop, busy with a rush job. The paper had gone into the mail on time and the usual Friday afternoon calm had descended upon the place. Fult didn't know where Lew had beat it to; the boss had gone home. Said he was going to bed. Looked sick enough to stay there.

But when Joe climbed the lower hill to Verriker's nondescript dwelling, he found Verriker stretched comfortably in bed, still dressed except for shoes and coat, collar and tie, and enjoying his pipe, a plate of Grimes Goldens, and Samuel Pepys equally.

"Naw, I'm not sick, Joe. Just tuckered out. It's been quite a week. I was kind of looking for you. What's new?"

Ralston bit into an apple. "Plenty, Ed, but most of it cancels and the rest doesn't make such good sense. Thought I'd run over the mess with you and then take another turn at that typing. Those *Ready or Nots*—I'm damned if I'm so sure they have any bearing at all on what's been happening."

"Maybe not, Joe, but I've been studying the lot—well, I made a few notes that may only add to your worries."

Verriker pawed about through a tangle of newspapers that covered his rumpled bed without finding his memoranda.

"First, before I forget it, Ed, who else in this town besides Cap Anderson might turn out a key?"

"Lots of woodshed tinkerers around. Ask Fult. He fixes us up around our shop. Ethel couldn't get her cellar door open after some visiting kid threw the key down the cistern, and Fult turned out a slick job."

"I've been thinking I ought to have a couple of spares—that's all." Joe threw what was left of his apple core into the brass kettle that served Verriker for an ash tray. No doll dishes for him, he explained to his daughter every time she criticized his domestic arrangements.

Joe found himself a box of matches in a torn carton handily kept on the window sill, and returned to his case. Briefly he reported the developments since their last conference. "Now, Ed," he concluded, "this is what has me chasing my tail:

"If Lydia killed her uncle and aunt and then killed herself, why didn't she keep the .32 to finish the job with? She was drowned, not shot.

"If Hawley found the gun in Dawson's room before anybody else appeared on the scene, was he so bent on killing himself that he took a time like that to steal a weapon to pop himself off with? If so, why did he wait for four days before he acted? Why did he stage the event in Alec Drummond's office and not his own study? Was it just sheer chance that he got up to Drummond's place without being seen? And why should he possess a key to the back entrance of Drummond's office?"

Ralston paused long enough to throw down on the bed the key he had taken from Hawley's ring.

Verriker's long fingers closed upon it. "Seems like Alec might know something about that, Joe. This the one you found on Tom? Fult could cut you one like it easy enough. Guess that's what was on your mind a few minutes ago."

Joe was still intent on his puzzle. "If Hawley committed suicide, then the reason might be, until another motive comes to light, that it was he who killed the Amberlees. There's a slight crack in his Sunday night alibi and he was out along Big Rock Road on Monday. And his motive for killing them will have to come to light, too. . . .

"If Hawley didn't kill the Amberlees, who did? I am not convinced that Lydia drowned herself. I am not convinced that Hawley shot himself."

Verriker made an abrupt, protesting gesture, but the younger man overrode him. "You see, someone could have admitted Hawley through the back entrance into Drummond's office. And dead fingers have been pressed on the handles of revolvers before this. The outside knob had been wiped clean as a whistle. I admit I bungled the inside knob and door frame, but it certainly looked like nothing else but suicide when I walked in. I've tested the key since. Mine and Hawley's prints were all I found.

"Now Drummond possessed the keys and it's not a complete impossibility that he could have got back to town during the time he says he was picking posies with Mother Nature on one of the hills, be-you-tiful hills of West Virginia. But why should he shoot Hawley with the same gun that killed the Amberlees? I regard it as a complete and utter impossibility for him to have had anything to do with the deaths of the three Amberlees. His alibi cannot be questioned. So—"

"So if Hawley did not commit suicide, I take it you're still looking for someone who can account for all four deaths. But, Joe, doesn't it look as if Tom must have killed himself?"

"That's the easiest way to look at it. I could get by with that answer, I suppose, if you back me up. . . . But here's another question that's eating me. If Hawley did not commit suicide, why was he murdered? Because he must have had something on somebody. Now who's the biggest, broadest target in this town? Alec Drummond, and you know that as surely as I do. Hawley was trying to see Drummond just before he got his and damn it all, Ed, Marta Bellifer was just across the hall the whole time! I'm going haywire."

"You're pretty good at answering your own questions. However, weren't you the young feller who said he thought he'd discard the *Ready or Not* warnings? Wait—let's take a look. What if Tom Hawley sent those messages?"

Verriker shuffled newspapers noisily and at last found a scribbled sheet of notes thrust between the pillow and its slip. He got up from the bed, and Ralston followed him to a table where the light fell clearly. The older man pulled an envelope from his coat hanging on a chair back. He shook from it the familiar sheets, four of them, bearing the warnings, and a flutter of papers, each partly filled with typed lines. He spread them all out on the table and took up his memoranda.

"Your first impression, Joe—mine too, as a matter of record—was that the typing on the warnings looked similar. Then the other night when you dumped your collection of samples on my desk, I realized that you were going about the job in a systematic, business-like way, and I suggested that you let me carry on. After all, I'd be more aware of type imperfections than you would. It's not been your field, and I've been at it, man and boy."

Joe Ralston started to interrupt, but did not succeed.

"So here's what I've got, Joe. I call my warning one, Marta's two, Drummond's three, Judith's four, and Dawson Amberlee's five, since that's the order they came to my attention. Now look at the samples. I've penciled on each its source and a number, one to five, if I could."

Joe picked up a typed sheet at random. It was scrawled with the word Bellifer, but it bore no number. The second one he seized was labeled Morgan and followed by the numbers one and two. Quickly he examined another, marked *Observer,* but without a number. The page that had

come from Hawley's typewriter was marked three and five.
A fifth sample from a typewriter with a worn purple ribbon announced its source as Bunting, and again there was
no number. Joe picked up one *Ready or Not* message after
another and tried to compare them with the numbered samples. He felt confused and uncertain.

"I see," he said at last. "You think that Drummond's
and Dawson Amberlee's warnings were typed on Hawley's
machine and yours and Mrs. Bellifer's on the one in Drummond's office. They still all look pretty much alike to me.
. . . And how about the one Judith got?"

"I've not identified it at all. You yourself remarked that
there were probably a couple of hundred typewriters in
town. There's no dealer here, so that source is out. Anyone
could have stepped up to a new machine on display and
typed out those few words. Not that what I've figured out
makes anything much easier for you."

"I'll say not." Joe's response was grim.

The editor gave him a little pat on his slumped shoulder
and went on. "I made notes here of what I based my conclusions on. The E on Tom Hawley's machine and the slight
nick in the crossbar of the G. The Drummond typewriter
shows the upper space of the A is beginning to clog with
dirt. Take a look."

Verriker handed Joe his notes. Again Ralston started to
say something. After an abortive start he came out with,
"Peggy Morgan's machine is quite new. She told me she
didn't allow anyone to touch it."

"Hawley's is the same make, but it's seen more service. I
suppose you noticed the fresh black ribbon?"

That was true; he had observed the new ribbon. But before he could make further comment, Verriker said, "Joe,
if Tom Hawley had a key to Drummond's office, the girl
would never have known that he helped himself to her
typewriter."

"There was a key in his pocket, all right. And no one else had access to the typewriter except Drummond and his secretary. She tells me Drummond never types—can't, was her word, I believe. But anyone could have used Hawley's machine. The parsonage is open to the whole town."

"So is the one in the *Observer* office, but it plainly doesn't check with any of the messages. Doc's is an ancient Smith-Premier. Even without the purple ribbon it would betray itself to a blind man. And Marta Bellifer's Corona she regards as a sacred cow. I can't tie up Judith Amberlee's warning yet, but the other four came from those two machines—that would stand in court, Joe. And it looks like poor Tom Hawley—"

"It looks like poor Joe Ralston to me, Ed. If Hawley was responsible for everything, nothing's going to have to stand up in court, which is a break for me. But for my own peace of mind, I want to be sure about Hawley. Damn it all, I liked the man! There'd have to be a motive."

"Any word from his wife, or any of his folks, or hers?" Verriker knocked out his pipe and regarded his worried colleague through half-shut eyes.

"No known relatives, except for Mrs. Hawley. The sanitarium wired that she was in no condition even to be informed of her husband's death. A mental case, I gather. Grace Church and the bishop are to see to the final arrangements."

"Poor old Tom Hawley. I'll bet he wouldn't come back if he could." Verriker sighed.

Ralston got to his feet briskly. There was a heavy burden of work ahead of him. He gathered together the papers that had told so convincing a story, and spoke again. "I'll take these back with me, Ed. I—I am indebted to you. I'm going to dig in on Hawley's alibis for Sunday evening and Monday. And another thing—I've been checking his phone calls, in and out, yesterday. He gave your office a ring just after twelve. Talk to you?"

"That's right, come to think. That blasted phone had me run ragged yesterday morning all the time I was trying to grind out a column. But Tom was just phoning in his sermon topics. That's all."

How that added up to suicide, Joe couldn't see, but he let it go.

Verriker slung himself back upon his tousled bed. As Ralston left the room he called after him. "Say, Joe, if you see that young squirt of a Lew Mason as you go back through town, send him up here to me. He's all set to work up a story that I think he'd better leave lay."

Ralston grunted a reply and banged the door behind him. Intent on his next step, he absently snapped off a twig from the mass of unkempt spirea bushes at the edge of Verriker's porch, stripping it leaf by, leaf as he strode on. He cast the bare stalk aside and reached for another, his thoughts piling chaotically. His sense of touch reported a difference and jerked his eyes to what he held in his hand. He dropped it as though it were a bit of white-hot steel.

"Where the devil did that stuff come from?" He swung about and retraced his last half dozen steps. There it was, growing along a boundary fence two houses below Verriker's. Bittersweet . . . its berries flaming in the level rays of the late afternoon sun.

                                    VII

Joe Ralston stalked on down the lower hill and into Main Street, somewhat embarrassed at his display of nerves. "All right," he ordered himself. "Go ahead and check in all the bittersweet items. Stuff's common as goldenrod in these parts, at that. A bowl of bittersweet on the altar rail at Grace Church last Sunday. A couple of berries on the floor of Peggy's room. Kate said that Peggy told her that someone she saw Sunday had a piece in his buttonhole. That would mean a man. She'd been with her boy friend, a lucky devil she calls Mack. She'd shared a seat with some kid from the high school—I could check that. She met Ed as he was going into church. I can check him, of course. She saw an unknown man carrying a bag—but she couldn't have seen a buttonhole bouquet on him. A doctor's bag . . . Um-mm. Kate ought to have something to tell me from Rena Bunting by now. And she saw Hawley and Doc both before I got there. Neither of 'em were decorated when I saw 'em. . . . Tom Hawley always liked that sort of touch. He could have. . . . Then that poor kid Lydia, and Drummond's bunch yesterday—gosh!"

The important thing, he still thought, was to get at Hawley's desk, but he'd better take the evening to do that. He'd spend the time before Kate would expect him for dinner seeing what some of the youngsters who had been at the six-thirty service at Grace on Sunday evening might tell him. The Ely kid ought to know who had been there, but to find him at this hour of the afternoon would probably take him out to the school athletic field.

A rakish car veered suddenly from Main Street towards the wharf and Joe was reminded of his commission. "Hey, Lew!" he bellowed.

The car screamed to a stop and Lew looked back as though hoping for another murder.

"Your boss wants to see you, p.d.q. He's down at the house."

For an instant Lew was disgruntled. This was the night that maybe Peggy Morgan would try out his speed boat, and he wanted to tune her up. Then with a business-before-pleasure expression he said, somewhat cryptically, "Oh, that . . . Okie-doke, Joe," and began to turn the car.

Ralston looked in at Ernst's. There was always a mob of high school kids there. "Anybody here know whether Howard Ely is up at the field tonight?" he inquired genially. A half dozen shrill voices informed him that Howard had to work. He had a job at Glaye's.

What Howard told him only sent him back to the drugstore. The crowd had finished their cokes and banana splits
and were dribbling through the door, to George Ernst's patent relief. With some finesse Ralston detached two girls
from the group and led them back to the last booth. Upon
invitation they decided upon chocolate malteds, and he
began some wary questioning.

Yes, they'd been at Young People's on Sunday night.
Elsie remembered distinctly that Reverend Hawley wasn't
there when they sang the first song, because she had to lead
the meeting and she was scared to death because if nobody
got up to speak it was just awful and Reverend Hawley
always did and if he shouldn't come, why she'd just have
died if there was one of those awful waits. And Margie
remembered too because . . .

Here both Elsie and Margie went into giggling in a big
way, and Joe deduced that Margie had been turning around
watching everyone who came in because that new boy, the
one whose dad had just been transferred to the refinery
from Oil City, had promised to come to the meeting. Reverend Hawley had come first. Elsie had her watch lying on
the table so as to know when to close the meeting, and it
was just exactly twenty minutes of seven when he slipped
in, and was she even glad to see him! She could call on him
to lead in prayer. . . . Oh, no, he hadn't come in from the
street door. From the other door that led to back of the
main auditorium, and he didn't have his hat and coat with
him.

Pondering on these items, Joe Ralston abandoned the
girls and took the quickest route to Grace Church. He
slipped into the coatroom where the pastor and choir members left their street clothes and went through a pantomime
of pulling off or on a top coat, first carefully checking the
minute hand of his watch. Then he walked at a smart rate
but by the most direct route possible up to the Amberlee
house. He entered, ran up the stairs, paused perceptibly

first at the door of Judith Amberlee's room and then at Dawson's, then ran down the stairway, and left the house. At the same brisk pace he made for the parsonage. He looked at his watch. Seven minutes and forty-three seconds.

If Howard Ely had dropped Hawley at the parsonage at half past six on Sunday evening and if Hawley had set off at once for the Amberlee house, accomplished what had certainly happened there shortly after six-thirty, and entered the young people's service at six-forty, the man had certainly cut it pretty fine. A margin of two minutes and seventeen seconds to cover the likely difference between Joe's pace and the preacher's, the necessity for obtaining and later disposing of the weapon, the problem of entering the Amberlee house, locating the position of the victims, shutting off the radio or the victrola, whichever was in full blast, leaving the house—though not by the front door, for that door had been locked with the key in place inside—hanging up his hat and top coat at the church, and entering his young people's service with face unflushed and unflurried manner . . . Margie had been quite sure too that there had been no sort of flower in the lapel of his coat. No, the idea was preposterous. Hawley could not have murdered the two Amberlees.

Yet there was a tie-up somewhere. There had to be. Hawley was dead and the same .32 had killed him that had done for the victims of Sunday night. He had known something which had driven him to his own death, either by his own act or another's.

Lydia . . . Was she the answer? Suppose Hawley had returned from his last service on Sunday evening to find Lydia at the parsonage, seeking refuge, distracted after her dreadful deed. That would account for Hawley's having the gun and for the agitated call he had made asking for Dawson Amberlee. He might have tried to spirit the girl away either that night or the next day. How readily Drummond's shack on the hillside might have occurred to him. But

Lydia, crazed and desperate, had wandered off from her hiding-place to find peace in the muddy waters of Big Rock.

A nice reconstruction, Ralston conceded, glooming in his office until his first assistant should relieve him and he could report for Kate's baked ham dinner, but it hardly covered Hawley's suicide, if that word was to stand. Two other ideas occurred to him. Suppose the clergyman, acting indeed as God's vicar, had not prevented Lydia's death by drowning. A tragic chapter would thus be closed with a minimum of hue and cry. Later, his life-long mold of character had found this assisting of divine providence had left him with an intolerable burden, and suicide had been the result. The other idea considered the possibility that a third person, who might have been guilty of the Amberlee shootings as well, came upon Lydia and was responsible for her death. Hawley, in that case, might have appeared in time to suspect someone or something, which had marked him down as the next victim.

Later, when the case was solved, how wrong he was, and yet how near the dreadful truth he had come just then was the chief reason for his stubborn refusal to accept a reappointment as town marshal of Bly's Landing.

Homeward bound at length, he again made his way up River Road. A car was parked before the Bellifer house. No doubt he'd had his nerve for nothing in suggesting to Mrs. Bellifer that her week-end in White Sulphur should be postponed. Joe stopped short and whistled. It was no car of the Bellifers'. It was the unmistakable, latest acquisition of Alec Drummond.

Ralston looked towards the house, hesitated, and went on. No one was on the sun porch. The front entrance was closed. He could see no plausible method of snooping.

Kate was waiting for him. Peggy was waiting too, but not for him. She was going out on the river with Lew Mason, she explained on the verge of bad temper, and after

Kate had been angel enough to pack a marvelous picnic supper, it was little enough for Lew to do to keep the date.

"He'll be along any time now. His boss called him in unexpectedly. It's really my fault for passing on the message to him." Joe grinned and wished that sudden death and the duties involving thereupon could let him offer himself as Lew's substitute.

However, before Kate and Joe had well begun on the ham and corn fritters, Lew came, full of apologies and bearing word from Verriker. He'd be in the *Observer* office for a while after coming down for the 7:31 mail and he'd like it if Joe could find a chance to drop around for a few minutes.

"That ought to give me time to eat my dinner in peace and hear what you've picked up, if anything."

"Which was one reason, Joe, that I suggested to Peggy that she and Lew start their evening with a picnic supper on the boat. The child is at my heels the instant she comes into the house. She's jumpy, and no wonder, after the two shocking experiences of this ghastly week."

"So you have some dirt to dish, have you? Go ahead." Joe sliced himself another choice bit of ham and gave his sister a hopeful look.

"Rena says the doctor had a fairly quiet day Sunday. He went out on a call a little after six but was back before eight, and that was all until he got the ring from the Amberlee house."

"Find out where he went?"

"Yes. Old Mrs. Prescott thought she was having one of her heart attacks. She's always more scared than in danger, and she dotes on Doctor Bunting."

"Um-m. Mrs. Prescott lives in the last house on the dead end of Sycamore Street."

"You told Peggy the man she saw was probably the doctor." Kate was making an effort to speak casually, but her fingers were twiddling a spoon. "It's just—just a coincidence, Joe. Not Dr. Bunting!"

"Whoa, Kate! Who said anything to make you jump to his rescue like that? Why not run over and see how the old lady is feeling?"

"Joe, I—I did. This afternoon. She says it was about a quarter after seven when she decided she was feeling too breathless to try to go to church, and when she opened the door to get a little fresh air there was the doctor going by the house. She called him in—he was a friend in need, she said—and he made her feel better right away. He stayed talking to her for maybe a half hour."

Kate looked at her brother miserably, but he demanded another cup of coffee and refused to express consternation, although he tucked away for later consideration the odd fact that Dr. Bunting had certainly not left his home in response to a telephone call from old Mrs. Prescott.

"And now, how about your first assignment, the beneficent Mrs. Bellifer?"

"I've dug in like everything, Joe, but since they came back here after those years in Texas, there certainly hasn't been a breath of talk. That was ten years ago, and she's been running the town along all lines of uplift so openly ever since, that if there had been anything to say it would have been said. She's a born leader, but she's not loved for herself alone. The copy-cats are impressed by her social gestures, and that's about all."

"Julian Bellifer's business take him to Texas?"

Kate nodded. "Manager or something big with one of the Drummond oil productions down there. They left town very suddenly."

"And when they came back, Julian went in as vice-president of the Mountain State Bank, didn't he? That was before Alec pulled out of it. I was about dry behind the ears by that time and beginning to take notice."

"Alec Drummond could have saved this town a lot of grief if he'd been behind the Mountain State five years ago."

"Water down the old 'Hio now, Kate. There was nothing Julian Bellifer could do to prevent the smash."

"Alec Drummond could have. Poor helpless Julian—the rest of us all know he was cleaned out and had to live on what his mother might dole out, but Marta always seemed to have plenty. She's said more than once that she had her own income. Ever since they came back from Texas, that is, and before the bank went under. But not before they left. Her people had nothing. Her father was a tool dresser and he died before she married Julian."

"Her own money since their return from Texas. Um-m . . . Maybe a little stake on a well that came in big. That's the way Alec Drummond got his start."

"Catch him handing a slice to anyone. Apparently he's never acquired a lady yet who made him come across."

"Plenty of scandal to hang on Drummond. That would have been a honey of an assignment, Kate."

Kate sniffed. Alec Drummond's ruthless career in industry and business as well as his open defiance of social convention needed neither investigation nor review.

"Let's see," Joe went on. "His first wife died just as she was about to divorce him. He divorced his second, and she's died since. There's been no official number three."

Kate sniffed again. "He keeps most of 'em out of Bly's Landing, thank goodness. And I'll say this much to his credit—he's behaved himself with Peggy. The child thinks he's perfection."

"That probably means he's interested elsewhere at present." Or that something's worrying him, he added mentally. Joe finished his lemon pie, and rose. It was time to get back on the job.

Verriker was waiting for him. Not with the inevitable *Times* at hand, not nursing his pipe, just waiting.

"What made you drag back here?" Ralston groused. "You look as though you should have stayed in bed."

"Something came up. Thought I'd talk to you. Just a sample of what I meant. . . ." He refused one of Joe's cigarettes and lapsed into silence until Joe's had burned a half inch of ash.

"Lew's a good kid," Verriker went on at last. "He's un-earthed quite a story. But I'm not going to let him run it. Maybe you can use it."

If Lew Mason had stumbled upon anything that had to do with the week's excitement, he would never have been so blithe and airy as he set off with Peggy from the presence of the town marshal. He was keen about his job and he'd have stuck to it, girl and speed boat notwithstanding. Joe's momentary expectation that something new had broken in his present tangle collapsed.

Until Ed Verriker's slow, even voice began again. "Lew's story might provide a pretty hot spot for Marta Bellifer, Joe. In my opinion, that is. Lew didn't quite get it added up the way I did.

"You recall my saying, Joe, that I've made it my business to forget a lot of things that I couldn't print. I'm afraid that was just my way of putting it. Trouble is, some things are damned hard to forget. . . .

"There was a time in this town—you were still in knee pants, likely—when there was a good bit between Marta Bellifer and Alec Drummond. No one was on to it, either. Marta's just about as slick as he is. . . . No one, except, after a while, Julian. He and Marta hadn't been married long; their girls were babies. And Marta, I guess, was beginning to be bored with the limitations of Julian's small salary. He was just a hand at the Mountain State. His mother had no time for Marta and wasn't handing over a penny extra. Drummond was in and out of town, already flying pretty high and piling up what he wanted. Marta gave him the eye, and there were carryin's on, but, as I said, they were careful. Marta would have divorced Julian at the drop of a hat, but Alec got fed up before long, and wasn't taking any.

"That much I know, because Julian came to me and broke down with the whole story before they left town. You're the first person, in all these years, Joe, that I've ever mentioned it to. But what I don't know is why Alec Drummond handed out a fat job to Julian Bellifer. You know Julian. Nice, decent chap, but not much gimp to him. It wasn't like Alec. He never gives anything away."

Thanks to Kate, Ralston did not need to interrupt with questions. All he said now was, "Should think you could take a guess about that, Ed."

"I can. I figure Marta had something on him—Alec was running circles around her for a while and that's a fact. She was an eyeful before she got so hippy. And she must have made him come across."

"Still makes him, maybe."

"I'm not—so—sure. Still, she might have wangled a key out of him."

"She speaks of her own income, I understand."

"I said she was smart. She certainly never reduced her own style much, even after Julian was washed up at the bank."

"How did Lew get on to all this?"

"He didn't, Joe. I've just been reminiscing. Lew's idea is that Mrs. B. was up to no good yesterday, while she says she was waiting for Hotchkiss."

"Sure, I could think that much myself. Point is, what does he know?"

"I've no reason to doubt the kid, and it's quite possible that in the excitement that mounted after the discovery of Hawley's death a casual impression was washed from his mind, so that he said nothing of it until this morning. As you know, he was with Miss Peggy almost the entire time that she was out of the office yesterday. They parted at the foot of the stairs and Lew crossed the street to Cardy's. In the second or so that he paused, watching the girl climb the stairs, he thought he heard the sound of typing coming from the open window above. He crossed the street and looked back again. Joe, he's almost ready to swear he saw a grayish figure moving through one of Drummond's rooms. The last room."

"Man or woman?"

"Nothing but an impression of something gray."

"Hawley wore a dark gray suit."

"It couldn't have been Hawley. Remember by that time
the young lady must have been entering the first of the
three rooms—that is, if you are taking a serious look at
Lew's vague impression. She would have heard the shot,
and anyway, Trasker's report settled it that he'd been dead
maybe a half hour when found. No, Lew says Mrs. B. was
wearing a gray dress."

"What the hell does he know about it?" Joe was remembering the vivid silk negligee in which she had talked to
him within the hour.

"Miss Peggy had mentioned it to him while they were
in the drugstore together. Trust a woman to know what
another one has on. It was some special sort of knit thing,
according to Lew, according to a highly clothes-conscious
young woman."

"See here, Ed, I can't see why you clamped down on Lew,
if that's all his story amounted to, unless you wanted me to
get the dope first. I know he's been wiring stuff to the AP
and that's all right—the town's made news this week."

Verriker looked across the cluttered desk at Ralston's
earnest, worried face. The hand that held his pipe relaxed
perceptibly. "It was Hawley who was found dead, not—
not Drummond. You could mix Marta with him, but why
should she kill Tom Hawley, or force him to take his own
life?"

"Or Dawson and Judith and Lydia? I got to account for
them all." Ralston rose abruptly. "Marta's been lying right
straight through, but I can put a little pressure on her now.
Ed, I wish you'd come along."

Verriker shook his head. "You can report to me later. I
don't feel up to Marta. And, Joe, my—er—fond recollec-
tions are to be used merely as pressure. I still think a lot of
Julian Bellifer."

"I'll be as discreet as possible, Ed. And don't forget that you elected yourself as bait. I don't want to come back and find that someone's pinged you."

Ralston strode off in the direction of River Road, fighting the temptation to postpone facing Mrs. Bellifer until he had organized more clearly these latest disclosures. Fortunately he permitted himself only one digression, else he would have missed Dr. Hotchkiss's final contribution to the case. Nor would he have seen Drummond's car. However, if he had gone on directly he might have seen for himself where the car came from.

He wasn't happy about the necessity for the digression. He swung across the street to the nearest public booth and rang up his friend Temple in Parkersburg, from whom he had received his first report concerning the typed *Ready or Not* messages. There was a little delay; he had to make a second call before he caught up with the chap.

"That you, Temple? This is Ralston, in Bly's Landing. . . . Sure, it came okay, and thanks a million. Listen, you said something about some sort of copies. Photostats, huh? . . . Rush 'em to me, Temple? Get 'em in the mail tonight. . . ."

Once more starting for River Road, he encountered Hotchkiss, evidently on his way to Cardy's. Still looking as though he hadn't liked the taste of his brief talk with Temple, Joe stopped the dentist and made a cautious inquiry.

Hotchkiss answered promptly. "Yes, indeed, Joe. I saw her at nine-thirty this morning. There was nothing wrong—just a little roughness at the edge of an earlier filling. Quite a natural mistake on her part."

Ralston moved on. He was reminding himself that Ed was right—Marta Bellifer was slick. If her trip to Hotchkiss's office on Thursday had been merely a blind, she'd been quick enough to protect herself by a professional inspection the next day. It was at that point that he looked up to see Alec Drummond passing him at the wheel of the shining car. Joe couldn't be positive, but he had a feeling that the car had just swung into Railroad Street from River Road.

Again his friend Bessie Peters admitted him to the Bellifer house. He asked for Mrs. Bellifer, and Bessie looked uncertain. "I'm afraid she's awful busy, but I'll go tell her who's here."

From the hall where he waited unobtrusively, he could tell that the girls had a noisy crowd in the living-room, and that Julian must be somewhere about too, judging by the cigar smoke.

Bessie summoned him. "She says to come on up if it's anyways important."

Marta Bellifer was in her office-boudoir, as she probably had termed it more than once. She was seated at a table, turning over papers. Almost as soon as he had noted with some disappointment that she was not wearing a gray dress, he observed the shocking change that had gripped her face since he last saw her. She had been disturbed and frightened then. Now she was haggard and despairing. After a murmured greeting, her next words were a bit firmer. "Bring me a glass of water, Bessie, and that will be all. I shall have to take more aspirin, I'm afraid."

There was silence until the maid returned with the water. Joe Ralston noticed the familiar-looking, small green bottle of white tablets, but for the time they remained untouched.

He gathered himself together. "Mrs. Bellifer, I feel that I should warn you. I want the truth and nothing but the truth. I could be justified in holding you as a material witness—at least."

She stared at him, almost as though she had not heard, her strong white fingers gripping the edge of the table. But she had heard, for she said after a long minute, "Close the door. I—I don't want . . ."

Joe backed against the door in response to her request and went on with his attack. "Alec Drummond has his reasons for protecting you, but—others are not so compelled. And whatever may have passed between you two today, Mrs. Bellifer, should dictate that frankness is your only safe course. I want nothing but the truth."

It was just a chance, he told Kate later. But he hit something.

"He told you!" Her words were a desperate wail.

"You tell me the truth. That's all I want. Is it a fact that you called Miss Amberlee last Sunday afternoon at four?"

She rallied a little under the unexpected harmlessness of that question. "Why, yes, I did. That's a fact."

"Is it a fact that you saw Lydia Amberlee at Mr. Hawley's door at five-thirty?"

"I—I thought it was Lydia. It—it might have been someone else."

"Where were you at six-thirty on Sunday evening?"

She caught the relation of that at once, but she answered without delay. "I was here in the house. Alone, unfortunately. As a matter of fact, I was writing letters at this very table."

"And Monday between one and two?" He chose those hours somewhat at random.

"In my dining-room. I had the program committee for luncheon. Ask Bessie."

"And later you took Miss Melody for a drive?"

"Yes, that's another—fact, to use your word."

"Can you swear that it was Hawley's car you passed on Big Rock Road?"

"No. But I can now swear that he since admitted to me that it was."

"And what was your reason for taking up the point with him?"

"I—I thought he ought to know that his car was seen."

"You mean you wanted him to know you had seen his car. I wonder what you got in exchange for that threat?"

She did not answer, nor did she give any hint that she was aware of the significance of his words.

His next was a statement, not a question. "On Thursday morning, before ten o'clock, you called Drummond at the Lodge. It interests me that you knew his private number." He was watching her, but her face was well under control. "And a little later you rang up Hawley."

"I wanted to know if he had a little time to run over the program schedule with me." Her fingers were again gripping the edge of the table.

"Yes, that would have served as an excuse. But when you went around to the parsonage, what did you say to him that sent him up to Drummond's office?"

Her eyes fell before his, fell upon the little green bottle of aspirin, but the glass of water still remained untouched. She said nothing.

"Maybe you talked about seeing his car on Monday?"

"Mr. Hawley was my pastor. It was—quite natural to speak to him of what was troubling me."

"And you found him prompt to extend—spiritual comfort, no doubt. And material aid as well?"

"I don't know." Her voice rose thinly and she reached blindly towards the green bottle. "After I left his study Thursday morning I never saw him again. If I only knew what he had done. . . ."

Ralston ignored the incipient hysteria. He went on, conversationally. "You know, Mrs. Bellifer, I still think it's sort of odd that with all the phoning you did on Thursday, you didn't give Dr. Hotchkiss a ring about that dental appointment. We all know you went up to his office at one o'clock and waited around for him quite a little while just at the time he's nearly always home for his lunch. And by the way, Doc tells me you hadn't lost a filling at all. Where's your key to Drummond's suite?"

She made no attempt at denial, but the question was apparently such a mortal one that she could scarcely gather herself together to make a reply. Her answer, in fact, came not in words. She fumbled at a drawer in the table and dragged out her handbag. Most of its contents were strewn across the table before she had shaken from it what Ralston had demanded. A key that looked, Joe was certain, exactly like the one that Peggy Morgan carried.

He examined it narrowly and slipped it into his vest pocket. He would have seen his way more clearly had she not been able to produce one. This was no crudely cut copy, like the one on Hawley's ring. This was as authentic as Drummond's and his secretary's, no matter how it had come into Marta Bellifer's possession.

"How long have you had it?" he asked.

"A long time. I've always had one." She spoke the words woodenly, as though she no longer cared.

"When did you last use it? Yesterday?"

"No—no! I don't know. . . . Not yesterday. I heard some-one there, and I was afraid— Now you know!"

"What did you hear?"

"Not Alec! I'm sure it wasn't Alec. He'd told me he had to go away. Someone moving around. And the typewriter. . . . That's all. It was after the noise from the train died away."

"No shot?"

She shook her head. "I wanted to go in. I had a right, Joe Ralston, to look for something, but there was someone there. . . ." She gave him a desperate look. "I've tried to help you. Believe me, it's been torture . . . But you—you must tell me!" Once more her voice rose unnaturally. "Did you find anything—a paper?"

"You mean on Hawley?" Her anguished eyes answered. "No, there was nothing that could possibly concern you." Joe spoke gently, reassuringly, but she found no comfort in that. "If you had sent him—asked him to get something for you, I do not believe that he succeeded. Did you give him a key like this?"

"This was the only one I had."

Ralston believed her. There was so little defiance left in her.

"Then it's true—what he said. . . ." She picked up the little bottle and shook out several of the aspirin tablets.

"What did Alec Drummond say?" He shot the question at her. "He was here this afternoon. I saw his car. And again this evening."

She shook her head wearily. "I—I don't have to tell you that. He's beat me at last. It's too late. . . ."

There was a quick flick of her white fingers and she picked up the glass of water. Joe Ralston got just one glimpse of her contorted face and blank eyes as she slumped across the table.

Part Four
"You Shall Be Caught"

I

Marta Bellifer died as Joe lifted her head from the table. He saw then what she had done under his very eyes. There was a second bottle, a much smaller one of unlabeled, clear glass that had been hidden in her handbag. The harmless aspirin tablets were still lying where she had shaken them out. What she had taken had come from the second phial, and it had worked with mortal swiftness. Joe paused only to pick up this tiny bottle and the glass of water half tilted from her fingers. He thrust them out of sight for the moment behind a bowl of asters and then opened the door and stepped into the hall.

Below he could hear Nancy and Elaine and their friends. He could smell the fragrance of Julian Bellifer's cigar and something that must be hot buttered popcorn. "Julian," he called, "Bellifer!"

There was no response from the carefree group below, but the grim urgence of his tone produced Bessie from around a door at the end of the hall. "Slip down and get Mr. Bellifer," he commanded. "Don't disturb the kids. Mrs. Bellifer's—sick."

For the time he let them all think it must have been a heart attack. As soon as Bessie reappeared in the wake of Julian Bellifer he directed her to call Dr. Bunting, but prompt as the doctor was, before his arrival both maid and

145

husband had discovered that the seizure was fatal. Bessie Peters kept her head admirably, and when the girls rushed upstairs, panic-stricken at their father's peremptory summons, she dispatched their guests as competently as Marta Bellifer could have done.

Bunting took one look at the dead woman's eyes, bent close over her, though in such a way that the others could not see exactly what he did, and then ordered them all from the room.

"I know what's happened," Ralston murmured in the doctor's ear. "You'll want me."

Julian Bellifer refused to go, understandably, and so he had to hear at once what the two had to say.

"Cyanide. Not heart at all." The doctor's blunt fingers pushed at the scattered aspirin. "Take it by mistake?"

Pityingly, Ralston killed the quick hope, that sprang in Julian Bellifer's eyes. "I'm afraid not, Doc. Look—" He indicated what he had hidden behind the purple and rose of the asters. "Right before my eyes—God! I thought she was reaching for an aspirin. Bessie can tell you that she spoke of aspirin as soon as I came in."

Bunting gave the little clear glass bottle an instant's professional examination. "That's the stuff. So it's suicide. Nothing for me to do. I'm damned sorry, Julian."

Ralston stood against the closed door, his arms folded across his chest, his eyes alert to interpret what he could from the baffled, confused look on Bellifer's face. His conclusion was, and he was afraid he was right, that whatever Bellifer had known of his wife's earlier secrets, he was at a loss now to understand her death.

"I guess we could slip out now," Bunting suggested with a significant nod toward Bellifer. "We can do a little necessary talking somewhere else. I'll have to notify Trasker."

"I'm sorry. I'll have to stay here." Not until Ralston crossed the room and laid his hand on Bellifer's shoulder could the dazed little man realize that the marshal was trying to explain something directly to him. "It's this way, Julian. I've got to take a look through things here, her papers and so on. I must refuse to let them be touched—by anyone, until I've seen for myself. There's a tie-up somewhere—all these things that have been happening this week, and it's up to me to do what I can. I don't mind your watching me, you and Doc, but if you'd rather go to the girls. . . . We won't move her till Trasker comes. That's a pure matter of form, you understand."

Whether he did or not, Bellifer dropped into a chair close to a couch upon which the doctor had already laid Marta's body. Bunting sniffed angrily, picked up the extension telephone on the table, and dispatched a message to the coroner. Bellifer paid no attention to the marshal's swift movements, but Bunting allowed nothing to escape him. "Looking all the time as though he'd like to wring my neck," Joe told Kate when the time for telling at last came.

Joe worked fast. The drawers in the table-desk, those in a small filing cabinet, masses of committee reports about gardens and better schools and proportional representation and medical missions and mothers' clinics. But nothing at all that might explain even one small detail of the mystery surrounding the violent deaths of five people in Bly's Landing in less than a week's time. There were no personal letters. Not even the contents of a small, locked dispatch box did anything more than verify something he already knew. The key that fitted the lock had been in Marta's purse, one of a fat cluster on a silver ring. The one already safely in his vest pocket had not been with those. . . . When he found the proper one and opened the box, it revealed a bundle of stock certificates. They were grade A securities, all of them Drummond-controlled interests, however she had become their owner, and their total was impressive. No wonder Marta Bellifer could refer casually to her own income.

As soon as his search was finished, Joe eased himself out. Before he left the house he took Bessie Peters aside

and bucked her up by a singular request. "I don't know
what will have to be done around here tonight—plenty, of
course; messages sent and all that, but I'll count it a personal favor if you can try and manage things so that nobody is deliberately reminded to get any word through to
Alec Drummond. Stick your eyes back in again, Bessie. You
know enough to keep your mouth shut."

He went directly home. Without a word of the calamity
he had just witnessed at the Bellifer house, he left Kate to
her placid enjoyment of a double-crostic, backed his car
out of the garage, and started off for an interview with Alec
Drummond. He intended planning his questions out in advance, for talking to Drummond would be quite different
from confronting a frightened, distraught woman already
on the verge of desperation, but he drove his roadster so
hard that he had reached the private road that led to the
Lodge before he had accomplished any ordered thinking.

The Lodge was lighted. There were no cars parked on the
curve that encircled the broad, low-lying building. Drummond must be at home, and alone, and Joe was thankful
for that.

He gave the door a vigorous thump and the man Tim
opened it at once. "Tell your boss that Marshal Ralston has
come up from town on a matter of important business."
He stepped inside; his title had registered duly upon Tim.
Without waiting, he followed his message into the long
common room where a fire snapped comfortably on the
hearth that filled the upper end.

Drummond rose at the sound of his steps and came to
meet him, his hand extended. "Glad to see you, Ralston.
Anything I can do? Tim, another glass."

The man was surprisingly affable.

When Tim had re-entered and again withdrawn, Joe
opened the session by sheering away from his main objective. "How about thumbing a ride yesterday afternoon just
after you left your car with Red?"

Drummond looked at him as if he had been addressed in Russian.

"You were seen. A car slowed up."

"Oh, that. . . . A young stringer with a U. of C. sticker on his suitcase climbed into a blue Plymouth just as I got alongside the telegraph pole that had been propping him up. Looked to me as if he might have been waiting for that particular car. It carried Missouri plates."

Drummond's report had come promptly, but by the time he completed it his jaw had set angrily.

"Um-m, I see. . . ." Indeed, Joe saw that the story more than covered the details that Red Gaynor's kid brother had contributed. He pulled some keys from his pocket and slid them from hand to hand.

"That's okay, I guess. What really brought me up here tonight was, I want to straighten out a little mess about keys. You gave me yours last night when I asked for them. These. . . ."—He tossed them upon the table at his elbow. "This is one I have just acquired tonight."

Drummond stretched out his hand and caught the key which Ralston threw across to him. "I see . . . from Miss Morgan, doubtless?"

"No, not Miss Morgan. From another lady."

"I congratulate you. You ran in better luck than I." Not only his tone but his face too expressed a satisfaction that was not assumed. However, if he wanted details, he did not ask for them.

"You led me to believe that there were only two keys for each of the three doors. Naturally, after this,"—and Joe nodded at the key still in Drummond's hand, "I am wondering how many more there are—to all the doors."

"No more. I am quite sure of that. You should scarcely have expected me to refer to this one."

"Then this one should be a—surprise, shall I say?" On his outstretched palm lay the key that he had found on Thomas Hawley. The gesture at last compelled Drummond

to rise from his chair. He bent over the unofficial duplicate, turned it over with his finger, picked it up and carried
it directly under the light where he compared it with the
companion he had given the marshal the night before.

"Where did you get it?" he demanded.

"I was thinking you might know."

Whether Joe intended it or not, his remark brought a
glitter of anger to Drummond's eyes. "I don't know what
you're trying to get at, but I don't like your approach.
You're being damned impudent. . . . I want to know about
this key."

"So do I. You've seen for yourself what it is: a rather
bad job of cutting, but it opens and locks the door that
leads from your private office to the back entrance of the
building. That's the way that Hawley got in yesterday
afternoon."

"Hawley! Preposterous . . ."

"Not at all for him to have come in by that entrance.
For him to possess the key—well, yes, I'm inclined to agree
with you."

"Then you mean he was admitted?"

"It's possible."

"Murder. Who . . . No—my God!"

It was not the crime, but a possible murderer that wrung
the words from Drummond.

For the time Joe Ralston ignored that gain. He went on
calmly, conversationally. "So I thought if we got together
about the keys, we might figure something out. Let's take
it this way: you've got your own bunch. Ever lose 'em or
mislay 'em, even for a short while?"

"No, they're always on me. You can take my word for
that."

"Um-m. You might not get the votes for being the ten
most popular men in Bly's Landing, but I've never heard
anybody call you a liar. Well, then there are the authentic
duplicates. The one to the first door you turned over to

your secretary. But Miss Morgan hasn't been with you very long. Maybe we can skip her, but how about her predecessors?"

"The answer to that one is that the lock on her door was changed the week she began work with me."

"That's my good luck. But not the other locks?"

"No."

"And naturally you took care of the—other lady's key at the same time."

There was not a flicker of response to that on Drummond's face.

Joe went doggedly on. "Your other duplicates you kept in the drawer you showed me—"

"And I kept that drawer locked—always."

"But perhaps you couldn't swear that you checked up on that locked drawer every day."

"I'm frequently away from the office for days at a time."

"And somebody else, and I know who as well as you do, had the key I've just returned to you. She could get in any time she wanted to—while Miss Morgan was out at noon, or at night. That was probably all right with you, or she wouldn't have had the key. I'll bet you she could have got into that locked drawer if she'd set her mind to it. Any idea why she'd have a copy made of the key to the back entrance?"

"Why don't you ask her yourself?"

Satisfied at last that no word had yet reached Drummond of what had occurred at the Bellifer house that evening, Ralston affected to be so lost in thought that he had not heard the challenge. "Maybe I'm guessing, Drummond, but just now I'm figuring that Hawley was bumped off. Now you could have let him in, only you weren't there, and besides, I can't see any sense to your fooling around with having an extra key made. . . ."

For that Drummond thanked him with an ironical lift of his eyebrows.

"And our lady friend could either have let him in or managed to provide him with this amateur job. Or—I've got an open mind—a third person found a way to get the key made, and knew why he wanted to use it."

"An open mind may only lead you far from the truth. I repeat—ask the lady."

There was something vindictive about Drummond's words.

"I'm afraid I can't do that—now. She's dead."

"Thank God!" The words slipped out, but a rigid control at once enveloped the man who had spoken them. He sat motionless, his eyes on Ralston. Joe stared back until he forced him into speech. "Did I—did I understand you?"

"I wouldn't know," Joe drawled. "I understood your comment, Drummond."

Again the two men measured one another in a long silence. It was Ralston who spoke first.

"I saw her die. She committed suicide—took poison right before my eyes. But Drummond, I don't think you can deny that you were responsible for her death."

Alec Drummond poured himself a drink, drank, set down the glass. "I'm not a liar, as you said. I'm damned glad she's dead."

Strangely, the words did not sound callous.

Joe intoned, "Ready or not, you shall be caught," but Drummond gave no sign. "So you won't be caught by Marta Bellifer."

"Nor will I have to catch her! It was about fifty-fifty between us. She broke first—that's all."

"Maybe that's not all." Ralston gave the last word a slight emphasis. "If I could be sure why she killed herself . . . Hers is the fifth unexplained death in Bly's Landing this week."

"I may have been flattering myself, at that." The words were jaunty, but Drummond was again watching Ralston closely, appraisingly.

"And I can't understand why Tom Hawley got his."

Drummond slipped his hand into an inner pocket and drew forth a folded paper. With eyes still on Ralston he slowly tore it across, once, twice, and again. He rose and stepped to the fire and watched the blaze eat the torn bits, completely, finally. He returned to his chair, poured himself a swallow of whisky, drank it. Then he began to speak.

"Marta Bellifer is dead. I still had what she wanted— what she might have got, had we met again. What I must have persuaded her she wasn't going to get. You saw what I did just now. It was not staged for your benefit; you merely chanced to witness an inevitable incident. It was no longer of value to anyone. No—don't ask me now!

"I could be tempted to fall in with your theory— I've been following your labored thinking. I could tell you that Marta hated that old Amberlee hussy. She knew—what Marta wished she didn't know. It was a case of one scandal against another, and the Amberlee skeleton kept Judith's mouth shut about other people's. But Marta loathed her. And killing the old woman might have necessitated going on with Dawson. Oh, if you'd dig in, you'd have no trouble finding reasons for Marta's knocking off the whole damn family, even the loony one.

"She thought she got the drop on the parson the other afternoon up along the Run, but why couldn't it have been the other way? He was there—she was there. Maybe he caught her. Sure, she had a key, and that makes her the most logical person to have tampered with my extra set. She wouldn't have stolen it outright; I'd have missed it too soon. But she could have managed to have a copy made. Say she slipped it to Hawley and got him up there on some pretext. She usually knew when I was out of town. . . . Well, she could have finished him off. No doubt you know that she had a weakness for detective fiction. She could have been on to all the tricks, fingerprints, making it look like suicide, and all that."

Drummond paused, as if expecting Ralston to accept or reject this hypothetical case against Marta Bellifer. But Joe stroked his chin in silence. It was good. Good enough, anyway. He wondered what Ed Verriker would make of it. Drummond didn't know about the .32, and Joe wasn't dragging that into it just now.

At length he said, "Well, maybe she could have killed the Amberlees and Hawley, but I'm damned if she shouldn't have gone gunning for you too, while she was at it."

"You're right, Ralston. It was one or the other of us, and she cracked up first. I don't mean that I'd have killed her—I've got what I wanted without committing murder, so far." Drummond made this statement coolly, but there was a deadly literalness about it that directed Joe's puzzled thoughts in a new direction.

Drummond rose and stood looking into the flames for a minute or two. Then he swung about, his hands thrust into his pockets, and his eyes bore steadily into Ralston's. "Understand this, young fellow. I admit that such a theory would be a well-deserved revenge upon Marta Bellifer. But I'm not taking any. In short, I don't believe one word of the fairy tale I've spun you. I agree with you—I am the only person she wanted to kill, and she didn't have the nerve. And now that she's out of my way, I'm standing by Marta. Let it ride the way it stacks up now. That crazy Lydia killed her aunt and uncle and then drowned herself. Hawley's a suicide. Or else pick yourself another villain."

"That's what I've set out to do."

Drummond paid no attention to this determined mutter. "What was between Marta and me in the past is in the past, a fact which she found hard to accept. I paid my share of the bill. She didn't. . . . Now that she's dead, nothing in the world can make me go over ancient history with anybody—and that goes for you, Ralston. And the one thing I'm going to do is to advise you, for your own good, not to hang a bunch of nasty crimes on Marta Bellifer."

"I'd just as soon lose my job."

"That sounded like a cheap threat, didn't it? You ought to know that wouldn't be my line. Only—keep me out of it! If you work on my wild theory that she was responsible, I'll be dragged in, and that I won't have. Marta was aiming for me with those Ready or Not messages. She was smart enough to scatter a bunch of them around, even one to herself and to an old innocent like Verriker. She was too much worried about what I was going to do, to undertake a mass killing of the Amberlees. Hawley might conceivably have picked up some gossip in the years that he's been in town that would have led him to wrestle with her for the good of her immortal soul, but I can't see him as the kind that would have killed himself because he lost out. No more than I can see Marta running to him for spiritual comfort when I—"

"When you issued your ultimatum to her."

"I see you've got the general idea. Well, I think we've about covered the ground." He glanced at his watch.

Joe Ralston rose tractably. "You've been a big help, Mr. Drummond. In fact, I've got a pretty good idea right now what I'm going to do next."

His host gave a tolerant laugh. "Smart fella, Joe."

II

After a night as near sleepless as Joe Ralston had ever spent, he came down to breakfast the next morning, grim and unhappy. Kate wanted to talk, for the news of Mrs. Bellifer's tragic death had seeped through the town shortly after his departure from the house the night before. Her brother's answers were so short, that after she had satisfied herself that he had indeed known what had occurred and had even been present himself, she took her cue patiently.

"It's been ghastly, this week," she sighed. "I do hope, Joe dear, that you can get away by the fifteenth. A little hunting up on Cheat Mountain is what you'll need."

"Hunting!" he groaned. "I'm having all of that I want for the rest of my life. I tell you, Kate, it makes me sick."

He pushed back his coffee and strode from the room. There were things he could do. The issue he must face could still be pushed away. He could ask Peggy—

She was coming down the stairs. He turned at the door and, ignoring her bright good morning, asked her a low question. When Drummond left the office at noon on Thursday, what sort of suit was he wearing?

"Tweeds. Awfully good looking."

"I mean color."

"Oh. A sort of brownish-gray mixture with a mere flick of rust. Stunning!"

"Um-m. I haven't your words for it, but you check my own recollection. More brown than gray, or more gray than brown?"

"Darkish brown, decidedly."

Joe went on with merely a nod of thanks. He'd seen Drummond himself on Thursday night, had talked to him, but for the life of him, ever since Verriker had reported Lew Mason's impression concerning a grayish figure moving through the third office, he had been unable to recall surely what Drummond had been wearing. It was ridiculous to suppose that the man had changed his clothes upon his return from Wheeling and before he had gone back to the Lodge, and now that Peggy's expert eye had reminded him, he could again see Drummond's tweed-clad arm pulling out a desk drawer and extending to him the duplicate keys. A brownish arm, not gray.

Drummond was out—that was certain. He'd have to accept that fact. The next thing was to see what was in the mail. Temple had promised to rush the copies up. They were there, but Joe tucked the thick envelope into his pocket. That could wait. . . . It would be such damning proof. He'd keep it for the clincher. In the meantime, maybe a miracle would happen. Maybe there would be an earthquake. If

Bly's Landing knew what a funk he was in, they'd run him out of town. Joe Ralston wished they would. . . .

Then he pulled himself together and set off at a brisk pace for his office in the town hall. Routine work having nothing to do with his big problem would steady his nerves. Or maybe that was just another attempt to sidestep.

If so, he sidestepped successfully for the next hour and a half. Then a wire from the Shoreham in Washington came in. Alec Drummond had been in and out of the hotel from the time he registered on Sunday until he checked out the next night. That was definitely that and Joe had known as much by the time he rolled into his garage the night before.

He pulled his telephone to him, allowed himself another instant of sick uncertainty, and then called the hospital in Marietta. It took longer than he expected, but he at last reached someone who told him with authority that Dr. Bunting had been in consultation with the chief of staff from eleven until twelve-thirty on Thursday, had lunched at the hospital, and then had stayed to observe an emergency thorocaplasty. He had not left until after two that afternoon.

His next job would have to be the key. He walked around to Cap Anderson's junk shop. Cap took frequent vacations, as he called them, and Joe caught himself hoping that the old boy's well-known thirst had already closed the shop for the week-end. But his familiar, tubby figure was limping through the maze of cast-off stovepipe and boxes of rusty locks which appeared to be his principal staple at the moment. With great cheer he settled himself for a good chin with the town marshal.

Throttling Cap's preliminary chat, Ralston at once produced the key, the one he called Hawley's. "You make this?" he demanded.

Cap pushed his spectacles into focus and peered critically at the key. "Don't reckon I did," he concluded, but without marked certainty. "That ain't no expert job, Joe, and me—well, I'm a reg'lar locksmith. Sure, sometimes I have to rush a job through, when I ain't feelin' so good, but I don't reco'nize nothin' about this here key. And you can take my word for one thing—see that there scratch, there on the finger piece? Whoever cut the key, didn't leave that. That's new and bright. Looks like to me somebody pulled it on—or off of a ring kinda careless or in a hurry."

"I think you're right there, Cap. Would you be willing to swear it wasn't your work?"

The official sound of that question cleared the old man's memory surprisingly and he became profanely certain that he had not made the key, had never seen it before, knew nothing about it. "Tell you what," he subsided at length, "whyn't you ask Fult Dodge. He's nothin' but a printer by trade, but he's picked up a right smart lot off a watchin' me. And it looks like a home-made job to me."

Joe hadn't needed telling from Cap Anderson. He'd known all along that he'd have to ask Fult.

Dr. Bunting's car was parked in front of the *Observer* office. That was another thing, Joe reminded himself. To be absolutely safe, he'd have to make a run out to Newt Gowdy's. Doc had been on his way there last Monday. About noon, he'd said. And away from home from six to eight on Sunday evening, according to his wife. And there was old Mrs. Prescott's evidence. . . .

Bunting and Verriker had their heads together in the front office. Joe gave them a business-like salute and strode on into the print shop. The boy was counting and stacking dodgers announcing next week's billings at the Regent. Fult rose from behind a small handpress in the far corner of the shop and said no, he wasn't rushed right now; he could take a few minutes off to talk. As he spoke he stripped off a lank, grayish garment, a long work-coat, soggy with fresh ink-stains.

"Inkin' them rollers finishes me up for the week, no matter what I got on. But Monday's clean clothes day, and the missus has a swell new washer. Hey, you, Butch! Rush them dodgers around to Nate's before his kids come bustin' in here after 'em. Nope, you can trot on home after that. Now, Joe, what's eatin' you? Some MAN WANTED—BIG CASH MONEY REWARD job, huh?"

"No, it's your other line this time, Fult. Take a look at this." He moved towards the rear window of the shop and lowered his voice. Fult was at his shoulder before he produced the key.

The printer picked it up and then gave Ralston a square look. "Well, what about it?"

"That's exactly my question to you, Fult. You cut it?"

The man nodded.

"Go ahead, Fult. I've got to have the whole story."

"Not much to tell, Joe, but at that it's darned queer. I've always sorta wondered. . . . I come back from dinner one day, oh, maybe two-three weeks ago. Everybody else out, except Ethel and I'd seen her a couple of squares ahead of me, so I knew for a fact she'd no more than got back to work. Well, on my desk here, right on top a bunch of fresh copy was layin' a key and a note. I kep' the note—you can see it for yourself. It just said to cut a copy, see, that night if I could, and to leave the two of 'em on my desk when I went home the next noon. So I did. . . . And when I come back in the next day, darned if there wasn't a nice new five-spot under that slug there."

"So you cut the key. . . . Didn't it occur to you that it sounded like funny business, a no-name job like that?"

"Who said it was no-name? Wait, I still got that note." Fult Dodge went straight to a small upper drawer in the grimy desk that had been demoted from use in the editorial quarters, unlocked it, and removed a layer of insurance papers, his union credentials, and something that might have been a flattened I.C.S. diploma. He handed Ralston a folded sheet of paper.

There it was, unmistakably. Dr. Bunting's letterhead and the characteristic typing of his old machine, even the worn purple ribbon. Joe read:

> "Fult,
> Fix me up with a spare for this. Instrument case in office, and so if you will rush it through tonight, I'll be much obliged. Will pick it up same place and time tomorrow. B."

The initial was signed, not typed, Joe noted dully.

"So I figured," Fult went on, slightly defensive, "that Doc didn't want much said about maybe a key missing to stuff like that in his office."

"Probably not. Ever ask any questions—Ethel or Doc or anybody?"

"Nope. Except Ethel, in a way. She'd been here when I left and came back just ahead of me, but she said nobody'd been in. I'm not one to stir up a woman's curiosity."

"And the next noon?"

"The boss and Ethel were both here when I come back and all I says was, had anybody been in to see me, and they both says no." Sharp as Fult Dodge was at checking copy even after Ethel Erbaugh's expert proofreading, excitement reduced him to free use of the vernacular.

"And were you the last one to leave for the noon hour?"

"Yep, I was. Awful busy that day. Left and came by the back way. Didn't even shuck off my work coat."

"And you never mentioned the matter to the doctor?"

Fult shook his head. "We don't doctor with Bunting. The missus goes to a chiropractor down in Parkersburg. But I might have some time, if I got a real good chance. Might yet. I'm curious, Joe, curious as hell."

"So am I, Fult, and for that reason you're going to keep still. And I'm going to keep this—for the time." Ralston picked up the note and slipped it safely into the same pocket that was still heavy with the unopened envelope received that morning from Temple. "You've got nothing to worry about, and I'll see that you get the note back again." He added to himself, "I hope to God you get it back again, before it's marked Exhibit XYZ. . . ."

He moved away from Fult's desk towards the outer room. "So long, I'll see about new letterheads later." That was for the benefit of whoever might have an ear cocked from the front room.

At the sound of his voice Dr. Bunting rose as if to go, but in spite of the invitation of Verriker's cocked eyebrow, Joe Ralston did not pause. He said, "Save some time for me after lunch, Ed. I'll catch up with you here or up at the house, just as you say."

"I'll look in at your office, Joe, on my way back from Mrs. Lukey's. How's that?"

"Just as you say, Ed. I'll be seeing you." He paused outside the door and surveyed the familiar busyness of Railroad Street. But rather blindly, for he could hear Dr. Bunting's hearty, distinct voice.

"There you go, Ed. Ready or not, I tell you you've got to pipe down. . . ."

III

"Ready or not . . ." Ralston could still hear the words, but what he stubbornly clung to was the image of Doc Bunting, clear and distinct. Doc in a new suit, its creases still sharp. Not the familiar, shapeless gray, a blue worsted. . . . Why, he didn't know when he'd seen Doc in anything but gray.

Funny how his mind refused to face the issue . . . how he grasped at any detail that led away. What he ought to do was ask Doc a point-blank question.

He walked on, his head bent and his mind sick with the ceaseless *why, why* that churned through it. Though he had left Bunting behind him in the *Observer* office, he found himself staring blankly at the doctor's door. "OUT—Back at 4 p.m.," he read almost as if he were figuring out words in a foreign language. He went on, unhappy and troubled.

Roused a few blocks farther on by an insistent greeting from a passer-by, he saw that he was near the parsonage. Its key was in his pocket and he entered the silent house. He could wrestle with one question: how had Hawley been lured to his death in Drummond's office?

Joe slumped in the preacher's study chair and examined that bit of his puzzle. The last report on Hawley was Peggy's, that he had called the office just at one, asking for Drummond, and had been told that he was out of town for the rest of the day. And not long before that he'd talked to Ed about his Sunday notices. Joe had checked those calls; he hadn't taken anything for granted.

Nothing except that it must be certain that Hawley had entered Drummond's rooms from the rear entrance. He'd just been informed by his secretary that Drummond was not there, and anyone in town could know about Peggy Morgan's noon schedule. All right then, Hawley had slipped into Drummond's suite surreptitiously because he had ascertained that no one was there. If he had agreed to do something for Marta Bellifer, what could he do for her there that she could not just as well have done for herself? Since Drummond himself had provided her with a key, he would not have been fool enough to have kept there the thing she had played so desperately to obtain, the folded paper which Alec Drummond had deliberately destroyed before his eyes the night before. Nor must he forget that all the while Marta herself had been just across the hall in the dentist's office. No one now living could ever know just what arrangement the two might have made. Marta had been at the parsonage that morning; it could all have been fixed up then.

All very well, but that was going to give him the answer he and Alec Drummond had already discarded. How easy,

how easy it would have been to put Marta Bellifer in a
nasty spot about Hawley's death if she had not chosen the
quickest way out. Maybe that was it exactly. . . .

Joe straightened in excitement and thumped his fist
soundlessly upon Hawley's desk. Could the preacher had
been merely the ruthless sacrifice of a pawn in order to
force Marta Bellifer to pay the piper? She had been threatened by the writer of the *Ready or Not* warnings. Hawley
had not. Joe's eyes swept again the litter of papers and
notes and letters that had so little to reveal to him. If Hawley had received a similar warning he had destroyed it and
said nothing. . . .

Much more likely that he had gone to Drummond's
office with the idea of being of service to Marta. She had
her own key; she would scarcely have provided another for
Hawley's use! That brought Doc in again and Doc would
have to stay out until 4 p.m. Well, then, Doc, or another,
could have provided the key that admitted Hawley, and
Doc, or another, could have known that all the time Marta
Bellifer was just across the hall waiting to be the logical suspect for causing Hawley's death. Hawley wouldn't have been
too much surprised to see Doc—or someone else. Marta Bellifer was always dragging people into breathless conferences.

And then, while the one-twenty freight thundered by
behind the Drummond Block, the shot had been fired, and
the vague, gray-clad figure seen by Lew had wiped the gun,
if that had been necessary, and had pressed it into Hawley's
hand and had slipped away again by the back door and
stairs. And he wouldn't have had far to go. . . .

Once more Joe Ralston slumped deep into Hawley's
sagging chair. If that was the way the answer was going
to come, what in God's name was he to do? Why? why?
why? There must be a reason for such an insane course. He
stirred wretchedly. That couldn't be the answer—insanity.
. . . Not yet could Joe force himself to the ultimate proof,
right in his pocket all the while.

There was still Doc Bunting. He needn't do anything till
he had a chance to sound out Doc a little more. He'd run
out to Newt Gowdy's. There was a loose end there that must
be tightened. And Drummond should be handled pretty
carefully. Surely nothing could happen to Drummond for
a few hours, but inevitably, there would be another. Ready
or not . . . .

Feeling like a fool, and a coward, Joe Ralston shook himself erect and left the parsonage. He glanced at his watch.
Verriker might be waiting for him at his own headquarters.
Ed would laugh at him; that's what made him feel the fool.
But the editor was no longer waiting for him. He'd been
in, one of the men reported, finished his cigar, and then a
call from the *Observer* had taken him off. Joe was to drop
in there, if he had time.

Instead, Joe got out his car and set off in search of Newt
Gowdy. Newt was cutting corn in the lower patch, his wife
said, but as she had been the patient

the doctor had come to see, Joe gleaned all that was
necessary from her with the able assistance of her reminis-
cent sister and mother-in-law. Sure, the doc had been out
on Monday, the last trip he had to make, too, seein' as how
the yaller pills he left for Rhody were that powerful strong.
. . . He'd come out early in the evenin'; they'd just got the
kitchen all redd up after dinner. It was pretty near one by
the shadders. Doc had set a spell after he'd seen for himself
that Rhody was feelin' right pert ag'in, an' they'd had a real
good visit. . . .

Joe's blood raced in premature relief. Doc Bunting's
story wasn't clicking. He'd said, close to noon. Gran'ma
Gowdy's time was significantly later. He checked and re-
checked the women's report, more and more hopeful that
he had found a flaw that could be made to deflect him
to Doc. Not until he was well on his way back down Big
Rock Road did the fatal confusion of standard and sun time
occur to him. The doctor's watch would agree with his and

Bly's Landing's time. The Gowdy farm ran according to the sun. There was no clock in the kitchen and they had no radio. Telling time by the shadders, at this season of the year, wouldn't throw Gran'ma Gowdy off enough to wreck Doc's story. Suppose Bunting had heard the Amberlee girl's voice "close to noon." He had gone right on to Newt Gowdy's, arrived within ten minutes easily, and had remained there chatting with the Gowdy women for at least an hour.

However, there was still the chance that on his way back . . . Certainly whatever had happened to Lydia had happened by that time, or not much later. Joe's list of questions for Doc grew.

It was not yet four when he returned to town, and he could see for himself that Bunting's car was not in its parking place. He braked his own savagely, and strode through his quarters to the inner niche whose STRICTLY PRIVATE was so seldom taken seriously by anyone in Bly's Landing. This time he shot the door bolt and then, grim and wretched, drew from his pocket, where all along it had felt as heavy as the albatross, the packet that had come from Temple that morning.

Photostatic reproductions of the five *Ready or Not* threats. He ranged them side by side and stared at them, at first scarcely able to focus his unwilling gaze. What he saw, at last, was not at all what he and Ed had seen when they had compared the originals with the assortment of typing samples the afternoon before.

Joe Ralston knew then, for sure. But what was he to do about it?

He wasn't just easy-going, good-natured Joe Ralston. He was the marshal of Bly's Landing and he had taken an oath of office. That was the answer. There could be no other.

When at last he emerged from his tiny office it might have been observed that he was looking strangely older. He strode past his somnolent clerk and out into the street, heading for Bunting's consulting room. Before he had gone half a block an incident occurred that, oddly enough, was to provide him, when the time came, with a missing bit of the whole unhappy jig-saw. A twittery little woman, her head turned to look at someone in a passing car, ran into him before he could sidestep. Gravely he begged Mrs. Bryant's pardon.

"Hello, Joe." She gave him a friendly beam. "Served me right for gawking. But I was hurrying along—I'm on my way down to meet the four o'clock bus. I'm expecting our Lester. My grandson, you know, Mary Ella's boy. He liked it here so—he was with us from the time school closed last May clear till the first of September, and Mary Ella promised that he could come back for a week-end before it got too cold. His grandpa and I have missed him like everything. He was a real help, carrying tourists' bags in and out. You know, Mr. Bryant really isn't fit to do so much lifting. Lester picked up a lot of dimes—expect that's why he was so willing to hang around when folks came and went. People will tip no matter what you say. I'm right glad, though, that he wasn't here this last week. He'd have wanted to be in the thick of our murders—dreadful, dreadful! Lester's that crazy about the G-man outfit Mary Ella bought him. . . ."

Joe edged along throughout this deluge, looking polite but paying little conscious attention, for he could now see that Doc's car was in its accustomed place.

Two patients were waiting. Ralston brushed by them and into the inner office whose half-open door revealed that the doctor had not yet emerged from the dwelling part of his house.

"You'll have to see me first," he announced bluntly, when Bunting stepped across a hallway, buttoning himself into a freshly laundered white coat. "It won't take long—I hope."

"The marshal is speaking, I gather," Bunting murmured, and closed the waiting-room door.

"Where had you been last Sunday evening when old Mrs. Prescott called you in? Don't bother to hit the ceiling."

The doctor's answer was prompt, mild, and impersonal—no urge to hit ceilings at all. "I'd been called about six to see a sick child up on Sycamore Street, one of the Archer tribe. Looked like it might be appendicitis, but it turned out to be persimmons."

"You were at Newt Gowdy's place on Monday between twelve and one. Where did you go from there?"

"A hound for detail, aren't you, Joe?" His face declared plainly that he had not forgotten the information he had already given. "Well, checking up's your job and I have nothing to be touchy about. After quite a little chin with the old gals, I drove on to the end of the road to see a man about a dog. My wife's got her new pooch—she's playing ball with him this minute, if you still yearn to check up."

"Lutter's kennels, eh? That's on the Clarksburg road."

"Just a quarter mile beyond where Big Rock Road comes in. I came back to town on the good road."

"Okay, Doc. I can skip that, I guess. Now, take a look at this."

Joe drew from his pocket Exhibit XYZ, commandeered from Fult Dodge, and handed the typed note to Bunting.

Quietly the doctor's facetiousness fell away from him. He gave the paper a careful examination and flicked it back across the table.

"That's damned peculiar, Joe."

"Why?"

"Because it's none of mine."

"I was afraid it wasn't."

"Want some evidence?"

"Whatever there is."

Bunting pointed to a worn, shabby case. "You can see it's no recent model, and it's the only thing that locks up in my outfit. I've carried it around this county for twenty years. I've never lost or even mislaid the keys. Here they are—" He pulled a bunch on a ring attached to a chain from his belt. "It would have been more sensible to keep them in separate places, but I never have."

"I'll take one of them, if you don't mind." Joe's voice sounded heavy in his own ears.

"I see. . . ." Joe wondered if he did as he caught the thin bit of metal Bunting detached and tossed across to him.

There was one more question. Joe Ralston did not know how to ask it. He backed awkwardly towards the door. "Thanks, Doc. I hope I won't need it long. I couldn't get much done without folks like you and Ed—"

"Anything I can do, of course—and I realize that Ed feels the same way, but—I say, Joe. . . ." Bunting checked himself and looked uncertain. "Well, we're both being frank. Ed won't play ball with himself. Don't run him too ragged with this damned mess of murder and sudden death. Excitement's not good for him. He oughtn't to be worried, but you know how Ed is—"

"And I go bellyachin' to him with every little mess I ought to clean up for myself. I get you, Doc."

IV

Since his talk with Fult Dodge at noon, Ralston had made a wide circuit. Now from Bunting's office he swung around so that once more he approached the *Observer* shop. The place should have been deserted so late on a Saturday afternoon, but the deliberate thump of the job press told him that Fult was still about. No matter how distinctly Doc had warned him, Joe felt that his half-way engagement with Verriker had been neglected. Perhaps he'd left a message for him with Fult.

Ethel Erbaugh, it appeared, had not yet pried herself away from her ledgers. "The boss is back with Fult," she called to him the instant she identified the figure that lounged at the door. "He's been wondering where you'd got to."

A minute later Verriker came through from the back room and the two slid into opposite chairs with Lew's desk between them. Ethel rather noticeably closed the door of her cubicle and attacked an adding machine. Mindful of Bunting's words, Joe gave Verriker's face an anxious survey. The old scout was looking seedy, no mistake. It was a good thing he was seeing the end of the mess.

"Nothing much to worry you with any more, Ed," he announced more cheerily than he felt. "Looks to me that I've got just about the right dope at last, unless you start popping it full of holes. As I see it, there's nothing much that we can do about it."

"Sez you. You're not by any chance a defeatist?" Ed's growl sounded comfortable. "Myself, I feel as if a little hole-popping might set me up—make me relish Mrs. Lukey's meat loaf and potato salad come supper time."

Joe plunged on. "There are a lot of damn fools in Bly's Landing, Ed, but only one prize villain, and he's the big-shot up at the Lodge. I think I know who peddled the *Ready or Not* notes, but I don't think that's so important. People who amuse themselves like that have their fun and call it a day without taking on murder. And of course one of them would be aimed at our friend, just mentioned. He saw a chance to turn a trick or two himself. You know you had the surprise of your life when he promptly passed on the news to you that he had received one of 'em. That wasn't what he would normally do, was it?"

Verriker shook his head. "No, Joe, it wasn't."

"I'm sorry about one thing, Ed—Lydia. Least said, soonest mended about that poor God-forsaken kid. That's just as the town thinks. She went off the deep end, cleaned up on those two old buzzards, and then drowned herself. But Marta Bellifer and Hawley, poor devil—they're something else again.

"Hawley's mistake was taking the gun and saying nothing about it when he discovered Amberlee's body. He was alone, you recall, while Peggy Morgan was at the phone and again when she went into her room for her dressing gown. I suppose he thought he was protecting old Dawson from the suspicion of murder and suicide. As I see it, Hawley had the gun with him when he sneaked up to Drummond's office to help Marta Bellifer out of a hole.

"Now Marta had got a warning note too. She wept on your shoulder at once, but can you imagine her not going as promptly to the one man she had a strangle hold on? I can't—not our Marta. And as soon as he knew she was trembling in her strapped sandals, he saw an out for himself. He could frame her, and if the law—meaning me—didn't catch on he could rub my nose in it till I had to act on the case against her. But she knew when she was licked and killed herself, which was no doubt a disappointment of sorts to her boy-friend. That he was perfectly willing to rub out old Tom Hawley to rid himself of Marta is quite in character, as I think you will yourself agree."

Joe stopped. Except for the steady pounding of Fult's press and the intermittent clatter that Ethel Erbaugh was making, the *Observer* office was quiet. Then Verriker gave a grunt of assent and waved his cigar as a signal for Joe to continue.

"I know about the telephone calls that went hither and yon Thursday morning, Ed. I know how he got a key to Hawley—very slick, that—not using one of his own. And his alibi's swell, but it's got to have a crack in it, and if you say so, I can pound away on that till kingdom come. But any case against him would last longer than that one that started when I was a kid—you know, that playboy that shot an architect or whoever he was.

"As I say, he could have got back to town all right. That right-of-way behind the Drummond Block's a very useful thoroughfare for those that think of such things. He knew from Marta just about what he'd find Hawley doing—doing it only because he truly wanted to help a lady in distress. Hawley had the gun, which was one up for the man who had followed him so quietly up that back stairway. He'd have used his own otherwise—he was prepared. But using other people for his own advantage is automatic with him. He's got where he is by that route. I doubt if Hawley did any more than pull the .32. He must have been completely flabbergasted to see the man who he'd just been told had left town for the rest of the day. It was snatched from his hand and turned on himself in a matter of seconds—and it was all over. All but staging the appearance of suicide. That would make it look all the worse for Marta when it would come out that she was keeping an exceedingly phony dental appointment right across the hall. Oh, he had Marta where he wanted her, all right. And then he was off again, down the back stairs, and up the tracks out of town. His alibi—"

"Still want to do a little cracking, don't you, Joe?"

"Otherwise he's in the clear, Ed. I had it out with him last night. Before my eyes he burned whatever it was that would have hanged him."

Verriker opened his eyes a little more widely, as if he had not quite understood Ralston's last words. "So that's why you say there's no use going on with it. I'm not so sure, Joe. If it could do Lydia any good . . . but I ought to feel just as outraged about the others as I would if he'd had a hand in her death. About Tom Hawley anyway. . . ." He stirred restlessly and fell silent for a moment. "Your case is weak, Joe, damned weak, and the state would be fighting his money and influence all the way through. You ought to have something that can be made to stick before you start and, boy, you may get it yet, if you keep at it and don't make a mistake too soon. I'm still a target. Maybe I can force him out in the open. It would be worth it. Let me think it over. . . ." Verriker closed his eyes. His face was like a death mask.

Dr. Bunting's veiled warning rested heavily upon Joe
Ralston. "Don't, Ed, don't—bother," he muttered. "What
in time's he got against you, anyway?"

"Plenty, plenty . . . And he knows I got one of the *Ready
or Nots*. You just let me think it over."

Fult Dodge's press had ceased its pounding. In a minute or so he came through the shop, a well-browned straw
hat clamped on his head and a newly lighted stogie in his
mouth. After an unexpected rush job, Fult was calling it a
day.

"'Night, boss," he called, but gave Joe no glance.

Verriker gestured amiably, without opening his eyes.

Ethel Erbaugh's door opened. She too was leaving. "I'm
mailing the rest of the statements, Ed. There's not a thing
for you to see to. Good night. Good night, Joe."

Again Verriker waved without changing his position. As
she slipped by him, Joe felt a slight pressure against his arm
and saw that she had thrust a bit of paper between it and
the table.

"'Night, Ethel. See you at the fire." And he shifted his
arm just enough to completely conceal the note, if that was
what it was.

A long five minutes ticked by. Not until the lull was
broken by the rumble of an arriving train and the clear hiss
of released steam, did either man stir.

"The 4:50's good and late," Joe observed, leaning forward on his elbows to look at the office clock. Ethel's note
was now safe in his palm. "So you think I might as well
keep pecking away at his alibi, huh?"

"Um-m, oh, that? Why not, Joe?" Verriker rose and
reached for his hat. "I'll have to start for Mrs. Lukey's. She
gets a little out of patience with me sometimes." He paused
and regarded the telephone. "Tell you what I want to do,
Joe. I'm going to have a talk with Drummond."

Without further explanation, he called for a number
and the connection went through. "Tim? Alec there? Let

me talk to him . . . Ed Verriker, Drummond. You coming down to town this evening? Kinda like to catch up with you somewhere. . . . Fine, fine. Any time suits me. . . ."

He dropped his hat on his head and started towards the door. Joe followed. "Says he'll look in here at nine-thirty. Going up to the house now, or back to the office?"

"Private?" Joe demanded.

Verriker looked at him as at a small boy teasing for a nickel. "You'd shut him up, don't you reckon?"

"I don't like the way you keep calling yourself a target."

"Too soon for fireworks, Joe. At that, you'd have your case. But it isn't going to be that simple. Say, do you know, I'm beginning to feel downright hungry. . . ."

Ralston loped along beside the older man, but nothing more was said on the subject of their solution of the murders. Every passer-by spoke to them both, and by the time Mrs. Lukey's boarding house was reached, Verriker had made a good start towards next week's news notes and personal items for the *Observer*. At Mrs. Lukey's, Joe asked to use the telephone, and when he had made a quite unnecessary call to tell Kate that he was on his way home for dinner, Verriker was at the table and well launched on a choice Hatfield-McCoy anecdote.

Taking the back way home, Joe managed his first look at the paper he had received so oddly from Ethel Erbaugh. He read, in her beautiful, characterless bookkeeper's script:

"Could I see you privately between seven and seven-thirty? At my house."

He took a second look at the note just before he reached his house. This time it was the paper upon which it was written that he examined. His excitement mounted. He held it up anxiously, but the fading autumn light was not sufficient to rely upon.

He hurried into the house and snatched just enough food to appease Kate. She and Peggy were both at peace with the world and hoping that Joe would be ready to talk.

Peggy's gambit concerned the jar of bittersweet she had just arranged to her own satisfaction in the Ralston hall.

"From that darling old-fashioned little brick cottage down on the same street where Mr. Verriker lives. There's a regular story-book old maid that lives there, but she's just as cute as a button. She announced that my stockings were too thin and that no lady ever put paint on her lips in her day, but she let me cut all the bittersweet I wanted. Mack will love it—he's coming down tonight. Kate took her a Kathleen Norris and some tomato preserves and I tagged along, and—oh, Kate, I must tell him, even if he is looking as cross as two sticks."

Joe was already folding his napkin, but he was finding it increasingly difficult to be heavily official with Peggy Morgan.

"Well?" He grinned. "Solved my murders?"

"Only wish I could, old dear. But I'm not bright. I've merely cleared away a little bother that's been hanging on ever since that dreadful Sunday night. You remember I said I had the feeling that I'd seen somebody with bittersweet that night and I couldn't quite focus it. Somebody else besides the boy who tried to sell it when the train stopped, I mean. And who do you think it was? I remembered this afternoon, just as clear as clear. It was nobody in the world but our own Mr. Verriker, with a bit in his buttonhole, on his way in to church. I was joking about going in with him just to show off my new hat. So that's out as a clue, if you ever honored it by calling it one."

"That's sure the way with most clues—they aren't, when you try to fit them in." Joe excused himself and rose. "Hard to say where I'll be tonight, Kate. I may be late."

V

Joe raced his car back along Railroad Street. The *Observer* office was dark. Halfway down Main Street he recognized

Verriker's familiar gait and heard his voice in friendly greeting. He was turning in at Cardy's to buy cigars. Nothing could happen yet. Lots of time before nine-thirty. Private or not, it was up to him to stand by Ed. . . . But it would be all right to take a little time off for Ethel Erbaugh.

He glanced at his watch. First he must stop at his own office, get the other note, and make his comparison in a good light.

Sickish excitement swept over him again when, behind closed doors, he pulled from the safe one of the clues that too certainly was a clue, and an inscrutable one so far, the note that had lain so inconspicuously against Peggy Morgan's pillow. Joe held it and Ethel's against the light. Not only were the sheets identical in size and texture, but they bore the same watermark. No other paper like it had been found in the Amberlee house. No way of identifying its source had as yet been discovered. Now he knew who had used another sheet of the same paper and almost certainly he knew where it had come from.

Placing the two sheets safely in a pocket memorandum book, Joe turned his car around the next corner and made for the Erbaugh house.

Ethel was waiting for him. "I asked you to stop here," she explained, "because this is the night my sister and her husband always go to the early show. And a little later somebody might've dropped in. I guess you'll think it's funny, seeing as I've always been one to mind her own business, but ever since the funeral—"

It was a promising beginning, but Joe risked an interruption. He felt impelled to press the sore spot. "Where did that paper come from that you wrote your note on?"

She gave him a strange look and then appeared relieved. "I used it on purpose. I was sort of hoping you'd notice it. From my own drawer in my desk. That's where I keep it."

He made no comment then on her strange remark. "Got much of it around?"

"Only one pad of it left and I'm getting down to the tail-end of that. Matter of fact, it was just two or three samples that came in—oh, maybe a couple of years ago. I cabbaged on to 'em, but it was too nice a paper to use for just scratch pads, so it's lasted me all this time."

"I see. . . ." But he didn't, exactly. "Now what was it about the funeral?"

"Lydia . . . That poor child—we were always extra nice to her down at the paper. Seemed to please Ed so. . . . I sat there during the service, thinking of Lydia and wondering—well, I guess I wasn't the only one. All the queer things that had come out and all. I suppose I knew as much as anyone on the outside—about the clues, I mean. Lew had been running in circles ever since it started to happen, and of course Ed was genu-winely concerned. He thought a lot of Lydia, you know. I hear things, but I'm not one to talk. And I see things too. You've been in and out of the office all week and I couldn't help but notice. That note she'd left on the Morgan girl's pillow—I'd seen it and it's been bothering me. That's what I was thinking about mostly. At the funeral."

Joe let her ramble, chiefly because he was not at all sure where she was going. After a pause she started afresh.

"You know, Ed coaxed her to peck at our typewriter whenever Dawson Amberlee would park her in the office, and I'd see that she had regular typing paper, not that sleazy copy stuff, and an eraser, and so on. One time—oh, easy a year ago, after Ed and Dawson went off to something or other going on up to the high school, she said she guessed she wouldn't stay any longer and could she leave a note. That's when I gave her two-three sheets off of my nice smooth pad. I don't know what she wrote or who to, only she didn't type it. She walked out of the office a few minutes later, and I continued to mind my own business, of which I had plenty. I remember, though, that when I put away the things she'd been working with there were a couple of sheets of what I call my paper not touched, and I put them back with my pad."

"And when the men came in?"

"'Lydia went away somewhere,' I called out, and I heard Ed say, 'Maybe this explains it,' and I saw he handed something over to Dawson Amberlee. It could have been a note, but I wouldn't know. That's all, but it worried me, kind of."

"What worried you about it, Miss Ethel?"

"Why, the paper being the same. It's my paper— I'd swear to that on a stack of Bibles."

"You won't have to on my account." But Joe Ralston thought of the judge and counsellors and jury that might have to listen to her testimony. "Suppose we do take a wild jump and say that Lydia's uncle kept her little message all this time and used it for reasons unknown to account temporarily at least for her absence last Sunday. He may have had good reason for sending her away from the house."

"But they say he was killed unaware." It wasn't easy to be illogical with Ethel Erbaugh. "Of course he might have been expecting some trouble-maker. I can see that."

"I'm afraid we'll never know a lot about what went on that afternoon and evening at the Amberlee house. Well, Miss Ethel, I'm sure much obliged to you for telling me all this. Up to now I had no sort of explanation for the note left on the pillow, but I must say you've given me an idea. You'll keep it under your hat? I'll have to use it in my own way."

"I told you once I wasn't one to talk. You did notice about the paper, too. I'll say Bly's Landing's got a real smart detective, after all."

"Sounds a bit left-handed, but thanks just the same."

From the Erbaugh house Ralston again made the circuit of the streets, lively with Saturday-night activity. There was a light now in the *Observer* office. Verriker was crouched over his desk, writing. Of Drummond Joe saw nothing. He turned his car up the road that led to the Lodge. He drove

along the private drive with dimmed lights but only until
he could see that the place was well lighted. There was still
plenty of time; it was not much after eight. Leaving his car
behind the last curve, he edged slowly along.

Drummond's Lincoln was parked near the entrance, but
in addition he satisfied himself that the man himself had
not yet finished a solitary dinner. He lurked in a laurel
thicket until he saw him rise from the table and enter the
long common room. Quickly shifting to another window he
was just in time to see Drummond close a desk drawer and
slip a gun into his pocket.

He might have expected that; in fact, he had. But he
did not wait to see more, He regained his car, turned it
cautiously, and then coasted down the drive. When he was
once again on the main road, he did not stop until he had
reached the edge of town. He pulled off at the first side
street and, with his car again pointed towards the highway,
waited, well hidden in the darkness.

The thirty-five minutes that went by added nothing
to his poise, but at last Drummond's big car flashed past.
Joe followed. He turned into Main Street in time to see
the Lincoln slow uncertainly at the Drummond Block, but
its driver evidently abandoned that idea. The car made an
abrupt left turn at Railroad Street. When Joe trundled by,
it was standing in front of the *Observer* office. He could see
the two men shaking hands. It was just nine o'clock.

He'd had time enough, he chided himself, to plan his
own procedure exactly but it took several minutes to get his
car out of sight and himself into the *Observer* office from
the back. He'd used his eyes while he'd interviewed Fult the
day before. At that, he made more noise than he should.

"What was that?" he heard Drummond growl.

"Creaky old shack, this dump of mine," Verriker assured
him without a glance towards the back room. It would be
just like Ed to cover up what he surely must suspect, that
Joe would never take the word "private" too seriously.

Then, suddenly, they were at it.

"So you're clear of Marta Bellifer at last, Alec, and a damned slick job, too. No bag holding for you. Never have done much of that, have you, Alec?"

"Ed, you must be drunk. You look like the wrath of God."

"God's justice—better phrase. And His justice will see that you hang for Tom Hawley's murder."

"You're crazy!"

"No, not crazy. Joe's got a right nice little case shaping up against you."

"That oaf. I know whose brain's been doing the work."

"I hope you will know—when it's too late. But about that case. Marta and you were due for a showdown and that silly *Ready or Not* threat gave you an idea. I know who wrote 'em—maybe you do too. Marta figured she'd expose you to the one man who'd feel that he'd have to do something about it, and she shenaniganned matters so that he'd join the rendezvous you'd promised her up in your office last Thursday. Poor Tom was a little bothered about what sort of hell Marta might let loose, and I reckon it was a sort of comfort to him to cart around the gun that he'd picked up beside Dawson Amberlee. That gun must have been a white elephant anyway—bet you he wished he'd never touched the thing. But it's helping with you all right. 'God works in a mysterious way. . . .'"

Joe Ralston could hear, but he could now see nothing, and he did not dare to shift his position. The instant that Verriker mentioned the .32 he could have sworn there was some sort of change in Drummond. Ed was touching up his own case against Drummond that he had laid before him late that afternoon, for his own good reasons, but Joe knew that he had been careful to keep the identity of the gun from Drummond when he talked to him on Thursday night and he could not recall now whether he had made that clear to Ed. No matter; Drummond was quick enough to see what that item might turn into.

"You managed your alibi well, Alec. You've got Joe pretty nearly stymied, but he still thinks maybe he can crack it. Better not underestimate Joe. So into your office you came, quite ready to handle Marta. But there was Tom Hawley. Handle him instead, and you'd have Marta on the hip forever and ever. Very neat, too, for even if it was settled as suicide, you could always make Marta understand that she had been responsible for Hawley's death. And if anyone said murder, our Joe, for instance, why, there she was—suspect number one, and you—you're on your way to Wheeling. She even obligingly kills herself. Phenomenal luck, Drummond. You've had a lot of it in your dirty, ruthless life, but now you've seen the end of it."

There was a stir. Joe was sure it was Drummond. Drummond with a gun in his pocket waiting for his hand. But Ed's voice went droning on.

"So at last you're going to be caught, Alec. Not because of Marta, not wholly because of poor Tom Hawley. But because of Julian Bellifer, that you made a helpless fool of, and his two daughters. Because of all the respectable citizens in this county that trusted their savings to your rotten bank you pulled away from so smartly. Because of men like my old friends Will Martin and Dan Clay. You didn't know I knew that, did you? They had first claim to that bonanza lease that made you a millionaire. But you got the lease. Dan died last spring. His address was the Tyler County poor farm. God knows whatever became of Will. Oh, I know—nobody can ever get you now for that rotten deal. Nor for the men your company police shot down when you had the strikers evicted from their filthy shacks. Even the courts backed you up on that. It's a great country. . . .

"And then there's the women—don't pretend to have a complete list myself, but I know about some. Remembers Elva Lacey, Alec? Nothing but a high school kid. She ran away and her mother doesn't know to this day what became of her. And that Polish girl in Pittsburgh. And your wife's nurse. And that stenographer you brought up from Tulsa. And the Drake girl. But most of all, Alec Drummond—God have mercy on your dirty soul! you're going to be caught now because of Lydia's mother, Esther Amberlee. My Esther, Drummond. Now you know."

There was the scrape of feet and a chair crashed over. Ralston flung open the door behind which he was hiding, poised for interference. He could see that Drummond had drawn his weapon, but the two men were struggling hand to hand. Whether Ed Verriker was armed he could not be sure, but Ed was clutching desperately at Drummond's right wrist. Joe leaped between them and the shot missed his out-flung arm so nearly as to scorch his coat sleeve.

Verriker was down, white and still. Drummond stood where he was, dazed. There was no sound but his heavy breathing. "Did—did you see what the fool tried to do?" he gasped. "My God!"

A splintered yellow groove across the table told where the bullet had lodged, but in spite of that, Ralston knelt in swift, anxious examination of the inert form. There was no wound.

"Quick, Drummond. There ought to be whisky somewhere. He's almost gone."

Drummond tugged at a pocket and produced a small flask. The stimulant dribbled back from the stiff, graying lips. Drummond was already at the telephone, barking profanely at the operator to get Bunting at once. Then he stood looking down at his gun that had landed under the overturned chair. He let it lie there. Joe pulled the faded seat cushion towards him and stuffed it clumsily under Ed Verriker's head, one hand still on the almost undetectable pulse. Once, when he pulled his eyes away from the death-stricken face of his old friend, he could tell that Drummond's control was well back in the saddle. But the man's inscrutable gaze told him nothing.

"How much did you hear?" Drummond's voice was soft.
"Everything."

"But did you see? Crazy, of course—I'll swear to that.
When he picked up that lump of lead, I acted accordingly
—you would have yourself. But he—he kept pulling my
gun down towards his own chest. Thank God the shot went
wild. But what was he trying to do?"

"I'm afraid I know. But why . . . why?"

There was the groan of bad brakes and the slam of a car
door. Dr. Bunting had been reached. The sound penetrated Verriker's ebbing consciousness. Joe bent still closer to
catch the blurred murmur.

"A target—that's what I said. And I guess he got me . . .
Let the column stand. No matter now—I shan't care."

VI

Joe Ralston let the column stand. He found it, folded under
the inkwell on Ed's desk, his own name neatly underscored
on the blank side of the uppermost sheet. Found it after
Doc Bunting had had the body removed and after Drummond had gone off in his gleaming car.

In the few seconds between the banging of the door of
Doc's car and his swift steps across the floor of the *Observer*
office, the two of them had acted with beautiful smoothness.
"The chair, the gun, the table. . . ." Joe breathed without
moving from Verriker's side. Drummond righted the chair,
dropped a paper from a stack of exchanges over the weapon
still lying beneath it, and laid his hat on the bullet's path
across the table. Then he stood, his back against the wall,
his arms folded across his chest, until Bunting announced
that Verriker was dead.

"Not surprised," he said, dropping his stethoscope. "He's
been on the ragged edge for some time, but he was a bad
patient. Only pretended to take what I prescribed. All this
excitement was too much for him. I warned him. Warned

you, too, Joe." His look was reproachful. "What was going on here tonight?"

Ralston looked Bunting straight in the eye. "Just talking things over. Ed was awfully keen about the damned mess we've been up against this week. I know what you said, Doc, but you just couldn't keep him off the subject. He just—passed out, Doc."

"He called me," Drummond said, and his voice shook a little, quite naturally, "and suggested that I drop in, if I came down this evening. He was afraid the big-town papers were playing up Bly's Landing in a way we wouldn't like. God, it all happened so a quick—"

Drummond said no more until, after what seemed like an endless time to Joe, the two were at last alone in the *Observer* office. Then he picked up his hat and looked at the scarred table.

"You've nothing on me, Ralston."

"No. Nothing on you. He had, but I haven't. . . ."

"Your case is solved."

"It's closed, thank God."

Drummond looked at the newspaper under the chair. "I'll be getting back up to the Lodge, then. I'm standing by, young fellow."

Joe nodded. "Take your gun along. You've killed no one with it."

Drummond picked it up and slipped it into his pocket. "His hand never touched it. There are just my own fingerprints. Good night."

Joe acted quickly then, for Lew Mason and Fult, too, might be barging in at any moment. He dug out the bullet and dropped it in his pocket. Then after a reckless jerk of his shoulders, he knocked over a stout, sharp copy spike and plumped a sizable pile of exchanges upon it and over the marred place on the table. He stalked over to the desk and looked until he found the folded copy sheets. Ed's column for next week's paper.

He saw what it was but he did not read it then nor there. He wanted to get off before he'd have to chew everything over with any of the *Observer* staff. Leaving the office in darkness and closing its door behind him, he made off up the deserted stretch of Railroad Street.

His own headquarters would be no retreat nor would his home. Hawley's study—that was the best place. He still had the key.

There at the pastoral desk, he laid out the folded pages of Ed Verriker's last column. Before he opened them he found a blank sheet of sermon paper and started to write. He headed it:

What I Think—What I Know—What I Can Prove

1. Ed knew from Doc that his number was up. I think it gave him an insane idea. But I don't think—not for a minute—that Ed was insane.

2. He wrote the *Ready or Not* letters. To his pet hates, obviously. And one to himself, just to be funny, perhaps. All of them on Hawley's typewriter, which anyone in town could get at. I never told him I had them photostated, not because I suspected anything then, but just to impress him later with not being as dumb as everybody took for granted I was. When he took the originals later, after they'd come back from Temple, he returned different ones to me and pointed out all sorts of interesting facts about the machines they'd been typed on. Or at least, Marta Bellifer's, Judith Amberlee's, and his own were substitutions. He could have typed two fresh copies on Peggy Morgan's machine while he was up there on Thursday. I don't know where the second for Judith came from; he said he hadn't identified that one yet. But why he went to all that trouble I don't know, except that he was out to get Drummond. It was a mistake, for it led me straight to him. And how I tried to hang it all on any one of the others involved. I'll never forget how sick I felt when the idea dawned on me. And I think he could

have planted the notes for the two Amberlees himself. He had the opportunity Sunday night, and I'd given the rooms a pretty thorough going-over myself without finding them.

3. What he told me about wanting to help Lydia I believe. I don't know what accounts for his passionate personal interest in the girl, but I suspect it has something to do with her mother—there's always been the question about her paternity, and then there's what he threw in Drummond's teeth tonight.

Could Ed have been her father? Somehow I can't believe that. He got Lydia away somehow on Sunday, or maybe she herself had come to the point of acting on his plan for her to go off on her own in Pittsburgh. Then he shot Judith and Dawson, but why I don't know, except what he said to Drummond. Ed himself told me all about Dawson's taste in music and he could have counted on the radio program being on or one of those loud records going. The .32 is easy. The Bryant grandson swiped it out of White's car and then got scared. Ed stood by him and sh-shushed it up—that explains what he wrote in his column the next week—but he kept the gun. And he carried it off with him after he had killed the Amberlees. To keep Lydia out of the mess as long as possible he put the note on Peggy Morgan's pillow, the old note that Dawson probably never took away from the *Observer* office. I think Ed must have been pretty sentimental about any little thing that was connected with Lydia. If Ethel Erbaugh hadn't been curious about the distinctive paper and possessive about it too, that would be one thing I never could have known. That's when the bittersweet berries fell from his buttonhole bouquet—when he was in Peggy's room. She'd found one of them by her dresser that evening before any of the excitement broke.

4. All day Monday Ed was scouting around hunting Lydia—so he said. I never checked his movements in any way. I know she must have been up in that picnic shack on Drummond's land and somebody else who left a little ash behind

was there too. Doc went by on the road below and so did
Hawley and Marta Bellifer, but those two were along after
her death must have occurred, and Doc's alibi's okay. I can't
believe Ed killed Lydia, but certainly he knew more about
what really happened to her out along Big Rock than I can
guess now.

5. Ed had sent Marta Bellifer and Drummond *Ready or
Not* warnings, and he got busy on them next. He had had
Fult make him a key—pretty, risky that was, in case Fult
ever got around to asking Doc questions. How he got hold
of Alec's spares I don't know. Maybe Drummond pulled
my leg about their never getting away from him. Ed must
have been trying to frame Alec, just as he tried tonight,
though how he could have reckoned on just what Drummond would do with himself when his car stalled on him
I don't see. He might have monkeyed with the wiring in
some way, but even then it would all have been too chancy.
Certainly he could have easily framed Marta, and maybe
she was the only one he was aiming at. At that, it would
have made a mess that was sure to drag in Drummond. All
those phone calls, Marta's and Hawley's, click well enough.
When Hawley called Ed he must have let slip something
that gave Ed the tip he was fixing to meet Marta up there.
I figure he could have slipped on Fult's gray cover-all and
hiked along the tracks from the back door of the *Observer*
office to the back stairs of the Drummond Block. Why he
deliberately shot poor Tom Hawley I don't know, but Marta
was just across the hall and really headed for Drummond's
office, so he was going to make her face the music, catch
her "ready or not." He left the .32, which indicates that he
himself had no further use for it. He could have done the
whole thing in five minutes, typing and all, and been back
at his own desk. It was a slack time at the *Observer*—he was
the only one not out on noon hour. I checked on that.

6. After that, I ran around in circles testing Drummond's
alibi, and why not? But it's sound enough. I thought that
through the other night. Seemingly I wasn't going after

Marta hard enough, and so he casually mentioned the story Lew was working on and handed me a slice of ancient scandal that I'd be sure to bite on, and there was I on Thursday evening, trying to worm something out of Marta Bellifer. She took the shortest way out—and he'd "caught" her.

7. That left Drummond. I was feeling pretty shot about Ed by that time, and after my talk with Drummond up at his place I felt worse, for I couldn't get away from the idea that he might get it next. Not that I was gushing with sympathy for Alec Drummond. . . . Still, I tried every little out today before I'd face the proof of those photostats. Then when I put my so-called case against Drummond before Ed this afternoon and heard him call Alec and arrange a meeting, I knew I couldn't sidestep much longer. Before God, I don't know but what I'd have let them have it out together without sticking in, if it hadn't been for Ethel Erbaugh. If she ever has to know the whole story, she'll probably never get over having helped to pin it all on Ed. Even Peggy Morgan forced me to keep right at it, with her dope about the bittersweet.

8. I think Ed wanted to keep me out of it tonight. He said Alec was coming at nine-thirty, but he made the office at nine sharp, and that's the hour they must have agreed on over the phone. If I had edged in a half hour later, I might have found Ed shot by a bullet that sooner or later could have been traced to Drummond's gun—I'd heard their appointment. There would have been only Drummond's word about Ed's goading him to attack and then struggling to force the gun against himself. Oh, he might have been cleared on a self-defense plea, but I reckon that Ed figured a lot of old scores would have been balanced by the mess he'd have got Drummond into.

9. But why Ed Verriker did all these things I don't know. While he was waiting for Drummond tonight he was writing his last column. The paragraphs should be pungent. I'm going to read his copy now. "Let the column stand"—that was his last request.

VII

The following Friday the *Observer* carried Ed Verriker's last
column, boxed on the first page. Kate Ralston agreed with
her brother that it was the fairest way to present the solution of the week of sensation and death to Bly's Landing,
but only Joe and Fult Dodge, who had it to set up, had read
the copy before the paper appeared. Lew stormed and then
sulked, but Alec Drummond pointedly asked no questions
and as pointedly never left town throughout the intervening
time. Meanwhile there was no question or doubt concerning the cause of Verriker's death; Bunting's prognosis had
emphasized exactly such outcome from undue exertion or
emotional strain. Bly's Landing was shocked and grieved—
Ed had been everybody's friend.

If Joe Ralston had thought that gossip and rumor would
have nothing more to feed upon after reading the last message of the editor of the *Observer*, he was of course mistaken. The paragraphs were obscure and cryptic except to
those directly concerned, but he let the town make of them
what they would. The case was closed.

They read:

Items of Old News

On a certain spring evening, some twenty-odd years ago,
Miss Esther Amberlee accepted a proposal of marriage made
to her by an ambitious newspaper man who loved her with
tender and passionate devotion.

Miss Judith Amberlee, unable to enjoy the fullness of
life herself, determined to make her young sister's life as
narrow and poisoned as her own. Esther was helpless against
the devilish machinations of Judith, ably assisted by the
cold and selfish indifference of her brother. The lover received a tragic note and after that he was never permitted
to see Esther again, or to hear from her—except once.

The editor of the local paper left Bly's Landing. He was
not, as the printed news at the time announced, acting as

foreign correspondent for a Washington newspaper. He was trying to find his sweetheart. He failed in that. The only clue he had was the grim phrase obliquely dropped by Dawson Amberlee, that she had been "put away."

The distracted lover returned to Bly's Landing to take up his old job—returned a year later, two days after the funeral of Esther Amberlee. She had died a suicide, leaving behind her a little nameless daughter. By some blessed miracle, considering the two implacable creatures whose pride and hypocritical righteousness had tortured her to death, she had managed to dispatch a last word to her lover—to the man, thank God, she had never ceased to love. She told him the truth about the baby girl and something of how callously and ruthlessly she had been victimized by the child's father. She told him the man's name—something no other person was ever to know. She wished the child could die—perhaps her courage would hold to take it with her into death. If it were only his, her lament was, the baby might be saved from a life with the two she most feared, her own brother and sister.

In time this newspaper man found a measure of peace and a certain quiet happiness. A good and noble woman helped him, became his wife and the mother of his own dearly beloved daughter. God bless them both. He stayed on in Bly's Landing because of Lydia Amberlee, even forced himself into the company of Dawson and Judith Amberlee at times, for her sake—and her mother's. But he could do so little for her. God help him—so little, so little!

Unvarnished Portraits

A certain person established himself in our town and became an economic overlord, financially and industrially. He also became our most hated man. I hated him most of all. I wanted to help God punish him.

Good women do much mischief. One such worked vigorously for our town's welfare and her own glory. May she rest in peace. Her own private lever for advancement and financial security was failing her, but that is not our affair. She annoyed me and I attempted to annoy her. Maybe I had some small share in hastening her end. I hope so.

Tom Hawley did not mind dying. Life had little real meaning for him. We were friends. We had long talks together and I know how empty everything was for him. He had been cast in the wrong part, but he no longer cared. I think he would have been glad to know how he was used in the end.

We couldn't get along in Bly's Landing without Doc Bunting. But he can't do a thing for a head-strong patient who won't take his pills. He'll find three untouched boxes full in the top drawer of my bureau.

Santa Clauses who put toy guns in kids' stockings, artists who draw comic strips, those who concoct movie and radio stories, and certainly we who fill the front page with scareheads, are doing something ugly to our children. Once or twice I have tried to help a little. A certain small boy swiped a man-sized gun and was about to have himself a time. I happened along at the right moment—for him, but I still think his mother and dad ought to worry a little. It may have been the wrong moment for me. I kept the gun.

Joe Ralston is a good police official and deserves reappointment. He has secured the evidence that will identify the puller of the strings of justice. He is shocked and unhappy at the truth he is facing, but he is going to see it through. I'm proud of Joe.

When a man sees the last chance of his lifetime approaching, he'd better take it. Even if it means trying to play God. . . . He has nothing to lose and there's the chance that old poisonous wrongs can be cleared away forever and the world left sweeter and cleaner. He can even have a good time doing it—most of it. That's the way it's been with me.

News Not in Last Week's Observer

Dawson and Judith Amberlee have decided to commit their niece Lydia to an asylum for the insane. They are tired of having her look at them with the eyes of her mother. And they know why that bothers them. So do I.

Several highly respected citizens of our town are a little uneasy over the anonymous letters they have just received. They are the work of one who because of his job has received many unsigned communications, but it is the writer's intention that theirs will worry them far more than he ever fretted over those that came to him. He borrowed an innocent typewriter for the job. Later he felt inspired to make some copies of his masterpiece. Typewriters temporarily inactive aren't hard to find. You can skip that detail, Joe.

Ed Verriker, owner and editor of the *Observer,* has arranged for Miss Lydia Amberlee to start a sane life of her own with good friends in another city. He is fearful, however, that her unnatural life in the Amberlee household has left a permanent mark upon her mind and spirit.

Lydia Amberlee came in great distress to the home of Ed Verriker towards the end of the afternoon of Sunday, September 26th. She had just learned of her relatives' contemplated action against herself. She remained under Verriker's roof until dawn of the following morning, when she was secretly removed to a secluded spot out along Big Rock Road. Her transfer to a safer haven is being planned for.

Because of this, something had to be done, and swiftly. The sudden death of Judith and Dawson Amberlee at the hands of Ed Verriker was the solution of the problem. She was now permanently freed of their perverted influence. A child of sin, they termed her. What were they?

When Ed Verriker met Miss Peggy Morgan, shortly afterward, he hoped most sincerely that she would not be the one to make the discovery that was awaiting someone up at the Amberlee house. He had counted on that experience coming

to the Amberlee maid, about breakfast time on Monday
morning. When Miss Peggy should find a note from Lydia,
which he had placed on her pillow, he saw no reason for
it to disturb her. He wanted most desperately to get Lydia
clear away.

Ed Verriker's gamble with Lydia was a hideous failure.
He attempted a plausible explanation to her of the tempo-
rary hiding place out on the Drummond hillside, but he
only precipitated a complete emotional collapse. In hysteria she fled from him down the trail and across the road
towards the run. He could not catch her. Doc knew what he
was talking about—that wild pursuit was nearly the end of
Verriker. By the time he regained consciousness, there was
no sign of Lydia. He knew then, as surely as he did the next
day when he went with Joe Ralston to reclaim the body,
what had happened.

On Monday night Ed Verriker made a brief business trip
to Pittsburgh, returning Tuesday noon. He satisfied himself
that no undue curiosity had been stirred by his tentative
arrangements for Lydia's stay there with friends, but chiefly
he used the interlude to get hold of himself and decide what
to do about further search for the girl. He began to see
that, no matter what, if she were found alive, most of Bly's
Landing would continue to believe that the poor child had
gone crazy and killed her aunt and uncle. The story would
follow her always. The state might "put her away." He had
done her no service. So he could not grieve for her death.
He could have spoken, but he had other work to do first.

From Tuesday noon on through Wednesday, Verriker
watched Joe Ralston work. More than one citizen of Bly's
Landing could have easily been enmeshed in what their marshal had already accomplished. It was not until Thursday
that Verriker saw a way to take another of his last chances.
A certain good woman for reasons of her own was arranging further interference with the private life of our most
prominent citizen. She convinced her pastor, the Reverend

Thomas Hawley, to join her at the designated place. She fancied that it was because of her chance knowledge of his presence along Big Rock Road on Monday that he acquiesced, but in this she was mistaken. Hawley called Verriker at noon and told him where he was going and why. It must have been a strange hunch; he knew nothing of Verriker's interest in the proceedings, but he trusted his friend. I can write that without remorse. It is my belief that Tom understands now.

Verriker misunderstood one point. He expected to find the Prominent Citizen there also. His plan was to time himself properly, go by the back way from his office to the rendezvous—he had his own key. I can pick locks, too, Alec— shoot his man and be out of sight before the lady entered. He could see her standing there over the body, gun in hand more than likely, just as Hawley would arrive. He himself would wear gloves, and if she was without them it would be the first time in the social history of Bly's Landing.

Because it amused him to do so, he slipped on his printer's cover-all, as he left the office, and also borrowed his abandoned felt hat hanging on the next nail. When he opened the back entrance to the Prominent Citizen's suite, sure enough, there was a man humped over the desk. The freight train was grinding by and the sound of his shot was thoroughly covered. As he fired, the man lifted his head, and he saw, too late, that he had made a tragic mistake. He forced the gun into Hawley's hand and attached the illicit key to his ring. That's how come the bright, fresh scratch, in case Joe Ralston wants to know. There were a few other odd chores too, but he was back in his own quarters fully ten minutes before the first alarm reached him.

Preview

In less than an hour now I shall undertake to rectify one of the mistakes I made Thursday. If my plans work out this time, I shall not know in life that they have succeeded, but just as I believe that Tom Hawley understands, I too believe that I shall know. I expect to be shot by Alec Drummond. He lied to Ralston when he declared that he never carried a gun. He always does. And he has not had an easy minute since he received a certain piece of mail a week ago. If I can keep Joe out of the way long enough, there will be only Drummond's word that he acted in self-defense. There will be his gun with his fingerprints on it. Joe won't be far off; he thinks my caller is coming at nine-thirty, I think he will be in time to hear the shot.

Why am I writing this, then? If my plan shouldn't work, I can kill Drummond with this matrix that Lew uses as a paper weight. In that case Joe will let me destroy this column if I can't get rid of it before he finds it. If nothing happens at all as I have planned it, I can always try again, though I know better even than Doc does that I haven't much time. If it does work, Joe gets the column, and Bly's Landing will enjoy reading the truth about Alec Drummond. I've started something he will never get away from.

READY OR NOT
YOU SHALL BE CAUGHT

And so you were, Judith Amberlee. You knew who killed you, and why. . . .

You too, Dawson Amberlee, and no one cares.

My poor Lydia . . . You were caught before you were born, and I was helpless to free you.

Tom Hawley, my friend, we often agreed that this world we live in doesn't make much sense.

Marta Bellifer, you gave yourself up.

And you lose if you win, Drummond.

THIS
MURDEROUS
SHAFT

Part One
Iowa, Late Spring

1

It was almost time for the bell. Charlotte and I would have
known as much without looking at our watches, because
Ellen Hawke had just entered the teachers' restroom and
vanished into the lavatory for her usual eleven-thirty gar-
gle. Poor old Ellen is our prophylactic pup. She oughtn't be
teaching in a public school with the germ complex she has.
Most of her colleagues think she shouldn't be teaching for
certain other good reasons.

I knew the period was nearly over for another reason. I
had three more papers to do and I never yet have been able
to check the second period's test in a so-called free period.
Charlotte stacked her accumulation of themes and slapped
her grade book down vindictively and got out her compact.
She'd just had a new permanent the Saturday before and she
was still worried about it. She cussed plaintively to herself
as she tried to size up the curl behind her left ear in a two-
inch square of mirror, the big looking glass being locked
up with Ellen. Then the door opened again and Nancy
Ray slipped in. She started toward the lavatory, but before
Charlotte or I could answer the question in her big brown
eyes the door from the hall opened again and Julia Meade
appeared. Julia is the biggest woman on our faculty and the
kindest and everybody always knows what's on her mind
and she asks, anybody, anywhere, what she wants to know.

"Here's the bride herself," she boomed, and made a swoop at little Nancy's hand. "If that isn't one gorgeous ring! When did you get it? You couldn't tell me those week-ends in Chicago weren't suspicious. Going to be married this summer, I'll bet. Well, one year teaching school won't ruin you, but it's plenty, and I'm telling you you're a lucky kid."

Nancy Ray doesn't know Julia Meade as we do. Besides, she's a polite child, and quite obediently she tried to catch up with Julia's string of comments. Charlotte and I remembered that once we had been polite children too and began to coo over the shiny new engagement ring. Just as Ellen Hawke emerged, patting her lips with a paper handkerchief and smelling to high heaven of the carbolized hand lotion she's addicted to, Julia began on Felicity Wendell, my Felicity.

"At that, for a pretty kid like you, just out of school yourself, to be getting engaged and married isn't news at all. It's just the natural course of events. Now when Felicity Wendell sprang her bombshell last summer, that was something! I'll not get a thrill like that again, not till old Elly here grabs off her new doctor."

Ellen giggled. She still does, heaven help her. Nancy was surrounded, having her ring admired and not minding much, naturally, though Julia's voice had swamped her mild admission of a June wedding.

"Felicity," she murmured. "What a lovely name. I hope I'll be happy too."

"She was our last faculty bride. Surely you've heard about that wild romance. Ask Peg—she'll give you the low-down. That was a real thrill. . . ." And she went right on giving Nancy the low-down herself.

"It happened last summer. After the NEA— I guess I'll give it a workout myself this year. It sure brought Flippity luck. She pops down to Mexico on one of those personally conducteds, all old-maid schoolteachers and such, and meets this man and he winds her all up and sweeps her off her feet and follows her right back home and marries her— bam! Just like that—and now she's living in a grand place in Virginia or somewhere, and not even Peg here knew anything about it till all the shootin' was over, and the B. of E. had the resignation of Felicity Wendell Howard. Peg hasn't recovered yet, have you, Peg? What do you hear from Flippity, Peg? Is she going to have a baby or anything?"

Nancy escaped to the johnny and Charlotte lined up to be next. The bell rang, but both Julia and Ellen Hawke paused at the outer door to hear what I had to say. They were joined there by Marian Cole, flushed and fractious after her session with tenth year boys.

"Felicity is fine and very happy. I haven't heard for a month because I just answered her last letter. That round with my throat left me way behind with everything."

"You're planning to go to see her, aren't you?" Charlotte asked.

"Just as soon as school closes, and I am looking forward to it. Felicity's not a very full letter writer, but she says she's saving everything to tell me and show me."

"Everything? Everybody would have been the more accurate word. She acquired a family as well as a husband, did she not? A spinster past her first youth usually has to satisfy herself with an elderly widower."

Marian Cole said that, of course, and as usual her frigid voice got under my skin.

"There's a runner starting in your stocking, Marian. And everybody is the right word, for of course I'm more interested in meeting Jordan Howard and his sons, all safely married and not living at home, if that comforts you any, than in seeing Felicity's house, a lovely old place overlooking the Ohio River—it's West Virginia, Julie. You're as hopeless about geography as the tenth-grade history kids."

"It's all right by me. I'd even wish for a bad cough or Bright's, if I were Felicity, and then she could spread herself. Widows have all the fun." Charlotte grinned at me, knowing that I never minded what she said. "Hurry up in there, Nancy. We've all got to go back to the mines."

"How old is this heart-throb of Flip's? I don't think you ever said."

Julia Meade was right. I hadn't broadcast everything I knew about Felicity Wendell's marriage and I wasn't going to begin now.

"Oh, between fifty-five and sixty, somewhere, and his health is excellent. Mourning would not become Felicity, blonde and beautiful though she is."

I moved toward the door, for the fourth period trig class was waiting and when I haven't that bunch of Indians tied down to tangents and cosines they're too much interested in throwing chalk down into the court. I pulled the door shut behind me, but not soon enough to miss, hearing Marian say something nasty about Miss Wendell's blonde beauty—if any.

School had been harder for me this year. I missed Felicity. I've taught at Grant High long enough to be on maximum salary and I like my job, some of the time. I have good and stimulating friends among the faculty, men as well as women. Charlotte Larsen is a joy and so is Beck Gratz, and I can argue at the drop of a hat with Joe Morris, but my dearest friend was Felicity Wendell, slight, vivid little Flippity. I could wring Julia Meade's neck, double chin and all, for appropriating my own name for Felicity. The fact that after I had first heard her using it my name for my friend had never again been uttered by me in anyone's hearing but Felicity's never registered on Julia's consciousness. It's useless to be subtle with Julie.

I was as surprised as anyone else at Grant High when Felicity married so suddenly and so unexpectedly, but I was genuinely glad that a woman as fine and sweet and feminine as she was not to spend the years of her life teaching

Macbeth and restrictive clauses to young barbarians. Because of our very real friendship I knew more than anyone else among the staff about Felicity Wendell. She wasn't a native of the town, for one thing, and she hadn't gone to the state university, as most of us had. She had no immediate family, perhaps a few widely scattered distant relatives. Her mother's family was Scandinavian, which accounted for her clear blonde coloring and blue eyes as well as for her very considerable reserve. Her father's people were New Englanders, but Felicity had been born in Seattle.

That's all I knew about her background, except for what state reports call our educational training, experience, and certification. She came to Grant to teach after I was well established there myself, and she had taught there for ten years when, at thirty-five, she had married Jordan Howard. A deep friendship had slowly grown between us, though we were neither the type to want to be on one another's neck. She had told me a little about one love affair she had lived through, and I think I was the only person in the system who knew about the three poems of hers that had been published in good magazines. I suspect few of my colleagues of reading verse in any sort of publication.

So, as I have said, I had missed my friend very much. My mind was full of her as I made my way through the corridors, crowded with clattering pupils, toward my classroom and a lesson in trigonometry. My most hopeless student was waiting for me at the door for his daily consultation about not being quite able to understand the assignment. Just as I turned to pull the door shut I caught a good whiff of the familiar antiseptic aura that always surrounds Ellen Hawke. There was a definite purpose in her pale eyes.

"I just thought I'd ask you privately, Miss Lenox, for fear I'd be misunderstood in the restroom." Her voice fell until it was almost inaudible. "Is Mrs. Howard well? Is she going to— I mean, it might be—"

I spoke up like a physician. "She is not pregnant, Miss Hawke. And it's none of our business if she should be. I'll tell her, however, of your concern."

That was a nasty one, for Miss Hawke and Miss Wendell had always got in one another's hair, though the badgering would be started by Ellen Hawke. She retaliated by a long and deliberate stare at my own gray hairs and then scuttled off down the hall.

Heaven help poor Flip now, I thought as I faced my class. By the end of the lunch period it will be a miscarriage or quints.

2

The next day, when I came home, there was a letter from Felicity. A thin one. They had all been short, even the one she wrote me the night before she married Jordan Howard. Nor had I received many since her marriage. She had told me about meeting Howard in her Mexico City hotel, how kind he had been when she was left behind inadvertently when the rest of the party set off to climb a mountain or view ruins or something else on the tourists' schedule, and how they had set off on a private sightseeing tour of their own, and how things had happened to both of them rather dizzily. He was in Mexico for business reasons, something about oil leases, but his home was in West Virginia along the Ohio River. He had been a widower for fifteen years; a sister of his wife's had been running his house for him and looking after his children, two of whom were now married. During most of this time he himself had not been home much. His business interests had been widely scattered. But now he had salvaged what was left after the hard times and wanted nothing more than to settle down and enjoy life and living. What he had to offer her was comfort and a modest degree of financial ease and all his love.

"But even before he had told me that, Margaret dear," Felicity had written in the letter she sent on the eve of her marriage, "my heart had gone out to him and I knew, deeply and truly, how he felt about me. So while everything is happening very swiftly, I do not think that I am making a mistake. A husband and a home and happiness— I am not so devoted to teaching as not to want that much out of life and I had thought those joys were not ever to be for me. . . ."

But I had wondered a little as the months went by after Felicity went to live at River View. The sister-in-law and ex-housekeeper was to continue to live with the Howards, but in quarters of her own, for the house was large and rambling. The second son was staying with her. Apparently he was unattached, though whether he was unmarried or divorced was not made clear to me. The other sons and their wives lived not far off in the small town that was Felicity's new post office address, Point Tyler. She said nothing about their attitude toward the new mistress of River View except that she liked the eldest son very much— he was like his father—and a comment about the wife of Chad, the youngest son. Her interest she evidently found a bit too pushing or exuberant. Felicity cannot be rushed.

The last letter I had had from her had been full of plans about my visit with her and I could tell that my welcome would be very real. In my answer, delayed longer than usual because of a nasty sick spell and the piling up of spring school work, I had assured her that as soon as the commencement duties were over I was taking to the road in my faithful Ford, headed straight for River View.

This thin letter waiting for me, then, was no doubt her last word about my arrival. Rejoicing that vacation and a delightful reunion lay ahead of me so soon, I kicked off my shoes and made myself comfortable in the peaceful oasis of my solitary quarters and slit open Felicity's letter.

Dear Margaret,

I have bad news to tell you, very shocking and
sad for me, and I know you will feel a share
of it with me. Jordan is dead. It happened last
week, very unexpectedly, and I can scarcely
believe it yet. Bartlett found him and the doctor said it was a heart attack. Jordan had told
me once, rather lightly, that his doctor had advised him to slow up and live longer, but even
Dr. Ammon had been quite sure there was no
serious condition to worry about.

    Everyone is being most kind and consider-
ate but I find myself confused and uncertain. I
must remain here at River View until a rather
dismaying lot of affairs is settled. In fact, I
have no other plans at present. I was so happy here, Margaret. But you will understand, I
know, that I shall have to wait to see you until
later on in the summer. You must come, dear,
but not now. I shall want and need you. Till
then, as ever,

                        Your loving Felicity.

Well! I felt at once that Felicity's new world had crashed
about her, but there was no use to speculate until I know
more about what the conditions of her widowhood would
be. I dashed off a note of love and sympathy and reassur-
ance and then dug in at a set of grades and averages.

On the first Monday of vacation Felicity's next letter came. She was very troubled and longing to see me,
she wrote, but she must still ask me to wait. A new will
had been produced, by which her husband had left almost
everything, the exceptions being very minor, to her. The
family was going to fight it, she more than suspected. It
was all the worse because his estate was much larger than
any of them had known. It was not because she wanted

the money—Felicity did not have to convince me of that. There was nothing grasping about her and her placid nature abhorred struggle. But the lawyers assured her that the will was sound and that the relatives could do nothing. Except make themselves unpleasant, she went on. They had had to be together so much. If only she could have River View to herself for even a short while, she could pull herself together, but family bickering and suspicion and even open antagonism were too much to cope with in the first freshness of her grief for Jordan. She had no clue to explain Bartlett's attitude, though she was sure that his aunt's presence accounted for much of it.

That would be Mrs. Sutton, the first wife's sister, who had been in charge of the establishment before Felicity's coming, I figured. It would be easy to guess that she had resented Jordan Howard's second marriage.

It was the closing paragraph of Felicity's letter that set me off and led to my decision.

"I'm afraid, Margaret, afraid of—I don't know what, except that the love of money is the root of evil always. I couldn't help worrying about the little bottle and then, the next time I looked it wasn't there. Since then Rhoda Sutton keeps looking at me. I'm being silly, I suppose, but I am alone against them. Jordan is dead. I knew nothing about his money but I knew his love. I want you, Margaret, and I shall have you here, if you will come, as soon as I can see my way. But not yet . . ."

The next day I set out for an unannounced appearance at River View. At least, I resolved, if I let her know that I am as near as Point Tyler, she'll be mighty glad to have me come the rest of the way.

Part Two
West Virginia, Wednesday, June 15

1

I like to jaunt through the countryside and try never to repeat a route, but this time I pushed straight on, cutting out Chicago, much as I could have used a shopping bout at Field's. Cincinnati tempted me too, but I kept steadily to US-50. All I knew about Point Tyler was that it was somewhere between Parkersburg and Wheeling. The farms were nothing after Iowa and Illinois, but I liked the rough, hilly country. Late in the afternoon after I had crossed the Ohio River I found myself entering a slack little town whose Rotary and Lions Clubs had cordially announced it to be Point Tyler.

My idea was to find a place to freshen up, make some discreet inquiries about River View, and then call Felicity by telephone. My first circuit of the town revealed a hot and stuffy little hotel too close to the railroad station, a tourist cabin place that might serve, but no tourists' lodgings, always my first choice in small towns, that appeared inviting.

I had stopped for a moment at the curb before pulling in to the biggest filling station when a smart coupé swung out from the pumps into the street. To my amazement I heard myself hailed and in a flash I recognized the speaker.

"Hey, Peg! Of all the damnedest times to see you! Stick around. I'll be back . . ."

That's what I thought I heard, anyway, but the voice and
the red head were unmistakable. It was Sally Anderson or
I would eat my sunglasses. I hadn't seen her since the last
summer I had spent at Columbia, five years before. She was
years younger than I and she was no schoolmarm bent on
summer credits, but she had been living in the same apartment where I had wedged myself that summer and we had
hit it off rather well. She had some sort of department store
job then; what she was doing in this West Virginia river
village now, heaven only knew.

There was something else that blurred in my mind too.
It must have been Sally who dashed out of the drug store
opposite and run across the street while I was cogitating
in the car. I realized now that the worried-looking young
woman with flaming red hair who had snapped out something to the attendant as she threw herself into the coupé
was she.

So I began my questions with her. "That car that just
pulled out, who was driving it?" I asked the service man.

"The Buick coop? That was Mrs. Howard. Mrs. Chad
Howard. She was in an awful hurry, on her way up to the
old Howard place."

"Is her first name Sally?" I asked weakly. "I thought I
recognized her, but I haven't seen her since she was married
and I certainly didn't know she lived here."

"Yes, ma'am, that's her name. Mrs. Sally Howard. Mighty
nice, friendly lady too. All I know is she didn't live here
before she got married to Chad. You're from away too, I
see. Iowa seems pretty far out west to most folks in this
town. But not me. I see cars from all over . . ."

I let him babble on, as he tested oil and rubbed the
windshield, my mind on the amazing fact that a gay, vigorous girl I had known as Sally Anderson of New York was
now undoubtedly one of my Felicity's step-daughters-in-law.

"If you'll tell me where she was going, I'll follow her. I
mustn't miss seeing her now that we've met so unexpectedly."

"Yes, ma'am. Kinda nice, ain't it, meeting up with an old pal like that? The Howard place, where she's headed for, ain't far up the road. Keep right ahead on this route here, number 62. It's just a little under three mile. You'll cross a bridge over the crick and the first road off to your left is the one. It's a private drive, but you can't miss it. There's a nice sign that says River View. That's what the Howards call their place. If you want, you might just as well wait here. Chad and his wife live here in town, a swell little place up on Terrace Drive."

"Thanks a lot," I cut him off. "I'll just tool around a bit and explore."

But I headed right out of town, determined to find River View and Sally and Felicity without more delay.

The gas man's directions were excellent. Route 62 followed the river picturesquely for about half the way and then I lost sight of it. I crossed the bridge and soon caught a glimpse of the branching road. On an ornamental iron standard braced in a stone entrance pillar was a rustic signboard lettered in gilt. River View, it read. Private. The winding drive I followed was perhaps

a scant half-mile long, but at the time it seemed longer because its grade rose noticeably and I was proceeding with both caution and curiosity. River View, apparently, was going to be quite a place, and this was my Felicity's home. Hers indeed, even though its master was dead.

I heard the noise just before reaching the last curve that would bring the house into sight, though, of course, at that time I didn't know how near I was to the end of the drive. Nor did I think anything about the noise, except that I heard it and wondered who had thrown what. It sounded like a not so heavy object crashing into the tangle of undergrowth that filled the ravine to my right.

I made another curve, the last one, and there were the house and the river and the view. Also, before my eye had scarcely caught the comfortable rambling lines, the glint of water, and the folds of wooded hills beyond, there was the car that I now knew was Sally's coupé. It was off the drive, parked tight in a tall wall of lilac, and I know now could not have been seen from the house.

Furthermore, there was Sally, bending over the baggage compartment at the rear. She must have been locking it. As I went into neutral she turned, and there I was a key in one hand and in the other a length of dirty cheesecloth. I shall not soon forget the look upon her face. Horror and fright and something nameless and grim.

"Stop! Wait!" she commanded, and then when she must have recognized me for the second time that late afternoon she shifted her position just enough to toss the duster through the open window of her car. "For God's sake, Peg, what are you doing here?"

"Followed you up, old dear, to see if it were really you. But principally to see Felicity Howard. She's a very dear friend of mine."

Sally pushed her bright hair off her forehead with the back of her hand. I saw a dirty mark then, but whether she had merely revealed it or her hand had just left it I could not tell.

"Felicity—you know Felicity! That makes it just perfect." The hand that had held the dirty duster opened and closed into a tense fist and a yelping, hysterical laugh half escaped her. Then she pulled herself together and looked backward as if to assure herself that the protecting wall of lilac was still there. "Of course. You're 'Margaret.' She mentioned the friend who would be her guest this summer. And you've come—now."

I was sure she was thinking fast about something and for an instant her eyes would not meet mine. The tense emotion that gripped her was getting me too, but when she spoke again she was calmer.

"Get out of your car, Peg, and slip over here to me. I don't want anyone to see you. I've got to tell you something pretty ghastly."

That brought me in a hurry.

She pushed me down upon the running board of her car and bent over me and whispered.

"I've just found her—Felicity. She's dead. She's—killed herself. We did it to her. Damn these Howards."

Her chin quivered and she began to cry soundlessly, but when she saw what her words were doing to me, she put her hands on my shoulders and braced me. I could feel the keys she still held pressing down into my flesh. That remained the only physical sensation I was conscious of.

"Stop it, Peg. Wait a minute. There's going to be a devil of a mess and maybe you're a godsend. Will you do what I say and not give yourself away? Will you do it? For Felicity, Peg?"

I didn't try to answer. My head was swimming. Sally went right on with her tense whispers without a word from me.

"Thank heaven I know you too. You've come to see me, Peg, not Felicity. Do you get it? They'll not know and I've got to have someone to help me. I'll tell you later what you don't understand . . . I'll tell you what I can. But first I've got to be sure. I don't think there's anyone here. I just walked in—and found her, and I dashed out to get Chad's flask. But she's dead. I know it. Come with me. You've got to. We'll have to do things."

She gave me a vigorous shake and darted off around the high mass of shrubbery across a stretch of lawn toward a side entrance to the house. I followed blindly, my knees like rubber. Something made me look up, but not soon enough. I could see nothing except the lower sills of the upper windows on that side of the house. Whether it was a slight sound or the flutter of a curtain or someone looking down at me I could not analyze then. But something made me look up.

Inside the door, in a sort of lobby on the ground level which was plainly not the main entrance to the house, Sally

stood waiting for me. The house was very still. My heart
was pounding. Sally's face was gray. It made her hair look
unreal. The dirty mark on her forehead was like another
eyebrow.

"She's in there." She flapped a hand vaguely. "In the
back living room. You've got to come with me." Her voice
was still a husky whisper.

She pulled me after her, up a couple of steps, around
the foot of a stairway, and along a hall to a half-open door.
I stumbled along like one in a nightmare into a generous, homey living room. I could see nothing at first except
quantities of chintz-covered chairs and sunlight and bowls
of flowers. There was a davenport at right angle to a fire-
place, and there Sally stood at the nearer end.

"There's not much blood, Peg. Please, you've got to
look."

Gripping the back of the davenport, I looked. The shot
had been directed toward her heart and there was no doubt
that my Felicity was dead. Her fine, lovely face and her
beautiful gold hair were untouched. Feeling unutterable
things, I looked upon my friend.

"I heard the shot. My God, if only I had stopped for gas
this morning."

That it was suicide seemed plain enough. On the floor
just below her drooping right hand lay a revolver.

"That's what she did it with," Sally whispered, and
stooped over the weapon.

"Don't touch it," I said, and I didn't whisper. Because
I teach math I've been accused of having a logical mind
and I was calling upon it to rescue me from the whirlpool
of shock and horror that would soon have engulfed me.
"Don't touch anything. There will have to be a coroner,
won't there? But first you must call a doctor. Was she alone
in this house? And what did you mean, you heard the shot?
It must have just happened." But I could not touch Flippity's arm to see if the body were still warm.

"The telephone's in the library. Let's get out of here."

We crossed the hall and entered a room directly opposite. Sally closed the door behind us. It was a man's room, full, of tall, old-fashioned bookcases with glass doors. The books behind them looked dark and heavy, like bound magazines or old encyclopedia sets. One wall was crowded with framed maps and there were shabby, leather-covered chairs. The telephone was on a desk that was as smooth and flat-topped and modern as an executive's in the offices of big business. Beyond one of those fountain pen sets and the telephone, there was nothing on it except a framed photograph of Felicity, a picture I had never seen.

Sally picked up the telephone. "I'll call Dr. Ammon. He'll know what to do. A pretty good old egg, Dr. Ammon." After a brief interval of crackling she breathed a sigh. "He's in, thank God."

She made her dreadful summons quite directly. She had just reached River View, she said, and found that Mrs. Howard had killed herself. Was she alone, the doctor must have asked, for I heard Sally calmly say, no, a friend was with her, a guest from out of town.

"He'll be right out," she reported. "He'll see about the coroner. You heard what I said, Peg. You're my guest. You came to see me, not Felicity."

"How do you know there's no one else here?" *If only I could have the place to myself . . .* Felicity had written.

"What do you think? If I heard the shot as I came across the lawn, Aunt Rhoda couldn't have missed it. You don't know our Aunt Rhoda. Anyway, this is her afternoon with the nature lovers and those gals are getting ready for a garden show. The devil himself can't keep up with Bart—his car may be out. I mean, I must look in the garage."

If that was a slip, I gave no sign that I had caught it.

"Chad and Allen wouldn't be here in any case," she went on as if checking a list, "and I think Lila is playing bridge. Of course, Adkins is on the place somewhere, but he's never inside and he's deaf as a post. The cook is at the dentist's, that I do know for sure, and the girl that's been housemaiding got mad at Aunt Rhoda the other day and walked out on Felicity."

I wanted to ask Sally more about hearing the shot and what it was that had brought her up here in such a hurry, but I knew that I'd be hearing what she'd say to the doctor in a very few minutes. It was more important to understand why I was to be Sally's newly arrived friend, not Felicity's.

"Before we go any further," I began, "tell me why I must do as you say. What is there that I don't know, except that my friend was broken by grief over her husband's death? What has been going on? Why do you, Sally Anderson Howard, need help?"

Sally pushed the telephone away and swung herself on the edge of the shining desk. I had sunk into one of the worn leather chairs. She hunched herself nearer and her eyes held mine steadily. "Listen, Peg . . ."

I listened, though not in the way she had meant. So did she. A door above had opened and closed. Slow, deliberate steps. There was someone coming down the stairs.

2

"Aunt Rhoda!" breathed Sally. "Try to take her in your stride."

The door opened and a flat, toneless voice addressed Sally. "What's going on down here? You woke me up. I've been in bed with one of my headaches."

Then she saw me. The big chair I had sunk into had its back to the door. Already I was prejudiced against Rhoda Sutton, in my whole-hearted partisanship of Felicity, and it would be easy for me to play her up as first villainess, but I must admit that there was nothing sinister about her appearance. Nothing, according to my first impression as I rose from my place and faced her, that bespoke personality of any sort. I learned later that she was over sixty, but her hair was still mousy. Her eyes were pale gray and her complexion slightly sallow. She was dressed as if to receive callers on a summer afternoon in a black and white figured sheer that looked expensive, and there were diamonds on her knobby fingers. The fingers were busy at glasses swinging from a silver chain about her neck and she moistened her thin lips as she stood there, looking me up and down. I couldn't see her as a domestic tyrant; her chin looked weak and her nose would not have adorned a silhouette.

Sally did not hesitate. "Something dreadful has happened, Aunt Rhoda. I shall have to show you."

"Yes, but who is this, please?" Her glasses at the end of their chain indicated me.

"My friend, Miss Lenox. My husband's aunt, Mrs. Sutton, Peg. She just arrived as I was leaving and I dragged her out here with me." Apparently it was Sally's lie I was to take in my stride, She rushed on, giving me no chance to speak. "Felicity is dead. In the living room, Aunt Rhoda. I have just called Dr. Ammon. Come, I want you to see."

Rhoda Sutton had not come any farther than the library door. She turned almost too quickly for me to see her face as Sally bluntly put the tragedy and started across the hall.

"You too, Peg," Sally muttered, and with a couple of long-legged strides managed to reach the living room door first. I knew that she meant to see how the woman would take the sight of what was awaiting her.

I followed them into the room and stood where I could watch them both. I was puzzled and uncertain about Sally's tactics. Rhoda Sutton's face tightened a little as she gazed downward at the davenport. That was all, except that after an instant she at last put on the spectacles she had been playing with. Sally was watching every move she made.

"Um-ph. That's our answer, Sally. I hope you're convinced." Then she craned her neck and I knew she was looking at the pistol lying on the floor. "That was Jordan's gun."

To my ears it sounded as if using other people's property was just what Rhoda Sutton would expect of her brother-in-law's wife.

"The doctor will be here any minute now. Will you stick around a minute with Peg? I'll have to move the car."

That's exactly what Sally said, and it sounded so natural and innocuous that I gave it no thought then, not even offering my keys if it was my car she was thinking of. She said nothing about my keys.

Sally vanished and I was there with Aunt Rhoda and my lifeless Felicity. Mrs. Sutton turned away from the body, ignoring me, and pulled at some flower stalks in the bowl on the nearest table. She hummed something tunelessly. I wanted to scream.

Instead I made conversation. Feminine instinct in a social crisis, no doubt.

"Your headache, Mrs. Sutton. This dreadful shock—couldn't I make you a cup of tea, or get you an aspirin?"

"I never drink tea. And no aspirin. Er—thank you. My headaches come on quickly, but if I can sleep, they soon pass. I was sleeping soundly when Sally's voice disturbed me."

I suppose that was meant for tact toward me, but thank heaven, someone made a clattering entrance from the back of the house.

"Peg? Aunt Rhoda? Where are you?"

Sally came in through the hall entrance to the front living room, a more formal apartment than the room behind it. "Dr. Ammon's getting out of his car now. Someone's with him. The coroner, I suppose. And Daisy will be back from town any minute now. Her nephew was to get her back in time for dinner, Felicity said." She bit her lip and there was a thick silence.

"Um-ph!" It was Mrs. Sutton who sniffed.

"Do you know where to get Bart, Aunt Rhoda?" Sally went on matter-of-factly. "The boys ought to be reached at once. Chad will be home by now." She glanced at her watch.

Dr. Ammon and his companion had entered the house. Their steps and voices were audible in the hall and Mrs. Sutton and Sally turned to meet them. There would be no telephoning done at the moment.

The older woman cut short the doctor's murmur of concern and regarded the second man as invisible. "In here, Dr. Ammon," she said, pulling aside the curtain. I thought she was going into the room herself, but she did not. However, she remained at the curtain and I think she could see through a fold of it. Sally and I stayed where we were. We could hear a little, not what was said, but movements and the sound of men's voices.

That part did not last long. Sally was restless. Mrs. Sutton hummed her monotone again. I tried not to feel anything. Then the two men parted the curtains and stepped into the room.

"There's no doubt," Dr. Ammon began professionally. "Mrs. Howard is dead. The shot penetrated the heart."

The coroner took over brusquely. "Every indication of suicide, but I'll have to ask you ladies the usual questions. How did you find her? Or were you with her when it happened?"

This was what I wanted to hear and it certainly was not my turn to speak. Mrs. Sutton gave Sally a waiting, interested look and then let her glasses swing from their chain.

Sally did not hesitate. "I drove out with my guest"— she nodded at me without looking at me—"just to pick up something I'd forgotten this morning, and as I started toward the house I heard what I thought sounded like a shot. I ran in and found her, just where you saw her. I suppose I screamed, I don't know, but it was too late. It was plain to see what she had done. I knew the cook was out of the house and I took for granted that Mrs. Sutton was away, and so as soon as my head cleared I ran back to the car.

Miss Lenox came back in with me and we both thought of
getting a doctor, and so I called Dr. Ammon. While we were
in the library at the telephone Aunt Rhoda came down.
She'd been sleeping and didn't know what happened. We
all went and looked at Felicity again and then you came.
That's all."

At this second mention of her name, Mrs. Sutton nodded slightly and wet her pale lips. Dr. Ammon gave another sympathetic murmur but let the coroner carry on. He
turned to Mrs. Sutton. "You heard the shot?"

"I was asleep in my own apartment, Mr. Paulding. I
was aroused by hearing people talking and I came down. I
found my nephew's wife, and—her friend." She said this as
if she would have preferred to say "this person," and Sally
arched her plucked black brows. "I was then told what had
occurred," Rhoda Sutton concluded.

"Mrs. Chad said something about you being away; I'd
like to get that straight."

Mrs. Sutton waited an instant but Sally did not speak.
The coroner looked at the older woman for his answer.

"I had expected to go to a meeting of the Garden Club
this afternoon. Sally knows the day very well. But a headache came on rather violently—" Her eyes turned toward
the doctor and he nodded again as if he had heard of the
headaches before. "I took one of your tablets and lay down."
This was addressed directly to the doctor. Already I was
certain that Mrs. Sutton disliked Paulding.

"So you didn't hear the shot but you did hear Mrs. Chad
and this lady here talking, eh? How about you now?" The
coroner swung to me. "You were out in the car, huh? Did
you hear it?"

"I heard no shot," I replied firmly. Sally, I knew without
looking at her, was holding her breath, but I was going to
tell no outright lies. "I had just set myself to enjoy the view
when Mrs. Howard asked me to come up to the house with
her. I could see she was upset, but she didn't tell me what

had happened. I'm a stranger here, I think I ought to tell you. I've never been in this house before. I don't know the family, except Mrs. Chad Howard. I knew her before she married Mr. Howard."

"And the poor dear had just rolled into town." That sounded as if so far Sally approved of my statement.

"From Iowa, I take it," said Paulding. "I noticed the car in the drive."

I said nothing which was smart of me. Smart of the coroner, too, to have noticed my license plates.

"Well, then, the next thing is—did any of you have any notion this way of doing things was on Mrs. Howard's mind?" Paulding looked at them all, skipping me. My statement must have sounded genuine.

No one spoke. After a long minute Dr. Ammon could not stand it. "Mr. Howard's death, just a few weeks ago, was a great shock, and I fear she had not been reacting from it normally. Her general health, however, appeared to me to be good. She had had no occasion to be my patient since her coming here, except for that last November when you all had colds. You recall, Mrs. Sutton?"

"It wasn't Mrs. Howard's health that led to this." The glasses were swinging again.

"Very sad, very shocking. Jordan Howard is greatly missed in Point Tyler." Coroner Paulding was evidently a leading noon-tide clubber. He sounded at that moment like the resolutions committee.

"Nor grief for Jordan's death."

After that remark, which to me sounded so malicious, there was an awkward silence. Apparently Sally was the only one who was not visibly disturbed by it. She spoke next.

"Felicity—Mrs. Howard had certainly not been herself since Dad's death. That's perfectly understandable. She was worried and unhappy, I'm sure, but she had said nothing to me. I was hoping she would—half expecting she would. I wish I'd talked to her without waiting—"

"Sally is the impulsive member of our family," Mr. Sutton spoke as if commenting on a six-year-old.

"Without waiting for what?" asked Paulding.

"For her to speak first," Sally replied gently. "I liked her so much."

Aunt Rhoda sniffed.

Paulding hurried on. "Now about the gun—where did she get it?"

"Aunt Rhoda said it was Dad's. I don't know." Sally left it there.

"My brother-in-law had one. Of course, his personal possessions were all in his wife's hands."

What I could have said then and there would have been a bombshell, but I did not say it. I was beginning to think that maybe Sally knew what she was doing.

"Um-m, I guess that's all for you folks right now. I'm going to the sheriff from here. Even when it's just plain suicide there's a certain amount of routine, you understand. And maybe I can get the boys here too. I'll have to be a little clearer about why she did it. You sent for Chad and Allen yet? And where's Bart? Telephone's in the library, you say?"

Paulding did not pause to have these questions answered. He started to leave the room.

"I'll give Chad a ring at the house." Sally was at his heels.

"If you'll just leave me have the phone first—the sheriff is sometimes a little hard to catch."

"Certainly, Mr. Paulding. It will be all right if Miss Lenox and I withdraw to the kitchen, won't it? Someone will have to break the news to the cook."

I followed Sally. Dr. Ammon remained with Mrs. Sutton in the front living room where a medical murmur began at once. The coroner went into the library and closed the door.

"Quick, here's our chance," breathed Sally. "I want to check up on something and they came before I could."

She ran through a shining, silent kitchen and out a back door. A bricked walk under a trellis led to a garage which we entered through a side door. There was space for three cars and three were there.

Sally whistled. "That's funny. Bart's car's here. And he never goes off the reservation under his own steam. And Lila's too. Which is funnier . . ." She moved around to the third car in the row, a smart, small sedan, and felt the hood. "The gal must have cut the bridge game. Her engine's cold."

I looked at her with a frank curiosity, for her eyes were narrowed in speculation. For the remaining car was not Sally's coupé; it was plainly the family model, an older, but well-cared-for car of expensive make.

She must have guessed my question, for she suddenly said, "I can't explain now, but don't mention my car. We came up in your car, see, and I'll be driving back with you, if and when—"

The sound of voices from behind and beyond the garage reached our ears at that instant, and we slipped out of the building by the door through which we had entered. Through the leafiness of the arbor we were just in time to see a man and woman coming along a path that apparently climbed upward from the direction of the river. They were laughing chummily as they started across the lawn toward the side door of the house.

Sally gave a queer gulp and I saw that her hands were knotted into hard fists. "Do you see that?" she whispered. "I'm glad you saw them too. Quick I'm going in. I want to see them stop laughing."

She darted through the kitchen and I thought she said over her shoulder, as if it were sufficient explanation, "It's Lila and Chad . . ."

They were in the hall as we entered and the newcomers were not laughing. Paulding was talking.

". . . been trying to locate you, Chad. Allen is on his way out now, Mrs. Howard. He said he'd leave word for you. I gathered he didn't understand you were here. I'm expecting the sheriff and Tom Nixon any minute. Take it easy Mrs. Howard. It's all over now."

I hovered discreetly in the background, for certainly this was no place for a stranger. For a moment no one was paying any attention to me and I tried to label the group. The doctor was still fussing about Mrs. Sutton, who didn't need his ministrations, for she had herself well in hand and was giving her attention to Lila Howard, Allen's wife, who was looking scared to death. She was a pretty person, very much the socially-minded, smalltown matron, not much younger than Felicity.

Chad—that would be Sally's husband, the youngest of Felicity's stepsons. He didn't look much like Sally's husband to me. I would have picked a domineering male for Sally. Allen's wife and Sally's husband—so that was the angle. And very possibly the explanation for Sally's peculiar behavior. But Sally wasn't blinking a red eyelash now.

"So glad you got here, Chad. This is rather a mess. Have you any idea where Bart is? Oh, here come more cars now. That's Daisy—I'll tell her." And Sally turned once more toward the service end of the house. Once more I followed.

A stout, middle-aged woman had just entered from the back door and lifted her arms to remove her hat. "Looks like a houseful for dinner again tonight, and me with my head drilled clean through. Two solid hours in the dentist's chair and he ain't through yet— Land sakes, Mis' Sally what's up?"

Sally told her, abruptly, and the woman seated herself. "The poor soul," she said heavily, "the poor little soul."

It sounded so genuine, this first word of selfless concern, that hot tears stung my eyes.

"The sheriff here too, you say, and a whole posse. Well, I'll just have to get out of this good dress and shoes before I can take hold. Never you mind about my end, Mis' Sally."

The door from the hall opened and a man I had not seen before stood there. "You're wanted, my dear Sally, by the law in full and dreadful panoply."

"In a sec, Bart. I've just been telling Daisy."

"Buck up, old girl. Come hell or high water, civilized man cannot live without cooks."

I do not think that Bart Howard had really seen me. As he stood in the shadow of the opened door, my impression of his appearance was not certain, but his mocking flippant voice repelled me. He stepped out of sight and Sally moved to join the family. I grabbed her arm. "What shall I do? Where can I go? Shan't I stay here?"

"In the library, Peg, if you'd rather. Only, for heaven's sake, stand by!"

She fairly pushed me into the library as she hurried by and I huddled in the nearest chair. The heavy door was half open and my chair was behind it. I could not be seen by the milling group in the hall, though I did not realize that. In fact, I daresay they had forgotten my presence, except Sally. But I could hear what was said, almost every word. The Howards had clear and distinct voices.

"You need not prolong this trying situation, Sheriff Floyd. What has happened speaks clearly for itself to us of the family." It was Rhoda Sutton who was talking. "Jordan Howard's widow has killed herself for a most excellent reason. We all know what it is."

There was a confused murmur and a man's voice in sharp warning. "Aunt Rhoda! Don't say another word."

"But I shall. It's my right. We have our proof. The case against her was complete."

A woman's high, hysterical laugh. Not Sally's. Probably Lila.

"You see, sheriff, Mrs. Howard had murdered her husband, and she knew that we had found her out."

3

Whatever Sally Howard's purpose might be in parking me in the library, I was listening for my own sake now, and Felicity's.

Sounds of hush-hush and polite consternation followed Rhoda Sutton's shocking statement and then came the voice of authority. I thought it must be one of the Howard sons who was speaking, but I was to discover in a few minutes that I was mistaken.

"You can prove what you say?"

"Certainly. Our discoveries and investigations had reached such an unmistakable point that we were about to confront the woman with our evidence and then get in touch with the proper authorities. . . . No, Dr. Ammon, no— I am quite calm. I know exactly what I am saying."

Like an *obligato* to Mrs. Sutton's flat, toneless voice ran the gulping sobs of a hysterical woman. That could not be Sally; it would have to be Lila Howard. I also heard the scratching of a match and then I caught the drifting smell of freshly burning tobacco.

"Aunt Rhoda! This is entirely unnecessary and dreadfully out of place. Felicity is dead."

"That's all very well, Allen, but you owe your father a son's duty—"

"I think that Floyd and I must insist on an explanation." Again this was my unidentified voice of authority, but I now knew that the speaker was not Dr. Ammon, nor the coroner, nor the sheriff. "It is the duty of the state to establish the motive for a suicide's death, and you have offered us a startling explanation for Mrs. Howard's deed. We shall have to consider the evidence."

"It's up to you and Floyd now, Tom. But there will have to be an inquest." That was Paulding, the coroner. He had mentioned someone named Tom Nixon, who was coming out with the sheriff. Well, this Nixon seemed to have his feet on the ground.

"Aunt Rhoda, it's all your fault." A woman's wail—Lila Howard's.

"Lila! For God's sake, what do you think you are saying?" That sounded like a husband to me.

"Oh, I don't mean— She killed herself, of course, but an inquest and courts and the awful publicity and the way everybody in town will talk. . . ." She relapsed into sniffles.

"Courts, my dear Lila," and the cool mocking voice was Bartlett Howard's, "did not appall you when it was a case of contesting the will."

"See here, we're all doing too much wild talking. Let Floyd and Nixon ask whatever questions are necessary."

"I agree with Allen," I heard Sally say. "And I'm sure these men understand that we're all upset."

"Only to be expected, Mrs. Howard." Sheriff Floyd's voice was kind. "Now, I gather that Doc here and Paulding got here first. I'd like to hear from them, as far as they'd got."

With brief competence the coroner stated what the doctor and he had done in the way of investigation. Bluntly and with not much tact he kept Dr. Ammon from maundering beyond a bare medical statement of how the shot had killed Felicity.

"They say the gun was Jordan Howard's and I guess his wife had easy access to it—seems no doubt about that," Paulding reported. "Mrs. Chad—she says she heard the shot as she was coming up toward the house and Mrs. Sutton says she was upstairs asleep and didn't hear it."

"I was asleep." I could hear Aunt Rhoda's abominable sniff, but perhaps I imagined that she accented her second word a bit defensively.

"I was just turning my mind to what might have led Mrs. Howard to take her life when I stopped to get word to you, Floyd, and then the rest of these folks came in. You can take over now, Tom, if you want."

It sounded to me as though everyone shifted his position a little and one person quite evidently rose from a chair and

began walking up and down. I could hear masculine heels
on polished wood. Then in an instant Tom Nixon's voice of
authority began.

"Suicide seems quite clear. Her fingerprints should show
up on the weapon, of course, and that's routine for us. Time
well established, too. Sally was outside and heard the shot.
Mrs. Sutton was upstairs and did not hear it. Now what can
you others tell me? Where were you?"

My presence was not being mentioned. Mrs. Sutton and
Sally and the doctor and Paulding knew I was there and
assuredly what the two men knew the other officials would
be told before long, but I was almost certain that the other
members of the family did not know of Sally's guest. I had
seen Chad and Lila as they came around the garage and Bart
at the kitchen door, but I did not think they had seen me.
What was Sally's game? Whatever it was, I did not count on
Aunt Rhoda's playing it long.

That's what flashed through my mind as I waited for
someone to start answering Nixon's question. Sally primed
the pump for him. I heard her say, "I ran out to the garage
to see what cars were in. Bart's was there, and Lila's."

"Oh, mine—I haven't been off the place, all day." Bart's
tone was airy. "I'd been down in the grove sketching ever
since lunch. I was planning to run down to town before
dinner, and on my way back to the house I fooled away a lot
of time with Adkins and then walked into—all this."

"When did you last see Mrs. Howard?"

"Felicity? Not since last night."

There was a sort of questioning murmur which I could
not make out, but I heard Mrs. Sutton's reply distinctly.

"Not at all, Tom Nixon. My nephew and I have our own
quarters and I see to his breakfast and lunch whenever he
wishes."

"I see. . . . And you, Mrs. Howard? Your car—you were
here at River View when this happened?"

"But I don't know when it happened, Tom. I drove up this afternoon and went down to the boat house. I had samples of stuff for new cushions for the launch and I wanted to make up my mind about color and all that. I was going up to Wheeling and shop tomorrow."

"Did you see anyone about the place when you came?"

"Not anyone. I drove the car into the garage and went right down to the boat house."

"About what time was it when you came?"

"Oh maybe almost three. I'm not certain."

"What happened to the bridge?" That was Sally, and I could guess that her sister-in-law would have used the phrase herself.

"Bridge? Oh, I called Terry and said I didn't feel like coming. It was all right; she understood."

"Understood what?" There was no menace in Nixon's question, but it was Mrs. Sutton who snapped an answer.

"It's only a short time since the death of my brother-in-law, Tom Nixon."

"Of course, of course. . . . Your errand at the launch wouldn't have kept you long?"

"No, oh no—but it was cool and pleasant down there and I relaxed with a magazine and I think I must have had a nap. It was five-thirty when I started up the path—"

"And met me. We came along together." That masculine voice would be Chad's and I wished that I could see Sally's face. "I'd been having a swim. I dropped off the truck as I came in from the Priddy lease and I was about to give Sally a ring and tell her I'd be staying for dinner."

"Come through this way as you went to the river?"

"No, I took the old trail from the road."

There was no comment or question about that and I decided that the geography of River View was well known to Floyd and Nixon.

"Well, as a sheer matter of record, when had you last seen Mrs. Howard?"

"Last night. Little family gathering out here last night, Tom."

"And you Mrs. Howard?" I noticed that Nixon addressed one daughter-in-law as Sally but did not call the other by her first name.

"Last night. Allen and I were here with the others."

"Now, Allen, you. I know you got here just after Floyd and I pulled in."

"That's right, Tom. I got the call from Paulding at my office and came right up. And I'd been right there all after-noon, just for the sake of your record. But I had seen Mrs. Howard since last night. She was in my office for a few minutes this morning, but when she saw how tied up I was she didn't stay. That was my mistake, I'm afraid. She was—I think she was troubled about something, but she said she couldn't wait for the half hour or so that I suggested. That damn school board—it does eat up my time. I meant to get in touch with her tonight."

There was a feminine rustle, but I had no way of know-ing which one of the women was reacting to his statement. Then came Sally's voice.

"You can talk to Daisy now too. She's back, but she was in at Dr. Ensley's most of the afternoon."

"Okay, Sally. I think we have most of the picture now, except for just what it was that impelled the poor woman to shoot herself. Now I suggest . . ."

Something about dinner and a little talk with the sheriff and the coroner must have been the substance of his sug-gestion, but the words were blurred by the sound of general movement. If any sort of private conference was to be held in the library, I did not want to be discovered there. The smell of freshly made coffee pulled me to the kitchen. My watch said it was seven o'clock and suddenly I was nervous.

What my hysteria needed was food. I slipped out of the library and vanished into the kitchen just in time, for the people were scattering. I don't know how I should have explained myself to Daisy, but she must have been in the dining room—I heard the rattle of china somewhere—so I kept on going, out the kitchen door and around the corner of the house. There I came upon a bricked terrace, bright with garden chairs and sun umbrellas. Someone's voice rose from the house behind me. It was Sally, and I think she was calling me. I flopped down upon the nearest chaise-longue and composed myself to look like Guest Idling with Magazine. There was no telling what story I'd be backing Sally up in this time.

Her voice came nearer, through French windows at my back. "There you are, Peg, poor dear. This has all been so dreadful—you'll never forget the reception I gave you to Point Tyler. . . ." I could tell by that line that she was not alone. "Allen, you must meet Miss Lenox. Peg's an old pal of mine from my New York days. Peg, this is Allen Howard, my brother-in-law—the head of the house since Dad's death."

I looked up into the face of a serious, worried man. In his middle thirties, I judged. I liked his handshake and I liked his quiet gray eyes. Felicity had liked him too, I recalled. She had written that he was the son most like his father. And she had gone to him that very morning, troubled about something. Disturbed so desperately that she could face life no longer. Perhaps Allen Howard would be on my side. Already I was thinking like that.

"Daisy has food ready, Peg, and Allen will mix you a drink if you want. It won't be long now. We can go back to town and you can get away from—all this. The men say it will be all right for me to go back because of you—and, Peg, am I glad for you!"

"You may have to come back, Sally, if Paulding and Floyd should insist on an inquest." Allen Howard's voice, was as quiet as his eyes. "Miss Lenox will understand that a family conference is unavoidable."

"I'm sorry—" I began.

"I'm sorry, too. Poor little Felicity."

From that time on, no matter what was to happen, I felt sure of Allen Howard.

"The others will be down soon, Peg, Let's go in now." With an imperious gesture which I took as a sign that Sally had hoped to avoid the others if she could, she retreated toward the dining room. Allen Howard followed us in.

The room was already occupied. The man standing at a sideboard shaking a mixer was thin and nervous and petulant. He looked a little like Allen.

"Peg, this is my other brother-in-law, Bartlett Howard, Bart, this is Peg Lenox. . . ." And once more I was identified as Sally's guest and only Sally's guest.

Bart Howard gave me a couple of darting glances that made me feel as if he thought that Sally had inexplicable tastes and then he set the shaker down on a waiting tray upon which was a plate piled high with sandwiches. He looked about as if in a bell-ringing mood.

Sally said, "Daisy's pretty busy, if it's she you want."

"I'll toddle in with it myself. Paulding and Company are still about and mewing plaintively for food. Lila's gone up with Aunt Rhoda. I'd say, Allen, that the family conference has already begun. And Sally, of course, always knows exactly where to put her finger on Chad."

Sally grimaced and gave Allen a side-long glance, but said nothing until the door had swung shut behind Bart and his elaborately balanced tray. "I ought to have a word with Chad before I leave," she murmured, heaping food upon a plate for me while I stiffened my morale with the black coffee.

"He's about somewhere, Sally. Shall I find him for you?" Without waiting for a reply Allen Howard followed his brother from the dining room.

"I hate to rush you, Peg, but we've got to work fast. I'm going to try some funny business with our car—just follow my lead. There—I hear Chad now. Come on!"

I wanted more food and I needed more coffee but I had to follow Sally. We emerged from the dining room into the main hall again. There were official voices, coming from the library and the sound of steps from the upper hall, but Sally was making for the two men standing at the front entrance, Allen and Chad Howard. Once again Sally said her piece about her old friend Peg Lenox's unexpected arrival. I was beginning to believe it myself.

"And so, Chad, I'm taking Peg back to the house, and then if you think I'll be needed out here again I'll run up with our car so that you'll have a way to get back without bothering anyone."

I looked at Chad Howard while she spoke and decided that his was the most negligible personality of the three brothers. He was the youngest; he lacked Allen's bearing and Bart's bad manners. Like the others, he was troubled and uneasy, but he gave me a friendly smile.

"I think you'd better come back, Sally," said Allen. "I'm sure Miss Lenox understands that the circumstances are somewhat unusual."

Chad mumbled something that ended with ". . . but just as you say, Sally," and we two started down the drive.

"Your car's exactly where you left it down here, Sally. Get going, and I'll talk. If I'm crazy, just say so. I won't mind."

But she said nothing after I'd backed and turned the car on the drive of rather inadequate width for one who suspected that the hillside drop on one side was a bit too abrupt for a guessing driver. We were perhaps half way to the main road when she said, "That's where I hid my car, down there under that hazel clump. I can't even see it, and I know where to look, so it's all right."

I slowed, thinking that she meant me to stop. "No. Peg, I'm not getting it now. You're driving me right back to town. You've been grand, Peg—marvelous, in fact, but I always knew what you were like."

I suppose she read the expression on my face, for she
gave me a sudden pleading pat. "I think you want to help
Felicity. That's what I'm counting on."

"You've put me in a position that I'm finding pretty intolerable, Sally. I believe I can say that I'm Felicity's 'next
friend,' and I've got to be told what this is all about. That's
all I'm promising—now."

"It's the will, Peg. It's Father Howard's will that's behind everything. He left everything to her—and they didn't
expect it. That's all. Aunt Rhoda's been fit to be tied, and
she's been at the boys and Lila. If only Felicity hadn't found
it herself.

"Yes, the new one. Godfrey Blair—he handled all of
Dad's legal business—produced the old one at once. The
one they all knew about. And everybody purred and Aunt
Rhoda even made a speech about Felicity's being very welcome to stay on at River View as long as she liked. Felicity
didn't seem to mind—I honestly think it never occurred
to her that she could make a just claim against the estate,
which any widow would be entitled to. They might have
known that Father Howard would never have been that
careless. He married Felicity because he had fallen in love
with her and no one can make me believe anything else."

"You're telling me," I snorted. "I knew Felicity Wendell.
She would have married no man for his money."

"Try telling that to Aunt Rhoda. Or even to my own
husband."

I promised myself that I should certainly make the trial.

"And then," Sally went on, "the very next day after the
grand will-reading scene, Felicity found the second will.
In an envelope of letters and things, keepsakes, I gather,
that Dad had put away. Just private things—her letters to
him before they were married. A perfectly good legal will
that completely changed the picture. She told them all at
once. Her sense of fair play, of course, but ever since Aunt

Rhoda's been calling her 'that brazen hussy.' And Felicity likewise had sense enough to take the thing right down to Blair, which was a damned good move, because between you and me and that stop-sign Aunt Rhoda was the sneak thief that ransacked Felicity's room."

That detail startled me so that I made a needless left swerve.

"Oh, yes. Life has been violent at River View ever since Dad's death. There was every sign of breaking and entering and Felicity's room was pretty well churned around, but there wasn't a thing missing and I don't believe Bart got around to reporting the incident to the sheriff's office. It happened in the early evening, a day or so after the new will appeared. Felicity was down with us for dinner and we brought her right back—she hadn't wanted to come. Aunt Rhoda was knitting on the terrace and Bart was out on the river and Daisy was down in the basement sorting laundry. Chad and I sat down with Aunt Rhoda and Felicity ran upstairs to get a sweater—it was coolish. She took one look at her room and dashed back frightened at the state she found things in. We all charged around at a brisk rate, particularly Aunt Rhoda, until I spilled the beans by saying it was a good thing that the will was safe anyway, as Felicity had left it with Blair that very afternoon. It was remarkable how calm and cool Aunt Rhoda was after that."

"You don't," I observed, "seem overly devoted to Aunt Rhoda."

"Well, what do you think of her?"

"Go on with your story."

"Turn at this next corner and drive to the end of the street. That's our dump. Leave your car in the drive. You'll have to take me back up the road."

I heard no more, until she had led me into a tricky little house, very modern age. It was all ours for the time. Her maid, Sally explained, lived in town and was never about in the evenings unless there were people in.

"You see, I've officially brought you back here, just as I said, in case anyone is noticing. I had to take the time to talk to you."

"Go on. You've barely scratched the surface."

"And I can only hit the high places now. As I said, this second will tore things. Everything to Felicity, nothing to the boys. Dad explained that he had started from scratch himself and it had been good for him. He believed there was something insidious that happened to people who wait- ed around to inherit money and he didn't want his sons to have that experience. The only one that hits is Bart, but— Furthermore, he said that he knew his wife would be fair and just when the time came for her to dispose of her property."

I gave an involuntary exclamation.

"You get my idea, I see. It was her death warrant." That was going far and fast, but I was letting Sally do the talking.

"The devil of it is that Dad left a far larger estate than we had any idea of. He had investments that even Allen knew nothing about. He was never one to put on much of a show and he talked like everyone else during the depression."

"But that preposterous charge against Felicity—for heaven's sake get to that." I had about reached my limit following Sally's lead.

"So you heard that. That's what I was hoping. I don't know . . . they've convinced themselves there were some queer things going on. Well, maybe there were. . . . The only thing I'm sure of now is that Felicity was driven to death. And that ought to end it. I mean, eventually, even if she inherited everything, the estate will surely be settled so that the family gets it."

I started an angry protest, but Sally silenced me. "Wait, Peg. I can guess what you're thinking and feeling, but we can't thresh it out now. I've got to get back to River View before they're on the watch for me. I kept you out there as long as I decently could because I wanted you to get some idea, and believe me, old girl, the only chance you have of getting back is for them to catch no inkling that you're directly concerned with Felicity. That's why I stuck to my story so hard. When I come back home this time I'll sit up all night talking but just now I can't take the chance. Now here's what I want you to do next—and I give you my word it will be the end for today. Take me in your car as far as the River View drive and then turn and get back here and run your car into our garage. I'll manage from that point."

"You're making it look as if this second trip is in your own car. What's the idea?" Sally wasn't so dumb that she couldn't tell the difference between cold suspicion and plain curiosity.

"I've got to make my story stick—about coming out with you in your car this afternoon. I'm holding out on them—for Felicity's sake. You're with me, Peg?"

We climbed into the car and backed out into the street.

4

As soon as Sally slipped out of my car and vanished up the River View drive, I turned and made swiftly for town and the house on Terrace Drive. Everything in the neighborhood was still safely dark and quiet. I made myself at home, as I had been directed to do, undressed, and stretched myself out on the guestroom bed.

A flash of headlights through my window interrupted my doze. A car was turning in from the street. That would be Sally and Chad returning from River View. There were sounds of domestic activity from below and once I thought I heard the tinkle of a telephone, but it was nearly a half hour before Sally knocked at my door. She came bearing food, for which I was grateful. "I'll be back," she said, "if you don't mind," and left me to my bowl of hot broth.

She reappeared, in rather dizzy pajamas, hunched herself at the foot of my bed, and shared her cigarettes. She

gave a long sigh and stared at me somberly. I rolled over to
reach a jar of cleansing cream from the dressing table and
pushed it at her.

"For heaven's sake, clean yourself up. That dirty mark is
still on your forehead. It's worried me ever since I caught
up with you this afternoon, up there at the end of the drive.
But it wasn't there when I met you at the filling station."

"So that's it. I knew you wouldn't miss much." She unscrewed the top of the jar obediently, gave the stuff a sniff,
and set it down. "Lavender . . . you're being your age, Peg.
There's to be an inquest. Tomorrow morning. Your name
wasn't mentioned—being called, I mean, so you don't have
to go. But I wish you would."

I said nothing, though I had no intention of staying
away.

"It's Aunt Rhoda's fault. She talked too much. And
Floyd has turned everything over to Tom Nixon, and he's
too smart. Even Allen couldn't stop him. He's tried to hold
them in all along. Bart sided with him, too, tonight, but it
wasn't any use."

"Whom do you mean by 'them,' Sally—the law or the
family?"

"Just what I told you before. Aunt Rhoda thinks
Father Howard's death wasn't natural and she's convinced
the boys—not Allen, really—and Lila that she can prove it."

"Not you?"

"Good Lord, no! At least, not Felicity."

"You have a doubt, then, about Mr. Howard's death?"

"I wish there'd been an autopsy, that's all."

"Felicity is dead now." I forced myself to say this.
"What's to be gained by establishing a preposterous motive
like that for her taking her own life? Or maybe you Howards like scandal and publicity. News pictures, you know,
and a flippant paragraph in *Time.*"

"Don't, Peg. . . . That's the way we all feel now. But Tom
Nixon heard what Aunt Rhoda said this afternoon, and Tom

can't be stopped. There will be questions tomorrow and no matter what we all agreed on tonight, Aunt Rhoda will answer, and then we'll all have to and it will end by being a field day for Point Tyler. And nothing gained. It's all over now."

But something irretrievably lost, something that Felicity had an eternal right to. I felt a cold, sullen anger possess me. I was here to fight for Felicity and I must not let emotion obscure my mind.

"Who is this Tom Nixon?" I asked impersonally with a gesture toward an ash tray. "The local Sherlock or a bright D.A. on the make?"

"He's bright enough, but he's no politician. He's the sheriff's chief deputy whenever any brain work's called for, but as far as I know his local reputation as a detective rests solely on his luck in nabbing a couple of car thieves. I really don't know a whole lot about the ins and outs of this town—off the record, I consider it a Godawful, lousy dump, but that's a dead secret from Point Tyler. I mean, I may not have the right slant on Tom Nixon, but I'd say he has a Round Table complex. A Doer of Good and a Righter of Wrong."

"Not a bad break for Felicity. That attitude plus brains."

A queer silence fell between us. Sally stared at me, but not as though she were really seeing me, and I looked back at her, seeing again the expression on her face as she crossed from the drugstore to her car that afternoon.

"By the way," I murmured at last, "how did you make out with your car?"

"Oh, I got by—I hope. The genuine, full-bodied snoopers don't live on Terrace Drive, thank goodness."

"I wish you'd tell me exactly what happened before I caught up with you this afternoon."

"I did tell you. Except that I'd really gone up hoping to have a heart-to-heart with Felicity. She hadn't taken to me much, you know. She was such a perfect lady, and that's

never been my line. And when I found—what I found in
the living room, well—it got me, Peg. I just wasn't very
calm, cool, and collected for a while. That's all."

She wasn't changing her story and so I let her think that
I was accepting it without question.

"What you must tell me, Sally, is why Mrs. Sutton
accused Felicity of murder."

"I told you why, Peg. She wants her share of Dad's money. Equally strong is her devotion to the boys, especially
Bart. She's been like their mother for years."

"That's motive, Sally. But what can she say that Felicity
did?"

"Polished him off with poison. That's what she says. You
see, Dad passed out quickly. They found him dead, and Dr.
Ammon said right off he wasn't surprised. He had a bad
heart condition that he had refused to worry the family
about. And so there was no question about anything off
color. Then after the new will was found and after it was
safely in Blair's possession too, Aunt Rhoda took to fretting
about a little infected scratch that Dad had been bothered
with for a couple of days before he died. It hadn't been
neglected at all and was well under control. But she kept
saying that maybe that had brought on the heart attack.
And then she found a bottle of stuff she said was poison
and a hypodermic needle. Found them where they'd been
hidden in such a queer way, all wrapped up in a small linen
towel that was Felicity's special property. I mean, not a
piece of the house linen."

I understood that detail only too well. Felicity had
always been fastidious about using quantities of small
linen hand towels. She'd even kept a drawer full at school.
No paper towels for Felicity. Furthermore, there was that
sentence in her last letter to me: *I couldn't help worrying
about the little bottle, and then the next time I looked it
wasn't there. . . .*

But I continued to hold out on Sally. "What would that amount to as evidence?" I demanded.

Sally pushed her red hair back and gave a weary shrug. "The queer thing that Aunt Rhoda did, or maybe it was a canny move, was to rush her find right down to the bank and into safety-deposit box that she rented especially for her bundle."

"Without showing it to any of you?"

"I don't think so; I'm sure not. Then she told her story to us all, separately and collectively, but not to Felicity until last night. We were all in on it by then, and Lila and Bart and even Chad seemed to think she had something. I frankly wasn't having any—that's why I thought Felicity would talk to me today—and Allen just tried to soothe everyone down. But Aunt Rhoda kept saying that the only settlement was to have Dad's body examined and the bottle and stuff tested for fingerprints."

"Felicity—?"

"She agreed with her there."

"It was Allen who was outraged at the idea of desecrating his father's body. That stymied us last night, and nothing was settled."

"Felicity tried to see her brother-in-law this morning. To persuade him to agree to an exhumation? That would be like her. . . . But before she could talk to him she—"

"You heard what Aunt Rhoda said, that her death proved she was on the right track."

I spoke slowly. "Felicity's death need not stop the proving. If she were willing to test the issue, I am too."

"No, Peg, no!" There was, or I thought there was, sharp fear in Sally's tense protest. "They mustn't do that. It—it seems so hideously unnecessary now."

I tried to meet her eyes, but the red head was buried on her knees and her thin fingers were writing through her hair. So I brought up another item that was on my mind. "Why should Felicity kill her husband? They were happy

together. I defy you all to deny that. She would rather have
had her husband than his money."

"You're right again, but Aunt Rhoda says she knows
there was another man."

"Bosh!" I laughed that one off. I knew about the only
other man in Felicity's life, but that story could concern
no one now living and I wasn't sharing it with any of the
Howards. "Who does she say he is?"

"She says she knows who he is."

"But not telling, eh?"

"Not telling—yet. How Father Howard put up with that
woman all these years— The boys are used to her. Chad
thinks I'm deliberately hostile."

Suddenly I wanted to ask Sally a lot of questions. Where
she had met Chad Howard. Why she had married him.
Whether their life together was going smoothly. Whether he
was making her unhappy about Lila. But I let my queries go.

Sally unfolded her long legs and stretched herself.

"It's all hours Peg, and we ought to relax before we have
to go through that damned inquest. It's going to be here in
town in one of Paulding's rooms. You slide in, just like an
idle spectator, and see how it adds up to you. Don't think
I'm just bats about Aunt Rhoda. She hated Felicity."

Sally knew what string to harp on with me. But all I said
was, "We'll see, in the morning."

"Here's hoping that Chad's sinus won't be playing the
devil tomorrow. He didn't dry his hair properly after that
swim. I'm quite an expert with nasal sprays these days, old
dear . . . Night!"

Was she telling me, I wondered, that Chad's story was
straight, or was she merely backing it up? I wished I could
have remembered for myself if his hair had been wet.

I went to sleep, but not until I had highly resolved to
tell Tom Nixon, Righter of Wrong, a large hunk of the
truth, and to be on the safe side, before the inquest, if I
could possibly manage to do it.

Part Three
Thursday, June 16

1

I thought I was being very clever the next morning, coming down promptly for breakfast and announcing that I was going to walk down through the town to the post office. Sally turned all her postal supplies over to me, and Chad offered to take any mail I had to get off directly down to the station, but I handed them a jumble about needing exercise and wanting to see the town and a non-existent nephew who collected postmarks, and set out. Chad Howard, by the way, showed a faint trace of sniffles, though I concluded that his hair was thin enough to have dried thoroughly in ten minutes of hot June sunshine.

I didn't take my car. My idea was that perhaps it might be wise not to remind anyone that he had noticed those Iowa plates scooting around the night before.

I'd be back at the house long before ten, I promised Sally. Ten was the hour set for the inquest. I found the post office easily enough. Point Tyler had recently had a sound member representing them in Washington. I'd ask someone in the post office, I decided, where to find Mr. Nixon. No one there could connect me yet with the trouble at River View. I passed Dr. Ammon's office on the way and also the Paulding Funeral Home, but I saw neither of the gentlemen who would surely have recognized me.

A postal clerk peered through little brass rods and gave me a full set of addresses for Tom Nixon, where he lived, where he ate, where he worked, and where the sheriff's office was. Kinda hard to tell about Tom. One thing, though, he hadn't been in for his mail yet, so he was probably still at Tony's Snack Bar. I'd passed that glass-fronted place, too, and had shuddered at its overemphasis on fish sandwiches.

I strolled back, counting on the glass front to reveal all, but none of the patrons could possibly be the man I wanted to talk to. True, I had not seen Nixon, only heard him talking, but surely two truckers and an old man with a beard couldn't be the Galahad Sally had sketched for me. So I crossed the street and went around a corner and up a flight of shabby wooden stairs to an office door marked THOMAS L. NIXON in fresh black capitals.

The office was unlocked, also unoccupied. I could tell nothing about its owner's business. If he was a lawyer, as I had taken for granted, there were no law books. If he was an insurance agent, he was strangely reticent about it; even the only wall hanging, a large calendar, advertised oil supplies, which meant nothing distinctive in that community. There was an inner door, upon which I promptly knocked. No answer. I turned the knob; it was locked. I sat down on a hard chair. There was nothing on the table but scratches and ancient ink stains, but on the floor beneath was a stack of magazines. They told me too much. They were all fairly recent numbers, but such an unassorted jumble, ranging from *True Confessions* and *Ranch Romances* to the *Saturday Review* and the *Atlantic*. No trade journals or professional monthlies. I leafed them over for about fifteen minutes.

There was nothing doing here. I'd try the sheriff's office next. That's where he'd naturally be with an inquest in the offing. I started down the wooden stairs and someone started up at the same time. I paused, expecting it to be Nixon, though I could not see clearly as the person was against the light. His figure did not look old, though he climbed slowly. He hesitated in deprecation as he drew even with me and removed his hat. He was noticeably bald. "I beg your pardon, madam," he said, and went on.

He was not Tom Nixon. The voices were miles apart. Nixon's had been crisp and vigorous and young; this man's was light and slow and professorial with no provincial overtone that I could identify.

At the foot of the flight I turned and looked up. He was standing looking at the lettered name on the door as if to assure himself that he had come to the right place. He turned his head and looked down at me, as if with growing curiosity, and then hastily stepped inside the office.

It was nearly nine-thirty by that time and I knew I ought to be getting back to Terrace Drive, but I had accomplished nothing and I was still determined to put a bug in Tom Nixon's ear. I blundered about until I found the sheriff's office, which, oddly, was not in the courthouse. In fact I wasn't sure at all that Point Tyler was a county seat.

A slick young man and a smart young typist confronted me there and agreed that Mr. Nixon was with the sheriff at the coroner's office. He might be in early in the afternoon, they said, but they didn't quite know. By the time I had worked my way through their polite endeavors the first of them was beginning the same business with another inquirer. It was the bald gentleman whom I had just left at the top of the steps leading to Nixon's office.

I don't think he saw me, but I heard that polished voice saying, "But I had an appointment. . . ." He must have mentioned his name or identified himself in some way or they may have known him, for the only other thing I heard was, "He's expecting you. Just ask for him at Paulding's."

I set out in a hurry, certain that Sally would be in a stew, but before I had gone far the Buick braked to a quick stop and Sally hailed me. "I told Chad we'd be sure to pick you up. Just turn yourself around and walk right in to Paulding's. They can't stop you. You can't sit with us, though."

Chad gave me a feeble but friendly smile as if to say you know how Sally is, and the Buick went on.

I followed directions and found myself in a back row on an inadequate undertaker's chair with time to wait before the inquest began. It was after ten and I wondered whether my bald friend's being expected by Nixon had anything to do with the delay. I looked about rather systematically but saw no one I recognized until the appearance of Coroner Paulding, who of course presided. The witnesses, apparently, were not to be auditors of the proceedings.

I can't give a verbatim transcript of the testimony—naturally I never had access to it, and I haven't that kind of super-memory. It was all rather informal and casual, though there was a jury, a collection of individuals who appeared perfectly normal and everyday to me. I'm a small-town gal myself. They showed no trace of Winesburg, Ohio, nor did they look like cartoons by Arno or Hokinson.

First, there was the routine matter of identification and cause of death, facts stated by Dr. Ammon. Sally was then summoned. She repeated in a clear, matter-of-fact way, her story of hearing a shot as she approached the house, of hurrying in and finding the body. She could not, of her own knowledge, identify the weapon. She knew of no reason for the deed, aside from the deceased's grief over the very recent death of her husband. Had that been a great shock to the deceased, she was asked. Yes, a great shock and a great loss. What, in her opinion, were the deceased's relations with her husband? I could see Sally give her red hair a toss and shrug her green-clad shoulders. They were very happy and completely congenial, she declared stoutly. That would be all, for the present, she was then told. Paulding who had done all the questioning so far, indicated that she was to retire to whatever waiting room she had come from.

Mrs. Sutton was next called. In pointed contrast to Sally's more than vivid sports ensemble she appeared in a black tailored outfit which sacrificed becomingness to her evident sense of what she considered appropriate. There was no expression on her flabby face.

She, too, repeated what she had told Paulding the afternoon before. She had heard no shot as she had been sleeping in her room. She had come down upon being disturbed by voices and had found her nephew's wife, Sally Howard, and a woman whom she did not know in the library. At that point I felt more than out-size, but no one turned to stare at me. Mrs. Sutton was relating, by the time I could forget myself again, that Mrs. Howard certainly had access to the gun, as she had taken possession of all her husband's property.

Now as to motive, the coroner began, but cleared his throat and drank half a glass of water while he checked himself by means of a memorandum before him. Mrs. Sutton's back—I could not see the witnesses faces—looked as if she could hardly wait to speak, but apparently the questions had been very carefully organized.

Did Mrs. Sutton consider that Jordan Howard's death had led to the deceased's deed? Absolutely. Why . . . But Paulding cut her off. Did she consider that the disposition of Jordan Howard's property had a bearing upon the deed? It certainly had . . . Again she was stopped. Had Mrs. Sutton, been named as a beneficiary under Howard's will? She had not. Everything had been left to Felicity Howard—everything! Then concern about her financial status could scarcely have forced the deceased to take her own life, could it?

Rhoda Sutton sniffed, but if she made verbal answer it was inaudible to the back row. Her next answers were more distinct. She lived at River View with deceased. She had her own apartments there and since her brother-in-law's death had kept to them pretty closely. Mrs. Howard's attitude had not been at all friendly at any time.

In that case, and Paulding quite ignored her last statement, since they were living under the same roof, could Mrs. Sutton testify that Mrs. Howard had been suffering from grief and depression over the loss of her husband? She had not been in Mrs. Howard's confidence concerning her feeling for her husband or anything else. But had she not observed signs and evidences of grief? Not what she would call signs of genuine, honest grief signs of a guilty conscience, if she was any judge.

The jury waited hopefully, but the coroner checked Mrs. Sutton with a traffic cop's gesture until the forefinger of his other hand had found the next question on his list. The cue he must have come upon relieved him vastly. Were there any questions that Sheriff Floyd or his deputy would like to put to the witness?

A big man sitting in the front row nodded, but it was the person next to him who rose. I did not need Paulding's murmur, "Go right ahead, Mr. Nixon," to know his identity. I heard the same voice I had listened to from the library the afternoon before say, "Thank you, Mr. Coroner. Just a point or two . . ."

And then he turned so that I could see his face and I knew at once that I had seen it before somewhere. That puzzled me so much that I almost lost what he was saying. I forced back for later consideration my surprise at the trace of familiarity I saw in his features—nothing more than a feeling that I might have seen him in the movies—to follow what was going on down in front.

When had Mrs. Sutton last seen Mrs. Howard alive, he asked. Yesterday morning, she replied, just before lunch, and Rhoda Sutton's voice was its most toneless. What were the circumstances of their meeting? She was in the garden, which had remained completely in her charge even after

Mrs. Howard's coming to River View. A thin note of triumph touched that statement. Mrs. Howard had come up the drive in the car—she did not know where she had been and did not inquire. When she had put the car into the garage she walked through the garden. Yes, she had stopped a minute or so but there had been no conversation. She had just stood and looked at her as she cut away spent rose blooms. Yes, she appeared to be in her normal state, looking sorry for herself, as well she might.

Mrs. Sutton had just stated, Nixon reminded her blandly, oblivious of the gaping jury, that she had not been in Mrs. Howard's confidence at any time on any matter. In that case it would be useless to question her concerning the reasons for Mrs. Howard's emotional state. Rhoda Sutton sniffed again and I imagined that the tilt of her stiff black hat indicated frustration, but then, I was a mass of prejudice against the woman.

Nixon went on to say to the coroner and to the jury that he knew they had not yet heard from the person duly qualified to testify concerning the late Jordan Howard's proposed disposal of his property and the actual terms of his last will, but he thought he might venture one question. Had not Mrs. Sutton herself expected a bequest from her late brother-in-law? She did not answer directly; it was no doubt an irregular question, but the mere asking had its effect. She said, with what I was pleased to call self-righteousness though it was no more than bare fact, that she had had charge of River View and the care of Howard's children since the death of their mother, her sister, more than fifteen years before. That, interpolated Paulding with a placating smile, was well known to all of Point Tyler.

Nixon's next question surprised everybody, I think. Had ammunition of any sort, to Mrs. Sutton's knowledge, been purchased by any member of the family, whether living at River View or not? To this Rhoda Sutton said flatly that she

didn't know. When had she last seen the weapon that had
caused Mrs. Howard's death? She could not recall. . . . Certainly not since her brother-in-law's death. Was it loaded?
Jordan had always said so, and for that reason she would
never open the drawer of his desk where she knew he kept
it. So she could not say of her own knowledge what had
been the condition of the weapon during this preceding
week, for instance? No, she could not. . . .

These last questions surprised me as much as anyone,
but they excited me and cheered me. Sally, I thought, had
not overestimated her Tom Nixon.

Mrs. Sutton was waved into disappearance. "For the
time," according to Paulding. A brisker tempo set in. One
after another, the others were called—first those living
at River View, Bartlett Howard and Daisy and the man
Adkins, whom I had not seen before.

As to motive for the suicide, Bart stated that his stepmother had been considerably upset even since she had
found his father's will, though why, he threw in airily, the
discovery that she would be sitting pretty should disturb a
widow as young and attractive as Felicity Howard, if they
cared for his opinion of her personal appearance, should
give her the jitters he could not fathom. Yes, his father and
Felicity had certainly been "that way" about each other.
Bart's tone implied a genial bless-you-my-children.

He was asked nothing about the two wills, but there
were some questions from Tom Nixon, about the gun. He
hadn't seen it for so long he couldn't remember when.
Sure, his father always kept it loaded. Yes, he had bought a
box of shells himself, early in the spring, with the idea of
doing a little target shooting, but he hadn't got around to it
yet. The box was untouched and could be found, if anyone
wanted to check on it, lying about somewhere in his own
room.

Daisy wanted to tell all about her dental sufferings, but
what the coroner and Nixon kept her to merely bore out

the fact that Mrs. Howard took her husband's death mighty hard. Daisy was worried about her. She wouldn't eat right and she looked so kinda lost. Yesterday she'd just pecked at her lunch and said that anything that Daisy planned for dinner that night would be all right, just so there'd be plenty if any of the family should be there. "And she went in the library and shut the door and that's the last I see of her. . . ." Daisy wept frankly.

They had trouble with Adkins, for he was frightfully deaf, though all he was asked was about Bartlett Howard's chat with him during the time that the excitement broke at the house. He was quite voluble about the time, incensed apparently that the accuracy of his watch should be questioned, which it wasn't. Not unless that item was a bit of subtlety on Tom Nixon's part. . . . At least, the impression that the jury got was that Adkins' watch was the dearest thing in life to him, against which he would back all comers, including the Naval Observatory in Washington.

Then came Lila Howard and Chad and Allen and Sally once more. The emphasis on their examination was wholly upon motive. They all agreed, though not with Sally's enthusiasm or Bart's flippancy, that Jordan Howard's second marriage had been a successful and happy one, that Mrs. Howard had been grief-stricken upon the death of her husband and deeply perturbed over her finding of the will.

Allen Howard went on record that his stepmother had declared to them all that she felt that the provisions of the will were unfair to the others. Nixon asked him whether any sort of compromise had been discussed among them. There had not been time enough for that, Allen replied. The new will had not yet been admitted to probate. Matters had to take their legal course, he said, but he felt sure that Mrs. Howard was not the sort of person who would have wished to cause dissension within a family. Was there a possibility of that, he was asked. He hedged a little at that and finally said that speaking for himself there would have been none. He was quite willing to abide by his father's wishes.

Each was questioned about the gun's being loaded. With the exception of Lila Howard, who declared she knew nothing about the gun owned by her father-in-law, they all affirmed that Jordan Howard had always said it was loaded and ready for use, but neither Chad nor Allen had had occasion to see the weapon for some months. The last time they had handled firearms themselves or brought supplies had been at the beginning of the hunting season the preceding autumn.

It was Sally who jerked the assemblage into vivid attention by nonchalantly admitting that she had bought a box of .32 shells two days before. For what purpose, Nixon demanded. "Oh, just for fun," she answered.

Pressed to make herself clearer, she plunged into voluminous details about a picnic she was planning. She thought that shooting at tin cans would be more fun than archery. I was to learn later that the young married set of Point Tyler's elite had lately gone ga-ga about bows and arrows and straw targets and that Sally had thrown that remark in just to get a rise out of a woman who was getting on her social nerves. She overshot herself of course, though my phrase is scarcely fortunate.

Nixon let her ramble on about the picnic and then put in with a sharp inquiry as to the present whereabouts of her arsenal. Somewhere about the house—her own house, she repeated—in the game room or maybe the garage.

More to the point than all this, or so I thought, was a direct question asked each of the three sons, but not put to the women. Had there been family discussion, Mrs. Howard being included in the group, of the terms of Howard's newly found will? There had, and no longer ago than the night before Felicity's death. Had the discussion been friendly? Allen said it was meant to be . . . Chad that everybody got edgy when they tried to explain investments to women . . .

and Bart that Felicity always let his aunt get in her hair.
. . . The three of them admitted, and of course none of
them heard what the others were testifying, that Felicity
had been quite nervous and upset by the time the family
discussion was over.

I was sure that Rhoda Sutton would be recalled, but she
was not. If I had been on the jury, I should not have been
satisfied with the scraps of information that were being
dished out, but they were all looking as if they had heard
of a juicy lot.

Floyd, Paulding, and Nixon went into a brief huddle
at this point, and then the coroner said that since there
had been so many references to the will, or wills, to make
it quite definite to the jury, he'd ask Mr. Godfrey Blair to
make a brief statement. A paunchy, pompous, and prosper-
ous (I'm sorry; if I taught English instead of math I could
write better—maybe) individual rose and mumbled about
two minutes' worth at the jury. All I heard was that he
didn't approve of what he was doing, but his explanation
about the terms of Jordan Howard's last will and testament
apparently captured the rapt attention of the jury.

Paulding next called Tom Nixon, who reported that the
weapon, a .32, had been duly examined for fingerprints and
that the only marks upon it corresponded with those taken
from Felicity Howard's fingers. As I listened to that, I went
absolutely cold.

Then came the big moment. One more witness, announced Paulding, and then he believed the jury would
have the complete picture. Mr. Wilson Markham . . . and
who should step forward but my bald-headed gentleman.
Aha, thought I, is this to be a demonstration of Tom Nix-
ons' smartness, or is Aunt Rhoda getting her oar in.

Mr. Wilson Markham was not identified specifically. At
least, not to me, for his reply to a suitable question that he
was well acquainted with both the late Mr. and Mrs. Howard and a frequent caller at River View only made me want

to know more about him. Felicity had never mentioned any such name in her letters to me. Indeed, as I thought about it, she had mentioned no one outside of the members of her husband's family and household.

When had, Mr. Markham last called at River View? Exactly one week ago this coming afternoon. He had seen no one except Mrs. Howard, not even the maid, for she served tea herself. Had Mrs. Howard mentioned any matter that might indicate that she was considering suicide? On the contrary, quite. . . . She had told him that she was afraid of firearms and that she would feel much more at ease as she attended to necessary business at her husband's desk if the revolver kept in one of its drawers were not loaded. In short, Mr. Markham stated that he had then and there removed the shells and taken them off in his pocket when he left. The empty gun had been returned to its customary place. Did Mr. Markham think that this request of the deceased—Paulding was putting the question—might have indicated a morbid sense of temptation to end her life and a—er—a desire to be protected from her own impulse? Very emphatically, Mr. Markham did not think of any such thing. Nor did I.

However, he wished to clear his conscience a little further. He had not seen Mrs. Howard after that, but he had talked to her over the telephone two days before her death, and on that occasion he had suggested to her that perhaps she had been somewhat foolish in removing a means of protection that a woman living in a rather remotely placed house might find herself glad to have. In short, he had advised her to ask one of the sons to reload the revolver for her. And had she followed his suggestion? Mr. Markham said he did not know. Had he any specific reason for making the suggestion to Mrs. Howard? She was not the only occupant of River View, Paulding reminded him. No specific reason, except that he realized that Mrs. Howard was a naturally timid person who was going through a lonely time. She felt alone, he expanded. Loneliness was not always dissipated by the presence of others. The other members of the household maintained separate quarters and River View was a large and rambling house. The maid had a third-floor room, he understood, and the gardener lived off the place and, moreover, was handicapped by deafness.

He surely seems to know River View, I thought. I was betting that Flippity had told him about her room's being ransacked, but that episode was not brought up.

That was all. Paulding attempted a summing up and did it wretchedly. There could be no doubt of suicide, however deceased had managed about reloading the weapon. As they had heard, her fingerprints had agreed with those found by the usual tests to be on the gun. Grief over her husband's death and a morbid depression had been established as the motive. It was all very regrettable, very sad, but such was life.

And such, the jury reported, was the way death had come to Felicity Howard.

I should have been among the first to leave Paulding's Funeral Home, as I had been sitting so near the door. But I loitered and let people jostle me a bit, thinking that Sally or Chad would be having me on their minds. None of the Howards emerged from the row of closed doors about the ornate entrance hall of the undertaker's establishment. One door opened and I heard someone step beside me. It was Tom Nixon.

"You wanted to see me," he whispered. "I shall expect you at my office at two-thirty this afternoon."

He stepped backward and the door closed.

2

It sounded like a command appearance and I should have been amenable, but I had changed my mind about the urgency of a conference with Tom Nixon since I had listened to Mr. Markham's statement at the inquest. The one thing that I had wanted Nixon to know had been taken care of, temporarily, and I had other plans for the afternoon. Perhaps if I could sidestep Sally and luncheon. . . .

The Chad Howards' Buick was still in its parking place. If they should catch up with me before I walked back to Terrace Drive and retrieved my own car,—no one would know except me what project of mine had been circumvented. I was hot and breathless by the time I reached Sally's house and I thought longingly of chilled salad and iced tea, but no one whom I could connect with the Howards had passed me. I made directly for the garage, but a voice from the kitchen hailed me. Sally's maid. I had forgotten about her.

"Are you Mis' Lenox, ma'am? Mis' Howard, she just called and lef' me a message to give you. They all had to go up to the Howard place for a while and she says for you just to make yourself at home, and I got some lunch ready for you."

Her last point was welcome, but I ate briskly, resolved to have a try at my project even though the presence of the Howards at River View might complicate matters. At any rate, I had until two-thirty and any family conference following sudden death and an inquest ought to last longer than that. I was not taking Tom Nixon's summons lightly, but if I could back up my story with a scrap of evidence all the better for me.

I told Norine—that was the maid—that I was going to go for a little ride and if Mrs. Howard called or returned to say that I was amusing myself and not to give me a thought. My little ride took me out Route 62 as fast as I could push my car. Nothing else was in sight as I turned off into the River View drive. I proceeded more cautiously then until I found the hazel clump where Sally had hidden the coupé. In the bright afternoon sunlight it was not such a perilous feat to maneuver the car from the drive to its shelter.

I meant to poke about there thoroughly, but that could wait until I returned. Somewhere between this spot and the place where I had come upon Sally the afternoon before I had heard something that sounded like an object thrown, and I was bent upon trying to locate the spot and the object. I hurried along the drive, well aware that driving and walking identical distances create confusing differences about time and space. Headed toward River View, I had the hazel clump to my left. The sound of the crashing object had come from my right and I had been just about to make a curve when I had heard the noise. The last curve before the cleared space of lawn was reached, I remembered.

The drive was all curves. The sensible thing was to work backwards and thus I would know which bend was the last one. I rounded three of them, with all the caution of an Indian scout, before a glimpse of the roof line and the glitter of sun on parked cars told me I had gone far enough. Then I went back as far as the curve preceding and advanced again, this time with my attention fixed upon the ravine to my right. Somewhere down in that thick viny tangle of undergrowth there might be something that ought to be found.

Poison ivy or no poison ivy, I clambered down and threshed about among the bushes and tree roots. I don't like snakes either, and things that buzz around my ears break down my morale. The lore of the deep woods is something I've always been glad to leave to the camper-outer, and so I had broken and bruised a dismaying number of twigs and leafy branches before I remembered that a falling object might have left just such a trail for me to see. It was too late to be wise then. The ravine or gully sloped steeply and I worked my way downward. Whatever it had been could very easily have rolled. One fact cheered me, provided I was searching in approximately the right place. The ground was damp enough to show my heel prints where there were no rock ledges nor spongy moss, and I saw no traces of others.

Then I found it—or rather, I found something. A dull grayish-white ball that I took for a harmless stone until I saw a line of stitching along one edge. I touched it and it was soft, but when I picked it up it was heavier than a rolled-up pair of gloves should be. I even thought about fingerprints, for I'd read how they could be shown up on fabrics and other unlikely surfaces, and was careful to jerk the roll apart by a gingerly pull at the seams. They were gardener's or houseworker's gloves, generous and baggy and stained from considerable use, though the original color must have been white or cream. Both gloves were wrongside out, except for the fingertips, as if they had been hastily and not easily drawn off, and the right one was wrapped about a stone and then in turn thrust into the left and its cuff turned back over the package Just the right size and weight to throw.

I attempted to roll the three articles back again as I had found them, but with no thought about destroying fingerprints this time. I dropped the bundle into my handbag and pulled myself upward to the drive. I don't know why I felt so satisfied, for the gloves told me nothing, except that they had not lain long where I had found them. They were not at all dampish to the touch, and the black earth upon which I had found them was far from dry.

Blowsy and breathing hard, I emerged upon the drive after assuring myself that the way was clear. I found my hazel clump and my car. I also found a man sitting on the running board. It was Adkins, the outside man, and I had the advantage, for he could not know who I was. That, it soon appeared, was the trouble. I was a trespasser. I couldn't read. I didn't believe in signs. I was on private property. And it wasn't the first time, neither. He'd seen them tire marks and oil spots. Breakin' down ditchin', tearin' up the ground. In short, I was to get the hell outa there, if I hadn't got stuck with the car. Women drivers. . . .

My mild apologies and attempts to identify myself as a True Lover of Nature were lost on Adkins, for I couldn't have made him hear even if he had ceased his enraged mumbling. I had to climb obediently into the car, but to my secret surprise and self-admiration saved my face by backing up and on to the road with a false move.

However, it was getting so near to half past two that I should have insufficient time to search the surroundings of Sally's hiding place. "Tearin' up the ground," Adkins had complained. If he meant anything more by that than the fairly harmless traces of the passage of Sally's car and mine, Adkins might find me trespassing again.

Just on the dot I entered Tom Nixon's office for the second time that day. The inner door was ajar and he swung it wide as I came in. He offered me a chair and seated himself in another. These two, a table with a covered typewriter on it, and some steel filing cabinets were the furnishings, with the addition of several interesting camera studies of the river thumbtacked on the wall. I was still without a clue to what this nondescript suite was an office for. And as I took a long look at this young man at close range, I was still convinced that I had seen his face before.

He opened the session by a question that for some reason startled me, "Have you mentioned this appointment to anyone, Miss Lenox?"

I shook my head and got back at him with two questions. "How do you know I am Miss Lenox, and how did you know that I had tried to see you this morning?"

He gave an easy little laugh and a prompt reply to my first question. "You are Sally Howard's guest. She's referred to you frequently in connection with this River View trouble. This morning she led me to think that you were at the inquest. I know everybody in town. You were the only stranger present."

Maybe I wanted to impress him with my own powers of observation. I said, "That man Markham must have mentioned that he saw me coming from here this morning." That was a sudden deduction on my part. Nixon let it fall without comment.

"I did not think it necessary to call you as a witness this morning," he went on. I liked his pleasant voice and his steady, bespectacled eyes very much. "But I do think it necessary to talk to you now. It was rather irregular—that performance this morning, and I'm not sure that we can say the matter's cleaned up. You're a stranger here and know little or nothing about the Howards, I understand. I'd like an unbiased account of what you saw and heard yesterday, if you please. Of course, everything's quite off the record now."

"That's just it," I burst out. "I know more than you think and I'm far from being unprejudiced and I'd like to tell you a lot of things." Apparently I had made my resolution quickly, but my angry grief for Felicity was just under the surface and I felt an instinctive trust in Tom Nixon's integrity. The false position I had been in ever since I had followed Sally into the living room at River View the afternoon before was intolerable to me and grossly, callously unfair to Felicity.

Nixon looked at me calmly. "So . . . I shall be very glad to listen."

My emotion thus checked, I proceeded to tell him about my friendship with Felicity Howard, why I had come to Point Tyler, how I had met Sally and followed her up to River View, the odd noise I had heard in the ravine, what she had told me when I caught up with her at the end of the drive, our entrance into the house, and all the succeeding activities in which I had had a part.

I paused for breath before going on with my latest endeavors along River View drive. "Is that all?" he asked politely.

"No, it's not all. I have two things to show you and one piece of information which no one else knows unless Felicity told that Markham man, and he didn't mention it before the jury this morning."

I opened my bag and first produced the rolled-up gloves folded inside one of my clean handkerchiefs. I explained how I had come upon them. "Maybe they account for the noise I heard, maybe not. I'm turning them over to you."

He opened my handkerchief, poked at the gloves a bit with a long forefinger, and said um-m-m.

Then I handed him Felicity's last letter to me, the letter that had sent me off to Point Tyler. "Read it," I commanded. "It worried me—and still does. Somebody was up to something up there at River View and I don't think it was Felicity."

He went through the letter twice, folded the double sheet, and put it back in its envelope. And again he said um-m-m.

"And this is what I know, Mr. Nixon—know to be a fact: Felicity Howard was afraid of any sort of shooting irons. She knew nothing about them. I heard her say, about a year ago at a faculty picnic, that she had never touched one in her life."

He asked me a question then. "Was your friend the sort of woman who made wills?"

I had to say that I did not know. Schoolteachers, I pointed out, did not accumulate estates, though insurance agents and investment men were always on their trail. She had no immediate family, no close relatives. She had kept up a health and accident policy—most teachers do—and she'd been interested in annuities. That was all I knew.

"I take it, Miss Lenox, from what you have said that you can scarcely make yourself believe that your friend committed suicide."

"And you can also take it," I broke in impatiently, "that I intend to clear her name from those utterly foul and outrageous accusations about having a guilty conscience because of her husband's death. That unspeakable woman. . . ."

"Don't misunderstand me, Miss Lenox. If there's any clearing up to be done, I intend to see to it. And I am very glad that you came to me so frankly and so promptly. The family—certain members of the family, rather—" He let that sentence trail off and started another one. "Now about Mrs. Howard—Sally Howard. There are too many Mrs. Howards to be conventional, Miss Lenox, and we're used to first-naming them. I note that you went only so far with Sally."

"I've reported exactly, Mr. Nixon. I wasn't sure—I'd like to be sure about Sally."

He frowned and looked off at the blank wall behind me, and again I fretted my mind about having seen his face somewhere before. I was about to settle the matter by a direct question when he spoke.

"About Sally—I'd like to clear that up, too. However, she handled you rather cleverly and I'm grateful for that. Keeping your connection with Felicity Howard from the others, I mean," he hurried to reassure me, for I suppose I looked as affronted as anyone does on being told he's been "handled." At that instant my question became unnecessary. The way he looked when his eyes twinkled told me where I had seen his picture—in a magazine I had confiscated from the sixth period study-hall boys, who were his ardent fans as Pedro Gunner. I wondered if Point Tyler knew and suspected they didn't.

"She's put you in an excellent position to help me, and I believe you are going to do it. I hope she hasn't given you too much of a background?"

"I think I'm just a dear old pal, so far."

"You're going to be a lady detective on the side. Let me plan a moment." He slipped a flat watch from his pocket and the lady detective pondered on the surprising item that Pedro Gunner, creator of an endless series of westerns, sported a Phi Beta Kappa key on his watch chain.

"I'm to join the family at River View before long, to hear their decision. You can throw it up to me later if I'm wrong, but I think Allen Howard is going to say go ahead with an exhumation. I hope so; it may bring our problem to a close before you and I get started. I'm going to slip

along now and give that hazel clump of yours a going-over.
I'm even hoping I'll meet up with Adkins. Maybe I'd better
suggest that you go back to Chad and Sally's and play
visiting fireman till you hear from me, even if you hear
from them first. It won't hurt you to relax a little and you'll
be more use to me not tied up in knots."

"A good rest with a rip-roaring western, say something
by Pedro Gunner, and I'll be a new woman."

His face went blank for an instant and then he burst
into a roar of delighted laughter. "Gosh, woman, keep it
dark. I've never been west of St. Louis."

I obeyed my new chief and returned to the house on
Terrace Drive.

Norine was shelling peas on the back porch. Mis' Howard hadn't come back yet, or called up neither. Did I want
lemonade or anything?

A bath and a rest, I told her, and while I had both, to my
physical and mental improvement, I could no more dismiss
from my thoughts what had happened and what might be
about to happen than I could forget to breathe.

The house was very still as the warm June afternoon
wore on. I tried not to be impatient, but I was ready for
action. The telephone bell was silent; not a car came to a
stop before the house or turned into the driveway. What
were Tom Nixon and his official confreres doing? Exhum-
ing? That was a process I could not picture except against
a background of midnight sky and flickering lantern light,
thanks to Wilkie Collins or some other Victorian worthy.
What were the Howards up to? Plotting in the River View
library? Manufacturing evidence? If only Tom Nixon would
call before Sally and Chad came back.

I heard the rattle of china and silver from below. Norine
was setting the table. That meant she was still expecting
Chad and Sally to return for dinner. I rose and dressed and
had just finished when the telephone pealed.

"It's for you. Miss Lenox, if you're fit to come down. I don't know who—some man," Norine called lustily.

It was Nixon. He wasted no time. "I'm calling from River View and I don't want to say much, but I think you'll get me. I wasn't wrong, and it's all over. Poison—no doubt. So it isn't all over, either. I think we agree there. I'm coming down to town now and I'll be dropping around, but I wanted you to hear before the others came. Stand by. . . ."

So it was to be Tom Nixon and me against the Howards. I was not even excluding Sally.

Part Four
Mainly Friday, June 17

1

Before I could get jittery about what attitude I should assume with Chad and Sally, their car rolled into the garage.

"How fresh you look, darling. We're wrecks, but if I go
up to change I'll never get down again, and anyway Norine
has a gorgeous shortcake just about ready." Sally flopped
into a chair and tried to give me a wan grin. "My dear,
we've been through absolute hell today, and maybe it's not
over."

"What do you mean, it's not over?" her husband demanded, busy with bottles and lemon slices. "We know now
that Aunt Rhoda was right all along, but unfortunately a
murderer can't die but once."

"Chad, don't . . ." Sally looked pleadingly at me, wretched
with sympathy. "Poor Peg hasn't the slightest idea of what's
happened."

Chad Howard half emptied his glass and set it down.
I was sure it wasn't the first he'd had lately. "Miss Lenox,
I'm delighted to be your host and all that, but we have just
had shocking information. My father was murdered three
weeks ago and it was his wife who did for him. Her suicide
yesterday saved the state an execution."

Sally's eyes were on me, hot and fearful with warning.
What I might have said I don't know, for I began to shake

with rage for Felicity's sake, but at that instant Chad Howard strode toward the door.

"Someone's coming. Who the devil—it's Nixon."

Tom Nixon did not wait to be invited in. "Thought
I'd find you two here. There's a point or so I'd like to
put to you—" He checked himself in well-acted surprise
and swung toward me. "Marg Lenox, by all that's holy! So
you're the girl friend that Sally's been babbling about." He
pumped my arm vigorously and managed to give me a pro-
ceed-with-caution signal. "You couldn't have crossed my
path at a better time. Does Sally know about your secret
vice?"

He turned again to the two Howards, both of whom
were looking dazed. I myself was feeling like three other
persons.

"She's an honest-to-God school ma'am, sure enough, but
after hours and during vacations, she goes in for private
investigations. I've seen her work—she's good!"

As a fictionist Tom Nixon's success was understandable.
Sally gave me a dismayed, uncertain look and then her
attention had to be diverted by Norine, who was bursting to communicate something about plenty for four. Chad
Howard picked up his glass and finished its contents. He
offered Nixon nothing. Holding the empty glass and thump-
ing the air with it, he said levelly, "The matter has just
been closed, Nixon. I don't care to have it rehashed. There
is nothing for a stranger to investigate."

"Oh, but you don't know—I came to tell you two something that can't fail to alter your feeling, Chad. And then
I interrupted myself when I saw Marg Lenox. You must all
forgive my exuberance."

Sally and Norine came out of their huddle at that point,
and the four of us found ourselves in the dining room. Nixon admitted that he couldn't resist shortcake and might as
well eat as he talked, but I noted that nothing significant
was said while Norine was within earshot. Nobody ate with

much heartiness except Nixon, and I presumed that the glass-fronted fish sandwiches accounted for his request for a meal in a family dining room.

Chad glowered at us all and looked like a spoiled adolescent. He was easily, I concluded, two years younger than Sally. If Lila Howard was philandering with her brother-in-law, she must be creating delusions of youth for herself. Judging cosmetically, she looked ten years older than Chad.

"Peg's so surprisingly versatile," Sally murmured once. "I recall now that she pored over a tome on criminal psychology that summer we met at Columbia. She said she was collating statistics, which sounded like mathematics to me. Have you really done detective work?"

"Not at all," I announced firmly. "I'm merely a fan of Mr. Nixon's. He cleared up a nasty mess at the Diamond Bar Ranch one summer not long ago. We all thought his name was Gunner. I was staying at one of those dude places."

I had something on Tom Nixon and I was telling him so, but with great seriousness he went on with my fairytale. "I'll have to tell you people about that case some day. But it was Marg here who found the missing bloodstain."

Chad Howard pushed his strawberry shortcake aside abruptly and Sally asked me pointedly if I recalled the little girl from Alabama who spent all her time answering letters from four distracted suitors left at home. At last we were back in the living room with a generous pot of coffee and Norine two closed doors to the rear.

"I couldn't resist the food, Sally, but I must get back to business now. Let's take Miss Lenox's presence for granted. She can be of real help, I assure you, and now that I know she's the person that is Sally's guest, I've a good idea of what she already knows about this affair. It has been established, Chad, that your father was murdered, and you and some others of your family feel certain that his wife was the responsible agent. If it should be proved that Felicity Howard was herself murdered, then what?"

Neither of the Howards spoke. I thought I might as well practice my role. Nixon's question had warmed my heart. "Then her murderer is likewise the murderer of Jordan Howard."

"The inquest says suicide—"

"You can't prove she was murdered! Or can you—?"

The two speeches tumbled against one another into a sharp silence. The first was Chad's, the second Sally's.

Tom Nixon let the silence lengthen, his eyes inscrutable behind his spectacles and the breeziness of manner that had marked his preposterous greeting of me entirely gone. "Never mind the inquest. Who murdered Jordan Howard is the problem now, and I'm beginning to think that the answer will prove that his wife was murdered also."

Chad Howard groped blindly for an ash tray. His fresh blond complexion had gone pasty and his eyes sought his wife's as if expecting her to take the lead. Her thin tanned fingers began to drum upon the arm of her chair. She said nothing.

Chad had made several attempts and then mumbled something about how could any evidence be found now.

Then Sally spoke, and she looked directly at Nixon as she did so. "Don't forget, Chad, about Aunt Rhoda's box. She put the evidence there."

I had passed that information on to Nixon that afternoon along with everything else, but he let Sally think it was news to him. The brisk questions he fired at her brought put again the fact that Rhoda Sutton had shown no one the bottle and needle. She had found them, Sally said, behind the old picture of Allen's graduating class that still hung in the back hall at River View.

"Are you people saying," I wanted to know, "that poison was injected into Jordan Howard's system through that infected scratch that had been worrying your aunt?"

Sally and Chad waited for Nixon to answer. He nodded and said, "Yes, that was the means and the method. The poison is known, no matter what is found in Mrs. Sutton's little bottle, upon which I venture to say there will be no fingerprints. Furthermore, and this is one of the things I came especially to say, I think I know how to trace the source of the poison."

Two brilliant spots of color blotched Sally's white face. They were not becoming. Chad tugged at a handkerchief and blew his nose. His hands were shaking. Sally's face as she came from the drugstore yesterday, I thought, and thanks to me, Tom knew exactly whom to ask first, and the man told and Sally thought he wouldn't. . . .

Neither of them said a word. The matter of the poison reached a dead end.

"The second thing I wanted to say is this—really, it's a question. Sally, do you mind getting me the box of shells you bought the other day?"

"Why, no, Tom, not at all. They're somewhere around. . . ." But it took effort for her to drag herself from her chair. She pulled out a wide flat drawer from a table and poked futilely among a litter of card packs and score pads. Chad's eyes following every move with a queer hopefulness. "Maybe in the gameroom," she murmured, and drifted out of the room.

Nixon followed her, but I stayed where I was. I was beginning to wonder about Chad Howard. He made several nervous wheels about the room, very conscious of the vague sounds that came from the basement. We heard the two mount stairs and go out toward the garage. Then, abruptly thrusting cigarettes upon me, he said, "I'm glad you really know Sally. You know she wouldn't—it's been tough, her feeling about Aunt Rhoda."

That didn't quite make sense, but I let him think it did. I said, "She liked your stepmother, too. That's a point."

"Thank heaven you were with her yesterday afternoon." And somehow I knew that Sally's peculiar performance with their Buick was unsuspected by her husband.

That's all we said. The others were gone a long time. When at last they re-entered the house Nixon was looking grim but satisfied, and Sally had herself well in hand. To tell the truth, I was somewhat puzzled by the look of quiet triumph in her eyes,

Chad looked the question I wanted to ask, and Sally said very jauntily, "Not a trace. I can't think where I put that box."

Her husband slumped in his chair and made no sign when Tom Nixon spoke from the doorway. "That's all for tonight. You understand that you've started something that I've got to go on with, Sally. You tell Marg what I want her to do."

After he had left, Sally crossed to Chad and gave him a wifely little shoulder pat. From her position behind him she raised her eyebrows at me. "Let's all get to bed as soon as we can. It's been a ghastly day and there's the funeral tomorrow. Take something up to read, Peg, if you like. I'll be in to see that you're comfortable."

I left them then, naturally, but there was no prolonged conference between husband and wife at that time. I heard them coming up and by the time I had got into a negligee Sally was in my room.

She stared at me and then laughed. "I suppose you've done the dirty on me, and yet I know I pushed you to it. You're no detective; Tom broke down and admitted that much. I realize you had to tell him about you and Felicity. I'm glad. He can do more with you than I can. He wants you to stay at the house tomorrow while we're at the cemetery. It will be the one time that you can have the place to yourself. You see?"

"I'm to look for something?"

"Through Felicity's things. And anything else that occurs to you—or to him, by that time. He doesn't trust me."

She said that last as if she were highly pleased with herself.

"What about the box of shells? You were gone such a long time."

"He'll tell you anyway. They weren't there. I knew they weren't. Tom knew they weren't. He had them in his pocket all the time. He'd found them this afternoon. I'd dug a hole and hidden them yesterday. Near where I'd stuck the car. You see, a lot of them weren't there. So now I'm suspect number one."

"That's what you think," I retorted somberly.

"It will serve. You detectives don't want your problem to be too simple."

"As Chad remarked to me, I'm glad I really know you, Sally."

"Did he say that?" There was a spontaneous eagerness about her words. "That helps, a lot. Maybe we're both fools, but I do love him. You see, Peg, Chad's such an old blunderbuss, but of course he didn't commit murder, and I'm sticking around and not caring what Tom thinks about me—in fact, I hope he does; it will give me a little more time."

I interrupted with schoolroom firmness. "I find your remarks singularly clear. What did Tom Nixon ask you about what had happened just before I caught up with you yesterday? He'll tell me anyway, so don't stall."

"I told him the truth, but I hope he doesn't believe it. The shells were in the car all the time, and when I found Felicity I dashed back to look, and then I thought it would be a good idea to hide the box."

"Sally, look at me. . . ." This was not necessary. Her gaze had never shifted. "You must have known that Chad was somewhere about."

"Not until I saw him with Lila, coming up from the boat house. But he had had the car the day before, after I bought the shells, and that morning, and he was the first one that Aunt Rhoda convinced. About Felicity, I mean. He was dreadfully cut up about his father's will. That was my fault, really. I've not liked it here at Point Tyler."

"Why did you hide the box?"

"Because I'd torn it open, silly. For no good reason at all, except that my mind was on that damned picnic And I didn't put them back—the couple I took out, and they got lost, or something."

"I think you're being pretty silly, Sally, and Tom Nixon will see right through you. He's working from the poison end. Whoever did that shot Felicity too. Unless Chad ties up somewhere with that stuff, why are you so hot and bothered? Tom will test the bullet, of course, though that won't prove anything about those from your box." I rambled on, decidedly mixed in my sketchy knowledge of ballistics.

But Sally wasn't listening. The instant I referred to the poison, she had changed. The bravado she had so gamely assumed slipped from her and I saw again the look in her eyes I had glimpsed when I had my first sight of her upon my arrival in Point Tyler.

She burst out into a frantic stream of speech. "But there is! There is a tie-up with the poison, and I'm scared green, Peg. I mean, Tom could make it tie up. Please, please, don't let him. . . . It's the hypodermic. Ours it gone. I've looked and looked and I can't find it. And Norine knows what I've been hunting for. I tried to buy one yesterday at the drugstore, but Tack didn't have one in stock and besides he said I'd have to have a prescription. Tack will remember. He'd do anything for Tom." She ran her fingers through her red hair and rocked her head from side to side.

"What of it?" I demanded. "What's a misplaced hypo? And why pick on Chad all the time or make these ridiculous attempts to divert suspicion to yourself? There are other members of the Howard family. There is your dear Aunt Rhoda. I'd like to know what else she knows about a needle and a bottle of whatever it is than that she found them and hasn't let anyone examine them—yet. She's the one that whooped it all up against Felicity. And let me tell you, Sally, if that woman was sound asleep in her room yesterday afternoon when you and I went into the house, then we're both of us sleep-walkers!"

2

At eleven o'clock the following morning, Friday, I found myself alone in the house at River View. There had been a brief and simple service for Felicity Howard at which I had been an inconspicuous attendant. That I was the most bereaved person present was for me alone to dwell upon. The beautiful decorum of the ancient phrases would have pleased Felicity, I comforted myself. But when the little procession of cars moved away toward a burial plot a mile or so below Point Tyler, I remained behind to serve my friend in another way. Tom Nixon had arranged the matter skillfully. Adkins had gone with the family to act as a pall-bearer and nothing would have induced Daisy to miss any part of the funeral.

So I could count on a certain amount of uninterrupted time. I had had a quiet word or two of instructions from Tom Nixon, but for myself I wanted to see something of the arrangements of the upper floor, particularly the rooms taken over by Mrs. Sutton and Bart.

They were, as I had suspected, on the side of the house we had approached from the drive. There were two bedrooms, a bath, a sitting room, and a square back hall that had been converted into a kitchenette. From any of the rooms except the bath there were exits that gave easy access to the rest of the house. On the other side of the main upper hall were the rooms that had been Felicity's and two smaller guest rooms. A short enclosed stairway at the back led to some finished attic rooms which of course were Daisy's quarters. There was another flight going down to the kitchen.

I went down those steps just to make sure, and it was while I stood at the foot of the steep flight that I noticed the funny little hole. It was a bullet hole, but I didn't know it. I stood staring at it absently, my heart heavy about Felicity, and then I thought, That gooey stuff that hardens like wood will soon fill that up. That's how I knew later that the planking surrounding the hole was smooth and unscratched when I stood there.

I prowled my way back through Aunt Rhoda's side of the house but saw nothing that gave me ideas, except concerning her taste in window hangings, which were many-layered and none too fresh, and that she loved trivia. Bart's room was as bare and unrevealing as an unoccupied hospital apartment and not much larger. On one wall there was a weird, badly drawn mural which had not yet progressed further than one thin wash of color. I wondered if Tom had done anything about his box of shells and decided that was his affair.

My chief business lay in Felicity's rooms. Her own bedroom was easy to identify. Familiar evidences of her personality were all about me and it was hard to keep myself steady for what I had to do. I held hard to the thought that I was there in her service.

"Don't lose time over the bureau drawers," Nixon had said. "They've been gone through. It's her desk that may be important. She kept that locked. Here are keys. She wouldn't mind your looking. . . ."

How or where he had obtained them I don't know. I stood before her dressing table, fingering bottles, and trays, and let myself imagine what could have happened yesterday. If someone else, not Sally, had shot Felicity that afternoon, Sally's arrival had certainly followed so immediately—"I heard the shot . . ."—that there would have been time only for the murderer to disappear. If obtaining and using her keys. had been one thing to be accomplished, then our appearance below had prevented that. Therefore, since Tom Nixon had given me the keys, the murderer had not yet had a chance to go through Felicity's desk. Provided, always, that the desk did hold something that bore upon events, which we did not know.

Suddenly my finger felt wet. I looked at it, saw nothing. But I smelled something. I did not need to wave the finger below my nose. It was Felicity's beloved and long used "Faded Flowers" cologne. I shut my eyes and made my finger go back to the place where I had first felt its wetness. There it was, about the stopper of the flask of "Faded Flowers."

But I had not removed the stopper. I shivered with quick fear and swung about defensively. The room was placid with sunshine; there was not a sound anywhere except a note or two of bird song in the maple beyond the windows.

Yet someone—someone had been at the bottle and not many minutes before. I knew as well as anyone how quickly a fluid like that, high in alcoholic content, would evaporate on a warm day.

The closet—would I be foolhardy to look? I opened the door wide and an electric light obligingly went on, only adding to my panic at first, and then I saw that there was nothing there except the proper furnishings of a lady's clothes-closet. The bathroom door was next in line, its door partly open. Nothing there. A connecting door led into another bedroom, dark and shadowy, for the shades were drawn. I went no further; I was still all gooseflesh.

However, after I had closed the bathroom door on Felicity's side. I felt proud of myself for thinking that, if someone had recently touched the cologne flask, there would surely be fingerprints other than mine, and I had only brushed the stopper. Using my handkerchief with care, I removed the bottle from the dressing table and set it on top of the desk.

Thank goodness, as I sat at the desk it was easy to see the door that led into the hall, and the bathroom door behind me was firmly closed. Tom Nixon had given me two keys. One let down the lid and also unlocked the drawers at my

knee. The other was smaller and must serve the compart-
ments inside the desk. The first thing I found nearly undid
me. It was my own picture, an enlarged, framed snapshot
and a remarkably clear though not flattering likeness. Felicity had taken it one October day when we had not gone
to a district convention. A blessed thing that give-away's
inside the desk and not out on top, I thought. Aunt Rhoda would surely have recognized me and Sally would have
identified it long ago. I slipped it into my bag, just in case.

I found nothing in the desk that mattered, though every
item spoke loudly of Felicity's careful ways. There was no
diary; there were no tied-up bundles of old letters; there
was no suicide note. Stationery for all purposes in delightful quantities. A little box for stamps. Her old brass letter
scale—I had given her that; I had bought it on Allen Street.
A new-looking address book, not the shabby blue-bound
one that I remembered. A household account book and one
for writing out a week's menus at a time. A few letters from
friends. My last one was among them and I recognized Julia
Meade's writing and Charlotte's on others.

The only thing I took, besides my own picture, was the
address book. There might possibly be something in it that
I could look into. What was sticking in my craw, of course,
was Rhoda Sutton's insinuation about another man. Preposterous idea. There couldn't have been anyone before her
marriage to Jordan Howard, and her devotion to him since
had surely been the real thing.

Then whatever happened to me, happened. I don't know
what—I just went out. There was a sense of smothering
blackness and I gurgled a scream. That's all I could report
later, except that I was positive that nothing had come at
me from the hall.

For all I knew, when I took hold again, it was the middle
of the next week. It wasn't. It was no more than ten minutes
later, for I managed to remember in time that I had heard
a clock striking as I slipped the address book into my bag.

I was down in the kitchen with a very wet face and more wetness trickling down my neck. I could see Daisy shakily filling a teakettle. I heard steps and a man's voice saying, "What the hell goes on?"

I tried to sit up and Tom Nixon bent over me. I had only one thought. "The bottle—the bottle on the desk? Is it still there?" I gasped.

He told me later he was wrong about what bottle I was babbling about, but he knew what I meant by the desk and vanished from my sight abruptly. I was still mopping my face with one of Daisy's dish towels and trying to make sense out of her exclamations when he returned.

"No bottle on the desk," he reported. "Here, drink this." He brought brandy from the dining room. "Now, what happened? Quick, before the others get back."

"I don't know. I was sitting at the desk and suddenly blackness descended and then I was down here—just now." I tried to make my expression tell him there was more to say privately, and then I saw my hand bag lying on the table before me.

"Give me that," I demanded, and opened it with hands that shook as mine rarely did. Everything was there. Its interior looked just as it had when I put the address book into it.

Tom Nixon turned from me to Daisy. "Now you—what do you know?

"Plenty, young man, plenty." And she poured forth a detailed stream of chronological narrative. She had gone to the cemetery in her nephew's car and coming back he had taken the short road and had gone pretty fast—Elvin had a grand new car—and she didn't mind anyway because she had luncheon to see to, though Mrs. Sutton hadn't been at all clear about how many would be back to eat, but she had plenty of chops and tomatoes for salad. So she had got back to the house in good time and the minute she set foot inside the kitchen she heard it—heard somebody fall as

clear as day. If there was one thing she did not believe in
and never had it was ghosts, and even if Mrs. Howard had
practically just that minute been buried and the noise was
right upstairs and all, she streaked it right up the back way
and through the hall and there she found her—her gesture
at me was possessive—layin' on the floor in Mis' Howard's
room with her head all wrapped up in that old brown bathrobe that Mr. Howard hadn't even wore all winter.

She yanked it off fast as she could though she never
would forget the way the belt tangled around her neck and
she got right to her feet. Apparently that was my neck and
feet. She got me downstairs—I was moanin' low and my
eyes were blank and stary—and then I fainted dead away
and she'd just brought me to when he come bustin' in the
kitchen door.

The instant Daisy reached her triumphant period Tom
Nixon vanished again. We could hear him going rapidly
through the house, doors opening and closing, stairs as-
cended and descended. I knew what he was doing and I
knew too what he would say when he reappeared.

"A pity I didn't get here a little sooner. I was only counting on getting here enough ahead of the others to connect
with you. Feeling better? No real damage?"

"I'm all right. Funny I can't remember about coming
downstairs. I must have been out completely. Never faint—"

We could hear cars making the last steep stretch of the
drive. "Here they come," Nixon said. "Daisy, you're to say
nothing about what has just happened. Not a word. Those
are orders—understand? They'll know I'm here; my car's
parked outside. Just say I'm in conference in the library
and I'm not to be disturbed for a little while. Will you
come, Miss Lenox, please?"

He closed the library door and stepped swiftly to a window, keeping well in the shelter of the hangings. "Bart and
Mrs. Sutton and Blair in the big car, and Lila and Allen
with Chad and Sally in Allen's. That makes it simpler."

I didn't know what or how. I was staring with a sickish return of gooseflesh at the brown flannel bathrobe which he had folded over one arm.

"It's so then," I mumbled, and pointed at the brown robe as he turned from the window.

"Every word, so far. An overturned chair by the desk—by the way, I closed and locked it and took the keys—and this thing in a tumbled heap on the floor. And no bottle of cyanide on the desk."

"It wasn't—it was perfume. That's how I knew someone else was there. I thought we could find fingerprints."

He didn't need to tear his hair or ask questions. I gave him a straightforward account of what had happened in Felicity's room—the sense of moisture on my finger as I touched the mouth of her bottle of "Faded Flowers," the cauld grue that gripped me, my inspection of the closet and bathroom, my unrewarding search of the desk.

When I had finished he looked to see if there were cigarettes in a cinnabar box on the desk and then pulled out a fresh pack from his pocket. Picking patiently at cellophane, revenue stamp, and silver paper, he checked off his comments.

"You're right about that stuff evaporating quickly. Someone had been at that bottle and not long before—surely not before the funeral started. And there would be fingerprints. That accounts for the attack on you. You were obviously going to make off with the bottle and then we would have known something for sure. So the bottle disappears and nothing else. But who was it and what would he, she, or it want to smell perfume for?

"The bathroom door was standing open when I dashed up to rescue the bottle—I thought of course you'd found more potassium cyanide. Whoever slung the bathrobe so neatly over your head grabbed the flask and left by way of the bathroom and the next bedroom. Yet Daisy was coming toward you from the back stairs. She got you down the

other way, though, and you must have been hard to steer
even if you were on your feet. By the time she got you to
the kitchen he, she, or it was safely away. Must have been
in that closet all the time."

That couldn't be, I protested. I'd looked.

All right, since I'd looked so carefully, had I noticed a
brown bathrobe hanging there?

"Daisy said it was Mr. Howard's."

"And I'll bet she'll know where and when she saw it last.
She's the only one I'd ask."

"I see—it has to be one of the Howards."

"You don't see at all, but you should. They were all down
in the front living room during the service, as you could
note for yourself. And they all—every one of them—went
off to the cemetery. Mine was the last car in the procession
and I can account for everybody. They return home just
now in a body, no one in a car by himself. So. . . ."

"So it couldn't have been one of the Howards."

With that new twist to ponder over, as well as being
knocked silly by my encounter with a brown bathrobe, it's
really not strange that I never thought of the neat little
hole in the second step from the top of the stairs leading
down to the kitchen.

3

I shared Daisy's chops and tomato salad with the rest of
the family. Nixon had eased himself out of the library and
Sally had promptly appeared and insisted that it was the
only thing to do. I felt sure that it was his idea. He had,
however, given me no further specific instructions.

It was not a pleasant meal. The Howard solidarity was
visibly cracking and in spite of the lawyer's presence and
mine I expected an outburst any minute. Lila and Mrs. Sutton checked up rather acidulously on the few people who
had been asked to attend the services, which had been listed

as strictly private. There were, according to them, people loitering about the cemetery who were there just because they had not been invited to the house. Their comments verified something I thought I was right about. Wilson Markham had been present at the house and at the burial also. I heard Lila say, "I know how you feel, Aunt Rhoda, but what else could we have done? Allen said he couldn't possibly not be asked, on account of Father Howard."

Chad and Allen Howard kept up a muffled exchange of question and answer with the lawyer. I could hear very little but I suspected that Blair was concerned about Felicity's distant relatives. No doubt I could have answered some of their queries, but I was not speaking out of turn. Chad, I noted, was seated next to Lila, but their attitude was typically in-lawish and I felt that Sally was a little fool to stare at them so fixedly. Bart, between me and his aunt, gave me his entire attention. It would be more accurate to say that he directed his clever barbs at me. He talked well on a dozen topics all a million miles from the immediate situation, but every time I attempted to ask him something about himself and his interests, I got nowhere.

Rhoda Sutton's ears must have caught something Blair was saying. She dropped her dessert fork with a clatter and announced in her flat, unpleasing voice, "That should be entirely unnecessary, Mr. Blair. A woman who murders her husband for profit has no rights. Her legal heirs could not possibly claim—"

"My dear Mrs. Sutton, the law—"

"Aunt Rhoda, please!"

Blair had interrupted Mrs. Sutton, but Allen Howard cut them both short. He let his fist drop soundlessly upon the table and went on. "Until Tom Nixon satisfies himself about my father's death it is dangerous for any of us to call his wife a murderer. Can't you understand?" Allen's face was white and worn.

Rhoda Sutton snapped her fingers, going back to the tactics she must have employed when the boys were youngsters. "She killed herself. That tells me enough."

"I yielded to you yesterday against my judgment. I'm admitting to you all that your suspicions were correct. My father was murdered. What you don't seem to realize is that the authorities are now engaged in investigating a murder. For the time, Felicity's suicide had no bearing upon that murder. Causes come before results. What I mean is, you're getting what you asked for, and you've got to like it."

"But we won't. What Allen is telling us. Aunt Rhoda darling, is that you and I as well as Felicity, to whom it now makes no difference, are equally suspect. You gave Felicity that infallible cure-all for scratches and mosquito bites and heat rash or what have you. She was the ministering angel, of course. And I found him. Maybe we'll have to shoot ourselves too." Bart rattled this off in an exaggerated undertone to his aunt, but we were all listening to every word long before he finished.

"Does Tom know all that?" Lila asked in a weak voice, looking at her husband. "I'm sure, when I called that morning Father Howard seemed just fine."

"So you were here, too. I'll tell Tom that myself," Bart jeered. "Too bad you didn't steal the new will while you were around."

"Bart!" There was anger in Allen Howard's voice. Chad lighted a cigarette. His hand was shaking just as it had the night before. "That was the day I drove to Wheeling, wasn't it, Sally?"

"You know very well you haven't forgotten what you were doing the day your father died."

Somehow, that sounded to me as though Sally were steadying her husband.

"So that's your alibi, Chad." Bart turned toward his brother, but his fingers were still stroking the Sutton wrist. "Bad, very bad. Always suspicious to produce an alibi before you're asked to. Don't you observe that big brother Allen isn't saying a word?"

Sally gave her chair a little forward jerk. "You forget that Aunt Rhoda has the evidence. When are you turning it over to Tom, Aunt Rhoda?"

I was waiting for the bottle and hypodermic needle to be mentioned, but certainly had not expected Sally to be the one to bring it up. Perhaps she was gamely meeting the inevitable. Maybe there was something in that Wheeling alibi that I didn't know about yet. Or she might have deliberately baited Rhoda Sutton.

This, last she accomplished beyond a doubt. Mrs. Sutton sniffed and her knobby fingers drummed upon the cloth, drummed until her nephew's eyes met hers. The nephew at the end of the table opposite her place, Allen Howard.

"If necessary, Sally, if necessary," she answered at last, and Chad drew hard upon his cigarette while Sally settled back into her chair. "For myself, the suicide is all the evidence I ask. A woman's intuition, Mr. Blair, should carry more legal weight. It's a plain case if ever there was one."

At that Godfrey Blair puffed himself up, which was not difficult, and attempted to be coy on the subject of the ladies, God Bless 'em. Tom Nixon saved us from much of that. He suddenly appeared in the doorway.

"Sorry to interrupt and all that, but I see you've about finished and there's a lot to be done this afternoon. If you will all come in to the library—"

He had enough chairs ready and he seated me as advantageously as he chose his own place. Rather impressively he asked me to take notes and pushed a pad of paper toward me. Across the top of the page was a light scribble. "Make it look like shorthand," I read. Sally's guest, Tom Nixon's private investigator, a stenographer—what next? More than anything else, I knew I was the person the Howards would like to turn out of the house.

"It is a fact," he began, "that Jordan Howard died because he was poisoned by an injection of potassium cyanide. It could have been absorbed directly into his system when a slightly infected mosquito bite was being treated with a soothing lotion. Or it is possible that a needle was used. The point has not yet been ruled upon finally."

He paused, as if to check upon the circle of set, unresponsive faces. I tried to believe that most of them were startled by his statement, but I could make nothing of Bart's expression nor of his aunt's.

"My facts about hypodermic needles are interesting. There were two found at River View in addition to the one—er—already mentioned. One had been left by Dr. Ammon for a regular prescribed purpose. The origin of the other, is obscure. The medicine cabinets of each of the other households were also equipped with needles. One of these is missing. And one of you made a rather frantic attempt the other day to buy one. There is likewise in safety deposit at the bank a small bottle of something and a needle wrapped up in a towel. At this time I ask Mrs. Sutton to turn over to me her key and full authorization to obtain access to this exhibit."

I made witless curves and scrolls diligently but by my own touch system, for my eyes were watching the Howards. The mention of Dr. Ammon had pleased Rhoda Sutton. Lila looked horrified when Tom brought in the other households, though I fully believe her first thought was as to when the upstart had ransacked her house. Sally, of course, was prepared for something of the sort. She did not turn a red-brown eyelash. Chad squirmed wretchedly and Bart looked as if he were going to say something. He did.

"Only one missing, Tom? Ours are still here then?"

"You will find no needles here now."

"Ah, the collector's urge," Bart murmured.

Allen whispered something to Blair which Nixon interpreted for his own purposes. "Your lawyer will tell you, Mrs. Sutton, that my request is quite regular."

She fumbled with her handkerchief and then with the chain that bore her glasses. "The key is in my bag. Will you get it for me, Allen? On the hall table, I think . . ." Allen Howard slipped obediently from the room and we waited silently for the few seconds that he was gone. Tom Nixon declared later that from his position he could watch every inch of his progress down the hall and back. Allen handed the bag to his aunt, who opened it and after a prolonged excavation of its contents produced a flat key. She laid it on the table and let Nixon pick it up for himself.

"I promise you," he said, "to let you know what I learn after my trip to the bank."

"Goody, goody!" jeered Bart.

"So much for that." Tom Nixon let the key fall from one palm into the other. "Now for the circumstances of the death. I have these facts from Dr. Ammon—"

"But we're to stop you if you're wrong." Bart, of course. Allen glowered at him.

"The doctor arrived within fifteen minutes after the telephone call from Bart found him with Mrs. Howard and Mrs. Sutton attempting first-aid measures. Bart had come upon his father half fallen from one of the chairs on the terrace, and since he could be stretched out there they had wisely not tried to move him."

I expected Bart to take a bow at this commendation but he had the decency to restrain himself. Tom went on.

"As Ammon was well aware of Mr. Howard's physical condition, he was not surprised that he had died so suddenly and he had no doubt in certifying the cause of death. Talking with Mrs. Howard, he satisfied himself that her husband had undergone no undue physical strain preceding the attack although he had, according to her, done an unusual amount of sputtering as he read the editorial page of his Pittsburg paper. She had last seen him alive about nine when she had insisted on applying a soothing lotion to an inflamed mosquito bite on his neck which had been bothering him for several days and which he had apparently scratched at during the night. He had then settled himself on the terrace with his papers and she went to her desk in her room to do some domestic bookkeeping.

"The doctor took a look at the bottle of lotion in the Howards' bathroom. It was entirely harmless and antiseptic. In fact, he recognized it as a preparation he had recommended to Mrs. Sutton."

"Aha, Aunt Rhoda, I told you so!" Bart interrupted softly.

"The appearance of the mosquito bite corresponded exactly with Mrs. Howard's account of its condition. It was in the primary stages of inflammation and had evidently been recently irritated as by scratching. Whoever was guilty of injecting poison had accomplished the deed skillfully. Those of you who are innocent should accept the fact that Dr. Ammon's mistake was a very natural one."

At that point Lila Howard shivered with nerves and I wished I had some way of getting across to Tom that it might help to ask her a question or two about that morning's events. Pushing him a note would be too obvious. I needn't have given it a thought.

"That's all I learned directly from Ammon. I gathered, however, that he knew no more concerning the whereabouts and activities of the other members of the household before Bart discovered his father than Mrs. Howard's statement about herself. I am now going to ask some questions."

He adjusted his spectacles and took a deliberate look around the group. They all appeared utterly wretched except Bart, who, just as deliberately as Tom Nixon, likewise surveyed the others. His amused detachment infuriated me. I was glad to have Tom begin with him.

"Bart, when did you last see your father alive?"

"Oh, that morning, definitely. Don't rush me—I think I can recall details, quite a lot of details." He placed fingertips to fingertips, pursed his lips, and gazed at the ceiling. His aunt, I noted, picked at the chain of her glasses and held her breath.

"Ah, yes . . . I had breakfast with my aunt in our rooms, quite as usual. The strawberries were oversweetened. Then I came downstairs to see about the mail, down the main stairs. Dad was coming up the drive with the mail. He'd gone out to meet Adkins, who'd gone for, it. The box is down at the road. He handed me the letters to sort—see how he trusted me!—and shook out his newspaper to glance at the headlines. The letters weren't many, about fifty-fifty between upstairs and down. The only one I drew was a bill—by the way, it isn't paid yet—but having been properly brought up I neglected to check the others. Dad asked me when I was going in to town and I said not before the noon train, my own taste being for the *Enquirer,* not that boiler-plate from Pittsburgh; and he said to remind Adkins about the asparagus beds. Then he started through the house to the terrace on the other side and Felicity called down to him to come upstairs for a poultice. He went up, obediently. Later, I found him on the terrace."

"Thank you," said Tom Nixon. "Your details were— uh—interesting. Now, where were you between that time and your discovery of your father?"

"Here and there, here and there. . . . But having established a reputation for detail, I see that I must oblige further. I went to the garage to see whether my car was dusty enough to have Adkins polish it. I went down to the boat house to look for a book I thought I had left in the launch. I hadn't. . . . I put in a half hour or more down there, meditating about my sins and making high resolutions. It was too early and too cold to swim, but with my physical well-being in mind I next indulged in exercise. I walked up the river by the low-water path, up beyond Cantling's boundary and then along the trail through the woods and back to our drive, and I shall admit before you ask me that I did not see a soul. When I reached the house again, I strolled through to the terrace, meaning to rest there for the length of a cigarette. I found Dad. I raised some sort

of alarm. Daisy and the other girl came running through
the dining room from the kitchen, and Felicity and Aunt
Rhoda both came from upstairs. Time: about ten-fifty."

"And your father's last commission? Adkins and the
asparagus?"

This question annoyed Bart Howard. "I did not see
Adkins. For all of me, the asparagus beds have gone to rack
and ruin."

"And now, Mrs. Sutton, I should like your account of
that morning."

The glasses clicked against the row of little buttons
down the front of her blouse and she began to talk promptly. Bart's irritating recital had certainly given the rest of
them plenty of time to order their reports.

"I last saw my brother-in-law alive about half past nine.
I was passing through the upper hall on my way to the back
stairs to go down to speak to Daisy. I recall that Mrs. Howard's door was closed, but Jordan's was open and I could see
him standing at his dresser. He was taking off his collar.
His wife was coming from the bathroom with a small bottle
in one hand. I did not speak but went on about my errand."

"And from then until you heard Bart's alarm?" Tom
prodded her.

"From the kitchen I returned to my rooms. I was busy
with some telephoning for a little while. Then I dusted
and looked over some curtains for any necessary mending
before they were laundered. By that time my hands needed
washing and I went into the bathroom for that purpose.
The bath in our own quarters, you understand." She nodded slightly at Bart to indicate whom the 'our' meant.

"That is why I happened to see that Felicity had left the
medicine cabinet door ajar when she came to get the lotion.
She had come in to ask me for witch hazel or aromatic
ammonia right after breakfast. Naturally, I had inquired
about the inflamed spot on Jordan's neck, and she had told
me that it was no better. Things like that worry me so. I

suggested that she use Dr. Ammon's lotion and told her where to find it. I was washing dishes at the time. If she had not left the door of the cabinet open, I should never have noticed that the case containing the hypodermic needle was open and the needle was missing. I thought nothing of it, really. My nephew is exceedingly careless."

"Wow! Take that, bad boy!" Bart murmured.

Beyond a doubt, Rhoda Sutton had decided not to sink or swim alone, for after that shaft for Bart her cool, flat voice continued. "When I emerged into the sitting room I found Lila there. I neglected to say that I thought I had heard some other footsteps while I was busy with my mending. Lila did not stay long, just a minute or two. She had run up to speak to me as she always does whenever she drops in at River View. She had on a new hat, didn't you, dear?"

Lila's face was white and set. She ignored Mrs. Sutton's question and Aunt Rhoda went on. "I admired of course—Lila has wonderful taste—and then she said she mustn't keep Allen waiting. I heard a car go down the drive very soon after that. I settled myself with a magazine and the next thing was I heard Bart calling."

Bart and Lila and Allen . . . Why should Sally have been so scared?

Tom Nixon reached across and picked up a sheet of my amazing hieroglyphics, studied it with gravity, and said, "You said you heard 'some other footsteps.' Make that point clearer, Mrs. Sutton, if you please."

"While I was dusting, Mrs. Howard came out of her room and went downstairs and I heard her coming back within a short time. She walked down the upper hall very quietly, I almost could say on tiptoe, and back into her own room."

"Did you see her, Mrs. Sutton?"

"No. No, I did not see her. But I always recognize footsteps. Besides, there was no one else it could have been."

"So you did not see Mrs. Howard between the time you last saw Mr. Howard and the moment you responded to Bart's call of distress?"

"No. We both came out of our rooms at almost the same instant. She reached Jordan a few steps ahead of me."

"I see . . ." Tom Nixon sighed. I hoped he saw what I saw—that the one person who could have known whether Rhoda Sutton was lying was now dead.

"Then when you heard Mrs. Allen Howard's steps below, you of course recognized them also?" he asked.

She had to say yes to that.

Inevitably the next question was, was she sure which set of steps she had heard first.

Mrs. Howard's—yes; Lila had come in afterward.

Tom Nixon swung to Lila Howard then, Lila, who had so obviously been anticipating a question since Bart's gibe during luncheon. Could she tell when she had arrived at River View that morning?

Sometime between ten and ten-thirty. Maybe Allen would remember more exactly.

Allen Howard said nothing and Nixon did not turn to him for corroboration.

"What was the purpose of your visit?" he demanded.

"Why, I just drove out with Allen." She laughed a little weak laugh. "It was a lovely morning. Allen was going to drop me at Mrs. Rudgate's on the way back. She'd just come home with her new baby. And I thought, while Allen asked Adkins about transplanting the iris, I'd run in to say good-morning to Father Howard. He was reading on the terrace."

"Did you know he was there?"

"No, of course not. I just walked into the house and through the hall. He was the first person I found. And he seemed just fine to me, just the same as usual."

"Had you any reason to expect otherwise?"

She looked appalled at that but answered reasonably. "Why, no! Only it wasn't so very long after that when he—you know. I hadn't even got home yet from Mrs. Rudgate's when the message came."

"All right. What else?"

"I talked to him a little bit, though I could see his attention was really on his newspaper, for he didn't say much, even when I told him about the fine report we had just received from Junior's school. And then I ran up to speak to Aunt Rhoda. Just as she told you."

"Did you see or hear anything of Mrs. Howard at that time?"

Lila shook her head.

"Did you see anything of Adkins, Mrs. Howard?"

"No. Allen was waiting for me in the car when I came downstairs and we drove right off."

Blair, who had not once interrupted this stream of question and answer, sighed a little as Tom said briskly, "Now, Allen, it's your turn. Did you see your father during that morning?"

There was an interminable pause before an answer came, and we were all looking at him before he replied, his head bent and his voice husky, "No. Not until I came back to see him dead."

"Had your trip out to River View been planned?"

Blair cleared his throat. Maybe it was a warning; I don't know. Allen answered normally, "We were talking about our garden at breakfast that morning and had made a mental note then to consult Adkins about moving the iris. I had a committee meeting that morning which was suddenly cancelled when I went up to the board room at the high school to attend it, so I swung by the house and picked up Lila and went on up to River View for that spare half-hour. That's all the planning there was to it."

"You had your consultation with Adkins, I suppose?"

"No, Nixon, I did not. I thought I heard the power mower, but I couldn't find the man. I went around to the kitchen and Daisy said she hadn't seen him since he brought up the mail. So I came back to the car and in a few minutes my wife joined me."

Tom spent a silent minute taking off his glasses and putting them on again. Allen volunteered a piece of information. "While I sat there in the car waiting, I checked the clock on the dash with my watch. I recall that it was ten-twenty-eight. So Lila's feeling about the time was fair enough."

In plain Arabic numerals I made elaborate note of that hour and then dropped my pencil as Tom Nixon addressed me.

"Miss Lenox, will you please step to the kitchen and ask Daisy to come in for a moment?"

Daisy followed me back into the library so eagerly that her dish towel came along too.

"We have been recalling events that occurred on the morning of Mr. Howard's death, and there are a couple of questions that I want you to answer, Daisy." Tom had risen politely as the woman entered and he kept shoving his chair at her until she settled herself in it.

"As if I could ever forget one single thing," she intoned lugubriously.

"Fine. . . fine. We're just putting everything together, that's all. You served breakfast that morning?"

"To the two of them, the boys' pa and the young missus. Omelette it was and hot muffins and new strawberry jam—"

"Everything as usual during breakfast? Mr. Howard seem like himself and all that?"

"Yes, sir. He surely went for them muffins."

"What did you see of him after that?

"He sputtered some about the mail and as I was clearing away after they'd et I see him start down the drive towards

Adkins, and then Mr. Bart, he come a-runnin' downstairs and stood chinnin' with his pa a little, and by that time I was out in my kitchen again. Thelma was in the livin' rooms with the vacuum."

"Thelma?" Tom interrupted.

"Sure. She hadn't quit yet." And Daisy gave Rhoda Sutton sniff for sniff.

"Did you see any more of Mr. Howard?"

"No, but I heard him. I couldn't say just when it was, but when I went out back to hang my towels in the sun, I heard that cane chair he always set in creak and give like and his newspapers a-rustlin'. Let's see now . . . That was after Mis' Sutton called down about the hot water."

Almost automatically I wrote: *hot water sterilizes* . . .

That startled me, but I don't think I missed much, for I heard Daisy explaining that she didn't know anything about Mis' Allen Howard being anywheres around, that after her dishes was done up she'd gone down cellar to put the new strawberry jam where it belonged. Yes, Mr. Allen, he had come around the back way, askin' for Adkins, who was one person she never even tried to keep tabs on.

"From which direction did Mr. Allen Howard come to the kitchen?" Tom asked.

"From around front. Where else could a body—"

"From which side of the house? That's what I mean."

Allen Howard's face reddened with anger and I thought Blair was about to pat his knee, but the hovering hand returned to pull again at his Masonic emblem.

Daisy was pondering. "Well, now you ask me, I don't know, for sure. I just looked up and there he was, askin' did we know where Adkins was at."

"We?"

"Thelma and me. She'd finished the cleaning' and was goin' to shell peas for me while she got off her feet for a while. He went back by the driveway side, though. I noticed him passin' the window."

"What did you see of Mrs. Howard that morning?"

"Not hide nor hair, from breakfast till we all come runnin' when Mr. Bart found his pa struck down. She had said, though, she'd be down about eleven with some meals written out. Mis' Howard, she kinda thought she had to do like that. Not that I cared—she was always so nice and easy-like if she had something wrote down that I didn't think was such a good idea."

"Now, Daisy, what do you remember about Mr. Bart Howard on that morning?"

Bart assumed a pose of mock anxiety and I scribbled: *find Thelma and ask her*. Aunt Rhoda's glasses clicked against her buttons again.

"Mr. Bart—he's one I never pay much attention to. He's always in and out. Seems like I saw him once down at the garage that morning, and then, of course, I could tell the way he called out that way that something was up. Thelma and me, we both run, and there he was, down on his knees by his pa's side. I'll never forget it, never!" She sighed in a luxury of recollection.

"Did you hear him come into the house?"

She shook her head. He was just there, by his pa, she repeated.

"Just one more question, Daisy, and thank you very much. Not counting this morning, where and when did you last see a brown flannel bathrobe that had been Mr. Jordan Howard's?"

She gulped over the secret that the question recalled to her but she remembered her promise. "That old brown one—it was hangin' in Mr. Howard's closet yesterday morning when I was straightenin' up after Paulding's man had taken her clo'es away."

The brown bathrobe startled them all. As Nixon's glance swung from face to face in the moment of heavy silence, I heard, and no doubt they all did, heavy steps crunching along the gravel below the library windows.

"That's all, Daisy," he said, "and will you please ask Adkins to wait for me in the kitchen. He's headed that way right now." Tom rose and made elaborate business of picking up my scattered sheets of notes. "You can see," he made the bland announcement, "how the matter is shaping up. Miss Lenox, will you come with me."

Five minutes later we were down the River View drive and turning toward Point Tyler. In the rumble of Tom Nixon's car Adkins crouched. A rather unwilling Adkins, whose mouth was settling into stubborn, sullen lines.

"He's so deaf," Tom whispered to me, "that I couldn't risk yelling at him up there."

4

It was hard work getting anything out of Adkins, but we got something. He conveniently did not hear what he did not want to answer, but Tom got around that by writing out the question and sticking it under his nose, which outraged him, for he did not want to go on record as being that deaf, and so at last we heard about the gloves.

But first I'm human enough to play myself up. Just as Tom's car rolled into town I said, "What's Thelma's other name? Norine mentioned a Thelma in one of her chatty moments yesterday. Norine is Sally's maid."

Tom muttered something at himself. "Thelma Jopp. And what do you bet somebody up there at River View is phoning her this minute and telling her what to remember? Just another thing I ought to be doing first."

"Swing around by Sally's," I suggested, "and I'll ask Norine."

Which he did. I ran around to the back door and found Norine giving herself a fresh and brilliant nail polish do. "Thelma? Sure, I had a card from her day before yesterday. She's out back of Webster Springs at her sister's. . . ."

I returned to the car with the sister's name, a post office address, and the satisfying supposition on Norine's part that she kinda thought Thelma wouldn't be in no hurry to get away because she'd been stepping out with a new boy friend down there. Furthermore, I'd given Norine a broad hint not to know where Thelma could be found for the next day or two.

"Webster Springs . . . pretty face. Ever been there?" Tom murmured. "Not so far away, either. . . ."

He took Adkins to his private quarters, not to the official cubicle next to the sheriff's rooms, doubtless so that the anticipated yelling could go forward more secretly. As I said, it was a trying interview.

Tom began with the morning of Jordan Howard's death. Adkins recalled readily enough how Mr. Howard came walking toward him to get the bundle of newspapers and letters, and he'd said something about thinning out the asparagus, just as if Adkins hadn't raised asparagus for the past thirty years.

Tom cocked an eyebrow at me and I cocked one back at him. Screwy bit number one for Master Bart.

Adkins had then gone down to the garden to get the peas he'd already picked for the house. He'd left them on the back porch and gone back to the garden to take another look at the tomato plants. Then he'd come back to his work-shack and had tinkered some with the power mower. No, he hadn't seen anything of Bart up to that time.

That last phrase was suggestive and Tom worked at it awhile, but all he got for sure was that Adkins hadn't seen or heard Bart at any time during the morning up until after Mr. Howard's, body had been found. But he'd had an idea he was somewhere about because he'd smelled him. Sure thing, he could tell the difference between cigar and cigarette smoke any time. He knew he was a leetle hard of hearing and he nor no one else could see anybody on the terrace from that lower stretch of grass where he'd taken the mower after he'd got that loose part tightened up just right, with that mess of blue spruce and all at the end of the terrace. He could tell, sure enough, by the smell that Mr. Howard was sitting there, reading and smoking one of them heavy cigars of his. And then, later, he'd smelled a cigarette. Mr. Howard never smoked 'em. Nor his wife nor Mis' Sutton, neither, as far's Adkins had ever noticed. Only Bart. Sure, it coulda been somebody else, somebody that didn't live there.

As for the time, it wasn't more'n two-three minutes after ten-thirty, because he'd looked at his watch at exactly half past ten and had figgered he'd get that piece of grass done by time to quit for dinner. I remembered, and so did Tom, the jealous faith that Adkins had in his timepiece, from his disturbance at the inquest.

He knew nothing of the brief call made by Allen and Lila. If Allen had been looking for him he hadn't hurt himself much, for he'd kept right on with the mower until sometime after eleven, when he'd become vaguely aware of something unusual going on at the house.

If Allen Howard was telling the truth about the time of his departure—there was small chance of shaking Adkins about his noting of the time—then it must have been Bart on the terrace with his father from ten to fifteen minutes sooner than he had stated in the library. Not that Tom took Adkins into his confidence that far.

He took him again over the events of the afternoon of Felicity's death. He had not been working anywheres near the house that afternoon. Sure, he recollected Bart Howard coming up from the river sometime or other and tryin' to chew the rag and keep him from his work, which was settin' some stones with a little cee-ment where the path washed out after every heavy rain, but, no sir, he could not tell just when that had been. Adkins had failed to look at his infallible watch.

He admitted he'd been kinda short with him, partly because the young feller always talked so's you were never sure what he was gettin' at and partly because he wouldn't give a straight answer to a straight question. Seems there was somebody tryin' to trespass on the River View land, and Bart, he wasn't givin' him no help at all. But Adkins had put up an extry length of bobbed wire where he thought they was comin' through and after the next day when he caught a strange lady—here he surveyed me at some length and Tom said I flushed guiltily—and sent her a-kitin' and got at them car marks off the drive, he hadn't had no more trouble. No, he hadn't found nothing out of the way down there where the trespassin' car had been run in—he just didn't like the idee of his ditch wall bein' broke down.

"Well, what did you do after that?" Tom brought him back.

Adkins had walked up the river path past the boat house clear to the upper line. No, sir, there wasn't nobody in swimmin'. And he'd come back by the side hill way, not by the drive, and he'd stopped in the garden to water the last batch of tomato plants he'd set out, and then Daisy had waved him up to the house and told him what had happened to Mis' Howard.

Tom Nixon took a little key from his bunch and unlocked one of the drawers of his writing table and pulled it out. Nether Adkins nor I could see what was in the drawer, but what he spread out on the table for the man's inspection was the pair of gloves that I had found.

"Look at 'em, Adkins," Tom shouted. "Ever see 'em before? Know whose they are?"

Adkins poked at them with what surely could have been called the horny hand of toil but showed no great interest or curiosity. "Them—yep, they look like Mis' Sutton's. See that there mark across the pa'ms. That was some rusty wire done that. She's a very determined woman. I told her she'd have to wait till I could get my clippers, but no, she twisted away at it like all possessed, irregardless of them new style work gloves she'd just bought her in Pittsburgh."

"You're sure, Adkins?"

"That's what I am, young feller. Me and Mis' Sutton spend right smart time together, long in the spring of the year. She's one woman that knows what a garden takes—and that's work."

Tom warned the old man to stick to his story, that he had a record of it—he waved in my direction, again labeling me as his secretary—and dismissed him. I was all set for a thorough pow-wow. I was seething with questions and bursting with theories. It appeared, however, that I was taking orders from a boss, just like a stenog.

"I'm assigning Thelma Jopp to you. If you start at once you can make Webster Springs in time for a late dinner, and I recommend the Busy Bee. You know the line of country to cover after all the listening in you've done. You'll probably have to stay all night. Get Thelma to tell you where. We can't stop to talk now. The case is one sweet mess of extraneous information, but maybe some of it will fade out into its real importance between now and tomorrow. My job, and I'm for it right now, is to get the bundle out of Mrs. Sutton's box. I'll have to take Floyd along to back me up, banks being what they are. You went up to River View this morning with Chad and Sally and came back with me, so your car's here. You take the way out of town that passes the end of Sally's street until you cut into US-50 and then straight on till you get there."

I had risen obediently. "You'll tell me one thing or I won't go. You said you'd soon know about Sally. But you didn't third-degree her at all in that after-lunch session."

"I do know about Sally. I know this: she and I were having a coke in the Owl Drugstore at the precise time that the monkey business was being done to Jordan Howard. So that's one alibi I don't have to check."

"And Chad?"

"When I plied her with the coke she admitted she was on the loose because her husband had gone to Wheeling."

"You said 'at the precise time.' Pretty sure, are you?"

"On your way, woman. Winchester's forty miles away."

"The road to Wheeling goes right by the River View drive."

With that as my parting shot I was off, thus losing my front-row seat for the scene at the bank.

5

The Busy Bee offered me a choice of roast pork, roast beef, or hot ham sandwiches, cream pies all topped with marshmallow for meringue, and ice cream from Clarksburg. I took toasted cheese on rye and coffee, which was extraordinarily good, and set to sizing up the help, as I should have to ask some questions if I was to find Thelma. The boss, I soon observed, knew everybody and was a friend to man, but he had a loud voice that excluded no one from the circle of confidences. However, that did not matter, for he knew all the right answers to my muted questions.

Sure, he knew that good-lookin' sister of Bug Reimer's wife. He was goin' to give her a job himself if she didn't get the place out at the Kanawha joint where the big busses were going to stop after the first of the month. He'd heard she was going steady with one of the boys on the pumps out there. Reimer's place. . . . Well now, that was quite a piece off good road, two turns off of it, but he'd sure do his best to keep me from gettin' lost.

The late June twilight was paling and there were thunderous mutters from the thickening mass of sunset clouds when I set out to demonstrate the Busy Bee itinerary. I became aware of a hunch stirring in the back of my mind, but usually I hold my impulses in low regard. Roadside signs were telling me about the Kenawha Trail, Truckers Welcome. Its charms lay dead ahead and the prescribed route to the Reimer place had sounded sadly involved! Why not stop to inquire for Thelma's steady? When the low-lying frame structure came into view, I swung my car upon the sweep of gravel flanked by the battery of red and yellow pumps. It was one of the luckiest moves in the whole sad, tangled affair,

I refuse to mix gasoline in my tank, but I told the brisk attendant to check the oil and water, and before I could grow cautious I said, "Are you the one whose girl's name is Thelma?"

The boy laughed. "Not me, ma'am. Pooch over there's the lucky guy."

He called him over to the car for me and retired politely, for the car needed nothing. "I'm from Point Tyler," I told him, "and I'd like very much to talk to Thelma Jopp. How could I manage it most quickly?"

Pooch was an earnest lad, matter-of-fact and serious. He rubbed the side of his nose with a greasy finger and came to a decision. "Why, ma'am, she'll be right here at nine o'clock. I couldn't get off any sooner tonight and I fixed it so's she would meet me here. But we'll just have time to make the second show and—"

"It's a date and you don't want it spoiled, of course. Maybe she'll get here a few minutes early." It was twenty minutes of nine by my watch. "I'll pull up out of the way and wait, on the chance."

That is how I happened to see the Buick. It was burning up the road and I guessed that it was headed toward the Reimer place. Whether Sally or Chad or both were in the car I had not seen, but I was not mistaken about the coupé. It would pass Thelma somewhere, and if she were recognized I might as well go back to Point Tyler at once.

However, I turned my car until it was well beyond the field of the most bustling activities of the Kanawha Trail and waited. Pooch kept an anxious eye upon me and the

clock and once he loped over to ask me awkwardly if it was
anything about a job in Point Tyler.

At eight minutes of nine a dusty car of some ten-year-old
vintage jerked to a stop on the opposite side of the road and
I heard a girl's gay voice say, "Thanks a million, Joe." Pooch's
head turned but his hands were full of hose and I was out
of the car and waiting by the time she had crossed the road.

"Are you Thelma Jopp? May I talk to you a few minutes while you're waiting? Pooch knows—it's all right with
him." I almost stuttered in my haste.

"Why, sure, I don't care if I do." Obligingly she accepted my invitation to climb into the car while we talked.

Thelma was young and pretty and, I rather suspected, flighty. It was not hard to see that she could easily be
"sassy" and walk out on any job supervised by Rhoda Sutton. For the interview I chose to be the well-known private
investigator that Tom Nixon had announced me to be and I
think I impressed the girl at once.

The preliminaries safely over, I asked her to recall as
carefully and fully as she could everything that she had
seen, heard, and done on the morning of Jordan Howard's
death.

"Gee, that was sure awful—that morning. I've been real
upset ever since. Daisy and I beat it outa the kitchen when
we heard Bart yell, and when Daisy said it looked to her
like he was gone, I was scared pink—"

I made her begin over again, with breakfast time.

"Well, it was the day for me to take the cleaner to the
hall and the two living rooms and I was supposed to get
through with it early, see, because none of 'em liked torn up
rooms, and—why, nothing happened. I was just runnin' the
vacuum and pushin' the waxer over the floors. I got done
in time to shell peas for Daisy. I was at that when Bart—"

"While you were cleaning, who came and went, up and
downstairs? That sort of thing. Do try to remember." Thelma's eye had found Pooch and I wanted her whole attention.

"It's been kind of a while back. Let's see now. . . . Bart came down and took mail from his father and ran right up again, seems like. Oh yes, and Mis' Howard, she called him up, Mr. Howard, I mean, and he came down again after a while with his collar off and a little pad of something on the back of his neck. I remember because I just caught a glimpse of him goin' down the hall towards the terrace and he put up his hand and felt of it, sorta."

Thelma stirred restlessly. Pooch had vanished within the gas station office. It was one minute of nine.

"Did you see anything of Mrs. Howard?" I prodded.

She shook her head. "I wasn't right out there in the hall all the time," she said with petulance, "and all them little doo-dads on the tables and around, it takes a long time to dust. And I had the phone to answer too."

"Oh, there were telephone calls?"

"Uh huh, always is. I guess I gotta go now. My boy friend's waitin' on me." She fumbled at the handle of the door.

Pooch was bearing down upon us. I stepped on my starter. "I'll take her in to town, Pooch," I called clubbily. "You follow."

6

My tactics, needless to say, did not please Thelma and she pouted for nearly half of the short distance back to town. I was uneasy about the Buick, too. It might be catching up with us at any minute and my Iowa plates stood out like a bandaged thumb. So I kept relentlessly at the matter of telephone calls.

One call had been a wrong number, Thelma at last was coaxed to recall. And one had been for Mr. Howard.

"Did you know who was calling?" I demanded.

"He said he was Mr. Markham and could he please speak to Mr. Howard. So I went back and told him. And, say, he was all right then. The last time I ever I saw him alive."

Her morbid interest in that memory dispelled the last of her bad temper.

"Could you gather any idea what the conversation was about?"

"No, huh uh. The phone's in the liberry, see. Only I did hear him say, 'Come on out. I'll be right here the rest of the morning.'"

"And did Mr. Markham come later?" This was a new bit.

"I wouldn't know. I didn't see him. The only car I noticed was Mr. Allen's, and Mrs. Allen, she come runnin' in and went through the hall. Darn—it's goin' to rain and me in my new white shoes."

Thunder had been rumbling nearer and nearer. There was a splatter of big drops on the windshield. That gave me a chance to slow down a little, though Pooch's car honked warningly just behind me. The lights of Webster Springs shone ahead and the road began to be a street.

"Listen, Thelma, this is terribly important and if you spoil your shoes, buy a new pair and send the bill to me, but I've got to hear more if there's more to tell."

But apparently there was not much more to tell, though Thelma was plainly taken with the idea of new shoes. I think she aspired to wedgies. She had finished her work with cleaner and dust cloth very soon after Lila Howard had come and had taken herself to the kitchen. She hadn't seen anything of Allen Howard. Of her own knowledge she couldn't even say that he was in the waiting car. She didn't know how long Lila had remained on the terrace. She didn't know that she had gone from there upstairs to Mrs. Sutton's rooms. And she was positive that Mrs. Howard had not come downstairs while she was working in the front of the house.

I drew up at the movie, let Pooch double park behind my parking place, and dashed through the rain to the ticket window. I could at least present the hijacked swain with two tickets for the show. And if the Buick should swoop by, maybe Pooch's car would conceal my license plates. I could not be sure that my strategy had been necessary, but by the time I had thrust the ticket strip into Pooch's reproachful hand and God-blessed my reunited children had made up my mind what I was going to do.

Rain or no rain, night trip over strange curves and hills labeled second-gear, through storm or moonlight, I was going back to Point Tyler and I meant to get there before the Buick made it.

It was a wild journey. The storm kept up with me all the way and grew worse. The lightning was a savage chartreuse that paled my headlights into insignificance between its flashes, and all the roads were ominously marked, "Slow— slippery when wet." And they were wet. The rain came in buckets. I had to stop for gas before I had made much distance along US-50 and the filling station's shelter had a tempting cheeriness that was hard to resist. Especially when I thought I saw the Buick whizz by. Even if it got back first, I told myself hopefully, I could prove something by its appearance, though that would mean stopping at the garage first. . . .

With the slim consolation that surely the Buick could not have seen Iowa drawn up at the pumps I ploughed on. I ran off the road once, but fortunately at a safe wide place where all I had to cope with was skiddy mud. I lost time there, and then the tortoise overtook the hare struggling with a flat somewhere on the last lap of the road that led into Point Tyler. All I could be sure of was that it was a Buick and a masculine figure, shapeless and unidentifiable in a dark raincoat, wrestling with a spare. Callously I passed by on the other side, and far enough over to splash through a wide puddle fast enough, I hoped, to obscure my Iowa signboard.

I felt as though I had been gripping the wheel all night, though to my amazement it was not yet quite half past twelve. My way lay by Sally's and Chad's. Their house was

the only one on the street still lighted. I had to be sure
about their car before I went on. I pulled up across the
street and well below their drive and scuttled through
the driving rain. The garage doors were closed. At the risk
of their banging in the wind I pried one open. I had to
know.

What I saw was an empty garage. Across the dry, oil-spot-
ted cement floor ran a double set of tire marks. Wet ones.
Very recently indeed a car had come into the garage and
apparently backed right out again. What the tread of the
Buick's tires was like I had no notion.

Well, that was all of that. Thanks to the thunder I got
the door fastened again without creating any disturbance.
I edged my way up to the living room windows. There were
Chad and Bart and Lila. Chad looked white and sullen.
Lila's face looked as if it needed lifting and her nose was
red. Bart was slumped comfortably in a big chair but one
foot was wagging nervously. There was a fourth, at the moment out of the room, for a cigarette was sending a pale
blue spiral up from an ash tray at the arm of an empty
chair. That would be Sally, surely. . . .

I could take no more time for that sort of espionage.
My motor stuttered uncertainly but kept on going, and I
turned the car into the main street of Point Tyler. If there
shouldn't be a light in Tom Nixon's office, I'd have to ask
an embarrassing question at the Glass Front, still shining
and doing business. But there was a light at one of the upper windows. I should have to climb the stairs to know for
sure whether it was Tom's.

The stair well echoed hollowly at my progress. It was
dark and smelly after the rain-fresh night without. I felt my
way upward. Just as I reached the top the door swung open,
releasing a wide band of light.

"My precious eye, it's you!" Tom's voice. I was too dazzled to see more than a black shape.

He pulled me inside and shut the door, locked it, too. "An almost drowned kitten, that's what you look like. Thought I sent you to Webster Springs."

"You don't sound glad to see me—" But I couldn't do the reproachful; I was too amazed at Tom Nixon's appearance. One eye had been quite thoroughly blacked and there was a dried trickle of blood from the nose down to the point of his chin. He saluted jauntily and the gesture directed my gaze from his battered countenance to a curious array upon the table.

"The prize," he said, "and I got it. If only I've marked the other fellow as plainly as he has done for me, I'll know more in the morning."

"A towel and a bottle and a hypodermic needle," I checked. "Looks like the whole collection. But why the battle?"

"Because they were not in safety-deposit at the bank. Because I was morally certain that Allen Howard had just returned the key to the Sutton bag this afternoon when I asked for it. Because I broke and entered, quite unlawfully. Because somebody caught up with me before I got away from his office with the loot."

"The Chad Howard car has been on my tail all the way there and back again. A car has recently left their garage. Chad and Lila and Bart are at Sally's now, if that's of any interest to you. And Thelma Jopp says Mr. Markham telephoned Jordan Howard that morning and he told him to come on out. But she doesn't know whether he did or not."

Maybe it registered. I could not tell at the time. Tom had turned again to the table and had set to work with something that blew powder over the array. That just shows that I didn't even recognize a fingerprint finding outfit when I saw one in action. He had a camera set up too.

"I accept the fact that the towel belonged to Mrs. Howard. There is a fancy F on it and it's been used until it's soft and thin. But the deadly cyanide solution is nothing but clear water, and what do you think of that? And the needle's empty. Um-m-m. . . ."

He worked gingerly for another minute while I dripped like a drain pipe just beyond his shoulder. He emitted a short, mournful whistle. "Nothing but smudges—no, here's one print."

He laid the needle carefully aside and twisted himself so that he could look up at me. "Markham? The devil you say!"

There was no telephone in this office of Tom Nixon's. I had already noticed that and accounted for it as this being the place where he could ride his fictional range without interruption. But someone was interrupting now. Heavy feet pounded up the wooden stairs and a heavy hand pounded at the door. It was nearly one o'clock, but we weren't a romantic-looking couple. Tom unlocked the door and I stood by in my dank coat and sodden shoes. Sheriff Floyd burst in.

"So you're here. Lordy, but I'm glad. Mrs. Sutton's just been murdered!"

7

"You can take my car," I volunteered, "but you'll have to let me drive."

We had wasted no time, and I recall that I was much impressed with Tom's orders. Between puffs he had got out of Floyd that a telephone call had just come through from River View. He had stopped only at Tom's lodgings and then had made for his office. Daisy had made the call and reported that she was alone in the house. She had just found the body and was scared to death.

Tom dispatched Floyd to rout out a couple of his men, but first to see without an instant's further delay whether Wilson Markham was where he should normally be at that hour. Both the Allen and Chad Howard households were also to be checked at once. "And keep an eye peeled for

Chad's Buick," he added, a detail which pleased me very much. "Then follow me out to River View. I'm on my way."

At that point I offered my car and the upshot of the argument about driving it was that I stuck with him all the way, which was all I wanted. Secretly I was glad to have him at the wheel, though I let him hear me mutter a little. He swung into Terrace Drive to see to that set-up himself and dispatched me for a swift reconnoiter when we had got as near the house as seemed safe, for the place was still lighted.

This time I could see only Lila and Chad. Bart had disappeared and I saw nothing of Sally, though there were cups and saucers and plates for three sitting about. Somehow, I had a feeling that she was there. There wasn't time to monkey with the garage doors again, but the few inches of dry cement close to the doors showed no fresh tire marks. Such was my report to Tom Nixon, and we began a breathless, slithering drive to River View.

I had no intention of wasting the time, short as it would be. "Will you tell me exactly what happened to you and the other fellow and where and when, or shall I tell you a few things? Not so much what's happened as some ideas."

"My end, in one sentence or thereabouts. The stuff wasn't in the bank box. I asked the boys at the bank some questions they kind of squirmed over. I had a hunch who had been there ahead of me. I paid a rather informal call at Allen Howard's office and got caught. It was dark and I didn't see who I hit or who hit me, but I got away with the bundle. Now make yours equally snappy."

"There are some things I'd like to know. Could you tell from the gloves whether someone had them on when the gun was fired? Did anyone know that Mr. Howard was thinking of drawing a new will? And that boy that drives Daisy back and forth, Elvin something or other, maybe he saw something. He brought her back from the funeral this morning, or yesterday—it's tomorrow morning by now, isn't it? Somebody was in the house besides me. Have you asked

Adkins whether he reloaded the gun for Felicity? And I'd still like to know for sure whether Chad's hair was wet the other afternoon and just when he got the lift on the truck. And it oughtn't to be hard to find out about Allen's being in his office all afternoon or Chad's going to Wheeling the morning his father died. If the mosquito bite was the port of entry for the poison, a lot depends on how fast the stuff worked. Was it a matter of minutes or hours?"

I talked fast but not as fast as Tom was pushing the car. Most of the time I kept my eyes screwed shut so that I shouldn't be tempted to squeal at the hazards. At that hour the road was all ours, which undoubtedly saved us from disaster. The rain was still a steady downpour. By the time I finished my hodge-podge of questions we were nearly at the top of the drive and Tom hadn't a chance to say much.

"Elimination does it, says you. Lady, lady, I sure hope so. . . . I'll try to get some answers for you, but not now. We're here!"

The car rocked to a stop and there was a spatter of gravel. The porch lights were on and the upper windows that corresponded to the Sutton apartment were blazing, though the downstairs looked dark. A shapeless figure wavered toward us. It was Daisy and she was whimpering with nerves.

"Take me away, take me away," she moaned. "I can't stay here alone."

"You're not alone now." But Tom couldn't stop to baby the cook. I added, "We need you now, Daisy. Come, get inside out of the rain and you'll feel better."

"Now, tell me, or better—show me. The others will be here soon enough." Tom wanted first go this time.

"Upstairs, in the back hall," Daisy managed to gulp and followed us fearfully as we made for the stairs. I didn't have to go, as Tom reminded me, but I wanted first go too.

We hurried up the front stairs and back through the hall to the back entry where Rhoda Sutton's kitchenette opened upon the stairs leading down to the service wing and up to Daisy's bedroom. There the body lay.

Rhoda Sutton was fully dressed, the same clothes I had seen at luncheon. They lay so precisely, so unrumpled that my first thought was that she had not fallen there. I was wrong about that, it developed, though Daisy's story did not immediately make it clear. And she had been shot, shot very neatly through the heart. There was a look of surprise upon her face and the fingers of her right hand were caught in the silver chain that bore her glasses. There was no sign of the weapon. And, thank heaven, there was not much blood.

There could be no doubt that she was dead, and as the proper officials were already on their way out, Tom Nixon got to work at once upon Daisy's story.

It did not help much, but it established the fact of murder beyond question. Daisy had been tired out after the big day and had gone to bed early, locking up the back of the house as she always did. She had gone to sleep at once and she was sleeping heavily when a loud noise waked her. She couldn't say for sure that it was the sound of a shot, but she found herself sitting upright in bed with the tail-end of a dream about a giant firecracker vanishing from her mind. Then she heard steps—that wasn't a dream, she insisted— and a door slammed and she heard someone, running from the back of the house toward the front, outside.

She had plumped herself out of bed by that time and turned on her light, and as soon as she could get her feet into something, she explained, never being one to walk in her bare feet, she had started downstairs. Her stairway door was shut and as she opened it and realized the back entry was lighted she had begun to call out, for the light ought to mean that Mrs. Sutton or Bart was about. But as soon as she rounded the door she saw Mrs. Sutton.

"And she didn't answer or nothing, and I knew she was dead—her eyes, glarin' like that—even before I saw where she'd been shot at. I screamed, I guess—I wouldn't know now, and there wasn't another sound anywheres, so I figured I was alone in the house with a corpse. I was scared to go on down to the kitchen, it was all dark down there, so I come on through to the front stairs. Mis' Sutton's rooms was all lighted and there wasn't nobody else there. I had enough sense left to know I had to phone and I couldn't have gone down into that dark liberry if you'd paid me, so I used the extension in her settin' room and then I went out on the front porch and waited. That's all I done."

"But whoever it was that got away—any more about him?" Tom demanded. "Was the porch light on? Was Bart here at all during the evening? When did he leave?"

Too many questions for the still shaken Daisy to cope with. Working more slowly, we learned that she herself had turned the porch light on. Did we expect her to wait out there in the dark? She hoped to tell us she'd have gone clean crazy. . . . She knew nothing more about who had got away, and she had no more idea than a kitten whether she had heard a car start right off. The thud of running feet away from the kitchen door—that was her last impression. She wasn't at all sure about Bart. He and his aunt had had a little supper together, and Daisy knew for a fact that Mrs. Sutton was reading in her sitting room when she closed up the kitchen and went to bed and that Bart was not there when she found her laying dead. He hardly ever spent an entire evening at River View. He almost always drove down to Point Tyler for a little while during the early evening. Nobody ever paid much attention to Bart's goings and comings.

We looked about the sitting room. It was not difficult to tell what Rhoda Sutton had been doing. A comfortable chair was drawn close beside a table upon which a high-powered lamp was lighted. An afternoon edition of a Wheeling newspaper was scattered about, almost sheet by sheet. Mrs. Sutton evidently read a paper as many women of her generation do. A piece of crochet work with the needle thrust through a ball of thread lay close to the base of the lamp. A garden magazine with the torn-off wrapper crushed between its pages was pushed a little way beyond the trailing crochet. There was a heavy glass candy jar half filled with flat hard peppermints and the lid was off the jar. There was a book by Temple Bailey between the cushions and the arm of the chair. There were two white handkerchiefs, one on the floor, as if it had slid from her lap, and the other, much crumpled, squeezed behind the book.

Said I, impressed by my deductive powers, "It looks to me as if she had found it hard work to settle down to anything this evening, as if she had tried first one thing and then another. She must have been nervous about something."

Tom grunted something that did not sound like amazement, but swinging headlights without and sharply drawn brakes indicated that our private survey was at an end. Sheriff Floyd had arrived and with him Dr. Ammon and Paulding and several other minor officials. They had no more than piled up on top of themselves in the lower hall with our group halfway down the stairs to meet them than another car swung up the drive and to a stop. Allen Howard hurried in at their heels.

"My God, what's going on now?" His face was strained and sharp with gray shadows.

Tom Nixon, commanding the situation from his height on the stairs, replied. "Mrs. Sutton has just been found—murdered."

Allen sat down, very suddenly, on a bench near the door. It was plain that his knees had buckled. "Poisoned?" he gasped.

Tom moved on downward to the level of the hall. "Go on up," he said quietly to Floyd. "You and Paulding and Ammon. She's lying in the back hall. You others, scatter around outside and see what you can see." All the while he kept his eyes on Allen Howard, white and miserable upon the bench. I could see as plainly as he that the man's face was unmarred by scratch or bruise.

Daisy had trailed back upstairs with the others. For a moment we three were alone. Tom stood in front of Allen. I collapsed on the bottom step and hugged my knees.

"What made you guess that your aunt had been poisoned, Allen?" Tom asked softly.

Allen shook himself and fumbled at a pocket, at last producing his cigarette case. Tom meticulously offered a lighted match. "Well?" he prompted.

"The stuff's gone from my office. I've just come from there. Somebody broke in and took it." Allen Howard's voice was almost firm, but his eyes clung to Tom's like a child's. I knew what Tom was suspecting, but I could not believe that Allen Howard was a guilty man. He looked so puzzled.

"The bundle you removed from the safety deposit, before the key was so obligingly turned over to me. That's one of the black marks against you, Allen."

"I didn't mean—" he faltered. "Things had gone a little farther than Aunt Rhoda— God! Do you mean she's—dead?"

"Things have gone so far that you'll have to help me, Allen, and your wisest course will be to give me a couple of straight answers. The fat's in the fire now. You went to the bank this morning before the funeral?"

Allen nodded.

"And parked the bundle in your office?"

Another nod.

"Did you unwrap it? Examine it?"

"No, I had no chance—I had no reason to."

"Why didn't you bring it out here to your aunt? You had got it at her request."

"Yes, yes. But I had no chance. There were people around in my office."

"Then you were with the family at the service and at the cemetery and back here again for lunch. And then we talked in the library. That much I'm clear about. What next? For you, I mean."

"After you went off we talked here for a while. Family stuff, all of us together. Then I got an important long-distance call relayed out here. Business, not personal, I had to get back to town to meet a man, and Lila and I left." He stopped as if he had finished.

"Was the bundle still in your office?"

"I didn't go back there. I met my man at, his room in the Dominion House and was with him until his train left at five-forty. Lila called me there about five-thirty and said they were all going to meet at Chad's. The family, I mean. But I—I didn't get there in time for Sally's supper." He paused abruptly, as if he had run himself into a cul-de-sac.

I wished I were sitting where I could signal to Tom. The best I could do was to shift my position warningly. It was time somebody was thinking about the Buick. My thought wave must have registered.

"You left town?" Tom's voice, was casual.

"Yes." Allen leaned sideways until he could drop his spent cigarette into the bronze base of an umbrella stand. He straightened up. "Look here, I'm going to tell you. I had a hunch about that girl who worked here until the last few weeks. I wanted to talk to her. Good God, Nixon, you don't suppose I liked the way things were stacking up here, do you? I grabbed Chad's car—it was parked near the hotel and I left word with old Billy at the door to tell him when he showed up. I didn't go back to my office at all. I made a quick trip out beyond Webster Springs. But it was a bad belt."

"You missed Thelma?" If Tom hadn't asked that one, I should have blurted it out myself.

"No. I caught up with her eventually; but she didn't know what I thought she might have known. I turned around and drove back—some trip! Had to change a tire and then to make time I took the old road across in spite of the heavy rain. Made it just after twelve. The others were still holding forth at Chad's and so I ran on downtown and up to my office. The door was standing open and my desk drawers were pulled out. The bundle was gone."

"So what?" I knew Tom was calculating times.

Allen sighed and looked toward the stairs. Sounds of official activity were drifting downward.

"That's about all. I sat there a little while, trying to think. I was uneasy about Aunt Rhoda. She'd said she was going to stay at home and enjoy a little quiet. I rang the house but got no answer, and so in a few minutes I shut things up and came down and got in the car. I cruised around, still trying to think, and then I came up here. It's easy to say now, but I was worried about Aunt Rhoda. That poison stuff—"

"You're sure you met no one or heard anything suspicious about your office?"

Allen Howard shook his head.

"You might as well tell me. You think you know who swiped the bundle."

The man's lips tightened to a thin line, then opened just enough to say. "I don't know." There was a faint hesitation that emphasized his last word.

The party that had gone upstairs must have completed the first stage of their work. We heard the sheriff's bluff voice say, "All right, boys, but give Tom a look first."

And Dr. Ammon was saying smoothly, "I agree with the coroner. Let us wait to do that by daylight."

Again Floyd, "No gun anywhere, but I'm on the record to say the bullet will be a .32. Hey, Tom, better come on up."

Allen Howard had risen stiffly from his bench. "A gun— not poison . . . thank God!"

8

I think that Tom must have heard what Allen Howard said, but the summons from above was imperative. He responded, two steps at a time. Without a glance at me, still huddled on the lower step, Allen slowly followed. After a second's indecision on my part, I hurried through the lower hall and into the kitchen. It was lighted by this time and the door to the back stairs stood open, but there was no one in sight. As if to account for my presence there, I went to a cupboard, selected a glass, and turned on the water at the sink for a drink. I wanted a front-row seat upstairs and I was plotting a way to get there.

It opened up, without further shenanigans on my part. I recognized Tom's voice, circumspect steps, and murmurs of interrogation and assent. Then suddenly a sharp exclamation.

"See here! What was it you found here?"

A babble of disclaimer and Floyd's heavy bass boomed out, "Looks fresh, too; Just dug out, huh?"

"Let her take a look, Floyd. She ought to know."

"On a stack of Bibles I tell you, it wasn't there before. I never had a chance to wipe them steps down till late this afternoon and there was no mess then," Daisy was protesting truculently.

Something came back to me in a flash and I began to guess. I scampered up the back stairs, but only part way. "Wait, let me see too."

What I saw was a sizable hole gouged out of the second step from the top and an untidy heap of shavings and chips, the whole spot-lighted by the hard glare from someone's flash.

"I know—I remember now. I mean, I can tell you one thing."

They all looked at me, Allen Howard as though he had never seen me before and Daisy with open resentment.

"Yesterday, right after the service, it was just a small neat hole." I caught Tom's eye. It would be up to him to explain what I was about at that time. "I remember I thought it could so easily be filled up with plastic wood. I never thought to mention it to you, I guess you know why. It didn't mean anything to me."

Daisy flounced away from the sheriff, who had been gripping her by the elbow.

"Then there's no use expecting her to have heard more'n the one shot." Floyd tried to look as though it had been Tom's idea all the time to make Daisy confess to having been aroused by two bangs instead of one.

Tom Nixon stood staring down at the gouged-out hole and whistling ". . . give me your answer true." He gave Daisy a sidewise grin. "Didn't dream anything about a mouse gnawing a big hunk of cheese, did you?"

"I'm sick and tired of being made fun of," Daisy snapped.

Rhoda Sutton's body had been laid upon her own bed. Tom indicated to Paulding and Floyd that their decision about waiting till daylight to take the next steps met with his approval, and those two officials with their subordinates made ready to depart. Two men were left to patrol at the front and back of the house. Daisy and I retreated to the kitchen and I suggested coffee to Daisy. Very shortly we heard Tom and Allen Howard on their way toward us from a final inspection of the front door. The coffee, started, Daisy scuttled back to her own realm to reappear later in an amazing blanketlike robe and with her pigtails concealed by a dark woolen cap. In that brief interim I heard Allen Howard say as they paused at the library door, "I must call Bart. You have no objection, Tom?"

Tom Nixon came on and lounged in the doorway, frankly listening. "He's calling Sally's house," he informed me soundlessly, "and not getting a prompt answer. . . . Ah, now he's getting someone."

But whomever he got he did not hold long, for Allen was with us in the kitchen inside of a minute or two. "Chad says Bart's on his way home now. I didn't tell Chad—they can wait till morning, can't they?"

He flung himself across a chair and pressed his forehead into his crossed arms along the back. "Just a minute," Tom murmured at me, and went out through the back door. I heard him speak briefly to the guard there and then his brisk steps went toward the front. In another minute he was reentering the kitchen just as Daisy, in her remarkable costume, came down the back stairs. Allen Howard had not shifted his position nor had I moved or spoken.

"When Bart comes, the boys will shove him right in," Tom announced cheerfully, and began to help Daisy with cups and saucers. As soon as she had debated which bottle of cream was the one to open, he blandly advised her to go back to bed. He hoped she wouldn't mind if she heard talking in the kitchen; he felt more at home there. Daisy yearned to wash the used cups, but we shooed her off at last.

Tom began with, "Bart ought to be up here by this time, don't you think, Allen?"

"I didn't ask Chad, but he might have taken Lila home. She might not have taken the car out. Night driving bothers her. It would only frighten her needlessly if I called there."

I took Allen's cup from him and managed to remind Tom as I passed him whom I had seen with my own eyes in Sally's living room on our way out to River View. He gave me a grain of a nod to say he didn't need to be reminded, thank you.

"See here, Allen, this is one screwy mess, but some things are going to be unscrewed before very long. I think I can promise you that. If you'll only stick to the truth, you and the others. . . . . We can get the lies out of the way in time, don't fool yourself about that, but it takes longer. You know now that your aunt was shot, not poisoned, and that fact has relieved you of a certain fear. I'd like a straight answer to this question: do you now feel obliged to shield the person who shot her?"

Allen Howard looked Tom steadily in the eye. "Before I answer that, I'm asking you one question. Is there any chance that my aunt committed suicide?"

"The evidence is indisputably against it. She was murdered."

"Then I want her murderer caught."

"And your father's?"

"God, yes!"

"And his wife's?"

Howard nodded wearily. "I felt they were wrong there," he murmured.

"You'll find them agreeing with you now. There might be a minority of one, at that," he added absently. "Now," he went on, "let's get this straight. What you told me a little while ago about your peregrinations this evening is the truth?"

"It is. But I did not kill my aunt."

"Who said that followed? Oh, I see—that last hour was pretty sketchy, I agree. However. . . . What I was getting at was this: of your own knowledge, then, you cannot alibi your brothers, or your wife, or your sister-in-law, can you?"

"I see. . . . No, I can't." His shoulders slumped.

"Don't try it out, hereafter. They'll have their own questions to answer." Tom looked up at the kitchen clock, pulled out his watch, and said, "See for yourself what time it's getting to be. Bart ought to be here."

White and miserable, Allen Howard tugged at his watch. His hand shook so that I was glad it was on a chain. "Maybe he's having trouble with his car," he managed to say.

"It's a thought," agreed Tom.

A long five minutes went by. I tightened a dripping faucet. The warmth of the hot water pipe felt good. I realized that my hands were icy. Daisy's kitchen filled with cigarette smoke. Then the telephone bell rang. Allen Howard rose, but Tom got to the door first. He closed the library door behind him. I think we both listened, but we could distinguish nothing. Tom reappeared very shortly. He made no comment about the telephone message.

June dawns come early. I had not even noticed that the heavy rain had dwindled to a drizzle. By the time the robins had begun their early morning chirping the gray light was

no longer dripping. The coming day would be clear. Almost
as if he had forgotten that we were still sitting there waiting with him, Tom had been making a series of notes on a
page torn from a blank order pad swinging on a cord beside
the door.

"I'm sorry," he said abruptly. "I needn't have made
martyrs out of you. Get a few hours sleep now, if you can.
Mrs. Howard's room—" He nodded at me. "And I hope
you'll be willing to stay here, Allen. Paulding will be up
here first thing, and since Bart's evidently stayed in town,
it's up to you."

At the mention of Bart, his brother cringed. I did not
wait to argue; I was stiff and groggy with fatigue. But before I could leave the kitchen, the next thing happened.
Someone pounded peremptorily at the back door. It was
one of the two men on outside duty.

"I've just been down to the boat house. The padlock's
hangin' loose and one of the skiffs is gone."

9

I'm not like Perry Mason's Della Street. I know when the
only thing that matters is sleep. At the guard's announcement about the boat Tom Nixon bolted from the kitchen
and I have a vague memory that Allen Howard trailed
after him, but I kept steadfastly on my way to the haven of
Felicity's room. I was so hypnotized by the thought of bed
that if the man had said he had three murderers tangled in
a fishnet down on the bank of the Ohio I shouldn't have
gone to see.

It was only half past eight when Daisy shook me awake.
"It's Tom Nixon on the telephone and he says you got to
talk to him. You can use the upstairs phone."

Tom's message was explicit but mystifying, and he rang
off as soon as he was sure I had understood and had agreed
to do what I was told. "You have an invitation for breakfast

which you must accept. Don't talk too much but let the spirit move you. Your host is Wilson Markham. . . . No need to go Emily Post about it. His rooms are behind his book shop. At nine, p.d.q. Step on it. . . . And when you tear yourself away, take a sneak up to my office."

My head felt like a sponge soaked in cold soup, but I endeavored to oblige. It was not until I had stumbled away from the telephone that I realized the instrument was in Mrs. Sutton's part of the house and that everything was neat and orderly and unoccupied. Paulding had indeed been there the first thing in the morning. In fact, there was no one at all about the place except Daisy, and if I were to keep my nine o'clock rendezvous I could not stop to check with her. But she had pressed my bedraggled dress, bless her.

The air was fresh and the sky was blue and my swift trip into Point Tyler served well as an eye opener. The trucks and cars I passed on the road, a khaki file of boy scouts hiking off for the day, a cheerful thumber with his college-stickered suitcase prominently displayed, all made it hard to believe the life I had led since the preceding morning, to go back no further. That Tom's invitation for me to breakfast with Wilson Markham had some tie-up with poison, shootings, and sudden death I must believe, but for the brief space of my airy journey I almost persuaded myself that I was traveling back to sane and everyday reality.

I had not yet discovered the book shop for myself but after what I had heard it was not hard to find. It was off the main street and close to the river, a shoe repair place on one side and an insurance and real estate office on the other, neither giving evidence of big business. Faded gilt paint announced *Old Books and Magazines—Americana,* and the one window displayed a bright fan of the latter and a dingy row of the first. There were also several old china plates in excellent condition and a damaged luster picture. The door said *Come In,* and I did. As I entered something like a bicycle bell tinkled from the rear and Mr. Wilson Markham promptly appeared.

His greeting was urbane. "This is truly kind of you, Miss Lenox. Our good friend Nixon assures me that you will not resent informality. I shall be ready for you almost at once. Will you sit here and look at my prints? Or perhaps you enjoy flowers? My small garden . . ."

He was headed toward a rear door through which I caught a glimpse of geranium red and delphinium blue, but a boiling-over sound from behind a curtain diverted him.

The garden would keep. I chose the shapeless chair and picked up a folio of beautifully mounted pages from Godey's, *circa* 1855. That was only a gesture, for I was curious about the living quarters of Wilson Markham. The shop had been narrow and dark; the room behind was large and square with a high ceiling. There were windows along one side and a door and another window on the garden side. The other two walls were stacked high with an assortment of old books. One end of a long, heavy work table had been cleared and laid for breakfast, a fine old damask towel, long and very wide, serving as a cloth. The rest of the table was littered with a dusty and jumbled collection of oddments among which bottles of ink, paste, paint, and shellac, each with an upthrust brush, polled heaviest. The curtained corner of the room evidently concealed his service quarters and a wide low couch covered with a dark blanket over which a gorgeous prayer rug was thrown must have served as his bed, for I noticed an edge of sheet hanging below the blanket. That was as far as I got with my inspection before he came back through the curtain with a coffee pot in one hand and a big glass pitcher of milk in the other.

I wish I could say that the breakfast was the most delectable I have ever eaten, but it was not. Whatever Wilson Markham's peculiar gifts might prove to be, they were not culinary. To offset the weak coffee and the lumpy oatmeal I can speak highly of the china cups that would have graced the American Wing and the satin-smooth old silver spoons. None of these pieces matched. I decided that my host was a magpie collector.

Working at an orange whose peel was hard and shrunken, I was about to make the obvious gambit of his interest in antiques, when he got down to brass tacks himself. "The bright young Nixon tells me, quite confidentially, you understand, that you were Mrs. Howard's dear friend. I think she would have named me as one also."

"Had you known Felicity before she came to live here?"

He sighed regretfully and whitened the top of his oatmeal with sugar from a bowl that I think was one of the rarer examples of Steigel. "True friendship is not always like the upward growth of the oak," he murmured. It sounded like a quotation to me, but anthologies of literary gems are not my field.

"Then you agree with me that she never would have committed suicide?"

"Quite beyond belief, Miss Lenox."

"I was grateful, more than I can say, for your statement at the inquest about her fear of a loaded revolver. I know exactly how she felt about guns. She couldn't have reloaded one herself. The question is: who did?"

"The same person, of course, who poisoned Jordan Howard."

"Yes, and who—" I gulped down some of the wretched coffee and finished blandly, "And who was that?"

Wilson Markham scraped his porringer delicately with his thin silver spoon. "I am not an orthodox person, Miss Lenox. A life for a life and all that—our friend will still be dead. Oh, I can understand the intellectual interest in solving a puzzle, but revenge is abhorrent to a civilized mind."

"A murderer on the loose is abhorrent to my low-grade mentality," I snapped.

"That is fear, Miss Lenox, the most powerful of the emotions, not a mental process."

I was afraid, suddenly and dreadfully afraid. I had already eaten most of my breakfast. I tried to have sense enough to tell myself that we had shared the same food.

"Do you mean to tell me," I demanded, "that you would do nothing to bring Felicity's murderer to ground?"

"I should never, actively or consciously, thwart justice, but I find no zest in the putting together of clues. And I am not beset by the fear that you admitted. The murderer has accomplished his purpose. There will be no more deaths." He added slowly, "'This murderous shaft that's shot hath—' lighted."

It all sounded very theatrical, but I was aware that he had not answered my question. I said, "Of course we know now one person who had nothing to do with it at all. Even a little narrowing helps."

There was a shade of question in his mild gray eyes and I suspected for an instant that I had talked too much, but his answer revealed that he knew what had last occurred. "Mrs. Sutton was antagonistic to Felicity, that is true, and it is my belief that she would have stopped at nothing. All others, except one, had no part in the business. That is the reason clues are so useless. I daresay the young Nixon's collection at this present moment points to all of us, including your blameless self. But come, you must see my garden."

He led the way to the back door and stepped ahead of me with a murmur of apology about bachelor housekeepers. Sweetpeas and snapdragons pulled my attention so promptly that I was only half aware that he had pulled at a couple of clothespins and let a dark mass plop to the ground just outside the door.

I walked on down an uneven brick path, damp and mossy, exquisite blooms to right and left. I could scarcely believe that Point Tyler's undistinguished, seedy Front Street lay just beyond the blank wall of a warehouse that formed one boundary line. What the rose trellises on the other concealed I could not tell. The garden was long and

narrow and the lower end where there was more air and sun
was given over to as fine a collection of hybrid roses as I
have ever seen outside the big show places.

"I have early spring bulbs, too. That's when my garden
delights me most. You should see it then. Our Mrs. Howard
. . ." He paused and caught my eye in understanding. "She
saw it last when the hyacinths were here. I believe I could
have persuaded her to come down to see the roses. She had
gone almost nowhere since her husband's death."

I stooped down to a perfect Gloire de Dijon, "Talk to
me about her, please. When did you last see her? What did
she say? How did she act? I've had to hide my interest and
concern since I came. Surely you understand what I want
to know."

We walked along the path toward a low brick wall from
which I began to suspect I would be shown a view of the
river. My sense of local geography was beginning to jell.
Sure enough, there was one angle that gave a glimpse of
murky water washing the end of an abandoned wharf. A
tangle of willow scrub hid everything else.

"The old ferry landing," Wilson Markham murmured.
"The new wharf boat is further down since the high water
of '37."

"You were here then?" I asked. "My guess is that this is
not your native state."

"Yes," he said. Apparently he was answering my question, not verifying my comment. "I am interested in old
books, as you may observe. I have found some fine eigh-
teenth century items among these West Virginia hills."

We settled our elbows comfortably upon the top of the
wall and he went on talking, dropping his words slowly,
gently. "Felicity was happy here, until her husband died. Do
not think otherwise. Jordan's will was a mistake, a ghastly
mistake. It loosed jealousies and greed and hatreds. I could
wish that she had not found it."

"You knew her husband well. Had he spoken to you of his plan? Did you know the new will had been made?"

"I have an orderly mind. I shall try not to forget your questions. I saw Felicity last the morning of her death. Ah, do not misunderstand. She did not see me and I had no opportunity to speak to her, but I saw her as she went in to Allen Howard's office. I remember thinking how like a flower she looked, like a mauve sweetpea, and her hair in gold tendrils. . . ."

"How perverse everything is," I burst out. "If you, or Allen, or Sally had only talked to her that day. If only I had called her up the minute I got to town that afternoon. We might have given her murderer no chance at her."

"You are not a fatalist then, Miss Lenox?"

"We might have been fated to save her, that's all I mean, if we'd co-operated better." I knew that sounded silly, but a mood of rebellion about Felicity was coming over me again.

There was a little silence. I gazed across at a distant hilltop, waiting for some more of my questions to be answered, but the faint trilling of a bell brought an end to our conversation.

"That will be someone in the shop. You will excuse me?"

I followed him back to the building and so saw one thing I had missed on my way out. In a clear sunny spot sat a pair of well-worn black oxfords, carefully stuffed with paper, I ran my finger across the leather; it was still damp. In a flash I was all curiosity about the wet something that had so casually been dropped from the clothesline. At the doorway, with Markham already trotting into the shop, I satisfied that curiosity. A coat and trousers, both garments sodden and smelly, as wet woolens always are.

I walked briskly through the living room and the shop, and my thanks and farewells were brief. I wanted to report to Tom Nixon at once. Fortunately, Mr. Markham was on his knees fumbling at a pile of old books for a customer who looked as if he didn't intend to buy anything.

I found Nixon alone and just about ready to leave. "Good," he greeted me, "I was thinking I might have to go around and collect you. I'm going to send you back to River View."

"Not till I tell you. I've just had a brain-wave or something. That Markham man has a suit out to dry and a pair of shoes, too. What was he up to last night?"

Tom gave me a queer look. "Neat, I calls it. How did you know his name is now on my list?"

"You sent me there this morning for some nefarious purpose, not because you thought I needed social life. Did Bart show up? Tell me everything."

"Bart had spent the night at Allen's house. Says his car lay down and died on him. You remember that Allen hedged about calling his place last night."

I nodded. "I suppose you're telling me that Bart's name is on your list."

"Yes, and Chad's and Markham's, if you must know. Bart did a lot of wandering around last night that I haven't checked back on as yet and he reports that he saw the old gentleman walking in the rain at a place that might indicate that he was coming in from the River View. Of course, I wouldn't know—not yet."

"So I did have a brain-wave, didn't I? But Chad and Bart—I don't see how they could. I saw them both, you know, between twelve and one."

"We'll do the speculating after I've checked and double-checked the times. There's to be an inquest, as soon as Paulding can fix it up. Meantime, I want you up at River View, and keep your eye peeled."

Part Five
Saturday and Sunday, June 18 and 19

1

After my return to River View nothing happened for a while. I circulated about the living rooms, ear cocked and eyes open, obeying Tom Nixon and hoping that my actions appeared natural and unstudied. Allen Howard remained in the library, slumped in the chair at the desk. He looked tired and worried. He called someone at his office to postpone an appointment and perhaps half an hour later rang his house to ask about Lila. "Asleep, eh? That's fine." That's all he said, and put the receiver back. A little while after that the bell rang, but the call was his. He answered someone's question by saying yes, the meeting was next week, in Pittsburgh. I'm no snooper; I was glad it was all so plain and innocent. I'm really no detective.

Meanwhile Bart very elaborately selected a book from the shelves in the middle living room and stretched out on a chair on the terrace. It looked like quite a tome and I checked later that it was *Decline of the West,* but he turned pages regularly and kept awake.

Almost as soon as Tom Nixon had left, Sally had muttered "bathroom" and vanished up the stairs. I heard water running and the faint thump of something automatic starting itself in the basement, but as yet she had not reappeared. I thought nothing of it.

Chad acted scared. Certainly he was nervous enough for one of Lila's sedatives. He frankly avoided Bart, but he kept hovering around the library door as if he wanted to talk to Allen, who ignored his presence. He trailed me about too, and at last when I had settled myself in a good strategic position in the living room he kicked a footstool into place and sat down more or less at my knee. He cleared his throat rather noticeably and said:

"I hope you don't mind my asking, Miss Lenox, but last night—where were you? You weren't there for dinner, you know, and you didn't come back to sleep."

"I'm sorry if you were worried—after all, I am your guest. But I was off doing a little spade work for Tom Nixon. I was later than I expected getting back—that hard rain, you remember. I was reporting to Tom when Floyd came for him about Mrs. Sutton and naturally I came on out here with him. As a matter of fact, except for one little errand I've been right here ever since, and don't I look it!" I smoothed my rumpled dress over my knees as if suddenly clothes-conscious.

Chad twisted himself into a new position on the stool and sighed. "I wish you had been there, that's all. I'd like to know what you would have thought. Lila and Bart—" He broke off and sighed again.

"Were they there?" I asked, all innocence.

"Yes, the four of us. Not Allen. But you heard what he said."

"He said he made off with your car. Did that bother you?" I might as well see what dovetailing could be done.

"No. Old Billy told me. But I had to walk up to the house. Sally was expecting you all, but you didn't show up and when she called Aunt Rhoda she said Bart was eating up here."

"So when he came the four of you had a long evening to talk things over. I should think you'd have appreciated that—it's all been so terrible." I was hoping he wasn't thinking much about my concern with the mess. "I'd say you ought to have been glad that I wasn't there. When did Bart come?"

"About ten—maybe before. It was storming and he ran his car in the garage, so he could have some light. But he's no good with car trouble."

"Oh, so that had already showed up?" I was wondering just how long wet tire marks would stay on cement. I had seen two sets at approximately twelve-thirty. Also an empty garage and Lila, Chad, and Bart in the living room. I'd have to go on with this as far as I could go.

"Was it all right when he was ready to leave—the car, I mean."

"He fumed so that I went out and had a look at it later. As a matter of fact, I ran it down to the shop and took care of his trouble or thought I did. Anyway, it seemed to be all right when he and Lila left."

Another something gained. Bart's car had come into and then out of the Chad Howard garage. I wanted to ask about times, but all I dared risk then was the lead he had just given me. At one I had seen Chad and Lila in the living room, but no one else.

"What time did they leave? I suppose we should have called your house as soon as we heard about Mrs. Sutton. We'd have caught you, perhaps, it's hard to think of everything."

"It must have been about one o'clock. We'd got to bed by the time someone called about Bart. I—I—" Chad's fingers twisted in their clasp about his thin knees and he hitched the footstool still closer. "Nixon should have told me then. Allen and Bart—always Allen and Bart. I'm the youngest, and I'm never allowed to forget it."

"There was really nothing to do and you'd all been through so much. They didn't tell Lila either. It was just because Bart was expected back."

His eyes grew intent and he leaned back an instant. "Did you call there—at Allen's?"

"Not that I know of. Your brother Allen got to River View before long and—"

"That's so. Allen never forgets Lila's nerves." There was something about that remark that should have pleased Sally, for it certainly did not suggest a romantic interest in his sister-in-law. "But if you had," he went on, and sought my eyes as he spoke, "you'd have known that Bart was there. Wouldn't you?" he insisted.

"Yes, and I'd have got a little more sleep." A fresh wave of fatigue swept over me at the thought of those hours of futile waiting in Daisy's kitchen. But I was still on duty according to Tom Dixon, and there was something that Chad had said . . . oh, yes!

"It's nice of you to wish I'd been with you last night. You were saying you wondered what I'd have thought. About what? But then your aunt's death has changed everything."

He looked at me blankly and then swallowed, but he was silent.

"I mean—Felicity Howard did not kill your aunt."

"You—you think it's all part of the same—oh, no! No, you're wrong there, Miss Lenox. It was a burglar—someone breaking in. Aunt Rhoda must have heard something—someone at the back and she started down. She was never afraid of anything. And the boat house broken open and the boat gone— No, it must have been someone from the outside."

"I agree. Certainly someone came from the outside. Your aunt and Daisy were alone in the house, and no one can accuse Daisy of being involved."

He shrugged his shoulders at that and twisted himself into a new knot on the stool. "About last night—we were talking things over, of course. Legally it's all so confused and Blair's so damned cagey. Even if Allen had been there he wouldn't have— Aunt Rhoda was right: Dad's money should be ours. Frankly, Miss Lenox, we were talking about what the set-up might be now that Felicity's out. Bart—and Sally, too—they think that even if she had no will—and how do we know but what she had some other lawyer, not Blair—" He discarded that tangle and started again. "Bart and Sally think maybe her relatives—we really don't know what claimants might appear."

I held on to myself. I must not reassure these Howards on that point. "I'm afraid questions like that are beyond me," I murmured politely. "I know nothing about law, but if your family lawyer says your father's last will will stand, I'm sure he ought to know, and then Felicity Howard's affairs will have to be administered in some legal fashion. Tangles like this take forever—that's all I do know."

"It will take a damned long time. That's just— God!" He buried his head in his hands and his shoulders writhed.

His nerves were getting me down. Rather shakily I said what a calmer moment would have advised against, for it was no change of subject. "And now there'll be your aunt's affairs to settle. I'll bet she had a will."

"Bart will get it all—you mark my words. She always said—" He pushed the stool back and stood up, smoothing his thin rumpled hair. But what Aunt Rhoda had always said I was not to learn, for at that moment Sally came down the stairs looking as if she needed my attention at once. The click-click of her heels must have warned Chad. At any rate, in the instant it took for my eyes to swing back from the descending Sally to him he had slipped from the room into the hall toward the kitchen. Well, Daisy was there and she'd report later.

"Peg," whispered Sally, "I've just noticed something queer. Upstairs. I'd like to know what you think."

I'd like to know what I'd think, too, but I was under direct instructions from Tom Nixon. "Can't you tell me first?" I faltered. "I ought to stay right here."

"Oh, I see— I get it. But there's no one down here to watch. Where's everybody?"

"Bart's on the terrace reading and Allen's in the library and Chad—he was right here a second ago. Wait, I'll see." I ran down the hall to the kitchen door and swung it just far enough to see. There he was, sitting on a table eating a cookie. Daisy was rolling pie crust. They didn't notice me at the door.

I came back to Sally. "You go up this way," I ordered, "and I'll take the back stairs. That'll work, I guess." Somehow, I wanted Chad to know I had gone upstairs.

I made my way along the upper corridor to Sally waiting at the head of the stairs. She opened the first door on the Aunt Rhoda side and went in. The living room looked just as it had the night before, but I knew that Tom had gone over everything. Sally looked about in distaste; Aunt Rhoda's clutter of trivia was not to her liking. On into the bedroom beyond. It was just as I had last seen it. There was the bathroom between this room and Bart's and that's where she led me.

"I was in here just now," she began, "and I got curious about the medicine cabinet. I can't help it— I can't get that missing hypo out of my mind. So I opened the cabinet— like this," and she pulled open the snugly fitting door, "and see—all those empty spots. Bottles are gone."

"What of it?" I refused to get excited over nothing. "Don't you realize that Tom Nixon collected a little of everything for that examination yesterday?" I could see for myself there was nothing much left but stuff labeled camphor and aromatic ammonia and witch hazel, an assortment of pill boxes, and a very dingy paper packet marked boric acid powder.

"Oh," she said, plainly disappointed at my attitude. "I suppose he did. And from the other bathroom too?"

"Felicity's? Let's take a look, if you want."

We left the bathroom by the hall door. Daisy's voice floated up from the kitchen. She was telling Chad about her teeth in such detail that her recital would not soon be finished. I led the way into Felicity's room where I had spent my brief night. The bed was just as I had left it. Plainly Daisy had had orders. My impulse was to make it then and there, for Felicity loathed disorder, but Sally marched on into the bathroom and I at her heels.

Except that there was no dust nor ancient odds and ends of medicaments, the cabinet there looked much like the other. Plenty of bare spots.

"You see, everything they thought might help has been cleared out, and maybe long before Felicity was openly accused."

"Peg, you make me shiver. I could have believed that Rhoda Sutton—but she's been killed too." Sally's eyes stared out of her white face. "It must have been someone breaking in—last night."

"Yes, it was—someone from outside last night." I had just said the same thing to Chad.

The door leading into Jordan Howard's room was closed. I opened it and stood looking in. It was dark and cool just as it had been the day that I hadn't gone in, the day I'd been smothered in the brown bathrobe. But I knew how thoroughly it had been searched after that experience of mine. I crossed to a window and pulled up the shade. I could just see the edge of the terrace steps. Bart was standing there lighting a cigarette. I knew that Adkins was raking the litter of last night's storm from the lawn and that a nameless deputy was supervising from the first curve of a drive.

I was at the window only an instant. A faint "Ouch!" from behind turned me back to Sally. She was picking or pulling something from the thick fringe of a tannish fur rug that led the way from the old-fashioned double bed to the bathroom door.

"It stuck my toe through these open shoes," she complained, and straightened up with something in her hand. "See."

I took it from her. It was a browned and withered flower on a short, hard bit of stem. It could easily have lain unnoticed, caught in the furry edge of the rug that so closely matched it in color.

"Just so it doesn't start a runner," I was beginning when I realized that the flower stem felt very hard indeed. "Why, look, there's a wire in it."

"A funeral flower," breathed Sally. "How in the world did one get up here? Now if I were only Lila dear I'd even recognize whose tribute it came from. Here, give me another look at it." She put out her hand to take it from me again, but thanks to Tom Nixon she didn't get it.

Allen Howard's rich, pleasant voice was calling me. "Miss Lenox, Miss Lenox! Are you somewhere about? Nixon is on the phone and wants to speak to you."

2

I thrust the withered flower into the pocket of my dress and hurried down. Sally followed me but slumped on the bottom step to stare moodily out across the lawn. Allen stood at the front door checking the hall clock with his watch after politely waving me toward the library. I was sure I could hear Daisy still talking in the kitchen.

Tom's message was reassuring. Acting on information received, he could now see that some things were going to be cleared up. I could be relieved from guard duty if I felt like freshening up down at Sally's. Allen was coming into town in any case and later in the afternoon maybe I could manage to run up to his office. I needn't be concerned about anything more at River View just now. The situation seemed well under control.

"Yeah," I scoffed. "Roped and tied should be your phrase."

"My little buckaroo!" He laughed and broke the connection.

I didn't need to be coaxed to leave River View. I broke the glad tidings to Sally, but instead of leaping at the chance to go with me she decided she'd wait until Chad was ready to go.

"Your car is here, Miss Lenox? I'll drive you down if you wish, but first I must—" Allen started through the living room toward the terrace and I heard him calling Bart. But according to Tom, that needn't concern me now.

So I got my rumpled self into my mud-splashed car without further argument. Sally bade me an absent farewell. "Norine's down there. She'll do anything you say and the place is all yours. Tell her I'll call about dinner."

Sally looked so forlorn waving at me from the doorway that I wished I could have told her something definitely cheering. Yet Nixon's words had been vague. However, he must have talked to Allen too, who certainly had not looked as if he had just learned more bad news, and what Allen had learned he would surely be telling his brothers and Sally by this time.

Norine was glad to see me, no doubt about that. She came running out to open the garage doors—how I had struggled with them in the rain the night before. She was bursting with curiosity, but she had more news for me than I for her.

"Poor Mis' Sutton," she mourned properly. "Such a nice lady, so stylish. Awful to get killed by a burglar like that. They found the boat a'ready he got away in."

"They have!" And I didn't need to act surprised.

"Yes sir, they have. I just heard it. Some kids swimmin' down at the island. Elvin Daum told me. Daisy up there's his aunt and so he knows."

Whether that followed logically I didn't care. Undoubtedly this was one of the developments behind Tom's message.

Norine's voice followed me upstairs. "And say, Miss Lenox, they was a phone call for you just before you come in. Tom Nixon, he says to tell you not before five o'clock. That's all he said; didn't hardly make sense to me."

"That's all right, Norine, thank you. I want a bath and fresh clothes." And I banged my door shut.

Not before five. That gave me a little margin of time to sort things out, though what would be the use of guessing at what I should soon be told. I was positive that Tom had been checking up on Bart's statement and my report of my nine o'clock appointment with that curious old gentleman, Mr. Wilson Markham. To that I had to add what Chad Howard had said—there were some odd angles to that—and Sally's discovery of the funeral flower.

After my session with the tub and Sally's de luxe bath powder, since she'd been so snooty about my own chaste lavender, I rescued the withered flower from its hiding place. It told me nothing. I hadn't even looked at the conventional mass of flowers that had surrounded Felicity as she lay awaiting burial. Lila would know, Sally had sneered. I didn't even know where Lila and Allen lived, but Norine could help there. Of course Sally might beat me to it at that, but I had the flower, not she. I glanced at my watch.

I'd been taking my time. I'd better not be late for Tom's command appearance, and anyway he might like to know about the flower before I barged around. I dug a white bag out of my suitcase, for I'd put myself into something cool and frilly and would have to change everything from my bulging standby. In the transfer part of the bulge was accounted for—Felicity's little address book and the snapshot of me I had taken from her desk. I always rather feel like tearing up pictures of me, but because this had been Felicity's I put it in my letter case.

The address book I had looked at only casually because it was so plainly a new one, belonging to Mrs. Jordan Howard, not to Miss Felicity Wendell. Automatically, however, I opened it at "L". Lenox was not listed, but why should it be? I flipped pages idly; there weren't many entries. But it gave me a queer little jealous jolt to see among the "H's" Ellen Hawke's name, complete with an address that I knew had been new only this spring. That stray fact kept digging at me as I went on clearing out stuff from my old bag. If Ellen Hawke had been hearing from Felicity, she certainly hadn't let on in any of our restroom conversation, and just as certainly I knew that I had never mentioned her in any of my letters to Felicity. That new address had not been furnished by me. I tried to recall the few letters I had found in her desk. There had been several from the Grant High crowd, but beyond recognizing the writing on a couple of the envelopes I had gone no further with them. Well, the desk was safely locked and Tom Nixon had the keys and if my curiosity got the better of me, no doubt Tom would let me do something about it.

It would not be before five if I dill-dallied longer, so off I went. Norine called after me that Mis' Howard had phoned that they were eating up at River View and for me to come up there if I wanted. "Or I'll fix you up something. I got a lot of cold fried chicken."

"Never mind, Norine. I'll be taken care of."

Tom Nixon was in his office and alone. There was an array of memo slips spread out before him and he was shuffling them about like a game. I waited for him to start, rather expecting a question or two about my afternoon at River View.

"At the present moment it looks like this," he began. "The missing boat from the Howard boat house showed up beached on the island just below town. Daisy's nephew Elvin Daum identified it and reported same to me, pronto.

Nothing in it but mud and water and only kids' fingerprints show up. No one, that is, neither Bart nor Adkins are
quite sure that it was there as late as yesterday. Bart uses
nothing but the launch and he hasn't had it out since Felicity's death. Adkins says the padlock was okay the last time
he was down there, which was night before last."

He pushed one card aside and picked up another.
"Markham was not at his place last night when I sent
around. No one stayed to watch—that's my fault—but he
was walking in the rain because he likes storms and darkness and that he turned in about one-thirty. His clothes
were so wet that he'd hung them out to dry, but pulled
them off the line, as you reported to me, so that the effect
of his garden would burst upon you unblemished by damp
woolens. They're still damp but not unduly muddy. And
they don't smell riverish, if you catch my idea. Maybe I can
test that, to be sure.

"And he checks Bart's story. They passed, just as Bart
said. But he says he doesn't recall meeting anyone else
while he was rambling about. It was late and raining cats
and dogs.

"There's a lot of junk in that place of his, including a
couple of old pistols, rusty and unloaded. He says he never
shoots for pleasure and hasn't even handled a modern shootin' iron for years except the day he unloaded Howard's .32
at Felicity's request. Rhoda Sutton was shot with a .32 and
in a short time now I'll know whether—"

He waved me to silence, for I was on the edge of my
chair. "Also, he frankly and freely stated that he did not
like Rhoda Sutton and that she did not like him. He and
Jordan Howard had always hit it off well, but it's only since
Howard's marriage that he'd felt sincerely welcome at River
View."

He selected another card and went on. "Don't say anything yet, not till I finish. I'm working backward. He was
at River View for Felicity's funeral and he started for the

cemetery with the others. In his own car, alone. He has an old A model, neat and well cared for, which he uses when he goes back in the hill country hunting up antiques. But he did not go to the cemetery, I checked with Daisy on that, and besides, her priceless nephew insists he passed Markham's old crate somewhere on the way back, though so far he's vague about details. Moreover, Markham blandly admits that he did not go to the cemetery with the others. Says he suddenly felt utterly unequal to it, turned out of the procession at the lower edge of town, and came back to his shop. Seems his car was behind mine, last in the line, as Paulding Brothers didn't think it looked as good as the others. Among his stuff at the shop I could neither smell 'Faded Flowers' nor see a bottle of it. Not that I'm an expert, but I'd fortified myself by a stop at the smell'um department at Dudley's drugstore."

After being twice warned I kept still about the funeral flower. It would be my turn sometime. Tom carefully replaced the card he had been waving at me and selected another.

"At the time that Felicity Howard was shot, Markham says he was at his shop—had been there all afternoon. Almost no customers, he says. Some dame in rather early looking for flower prints to use in a guestroom. A stranger passing through town who stopped to ask about McGuffey readers. He hadn't any old enough that he'd part with, but he did sell the chap an old arithmetic. Markham says this was sometime after four. Felicity was shot close to half past.

"Next step backwards and we come to the morning of Jordan Howard's death. Thelma's right. He did phone River View that morning and talked to Howard. He'd run across an old map he thought Howard would like and Howard told him to come up with it, but there was no set appointment. People kept dropping in all morning and one of them later on brought the big news that Howard had just passed out with a heart attack, and naturally that was all he ever did

about the map. I might add that the old boy has nothing that looks like a medicine cabinet. Shaving cream and
mouth-wash and bunion pads and that's all."

Tom put the card back in its line and straightened the
whole layout methodically. I kept wondering what was on
the others. He had used only four so far. Then he began to
polish his glasses.

"Now what do you think? Am I crazy? Shall I go ahead
and tangle Wilson Markham in all this? Some of it could be
tightened rather uncomfortably."

"Not without a motive. Why would he do any of it?"

"That's exactly what I do not know. Suppose he did
shoot Mrs. Sutton. That's all I have to work up against
him. He admits he didn't like her, but he's not unique in
that. She could have been shot for that any time these last
twenty years. His story about walking in the rain is wacky
and his clothes are very, very wet."

"Can he swim?" I asked.

"Yes, he can swim. He is also sixty-five years old."

"But he took the boat and rowed or floated down the
river and maybe just swam in to the bottom of his own garden. How did he get up there? Walk?"

Tom made a careful note on a fresh card before he answered. "Could have. And he knows his way around the
place all right. But there should have been traces of wet,
muddy feet through Daisy's kitchen and on the back stairs.
I hope my treasured assistant noticed that there was nothing of the sort. The path down to the boat house is all
gravel." Tom was apparently thinking aloud.

"He might not have liked what Mrs. Sutton was saying
about Felicity and another man. Not that I believe that for
a minute myself."

"We don't *know,* though."

I made myself sound cool and objective. "If he had felt
that way about Felicity he'd never have killed her *after*

Jordan Howard was out of the way. But if he had felt that way, he might have gone after the one who did shoot her."

"I'm with you there, Marg. I was sure it was Rhoda Sutton who did that. But now— See here, what if it's established that the bullets come from the same .32?" He gave me a narrow look.

"All I can see is this: I don't much care about Mrs. Sutton. I want to know who killed Felicity and I want it proved that she did not kill her husband. And the two deaths that ought to link don't, and the two that do—or may—don't. Oh, I'm getting all mixed up. I mean, even if you do make a case against this old man, that will only be for killing Mrs. Sutton, and I want Felicity—" I had to stop for I was going to cry.

"You've got something there, Marg. Those last two deaths will tie up— I've a deep-down hunch they will. When Floyd's report comes in, I can go ahead with all the funny stuff I have against Markham. The only crack in it is that two methods were used, poison and shooting. If one person is guilty of all three, you'd think there'd have been three poisonings or three shootings."

"Not if Mrs. Sutton was the one. Oh, I know someone else had to be in it to shoot her, but she made such a point of getting poison bottles, or anyway—bottles, out of the way, and Felicity's death did look like suicide." That incoherent speech made me think of the survey that Sally and I had made that afternoon. Tom was whistling soundlessly over his row of cards, not much impressed with my maunderings.

"You've got all the stuff, haven't you?" I demanded. "The mosquito bite lotion and everything. Lots of bottles are gone from the medicine cabinets."

"Yes, oh yes. Aunt Rhoda's cabinet had plenty. Doc Ammon was always writing her prescriptions. But much could have happened to anything like that between the morning that Howard passed out and the time she began to dish the dirt. Even the bottle in the bank vault was tampered with, thanks to that civic leader, Allen Howard."

"What about the others? Are you so sure that the family's clear? They had motive, all right."

"Not at all sure about Aunt Rhoda, but who killed her? I'll be roped and tied"—and he cocked an eyebrow at me— "if that's an entirely separate crime. But listen, last night at the proper time Lila Howard and Sally and Chad and Bart were all together here in town, and you and Allen were chasing each other back from Webster Springs."

"I'm not so sure about all that. Both Chad and Bart were out at various times fussing with Bart's car, and where did your men catch up with Allen?"

"They didn't. You heard what he said, that he got back about twelve, found his office a mess, cruised around a while worrying about his aunt, and then drove up to River View on his own. Don't worry; I'll check times carefully for everyone between twelve and one."

So I went over again with him my observations about the wet tire marks and what Chad had said, and Tom told me that there was evidence that Bart had finished the night on the davenport in Lila's living room after futile efforts to start his car, though there was no one but Lila to back up his statement. And the car had started all right in the morning. Bart had come up to River View in it.

His mention of Lila's house again reminded me of what I had in my bag, wrapped in a piece of cleansing tissue. I produced the withered funeral flower and reported its finding in careful detail. He agreed that it might help to ask Lila about it and told me where to find the Allen Howard house.

"She may be up at the other place by this time, however. In any case talk to her alone. I've got an open mind, but I don't see what it can possibly indicate."

"Another thing. Even if Lila is here, I'd like to go back to River View and I want the keys to Felicity's desk. There were some letters there that I'd like to look at again."

"Everything's just as I left it, but I found nothing in the desk that helped me."

But he did not insist on explanations for my interest. I took the keys and rose to go. "What next for you? I'll probably come back with Sally and Chad. I'd certainly prefer sleeping at their place tonight, but I may have something to report."

"I'll catch up with you somewhere," he promised. "I'm staying right here for the present—waiting for a ballistics report."

He was shuffling cards about as I went out the door.

3

A very proper maid, a colored girl, admitted me at the Allen Howards'. Everything about the place bespoke prosperity. Yes, Mrs. Howard was in. She was having a tray in her room and possibly could not be disturbed, but she would tell her who wished to see her.

"Tell her I've come for a little advice," I suggested to the maid. That may have done it, for without delay I found myself entering a mauve and ivory bedroom where Lila was looking decorative on a be-pillowed chaise-longue. The maid removed the tray, shifted the position of an electric fan, and departed.

I murmured something sympathetic and deprecated my intrusion. Lila Howard smiled faintly and said nothing. So I went directly to the point.

"I'd like your help about something connected with Mrs. Howard's funeral the other day. It's about the flowers. There, were quantities, naturally, but I'm sure you took some note of them—who sent what, I mean."

"Why, yes, I did. It all seemed to worry poor Aunt Rhoda so—I understood that, so naturally I took over the lists and told her I'd see to the notes of thanks and so on. I'm the only one really, for Sally—Aunt Rhoda would want me, I know. Oh dear, it's all so hideous— I've been flat on my back all day. But Allen said the arrangements could wait until tomorrow."

But I wanted to talk about Felicity, not Rhoda Sutton. I produced my withered flower. "Do you recall any funeral piece with these in it? You see, I can't even name it properly, as you doubtless can." I knew that Lila was a garden clubber.

"White bergamot—most unusual," she cooed. "They're never in the commercial greenhouses. I had some once, when I had my wildflower grotto. Um-m, let me think . . . the flowers were mainly glads and snaps. Some asters and button dahlias. The florists are always ahead of season. Allen ordered roses for the family—he would. But I told him to see to it himself."

She needn't have said that. I knew she'd spend no personal thoughtfulness on my Felicity. "The I flower is wired, you see. It must have been a set piece."

"Yes, I'm trying to think. Azalea mums—I'm connecting it with those—in an ivory basket with a pale pink bow. And asters, I think. No, that was from the Women's Guild at Trinity. There was no bergamot in that, I'm sure. With white glads—that's it. Now, where's my list? Oh, dear . . ." She pawed helplessly among the pillows and at last rang for the maid.

"Hester, my bag—the black and white petit point. You remember what I wore the day of Mrs. Jordan Howard's funeral. No, look in that other drawer. That's it." She produced a folded list and ran a rose-tipped finger down its items. "Um-m . . . Mr. and Mrs. James, the Cardo family, Dr. and Mrs. Ammon. It was really because of Father Howard, of course. None of these people knew Felicity, scarcely.

Garden flowers from Wilson Markham. He brought them up himself, but I listed them with the others, of course. Yes, here it is. . . . Basket of white glads and azalea mums with something—I've scribbled so, but I'm sure I meant it for bergamot. They were from Dan and Ruth Thatcher. He's the high school principal. My husband's on the school board, you see."

Drat the woman, she wouldn't admit that anything had been sent for Felicity's sake. I'd have to ask something about the high school principal. I was winding myself up, but Lila was babbling on.

"I remember now. Old Mr. Markham had just arrived with his bouquet and he admired the Thatcher basket. They say he gardens, but I've never seen his place. And he broke off one of the flowers and held it in his hand. Of course, I never said a word—it was scarcely the place—but he's always a law unto himself."

I didn't want Lila to ask how I had come by the flower, but there was one more question I had to ask. "When did this happen? I mean, when did these flowers come?"

"The morning of the funeral. Daisy had carried some boxes upstairs before I got there and I'd just finished putting everything in place."

So. . . . That fact might change the picture, but I decided to rely on Daisy for further information.

I thanked Lila fulsomely, wished her nerves well, and withdrew. Tom Nixon could ask his own questions about the night before. But downstairs as Hester saw me to the door, my resolution weakened. "You must have had far from a quiet night here last night. Too bad to be so disturbed."

"I was not disturbed, ma'am. And Mr. Howard did not phone down about his aunt's death. After Miss Lila came in last night, I got my rest just as usual. But Mr. Bart would have only had to call and I'd have had the guestroom ready for him in no time."

"That's right. I heard him say he slept here on a daven-port."

"Yes ma'am, he did so. Mr. Howard, he was out of town on business. I reckon the phone call was for him about his aunt. The bell woke me and I came down and answered— that was before Miss Lila and Mr. Bart got in, but of course I had no idea what it was about. They wouldn't leave a message and all I could say was that Mrs. Howard was up at Mr. Chad's and that Mr. Howard was out of town and hadn't said when he'd be back."

That call was surely the check-up Tom had ordered as soon as he had heard of Rhoda Sutton's murder. Allen apparently had not come home but was still "cruising around, worrying," as he had said. Well, that might turn out to be just too bad for him.

As I turned my car in the direction of River View, I set myself to pondering on some odd items. Tom had broken into Allen's office to get the bundle that hadn't been in the bank vault. At that time Allen was still on the rain-swept road from Webster Springs, Tom had tangled with someone in the office, someone who didn't want him to examine that mysterious bottle. That someone could not have been Allen, but whoever it was ought to show some mark of the scuffle, for Tom certainly was not unscathed. Yet neither Chad nor Bart was visibly battered. I could be positive about Chad, for his face had been thrust before me during his session at my knee. But what about Wilson Markham? I had seen him that morning myself and I could recall neither bruise nor scratch. Allen had been scared about the poison in the bot-tle, "worried" about his aunt, and quite prepared to hear that poison had caused her death. Very definitely he had shown relief when he learned that she had been shot.

Yet the bottle, which someone else had not been able to keep from Tom Nixon, contained nothing but water. And a fingerprint. Tom had said nothing more about that finger-print. But he wouldn't be skipping it. Probably that and a lot more were on those cards of his.

There was an entirely different atmosphere at River View. Nothing gay, naturally, with another inquest imminent and another funeral being planned, but the strain and tension were less evident. Daisy ushered me into the dining room where the three Howard brothers and Sally were at the table. Apparently none of them except Allen had left the house since my departure. However, little was said about the last turn of affairs beyond Sally's comment that the excitement now seemed to be directed against poor old Wilson Markham, but she supposed I'd heard all about that from Tom. The men excused themselves shortly and went out to the terrace with cigars, Allen reminding Sally that the minister from Trinity was to call and would she please be available.

All that suited my plans, because I wanted another look at Felicity's desk without supervision, even Sally's. So I dawdled over my dessert and drank more iced tea than I wanted and encouraged Sally to talk about Wilson Markham.

"Tom's waiting for a ballistics report—whatever that is," I said. "If it comes through the way he expects it to, the old gentleman's going to have it put to him, though I think the case is weak, myself."

Sally's look was a protest but not in behalf of Wilson Markham.

"No motive," I explained. "Unless you people know of something."

"Maybe Aunt Rhoda's mind wasn't so nasty after all. He certainly spent more time up here after Felicity came than ever before. And don't get your back up, Peg. There was nothing as far as she was concerned, but who knows what was in the old coot's mind?"

"Not shooting Felicity, surely, if he felt that way about her. But he could have been prowling about up here last night, and that's what Tom's starting with."

"If he gets him for Aunt Rhoda's death, then that would end it. And, Peg, surely you realize what that means for us. I'm a Howard, too." There was nothing flippant or detached about Sally's pleading voice.

"I know, Sally. I understand how you feel. It's all so dreadful and hideous. Somebody killed three people and one of them was dearer to me than to any of you. Wilson Markham's nothing to me, only I want it to come out that Felicity had nothing to do with her husband's death—nothing."

"Peg, let me tell you what I think really could have happened. It might all have been an accident, the poison that killed Dad Howard. Don't you see that it might? Felicity got the wrong bottle and never knew it, and then Aunt Rhoda guessed and she was so mad about the will that she didn't care what she said—oh, don't forget I know all about Aunt Rhoda. All the boys can think of is she was always good to them, but she could be a devil! She resented every one of us who married into the family. Lila got the best break, but that was because Lila always ran to her with everything. And so I cheerfully agree that she would have been capable of hounding an innocent woman to suicide. It's likely that Felicity might have confided in a sympathetic friend like Markham, and then he goes to pieces and kills Aunt Rhoda because of what she'd driven Felicity to do. It could have happened that way—it could have! Don't you see it, Peg?"

Sally was pacing the dining room floor and all the nervous tautness was back.

Her argument was so nearly parallel to my own that I had propounded to Tom Nixon that I could have said, "That's just what I think—almost!" Except that I knew that Felicity would have been physically, mentally, emotionally unable to turn a weapon against herself. So instead I said, "Even that would take some proving, Sally. Proving about the poison and all that. And there's some funny business about the bottle that Tom's working on. If Rhoda Sutton was responsible for that, then she really killed your father-in-law. I intend to clear Felicity—that's all."

"I don't care at all—about Aunt Rhoda. God, how I hate this town!" She clenched her fists high above her head and swung away, staring out across the terrace. "After, this, surely—we'll get away. Chad will leave the damned town now." Then she sank again into the chair across from mine. "No, Aunt Rhoda could have been into it up to her neck for all I really care, but someone killed her, and it couldn't have been any of us."

That was it, as I'd been aware all along. Just so it was none of them, the Howards, they'd not much care what sort of trumpery case was stacked up against an eccentric, harmless old man. Well, maybe not so harmless. Who knew yet? But a few bits of suspicious circumstance were a long way from being proof that would stand in court.

Then the doorbell rang and Daisy bustled forward and back to the dining room and the terrace announcing a reverend arrival, and Sally, muttering "old pious whiskers," meekly followed Chad and Allen into the front of the house. Bart, I noticed, remained on the terrace. It was my chance to slip upstairs.

I found Felicity's desk apparently just as I had left it at the moment the brown bathrobe had been thrown over my head. If Tom Nixon had gone over its contents also, he had churned nothing around. It was those few, fairly recent letters that I wanted to examine. I had given them only a casual look before and had read none of them. As I recalled, they were mainly from the gang at school. There was my own last one and one from Charlotte and two greeting cards from Julia Meade among them. But it was finding Ellen Hawke's new address in Felicity's book that had impressed me as odd, and I felt there should be a letter from the lady somewhere. But all I found was an empty envelope. The address was typed, which was the reason I'd had no memory of Ellen's up-and-down writing, which I surely would have recognized the first time. The return address was her new one, so Felicity had had a letter from Ellen Hawke.

Now there was absolutely nothing about that to impress me, except that I'd have said that Ellen Hawke would surely have mentioned hearing from the latest faculty bride, she being the kind of old gal she is. And Felicity had answered the letter. The back of the envelope more her usual neat little notation: Ans. 5-9. That meant that early in May Ellen had had a letter from Felicity Howard. Furthermore, Felicity had entered Ellen's address in what I called her new address book, as if she might have need of it again. But somehow, I kept on thinking the whole thing a little odd, out of character for both of them.

Before I left the upper floor I repeated the inspection of the bathroom cabinets that I had made with Sally that afternoon. I knew that whatever pertained to the case had been safely removed days before, but I stood looking at the three neat shelves that had been used by Felicity, wondering whether that could have been what happened—Sally's theory that the medicine applied to Jordan Howard's neck might have accidentally been the fatal poison instead of the soothing lotion.

I could hear Daisy washing dishes and there was something I wanted to take up with Daisy. The reverend gentleman whose whiskers Sally had described as pious would not detain the others forever, and so while time served I slipped down the back stairs to talk to Daisy.

"I'm hoping there's something you remember, Daisy," I began after a preliminary inquiry about the present state of her dental troubles. "It's about the flowers that came for Mrs. Howard's funeral. Mrs. Allen Howard tells me that you had carried some unopened boxes upstairs and that she arranged them the morning of the funeral."

"Yes'm, that's right. Mis' Lila, she was set on seein' everything that come herself, not that I couldn't have been trusted to put all them little cards to a side, and Mis' Sutton, she wouldn't touch a thing, and there was no place to put them big packages down here—I tried keepin' 'em out here but I got to have room to turn round—and so I just took 'em upstairs in the one room I knew nobody'd care about, Mr. Howard's bedroom."

"Did you open anything up there?"

"Not me, I didn't. Not a thing. I told you Mis' Lila—"

"Did she open them up there before she carried the flowers downstairs."

"She must of. Anyways, there was boxes and tissue paper and bits of fern all over. I got it cleared away before the service, though."

I had stood looking into that darkened room that morning just after they had left for the cemetery. It was certainly tidy by then. But a bit of broken flower stem might have caught in the edge of the rug and remained there unnoticed until this afternoon when Sally had felt it through her toeless shoe. There seemed no sure way of proving that it had been carried there by Wilson Markham and dropped by him before or after the brown bathrobe had been thrown over my head.

4

I went on into the library then, for sounds of decorous conversation were moving from the living room toward the hall. The outer door closed and I heard Sally say in a tired voice, "I'll find Peg and tell her we're leaving." I made myself evident and was informed that everybody needed rest. Sally and Chad and I were to go back to town, and Allen too, to tell Lila what the plans were for services for Aunt Rhoda, but he was coming back to stay in the River View house with Bart and Daisy.

There were too many cars, but they all had to be used, so there was quite a procession down the drive and into Point Tyler. Sally chose to go with Chad in their Buick; I followed, and Allen came last, for he'd want a car to come back in. I was just as glad not to have to talk to anyone on

the way in, though it would have been more like Sally to
pile in with me.

The Buick and the Ford turned into Terrace Drive and
that was the last I saw of Allen Howard that night, so I
can't say whether or not he kept to his announced schedule.
Maybe Tom Nixon talked to him; I don't know. I know that
both Sally and Chad slumped into silence in their living
room and that it seemed tactful to leave them. I was rather
expecting to hear from Tom, and I left my door slightly ajar
to be alert to door or telephone bells. That's how I know
what my host and hostess did very little talking. Chad must
have turned the radio on, for I heard a familiar urgent
expository voice and then Sally's sharp, "For heaven's sake,
Chad, not that tripe . . ." and then silence.

So I wrote a letter. I wrote to Charlotte. I explained
little, even though our home papers might not have carried
much about the sudden deaths in a remote West Virginia
town. Charlotte would not be surprised to hear that I had
gone on to attend Felicity's funeral, and I knew that I could
rely upon her discretion in doing what I wanted her to do.
I felt that I had to know about the letters that had passed
between Ellen Hawke and Felicity. So I asked her to hunt
up Ellen, who I knew never left town until hay fever time,
tell her of Felicity's death, and ask if she knew where to address her—shape her story any way so that it would sound
like a natural inquiry and not bring me into it directly—
and report at once to me anything that Ellen might say.

I don't know what I expected, but I couldn't dismiss the
feeling I had about those letters. I had just stuck a row of
stamps for special delivery, air mail, on the envelope when
the telephone rang. It was for me, Sally called.

"Just listen and don't say much," Tom Nixon cautioned
when I got to the receiver. "I'd like to talk to you tonight
without arousing anyone's curiosity. Do you think you can
get away?"

"Yes." My letter was ready to mail.

"Fine. Start down toward town and I'll pick you up."

"All right."

"Sally recognized my voice, so just say that I called to tell you that I've got the old man on a spot right. . . . And I have, no foolin'."

"You have! That sounds fine. . . . Sally and Chad will want to know. . . ." That was strictly for their benefit, for they were listening.

"Within ten minutes, then. . . ."

"Good night and thanks for calling."

"That was Tom Nixon," I reported promptly. "He says the case against Mr. Markham is shaping right up, but he couldn't give me any details. He thought we'd like to know."

I perched on the end of the davenport as if that were all that was on my mind. Chad yawned and looked limper than ever and Sally sighed in relief.

"What you two need is sleep. Let's all turn in and catch up with ourselves—tomorrow will have its excitements. Tom sounded as if it might be the beginning of the end." I rose and started toward the stairs, "Oh, I forgot—my letter, I've written one that just must go. I'll slip down and mail it at the station. No, Chad, don't bother—the walk will be just what I need. And don't wait for me to come back either; you both look all in." When I came back downstairs with my letter Sally was already turning out lights and Chad was in the kitchen locking up. "If you're sure you won't let me take it for you—just bang the front door when you come in."

So I got away. Three squares along my way down Terrace Drive I met Tom in his car and we tooled around the streets of Point Tyler, though first I insisted on mailing my letter, about which I said nothing to Tom.

"I've spent the evening talking to Markham," he reported. "I can't make him out, but I'm convinced he's involved in the affair—in some of it. I'm so convinced that I've a man on duty watching him, though I don't believe he'll try to skip out."

"That will suit the Howards just fine."

"You've noticed that? But I'm still without a motive, though he freely states he'd have done anything to help Felicity Howard. Circumstantial evidence—yes, a deadly amount of it."

"Do tell me what he said and so draw to a point. And what about that ballistics report you were panting for?"

"It came through all right and it is all right, believe you me. I hope your eyes bug out. Listen—you may be a bright gal and all that, but old Pedro Gunner thinks you swallowed something pretty thick. How come Rhoda Sutton could be shot with the .32 found by Felicity when I had it all along, exhibit A?"

I gasped. No use to deny it now; he'd never believe me. And I hadn't taken into account the fact that two guns had been used. But the second one had not been left by Rhoda Sutton's body. My only solace was that I had never posed as a Master Mind. I let him gloat and murmured meekly that of course she couldn't . . .

"But she was! I mean, the gun found by Felicity Howard was her husband's, but the bullet that killed her came from another .32 as yet missing, and the bullet that killed Rhoda Sutton came from the same missing gun. How you like that?"

"So the same murderer killed them both." I was almost weeping at this definite clearing of Felicity, evidence that would have to be accepted as my conviction about her temperament never would have been. "And I'll bet that horrible Rhoda Sutton put the other gun there as evidence of her case against Flippity." I was hardly aware that I had used her pet name for the first time since my arrival in Point Tyler.

Tom Nixon's response startled me. "Her murderer probably was the one who placed it there. That person was not Rhoda Sutton."

"Then you must mean it's Mr. Markham, though I can't see why he would kill Felicity. Go on; tell me."

"His story about last night's full of holes. He could have been rambling around in the rain, all wet and innocent, but his only witness is Bart Howard, and the time they passed doesn't establish a thing." Tom paused briefly. "For either of them. He's a good walker. He could have made it up to River View, and if he did, surely I'll run on to someone who saw him on the way. That road's a highway and never untraveled for long. He was not at his place after Floyd found us last night. He couldn't have been, if he'd just finished shooting Rhoda. He'd have been leaving River View by boat, for Daisy's disturbance meant that she'd be phoning an alarm, and he'd be meeting cars from town if he tried to get away by road. So he took the boat and then swam ashore. You see, I took his wet clothes and I've tested them for river sediment. Not conclusive, however. And something else, too. Four cartridges in a coat pocket. Four, not six. He explains that. Says when he unloaded the gun for Mrs. Howard, he dropped them in his pocket and forgot they were there. Says maybe there were only four in the gun. It's hard to tell—they've been soaked, but one will be discharged from Jordan Howard's .32 to test the markings."

"I don't see that that will prove a thing. All bullets of the same size look alike before they're shot."

"Right. And we haven't found the missing gun. But the story was that Howard's gun was fully loaded, so there should have been six slugs in his pocket, unless he used 'em in the other gun."

"He might have had a hole in his pocket. And you've never said whether Bart's box of ammunition was accounted for. I know you must have looked for it."

"You bet I did, and it was there. Intact. And Adkins vows he never saw Howard's .32, let alone reload it for Felicity."

"Look here, Tom, I'm not a smart gal, but you've got three bullets to account for. What about the one that was dug out of the back stairs?"

"It's gone, that's what about it, and so there's no way of telling what gun it was shot from. Anyway, if it was one of the two missing from the unloading of Howard's .32, there'd still be another to account for. Of course there's a chance that Markham's right about there being only four in the gun to begin with. No, it looks better to me to say those two missing bullets were used on Mrs. Howard and Mrs. Sutton. But to come back to my report—" It seemed to me that Tom was in a hurry to get off the bullet subject.

"As I've already told you, the old man freely admits that he did not go to the cemetery but turned off at his place. Now Daisy's Elvin's memory has been jogged a bit by me and he is as sure as cross-his-heart-and-hope-to-die that he passed Markham's car coming into town from the River View direction as he was bringing his Aunt Daisy back. I hinted at this fact to the old boy, but he insists that the 'young jackanapes'—I'm quoting Markham—is entirely mistaken. Boys like Elvin have a photographic eye for recognizing cars."

"The flower—I must tell you about the flower." I repeated what I had learned from Lila and Daisy. "So ask him about the flower he broke off—Lila saw him and I'm sure she didn't make it up. And there it was caught in the rug today—I saw that. And someone was up there that morning, and it could have been Mr. Markham, but what was he after?"

"A bottle of 'Faded Flowers.' So what? Well, your funeral sprig is surely something else to go on with. You've still got it, I hope?"

"Yes, in my bag in my room at Sally's. Is that all he I said? Do go on. I ought to be getting back to Terrace Drive."

"He has no real alibi for the afternoon of Felicity's death. His story about customer number one is okay. She turned out to be Mrs. Lew Graycie, but customer number two could be nothing but thin air, a stranger driving through town who bought an old arithmetic. No way to check up on that. If only Markham's one neighbor hadn't chosen this month to be away from home, I'd know something. It's nothing to you, but the woman in the brick cottage across the street is Point Tyler's prize snooper, who sees all and knows all. She's in Texas, welcoming a new grandchild, and Markham's comings and goings have been unsupervised."

"So you reason he could have come up to River View that afternoon. Surely Sally would have remembered passing him—no, she heard the shot. He couldn't have had his car, for we'd have been bound to see some trace of it. And Lila was in the boat house and Chad was swimming and Bart and Adkins were somewhere on the place. I just don't see how he could have vanished."

"What you really mean is that for some reason you can't accept the man as the murderer of your friend. If you had only heard the shot— Well, suppose I tell you that there is an old road along the river that dead-ends at the lower edge of the River View property. I've found traces of a car having been parked there—no, nothing as conclusive as tire marks, but the treads of Markham's are worn pretty smooth. That might indicate that he'd been there and how he got away without being seen."

I sighed. It seemed like a lot of guesswork to me. "I suppose you examined his car today and can prove it wasn't out in the weather last night."

"Exactly. It's dusty and quite unmarked by rain."

"But there's a lot more you've got to fit in. Who tried to get the bottle last night? Whose fingerprint is on it? And what became of the stuff that had been in it? What about Bart's car? Was it really acting up? Chad was out in it, and Bart too, and who can tell for sure that Bart stayed put on Lila's davenport? And Allen didn't go home and he wasn't at Sally's and the Buick could have got him out to River View and back again easily in the time he accounts for so vaguely. You said you were going to check up on everybody. Have you? And those gloves—"

"Lady, lady, you ask more questions than I can answer unless you can think of a good story to tell Sally and Chad. That is, if you're really worried about getting back from your letter-mailing expedition."

That was a point, though if they asked I intended to tell them frankly that I'd run into Tom at the station and he'd dared me to take a midnight ride. But the house was dark and quiet when I sneaked in a few minutes later. I snapped the lock after me, took off my shoes, and crept up the stairs in my stocking feet. Tom had promised to tell me the rest the next day—he intimated that everything else was negative—and besides, I was too tired by then to get anything straight.

There was a dim light coming from the hall above, which I thought was a night lamp until I got there and realized it was coming from Sally's vanity. Their door if was open and I could hear deep regular breathing. Another cautious step in the direction of my own room, and I could see the lower ends of the twin beds. Covers were tossed back over one. Only one was occupied. I craned my neck shamelessly. Chad was lying there, sound asleep. Sally was not there.

And the night light on the vanity shone down distinctly upon a bottle of "Faded Flowers."

I scurried soundlessly on into my room, half expecting to find Sally there, waiting for me. But my room was just as I had left it. In the bathroom, of course. But that door had been standing open. From the head of the stairs I had seen that it was dark and empty. I jerked off my clothes and made ready for bed, even negotiating a personal foray to the bathroom, which of course I lighted. No signs of Sally, and Chad still sleeping alone in his dimly lighted room. I had no further thought of searching the house; it was small and compact. But where had she gone? And why?

I lay tense in my bed, quite unable to sleep. It seemed hours, but at last I heard the sound of a lower door being

stealthily opened—the kitchen door, I thought. Quiet footsteps coming up. The other bedroom door closing. Nothing
more. But I knew that Sally had come back. I looked at my
watch. It was only a scant three quarters of an hour since
my own belated return. I yawned deliciously and drifted
off. But the last conscious thought I had was, for all I really knew that bottle of "Faded Flowers" had always been
on Sally's vanity. She always had gallons of stuff in bottles.

5

So much happened the next day it's a wonder I can tell
it straight, from Sally's cool comments at breakfast to my
long-distance call from Iowa that night.

We all slept late. Norine's brisk call, "I got a batch of
biscuits coming out of the oven, Mis' Howard," roused me,
and then I heard Sally's heels clicking down. As soon as
Chad went down, I got up, and even though Sally called up
an offer of breakfast in bed I preferred to have my share of
the hot biscuits and honey in their company.

Sally looked haggard but acted and talked quite her usual self. Chad was quiet, but his jumpy nerves were gone. I
knew he'd had a good night's sleep. I said something polite about sleep having been good for all of us and Sally
said yes, she'd certainly been dead to the world—she hadn't
even heard me come back from mailing my letter. I knew
that was true enough, but I said I hoped I hadn't disturbed
anybody. I'd tried to be as quiet as a mouse. She said she'd
made Chad take a sedative—they'd both taken one, and
she'd hoped I'd see the bottle in the bathroom. She'd meant
to speak of it. I said an aspirin was all I ever needed.

"And I bet even that makes you feel depraved—you
school teachers." Sally will always think teachers are screwy
after that summer's experience with the Columbia bunch,
and I must admit she has something to go on.

She chatted on, pouring second cups all the way around. "We'll be pretty well tied up today, I suppose. Allen thinks Lila and I ought to be on duty up at the house. We want everything private, of course, but Lila—well, Tom Nixon may have something to say." She was, I gathered, talking about arrangements for Rhoda Sutton's funeral. "I'm sure the worst is over, though. That's what he meant last night, when he talked to you. I suppose he'll tell you more today. If he does, you'll come across, won't you, Peg?"

"The Howard family should be informed of everything and will be, I'm sure, if anything decisive develops. And from what he said last night, something must be shaping up."

Chad pushed back his chair, as though he wished the subject had not been brought up. "Markham's a phony, if there ever was one. Always slipping in and out of the place up there. Adkins didn't like it, but whatever Dad said went with him."

I wanted something more said about that, but Chad excused himself and left the house shortly, even if it was Sunday, for an essential hour at his office before the family duties claimed him, and Sally said she had some plans to make with Norine. Whatever it was that Adkins didn't like could be put on the list for Tom to ask about.

Like a proper guest, I merged into the background for a while until I heard Sally answering the telephone with a "Why, yes, but not for another hour maybe. . . . Very well, we'll wait here."

She came on upstairs saying, "I've got to take time off for a manicure. Let's do nails together, Peg. We're to stay here anyway, until Tom comes or calls again. All this importance is going to his head. He doesn't even say please, just pushes us around."

I followed her into her room and watched her produce a professional array of stuff for a manicure. "My nails are a sight," she murmured. "When I pick flowers I always start to weed and then I'm grubby. See—" Her fingers were earth-stained, but I also noted that she had two broken nails. "Take your choice. Peg. I've got all the violent shades, but nothing pale-pink or pearly. Try a little Helmet Red—you're a million miles from chalk and blackboards."

But as she scrubbed and filed I hovered over her array of perfume bottles. "Sally, my love, I'd expect to find quarts of *femme fatale* stuff here, but something as ladylike and prim as this 'Faded Flowers'—how come?"

"Help yourself. I never use it. As a matter of fact, Felicity gave me that for my birthday." But the bottle was half empty, just as the one that had vanished from Felicity's dressing-table had been. I said nothing except, "Um-m, it's nice," and waved the stopper under my nose.

"Lucy should be doing this job," observed Sally, frowning at one of the broken nails, "but I can't risk the local Beauty Shoppe till some of the excitement dies down. As I've said before, Peg, there are times when this town gets me down."

"Which reminds me, Sally, I'm bursting with vulgar curiosity. How did you come to marry Chad, anyway, and come here to live?"

"A question I often ask myself, old dear. Met him in New York, of course. He was on for the motor show—you know he runs the biggest agency here. He was with some people at a place on 53rd one night and I was with some other people and somebody knew somebody else and the two groups melted together and there we were. He liked me right away and I thought he was sort of sweet, and he was—and is, and he kinda stuck around. I was so fed up with my job just then that I didn't mind at all when he explained about his business being off somewhere in a little town. I didn't know much about little towns—and God knows, I don't yet. But Chad's always saying he'll get out sometime. Now that his father's dead. . . ." She fell silent. "You realize, don't you, that Papa had the mostest of the money?"

"So this business of the wills does make a lot of differ-ence," I said.

"It means we stay right here running a small-town agen-cy and repair shop, and I'll have to be like Lila, and like it. Only I can't be, and I don't like it. There isn't much mon-ey in it, for one thing. I could do better for myself, right now, in New York. I was good at my job and all this styling has boomed since then. Chad is—oh, I love him and he's all right, but he's not as clever as Bart nor the sound busi-ness man that Allen is, and I know it. If I must let down my hair—" She waved a finished hand and sighed. "I say, Peg—"

"Well, what?"

"Don't think me ghoulish or anything, but you knew Felicity. What will become of the money? Will there be relatives bobbing up?"

"As far as I know, no one immediate. No one has said anything to me about her leaving a will, and if an estate has to be administered, they advertise for heirs, I believe, and claimants always turn up, and it will take ages. That much I do know."

Sally sighed again and began to put away her imple-ments. "However the mess turns out, I'm betting that Lila will be queening it from River View. Allen would be fool enough to buy the place. She longs for a station wagon."

"And Bart?" I asked.

"Bart will lie low. He'd better—"

Whether that was a threat or an observation I was not to learn, for a car honked peremptorily from the street below and Sally dashed downstairs. I followed as soon as I caught the sound of Tom Nixon's voice.

"I thought you'd like to know what's just turned up. The missing gun. It's a .32, anyway, and the necessary tests will soon be under way. The hot stuff is that it was buried in Wilson Markham's garden."

Sally clapped her hands as if in applause and Tom blinked at her resplendent polish.

I opened my mouth but before I could speak he added, "Yep, the old boy reported the find himself, which seems a bit odd, and he swears almost with tears in his eyes that he would never have ruined his Canterbury chimes or whatever they are. However—"

I interrupted. "Why, only at breakfast Chad was saying that he was always up to queer things at River View. I do believe you're on the right track, Tom." I hoped he understood what I was passing on to him. He gave me a quick, level look and said, "Lots of loose ends yet, but we're getting somewhere. I'll have more to report later. You're going up to River View, I understand. I'll be seeing you there. Oh, yes—about the inquest. Paulding can take it in the morning early, before the funeral. Marg has to attend and Daisy, but the rest of you won't be called." He made off as suddenly as he had arrived.

We made ourselves ready for what would probably be a day at River View and set off in my car, as Chad had the Buick. Sally had little to say other than hostesslike comments on the local landmarks, but she did no more sighing.

The big house high above the river was in decorous silence and shining order when we arrived. Adkins in a clean Sunday shirt was gloomily surveying Mrs. Sutton's garden and Daisy was at work in the kitchen. There was no sign of Bart. Allen, Daisy said, had gone in after Lila. Their arrival followed ours within ten minutes. I hardly knew what I was expected to do. Sooner or later I hoped to be allowed to pack up Felicity's personal effects and yet I realized that there would probably be legal reasons why nothing could be touched now, even if there were not a Lila to cope with.

As soon as Lila had given the lower floor a critical once-over, she mounted to Rhoda Sutton's apartment. Allen

invited Sally to accompany her, a proposal she declined.
Lila purred in pleased approval. She knew what Aunt Rhoda
would want, she murmured.

"Grave clothes," Sally muttered, and selected a magazine.

As soon as Lila went up Bart came down, greeted us
casually, and asked whether anyone had stopped at the
post office for mail. Then Chad drove up, looking full of
news. It appeared that he had just learned about the gun in
Markham's garden—from Tom Nixon, of course, but Sally
and I already had heard about that. And so had Allen, it
developed. Tom had certainly made the rounds. Thus it was
news only to Bart, who made no comment other than an
unimpressed grunt from behind his newspaper.

Time dragged on. Lila reappeared bearing a couple of
cardboard boxes and asked Allen what about getting them
down to Paulding's. He said after lunch would be time
enough and Lila went out to speak to Daisy, about lunch
presumably. I had the feeling that something was on Allen
Howard's mind, which my presence was keeping there. Several times he drew a letter from his pocket and then put
it back, so at last I wandered off into the library to see if
anything would happen, but I thought it would look a bit
pointed if I closed the door. There was a prompt murmur of
voices. I didn't want to hear, goodness knows, and I didn't
try to, but in a few minutes I heard Sally in clear protest.

"But, Allen, I insist. I want Peg to know. She ought to
know. Peg! Peg, please come here."

So I joined the family, as meechingly as my nature per-
mits. Lila glared at me distastefully and Sally was leaning
forward from her chair, all tense excitement again. Chad
and Bart rose politely as I entered, and as Bart seated me
with exaggerated courtesy he gave me what I swear was a
slight, malicious wink. Allen continued to stand, like the
chairman of a meeting, with an open letter in his hand.

"I'm sure, Miss Lenox," he began in his steady pleasant voice, "that it's quite unnecessary to inflict these family matters upon you, but then, there's really no reason to refuse Sally's—er—request. She—er—we all are, naturally, a bit edgy because of what we are going through."

"It's about Felicity. Tell her, Allen. Don't talk around so," Sally commanded.

"This letter—in the mail this morning. I stopped at the post office. It was my duty to take charge of it." That, I thought, was directed at Bart, who murmured something unintelligible and lighted a cigarette.

"The letter is a brief communication from a person quite unknown to me, a lawyer in Des Moines. He states that a news item of the death of Mrs. Jordan Howard has come to his attention and that he wishes to inform whoever should be concerned that he has in his files a will drawn by her before the date of her marriage. In case no later testament is at hand, anyone officially in charge here may take the matter up with him at any time."

I made at sudden resolution. It was time to speak. There was no reason at all to keep on concealing my connection with Felicity. And so I told them. I couldn't figure out how Sally took my revelation, but Chad's foot began to swing nervously and Bart raised cynical eyebrows. Allen listened gravely without antagonism and said nothing, largely because of the torrent of speech from Lila.

"I told you so—I told you so. She'll dispose of everything. You must start at once, Allen. Break the will—you must. Your father's property belongs to you—and the boys, of course."

"There are three of us, dear Lila. So glad you remembered," Bart drawled.

Allen's firm composure prevailed. "Just a minute, my dear. One will at a time. I should like to ask Miss Lenox some questions. In the circumstances, I for one, welcome the presence of someone belonging, so to speak, to my father's wife. I assure you it distressed me to think of her being so alone."

To me it sounded genuine and I turned to him gladly. "Anything at all, Mr. Howard. Felicity Wendell was my dear friend."

"Did you, by any chance, know of this will?"

I did not, but I told him I knew of the law firm in Des Moines and that it was respectability itself.

"There is no need to anticipate—we shall know in due time what it provides. You understand that we are not yet certain about a later will. I should be inclined to think that if she made one, she'd have made another, after her marriage."

"After your father's death, more likely," Lila put in. "Fond as we were of one another, she was reserved about her affairs. I mean, she never poured out details. Certainly she wasn't haphazard about business matters. I should say, if she had made another will, she would have informed the Des Moines lawyer."

"That's a point, yes. Now, Miss Lenox, do you know anything of her people? My father told us at the time of the marriage that she had no close relatives."

"I know of none. Her parents were dead and she'd been an only child. But it's likely that distant connections of some sort might be heard from, if an estate is to be settled." I said that purposely to annoy Lila.

"Yes, very likely. Well, I shall turn this letter over to Blair."

Lila broke in fretfully. "Allen, are you sure you've looked everywhere? You should insist that Nixon give you those keys."

I knew what keys she meant and I also knew there was no will in Felicity's desk, but it was for Allen Howard to speak.

"My dear, I have Tom's word that nothing was found that pertains to our problems. And Blair is quite definite about having done no business for Felicity herself, though I admit there's still a chance that something may yet be found. In any event, we know now that a will exists, and how that may complicate matters— And by the way, Miss Lenox, I should like to ask one favor. When the proper time comes, if you will be so good as to take charge of packing Felicity's personal effects—"

I jumped at that chance so promptly that I didn't even let him finish, though it was easy to see the others were not seconding Allen's request. However, Daisy announced lunch at that point and any rising friction was allayed for the time.

Before we had finished, Tom Nixon arrived. He appeared at the doorway just long enough to say that as soon as we were ready he wished to see us all in the front living room. Mr. Wilson Markham had come up with him to make a statement that it was our right to hear.

6

So there we were, the five Howards, Tom and I, and Wilson Markham, ranged in a grave circle in the formal elegance of the front living room. I noticed at once that the old man looked pale and determined and I felt a sudden rush of pity mingled with recoil from the whole miserable business, no matter what we were going to hear. I almost wished I had minded my own business and stayed in Iowa, as Felicity had wished me to do. But I was Felicity's next friend and she still needed me.

Tom glanced around the circle of waiting, inscrutable faces and began to speak. "Mr. Markham and I have had some very frank talk and certain matters are now very clear. He wishes to tell you himself something that I know you will find quite conclusive. And then—well, I'm afraid the next move will be inevitable. Go ahead, Mr. Markham, if you please."

The old gentlemen straightened himself in his chair. His hands, quite steady, lay relaxed along the arms. One long thin finger tapped soundlessly for an instant upon the upholstery. He did not look at anyone directly, except once or twice at Tom.

"I feel that I must tell you that it was I who killed Rhoda Sutton, but I must also tell you the reason that I did so."

Lila started to scream, but Allen gripped her arm hard. Sally let out a long gasp and Chad huddled forward, his head thrust out, as if he were deaf. Bart's cigarette burned down to his fingers and he jerked at the pain. But Tom held us all with a commanding gesture and Markham went on.

"You see, Mrs. Sutton murdered Felicity Howard and I could not let that pass."

Tom gave a quick glance at Allen, whose face was utterly blank.

"I stood it as long as I could and then I acted as executioner. She was a poisonous woman—I never liked her."

Sally gulped at that and I expected hysterics.

As if explaining, he added gently, "I did not find it hard to do, you understand. It seemed the most direct way to silence her groundless accusations. The law's delays are interminable and I found it impossible to wait. So, after reaching my irrevocable conclusion, I walked up here the other night. I knew it was likely she was alone, that we would not be disturbed. I know this place well—she was my friend's wife. I had keys—a shop like mine contains a heterogeneous mixture. It provided me with the necessary weapon also, as Mr. Nixon now knows. I entered and started up the back stairs. Rhoda Sutton's ears were good; she heard me and I was forced to act more quickly than I had planned. I intended to tell her what was about to happen and why. I then left at once, for I confess that I had forgotten the presence of the cook and I heard her stirring above. I had planned to leave by the river and that worked out very smoothly. The boat got away from me, just as I had also planned, but it was a warm night and the soaking did me no harm.

"Naturally, I was human enough to have hoped not to be involved. But it appears that I was a bit careless about my wet clothes, as a certain observant guest of mine noted, and Tom Nixon pointed out a number of other things to me, and after all, I had accomplished my purpose. It was histrionic of me to bury the gun and then find it myself, but you see I'm not experienced in these matters."

He stopped speaking, just as if there were no more to be said. Bart made a quick harsh sound and Sally's tight fists slowly unclinched, revealing those atrociously painted nails. Allen fumbled at his collar, but Tom prompted quietly, as though the story had been carefully rehearsed, "Go on, Mr. Markham. About the flower, you know."

"Oh, yes, the flower. I'm truly sorry that was necessary, Miss Lenox. I tried particularly not to hurt you. I did not realize at the time that I had dropped the flower, the little sprig I had broken from one of the bouquets, just as a keepsake. I had been deeply drawn to Felicity Howard. She was kind to me and understanding, a fine, lovely woman."

Lila sniffed at that, too horribly in the style of the unlamented Rhoda Sutton. Even Wilson Markham noticed it. "No, not that," he murmured. "Certainly not that, though I know I cannot control your thoughts." His eyes rested so unwaveringly upon Lila Howard that she shivered and squeaked out a little protesting whimper.

Then he went on, his voice still steady and normal. "You must know that I came back here instead of going to Felicity's burial. I was sure I would have the place to myself—I had no way of knowing about Miss Lenox, you see. I knew that Felicity Howard had been murdered and I hoped to find some evidence. I must have dropped the flower sprig then. Tom says it was found caught under a rug in Jordan's room. Well, I had slipped in there when I realized that someone else was about, but all I know about the flower is

that when I got back to my own apartment I did not have
it. I thought nothing further of it until Tom and I got to
talking things over."

"But the bottle of cologne, Mr. Markham?" I hardly
knew I asked the question.

"Odd of me, wasn't it? As I said, I'm not practiced in
these matters. I had gone through the room, conscious of
its being—her room, and I'm old-fashioned and sentimental,
no doubt. In short, I had let a little of the fragrance in the
bottle make more vivid to me the living woman—I did not
want to remember her lying in her coffin. And as I stood
there in the darkness of the adjoining room and watched
what then was a strange woman to me—yourself, Miss
Lenox—make a peculiar discovery about the bottle and then
remove it carefully as if for further investigation, I realized
that it would show my fingerprints and so—I acted as I did.
I am indeed sorry that I was forced to subject you to such
an unpleasant experience. The bottle very shortly there-
after went into the river. Tom has all the data on that."

It all sounded possible, but my head was swimming.
What Bart said steadied me. "And the evidence you hoped
to find, Markham? What luck, may I ask?"

"Something, yes. A bullet hole in the back stairs. But I
could do nothing then. Miss Lenox's presence forced me to
get away. It was a good thing I had used the old road, or I
should have met Daisy and her young relative returning. As
a matter of record, Tom reports that the lad did observe me
coming back into town."

Allen Howard at last got out a comment. "You have accused my aunt of a crime. What evidence have you for such
a charge?"

"The bullet hole, for one thing. Didn't I say that when
I entered the house the other night Rhoda Sutton heard me
at once? She was at work upon the back stairs, digging out
a bullet. I got it before I left. Nixon has it now."

"Ridiculous. No proof at all. You killed her yourself."

"No, I did not kill Felicity Howard."

Maybe I was the only one in the group who believed him, though he certainly had not proved his charge against Rhoda Sutton.

A point which Bart Howard promptly took up. "You'll have to do better than that, Markham," he finished.

"I can, if it's necessary," he replied. "Mr. Nixon has no evidence at all that I was here at the time of Mrs. Howard's death, though other people were. Nor could I possibly be involved in the events that occurred the morning that my friend Jordan Howard died."

A queer silence fell. It was as if each one of the family, were facing the situation as it concerned himself. As for me, I was thinking that Tom Nixon possessed evidence that both Felicity and Rhoda Sutton had been shot by the same gun. What on earth was he up to? And how contradictory was this confession of Wilson Markham's to his calm detachment about revenge in our conversation the preceding morning.

"Aunt Rhoda hated Felicity—we all know she did," Sally said at last. "She can't answer now for what she did or did not do. That wouldn't have to be argued, would it, Allen? I mean, in a trial now—now that Mr. Markham has said what he has."

I could see how she was putting the matter to the others. Allen turned to Tom as though he wanted him to answer, but Tom said nothing.

"But if you want to know what I really think," Sally went on impetuously, "Aunt Rhoda deliberately framed Felicity, from the poison in the bottle of lotion to making it look like suicide when Felicity was shot."

"Sally Howard, how perfectly vile!" Lila blazed, and Allen shook his head in protest. Chad turned a shocked, unbelieving face to his wife.

It was Bart who smoothly dropped the point. "I gather, Nixon, that you are prepared to act upon Markham's statement."

Tom's nod of assent was solemn.

"Then by all means proceed with the case against the man for his self-confessed murder of my aunt. We shall give you every assistance." For the first time I caught a faint likeness to his older brother. He had been Rhoda Sutton's favorite and her dreadful death had surely touched him more profoundly that he had shown so far I until now. Yet he had listened to Sally's accusations without apparent emotion.

"I believe, Mr. Nixon, that that is all that I need to say." A calm reminder from Wilson Markham.

Tom rose. "I have only to add that Markham is being held, of course, but nothing public will be done until after Mrs. Sutton's funeral, unless you insist." His eyes queried Allen Howard. "The inquest in the morning will come to a speedy adjournment until later."

"No, oh no. Much better to wait. I—we appreciate your consideration of the family. The publicity that we shall have to face—" He drew out a handkerchief and mopped his forehead. Hesitantly he followed Tom and the old man, who were moving toward the door. I rose too and slipped out after them.

"I may need to see you later, Miss Lenox," Tom said, the formality for Allen's benefit. "You will remain here." I took it as an order and nodded my answer.

Allen opened the door and watched Markham descend the steps to Tom's car. Perhaps he suspected the old fellow would attempt an escape. It all seemed casual and unreal to me. As Tom passed me I managed to whisper, "What does it mean?"

"I know you don't want to believe a word of it, but I'm I telling you, you'd better!"

7

I followed Allen back into the living room where the others were just as we had left them. My being there was now creating no resentment.

"In my opinion," said Allen, "the first thing to do now is to call Blair and ask him to come out here. He must see that letter from Des Moines and we should be guided by his advice in the Markham matter. The old chap will probably plead insanity."

"Why, Allen, you talk as though you didn't want—"

He cut Lila off. "I want a minimum of publicity. That's what we all want, surely."

"Publicity is what we'll get, and plenty of it. We can't stay barricaded here forever. I shan't, I assure you," Bart announced.

"And what will you use for money?" That was Lila, and there was deliberate sweetness in her tone.

"Borrow on my expectations, my lamb. Or go off to the foreign wars. 'A soldier of the legion—'"

"'—lay dying in Algiers.'" Sally and I finished it together.

"No more dying, please. But I shan't hang around here for the next decade waiting for a tangled estate to be settled. I shall leave that to Chad and Allen and their—er—canny helpmates." Bart was rapidly returning to his normal manner.

"You might as well know now as after the funeral, though Blair needn't know I've mentioned it. Aunt Rhoda has a will and I can foresee no difficulty about that." There was something almost placating about Allen's words. "She had very little of her own, as you well know, but she's left her few bonds to Bart and all her personal effects to Lila."

Chad flushed a little but Bart carefully said nothing. Sally gave me an infinitesimal nod, all of which Allen noted. He went on in a hurry. "Of course she expected to make other arrangements if—" He stopped abruptly.

"If Father Howard's first will had held," Sally finished. "That fit in with my idea neatly, thank you, Allen. She wanted Felicity out of the way before he got around to changing his will. But he'd taken care of that without her knowledge."

"Fortunately or unfortunately, Sally?"

"That's not for an in-law to say, Bart. She didn't know—that's sure. She'd never have killed her brother-in-law merely to hand over his property to his widow she hated."

"Sally, that's quite enough. This is getting us nowhere." Allen was quite the head of the house. "I'm calling Blair now, and Paulding's too. They can send someone out for those boxes. And, Lila, I think you should lie down."

He left for the telephone in the library and Chad tagged after him. Lila dragged herself upstairs. Bart settled himself in another, more comfortable chair and gave himself over to meditation. I went on through the middle living room toward the terrace and Sally followed me uncertainly.

"I think I'll stay in here, if you don't mind," she called to me, "Chad may want me, and I—I don't feel like talking."

I didn't either. I'd had about enough of the Howard bickering. I wanted to think, to sort things out.

I wanted particularly to consider the one thing I could not fit in, unless Tom Nixon had been handing me a line. He had called me out last night to tell me in high triumph that the shots that had ended the lives of both Felicity and Rhoda Sutton had come from the same weapon. This afternoon he had ignored that fact completely, and Markham had stated that the gun he used had come into his possession quite normally in the course of his junk shop business. When Tom talked to me the gun was still missing. This morning Markham himself recovered it from his own garden. The old man must be crazy, digging it up himself and presenting it to Tom. The tests must have gone right though, or he'd never have produced Markham and his story this afternoon. He had a lot to tell me. He must have had a busy morning.

I stirred comfortably on my long sun chair and looked out across the river. There had been nothing but silence from the house behind me. I learned later that Blair had come up in obedient haste and that he and Allen talked at length behind the library door. Now Sally appeared to call me to the telephone.

"Paulding's men are here, too," she said. "Everything will be ready before long—in there." She gestured wanly toward the front living room and I knew that meant that a second coffin was being placed there. "Bart's got the right idea—to get away as soon as we can. I need a drink, I guess."

Allen and the lawyer withdrew from the library as I entered. Maybe it was courtesy; maybe their conference was at an end. It was nothing to me and I closed the door. I hoped it was Tom Nixon and it was.

"Excuse yourself and come in to town," he said. "I'll stand you to dinner."

"Fish sandwiches? I don't like 'em."

"You'll eat 'em—you'll be so held by my answers to all the questions you're going to ask me."

"I'm glad you're prepared. My question are all ready. I'll be down."

"I'll pick you up at Sally's. . . ."

An occasion, evidently, not a street-corner rendezvous.

"You'll be glad to get rid of me, I know," I explained to Sally. "You'll be having some people the family will have to see, and I'm no help at all with that."

"Yes—no. Aunt Rhoda has always lived here and there are a few old friends that Allen and Lila insist on seeing, but the service tomorrow is to be strictly family, thank God. But you've been wonderful, Peg."

I was glad to get away. The house in town was cool and quiet. By the time I had bathed and changed, confining my mental processes to nothing more serious than dusting powder and a careful hair-do, I decided I felt more human than I had since my arrival in Point Tyler.

Tom drove me back up in the hills to a delightful home-cooking place and plied me with fried chicken, corn fritters, and iced coffee. Of course we talked and at great length. Nor did I have to bring up the subject or fish for information.

"I know it looks screwy as hell, Marg, but I think I'm going to accomplish something. And don't fool yourself, the old chap's a stout fellow."

"But he confessed—"

"Sure he did, but let me tell you about this morning. He found the gun, bright and early, and reported the same to me. Neither of us knows how it got there, but he's convinced his precious garden was undisturbed last night, and I know that the whole place had been gone over inside and out without finding a thing. By the time I got there it had his prints on it, right enough, nice fresh ones, but no others. And it is the gun that killed both women."

"I thought you said you had a man watching."

"I had, but not such a hot number, between you and me. Jud said he hadn't seen a thing."

"What sort of marks round about? Surely there must have been something. The ground would still have been damp after the downpour the night before."

"Nothing much to be sure about. Some plain traces of Markham's shoes, the ones he was then wearing, and some vague ones that could be his too. Or 'most anyone's whose feet were normal in size. No heel prints. Are you guessing anything?"

"No-o, and I'm afraid I don't want to. But I guess I'll have to tell you that Sally was out of the house somewhere last night while I was out with you. She doesn't know I know."

"So? Could be, but—well, I'll fit that in later, if I have to. I want to go on with the Markham set-up. As soon as I am positive about the gun being the right one, I went to work on him. At first he denied everything, not so much as though he was scared, more as if it wasn't any of my business what he chose to do. Then I happened to say that I knew there were three murders to be explained, and that tore it. You mean, he said, you don't believe Felicity How-ard killed herself? No, I told him, and if she was involved in her husband's death, it was an innocent action on her part. Someone else made all the arrangements."

I choked up at that and Tom patted my hand. "You see," he whispered, "I'm hoping it's going to come out right for you."

I wiped my eyes. "Go on," I begged.

"So then the old boy said, 'If you will assure me that Mrs. Howard's name will be completely cleared, I shall make a statement to you that can solve the problem.' But believe me, I had to do some assuring before he would go on. He *knew,* he said, and he was positive as you are, Marg, that Felicity Howard would never have committed suicide. He gets beside himself at the thought. He accuses Rhoda Sutton of everything, though Howard's death itself he's quite calm about. But he admits he has no real evidence. So first he told me about coming back to the house in the hope of finding something while everyone was at the cemetery. He found the bullet hole in the back stairway and then you sidetracked him.

"The bullet hole does not point to Rhoda in itself, but I didn't say anything except to remind him that he was the person who had removed the load from Howard's revolver. His own story for that.

"'So you do see, she could not have killed herself. Rhoda Sutton murdered her, and I—I killed her.' Just like that he said it."

"You don't believe it, Tom, do you?"

"No, Marg. But it could be, and he admitted it."

"Why did you let him?"

"I shouldn't think I'd have to tell you. I think I'm going to catch the real murderer. The Howards were feeling pretty good, weren't they? After we left, sighs of relief and nothing to worry about now, huh?"

"Don't underestimate the Howards, any of 'em." I was surprised at the bitterness in my tone.

"I'm not merely waiting for someone to give himself away, Marg. I've got ideas, and I'm going to act. Surely you know that everything's not accounted for. But I've got a little time now, and suspicions have been allayed."

"I hope to goodness you've got ideas about poison disappearing from a bottle of mosquito-bite lotion and about gardening gloves and all the rest of it. And the alibis. Everybody was around and nobody was around, and all three of the Howard men were in and out and here and there the night Rhoda was shot. And I shouldn't be surprised to hear that nothing much was wrong with Bart's car—"

"How right you are. There wasn't. I've got that cleaned up already. Just another secret you know nothing about, if anyone's curious, but it would be nice to know who's curious. And Sally was out prowling last night. I wish I'd seen her. Was she wearing heels?"

I'm afraid I looked blank. It took me a minute to see the point of his question. "I heard no heels, but she was wearing dress pumps when we broke up last night. She has all sorts of shoes."

"Pretty feet, Sally has, and big enough for her height. Pretty hands, too. That stuff she uses on 'em sure catches the eye."

I didn't want to say it but I did. "She gave herself a thorough manicure this morning, right after breakfast. Her nails were a sight, really. Two bad breaks. She said she'd been weeding."

I don't know what that might have led to, for at that moment Mrs. Home Cooking emerged from her kitchen and interrupted us. "Are you a Mr. Nixon from Point Tyler?" She asked. "It's the phone. They're trying to locate the lady that's with you. It's long distance, seems like."

It was a wretched place to talk, that wall telephone in a dark passage way loud with the clatter of dishes from the kitchen, but the connection was made at last. I realized, of course before I got my "party" that the call was coming from home and I expected it would be Charlotte's voice that I would hear. But it wasn't; it was Ellen Hawke.

"Charlotte Larsen has just left. I guessed right away what she was up in the air about—there was quite an item in this morning's *Gazette* about poor Felicity Wendell, and I thought maybe I'd better talk to you myself. The paper said she had no near relatives, but I happen to know that's not so. I wrote to Felicity myself about it. Yes, a father, if you please, in a way . . . I ought to know. He's a kind of connection of mine, by marriage. I don't mind saying that my family were never particularly proud of the fact. To tell you the truth, I never knew a thing about it until this spring. Easter holidays, remember, I went to see a cousin of mine in St. Louis and we got to talking. And when I came home, I wrote to Felicity. I thought she might like to know. . . . She wrote me a pretty snippy letter . . ."

Again I tried to interrupt. "Who is he? Where can he be reached?"

"That I don't know—where he is, but I'd say he'd turn up, if Felicity's left anything. His name's not the same as hers, if you know what I mean. His name's Markham—Wilson Markham. Maybe my cousin would know—"

But I had broken the connection. I turned to Tom, who had been shamelessly hovering in the doorway. "The motive—I think it's come to light."

Part Six
Monday and Tuesday, June 20 and 21

1

We returned to Point Tyler at once. Tom was depressed and silent. His faked case against Markham Wilson was going to hold up after all and now it was his turn not to want to believe it. But somehow, I believed it. A father would do a thing like that for a daughter like Felicity, even though the relationship were illegal. For I did not doubt Ellen Hawke's story. I knew Ellen. She never made things up and she never failed to trace any unsavory detail as far as she could hound it and she never forgot an iota of a scandalous story. My use of words like that shows how quickly I had accepted the impression she had called from Iowa to give me.

"What I can't see," I burst out as we went speeding through the summer darkness, "is that Felicity did anything about what Ellen Hawke told her. I'd say she didn't believe it. Certainly her reply to Ellen gave that gal no satisfaction. And she never hinted a thing to me."

I recalled how few letters had passed between us from spring vacation on. "She might have told me, though, if—"

"That may all come out, Marg, when we talk to the old man. If the story's true, I don't expect him to deny it. I'd like to check what your girl friend told you, though. It might look more regular."

"Can do. There is a cousin in St. Louis. They all go in for family reunions and fifth cousins twice removed and stuff like that. But I think he'll tell you everything you want to know. Are you going to see him tonight?"

"No-o, I hardly think so. There's something else I want to do before he verifies the story. I'm going to take you back to Sally's." He hesitated a little, but he did not tell me what it was he wanted to do. "If I thought there was any chance of not finding a lot of other people up at River View, I'd be almost tempted to run you right up there. In any case, I want the family to hear about Markham's relation to Felicity as soon as I know for sure that he'll admit it."

"Shall I say anything to Sally about it tonight? They'll be back for the night, I'm sure."

Again he hesitated. "No-o, better not. I want them all to hear, you see, but I'd like to know how Markham takes it first. Tell you what, Marg. If it can possibly be managed, I want you to sit in on my interview with the old gentleman. The inquest's the first thing tomorrow morning, but it will be just a perfunctory opener. None of this hot stuff is going to come out till later. After that we'll talk to Markham and then maybe before the funeral service you can spill the news to the family. They'll like it, what?"

The odd hour at which the Sutton inquest was held had been necessary for some reason connected with Paulding's business as well as for the reason of the intervening Sunday. The result was fortunate, if only that there were few curious outsiders present. The routine was well managed. There was no question that it was murder, and all that Tom wanted for the moment was a postponement. Godfrey Blair was present to look out for the family interests, but none of the Howards was called to testify. Daisy and Dr. Ammon, the sheriff and Tom and I were heard from. Daisy was the chief witness and her loquaciousness was skillfully curbed. It was quickly established that she and Mrs. Sutton had been alone in the house, that Daisy had been wakened by the sound of a shot followed by running feet without, that she had come down from her third-floor room to find Mrs.

Sutton lying in the back hallway, and that she had promptly telephoned for help.

The discovery of the missing boat was duly entered, both its disappearance and recovery early the next afternoon. A few ponderous questions from Paulding led to Tom's statement that the island had been carefully searched but with no positive results and that he was still waiting to receive some essential reports that he expected would bear directly upon the affair. An adjournment until a later date was then in order, and that was that.

I oozed out at once and headed toward Markham's shop, as I had been instructed to do. If the Howards assumed that Wilson Markham's present address was the local hoosegow, they were assuming too much. There was nothing to indicate that the run-down place was under surveillance, though I could easily be wrong about that. Tom's car without announced that he was already there. No one was in the shop. I walked back into Markham's living quarters. No one about. The two men were in the garden blandly admiring posies.

"Ah, Miss Lenox! Good morning. I'm glad to have you here again." Quite as though nothing much had happened since I had last surveyed his garden. "You have something to tell me, Nixon says. Shan't we sit here? It's delightfully cool in the shade. These old canvas chairs may not look elegant, but I promise you, they're comfortable."

With that sort of preamble I was to confront him with Ellen Hawke's information. Tom signaled me to take the lead. I think it was Markham's old-fashioned courtesy that affected my own manner. Tom accused me later of sounding quite like an old-maid schoolteacher, but I thought I was being calm and dignified.

"Felicity Howard was my dear friend. You have been informed of that and understand that my concern in this matter of her death is genuine and very proper. I knew her all these years as Felicity Wendell. Last night I received information that she was your daughter. Is that true, Mr. Markham?"

He looked off across the river to the Ohio hills and smiled a little, proudly. Then his eyes met ours, first Tom's and then mine, and they were very steady. "Yes," he said. "It is true. She was my daughter. So—you understand."

"I can understand, yes—that it might have been unbearable to have foul things said of her. But—"

"That is what I mean, Miss Lenox. I had persuaded her to keep our secret before—and I thought it unnecessary to reveal it since her death. But if others know . . ." He shook his head wearily, as if he had been bested.

"So she knew who you were. Had she known it before she came here, or did you tell her?"

"No, to both questions, Miss Lenox. She told me about it herself, in the spring. She wanted to—" His voice quivered a little. "But I persuaded her not to speak, even to Jordan Howard. Perhaps that was a mistake, though surely none of them knew—or guessed. No, they would never have kept silent. It would only have been a new way to torture Felicity. My side of the story would have appeared dishonorable. I have a share in the story, I assure you."

"Could you prove it?" He gave me a quick look that reached my heart. "Oh, I don't mean that, Mr. Markham. I mean, how did you know what Felicity told you was true? Did you know her all along?"

"I knew nothing. I suspected nothing. But from the first time I saw her, when she came here as Jordan's wife, I was reminded of—her mother. We grew to be friends. We had many tastes in common, and she was always a little lonely, except for her husband's devotion. The marriage was not a mistake in itself, Miss Lenox." He shot that at me almost argumentatively. "But the others resented her, as so often happens. No, we knew nothing until a few months ago. Then she came to me and asked whether I had ever known a girl named Frances Dunroy. As soon as she spoke the name I knew.

"She told me Frances Dunroy was her mother and that her mother had told her before she died that the man she had always called her father and whom she had always loved as a father was not her own father. However, she had refused to give her the name of this man, insisted that she did not know his real name, which was, God help me, the truth. I was in trouble with my own people at the time I met Frances and I played the part of a romantic young fool, though I was old enough to know better. Frances and I loved one another very much and we planned to be married. I give you my word—we were to be married, but my family, and hers too—we were separated very successfully. Frances had always been regarded as a child by her parents and dominated by them, and I—I had broken away from mine and played the prodigal. I may say that I never returned—to be feasted and forgiven, that is. But I could not find Frances, thanks to the upright Dunroys, and she did not know my real name. And I could not know about the child . . ."

He cleared his throat and went on with a hint of apology. "But the details of that old story are not vital to you now. Forgive me for digressing. To return to Felicity's talk with me: she asked me then whether I was this man. I told her that I had no knowledge that I was the father of Frances Dunroy's child, but knowing Frances I could not believe that any other man was, since there was no question that the man who later became her husband was Felicity's father.

"I asked her in my turn why she had come to me. She told me that she had received a letter from a family connection of the Markhams who apparently had unearthed the story of the black sheep's vain search for a young woman named Dunroy, to make an honest woman of her. You see, I had crawled back to my father once, for at that time I was frantic for money to continue my hunt for Frances.

This kind soul had written Felicity that an in-law cousin years later had met a Mrs. Wendell on the West Coast who had told her casually that her name before she was married had been Frances Dunroy and that in mulling over family history and old times generally they'd come to the conclusion that this was the girl that somebody or other's Cousin Wilson had stormed the castle about so many years before. She just wondered, this friend had written, if Felicity could help them out with any information."

I pawed the air at that, for I could so easily picture the gusto with which Ellen Hawke had nosed down that ancient bit of family scandal.

"Felicity came to me at once with her question, for my name was Wilson Markham. I asked her then who had given her her name, Felicity. She told me that it was her mother's choice and that she had always been proud of it, and still was. That told me everything I wanted to know . . .

"But there was much to be said between us, just the same. I need not go into that. She told me that her mother's life with James Wendell had been serene and happy and that she herself would always remember him as a loving father, but that it was a deep satisfaction to her to know the truth. She was a little disturbed, I could see, about our present relationship, but I begged her to let it rest between us. Jordan Howard was already my good friend and it would be only natural for his new wife to be included in that friendship. And, as far as I know, our secret remained our secret."

He stopped as if he had no more to say. I looked at Tom Nixon, for I felt that the next step was up to him. He rose to his feet and stalked up and down the garden, scowling at the flowers.

"And so what?" he burst out. "My problem's still to be solved. I know you did not kill Rhoda Sutton, but I've let you go on record with your story and you've just now presented us with a motive that will hold like glue. And,

Markham, I want the Howards to know what it is. Will you do that one more thing for your daughter?"

The old man folded his hands and looked off at the clouds for an instant. "Yes, Tom, you know I will. I have already made my decision. My solution is a good one."

Tom drew out his watch. "Okay, Marg. Beat it up to River View and do your stuff."

2

At River View I made a decorous entrance just as Lila and Sally were descending the stairs to join the men in the library. I followed them, and there was no need for me to counterfeit nervous excitement, for I was all on edge. It seemed so unspeakably not the time and place to let fall my news, but Tom's orders were orders.

"Whatever's the matter, Peg?" Sally demanded. "You're jittering."

"The most amazing fact has just come to light. I've got to tell you—you've a right to know. Wilson Markham killed—did what he did, because he's Felicity's father."

It was a jolt all right, but surprise was all I could be sure of. I had just started to answer questions when we were called to the front living room for the service. It was humanely brief. I kept my attention on the mourners, as I knew I was expected to do. Lila wept softly throughout and so did Daisy, who of course was included in the group. Allen sat like a man of stone. Sally's face was composed and quiet, but her toes kept curling beneath the slits of her slippers. High-heeled shoes again, I thought. She's worn nothing else but. I must look to see if she really owns any flat ones. Chad's expression was as inscrutable as his older brother's, but Bart's lips never stopped twitching.

Then that part was over and the trip to the cemetery began. I went along. Curtains stirred at every window as we

passed through Point Tyler and there were plenty of distant
observers at Willow Grove. Since I'd come up to River View
in my own car, maybe the family had circumvented me by
letting me use it in the procession with only Daisy as passenger. So I had to drive her back to River View. But that
was all right with me: Tom's directions had gone no further.
The family group broke up anyway, for both the Allens and
the Chads turned toward their own houses as we came back.

"And never a word to me," lamented Daisy, "about what's
going to become of me now. It's goin' on fifteen years I
been up at that house. Mis' Sutton, she wasn't always easy
to work for, but we got along. I got used to her. That big
house an' all, I wonder what the boy'll do with it. Bart
now—he's a queer one, but him an' me, we got along fine.
You any idea what'll happen now?"

Certainly I had no idea what was going to happen now
and I had no intention of discussing the tangled legal situation with Daisy. I told her, however, that as soon as it
could be arranged I was to pack up Mrs. Howard's personal
possessions.

"She was real sweet, Mis' Howard, was, but they was all
agin her before they ever set eyes on her. I'll never forget
the time their Pa's letter come, about his gettin' married
again. They was all up to the house for dinner and if they
didn't chew the rag!"

"It was hard for Mrs. Howard, coming into a family of
strangers who naturally resented her presence."

"I'll say. . . . And that Bart—I declare he done just what
he told 'em he would."

"What was that?" My interest was real now.

"That night, he talked kinda silly like—he always does.
Told 'em not to worry, he'd fix it so they kep' the money,
an' that they could always depend on their Aunt Rhoda.
I declare, Miss Lenox, that boy'll sure miss his aunt. He
always had her eatin' right outa his hand."

"But what did he do that he said he would do?"

"Oh, that—" Daisy gave a kind of embarrassed titter. "It didn't really get him nowhere, not with a lady like Mis' Howard. But he said he'd play up to her like and get her so fond of him she'd see that he got everything that was comin' to him. An' he tried it, I guess, when he didn't think no one was around."

"Just what did he do, Daisy?"

"Oh, jus' fool around, talkin' at her, an' moonin'. But Mis' Howard, I don't think she took to him much. She got so she kep' outa his way, if they was to be alone together. I declare, Miss Lenox, I never felt so sorry for anyone in my life as her when Mr. Howard died. She went around lookin' scared the whole time. The only person she ever looked real glad to see was that old coot Markham. Mis' Sutton, she oughtn't to've said what she did."

"What did she say?"

"Makin' out that Mis' Howard was takin' notice a'ready. An' him only bein' friendly an' respectful, good friends as him an' Mr. Howard had always been. Mis' Howard didn't know how to answer her. I'da give her a piece of my mind. Well, here we are, back again, same day we left. Thanks an' all for the lift. Come up any time, Miss Lenox, an' if there's anything I can do to help. . . ."

Maybe she hadn't helped any, but I certainly drove back to Point Tyler fuming at the Howards and wishing that since it could no longer be Rhoda Sutton it would be Bart that Tom was gunning for.

I drove up and down the two main streets of Point Tyler, but I saw no sign of Tom. There was a strange man lounging in front of Markham's shop whom I guessed to be a deputy guard, in case any of the Howards had discovered that the old man was not yet in jail. There was no one in sight at Allen's house, but I thought I recognized Mr. Blair turning up the stairway that led to Allen's offices. I had no idea what might have become of Bart—the last I'd seen of him was with Lila in the car. So I returned to Terrace Drive.

A little later a call came for me. It was Tom Nixon. "Stick around up there tonight, will you? There's a little job I think I'll have to ask you to do."

3

The little job proved to be weird.

"I've done a little bit of timing," Tom explained, as soon as he had called on the pretext of taking me to a late movie and we left the house, "but I want to check it with you, and in your car, if you don't mind. Yours will go more like the others. Several matters have come to a nice boil this afternoon, but this job must be done before I can talk."

My car was already garaged, but we ran it out and away with no undue noise. Tom's car, I observed, was parked along the curb two houses beyond. Tom directed me to make a memo of my mileage and to note the exact time. He did the driving without asking me. He went directly down Terrace Drive to the main street and turned into Route 62 toward River View, and he drove fast. Up the winding drive we sped, and at the last turn before sighting the house he snapped off the lights. He rolled on to the space in the back before the big garage there and turned again so that we could have started right down the drive, all without losing a minute. He swung open the door and told me to jump out and follow him. He ran down the path to the boat house. The door had a new padlock on it. He produced a key and unlocked it. It opened at once, but for some reason he fiddled at the lock for a little longer time. There was a sliding door along the water side, something like those disappearing garage doors. Bolts on the inside closed it securely to prevent any intruder from the river getting at the boats from that direction, but a few seconds were all that were needed to push the bolts back and roll up the wide door.

He used a flashlight as he worked and I could see for myself what the boat house contained. For all my concern in the events that had occurred at River View since my arrival, this was my first inspection of the boat house. There was the launch, a trim, de luxe little job, and besides there were two ordinary rowboats, one much shabbier and older than the other. No oars were in the rowlocks, but there were several pairs in racks along the wall to my right. I knew so little about watercraft that I thought this was unusual. However, Tom paid no attention to oars. He slipped a chain from a staple and pushed out the shabby gray boat with a vigorous, mighty shove.

Then he grabbed my hand and dashed back up the path toward the house. I was right at his heels as he reached the kitchen door. He unlocked it with a key already in his hand and we stepped into the kitchen. A low-powered light was on, but there was no sign of Daisy. I think I tried to re-call then whether I had noticed lights anywhere else in the house. I thought not. Tom made at once for the back stairs, knelt at the step where the bullet had been dug out, and went through a mysterious pantomime.

"Go on up," he whispered fiercely; "See, I've turned the hall lights on. Chase yourself into Rhoda Sutton's sitting room and when you hear a queer little gnawing noise come right back to the head of the stairs and I'll shoot you. You know—I'm reenacting. There's nothing to it. Gosh, do I have to explain to a panty-waist!"

He didn't; I think he had me hypnotized. But it was no fun. I even made myself sit down in Rhoda Sutton's rock-er. My heart pounded so, I couldn't hear a thing. Then I caught it, a faint scratching from the back stairway. I fol-lowed the sound, as no doubt Rhoda Sutton had done, and there was Tom kneeling on a step and looking up at me. His dumbshow at the place where the bullet had been dug out ceased. He rose to his feet and started toward me, drawing a gun from his pocket.

"It's just a blank," he said calmly, "but I've got to shoot, so that Daisy will hear."

He told me later that I screwed my eyes tight and huddled in terror, but he kept talking softly right through the terrific bang that promptly followed.

"Come on now. You're all right. Now we make our getaway. That's Daisy shuffling about up there. Don't you hear her? She's just helping out—I've promised her heart's desire—I think she'll settle for a new hat. Hurry now. She heard someone running, remember?"

So we ran. Ran out of the kitchen and jumped into the car. Off we went down the drive. A shadowy someone waved at us as we took the first curve.

"Who's that?" I gasped.

"Just Adkins. He's on my staff too, tonight. He meant that he's seen no one else about."

It was as pretty much down grade all the way back to town, but at that my old Iowa car burned the wind. I was still too breathless to talk, but Tom called it intelligent cooperation. We flew along Terrace Drive and stopped outside the house.

"Check the exact time at once." He turned his flash on my watchface and read the mileage gauge to me.

I subtracted with pencil and paper, for mental arithmetic was beyond me at that point, even if I do earn my living teaching algebra and trig. "Twenty-three minutes, forty-one seconds. I can't believe it."

"And one minute and nineteen seconds to the good, if I can believe Mrs. Allen Howard. Maybe we needn't have rushed so." Quite as though seventy-nine seconds would have added to the leisure of what I had just gone through. "It was seven miles, two-tenths," he added.

Naturally I assumed that the little job had been completed and I moaned in protest when he said, "Now for act two. We're going back."

And back we went, this time at a more normal pace.

I began to splutter questions, but Tom was not responsive. "Wait," he said. "You'll see. I'm doing what you want me to do—trying to catch whoever killed your friend, and, by the great horn spoon, it's beginning to look as though a smart guy is not going to be quite smart enough. But I'm not sure yet. Can you swim?"

"Why, yes, in a pool. In the deep end, even."

"Good enough. Can you row?"

"No-o—" My feet began to feel chilly.

"You can take 'em anyway, in case you get caught. Elvin will be on the lookout and you won't need to do a thing but stay in the boat."

"Will you kindly tell me what sort of guinea pig you're going to make of me? And am I to like it or else?"

"You won't like it, I'm afraid, but I think you're going to do it because you've got a big stake in what is going on, and there's no one else to use without running the risk of getting the wind up. Elvin's helping, but he already has an assignment, and I can't be doing two things at one time. So you're going to be a first-class sport and get in that other boat and let yourself drift down the river. No oars were missing the other night, so I have to figure it without 'em. But if you should get stuck or caught or need to shove yourself around any, you'd better have 'em, and this flashlight."

By this time we were back at River View. The shadowy Adkins was still on guard, but Tom did not stop to speak to him. The house was quiet and dark except for the same light in the kitchen.

"That's the only condition Daisy made," Tom chuckled, "That there'd be a light there if she had to come down. She's locked in her room and my bet is that she's gone to sleep."

"If I know Daisy she's hanging out her window this minute not missing a trick."

But we took no time to see. Again Tom hurried me down the path and into the boat house. He helped me into the remaining rowboat. "Here's the flash. Use it whenever you wish but don't make signals. There's always a certain amount of traffic along the road on the Ohio side. But you'll be surprised how much you can see by the stars of the summer night."

The idiot actually tried to sing those last words, but I was speechless, whether from sheer funk at the thought of the ordeal he was so nonchalantly arranging for me or from rage at being pushed around with so little explanation, I couldn't have said. There was no time to analyze emotions.

"Now listen," he went on, preparing to shove the boat out into the current, "here's the only thing you have to do. Watch the bank to your left. You'll pass two lights and the third one means you've reached the upper edge of town, see. As soon as you pick it up, begin winking your flash. One, two, three, pause—one, two, three, pause. Yes, like that. And Elvin will row out to meet you, or maybe I will. That's all there is to it. Except to note the exact time now and the exact time you reach the street Elvin will guide you to. He won't let you loiter. Take a look at your watch, and off you go. Atta girl!"

The skiff bobbed a little and then swung into the current, and there I was, floating down the Old 'Hio. I sat humped up on the middle seat, my hands gripping its edge as though I could by that force alone turn the little boat back to safe haven in the Howard boat house. I could see nothing at first. Velvet blackness all around me and starry sky above. No sense of motion, even. Only the dank smell of the river. I was still scared and very, very angry. But nothing happened and before long I began to relax a little and use my head. I was going somewhere, I decided. The shore to my left was an unrecognizable dark mass, but far to the right I could see an occasional swift glimmer of light that must come from cars on the road to Marietta. It was a windless night, cloudless and beautiful, but not warm out on the river, and I was glad for the sweater that Tom had taken from the railing of the launch and tossed across my shoulders. I loosened my hand from its tense clutching of the seat and experimented with the flash. The boat had not yet sprung a leak and the oars were firmly in place and there were vast stretches of still, black water all around me. It wasn't such a good idea to do much fooling with the light, I realized, for when I snapped it off I felt that I had gone into a bottomless pit of inky blackness and it seemed ages before I could see by starlight again. But the stars were there and now and then a ripple reflected their pale distant shining.

With only a long-ago reading of Huck Finn to go by, I expected sandbars, island hide-outs, lone night fishermen, sternwheelers—anything, but nothing happened. The first of the shore beacons came into view. By daylight it would have been nothing but a lantern hanging on a securely placed pole, but for all I knew then it was under the constant supervision of a detail of coast guards and I cowered lower as my boat slipped by. Once a car on the farther shore swept close to the water's edge and its lights went out. Again I was prepared for anything, but all that amounted to was the thin faint sound of radio music. "Boy's met girl," I told myself.

By the time I passed the second light I was almost normally calm and even beginning to savor my unusual experience for its own sake. The current evidently was nearer the West Virginia side and so far nothing hazardous had diverted my course. Once something bumped the side of the skiff and my heart leaped into my mouth, but the flash revealed only a floating bit of timber.

At last the third light shone out, a faint wavering pencil that scarcely marked the water at all. One, two, three, my flash winked—one, two three. I must be sure to wait between the winks. One, two, three . . .

I looked through the darkness at the left bank so hard that my eyes felt stretched out of shape. I could see other lights now, small and bright and high, and one in a quick swinging flash that was gone as soon as I caught it. It must

have been a car. "Close to the upper end of town," Tom
had said. So maybe those other steady little lights were
shining from people's houses. I kept on winking my flash,
one, two, three, pause, but I was still looking too high. I
heard sounds before I saw anything, sounds of oars dipping
skillfully, and then a low cheery voice, strange to me. "I'm
comin', Miss Lenox, ma'am."

It was the admirable Elvin. When I had thrown the
painter to him and he had hitched me fast to his own skiff,
he told me that he had answered my signal at once, but, as I
said, I had been looking too high. Before I knew it, he had
beached his boat and was pulling mine safely up beside it,
and I was on dry land once more.

"Tom said we wasn't to lose any time, so if you don't
mind hurryin'—" And he set off up the bank, with me in
his wake. It was steep and rough and we were not on a path;
that was all I could be sure of. We had made perhaps fifteen
or twenty yards when a blinding light from a source quite
close to my left was suddenly swung first at my guide and
then at me. It was followed at once by another, whiter flare
and a soft plop. Then pitch blackness. I heard swift steps
crashing off.

Elvin had not been using his flashlight, being evidently quite familiar with the terrain, and mine was clutched
backward in my hand, but his was out of his pocket before
I had clumsily righted mine. Its glow was feeble compared
to the brilliance that had dazzled in our eyes and the beam
discovered nothing. Whoever it was who had been so interested in our landing had not paused and had certainly made
time. The sound of his departure was already distant.

"For the lova Mike," Elvin grunted. "Guess there's
nothin' for us to do but keep on goin', like Tom said."

Breathless and shaken, I shortly found myself at the top
of the bank. "Crawl through here," Elvin directed, and I
wriggled under some strands of barbed wire and stood upright. The neatly painted blank wall of a low building was

before me, as the flash obligingly revealed. "Come on, we can't stop yet, but no lights now and don't make no noise."

I followed Elvin around the corner of the building and into a graveled driveway that led toward a street. The house to our right was well lighted and no doubt occupied, though I was too busy negotiating the gravel without crunching it to look through windows. It was only when we had reached the street and our progress was checked for a brief reconnoiter from the shelter of a clump of evergreens that I recognized that the house was Allen and Lila Howard's.

"Come on now," and Elvin breathed damply down my neck, "just like we was walkin' along together."

So we walked along together, but briskly, across the street, down to the next corner, and up that street another square and a half.

"Now you're to look at your watch again, and that's all." There was unmistakable regret in the boy's words. "Course, you don't have to stay here. I guess you could go to Tom Nixon's office if you'd want to."

Carefully I noted the exact time, but the end of my trek claimed my whole attention. We were standing at an alleyway by the corner of an establishment, closed and darkened now, plainly labelled Point Tyler Motormart, Chad R. Howard, Prop.

4

Elvin, it appeared, was pleased to accompany me further. In silence we walked on to the main street and along it, past the fish sandwich place toward Tom's office. I stared for some seconds at a car parked near his stairway before I recognized it as my own. As we approached it, the door swung open and there was Tom.

"I thought you might show up if I waited long enough," he said, "Well, kid, how'd you make it?"

"Okay. She slipped by at—lessee now." And he drew a grimy slip of paper from the pocket of his shirt and thrust it under my dashboard lights. "At twelve minutes after eleven bells. So then I beat it up where you said and waited, and sure enough, she comes floatin' down and gives the signal, and we didn't waste a second, except maybe when that bum tried to see who we was."

"Not trying to kid me, is he?" Tom's voice was wary.

"No, it happened all right, but I'm going to get in the car and sit down if you have nothing better to suggest. I'm all wobbly."

Tom dispatched Elvin for coffee and hamburgers from the Glass Front and got me upstairs to his office. "We'll get together on this as soon as I can get rid of the kid," he promised, "but I mustn't hurt his feelings—he's been darned useful."

"My feelings have already been hurt and if I haven't been used for some nefarious purpose I don't know what to call it, and the dampness has ruined my wave, and barbed wire's snagged my new nylons, and I've been drifting in deadly peril down the Ohio River—but don't give me a thought."

Tom grinned at me and patted my shoulder. "I've given you a yarn you'll relate to your dying day, and besides, you're a grand sport. Here's Elvin with coffee that's a lot better than if I'd made it myself—or you, either—and it will make a new woman of you."

When I got back to Point Tyler Sally was still up, waiting for me and nervously curious as to what I had been up to. Chad, she said, had gone to bed long since. It was much too late to blame the movies; besides, I hadn't the faintest idea what picture I should have seen. So I said Tom Nixon had taken me for a little boat ride and we'd got to talking.

"Allen was here," she reported while I undressed. "He says it will be all right for you to take care of Felicity's things tomorrow. I told him you were tired of hanging around here." And she laughed shamelessly. "So I said we'd go up in the morning."

The bright sunshine of the next morning made us all appear normal and sane. After some discussion between Sally and Chad as to our morning's plans it was decided that Chad would run us up to River View and come back for us when we were ready to return. When we arrived at River View, Bart was breakfasting in state under Daisy's supervision. I made my way upstairs and set to work in Felicity's room. However, Sally followed me before long and introduced me to the trunk room where we found a wardrobe trunk that I knew had belonged to Felicity and Sally pointed out another newer one that she was sure had come back from the honeymoon.

We did not talk much. Sally sat and watched me fold dresses and sort under things, her fingers locked around a knee and her eyes set and hard, as though her mind were not at all on what I was doing. Within the hour Lila and Allen drove up, and I had a distinct feeling that though I had been told to do what I was doing no one in the family was quite willing for me to do it without being watched. No one but Bart, perhaps, for from a window I saw him strolling idly about the grounds.

Sally went down to see what had brought the Allen Howards, but she came right back up again, reporting that Allen was going through his father's papers in the library and that Lila was snooping through the dining room linen. "And some of that stuff was Felicity's, if you want to know," she murmured, and then resumed her blank air of abstraction. I saw no one else approach the house.

After a half-hour or so of this, during which time the only remark that Sally made was, "I suppose her desk has been searched for the will they're afraid she made," and my response was, "It's locked. Tom still has the key," she at last jumped to her feet and ran her fingers through her red hair.

"I can't stand this. I'm going swimming. Tell Chad to wait if he comes." And she dashed from the room and down the back stairs.

But in a minute or two I saw her joining Bart and they walked out of my sight around the house. "I don't care," I thought. "It's up to Floyd and Tom now, and if they're not here to attend to their business, there's nothing I can do about it." And I began to fold the contents of another drawer.

The house was quiet and as I sorted and packed the quantities of exquisite new lingerie that must have been purchased since Felicity's marriage, I got to thinking about the tangle of the wills. Allen Howard, I was willing to bet, was once more searching for something to settle their uncertainty about Felicity's disposal of their father's estate. He had willed everything to her, and unless she had acted since her discovery of that will, her pre-marriage document safely filed in a Des Moines law office would almost certainly control a handsome inheritance. Of course the family might now have a better chance of contesting, and they'd do exactly that, but how a charge of murder and a possible conviction would affect the outcome I could only guess. An unsavory struggle like that would not be worth the prize— the long-drawn-out publicity, the disgraced family name, the consciousness of guilt.

I looked out of the window again, for I could not forget that Bart and Sally had vanished in the direction of the river, and that's when I noticed the car. It wasn't Tom's roadster nor Chad's Buick; it was a strange car to me. I saw no one except Adkins grubbing in a flower bed, and I heard no extra sounds within the house.

I resumed my work, for Sally and Chad were clearly expecting me to finish in time to go back to Point Tyler for lunch on Terrace Drive. I wondered what would become of Felicity's things, her dresses, her intimate possessions, the contents of her desk, the linen that Sally had spoken of, the silver I knew she had owned, the few choice pieces of antique china. I recalled the vase in the living room that I had identified on that dreadful afternoon when Sally had pushed me in to see Felicity lying dead. All that I was doing was packing; nothing could be removed yet or disposed of until the matter of the wills was settled. I wished with all my heart that Allen or Blair would find a new will. I knew Felicity well enough to feel sure that she would have dealt justly with the Howards. Nor would she have ignored her newly identified father. He and I alone would treasure and care for anything that had belonged to Felicity.

With my mind so thoroughly absorbed in thoughts like these, it was some time before I became aware of the sound of voices. Not loud, quite near. The door to the hall was standing open. My presence was in no sense furtive. I stepped to the door and looked out. No one was in sight, but I could hear the talking more distinctly. Someone was across the hall in Rhoda Sutton's sitting room. That door was ajar. At that instant I recognized the voice that was speaking. It was Tom Nixon's.

"Your alibi for the morning is out—washed up. And you had to see your father—make another desperate plea. Your brother had let you down and there was no more time. His answer was no, of course, or you wouldn't have killed him in that cowardly way."

I tiptoed back out of range indistinctly and stood rigid in the midst of box lids and tissue paper. There was an answering voice in a snarl of protest and then Tom's again. I could hear, in spite of my scruples.

"Oh, yes, you were, Lila put me on to it. You thought she was alone and you thought it was easy to fake a suicide. But your aunt caught you and that's what really did for you, since it was you and not—"

A door banged below and Daisy's strident voice called, "Adkins, oh A-a-adkins! Come here at once, can't you?"

I had to hear more, no matter how I had been brought up. I advanced to the door, halfway down the hall, but I couldn't distinguish what the second person was saying. It was a scared voice and back-to-the-wall. But Tom sounded easy and sure of himself.

"So you dropped the gloves and got away to turn up later with the others. You took a chance on that alibi, and it almost worked, but not quite. And Sally suspected, for she found the gloves and did the best she could to clear the scene. But your aunt gave you no peace, and you know why. She held an ace against you, down in the bank vault, and you had to work fast when you realized that she was going to force the appearance of that bottle. It wasn't hard, though, to get the key and put it back again, and the bank people think you Howards own the place. It was worse the next time— Oh, no, you won't. Floyd's waiting for you, just as soon as I finish."

Somehow that startled me so much that I gave a quick survey up and down the hall, expecting to see Floyd lurking in ambush, and consequently I missed what was said next.

"I gave you a good one all right, though I must admit you nearly knocked me out. However, I kept the bottle and, just to keep the record straight I've still got it. Nice piece of evidence. And to make it harder to take, I'll tell you that I didn't know then who I'd met up with. But I've run across another nice piece of evidence since and it's got your name on it, don't worry. So you had to kill Aunt Rhoda. And that wasn't hard either—a real pleasure in the spot you were in. It took some slick timing, but you managed. The other car's lighter than yours and much faster, and there wasn't a thing wrong with it, as we all know. The Howards have everything right in the family, even a quite empty auto shop. The only trouble was that the girls' stories about the times didn't quite jibe, though I must say that they did their best to oblige. Family solidarity, I'll say! Even with the gun—"

I was leaning forward so far that I almost lost my balance, for the protesting voice was clearer now and I wanted to be sure. Bart's lazy mockery was missing; the thin husky tone sounded slightly reasonable.

"—nothing whatever about the gun. Why should I? You already have a confession for that. Act on it."

"Yes, the gun that Wilson Markham did not bury in his garden. A confession that was pure moonshine— that's why the old fellow will continue to putter about in his shop. But, oh, while it lasted, weren't you all pleased. Particularly you, since you were the one who knew so well that it was all poppycock! But it led you to do exactly what I wanted you to do, and that's why I'm deeply indebted to an old man's last service for his daughter. He wasn't arrested and you knew it, and you also knew I was up to something that you weren't just sure about, and you were right on hand last night to find out. Only I found out, with a camera."

The words were scarcely out of Tom's mouth before the crash came and a growl of frustrated rage and hatred that made the little hairs on the back of my neck rise. "Floyd! Floyd!" I heard Tom call and heavy steps pounded forward from the back hallway. But I got there first to see a tangled mass of arms and legs writhing on the floor. One hand snatched at a doorstop—a ridiculously decorated object like all of Rhoda Sutton's stuff; I can still see a yellow oilcloth doo-dad that the fingers first grasped—and gripped it hard and raised it. It was coming down on Tom Nixon's head.

Well, I stopped that. At least, Tom has given me public credit for so saving him a bashed-in skull. I seized the wrist and held it fast. Floyd was puffing and blowing over us all by that time and helped Tom to entangle himself.

"Got him, huh? Nice work," he grunted.

I was still holding the murderer's wrist. It was Chad Howard's.

5

There were sounds of an aroused household and we had only a few seconds before Lila and then Allen were at the head of the stairs.

"My God, Nixon, what do you mean by this?" Allen Howard strode into the room. Floyd shifted his position on

the prostrate Chad, who whimpered a little like a child but
lay motionless with closed eyes.

"You're hurting him," Lila complained. "Whatever happened? I thought I heard someone fall."

Tom straightened himself and flexed a wrist that had
had rough treatment. "Howard," he said in a slow, regretful
tone, "I've caught the murderer. I'm sorry, but the mess is
still all in the family. Floyd has the warrant ready to serve."

The sheriff nodded his head solemnly and fished in a
pocket for a pair of handcuffs. "It's so, I guess. Tom's got
him right. I give him full credit. We'll have to take him in
to town."

"No—no, he's hurt—he's dying." And Lila dropped on
her knees beside him. I couldn't tell even then how deep
her concern went; I had always had the feeling that Lila
Howard's interest in her younger brother-in-law had not
exceeded her own first principle of playing safe.

Certainly her husband took her behavior as natural.
He stood where he had first halted, his arms folded and
his head down. Even Floyd's reply to Lila's protests—"He's
okay, Mis' Howard. Just the wind knocked outa him"—did
not seem to reach his attention. At last he shook himself
and addressed Tom.

"Very well. Play it through, if you must. But be assured
we shall take the usual steps in his behalf."

I saw the look in his eyes and that, more than anything
that I myself knew, or had heard or seen, convinced me that
Tom had not made a mistake.

Daisy had crowded into the room by that time and
Adkins too, but still there was no sign of Sally and Bart. I
was shaking with cold dread. The handcuffs were snapped
on and Chad was pulled to his feet. Tom gave Floyd a slight
nod and the sheriff moved toward the door with his prison-
er. Chad was still groggy and apathetic, but by the time he
had been propelled to the head of the stairs he was crying
weakly and mumbling wild denials. Save for that there was

nothing from the others but shocked silence. As if they had known all the time.

The rest of us moved slowly down the stairs, but well behind the three men. "Do something, Allen. Why don't you do something?" Lila wailed. "You've got to!"

He shook his head vaguely, but before Tom reached the front door he spoke brusquely, "Nixon, if it's not necessary for you to go, stay here and put this thing to me. That's all I'm asking now. Adkins can drive your car." Yet for all his brusqueness that look of acceptance was still in his eyes.

"Very well, Howard," Tom replied quietly. "Floyd won't need your man. He brought a couple of extras with him."

We clotted at the doorway as someone started the strange car I had seen from Felicity's window and moved it to the spot where Floyd was waiting, his free arm supporting the drooping Chad. The car started slowly away. There was a rush of running feet around from the back of the house and Sally leaped upon the running board.

"Chad, Chad—wait! I'm going with you."

And then I cried.

We backed down the hall again following Allen to the library. As we reached the door, Bart raced in through the kitchen. "Has she gone—Sally? God, she was right! She knew you were going to get him."

He sank into a chair and gave Allen a look of utter misery, and for the first time since I had met him I knew that at last Bart Howard was being genuine.

"I should say," Tom spoke softly, "that there isn't much that you don't know."

"I know—very little. Surely you have evidence, Nixon. We have a right to hear it." Allen had resumed his usual calm. He pulled forward a chair and seated his wife with grave politeness.

"Evidence is properly produced at a trial, Howard, and mine will be, but I am willing to answer questions, in reason, and to explain to you what led to this."

So he told them.

"One of the facts you know, Howard, is that your brother has always felt slighted. You were the oldest and everything you did was always right. I mean just that, Allen. You have been the successful, wholly trustworthy, admirable eldest son. Your character and position in the community are without blemish, but you have often been worried about your brothers. Bart has been the spoiled one whose way has always been made easy, largely because of the devoted championship of Mrs. Sutton. Chad shifted for himself and everything that he attempted always went a little haywire. You and your father were forever shaking your heads a little bit over anything he proposed, and more than once you pulled him out of a hole. You helped get the agency going yourself before you turned it over to him, but since then— well, I have made it my business to find out what the present state of affairs is and that your father had laid down an ultimatum. He'd have to rescue himself and pay for his own business mistakes.

"All this was burning Chad up. He'd always been made to feel inferior and he was quite convinced that he never got a break. Then too his wife—Sally was very unhappy here and was at Chad continually to pull up and get away. He had promised her he would do so, though he had no way of keeping that promise."

Tom paused abruptly and I wondered whether he were thinking of the slightly adolescent situation that had been brewing between Lila and Chad. There was really no need to bring it up and I was glad for Allen's sake that he made no mention of it.

"Some of that is quite true, Nixon." Allen spoke slowly. "But it will scarcely hold water as a motive, if that's what you think you are establishing. I did everything to help my brother, Why, only the very morning that Dad died—"

"You were discussing Chad's financial difficulties with your father, weren't you? And you passed on to him as you were leaving your father's unchanged determination to make him hoe his own row. Well, he came on in, slipped upstairs to your aunt's bathroom, dosed the lotion liberally with cyanide crystals, brought the mixture down, and mopped his father's neck with it—a nice filial attention. And then he sped on his way to Wheeling. Dr. Ammon is now of the opinion that was the method of introducing the poison into the blood stream."

Allen groaned and buried his head in his hands. Bart was the color of putty. The words came through his clenched teeth, "What in hell did he do with the stuff? I looked—after I found him."

"He took it away with him, I have every reason to believe. But here's where someone else enters the scene to play a part equally criminal—your aunt, Rhoda Sutton. She hated your father's new wife and she at once seized upon a way to discredit her. I give her credit for doing some shrewd guessing, but I think in one particular she must have guessed wrong. Perhaps Bart can throw some light on that point. However, because of some slight disarray in her medicine cabinet she guessed poison at once. Her larger bottle of lotion was missing, the one that Chad had taken, but the smaller one that she had turned over to Felicity was where it had last been used, in the Howards' bathroom. She appropriated it at once. Miss Lenox has a letter from her friend telling about the mysterious disappearance of the little bottle. In due time, as you know, Mrs. Sutton 'found' the bottle wrapped in one of Mrs. Howard's towels together with a hypodermic needle which she considered a necessary adjunct. The bottle she 'found' you may be sure she laced well with cyanide and promptly and secretly placed it in the box at the bank to produce when and if she needed it.

"Then Felicity Howard came across her husband's new will and whatever help Chad had hoped from his father's death was nullified. None of you liked it, but it must have been a bleak moment for Chad. But here was his Aunt

Rhoda, whose favorite he had never been, solving the problem for him by all sorts of insinuations against his young stepmother. There was much family talk, which it is useless for any of you to deny. Daisy will make an unshakable witness. Much discussion and speculation about contesting the will and even what Mrs. Howard would do with the money when it came her time to leave it. But none of that would be fast enough to meet your brother's immediate needs and it occurred to him that to wipe her out right then would not only demonstrate that your aunt's suspicions were correct but might also make the family's claim on the estate the stronger. He could borrow on his expectations.

"Chad worked that one out very carefully and he probably would have been successful if he had only known that his aunt was in the house. From that time on she ceased to be the passive ally she had unconsciously been until then, even though she publicly harped on Felicity's suicide as clear proof of her guilt. But Chad's actions—he arranged his work that afternoon so that he was in the vicinity and he slipped quietly into the house with a .32 ready for action.

"With a fake suicide in mind he helped himself to Mrs. Sutton's gardening gloves that she made a habit of keeping on a shelf on the back porch, and he also procured and reloaded his father's gun from the drawer here where you all knew it was kept. Sally probably told the truth about her box of shells—that when she realized how an opened box would look, she threw away some more and then got panicky and tried to hide the box. Chad would have taken just enough to load his father's .32, so I'm not inclined to think she's covering up for him in this instance. No matter where he might have come upon his victim, he would have committed the deed he was keyed to do, but it must have been easier than he expected, because she was undoubtedly asleep on the living room couch when he shot her. He marked the gun from the library with her fingerprints and placed it where it would naturally have fallen from her hand. In his general innocence of detective procedure or the excitement that surely gripped him, he never thought that the bullet from one gun would not tally with the barrel of another.

"The shot had, of course, aroused Mrs. Sutton and at that point he undoubtedly heard her stirring overhead. Heard someone—he couldn't have been sure who it was. He dropped the gloves and fled toward the back of the house. Someone was coming down the back hallway toward the stairs. Completely losing his head, he fired a shot at random which lodged in the step and raced from the house down toward the river. His aunt saw his flight, and the use she put her knowledge to made her murder inevitable."

Bart jumped to his feet and strode to a window, his shoulders shaking with emotion. "She thought she was helping me," he muttered.

"Did she think it was you?" Lila demanded.

"No, Mrs. Howard," Tom replied. "She saw Chad, but later she attempted to make a deal with Chad for Bart's benefit. That's so, isn't it, Bart?"

"I'm not talking," he growled.

"It was the second shot that Sally heard, not the first. No matter what she said, or may say, Sally had come up that afternoon on Chad's trail. She was frantic with worry about her husband's affairs and had been for some weeks. She found Felicity lying as Chad left her and realized at once that except for the tell-tale gloves it looked liked sui-cide. She snatched up the gloves and ran out again to her car. She was acting without thinking and she might have done a dozen things with the gloves. What she did was to wrap them around a stone from the edge of the driveway and hurl them from her as she ran. Sally's got a good throw-ing arm. If Miss Lenox had not heard the sound of their fall into the ravine, we probably would never have known anything about the gloves. That's how come the smudge of dirt on her forehead, Marg," he parenthesized at me. "She always runs her fingers through her hair when she's upset."

"And so, scarcely knowing what she was doing, Sally played her part that afternoon and willy-nilly forced Miss Lenox into one also. Meanwhile, Chad was completing his alibi, going for a swim, meeting Lila at the boat house. I've not had any reason to doubt her account of herself that afternoon, except for one item which I think she will tell me now."

Tom turned to Lila. She bit her lips and looked at her husband for a cue, but his head was bent. "I don't know anything—more. I oughtn't to say anything against Chad."

"You waited for him to come back from his swim, didn't you?"

She nodded.

"To come back, Mrs. Howard. Then you saw him go past the boat house?"

Again she nodded.

"So you see he didn't do what he said—go down the old path from the road. I told him his alibi had a crack in it. The guy that drives the truck he said he came in on will make another good witness.

"But again nothing happened, apparently," Tom went on patiently. "Except that Miss Lenox and Wilson Markham insisted that Felicity would never have touched any kind of weapon that goes off with a bang. Marg suspected murder at once, and when the gun was tested, after the p.m. on your father, we knew we had two murders to solve. The third one made it easier, but I think we should have worked things out even if Chad had not turned on his aunt. He knew very shortly that she had seen him leaving the house and furthermore she told him that she had the evidence of poison he had used in his father's death. Perhaps she had only suspected him of that deed, but now she felt certain enough to accuse him. He knew her story about the bottle was a lie, but there was no way to prove it without giving himself away. She may have told him that his fingerprints would show up on the bottle. At any rate, he felt that the second bottle must be disposed of and he conceived the bright idea of stymying Aunt Rhoda's game by substituting a harmless bottle for the one in the bank. Then when he knew it was to be produced for what it was worth, he got jittery again about fingerprints and tried to get hold of the bundle—this time no doubt it would have vanished forever. But he tangled with me and I won."

Tom shifted his position and squinted through his glasses at the ceiling. "It's a funny thing—he needn't have worried about fingerprints. There was one on the bottle, an old one of Rhoda Sutton's. He'd have been in the clear there, but he was getting scared. As I say, he ran into me up there in Allen's office. I had a vague idea even then, but not enough for an accusation. And I had to be sure. That's when I thought how swell it would have been if I had been able to catch whoever it was by camera. I thought out a possible way to trap him and used Marg here as a kind of come-on, and by heck, I caught him!"

"You might at least have played fair," Lila complained. Now that the whole thing had burst in their faces, she was surprisingly childish in all her comments.

"But Aunt Rhoda—surely not that night," Allen mumbled almost indistinguishably.

"Yes, that night. He still felt there was a chance that the tangle of the wills might work out in your favor—and for all I know of law, it may, though it won't do the poor devil any good now—but his aunt was going to hold him up for most of his shares as the price of her silence and it would have gone to Bart, he well knew, and so there was the only way out for him.

"Rather oddly you, Allen, appropriated his car that evening and paralleled Marg's run to Webster Springs. You wanted to make sure that Thelma Jopp had not observed your brief chat with your father and whether Chad had come in afterwards, as you suspected he might have done. Thelma, unfortunately for our side, hadn't seen either of you.

"On the whole your taking the Buick was to Chad's advantage, for if a car was recognized it wouldn't be his. During the course of the evening Bart and he were in and out of his place any number of times and he seized a chance to tinker with Bart's car just enough to make his brother notice that something wasn't working right. You'll all admit that Bart never touches his car except to drive it and that Chad's the one to whom motors are all in the day's work. So when Bart reported a spot of trouble it was perfectly natural for Chad to say he'd see what he could do. That's when he made the trip to Allen's office to try to get the bottle. My interference only made him more desperate to get the matter settled.

"He came back to his own house—stop me if I'm wrong, Lila. You and Sally and Marg all did your share of establishing times, though at one point Sally told me a deliberate lie, poor kid—so he came back home and reported that he'd have to run the car into the shop but would soon have it okay. That accounted for the half-hour's absence when he was burning up the road to River View, bursting open the boat house door and thrusting a skiff out into the river with the idea of laying a false trail, slipping into the, house and up the back stairs, where he came upon his aunt and shot her. He got back home just before Marg made her first observation."

"You can't prove a thing by me." The first sound from Bart for many minutes. It was evident that he now had a firmer grip on himself. "I sat there at Sally's half asleep and I've no idea when he left or came back."

"But I have, and it all clicks. You separated shortly afterwards," Tom went on, "and that night none of you except Allen and of course Chad knew that your aunt had been killed. Chad must not have done much sleeping, waiting for the alarm to reach him, but as the dark hours of the night wore on and nothing happened except a phone call about Bart, he must have felt that he had pulled it off.

"Then came the perfect solution—the villain was no other than old Wilson Markham. Make no mistake, the old gentlemen was willing to serve as scapegoat as a kind of expiation he owed his daughter, but the story he told of that night was built to fit the facts we had, and I knew at once by the eager way you all swallowed it that you were well pleased with the answer. There were so many loose ends that none of you dared to mention. So I kept right on figuring which one of you was guilty.

"You see, Chad still had the gun, and if Sally hadn't made one last fool attempt to help her husband—well, I knew she'd never have made that trip to Markham's garden for anyone's sake but Chad's. She didn't know in so many words, but she was in the best position to suspect that her husband was guilty, and so she's made herself technically a *post facto* accomplice."

"No she didn't know," Bart groaned, "but she was afraid she knew—and she went with him."

This murderous shaft that's shot hath not yet lighted. . . . Sally too!

"Well, that's about all I have to say." Tom rose. "I should be getting back to town."

"It's not quite all, Nixon." And Allen rose to his feet. "I'd like to tell the others—" and apparently his glance included me—"in your hearing one additional fact. Blair and I are convinced that Mrs. Howard made no subsequent will to set aside the one she had drawn before her marriage. A copy of that one has duly reached us. It is brief and undeniably clear. The chief provision in it reads: '. . . All that I am possessed of at the time of my death to my friend, Margaret Lenox.'"

So that's the reason that I too came to loathe Point Tyler and wish that I had never heard of the Howards and their property. So far, however, I've not been murdered.

MURDER RINGS TWICE

Chapter One
I Accommodate a Tourist

I have been advised to get it out of my system by writing it down—what occurred at the Dark Lantern during the third week of June. I can see now that to be strictly chronological I must not start with the frightened girl in the rumble of the muddy yellow roadster. The strange web of events that was to tighten about the Dark Lantern, the tourist camp at the junction of US40 and the State Line Pike, and the old Newagen farm, opened with the comments of one of my dinner parties that Tuesday evening.

Perhaps I should explain first that I was understudying for my lifelong friend, Ella Brookfield, who for several seasons had been running a roadside luncheon, tea and dinner place which she called the Dark Lantern for no better reason than that she had found one in the basement of the place. My name is Sara Fergus and I once earned my living teaching school. Ella had just had an ultimatum from her doctor about an operation. She explained that she had an excellent cook and a reliable headwaitress, and would I please for the sake of auld lang syne, et cetera, et cetera, carry on.

So much for the reason that I happened to be in charge at the Dark Lantern when all the shootin' began. . . .

With one good broad jump that brings me to Tuesday evening, June 19. We had two special parties that night and an average number of casual droppers-in, both highway tourists and people motoring out from Dayfield, the nearest city of any size. It was one of the special dinner parties that spoke the prologue for the melodrama that was about to start, though I had no idea of its significance at the time. It was not until after I was startled by the anonymous telephone call that I caught the faint click of events shifting neatly into place.

This is the snatch of talk that I heard:

A tall plumpish blonde: "I tell you, I've seen him before—somewhere."

A bilious-looking man who had been eating greedily: "People don't travel incog in this land of the free and easy."

The handsomest man at the table: "He's here for a purpose—that's my guess."

A little brunette of the cute type: "I don't know yet whom you're talking about, but why not ask him and then let's all talk about me?"

The plumpish blonde again: "His picture somewhere— or maybe in the movies. It worries me somehow."

A patient-looking man, quite bald, his voice registering an infinite boredom: "A murder has no doubt been committed somewhere. The fellow is never seen except when an unexplained death calls him out."

The rest of them, the women's voices screeching unpleasantly: "What! Murder—"

At that point Lola, the head waitress, beckoned to me and I moved away from the alcove where the party was seated, but I was just curious enough to check up as to whom they were discussing. There were only three tables, all within range of the group in the alcove. One was a family party complete with grandpa, auntie and a high-chaired Junior. Another was occupied by two elderly businesswomen, rather regular diners at the Dark Lantern, who always made punctilious inquiries about Miss Brookfield's health. That left a singleton, a man with an interesting face, who looked more like a hiker than a motorist.

I meant to speak to the man when he paid his check, but a minor crisis in the kitchen deprived me of my chance. My hunch that he was a walker and not a motorist went unverified.

That, as I have said, was the prologue to murder on 40, though I was not to identify it as such for several days.

By a quarter of nine all the diners had gone. I went out to the entrance of the drive to turn off the light in the lantern that illuminates the sign beckoning transients to pause at the Dark Lantern. The evening had been a bit overcast, but because it was so close upon the summer solstice there was still light enough to see everything quite plainly. I snapped off the switch, for we wanted no more custom that night, and stood for a moment looking off across the quiet gold of the wheat fields sparked with fireflies.

For two or three minutes the road was empty and quiet, always noteworthy, for 40 is a national thoroughfare. But in the still evening air I could hear the screech of brakes and the crunch of gravel at the junction filling station just out of sight beyond a slight curve. Even more plainly I could hear a blatant radio. That would be someone at the tourist camp.

Just two or three minutes of empty roadway, and then a car swooped swiftly from the east. It slowed a bit in response to the highway sign about the curve, and that is how I happened to observe that the car was yellow, a roadster, and so muddy that I could not be at all sure of the license plate except that it was not an Ohio one. There were two men in the car. Something or other impressed me about the one at the wheel, but I did not work it out. I was more interested in the girl.

For in the rumble seat there crouched a girl with a thin, frightened face. She was leaning forward almost as though she were trying to hear whatever might be said by the two men. That is merely what I thought, but the next bit actually occurred. As the car slipped by, the girl made a quick

stealthy gesture and a little bundle of something slid over
the side of the car, bounced from the fender, and swirled to
the side of the road. The girl continued to strain forward,
even the line of her shoulders bespeaking fear, and the muddy yellow roadster made the curve and vanished. I listened,
but I could not be sure whether it had merely paused at the
crossing or had drawn up to a dead stop at the gas pumps.

I did the altogether natural and human thing. I stepped
from behind the board that holds Ella's sign and went in
search of whatever had been thrown overboard. I found it,
too: a little cottony bundle, like a tightly rolled garment
of small size. It was now too dark to examine it adequately,
nor was the side of the road an ideal place. I entered the
hall all set to examine my prize at once, but one of the girls
was in difficulties about her time off and I thrust the little
bundle back into a pigeonhole of Ella's desk, now temporarily mine, and hurried out of the tiny office.

Something else called me back to the front door after
I had settled the waitress. I stood there, just outside the
screen door, wondering about extra tables for the shadier
end. Suddenly a lightish shadow darted by around the west
end of the veranda and up the steps.

It was the thin, frightened girl.

"May I go inside, please—just for a minute—while I tell
you?" I opened the screen door in invitation. With swift
lithe grace she entered.

"May I stay here tonight? I have no money. And nobody
must know that I am here."

I agreed with my common sense that that sounded
preposterous, and rallied my caution in behalf of the contents of Ella's cash register. At the same instant my eye
caught the glint of a tiny bit of something pinned on the
girl's sweater pocket. It was a piece of collegiate insignia.
I am not at all the old grad type, but the Greek letters on
her pin identified the girl for me sufficiently to weaken my
sensible decision.

"Your line sounds somewhat mysterious," I replied, "and I really ought to take a good look at you first—"

I never finished what I was starting to say, for heavy steps thudded up the drive to the porch. I turned in inquiry and the girl disappeared in the darkness of the lounge, but I caught a trace of a frantic whisper:

"Please! Say I'm not here!"

A thick-set but pale-faced man with curiously blank eyes stood at the door. "Pardon me, madam, but did someone just come in here? I'm looking for my sister. I think she strolled down the road while the boy at the gas station was putting air in the tires. We're ready to start now."

The man, I decided, must have been the one at the right in the yellow car, for he was very definitely not the driver. That he was not the girl's brother I knew in a flash. His words were polite enough, but there was a non-Ohio cast to his voice and something that I felt still more notice-ably—a lack of breeding. And this last my frightened young lady had, and a genuine middle-western accent besides. So I heard myself saying in quiet, faintly surprised tones:

"No one has been here for an hour. Our dining-room is now closed—I'm sorry."

He looked as if violent language was coming and he tried to open the screen. Then he said with an extra lather of forced politeness, "Are you sure, madam? She was seen coming this way."

"Quite sure." My insistence was calm and utterly indif-ferent, or so I prided myself. "The inn is closing for the night. We have no accommodations for lodgers."

All the time his strangely dead eyes were checking my statements. If the girl had dropped any personal belongings in her precipitous entry, my play-acting would be reduced to farce.

"Sorry to have troubled you, madam. She's probably back at the car by this time."

I kept my eye on him. When he reached the road he neither paused nor looked back, but turned at once to the right and walked smartly off toward the crossroads. I could no longer hear his steps, but a passing car or two showed him up distinctly as their headlights swung at the curve.

I could hear something else, though, more and more plainly. The breathing of the frightened girl. I knew by the sound of the convulsive inhalations that she was still terror-stricken.

"He's gone. Back along the road toward the crossing."

"Oh, thank you—thank you! You'll never know how heavenly good you were." It was a voice only. She still lurked in the darkness.

"Certainly I shall never know—unless you explain yourself a little. I'm afraid I'm going to insist upon that."

"Of course, of course. But first—will you—oh, please will you let me stay here tonight? And can you take me somewhere where no one can see in? He'll be back—oh, I'm afraid he'll come back. Then I'll tell you—I'll tell you what I can."

I must repeat: I was strongly in the grip of a hunch that this was a Perfectly Nice Girl. At that, my line of action was scarcely rational . . .

I said, "Very well. Provided you can give me some sort of convincing explanation of your presence here, you may stay. If we go upstairs at once, no one can see us. There—to your right. As soon as you've started up, I'll switch off this light and follow you."

The Dark Lantern is a story-and-a-half house. There are only two small bedrooms and a bath on the second floor. I had been using the back bedroom and it was there that I led my visitor.

"Now," I ordered, "let me take a look at you."

"A pig in a poke," she murmured as she squared toward me.

I sensed an immediate change in her mood. Fear had given way to a calmness which had something of calculating thought behind it.

My survey tallied with my initial impression. Whatever sort of jam she was in, here was a Nice Girl.

She seemed to know when I was ready for her to speak. She cocked one eyebrow engagingly and gave me a faint smile.

"I am Mary McCann," she told me, "and I've been doing a reprehensible but delightful thing. I've been hitch-hiking." Her eyes left mine for an instant. "I go to Greenwater College—where we get along on a shoestring, you know—and I thought I'd get a job in Chicago for the summer. So of course I had to thumb my way to get there—no one has any money at the end of school. I should have known better than to take a chance with two men, but I did. They were driving right on through to Chicago tonight, but I decided that it would be better for me to drop off, and so when they stopped for gas, I made an excuse about the restroom and then disappeared. That's all."

"No," I said, "not quite all. You were badly frightened when you stumbled up to the porch, and you were scared to death when the man came in search of you. Why was that? And why must no one know you are here? And I saw—"

I was just about to blurt out that I had seen her throw a parcel out of the car when I caught myself.

She gave me a sort of sisters-under-the-skin smile. "You know how men are. It was my fault, of course. I had been giving them a hard-boiled line and they thought—they thought— Well, I knew when things had gone far enough. I had to get away from them before it got any later."

She turned a slow, embarrassed red, but it was such an honest blush that I felt surer than ever that I was right about Mary McCann.

"Very well," said I. "We'll let it go at that. And now let's get to bed—" I stopped in sudden embarrassment. I had forgotten entirely that for the present there was but one bed, and that a single one, available at the Dark Lantern. Ella's mattress had been sent back to the factory for repairs

while she was at the hospital. I began explanations to Mary
McCann, but she was not concerned.

"I can sleep on the floor," she declared. "Or did I or
didn't I stumble against a davenport down in the room
where I hid? That would be swell. Only let's not turn any
lights on. My persistent boy-friend might come snooping
around again."

"I thought you said they were driving straight on to
Chicago." I had to say that.

"That's what they said," she agreed without a quiver.
"It's only that I've let my nerves run away with me. But I'll
sleep on the stair rail if your heavenly kindness will only
run to a bath and a long drink of cold water."

I turned over the bathroom to Mary McCann and promised her sandwiches and milk when she had finished, and
went on to see what I could do about a bed. There were
plenty of blankets and I decided to let the girl take her
choice. She could sleep on the floor in Ella's room or she
could wrap herself up on the davenport in the lounge if she
wished. Then I slipped downstairs to the icebox. If anyone
were spying on me, it would certainly look like my own
midnight lunch I was assembling.

As I got to the head of the stairs with my tray, Mary
McCann opened the bathroom door and called out, "Mind
if I come out in just a combination? I'm traveling light, you
know. The bath was grand and I'm a new woman."

There she stood in a delectable pinky thing, looking like
a still Nicer Girl. I felt quite sure that I had not been rash
in taking her in. I thrust the tray upon her and hurried off
to my own room. I could do something about a nightgown.
I returned with my very best one—any woman produces
her best in such an emergency; that's one of my pet observations about my sisters—and an apology about my never
having taken to pajamas for sleeping. College girls live in
pajamas, I've gathered.

I deliberately thought up the remark about the pajamas to cover my amazement over something Mary McCann did while I was in my room getting my lace nightie. I chanced to catch her swift gesture through the crack of my door. She had something in her hand that looked like a letter or a folded paper, and she stooped and pushed it under the hall runner. When I emerged with the gown over my arm she was drinking milk thirstily and she gave me a friendly signal with what was left of the sandwich.

But all I said was something inane about pajamas. She giggled appreciatively and finished the sandwich while I went on to explain about the blankets.

She chose the floor in Ella's room and called out to me sleepily within a few minutes, "Good night, you heavenly person. I'll wash dishes for you in the morning, or something. Anything except peel potatoes. I loathe that."

I have now to relate that I went to sleep at once. I always do. I'm that kind of person. I grant that it was unbelievable of me after everything that had happened. I must also confess that for the time being I had completely forgotten about the queer little bundle that I had tucked into the desk downstairs. Yet I had not forgotten about whatever it was that Mary McCann had slipped under the rug just outside my door, but I had to be sure that the girl was asleep before I could investigate that. Meantime I dropped off soundly.

I woke once during the night, as I always do. Nothing had disturbed me. It's just a physical habit. At first my mind was blank about my overnight guest. Almost like a sleepwalker I went to the bathroom, and there things began to come back to me. There were slight traces of the late bath that had been taken, but none of the girl's clothes were about. I listened. Everything was normally and reassuringly quiet. I peered out of the bathroom window. The night had not cleared and it was difficult to see anything. There was not a sound—at first . . .

And then I heard a slight something. Even before I could identify it I saw something which I had not the slightest trouble in recognizing. The girl—Mary McCann. And she was returning to the house.

I looked at my watch. It was ten minutes after three. I kept my eyes on her until she got so close to the house that I could no longer see her from the upper window. She was moving swiftly, but not running. As near as I could tell, she was wearing a long dark coat.

When I could no longer see her I stepped to the head of the stairs and listened. I could hear the kitchen door quietly closed and then the faint shuffle of steps. I heard the davenport creak reassuringly. It was clear that Mary McCann was curling herself comfortably into place. I stood there alert and still somewhat uncertain, until I could distinguish faint regular sounds, the breathing of one who is falling asleep.

Only then did I stir from my place at the head of the stairs. Stealthily I moved into Ella's room. I snapped on a light and saw that the blanket bed on the floor had been considerably reduced. That puzzled me for an instant until I concluded that the bed on the floor had evidently grown uncomfortable before the expedition into the night and that she must have transferred the blankets and herself down to the davenport before her departure. The way in which she had just now settled herself upon the davenport was not at all experimental. I looked about the room for her clothes. They were not there.

I retreated towards my own room, quite resolved to think out a course of action for morning. At the head of the stairs I paused again and listened. Not a sound from the room below. I must repeat that I had by no means forgotten whatever it was that the girl had slipped under the rug in the hall. As I passed the spot I stooped and groped about with my hand. I scarcely expected it to be there, but it was—a thinnish manila envelope about five by seven inches.

Behind my own closed doors I examined it. The envelope was blank and tightly sealed. There was something inside, and at last I held it up before the light. At first I could see nothing except where the edges of the enclosure were. And then I began to see heavy black printed letters, like a heading of some sort. With a cold fascination I worked the thing out until I was fairly sure of these words:

CERTIFICADO DE DEFUNCION

That was quite enough, and I stopped, thoroughly ashamed of myself. I returned the sealed envelope to the hiding place where Mary McCann had left it, and once more put myself to bed, but I could not forget that there was a death certificate under the hall rug. I lay awake conscientiously until everything began to gray with the dawn and then again I slept heavily.

That was all that happened that night—so I thought.

Chapter Two
I Meet an Inquiring Reporter

But much more was to happen the next day, the twentieth of June. I rose at my usual time and moved briskly about, thinking thus tactfully to rouse my guest. We'd breakfast together, and if I could manage it I knew what the subject for conversation would be. Sometimes Viney arrives early enough to make me a pan of muffins, which she adores doing, and sometimes I make coffee and toast for myself. After breakfast I check menus and do the ordering for the next day. Lola comes on at nine-thirty, and the day's routine at the Dark Lantern is under way.

I looked into Ella's room as I went by. It was just as I had last seen it at about twenty minutes after three that morning. I let my heels pound down the steps and pushed wide the door to the lounge with a cheerful good morning.

Mary McCann was not there.

I went to the kitchen and looked about, more conscious of irritation than anything else. That's how I came to notice the towel. It was one of the dishtowels that as usual had been rinsed and hung behind the stoves, but this one was now trailing from the edge of the sink. I picked it up. It was dampish. I shook it out. One end was clean and unmarked, but the other was colored with something still faintly reddish, like a bloodstain that had been washed out before it set. Yes, I thought of bloodstains at once.

I seized the towel and retreated to the lounge. It was almost time for Viney and I had no explanations that sounded sensible. If I saw no more of the girl, what was the use of letting Viney ask questions? I folded the blankets in a pile to take upstairs and plumped up the davenport pillows. I shook out my nightgown critically—the lace on it is real and I shall never own another as lovely at the rate I'm being paid by a grateful public.

I saw the stains at once. Unmistakably blood this time, already dried and brown. The lace that forms the left shoulder strap was definitely marked, and further examination revealed faint traces on the inner side of the back that somehow suggested scratches.

Loaded with the blankets, gown, and towel, I turned at the door to be sure that I was leaving no sign of my informal guest. I had cleared away expertly, I was positive. Back upstairs I hurried, thankful that Viney was a bit late. The blankets were dumped back into their cedar box. I could not attempt a rush job on my precious lace gown, so I rolled it up and thrust it down into my knitting bag. The dishtowel I put to soak in the bathroom bowl, and gathered up the towels that Mary McCann had used and tossed them in the laundry hamper. There could be nothing give-away about a few extra towels.

Then I thought of the sealed envelope which I had returned to its hiding place. I threw back the runner, but no manila envelope lay revealed. It was as gone as Mary McCann.

By this time I was more incensed than irritated. If the envelope had vanished it could only mean that the girl had sneaked back upstairs after I had fallen into my last sleep. Certainly she had done a lot of coming and going; furthermore, she had meant to disappear.

I rinsed out the dish towel and satisfied myself that the faint discoloration had entirely left the fabric. It would be wiser, I thought, to return it to the rack behind the stoves.

I could invent a good explanation for Viney if necessary. That done, there was a good ten minutes in the clear before Viney came, and by that time my coffee was perking and I had the house opened for the day. If only I'd washed the plate and glass instead—

Viney, it soon developed, was so full of news that damp dish towels, sandwich plates and milky glasses could have been thrust at her from all sides and she would not have been interested.

Something terrible had happened at the tourist camp, she began to shout at me. Viney is a grand cook, but her voice is not that described as an excellent thing in woman.

"Seems like they found a dead man up there," she continued in her own sonorous style. "In one of them little houses, you know, where folks sleep all night. That's what kept me a little this morning, Jed stallin' around up there as we come by. But shucks, Jed says it's likely the nearest he'll ever get to a murder and he oughtn't to lose his chance."

Jed is Viney's brother-in-law and she, I suspect, helps to support him in the large and elegant leisure that is his.

"Murder!" I echoed.

"Yes'm, Miss Fergus. Alec Porter and that red-headed kid at the gas station, the both of 'em is sure it's murder. They was a knife stickin' right out of his back. I didn't see it, though." A story never grows under Viney's telling.

"That's the danger with a tourist camp," I replied. "All sorts of riff-raff and no way to be choosy."

"Riff-raff, hr-rmph!" Viney scoffed. "Jed says he had a bunch of money on him and a finger ring—not a diamond, though," she qualified with her usual care. "And his car was a Packard."

"But who found him? And how did they happen to find him? And have they sent for the police?"

It was like Viney to correct my errors first. "This ain't no town, Miss Fergus. But Ike Harvey—he's our sheriff—

he'll turn the job over to Steve Ellender, the poor kid."
This comment meant nothing at all to me.

"But who found him?" I insisted.

"Alec Porter should have—it's his place—but seems like
some little tyke, runnin' around the camp while its folks
was packin' to be off, barged right in on the corpse and
then nearly had a spasm."

"And had the person who did it already gone away?"

"Yes'm, Miss Fergus. How in time am I ever goin' to
strip veal without my other knife, I'd like to know? . . .
He'd had a light night, Alec says, and most of the cars had
already pulled out. But he asked them that was left, the
outfit with the youngster and a couple of others, to stay till
Steve got there—"

"Steve?"

"Steve's nothin' but a kid, but he's real bright and a awful hard worker. Ike and that Downing feller always puts
it up to Steve. Say, Miss Fergus, you ain't took my other
knife?"

I once more assured Viney that I never touched her pet
utensils, and prepared to type the menus for the day. If
Viney continued her revelations I'd have no trouble hearing
her above the clatter of the typewriter keys.

"Dumb funny thing about that knife," I heard her mutter. "I bet you that Lola— Anyways, whoever done it, he
didn't go off in the car. Jed seen the car hisself. A good car,
he says."

"What make?" I asked a bit absently. "Oh, yes, I remember you said it was a Packard."

"Yes'm, Miss Fergus, with just one seat to it and a little
extry one behind. A yellow auto."

I knew then just as surely as I know now, after the trial
and everything, that I was in for something. Yet I was fool
enough to think that I could keep things to myself.

I finished the menus—such a mess of them as I made
after hearing about the yellow roadster. Then—and only

then, for I was determined not to get hysterical—I reached
across the desk and pulled out the little cottony bundle I
had thrust there the evening before. Perhaps I'd better not
examine it there, I thought, and marched sedately up to my
room and closed the door.

There was no wrapping; the bundle was held together
by a couple of common pins. What the pins fastened was
blue, not cotton but linen, and when shaken out proved to
be a boy's suit—the sort of outfit a small boy wears in hot
weather. Microscopic pants and a jumper all in one piece.
No sleeves. The whole piped with white linen. There were
midget pockets and across the left upper one was embroi-
dered a name. *Tommy* . . . I looked twice at the embroidery.
It was not machine work, but something that had been added by an expert hand. I say added because there were unmistakable wrinkles about the pocket labeled *Tommy,* wrinkles and creases and needle pricks and even the faint traces
of a penciled guide that the embroiderer had followed. Yet
the suit was not new. It was not at all shabby, but it had
seen service.

Wrapped within the linen suit were other articles, equally worn. There was a blue linen beret matching the suit.
There was an undergarment of fine white cotton that to my
uninitiated eye—I have no nephews—looked to be nothing
but trunks and crisscrossing straps. There was a pair of
elkskin barefoot sandals. That was all. Everything was of
excellent quality. They would fit a four-year-old I decided
weightily. I searched every article again, for labels. There
was nothing of the sort, yet I could not be certain that the
clothing was hand-made.

So this was my clue. I felt relieved. A boy's blue linen
play suit could have nothing to do with murder in a tourist cabin. I rolled the bundle up again and deposited it for
safekeeping in my knitting bag. That made me think once
more of my bloodstained nightgown. Well, I should have to
wait until the end of the day to deal with that.

I had to get back to my job. The Dark Lantern does not quite run itself. I did some ordering—went over the mail—wrote some checks—took care of telephone reservations—discussed salads with Lola—cut ascension lilies and delphinium for the big bowls—and all the time I was wrestling with an almost irresistible temptation to slip away to find out for myself what was going on at Alec Porter's tourist camp.

Stay out of it, stay out of it—I told myself sharply. No one knows the girl was here last night. You have no right to take chances with Ella's business, sick as she is. And anyway, it's just your feverish imagination that connects Mary McCann with a man found dead in a tourist's shack.

Stay out of it. . . Well, so I did—for about two and a half hours longer.

The luncheon period at the Dark Lantern swung along, and soon I was too busy for inner debate. There were a dozen dieting matrons in prints and chiffons who were to play bridge afterwards in the lounge, and their wants kept both Lola and me on the jump.

Just as the last check was presented and I was deciding that business had about run its course until the dinner period, another guest arrived. Something told me at once that here was a reporter from a Dayfield paper. The woman was smart and up-and-coming, clearly nobody's fool. I resolved to give her no chance to question me—women have more subtle ways of gleaning information than have men—and withdrew discreetly to the kitchen. When I think how we two got together before the week was out—

The kitchen was hot and too odorous and noisy with dishwashing, but I loitered uncertainly. Viney was making pies, green-apple and fresh raspberry, and I watched her with admiration, for the woman is an artist; but she was not pleased, and I knew that her opinion was that I should be minding my business at the front of the house.

Consequently, I seized upon the first item for comment that took my eye.

"Why, Delphine hasn't called for the basket yet, has she?"

"No'm, Miss Fergus, she ain't, but I got the milk and bowl of salad back in the ice-box, don't worry. That lazy good-for-nothin' and the woman she works for, the both of 'em, them's the kind that sleeps all day. Nobody ever seen 'em stirrin' around. Not that Delphine's ever been as slow as this before." Viney's passion for accuracy was functioning normally.

Lola beckoned to me. The bridge-playing ladies had thought of something else they wanted. I assuaged them mechanically, thinking idly of what I had hitherto considered the only mystery afforded by the environs of the Dark Lantern—the picturesque Delphine. I had always meant to trail Delphine to see exactly where she went. Both Ella and Viney had told me, but I had a secret hope that Delphine was more interesting than their accounts would indicate.

In the first place, Delphine looked exactly like a musical comedy quadroon from New Orleans. They don't really come that way, I know, but she looked the part, most decoratively. It would date me hopelessly, I am well aware, to say that she was my idea of Cassie—Legree's Cassie, always one of my favorite storybook people. She was tall and slender and languorously graceful; her eyes dark and always half shut and I liked to call them tragic; her skin was a warm yellow that was almost ivory. I could never be sure about her hair, for she always appeared in a plain wide-brimmed hat with a deep tight-fitting crown, but I could easily imagine it was straight and worn parted in the center and drawn closely back around her head. To my delight, large red-gold hoops swung from her ears. Otherwise her costume was not at all in character, for she was always attired in a glistening white cover-all much like a nurse's uniform, buttoned high at the throat and long-sleeved.

Now that I've digressed with such a long description of Delphine, I may as well make the explanation complete. All that we knew—all that even Viney knew—was that Delphine "did for" an elderly invalid who had gone into retreat at the old Newagen farm, a half mile or more back from the Dark Lantern in what was called locally the Old Cut. Early in April Delphine had appeared and, speaking for her employer, had made arrangements with Ella to call for a basket of prepared food every day at noon. The quantity stipulated could serve two people amply, but it was to be plain and simple, soups and plenty of vegetables, custards and other milk puddings, chicken and sometimes a little fish—the usual uninteresting diet of an invalid.

Every day at noon Delphine would appear at the kitchen door, hand in an empty basket, receive a filled one from Viney, and stride off across the fields to the point where her path dipped into the Old Cut. Once a week she would demand the lady in charge and deliver a small sealed envelope, exactly like a pay envelope. It always contained the exact amount agreed upon in new money—dollar bills.

That—so far—was the mystery of Delphine. I was still thinking about her and it when, after placating the bridge-players, I looked in upon the dining-room hoping to find it empty. But my friend, the reporter, was still there.

She put down her coffee cup and beckoned to me. I could do nothing but advance toward her table.

"Sit down a minute, won't you? I'd like a little help and may be you can give it to me. And won't you join me?" She offered me a cigarette.

"I'm Georgia Paxton and I've been sent here on a story, and I'm afraid I'm sunk."

Now, I ask you, didn't that sound like the tourist camp murder? I could feel myself stiffen, but the woman went right on.

"I'm hunting a farmhouse that seems to be off the beaten path. I've had my car up I don't know how many impossible lanes, but I must be hopelessly stupid about following the directions of the natives. It's called the Newagen farm, I believe. Have you ever heard of it, or have I lost it completely?"

"Yes, I've heard of it," I admitted in rather patent relief, "and it's not so very far from here, but as far as I know you'll have to walk. I'm no authority on the neighborhood, however. There's probably a road in from the other side."

"I'd prefer to sneak up on the place, if I could," Mrs. Paxton stated, and then laughed frankly at my raised eyebrows.

I believe she would have told me more, but at that moment a stentorian summons from Viney commanded me. "Miss Fergus, come here once, please, ma'am!"

To keep those ample tones from arousing the bridge-players, I excused myself and fled to the kitchen. Viney waylaid me in the cupboard room with an ominous whisper. She can whisper upon occasion.

"Miss Fergus, Steve's here, and he wants to talk to you. And what in time do you think?" She attempted a sympathetic pat upon my shoulder, a gesture which should have warned me. "Steve's found our knife!"

Chapter Three
I Look at a Dead Man

Ever the efficient businesswoman, my first comment was:
"Tell Lola to take the desk. There's a woman just ready to
leave. Now, who wants to see me and where is he?"

"It's the sheriff's young man, Miss Fergus, our Steve
Ellender from over to Portage, and he wants to know about
the murder. He's in the kitchen."

I advanced to meet the law. I wanted to know about the
murder too.

A pleasant-faced young fellow still in his twenties stood
at a window as if studying the rear approaches to the inn.
He turned as he heard me and smiled. It was a charming
smile, and I hope that I smiled back. He fingered the lapel
of his coat as though he were about to reveal a badge.

"My name is Ellender," he introduced himself. "I'm from
the prosecutor's office. I can say that I'm speaking for Sheriff Harvey as well. Is there a quiet place where I can talk to
you? I understand you are the manager."

On the chance that Mrs. Paxton would have taken herself off, I led the way back through the cupboard room and
across the dining-room to a corner table. "This is the best I
can do," I explained. "We won't be disturbed at this hour."

I caught a glimpse of Mrs. Paxton stepping into a trim
coupé. I recalled too late that I had given her no very specific directions for reaching the Newagen farm. I seated

myself and no doubt disappointed the young upholder of the law by not facing the light.

"First," said he, "tell me your exact relation to this place. The woman in the kitchen attempted an explanation that balled us both up."

I explained myself and my friend Ella Brookfield's illness and all the rest of it, and Steve Ellender nodded agreement.

"I see—that rates you as number one boss. I take it that you have already heard that a man was killed sometime last night at Alec Porter's camp, just west of here. This is what killed him . . ."

Like a magician performing a trick he produced a knife which he displayed on the table between us. Viney was right. Our knife had been found.

"Your woman in the kitchen has already identified this knife as belonging to the inn here," the young man resumed. "She tells me it was in its usual place when she left last night, about nine o'clock. I want to hear what you can tell me about it." This time he did not smile at me.

I gave him as grave and steady a look as he was bending upon me. "I know nothing at all about the knife, except that it appears to be one of a set in constant use in our kitchen."

"Were you alone here last night?"

I was not expecting the inevitable question so bluntly, nor so soon, and I must confess that I quibbled. "The staff leaves when their work is finished, and since Miss Brookfield's illness, that means that I am alone. I've not minded that; I'm not afraid."

He persisted. "And were you alone last night?"

"Well, I'll tell you," I began with an air of bright obligingness.

And then I told him about the man who had been looking for Mary McCann. I described him and said that I should recognize him if I were to see him again.

"Not a chance, Miss Fergus. You have just described, quite plainly, the man who was stabbed in the back with this knife—of yours." He added the last two words after a deliberate pause.

I gave an appropriate shudder and waited. I had nothing more to volunteer, though there were plenty of questions I wanted to ask. I was about to take them up when he smiled at me, almost apologetically.

"Could you establish an alibi for yourself for last night?"

"Only my word," I proclaimed, no doubt proudly, "that I was here in this place all night and asleep for the most part, I had no cause for alarm after the prowler left. And he did leave . . ." I told about his making off up the road. Rather neat, I thought. I hadn't lied yet about Mary Mc-Cann—at least, not in so many words. I decided to edge in with some questions of my own.

"The man who came here last night—the man who was killed—who was he?"

"We are not yet certain of his identity," Ellender replied. "Several names were found on him, all or none of which he might have used. Here—let me read them to you. Maybe one of them will click."

He said this ingenuously, but I had a nasty feeling that he was watching my expression with the well-known gimlet eye.

"Peter Hughes . . . J. C. Smith . . . Gibson Breck . . . No addresses at all."

The names told me nothing, and Ellender recognized the fact.

"But they're something to go on," I offered fatuously. "And surely you have other clues?"

"Yes." He gave me a steady look, which left me a bit chilled. "Yes, there are—other clues."

"Do you know when he was killed?" I asked.

"Not officially. The coroner's first guess, something between midnight and three a.m., will probably be established."

I thought of Mary McCann, of her strange return from elsewhere at ten minutes after three. I was afraid the young detective was reading my mind, so perhaps I overdid the nonchalance.

"Viney is my authority for the statement that the murdered man was driving a Packard with a rumble. I believe I may have seen that car last night, about a quarter of nine. A muddy yellow car went by. There were two men in the front and a girl in the rumble. I suppose that's the reason I noticed it. The girl alone in the back looked a bit odd."

The young man was smiling at me fondly. "I felt sure you might have something to tell me, Miss Fergus. Two men and a girl. Could you describe them?"

"No, I'm afraid not." I was decently regretful. "It was dusk and the car was going at a fairly good speed. Two men and a girl in the rumble. A yellow car, mud-splashed, with an out-of-state license. That's positively all I can report."

He was silent for a minute, his lips pursed as though he had some intention of whistling. "My most promising clue," he said slowly, "is the knife that came from your kitchen. I wish you could explain that knife, Miss Fergus."

"I recognize that it belongs to the inn, but I feel no burden of responsibility about explaining it," I announced in what might be called my schoolroom style. "Its presence in the murdered man's back is a complete mystery to me."

"Are you quite sure, Miss Fergus, that you saw nothing of the girl?"

My test was upon me. "There was a girl in the rumble," I repeated. "I'm afraid that's all I can tell you." Direct lying I found to be a grim business.

Steve Ellender's face lost much of its youthfulness. "I'm sorry," he said. There was a brief interval. Then he spoke again. "Your cook tells me that you never drink milk."

My mind raced furiously. Viney's passion for accuracy had betrayed me. Why, oh, why hadn't I washed and put away the plate and glass which had held Mary McCann's late lunch?

"Well," I managed to say as facetiously as possible, "hardly ever. Viney hasn't known me long."

"No one around here has known you long. Miss Fergus."

The way I felt when I heard those words from the lips of that mild-looking, steady-eyed young upholder of the law wasn't any fun, but I succeeded in listening to them blandly.

"The plate and glass will be checked for prints, of course," he murmured, but still I failed to break down and confess, if that was what he was trying to accomplish. In fact, I believe I forced him to lead a trump, which was to startle me more than I let him know.

"Your cook—Viney, you call her?—has identified a raincoat hanging by the kitchen door as yours." He paused in interrogation.

"Yes," I admitted, "I believe there is an old coat of mine hanging there."

"When did you wear it last, Miss Fergus?"

"When did it rain last? I never wear it at any other time. Last Saturday, wasn't it?"

"I have to tell you that your coat is quite curiously marked. Viney states that last night when she left the coat was in its usual condition. She has explained to me that she considered wearing it herself last night, with your permission, of course, for she thought when she left that she might get caught in a shower. It was quite cloudy, as you may recall."

He made this statement dispassionately, but a kind of chill bit into me. I knew so well how correct in detail Viney's information was.

"You astound me, Mr. Ellender," I said in a suspiciously faint voice. "I have nothing at all to say because I haven't the faintest idea what it means. I should like"—and I spoke more positively—"to see the raincoat."

"I can arrange that," he replied.

For a few seconds he sat and looked at me. He was not convinced, that was evident, but I bore his inspection stolidly.

"I take it," I said at last, "that you regard the inn and me as being connected with the case. We are to be investigated?"

"You are already being investigated."

"If I can be of any help, I shall be very glad," I murmured conventionally. "I wish that I could explain about the knife and the coat."

"I wish you would," he returned. He glanced at his watch and rose to go. "There's one other point, Miss Fergus. I must ask you to view the body. I can have you back within a hour and a half."

"Very well. If I must, I must, and I should prefer to go now than nearer the dinner hour. But I must speak to Viney first."

Steve Ellender followed me into the kitchen and stood by gravely during my colloquy with Viney, who was almost beside herself with curiosity. My eyes strayed to the raincoat in spite of myself. It was still hanging where it always had. I brought up the matter of my own accord.

"Marks on this coat?" I demanded and stretched out my arm to grasp the garment for inspection.

But Ellender forestalled me and held it out for me to look at, but not to hold in my own hands. I wonder what damage he expected me to wreak upon it . . .

He turned the raincoat slightly, and there, just below the left shoulder was a smooth cut rather than a tear in the cravenetted surface of the coat. It was almost three inches long and looked as if it had been made by a sharp-edged means—a knife. I thought of my lace nightgown. The blood stains had been on the left shoulder strap.

We went to the county coroner's office. I shall not dwell on what followed. I was bidden to look upon the face of a dead man. I heard myself saying yes, this was the man who had stepped up to the inn door the evening before.

That was all of that, thank heaven . . . There was a brief colloquy between the prosecutor's young man and the coroner, to which I listened with indifference, upon the part of the participants. The man had been dead at least eight hours when examined, which meant he had met death about two o'clock. The knife thrust had been a savage one. The heart had been pierced and death had ensued at once. How could a slight girl have struck such a terrible blow? I triumphed silently.

The run back to the Dark Lantern was accompanied by no more conversation than upon our first journey. I preferred not to start anything that might lead to Mary McCann. I had a dreadful feeling that the young detective already knew more about Mary McCann than I thought he did.

He had turned into the drive at the inn and was beginning a perfunctory apology for the necessity of the expedition which had just ended when a small car furiously driven swung in behind us so suddenly that a collision seemed inevitable. But the brakes of the oncoming coupé were in excellent condition.

"Officer! I must speak to Steve Ellender at once!"

It was a woman's voice. I recognized both it and the coupé. Georgia Paxton stepped out and advanced toward us.

"They sent me after you from the camp," she panted. "You had just passed. There's a dead man down at the Newagen place. I found him. Another murder!"

Chapter Four
I View the Second Body

I must now become a second-hand narrator. What Georgia Paxton discovered at the Newagen farm and what happened after she returned there with Steve Ellender she herself told me.

After leaving the Dark Lantern Georgia had lost a lot of time but had at last found the Newagen farm. She parked her car with the growing impression that the place was surely deserted. She advanced to the front door which, oddly, stood partly open. She knocked. No one came. She knocked again—and again. At last, because the door was ajar, she walked in. There was no one on the ground floor nor anything alarming to be seen. Everything was in reasonable order.

Now that she was in the house, said she, why not make her survey complete? She went upstairs. There were three rooms. The first one was unused except for a general clutter of abandoned furniture. The second room showed plain traces of recent normal occupancy, but there was no one there. The third room opened from the second, and it was there that Georgia Paxton found the body.

She retreated screaming from the sight, for it was only too clear that the man had been murdered. She pulled herself together then and forced herself to a more intelligent course. She went back into the room and took a long photographic look at the man a-sprawl on the floor at the foot of the bed. There was a knife sticking from his back. A wooden-handled knife.

She could not see his face except for the line of freshly shaven chin. His clothes were those of the custom-fitted hiker, and the one hand that she could see was tanned but smooth and well cared for. There was what looked like a recent inkstain on the middle finger.

She backed to the door and again tried to check up on what was visible to her eye. There was nothing that announced itself as a clue. There was a single bed, a painted dresser, a chair. That was all the furniture. Upon the dresser was an amazing array of cosmetics, bottles and boxes, expensive brands. There were no women's clothes anywhere—nor men's, for that matter.

Then she had fled the place, tried to telephone from the gas station, and had caught up with Ellender as he was returning me to the Dark Lantern.

As I said, Ellender went off immediately to the Old Cut, taking Mrs. Paxton with him. On the way she told him her story. He did not ask her many questions beyond wanting to know what had taken her to the Newagen farm. She showed him her newspaper credentials and said she had been sent to interview the occupant, as the paper had a tip that an internationally known novelist was staying there.

Arrived at the farm, Georgia Paxton reported that the detective did little more in the room where the body lay than she had done. Elsewhere in the house, however, he poked about inquisitively and verified her impression that there were no clothes anywhere, upstairs or down. There was nothing to indicate the recent presence of anyone from the great world, aside from the astonishing collection of face creams and lotions. Ellender turned quizzically upon her as he picked up an ancient copy of *Capper's Weekly*.

"I don't quite believe in your international novelist."

Georgia Paxton said she stepped back into the kitchen and opened the doors of an old-fashioned wooden cupboard. There was nothing to see but dishes—heavy, shabby

plates and cups. Under a napkin in a basket were several
pieces of china quite different in quality, a detail which I
found of considerable personal interest. She went to the
coal range; it still felt faintly warm. She lifted a lid and together she and Ellender examined what they found among
the ashes. There were no papers or letter charred beyond
recognition, only empty boxes and cartons—breakfast food,
cereals, rice, barley, oatmeal, stuff like that.

By that time other officials began to arrive: Sheriff Harvey with a retinue of deputies, the coroner, and a solid citizen who was County Prosecutor Downing, all quite willing
to follow Ellender's lead. The body was officially examined
and searched. The knife was withdrawn and possible finger
prints properly protected. The victim's pockets contained
the usual articles. When Georgia Paxton saw Ellender looking at cards and an identification slip in a leather case, she
asked a few direct questions.

"Who is he? You've found his name, haven't you?"

"The cards say *Laurence Gregory*—a club address in New
York."

"Laurence Gregory! What a story!"

"What do you know about him?" Ellender demanded.

"How delicious for me to tell you who Laurence Gregory
is. Haven't you heard of the Jonas Craig will, or the Nich-
olas murder, to mention only the Ohio cases?"

Georgia said he blushed in real embarrassment, but with
considerable dignity admitted that the name meant nothing to him. He was willing to suspect that Gregory might
possibly be an operative connected with one of the eastern
private agencies.

She let it go at that, she said.

Naturally, Steve Ellender did not. He sent wires east-
ward at once—he told me later that his first idea was that
the real Laurence Gregory would be found placidly following his daily round and that the dead man would prove to
be an imposter.

And then the young man set to work to find those in
the community who might have seen the murdered man.
That brought him to me. By that time the dinner hour at
the Dark Lantern was over; in fact, it was about the same
time that I had seen the yellow Packard the evening before.
Steve Ellender's forecast had been sound. We had been doing heavy business and the curious were still inclined to
loiter.

I listened to his official description of the victim.

"A man who sounds like that was here for dinner last
night. He was alone. He sat there—at that table." I pointed. "I had a reason for becoming quite interested in him."
I paused.

Steve Ellender was patient with my dramatics. "And that
reason?" he urged.

"A comment made about him by one of a party of diners." I repeated what I had overhead, ending with the sinister interpretation put upon his presence by the bald-headed
man.

"Hmm—that would point—" he murmured. From what
Georgia had said, I knew to what or to whom it would
point. Ellender had been careful not to mention to me the
victim's possible identity. "I'd like the names of those people."

"The reservation was made by a Mrs. Carson Bray; that's
the best I can do."

He made a note of the name and was reasonable about
my lack of other information. "And from what those people said you attempted to identify the subject of their remarks." He returned to my story.

"Yes, and I am quite sure I spotted him. The man dining
alone looked like the one you have been describing to me.
I tried to find out when he left whether he had come in a
car. I thought not. There was something about his clothes
that suggested the hiker—but not the hitch-hiker."

"Perhaps he was a cyclist."

I paid no attention to that comment. "Something inter-rupted me—I did not see him leave. Lola might have—or maybe you've already talked to her."

I didn't quite like the way he looked at me when I said that, but his voice sounded friendly when he spoke. "Well, Miss Fergus, it adds up to this—I'll have to ask you to take a look at him."

"Not again," I wailed. "Remember I'm staying here alone of nights." I consider that I was entitled to a qualm or two.

"I'd be delighted to post a guard." He made the offer with a quickness which I did not regard as suspicious until I had almost accepted it. What if Mary McCann should come back?

It developed, however, that I need not be taken to my second inspection of the dead until the next morning. Steve Ellender had other matters to discuss with me at the mo-ment.

"What can you tell me of the Newagen place? Know who's been living there?"

"I can tell you of one set of facts which is beginning to impress me as—er—well, odd." Relieved that on this topic I had nothing to conceal, I related to him what I knew of Delphine and the arrangement that had been made about the daily supply of food. I worked to the climax of her non-appearance that day for her basket.

"By the way, your Delphine never rode a bike, by any chance?"

Delphine on a bicycle—curiouser and curiouser. I mean, I was beginning to wonder about the bicycle *motif*.

"Well—suppose we leave it that if anything—anything at all occurs in the night, you call my office at once. Some-body will be there to answer."

I went to bed, or rather retired to my room. I suppose I was too tense to sleep. I tried to sort things over mentally, but I could make neither head nor tail of any of the events of the last two days; I came to a determined conclusion about only one point: I was going to "find" the bundle of little boy's clothes. I could not tell how I had actually found it; that would betray Mary McCann. So I must think out a way to produce the bundle in the most realistic manner.

Surprisingly early the next morning Steve Ellender appeared. I had just poured my first cup of coffee when his rakish, almost paintless car announced itself. He made no attempt to conceal his impatience to hurry me off, but I drank my usual two cups just the same.

I don't believe that familiarity breeds contempt nor that you can get used to anything if it lasts long enough . . . It was a nerve-wracking business having to look down upon that dead face, and I hope I shall never have to do such a thing again as long as I live.

Yes, I said at once. Yes, it was the same man, but almost as I spoke I was not sure. There was something about the line of the jaw, and then I noticed his hands. I was certain enough about the hands to speak firmly.

"The man who dined at the Dark Lantern did not have hands like these. He was lighting a cigarette as I passed his table, and somehow they registered. See—these are manicured. The man at the table had very short nails and thick cuticle. You can't grow fingernails overnight."

"A nice point," agreed Steve Ellender. "Now if you will just take a look at his clothes—"

I fell down there. I could be sure of nothing except that the man at the inn had worn fairly similar clothing. My conclusion was, and Ellender gravely accepted it, that this was the body of a different man.

"I picked up your waitress last night and she's even more positive than you, Miss Fergus, that this is another man. She says your customer had very stylish gold-tipped cigarettes."

I tried to recall, for my own satisfaction. I could see the hands holding a lighter, snapping it into flame, but I couldn't see a gold-tipped cigarette. I had to let Lola take her bow alone.

Ellender drove me back to the inn at once. There was no attempt at making conversation from either of us. I had something to stage and I was growing miserably nervous about it, and no doubt the detective had plenty on his mind.

"Well, so much is so much," he said as he opened the door of his car and helped me to alight. "My next interview is with your Mrs. Carson Bray. Wish me luck."

"Of course," said I brightly, with a bland gaze about my domain. "Why, whatever in the world—" I exclaimed, and pointed at a small object, carefully planted by my own hand at dawn's early light. "Looks like somebody's dropped something."

I walked toward the edge of the barberry border and poked at it with the toe of my shoe and then stooped and picked it up. If ever I wished for the schoolteacher's eyes in the back of her head I did then, but I had to go on with my role without knowing how my audience was taking it. I fingered the package gingerly and refused to let myself say, "Maybe it's a clue . . ." I was resolved not to be obvious.

"What's in it?" Steve demanded helpfully.

"I—I don't know," was my foolish reply. "It's—it's fastened with a pin."

Forthwith I pulled it out and shook out the bundle. "Clothes. Clothes for a little boy. See—" And I held up a garment at random.

Ellender poked about among the things for a minute, but gave no special sign of interest. "Lost out of a passing car, no doubt," he concluded. "You might keep 'em handy in case there are any inquiries. Well, stand by, if I need your help again." He started his disreputable car and was off.

Chapter Five
I Read the Papers

Viney was already at work, laden with gossip or news, as one chose to rate it. "Jed's wife seen Delphine yesterday," she bellowed as soon as I entered the kitchen.

Lest it be thought that Jed's wife is Viney's sister and that hers is a needlessly formal mode of address, I should explain that Jed's wife is Viney's sister's successor. According to Viney, she'd always kinda liked Jed and there was no sense in holdin' hard feelings after the divorce. So much for domestic history.

"Saw Delphine! When? That might be important."

"Yesterday morning just before eleven. She see her drive by and turn into the pike. She come on this way."

"How did she know it was Delphine?" I asked.

"Seen her. Plain as day. In that white get-up, just like she comes here."

"Driving a car?"

"Yes, ma'am, drivin' a little car. Jed's wife, she didn't know just what kind of a car it was except it was a little coupé, not so new—not shiny new anyways."

"Viney, I think Mr. Ellender ought to be told what your sister-in-law saw."

"Sure indeed, Miss Fergus. That's just what Jed said. He was fixin' to call Steve soon as he got to work. We ain't got no phone yet."

I was still engrossed in thinking over this item when Lola arrived, and Lola, thank goodness, brought in a bundle of newspapers.

The boldest headlines of the morning editions were devoted to the Laurence Gregory angle, but all it amounted to, in spite of the space the story occupied, was that the famous investigator could be reached neither at his office nor at his apartment. It was thought that he was working on a case, but as his secretary was fishing somewhere in the Adirondacks, nothing had yet been verified.

The question I had myself created only that morning was not yet in newsprint. The identity of the man slain at the Newagen farm with that of my mysterious diner on the evening of the nineteenth was now Ellender's business.

Ellender's cryptic allusions to a bicycle were no longer a mystery. I read that in a shed on the Newagen property a brand-new wheel had been found, a man's model. It had been tested for fingerprints, but nothing was said about results. There was no license on the bicycle. Dealers in Dayfield and surrounding towns were being canvassed.

There was plenty in the papers about the knife from the Dark Lantern kitchen, but just as much about the second knife, which came, the officer in charge stated, from the Newagen kitchen. Much was hinted about fingerprints, but no definite statements made.

One of the last parties of lunchers to arrive brought with them a screaming extra, and from what I could make out of the headlines I was wild to get it in my hands. There was something about Delphine and a bill of sale for an automobile, and also a phrase about SECRETARY EN ROUTE BY PLANE. I should have asked for the paper had I not seen it tossed aside as the group rose from their table. I swooped down upon the sheet at once and nonchalantly tucked it behind a tray on the plate rail.

The crowd had thinned enough by that time for me to read the paper, but before I could retrieve it not too openly matters took another twist—two twists, in fact.

A woman whom I had not recognized and to whom I had paid little attention finished her meal and bore down upon me with her check. "You won't mind if I wait here, or is the lounge to be in use? I was here yesterday, you know, and I found something that I've got to show to the police. He'll be here, he said, between two and two-thirty. So I won't have long to wait now. Men are supposed to be more dependable about dates than women, aren't they?"

"The police? Here? You found something? Who is coming here?" I knew I was stammering inanely, but I was startled.

"I guess I don't exactly know his right title." She laughed fondly. "His name's Ellis or something." She moved on and into the ladies' room, vanity case already open.

I was still at the cashier's desk and about to lock the cash register after the last of the lunchers when the service door swung open and a second woman made straight for me. I had no notion who she was, except that she could scarcely be a prospective patron, but there could not be the slightest doubt that she was in a highly exasperated state of mind.

"Viney says it's all right for me to use your phone. There's a reporter hanging on to ours, and I got to get through to Steve. Bet you a cent I can tell that kid something about the murder he don't know yet. Whereabouts is it at?"

At that moment Steve Ellender chose to make his entrance. Girlfriend-in-waiting number one was probably doing lip-stick duty again, for she did not emerge from the lounge to greet him, which gave girl-friend number two her chance.

"Listen here, Steve, I got something on this murder business and it ain't right you shouldn't hear about it. You know me, I guess—Mrs. Alec Porter over at the cabins—"

I saw Steve come to attention at that; furthermore, I saw him shoot me a glance that suggested exit, but they were the intruders, not I.

"Just a moment, Mrs. Porter," he begged. "Let's sit down here and be comfortable. I'm delighted to have this chance to talk to you. Alec explained where you were yesterday morning. He said you'd left before anyone knew what had happened."

His comment was merely polite and certainly without insinuation, but it infuriated her none the less.

"And if by that you think you can accuse me, you young whippersnapper—"

The young whippersnapper turned on the full force of his charm and finally soothed her to the point that she consented to be seated at one of our small tables.

"Now then, Mrs. Porter—but wait. I shan't want to be interrupted. Miss Fergus—" and he raised his voice as though my attention would have to be dragged to their *tete-à-tete*—"is there anyone waiting to see me?"

There was, I told him. In the lounge. A billowy lady who had acted mysterious about her business. Let him read that, I thought, into a declaration that I had failed to find out what she had come for.

Ellender strode to the lounge and looked in, murmured something pleasantly, and returned to his place opposite the impatient Mrs. Porter.

"And now, if you please, I'd be glad to hear your statement."

"Well, I was up early yesterday morning. I'd set the alarm for five, but I got up before it went off. I'd heard there was a detour beyond Rushville and I wanted to give myself plenty of time. It wasn't very light yet while I was dressing, and I run up the shade so's I could get what there was without turning on a light. A light turned on sudden always wakes Alec right up. That's how I come to see what I did, I guess. Anyways, I kind of noticed that with the curtain 'way up I could see across almost as far as Miss Brookfield's place."

At that point I broke out into gooseflesh, and I'm sure that young devil knew what was happening to me.

Mrs. Porter continued stolidly. "And then, just as I was pinning down my hairnet, I saw this girl. She was running along the path. You can easy see for yourself there's a path that makes a short cut from the State Line Pike clear up here to Miss Brookfield's, and this girl, she was coming towards the Pike."

Ellender nodded, but said nothing. I know I must have looked far too interested, but I was spellbound.

"But that ain't the whole of it," she resumed. "This girl—of course I couldn't see her very plain—she slipped right across the road and down along the row of cabins. I couldn't see whereabout she went after that. Fact is, I didn't give it another thought, for I was hurrying to get off and didn't have no idea that anything terrible had happened. I just sort of took for granted that she belonged to one of our tourist parties, but when I heard about the murder and all, I checked back in my mind and I knew very well that up to the time I went to bed on Tuesday night there was no girl like that in any of our cabins. I have to keep my eyes open, you know . . .

"So the minute I got back today I asked Alec, and he said no, the only party that turned in that night after I went to bed was this one that the murder happened to, and there was just the two men. No girl at all, Alec said. So I got to wondering whether that girl didn't come across from here to our camp just on purpose to kill that poor soul. I kind of thought I ought to tell you."

"Quite right, Mrs. Porter. You did exactly what you should have done."

If Steve had not replied with such prompt smoothness I suppose I should have made a fool of myself by blurting out something about the man having been killed much earlier than the hour at which Mrs. Porter had seen the girl. Steve Ellender knew that well enough, and he had his own way of handling both Mrs. Porter and Miss Fergus.

"Mrs. Porter, did you see this girl come from the inn?"

At that, my state was febrile.

"I told you I saw her on the path." Her answer reduced my temperature, but only for a second. "But if you want to walk yourself along the path, you'd see she'd have a pretty hard time finding any other place to come from. But I don't know where she hailed from—don't ask me," she disclaimed, after neatly putting me on what I have heard called a hot spot.

Ellender had finished with her. When she had been thanked, commended, and dismissed, I expected he would swing to me. So I felt somewhat put in my place when Steve said, "Just a minute, Miss Fergus, if you please. Mrs. Rockey won't take long, and then we'll get together."

He disappeared into the lounge. I heard the sound of voices, but I could distinguish no words. To show how coolly I could await the issue I shook out the noon extra of the Dayfield paper that I had salvaged during the luncheon hour and brought myself up to date with the press account of the case.

So deep was I in the news reports that I was almost unaware that Steve Ellender was saying goodbye to his friend Mrs. Rockey. He turned on his heel and marched directly to me.

"Wouldn't you like to see what was found here yesterday noon—found right there in that room?" He poked his head forward to indicate the lounge.

I stared up at him and waited.

He withdrew his hand from his coat pocket, extended it toward me, and unfolded his fingers.

My eyes felt themselves pulled downward to what was lying on his palm.

Chapter Six
I Face a Search Warrant

I believe that at this time Steve Ellender credited me with being a consummate actress. My portrayal of one completely surprised and nonplused was effective because it was genuine, though the stern youth who confronted me judged it the perfection of art.

I peered at the object lying on his outstretched palm. It looked like a tiny metal plate and a bit of chain.

"But what is it?" I fixed my puzzled eyes on his accusing ones.

"What is it?" he mocked. "That's good . . . Well, take a look."

I accepted his invitation. The object that I examined was an identification disk. I am no expert, but I was quite sure that the metal that composed it was not silver nor steel but platinum. The chain was fine and short, the whole gadget so small that never could it have encircled adult ankle or wrist. The name on the plate was Thomas Spade Neill.

Thomas—Tommy! Little boy's clothes marked Tommy—I got only that far, but the law could wait no longer.

"Where is the boy, Sara Fergus?"

His tone of righteous wrath infuriated me "You are making a fool of yourself, young man. I haven't the slightest idea what it's all about. You've got off on the wrong foot about something."

"I'm fed up with your stalling. And remember there's no gallery of fans for kidnapers. The public wants action and gets it quick. One word from me, and police and federal men and detectives all over the world—gosh, to think of its breaking on me!"

He paused and swallowed painfully. His face was clammy with perspiration.

"You're crazy," I retorted stoutly. "I know nothing of a kidnaped child."

"The disk that was on the Neill child when he—er—disappeared was found ingeniously hidden in this house, and that bundle of clothes— Quite a line you handed me about them. That fact alone could enrage a mob to the lynching point."

I was appalled, but my back was still up and I snapped, "Where was this chain found? And who found it? I mean—who is this fat woman that you trust her so implicitly?" I had to let fly at someone; the gibe at Mrs. Rockey's cushiony figure released a little emotion.

"I'm the one to worry about Mrs. Rockey's statement—her integrity is not your business. She found the nameplate when she emptied the pencil sharpener."

If he expected his information to break me down he was mistaken. It was fantastic and meaningless to me, but I said nothing. I puzzled it out later, of course, and in time learned that I wasn't so far wrong.

I thought the worst had happened, short of the lynching he so pleasantly hinted at, but it hadn't. I was plain scared when he drew a paper from an inner pocket and mumbled something about a search warrant.

They found nothing. There was nothing to find. The only thing removed by the searchers was the bundle of clothes. Ellender's morning indifference toward the garments had vanished since his interview with Mrs. Rockey.

"Miss Fergus, I could arrest you this minute as an accessory after the fact—and I could hold you. Such a course appears inevitable. That's not a threat; it's a prognosis. Think it over . . . Pick out your lawyer. Do a little financial planning about bail. Only don't be such a fool as to try to get away. You're being watched, you know. I've got quite a lot on you. The knife—and the raincoat—and the fingerprints on the glass—and Tommy's clothes—and the chain in the pencil sharpener. I'll say it's a lot."

"If that's your opinion," I was able to reply, "I know enough to say that I have nothing to say. And thanks for the hint about a lawyer."

He bowed slightly, but with no more grace than a small boy at Saturday afternoon dancing class. And then I did what he was probably counting on. I brought up the subject of Mary McCann myself, or what amounted to the same thing.

"Fingerprints on a glass?" I queried. "I wish I knew what you meant by that."

"Fingerprints on a glass from which milk had been drunk and fingerprints on the bottom of a small plate too—fingerprints that aren't yours, Miss Fergus, nor Viney's, though yours are there too, nice neat ones. Yet you were here quite alone on Tuesday night, you tell me . . . And these same fingerprints are coming to light in other interesting places. You followed Mrs. Porter's story with the keenest attention, too, I observed. Just one of the gang, Miss Fergus, one of the gang . . . Think it over. I'm off to hear others talk who are more chatty than you are at the present moment. I'll be seeing you!"

If that was to be his exit line it did not quite come off, for the telephone bell rang and he snatched at the receiver as though it was sure to be his call.

It was . . . A tiny voice crackled and snapped a message at him. I was probably rewarded for not trying to listen, for a second later Ellender bawled a relay toward a deputy still loafing in the drive.

"Hey, you, Pete! Drop around at the field in time for the seven-fifty plane this evening. The word is that Gregory's secretary is likely to have made it. If he did, give me a ring and I'll tell you where to park him."

Pete went off in one direction and Ellender in another, and I betook myself in the brief interval that was mine into the lounge.

I was pretty much in a state of nerves and was just about to resort to a cup of strong tea when my savior appeared. Georgia Paxton, no other.

"I've had no lunch and it's too early for dinner, but I'm starving. Can't you rustle me a high tea or an advance lot of whatever's being dished up for dinner tonight and sit down and talk to me while I eat it?" she demanded, plopping herself into a seat and snapping open her cigarette case. "It's about time the star witness gets an interview all to herself, anyway."

"Interviews!" I snorted. "If there's any interviewing being done, I want to do it, and you're it. Before I'm accused of any more crimes, I'd like the synopsis of the previous chapters, or a scenario or something. I've been reduced to reading the papers for information about murders committed practically next door."

"There, there, old dear! Drink your tea—you ought to lace it with rum, in your state. The papers haven't earmarked you as first murderer—yet. That fresh young sleuth is holding out on us, is he? Better tell Georgie all about it."

"Who are the Neills?" I countered. "Is there a scion named Thomas Spade?"

Mrs. Paxton put down the chicken bone she had been gnawing and wiped her fingers on her napkin. *"The* Neills? Tommy Neill? The Neills! Woman, what are you trying to tell me?"

"I'm asking you . . ."

"Thomas What's-his-name Neill—Tommy Neill! How did you guess?"

"I've guessed nothing. Why does that name set everybody off?"

"Don't you really recognize the name? Old Tom Spade was one of the bandit barons who cleaned up rather odorously in the days of Big Business. He's dead long since. Most of this ill-got ten millions went to his daughter Margot, who married a far more socially important person named Neill—a Philadelphia family. They lived here in Dayfield for a year or so after they were married. Young Neill was given some sort of a complimentary vice-presidency. They went back East and not long after there was a divorce. There was one child, a boy named after Grandfather Spade. The little chap died about a year ago."

"Then," said I, "if the boy is dead there's nothing to get excited about." As plain as day I could see CERTIFICADO DE DEFUNCION through a thick manila envelope.

"And yet you were pretty well steamed up a few minutes ago. Why not tell me the straight of it?"

I told her first about the platinum chain and disk that had been found in the pencil sharpener. And then I told her about the bundle of clothes.

"Ellender doesn't quite understand about the clothes," I explained. "I let him think that I'd found them just that minute. As a matter of fact, I picked the bundle up on Tuesday evening. I saw the car go by—the Packard, you know. I'm pretty sure the bundle was thrown from that car—"

She tried to interrupt me at that. Her disapproval was plain, but I hurried on.

"I never got around to examining the parcel until the next day. Of course I should have turned them over at once, but I didn't—and now Ellender thinks I know something about the child they belong to—and I don't!"

"I'll say you walked yourself right into trouble—and I'll say you must have had a reason—still have it, too—for not telling him they had been thrown overboard from the yellow roadster. And you're not telling me, either?"

She waited, but I said nothing.

"Just as you say . . . Have you put any of the twos and twos together? I have—and I'm beginning to fancy myself as a lady detective rather than the superlative special correspondent that I undoubtedly am."

"But you said the little boy was dead."

"Haven't you yourself just told me that your bright young man used the word disappearance? Here's my theory: what if the Neill child is not dead at all, but has been kidnaped?"

"Steve Ellender didn't talk as though the police knew about the case."

"He's smart, but I wonder—I wonder if he knows, or just guessed about the child. Lord, what a story!"

This from the newspaper woman who had just announced her intention of turning detective—

"So you think these two murders here link up with Tommy Neill, if he's kidnaped and not dead? Couldn't you find out about the child's death? That's something that can't be faked very easily."

"If the boy is not dead, where has he been kept for a year? Where is he now? Why has everything sort of come to a head right here? Oh, do you suppose—" I broke off to consider in silence the startling idea that had just come to me.

Georgia Paxton may not have been listening to me. Apparently she began to think aloud. "And here's another thing. The man I discovered at the farmhouse yesterday afternoon is in all probability Laurence Gregory, just about tops for private dicks. That's the kind the Neills would use. He must have been on a pretty hot trail. Do you suppose—" And she too lapsed into silence.

I took a chance. "That's exactly what I think. Delphine's elderly invalid. The plain, wholesome food. The boxes of cereal stuffed in the range. The rumble seat. But I wish you'd tell me just one thing."

"The rumble seat? I don't get that."

"Delphine's car. The child's been concealed at the New-agen place during these last weeks. Yesterday morning when Delphine drove off she had him hidden in the rumble, at least until she got beyond the gas station. If you've read the noon editions you know what I'm talking about."

"I'll bet the kid's been killed too," she said somberly. "But who does that leave to kill Gregory?"

"If the man you found was Gregory," I corrected. "Why, Delphine, I should say. Before she left."

"No, he hadn't been dead that long when I found him."

"Just a sample of what I meant when I said I had to depend upon headlines for what I know about the case. What is the official report about the time of his death?"

"The coroner says not much more than an hour before I found him."

"And Delphine left before noon. Why don't they get her and make her talk? She oughn't to be hard to trace."

"She's a noticeable person, from what you say. Something will break. But I don't know—about the child."

"He might be all right," I comforted.

"I don't mean that." She shook her head impatiently. "I saw the house, you know. Frankly, I can't believe that a youngster under six could have been kept there all this time and no trace remain. I've a good notion to go back there right now and see for myself."

She rose to go, but I was determined to make one more effort to pin her down on a certain matter. "Mrs. Paxton," I demanded, "just exactly what took you to the Newagen farm yesterday?"

"That," said she, "is a question I'll answer when you tell me just exactly why you haven't made yourself clear about the bundle of clothes."

"Check!"

"Quite."

"And I'm not weakening," I went on, "when I suggest to you that while I have no doubt that the identification tag so strangely found right here in this house is an authentic and genuine clue, I'm not at all sold on the clothes. They may have been provided for the child, but from what you tell me of his family, they are not the sort that actually belonged to him."

"So? It's a thought, but—does it help?"

"And I'm going to tell you something else, too, though you don't deserve it. They're expecting Laurence Gregory's secretary to arrive by plane tonight. At a quarter of eight."

She turned just as she was going out of the door, apparently bound to carry out her resolution about the Newagen farm at once. "Thanks! Thanks loads. You are a dear, Sara Fergus. I'll do as much for you some time."

"Do it now," I called after her. "What I'd especially like to see is a catalogue of Greenwater College."

"Bless the schoolteacher's heart! That's easy."

Chapter Seven
I Answer the Telephone

Diners were already beginning to arrive, but nevertheless I dispatched Lola to the gas station to buy the evening papers. I carried on in Lola's place and it seemed to me that she was gone longer than should have been necessary, but at last I saw her thrust her head around the service door. She was wide-eyed and pale with excitement. Leaving a party of six still debating the merits of melonball cocktails versus jellied consommé, I dashed out to meet her.

She stuttered over her news, and small wonder. "I got you the papers all right, Miss Fergus, but what do you think? I was just starting to beat it back here when she showed up. Delphine, Miss Fergus! She drove right up to the pump and stopped her car. Joe nearly sprained himself getting to the phone to call up Steve Ellender, but I don't know how they made out keeping her there. I was crazy to stay and yet kind of scared to, at that.—Sure, I'll be right out." This to the frantic appeal of one of the extra waitresses, who was being besieged by impatient customers.

I spread the newspapers Lola had brought me upon the cashier's desk when a persistent honking from the drive summoned me.

It was Georgia Paxton and she had the gleam of triumph in her eye. "I can't stop if I'm to make the field and welcome Laurence Gregory's secretary, but I simply couldn't wait to tell you, or rather, to show you. See, look at this!"

She displayed a calendar, a gaudy lithograph of Daddy, Mummy and the Little One basking about the hearth, the trio presumably caroling, "Keep the home fires burning," for music bars and notes and carefully syllabled words encircled the whole. In other words, it was merely another one of the calendars issued by a local coal company; there was one of the same crop hanging on the kitchen wall of the Dark Lantern.

My expression probably indicated an abridged version of the above comment, for Mrs. Paxton exclaimed, "Silly, don't you get it? See those marked dates. The nineteenth and the twentieth and the twenty-second. That's tomorrow! Who goes on the spot tomorrow? I ask you!"

"You mean somebody else is going to be murdered tomorrow?" And I shan't deny that my backbone went icy.

"Shudder if you must—all I know is that this calendar was hanging behind the range in the Newagen kitchen. Right before our eyes, and the young smartie never noticed it. He cleaned out all the ashes and stuff from the range, but paid no attention to this. I must have," she boasted, "or why should I have sent myself back there to chase down a faint impression of something? I calls it a clue."

She had thrust the calendar into my hands and I stood staring at it. The leaf topping the pad was June and the three dates were ringed in ink. The light where we were was not good enough to reveal more than that, but in fairness to myself I shall state that I said:

"Funny, isn't it, that this year's calendar should be hanging in a house that hasn't been occupied except for the last month or two? People don't acquire calendars in June."

"Which means that you call it a clue also. We'll go into a huddle later, old dear. I'm off to the field. I'll give you a ring before bedtime—if I can." She snatched back her calendar, stepped on the gas, and was out of the driveway before I had a chance to report the news about Delphine.

No doubt Georgia would be telling me by the time I next talked with her.

Business at the inn slackened after nine and I began to listen rather steadily for the promised call from Georgia Paxton. But the telephone did not speak. Lola and Viney finished their work and left. Lights were turned down and doors locked. I was restless. There was so much that I wanted to know . . . I determined to return Mrs. Potter's call.

The Porter house was well lighted. I walked around toward the kitchen where I found Mrs. Porter shaping hamburger steak into cakes. It was a staple in her sandwich line. I threw myself on her sympathy at once; an excellent approach, I've learned.

"You don't mind, I hope, trying to cheer me up. I declare, all these terrible things happening around here are getting on my nerves. I'm all alone at the inn, you know."

Mrs. Porter sniffed. I could be good and thankful that I didn't have to play jailer to the murderer herself.

I exclaimed properly over that lead and begged for more.

"That's exactly what Alec's let himself in for," she went on, slicing onion over her frying hamburger. "She's upstairs this minute, instead of in the lock-up where she'd ought to be. Not that I was supposed to have any say about it." She sniffed again.

"Delphine, of course! Lola told me she had come back. But why didn't they arrest her? Did they tell her about the man at the Newagen place?"

"Arrest her! I ask you . . . How should I know what they asked her, for all they had her right in my own parlor talking to her? Seems like there was no good place at the gas station and so Steve traipsed her over here. You heard about her driving off somewheres yesterday morning? That was in the papers, I guess. Well, of course, Joe and some woman did see her go, and Joe Teaberry's a nice clean boy who'd have no reason to lie about it, so that much is straight. I didn't hear Steve and them talking to her, but they was at it good and proper for over an hour, and then Steve said something to Alec, and Alec come and told me to see if the attic room was ready.

"It was ready good enough for her, but after she went up I followed along to see if there was anything I could do, and didn't she begin to talk a blue streak! She acted like it was a joke, kind of, that they wouldn't let her go back to the farm. There was some things she wanted, she said, not her clothes—she had some in a little bag with her and they'd even searched it, she said, so they knew she was telling the truth. 'And I suppose I'll be locked up in this room,' she says, going over to the window and looking out.

"I showed her the key on the inside of her door and she laughed a little and said the whole thing made her furious. She'd done nothing but mind her own business and here she finds herself treated like a criminal. Why didn't they find Miss Longwell and ask her what had happened at the farm—"

"Miss Longwell? What did Delphine say about Miss Longwell?" I might be getting this story in a garbled second-hand version, but there was more than one detail that struck me as curious.

"She said this lady's a famous author, but that she didn't know her name—her writing name. She was taking a rest cure because she'd broke down and nobody was supposed to know where she was at. Miss Longwell was a sick woman, she said, and was probably wandering about, out of her head. They ought to be out looking for her, instead of asking her—Delphine, see—all these fool questions."

"And did you believe all this stuff Delphine told you?" I scoffed.

"I just listened. Does any woman good to talk when she's all worked up. She says they're welcome to check everything she says. Her friend in Indianapolis will soon

convince them that she couldn't have had anything to do
with a murder."

"Then her story is that she left her invalid, Miss Longwell, alone when she departed for her little holiday. I wonder . . ." I was thinking of the food that Delphine had not
called for on Wednesday, but I did not enlighten Mrs. Porter that I thought it odd that nothing had been left in the
house for the invalid to eat.

Declaring myself much reassured, I said my good nights
to Mrs. Porter and set out for the inn. No doubt as punishment for pretending to Mrs. Porter that I was nervous when
actually it was curiosity that possessed me, I found myself distinctly jittery before I had gone a half dozen steps.
The prospect of re-entering the Dark Lantern alone had
me scared almost silly. Like a rescuing angel, Joe presented himself. He had just closed the station and locked the
pumps for the night and he said, sure, he'd be glad to give
me a lift back to the inn. The distance was infinitesimal,
but his callow masculine vanity expanded immediately.
He delivered me with a flourish to the very doorstone and
even stepped inside and turned on all the lights. That little
interlude gave me an opening for a question.

"Mrs. Porter's just been telling me about the woman
who works at the Newagen place, and I think you're the one
that ought to have the medal. How in the world did you
manage to keep her at the station till you got Mr. Ellender
there? That took finesse, I should imagine."

"No'm, not any of that. Just used my head, that's all it
took. Seems she couldn't get her car to start after I'd filled
her tank . . . Seems like the more I fussed around, the balk-
ier it got, too. I took a chance, though—no telling what a
woman really knows about a car these days. But it worked."
He spoke with huge satisfaction.

"What worked?"

"Just shut off the feed-line temporarily—that's all I
done. I even swore at myself most uncomplimentary when

I finally located her trouble. That was when I seen Steve's car coming. I kinda think she'd caught on by then, but it was too late to do her any good. And I put in another lick for Steve, too."

Joe was boasting now, but I obliged with the necessary question.

"I got a look at the mileage on her car. Boy, it has been run plenty since she bought it off that second-hand dealer, if he's telling the truth about what it had on it when he made the sale. What's eatin' me is how she piled it up without ever doing no business with us . . . Well, you just lock the door good and tight and you'll be all okay. Good night!"

I switched off the lights and got upstairs without dawdling. My common sense had rallied and now that I was again inside my familiar quarters I was no longer nervous. At least I thought I wasn't, yet the shrill peal of the telephone bell that cut through the silence of the house before I had more than stepped out of my pumps and into my bedroom slippers nearly jerked me out of my skin.

There is no telephone extension on the upper floor. The bell rang again urgently. I fled down to answer it. After all, it was probably Georgia Paxton with a juicy bit.

It wasn't Georgia. I didn't know who it was. The voice was deep and not quite natural. I believed I had never heard it before.

"Miss Fergus? Merely a friendly warning . . . Gregory dined alone at your place on Tuesday. He's dead now . . ."

The voice broke oddly. There was a click and silence. The connection had been broken.

Chapter Eight
I Mail a Letter

I slept wretchedly that night. I suppose it was the telephone call. It didn't make sense.

By the time that morning came, I was prepared to hear that Delphine had made her getaway. I heard nothing of the sort, for the excellent reason that such an event had not occurred.

The Dark Lantern is served by rural mail delivery, and conveniently enough it is near the beginning of the carrier's route, so that we do not have to waste much of the morning waiting for mail. In the box that morning I found a generous envelope containing a catalogue of Greenwater College. Good old Georgia, she had not forgotten.

In my day college catalogues were always complete with names and addresses of students neatly arranged by classes and courses. Greenwater has gone more modern than that, but at last I found the list I wanted. With a marked return of last night's jitters, I ran my finger down the M's. There it was, just as the child had said—McCann, Mary . . . Home address, Perry, Michigan.

I went to the inn's reference collection of highway maps and discovered that such a town was indeed to be found and that it would be just as simple for a traveler in our immediate neighborhood to go northward into Michigan as westward toward Chicago. Very well, I would address Mary McCann at her home town and see what happened.

I composed my letter—I decided against telegrams as too open to official inspection.

When I write a letter I itch to mail it at once. As the Dayfield-bound bus had just passed, an immediate dispatch of my letter meant a trip to Clear Portage. I could and did concoct some camouflaging errands. I half expected to be stopped as I openly departed from the inn. Nothing happened, and I bought my special delivery stamp and mailed my letter in the Clear Portage post-office without feeling like a marked woman.

There was, I learned, a gap in the bus schedule that would keep me in town longer than my responsibilities at the inn should allow. In the meantime there was a little marketing I could do. When I regained the street the problem of my return to the Dark Lantern settled itself. A raucous blast from a motor horn called me. It was Georgia Paxton's coupé, but the person I saw first was not Georgia.

A distinguished-looking man about my own age was regarding me with intense and flattering interest. Then Georgia's voice reached me.

"My dear Sally, here is a gentleman who wishes to be presented . . . This is Mr. William Pryde, Miss Fergus, Laurence Gregory's partner, who arrived by plane last night."

"Once more I correct you, Mrs. Paxton—not partner, merely a secretary. How do you do, Miss Fergus?"

The voice was completely Bostonian.

Georgia's tongue raced on. "I'm about to deliver Mr. Pryde to Steve's office, and if you don't mind meeting me there—say, in ten minutes, I'll run you back to the inn and we can put two and two together." She turned to the man at her side. "Sally Fergus and I have ideas about murder that will confound you professionals."

Mr. Pryde murmured something politely.

"I say, there goes Steve this minute. We mustn't twaddle here. Don't forget, Sally—be seeing you!" Georgia started her car with a jerk, and I looked along the street just in time to see the paint-worn runabout that carried official county plates disappear around the next corner. Steve had a passenger, and if I was not mistaken that passenger was Delphine.

I had one or two other errands that I saw to methodically and which neatly filled the ten minutes which Georgia Paxton had stipulated. Then I too rounded the corner into the side street where Steve Ellender maintained an independent office.

Georgia's car was parked at the curb, but she and William Pryde were nowhere about. Lounging rather pointedly at an inner doorway was my friend Pete, and in plain view through the door was Delphine, seated on a stiff, hard chair but deporting herself with the poise of a tragedy queen.

"I'm to wait here for Mrs. Paxton," I tossed in explanation to Pete and passed determinedly on into the inner room.

"Why, Delphine," I exclaimed without too much pretense of surprise, "where have you been? We've seen nothing of you at the inn for two days."

Which was nothing to boast of as a gambit, except that I gained a reply.

"But you've been reading the papers, haven't you? I have been away, and now I am supposed to know exactly who has been killed—and who has committed murder."

"Oh—did you? I mean—did you have to look at the dead man too? I did—it was horrible." I thought the sisters-under-the-skin note was my best approach, but the results were meager.

"I could tell them nothing. I had never seen him—nor the other." Her manner was cold and indifferent, but there was a trace of strain and physical weariness in her voice.

I persisted briskly. "What a dreadful situation your employer left for you. The police think you just have to tell them something, don't they?"

She shrugged faintly, and again I was reminded of my old love Cassie. "She—they will never find her. Except dead!"

"What do you mean? Why do you say that?" My protest was unforced. There was something dreadfully final about her last two words.

"The dead reveal nothing."

I shivered. I could not help it. It was as though clammy spirit hands had groped for mine. "But surely, what you suspect—what you fear—you have told that to the police?"

She sighed and her eyelids fell for an instant over her somber dark eyes. "It is to be hoped that they will search for the poor lady."

"What sort of woman was she, Delphine? No one around here ever saw her, you know."

I thought for a moment that my question was to go unanswered. Then she spoke. "Madame had no wish for society. She had left her world."

"A very famous writer, I understand. I'd recognize the name she used, I'm sure, if you'd mention it."

"Madame did not wish it known. Nor did she deliver her secret to me."

"But surely—" I was about to refer to the strange absence of food in the Newagen house, a fact which clung stubbornly in my mind. What was the famous invalid to eat while Delphine was gone? I had no chance to trap Delphine, provided she were vulnerable on this point, for a cautious cough from Pete warned me of the return of Steve Ellender.

It was obvious that something had developed. Georgia Paxton looked triumphant; Mr. Pryde looked shocked in a grave, decorous fashion; Steve Ellender looked as one might who had just found it necessary to swap horses in the middle of a stream. He spoke first.

"I accept without question your identification of Laurence Gregory, Mr. Pryde, but you will understand that your recognition of the other body, the first victim, ought to be checked at once. What else can you tell me that might throw a little light on the matter?"

"Not much, I'm sorry. The man called at Mr. Gregory's office about three weeks ago, without an appointment. The name he gave me was Smith—J. C. Smith, and naturally I was inclined to suspect that he was not using his real name. He would not tell me his business, nor was he willing to return at another time which I offered to arrange for him. He waited for perhaps an hour on the chance that Mr. Gregory would see him. A spare fifteen minutes opened up, and I sent Smith in. I do not know how long he remained, for I left the office on an errand. Mr. Gregory made no comment at all to me about the man's business, nor was he entered as a client."

"Perhaps, Mr. Pryde, you can recall something that Gregory said or did after his visitor left that might be the result of their talk?"

"I'm sorry . . . I believe I am recalling with accuracy the events of that afternoon. When I returned to the office Mr. Gregory was conferring with the client next on his appointment list. The interview was prolonged; Mr. Gregory saw no one else that day. When this last client left, he turned over to me some papers she had brought and the notes he had made during their talk—a matter of routine duty for me, you understand. Then he asked me for a map and returned to his own desk. Within another half hour he had left. Nothing was said about the man Smith."

"Um-m, he asked you for a map . . . What kind of map? An atlas?"

"No. He asked for an AAA map of the northeastern states and—I say!" Mr. Pryde whipped off his glasses with a movement so vigorous as to suggest excitement. "I'm no detective, but there is something which has just now taken on new meaning. Before I left that day, I went into Mr. Gregory's office as I always do to see that nothing had been left lying about which should be in the files or the safe— you understand—and the map that I had taken in to him was spread open on his desk. There was a mark on it."

We were all touched with William Pryde's excitement, but he needed no prompting to continue.

"A ring in blue crayon around a certain point—the place where highway US40 is crossed by this other road, whatever its number is. Mrs. Paxton showed me the very place this morning—the camp where Smith was killed."

"I thought you could tell me something that would help," Ellender drawled. "That is, if you are sure the map was unmarked when you gave it to Gregory."

"I can say that it was crisp and unused when I took it from the file. It was a new issue that I had recently acquired from the automobile club. Another matter of routine."

"Smith left no address?"

"Not with me."

"What would be your guess—was Smith a New Yorker or clearly from out of town?"

I completely forgot my role of unobtrusive listener. "I told you that I would recognize the man's voice if I should hear it again. It was definitely—Al Smithish."

"I agree with Miss Fergus. Quite an apt description of the man's voice." Mr. Pryde's friendly nod compensated for young Steve's look of annoyance. After all, only the day before he had been hurling words like lynching and kidnaper at me.

"Not a chance," he groused, "but I'll give it a workout. Photographs, description, name, which may turn out to be genuine, accent—those boys in Center Street might come through with something. And now, Pryde, I want you to give this woman the once-over." A slight inclination of his head indicated the closed door behind which Pete was presumably guarding Delphine. "And then I must insist that you make yourself a little clearer about the case that called Gregory to these parts."

That puzzled me, for I considered that Mr. Pryde had been very clear indeed in his statements that he knew nothing about Smith's business, but this time it was Georgia Paxton who spoke out of turn.

"Is it true, Mr. Ellender, that Delphine has an alibi?"

"Her statements are being checked right now," he admitted, a bit grudgingly, I thought.

"What I really mean is—did she say anything about the woman she works for?"

Ellender's yes was curt.

"What did she say?"

If I had doubted Mrs. Porter's story of what Delphine had revealed in her first interrogation I was reassured, for the detective's concise statement contained no information that was new to me. When he repeated her explanation that she had gone to Indianapolis because her employer had given her a couple of days off, Georgia Paxton leaned forward impressively and with a gesture interrupted him.

"But how could Delphine say that? You see—I made that woman up!"

Steve Ellender blinked. "I guess—I guess I just don't get it," he mumbled. "Would you mind saying it again?"

"The famous writer incog. The celebrity in retreat. All that isn't so. Oh, I admit that I said something of the sort"—and she gave me a swift side glance—"because it was impossible for me to give the real reason for my errand to the Newagen farm. Never mind that just now," she hurried on as Ellender showed signs of turning heavily official. "What do you want to bet that Delphine's alibi turns out to be phony?"

There was a little interval of silence. I was tense with excitement and I should say the others were too. At that, I was the first to speak.

"If she left her precious invalid in good faith, she'd have arranged about her food. I don't believe there was a soul in the house when she drove away. She just snatched at your story—she must have seen the newspapers. And it's going to trap her."

"About one chance in a billion, I should venture," Pryde offered judicially, "that Mrs. Paxton's alleged reasons for going to the farm should have coincided with an existing condition there."

"What she didn't know—and will not be told yet, understand—is that you are in a position to deny your own story." Ellender spoke slowly as though he were thinking out each word. "Delphine knew, let's say, that there was no such woman at the Newagen farm, but she must for some reason have gambled on the chance that you thought there was. My guess this minute is that her Miss Alicia Longwell is nothing but thin air, but a very convenient scapegoat for the real murderer."

"I got that far myself when I said her alibi would turn out to be made for the occasion," Mrs. Paxton jeered. I expected her to be annihilated, but Ellender merely grinned at her amiably.

"Until then and if—anyway, you've given me exactly what I did not have, sufficient grounds for holding her." He scrambled about among the mass of papers on his desk and began to write. "And," he said, as document in hand, he advanced toward the inner door, "it may not be long before others will join her."

Chapter Nine
I Break and Enter

I had lunch at the Dark Lantern, where necessary duties kept me fully occupied until well past the middle of the afternoon. Then, at my first breathing spell, I proceeded to gratify a desire that had been growing stronger and stronger. I wanted to see for myself what the Newagen place looked like.

I went out through the kitchen, loitered along the strip of herb garden long enough to assure myself that no watcher of my movements was about, and then I sauntered off along the path that I had seen Delphine follow so many times.

I hurried along with jaunty spirit. Then I caught first the pungent fragrance of a pipe and after that I heard heavy steps, slightly uneven, crunching through gravel. The steps were approaching, not receding. I heard a door screech open and then another, undistinguishable noise.

I edged myself nearer, glad that I was wearing green linen. There's something to be said for protective coloring. I could see the house now, as deserted-looking as Georgia had described it to me. Between the house and the fence I was following, unsightly outbuildings sprawled. The nearest one to me was a floorless shed before which was sitting my pipe smoker. Evidently he had just slid back the door and pulled out the bench upon which he had seated himself. That would account for the unidentified sound I had heard. I was not sure I had seen him before, but surely that was a shiny badge in plain view upon his blue shirt.

The deputy smoking on the bench could see me if I attempted to reach the house from this point. I plunged back into the undergrowth and back along another arc. This time I could no longer see the scout, for I was now on the far side of the farmhouse.

There was no door on this side and only three windows. Two were near the front and in all likelihood belonged to the best room. They were closed and blank, and dismal blue shades were pulled tightly down behind them. The third window was nearer the back of the house and was so much smaller than the others that I guessed it to give upon the kitchen or perhaps a pantry.

I did not hesitate. The smaller window was farther from the ground than I expected, but I managed to get a firm grip on the frame and gave it as hard a shove upward as my height would permit. It was quite like taking one more step upwards in the darkness when you are already at the top of the flight; I mean, the window was not locked and would have yielded to a child's strength.

I'm no athlete and I suspect I'm overweight, but at last I hoisted myself to the sill. I'd snagged my green dress and broken two fingernails, but there I was, astride the sill and one foot planted on solid flooring. Another series of awkward maneuvers and I had my head and shoulders through the window.

I was in a pantry or a storeroom, but an almost empty one. All that I could see on the shelves were dusty jelly glasses and fruit jars. I tiptoed across to the door and slowly turned the knob, but the door would not open. I squinted along the frame and at last satisfied myself that it was not a lock but a bolt that was keeping me from any further inspection of the Newagen house.

I felt ridiculously let down. There was nothing to do but to crawl back out of the window. No wonder it had been left open if the door beyond was so stoutly barred. More likely, the door had been bolted because the window had no lock.

I looked about me once more. Nothing but cobwebby pots and jars, and a blunted bit of chalk. Trust a school teacher to spot an end of chalk.

Then my head jerked backward and my body stiffened. There were footsteps overhead, cautious and furtive, but unmistakable footsteps. Furthermore, I chose that particular second to recall that there had been three encircled dates on the calendar and this was the twenty-second—the third one. Hadn't I even been fool enough to say to Georgia, "Who's going to be murdered on the twenty-second?"

Goose-flesh, cold sweat, heart in my mouth, blood running cold—I promptly had every one of the time-honored symptoms of a first-class case of jitters. The footsteps did not cease, though they grew briefly fainter. When they strengthened again they were coming downstairs and now I could detect something about them that sounded masculine. I had not moved a muscle; I was rigid with fright. The footsteps were coming nearer. They were entering the kitchen. They were coming directly toward the pantry door. And this was the twenty-second . . .

With one mad impossible scramble I thrust myself over the sill and made ready to jump to the ground. Someone was at the bolt. It was being drawn. For an instant I poised motionless as if held by the invisible presence on the other side of the door. Frantically I pulled my gaze away from the panel and rested it upon the wavering chalked letters that were scrawled along the side of the lowest shelf. The letters were meaningless, but there was an attempt at illustration, an animal with an undue length of tail.

All this in a split second; then the door gave. I leaped to the ground, my knees and wrists getting the worst of it. I heard someone at the window above me, but I did not dare turn to look. I ran. There was an explosive crack behind me and a spit of something stung my cheek. I screamed and kept on running, conscious only as I rounded the back of the house that the alarmed guard at the shed door looked like an army with banners.

I had been shot at, though I did not realize yet that that was what had happened. The deputy had heard the shot and my screams; he yelled something unintelligible at me. I gasped out, "Someone—someone's in the house," and raced for the shelter of the shed. I was scared silly, and I have no shame in declaring the fact.

The guard disappeared around the corner of the house. I did not even try to see what might be happening, but I know I heard nothing. After no more than ten minutes the man came shambling back. By that time my tremors had slackened so that I could answer questions.

The deputy did not ask me who I was; he seemed to know that. He demanded to be told how I knew someone was in the house. Because I was inside myself, I explained, and had heard with my own ears. I went on to tell about the bolted pantry door and the approach of the unknown and how I had escaped through the window.

"Yes, but didn't you see the feller?" my champion interrupted. "He took a shot at you, I ain't denyin' that. Got the slug right here, s'matter of fact," and he gave a loving pat to something cradled in the palm of his hand.

"No, I didn't see him. Did you?"

He looked surprised at my direct question and then admitted reluctantly that the intruder had disappeared, but, he added, he might return and therefore it was more than ever up to him to stay on guard.

I retraced my way to the inn with barely time enough to change my battle-scarred linen before the dinner duties began. Lola found a minute to tell me that Mrs. Paxton had called me on the telephone and that her message was that I should hold everything—she'd be out later.

Chapter Ten
I Puncture a Theory

Georgia Paxton came galloping in. She greeted us with a beatific wave of the hand.

"For once, old dears, please note that little Georgia does not demand food, not even coffee. What she craves is conversation."

Just the same I sent out for another pot of coffee and traded filled ash trays for empty ones before assuming my post of rapt attention.

"I'm about to break down and tell you all because I've got a perfectly swell theory that I want to spring on the boy wonder and I suspect it's going to need some rehearsing. I won't keep you in suspense another second: I think that Delphine is Tommy Neill's mother in disguise . . . What, no prolonged cheers?"

"What bearing has such a startling hypothesis upon the murder of Laurence Gregory or the man Smith?" Mr. Pryde asked.

"It's this way, see . . . The Neills have been divorced for some time and Roscoe Neill was granted the custody of the child. What the low-down on the case was I don't know, except that there was no alimony involved. Margot Neill didn't need it, of course—she's lousy with undepressed securities, and the Neill interests have been pretty much shot since 1929. The Neills lived in Dayfield for a little while after the marriage, but since they left no one here

knows much about their affairs directly. We heard, of
course, that the child had died, about a year ago. One day
last week a hit of gossip floated past my ears to the effect
that Margot Neill had said the little boy was not dead at
all—that the story was all a device to make her give over
her efforts to regain possession of her child.

"I spent three days running that story down, and I'm
telling you there was nothing to it. I mean I couldn't corral
a single fact, not even where to find Margot Neill. Since
the divorce she's apparently dropped out of everything. Yet
this queer rumor about the child had got into circulation
somehow. Then on Monday morning of this week in my mail
there was a letter—anonymous, and just one line of typing.

"'An unannounced call at the Newagen farm will answer
your questions.'

"That's all it said. Why I felt so sure that crazy message
had to do with my Margot Neill story I can't tell you—
just plain dumb hunch. I floundered around trying to find
out where the Newagen farm was without asking too many
questions and it wasn't until Wednesday noon that I got
into the right neighborhood. By that time I had a story
ready to serve as a reason for my call there, and as I remember I tried it out on Sally and it went over well enough.

"You know what I found at the farm. When I realized
that the murdered man was very likely none other than the
great Gregory, I gave over my wild goose chase of an apparently baseless rumor for something that was not only real
news but a big story as well. I explained myself to Ellender
by the same story I had told Sally and he took it for what
it was worth."

An imperious gesture checked us both. "I know what
you're going to say . . . That anonymous note was important and should have been turned over to the police. Well,
my dears, it was. All I needed to tell Ellender was that
the questions mentioned in the message had to do with a

possible celebrity in retreat at the Newagen place. It clicked neatly, you see. The usual things have been done—tracing the paper and identifying the machine that did the typing—but they haven't got anywhere with that yet. Ellender—give the boy credit—put his finger on the weak spot at once. I even had a vague feeling about it myself. Suppose someone for reasons unknown wanted me to go to the farmhouse. My appearance there could not possibly be timed. Actually it took me from Monday morning until Wednesday afternoon to present myself. In short, I can't believe that I was intended to prevent a murder or meant to be the one to discover it."

"Do you mean that Ellender believes your anonymous note has no bearing at all upon Gregory's murder?" William Pryde demanded.

"Not at all, only he couldn't see that it was getting him anywhere, unless something should break about the writer of the note. With me it was different. I knew my real reasons for going to the Newagen house and I decided to sit tight until the Laurence Gregory part was settled one way or another. To know what business had brought him here might clear everything up. In the meantime it would be my job to find out something else, but I'll get to that in a minute. I sent off a couple of telegrams and had a long-distance conversation and ran around town asking outrageous questions in a perfectly nice way, but they didn't get me anywhere at all.

"Now, don't forget that I had been with the first group that examined the house and what I saw should have meant more to me than it did. Those were not cut-rate cosmetics in that bedroom . . . Then Sally's report on Delphine came out, but still nothing clicked. As I said, I kept trying to be told things by people. I should have known before Sally wept on my shoulder about the identification disk—"

"I did not," I protested.

"All right. Let's say you were highly agitated, and let it go at that. I was terribly excited myself, for I knew that the Neills were certainly mixed up in it some way. The only catch was that it couldn't be just my private lead much longer, for Ellender had the name tag and would go to work toward the Neill angle at once. Well, Sally and I sketched out a theory then and there, and I rushed off to take another look at the farmhouse."

I interrupted again, with great firmness. "But, Georgia, you said that you did not believe that a child had been kept in the house."

"Nor do I believe it yet. Listen, I'm getting closer to my theory, my new theory. I had had no success tracking down this wild story about Margot Neill's saying the child was not dead. Anyway, the fundamental thing to do was to establish the fact of the boy's death, so I took it upon myself to do the next and logical thing. I wired Roscoe Neill about his son's death—date, place, cause, burial—the whole works. I got no answer. I wired again. No answer. I called him by long distance and was told what I had already dimly suspected; he was not at home but was expected within the next twenty-four hours.

"Well, I had no facts as yet, but I could still theorize . . . And I did—all last night—but I might just as well have used the time for good sound slumber, for I got no further than my first conviction that no child had spent even a short time in the Newagen house. But this morning, bright and early, I got a wire from Roscoe Neill."

Neither William Pryde nor I interrupted that climax. My mind was milling with the strange contradiction of a death certificate that had been hidden under my hall rug coupled with a tipsy row of downhill chalk marks in the Newagen pantry.

Georgia went on at once without any posing in the spotlight of our astonishment. "Neill's wire said he'd be in town by noon and would I get in touch with him at once."

"Then that's whom you called from Ellender's office?" I asked.

She nodded. "He asked me to see him at two o'clock, but then I saw Delphine for the first time this morning. I asked Ellender about her alibi and then handed him my hot one about my famous writer in retreat being all moonshine. Of course, I knew he'd crack down on me the minute he could get around to it, but I knew also I could take a chance on being ready for him by that time. I had to talk sassy to him, but I got away to keep my appointment with Roscoe Neill.

"Believe me, my dears, Roscoe Neill is a grand person—and do I feel sorry for him! I blurted out everything to him—I mean all about the wild story I had heard about Margot Neill's expecting to regain the child. He looked like death, but he pulled himself together and told me the inside story. He has every reason to believe the boy is dead, but—he can't prove it! Oh, it's a pitiful story . . .

"It happened soon after the divorce. He had the custody of the child and he left at once for an extended trip down into Mexico. He took the little boy with him. Of course, it was an ill-advised thing to do—I could see for myself that the man is ridden with remorse. Well, he left the child somewhere at one point and went off for a two days' prospecting jaunt. He was delayed a third day by a torrential rain and when he got back to the coast village where he had left his son in charge of a very reliable native woman, he had to be told that the child was drowned. You can guess the rest—the boy's body was not recovered.

"So that's the reason the announcements in the papers here were so meager. I asked him if he felt so certain that his son was dead now that what's happened here indicates a kidnaping angle to the case, and he said he did. He said he could never have left San Cristobal if he had not been completely convinced that the little boy was dead. Then I asked him what he thought this situation here meant, and he said he believed it was an attempt to extort money from the child's mother.

"'Extortion is a crime,' I pointed out, 'and it is your duty to prevent it. Of course you will get in touch with the child's mother at once?'

"That was what I wanted to know more than anything, you understand—whether he knew where Margot Neill was, and for a moment I thought I had drawn a blank. Then he said with some embarrassment that he did not know exactly where Mrs. Neill could be reached, but that he would get in touch with his lawyer at once. He added that the last definite knowledge he had had concerning her was that she was suffering from a severe nervous collapse and had gone to a sanitarium to recuperate.

"'In that case,' I plunged in to say, 'she must not be victimized by false hopes concerning the little boy.'

"'Certainly not,' he agreed. 'I shall act at once. All the information I have is at the immediate service of the local authorities.' And with that he pulled the telephone toward him and asked for the long-distance operator."

"Mr. Neill had to use long distance to call Ellender?"

Georgia patiently pointed out that Dayfield was in one county and Clear Portage and Attica in another.

"Oh, I—I see," Pryde replied blankly.

"So you went out to see Delphine," I prompted.

"Yes. So I talked to her—or at her—but I didn't get anywhere at all. She kept telling the same story about taking care of a great celeb in retreat at the Newagen farm and all that, and I let her tie herself up tight in that yarn without any side remarks from me, the author of it."

It was William Pryde who interrupted. "Why not ask Neill about the Newagen place?"

"I shall—the minute I get his ear again. But you see, he'd gone off on this tour of inspection. And—that's an idea! I don't believe he'd ever heard of the place, because the reason he had to be personally conducted this afternoon

was that he had no idea where this remote farmhouse was.
If he'd only had sense enough to ask me! I was the original
trail-blazer the other afternoon." She paused and cringed
a bit. The memory of that Wednesday afternoon discovery
could chill even her professional sprightliness. But not for
long. "But, little ones, you haven't heard it all yet. Didn't
Roscoe Neill walk right into a thrill there himself!"

My increasing feeling of suspicion and chagrin vented
itself in a carping, "But I thought you hadn't seen him
since he left for his interview with the country officials."

"I haven't, but one of our reporters picked up the story
right away. It will be in the morning editions. Someone
was prowling about in the Newagen house and Roscoe Neill
almost caught him."

"Hm-m, that's nothing." I dismissed my resolution airily.
"The prowler shot at me!"

"Neill shot at the prowler, but he jumped out of a back
window and got away. What are you talking about, Sally
Fergus?"

I suppose my face ruined the coup I had attempted.

"Don't tell me you were the murderer revisiting the
scene of his crime?" she moaned. "How perfectly flat!"

I recounted what had happened to me.

William Pryde snuffed out a cigarette very carefully
indeed and offered a mild remark.

"A comedy of errors, Miss Fergus; Mr. Neill and you
each believing he had encountered a sinister actor in this
tragic crime. A very disagreeable experience for you," William Pryde sympathized properly.

"Chalk marks," Georgia mused.

"You know what a kid does with a piece of chalk—no
grown person could possibly imitate the way their letters
straggle. And just the right height too for a four or five-
year-old. All over the side of the lower shelf like a black-
board. It looked like writing, but it wasn't. Flattish O's and

a lot of wabbly 5's, but no words. Pictures though—I think they were meant to be Mickey Mouses."

There was a little time of silence. Perhaps a small boy shut up in the pantry of the Newagen house amusing himself had become as real to the others as he had to me.

"I followed Steve Ellender into that pantry on Wednesday afternoon, but I admit I didn't see the chalk marks. Steve might have; he stood staring around quite awhile. I saw the dusty jars and glasses and let it go at that."

"I don't think anyone would have noticed the scribblings except from the window side of the pantry," I explained, recalling my last frantic backward look from the window sill.

"All right, let's say that the boy was being held at the farm all these weeks since you've been doing business with Delphine." Georgia Paxton proceeded briskly as if she had found a new path. "There was no child there on Wednesday when I arrived on the scene, that's certain. Delphine had departed at eleven, before Gregory was killed—also a fact. Let's even say that the child was hidden in the rumble of her car, a gruesome detail that apparently delights our Sally. Now the child would be either alive or dead—"

"And she calls me gruesome," I wailed.

"In either case, her reason for leaving was clearly to dispose of the boy—or his body. She did so, for back she comes late yesterday and quite ready to make use of a story she could have got only by reading the papers—my own exclusive release about the famous writer in seclusion—and yet she confesses complete astonishment at and ignorance of what had happened in the neighborhood. Steve's had her traced, of course, or is working on the job, and certainly he can't fail to find out where she went and what she did."

"That mess of make-up was the only thing she left behind," I suggested, and Georgia's face took on a determined expression.

"That reminds me," Pryde said. "No doubt Mrs. Paxton has already acquired this detail, but you, Miss Fergus, will perhaps be interested. It concerns the car driven by

Delphine Thibault. A second-hand car, it has been learned. No one in the vicinity was aware that there was a car at the Newagen farm, although Ellender verified its presence in the shed where it was garaged. But this is the point. The mileage was checked upon her return yesterday and the figure compared with the mileage officially on record at the time the car was sold. According to the difference in the figures, the car has been driven nearly three thousand miles since its purchase about a month ago."

Georgia whistled like a boy. I was petty enough to be pleased that this item of information was newer to her than to me, thanks to Joe. "I suppose she drove at night." My conclusion was matter of fact. "We saw her here only at noon, you know. But she never missed a day, until the Wednesday of this week."

Georgia rose to her feet. "You may have nothing in the world to do but to run a tea room, but this is Friday night and there's Sunday's column. Going back to town for the night, Mr. Pryde? Might as well run in with me."

I was curiously aware that there was something very much on William Pryde's mind. "Do you suppose it's too late for me to look up Mr. Neill? Gregory was consulted, you know, and a word from him might clear up everything . . ."

Georgia gave him no attention. "Isn't Sally wonderful, staying here all alone? We'll be the first to break in, come dawn's early light, darling. I promise you, no unfriendly hand will paw your clues about. 'Night!"

William Pryde lingered, an attempt, I suspect, to atone for the bloodthirstiness of Georgia's farewell, but I sent him trotting after her in high and not entirely assumed indifference.

For I was not proud of myself. . . . The instant that Georgia Paxton had related that Tommy Neill had been drowned in Mexico I could see again those horrible letters, CERTIFICADO DE DEFUNCION. There was something terribly wrong somewhere, and I, Sara Fergus, had not simplified the problem by my stubborn policy of silence.

Chapter Eleven
I Call on Mrs. Rockey

It was Saturday, June 23rd, and I rose to find the outer scene drenched with a cool persistent rain we had not yet had enough searing heat to appreciate. As I dressed I was conscious of a strong feeling of calmness and poise. How hot and bothered we had all been last night. . . . And just then my idea about Mrs. Rockey popped out.

Mrs. Rockey had played bridge at the Dark Lantern on Wednesday afternoon. She had been moved to empty the pencil sharpener. She had found within it the Neill's child identification disk. She had not, as far as we knew, called the attention of any of the other players to her find. As far as we knew. That was part of my idea. Well, why not look up Mrs. Rockey on my own? . . . Just what did she or some of her friends know about the Neill child? She knew something. . . . That was the rest of my idea and it set me up on end.

I buttered a third muffin and reached for the marmalade. The telephone rang.

"Just you set still," Viney commanded. "I'll answer."

She was in the cupboard room at the time and I heard her creak on toward the telephone in the hall.

"It's you, Miss Fergus," she trumpeted back at me. "Long distance."

I took over the telephone and for an instant there was a singing silence. Then the flat nasal tones of the operator. "Ready, Perry? Here's your party. . . ."

For another instant my ears did not know what they had heard. Perry. Perry, Michigan. Mary McCann!

Then came a thin, distinct voice. A young voice. A girl's voice. "Is this Sara Fergus?"

"Yes. Who are you?"

"I got a letter from you last night. A special. You've got me wrong. I was never—"

"Stop. Please stop. I can't talk to you now—where I am. Tell me how I can call you. Let me call you. In a little while, from another place."

There was something that sounded like a sniff and a giggle. "Okay. Just call me here. I'll be on all morning."

"The same name?" I breathed. I knew Viney was listening.

"Sure, the same name. Just ask for—"

"Stop! Don't say it," I commanded. "It was your name on the envelope, wasn't it?"

"Sure, Ma—"

"I'll call you later. Goodbye!"

I rather fancied myself. Surely anyone listening in had not learned much. I now had two excellent reasons for going in to Dayfield, and my first problem would be to get there without being followed. I felt equal to the situation.

Thanks to the weather I got away from the inn slickly. At nine I was standing on the porch, ears cocked for the deep honk of the bus. As it rounded the curve to the west, I scrambled wildly across the road flapping a half-open umbrella at the driver. I settled myself on a back seat so that I could watch accompanying traffic more easily. The only car that kept stubborn pace was a T-model bearing a Dunker farmer and his vegetables to market.

When I alighted in Dayfield, I made at once for the nearest cut-rate drug store, one that showed a steady stream of custom, and put in a call to Perry. I wished to speak to the long-distance operator, I explained. I recognized the answering voice at once; again I was saved from mentioning the name I was so strangely determined to protect.

"This is Sara Fergus. Now will you explain yourself?"

"Explain myself yourself! I didn't start this mystery," and she laughed. I knew by her laugh that she had not a worry in the world.

"Your name is the same as that in my letter?"

"That's right."

"Do you attend Greenwater College?"

"Yes. I'm a junior."

"When did you leave the college?"

"Why, last week. Thursday."

"When did you get home?"

"The same day. About six that evening."

"Where were you on Tuesday of this week?"

"Right here where I am this minute. I stepped right into a job in the telephone office."

"I see . . . And where were you that night?"

"Same place. An extra trick of night duty."

"Then that means that you can readily prove your statements?"

"It sure does! And say, Sara Fergus or whoever you are, what do you think I'm mixed up in?"

"Nothing. Nothing at all, but somebody else is . . . Have you been reading the papers?"

"Sure—the *Beantown Bugle*," and again the girl laughed. The carefree note cleared her completely in my mind.

"The papers might give you an idea. But don't talk too much, unless you want to get mixed up in something pretty nasty. And forget my letter. Burn it."

"You're telling me?"

That was all. I left the drug store at once, even though there was another call I wanted to make. Another public booth would be safer. Why I expected an army of sleuths on my trail, I don't know, but I felt smartly cautious.

The rain was still drumming stubbornly. This time I telephoned from a hotel lobby. It made no difference now who saw or heard me. I called the paper that made use of

the talents of Georgia Paxton, though I had only the fog-
giest notion of her schedule or duties. Fortunately she was
somewhere about and promptly I heard her rich, sure voice.
Would she let me talk to her somewhere? I had an idea. . . .

Would she! Just name the place. . . .

Within ten minutes Georgia Paxton met me at the hotel
from which I had telephoned. It was too early for lunch by
far, so we settled ourselves in a deserted writing-room. I
proceeded to unfold myself to her. Mrs. Rockey's concern
over the name-tag would bear looking into. Georgia Paxton
got my point at once.

"There's something there that's worth finding out," she
declared. "I'll bet an inflated nickel there is. She rates a
call, Sally, old dear, and you and I are just the girls to drop
in on her and catch her in the midst of her Saturday baking.
What if she does make a specialty of bridge luncheons—she
won't be on her way yet. Come on!"

As we paused under the canopy at the main entrance to
unfurl umbrellas, I asked dubiously, "Are we walking?"

"No, darling, but we're going back to the shop first. I
want a look at the morgue."

My associations with that word were unpleasant, but I
splashed along in Georgia's wake obediently. The *Record*
office was only around a corner and by the time we arrived
I had recalled that newspaper morgues were not gruesome.
All that Georgia said was:

"Of course, there's every chance that the bright-eyed
boy wonder has her sewed up tight, but I've got a way with
me myself. I know what kind of apples Eve likes best. If you
wait here no one will wonder about you."

She parked me in a lobby by a chilly marble counter
behind which a pretty girl was taking in classified advertising. In two shakes she was back, snapping the clasps of her
capacious handbag with evident satisfaction.

This time we climbed into a taxi. The address she mumbled at the driver would probably have meant nothing to

me if I had caught it. During our run she did not discuss strategy with me nor did she give me a chance to do so. We alighted at last before a stucco cottage that started out Spanish but crowned itself with a weird imitation of thatch.

As she pressed the doorbell she said, "Do you want to start the ball rolling?"

There was no warm urgency in her tone and I obligingly replied, "Not if you have a good opening line."

"That's for you to say, but give me a chance."

Mrs. Rockey answered the door herself. She was not befloured, but she was rubber-gloved and a heavy black net was being used to resuscitate a wave. Yet she was more at ease than she had been when I last saw her.

"We're from the *Record,* Mrs. Rockey. The society editor sent me out to inquire about a photograph. You're chairman of an important committee for the Federation garden party, aren't you?" Mrs. Paxton beamed upon her fondly.

Really, it was too easy. Not that I recognized at once the strength of the bait that Georgia used. The woman melted, positively melted before us, yet she knew her way around at that. The first thing she said was:

"But it's too late for tomorrow's paper, isn't it?"

"Quite. But the more prominent people are being saved for next Sunday's paper."

"Tickets are important," Mrs. Rockey murmured complacently. Her eyes wandered toward a large framed photograph ranged in state on the radio. It was clearly an "art study" of Mrs. Rockey.

Georgia pushed her opening expertly. "Your sort of publicity is much pleasanter than the kind poor Miss Fergus has been getting. You remember meeting Miss Fergus, don't you? You were one of Mrs. Upton's guests at the Dark Lantern, our society editor tells me."

"Yes, indeed. I remembered the face perfectly—I never forget a face, but I didn't just catch the name," gurgled Mrs. Rockey.

"Tell me," I begged prettily, "did the ladies of your party know that afternoon of the dreadful excitement we were having?"

"No, we didn't," she began impressively, "or do you think we could have kept our minds on contract? It was all I could do—"

She stopped with a gulp and blinked her pale blue eyes. Georgia swung her gaze rather pointedly away from Mrs. Rockey's embarrassment toward the framed photograph on the radio.

"You mean when you found the little jigger in the pencil sharpener? I knew very well you hadn't spread the news about that to anyone—except to Mr. Ellender. Of course, we knew—it's all in the day's work with us."

As the purport of Georgia's words sank into her gelatinous mind, Mrs. Rockey looked relieved.

"Did you know right then that you had found something important? Mr. Ellender showed it to me at once, you know."

"Oh!" The syllable wavered a bit as she again considered my status and then she went on more confidently, "Well, I was terribly curious and, of course, deeply interested personally—and it wasn't any of their business anyway."

"Certainly not," snapped Georgia. "A thing like that would be all over town in no time."

Whether she knew what she was talking about was a mystery to me, but I considered it a fine line in any case. Furthermore, it worked.

"Besides, I had promised my sister not to breathe a word about poor Mrs. Neill."

Plump! the prize had fallen square into our laps.

"It was terribly smart of you to go to Mr. Ellender the next day instead of the police here in town. Or did you get in touch with your sister first?"

"No-o. I'd have given anything to have talked with Mabel that night, but you see, I didn't know where they were. The last letter I had she said they were trying a new place and that Mrs. Neill wouldn't hear of anything but Mabel going with her. She's been on the case so long, you know."

"I see . . . Your sister is a trained nurse?"

The pattern was taking shape, but still I forebore to touch the pieces.

Georgia went on smoothly. "And your sister had written you enough about the situation so that you understood at once the importance of what you had found? How fortunate!"

"Oh, no. Mabel never writes long letters. She told me when she first began to worry about it."

"And when was that, Mrs. Rockey?"

"Let's see . . . She got off to go to Uncle Ben Brockman's funeral. That was early in May. He was buried out at Hanging Rock and we had a real good visit driving over."

Georgia took a deep breath and made the plunge. "That was just about the time Mrs. Neill got her first hint about the little boy, wasn't it?"

I swear, Mrs. Rockey looked relieved to find we knew so much. "Must have been," she replied readily. "Mabel was all steamed up about it, for nothing happened to Mrs. Neill that she didn't know about. It did her good to talk to me."

I ventured another comment. "Surely she must have told you just how the first approach to Mrs. Neill was made. I'd love to get that straight."

"A woman phoned. Didn't say who she was or anything. All she said was how sure was she that her little boy was really dead."

"Where did this happen?" Both of us spoke in unison.

"Right at the house," answered Mrs. Rockey with disconcerning naivete. "Mabel said, if only she'd got the phone call first—but she'd stepped out to mail a letter, and the cousin was laid up with a cold that day, and so the mischief was all done before either of them knew it. The poor woman in the condition she was and all, once that idea had been put into her head—well, she's in a sanitarium somewhere this minute, and you know what that means. It got Mabel, too, I could see that. But then, she always lives and dies with her patients."

I was scarcely listening. Something she had said had sent me off. A cousin? Would it do any good to ask Mrs. Rockey more about this cousin of Mrs. Neill's?

"There were more messages?" Georgia was keeping at it.

"Yes, over the phone. And once a woman came and left that little chain. Nobody was around that time but Mrs. Neill. Seems like they sort of watched to see when everybody was away. That's what Mabel thinks."

"I see . . . Your sister saw the tag and chain after they were received and described them to you, and that's how you came to act so promptly the other day. What about the woman? Any idea what she looked like?"

"No-o. Mabel said Mrs. Neill had an awful spell afterwards. And since then, all she's said in her letters is that they were still worried about I-knew-what and that she guessed they'd have to take Mrs. Neill away for some special treatments. You see, Mabel is always pretty careful about what she tells me on account of my living right here where Mrs. Neill had been known—not that she couldn't trust me, and did!"

"That's very evident, Mrs. Rockey." Georgia's praise was fulsome, but she hesitated just long enough to give me my chance.

"This cousin of Mrs. Neill's—what was her name, did you say? She knows about these messages too?"

"I don't know as Mabel ever mentioned her name. She's hardly more than a girl, but she tends to lots of business for Mrs. Neill since she hasn't been so well. Mrs. Neill's got millions, Mabel says. Yes, I suppose the cousin would know about whatever was worrying Mrs. Neill as soon as Mabel would."

"Is this cousin with your sister and Mrs. Neill now—wherever it is they are?"

"I don't know . . . I wouldn't know . . ." This last statement sounded uncertain, and Mrs. Rockey's too plump hands began to twist the rubber gloves lying in her lap.

Georgia might have let me ask my next question myself, but she did not. "You don't know where your sister took Mrs. Neill, but of course you know where they were before they left, don't you?"

"In Cleveland. She took a house in Shaker Heights early last fall, but they were gone most of the winter. Out West. In Tucson."

"Could they have gone back there?" I asked hopefully.

"Oh, no. You see, Mabel called me up on Thursday night."

That took Georgia Paxton by surprise but not me. "I thought so, Mrs. Rockey. By that time your sister had seen the papers. I suppose you told her then what you had found out and what you had done."

Mrs. Rockey nodded unhappily and I noted the stubborn line at her chin. It was going to take tact to end the interview successfully.

"I know she thought you had done the right thing." I knew better than to ask where the call had come from. If an up-and-coming newspaper and an efficient police system could not find that out for themselves, it was just too bad.

Georgia must have reasoned in the same way, for she wisely repeated a former comment. "I still say it was terribly smart of you to go to Ellender directly. When you got home Wednesday after Mrs. Upton's party, did you read the papers?"

"Indeed I did. You see, it was this way. We didn't know until we were leaving the Dark Lantern about the murder, and then we didn't get the straight of it so good, so I guess every one of us found out from an evening paper as fast as we could. I know I did."

"And what you read in the paper made you realize that what you knew about Mrs. Neill's little boy had a bearing upon the murder in the tourist camp." Georgia did not allow her voice to sound too triumphant, but judging by my own feelings we had taken our last possible hurdle with Mrs. Rockey. "You told Mr. Ellender just what it was, of course."

"He came right to me as soon as you left on Thursday, Mrs. Rockey," I confessed. "He felt I was entitled to know what had happened in my own house, but he didn't tell me that detail. I'd love to know just what it was."

Georgia gave me tops for that speech. I was rather proud of it myself.

"I would never have given the murder news a second look—detective stories make me nervous, but it was the part about the yellow Packard. Mabel had told me about the man who came in a yellow car."

Chapter Twelve
I Consider Fingerprints

My head was still swimming by the time a taxi picked us up at the corner drug store where we stopped to put in a call for one.

Naturally, we had pounced upon Mrs. Rockey's statement about the yellow Packard. Mabel, she told us, had walked down to a drug store on an errand—this was quite definitely at the Shaker Heights house—and as she returned she saw a man leaving the house. A strange man; she had never seen him before; rather heavy-set. He had climbed into a yellow car standing at the curb and had driven off. Mrs. Neill was locked in her room having hysterics. In getting her calmed, Mabel had picked up a pretty good idea of what had happened. The man had seen her Tommy, and his advice was—do what she'd be told and ask no questions and she'd have the boy again. By that time Mrs. Neill's cousin had come in—she'd been out somewhere too—and it took both of them to handle the poor woman. And all this had happened less than three weeks ago. Mabel had mentioned it in her last letter.

At the drug store I stared silently at a gaudy display of magazines and Georgia gave her rapt contemplation to a shaving soap poster, which seemingly inspired her to say just as the taxi drew up, "The cousin sounds interesting, what?"

Just how interesting to me I gave no sign.

On our way back to the *Record* building we grew more communicative. "I can manage the long-distance call from Mabel," Georgia announced with confidence. "Her name's Turvene, by the way. Dear Mabel—how I long to meet her. And getting the Cleveland address is an easy matter too. Something ought to come from that."

"You'll tell me, won't you, what you find out? I've got an idea—"

"I thought so." Georgia's voice was grim and not particularly approving, but I said no more and she did not coax me.

Arrived at the *Record* entrance, she hade me follow her. "I've got to break the news to Addie Trevor about this picture. She'll run it next Sunday, if I have to buck the Junior League in toto. And then while we're waiting for action on the phone call we'll grab ourselves a bite of lunch. Wait here—I won't be long."

She shoved me into an empty chair at a desk that must have belonged to a sports editor, judging by the mess that covered it. It was the first time in my life that I had been so informally in a newspaper city room, and for a few minutes my mind wandered from the amazing interview we had had with Mrs. Rockey. Then a brisk and whistling boy came through the clattering room leaving ink-fragrant papers on each desk, noon editions of the *Record*. The headlines leaped at me.

FINGERPRINTS SHOW MURDERER AT INN
MANAGER SUSPICIOUSLY SILENT
NATION-WIDE SEARCH FOR GIRL IN MURDER CAR

The story that followed was built upon the official reports of the findings of the fingerprint experts. I suppose no reader with the exception of the mysterious unknowns in the case learned more from it than I did. My eyes raced along the lines. The authorities studying the prints knew this much:

A bewildering maze of marks had been found on the Packard. There was one clear set on the door frame by the driver's seat which checked exactly with those of Smith, the murdered man; but there was nothing on the wheel, which indicated that the driver, either Smith or his unknown companion, drove gloved. The attendants at the gas station were certain that Smith was not at the wheel when the car pulled up at their pumps. Several sets of prints showed up about the well of the rumble seat, but none was Smith's. A girl had been seated in the rumble when the car stopped at the filling station. She had immediately disappeared.

On the knife with which Smith had been stabbed appeared one recognizable print and some blundered smudges superimposed upon others. The clear print was identical with one found on the rumble. The knife had been traced to the kitchen of the Dark Lantern.

Badly smudged prints had also been found in cabin eight at the Porter tourist camp. However, one clear set had appeared on the frame of a recently painted door. This set again corresponded with the one plain print on the knife and those on the edge of the rumble.

On the second knife, the one that had been used to kill Laurence Gregory, the well-known et cetera, et cetera, which was believed to have come from the Newagen kitchen, only useless blurs had shown up. Most of the prints picked out at the farmhouse were those of Delphine Thibault, who had been employed at the place.

(Wracked as I was by this indisputable report, I detected a certain interesting reservation in the passage about the Newagen prints. What other prints besides Delphine's had been revealed?)

On three objects found on the premises of the Dark Lantern—and as I read this whatever glands they are that betray guilt kicked up an unendurable row—the same tell-tale prints found on the rumble, the first knife, and the painty edge of the door at the tourist cabin had been discovered.

On two of these objects appeared other clear prints, already identified by the investigator in charge of the case.

(My prints. They might as well have been labeled. On the glass and plate, I told myself stonily.)

The third object—the reticence about naming these objects annoyed me—also showed other prints, but it was likely that the maker of them could be cleared completely from any guilty connection with either of the murders.

Then Georgia Paxton breezed in. "And is Addie Trevor fit to be tied!" she chortled. "Listen, old dear, I've already got the Shaker Heights address, though no particular idea at the moment what to do with it. You're welcome, if it will do you any good—1066 Cottonwood Drive. I looked up Mabel Turvene too, but the only one listed is a stenographer, so that's not our Mabel. By good luck a new directory had just come in. Anyway, I'm betting that Mabel uses Mrs. Neill's address. She sounds like a fixture in the entourage. Getting the low-down from the telephone company is something else again, but it's coming. Trust Georgie's finesse. And now for food. You look all gone or something, Sally, my pet."

"Look," I said feebly. "I'm in the paper."

"Of course you are, darling. You'll be getting bids from Hollywood before you're through." She scanned the paper with a swift and practiced eye. "You're a tight-mouthed wretch and it serves you right. Come on. You need a drink. I know a quiet place where you won't be lynched on sight."

"No, Georgia Paxton. I'm going back to the inn at once. I've got to think things out."

Back at the inn, by the time Viney and I had come out of our huddle about food supplies, Steve Ellender had arrived. His bland boyishness was not especially evident and he indicated rather plainly that he wished to interview me in the lounge. After I had preceded him, he closed the door with considerable ceremony. Without a doubt it was time for me to rally around my story.

His first question took me completely by surprise. "Why did the telephone call from Perry so perturb you this morning, Miss Fergus?"

Viney! Could I imagine her answering Ellender's questions about me without a deluge of detail too painfully accurate? Not Viney!

I thought of a half dozen answers to his question, all of them lies, and then managed to say, "It was of no importance. In fact, I have no idea who was trying to talk to me."

"So it wasn't an important call. Why then did you make a return call to Perry?"

His question hung there, demanding an answer. I gulped miserably and stammered something about business for Miss Brookfield.

"You're telling me that! Okay, I can check up easily enough." He appeared to dismiss the subject, for he lounged across the room to the window where once had been screwed a pencil sharpener and stood staring down at the scars that had been left.

He swung around. My moment was upon me. Since the window was behind him, I had to face the light.

"Miss Fergus, who was here with you on Tuesday night?"

"Between forty and fifty people dined here that evening. I have no possible way of identifying them all by name."

"Don't be funny. You know very well what I mean. You did not spend the night here alone."

"All right. You tell me. I thought I was alone. Except for the prowler, whom I have already reported to you."

"Two sets of fingerprints show up on the plate and glass you have admitted using for a late lunch on Tuesday night. One set is plainly yours. Whose is the other?"

I became Miss Fergus, the schoolteacher. "Listen, young man. This is a public eating place. The dishes used here are handled by hundreds of people, all strangers to me, except for the staff. I can't be held responsible for fingerprints."

"At that I can hardly believe you picked a dirty glass and plate for your milk and sandwich."

I sighed patiently. "The best of maids is regrettably careless. It takes time to polish glass."

"Your maid. You have more than one—" He made some sort of note.

I said nothing, for his remark had not sounded like a question. Besides, I felt cheap dragging in the girls. As a matter of fact, I learned later that from Viney on down, the staff looked upon the fingerprint-taking as one of their big moments.

However, I had more need to worry about myself, for the next thing Ellender said was, "But the odd thing about it, Miss Fergus, is that these unidentified prints are now and then superimposed upon your own."

"I don't understand it," I said darkly.

"The Latin super—above, upon, on top of; impono—"

"Oh, teach your grandmother to suck eggs!"

Then we both laughed.

His face sobered almost instantly. "I don't want to deceive you, Miss Fergus. Your situation is serious. These prints are definitely linked with the murder that was committed in the tourist cabin—committed by means of a knife which came from your kitchen. How can you let yourself be involved in a thing like that? In spite of your blameless record"—I thought of the checking up that had been done on me, Sara Fergus!—"I can hold you as an accessory to that murder, an accessory both before and after the fact."

"That would make me an accomplice, wouldn't it?" I murmured.

"That's a good word, too."

"Mr. Ellender"—and I leaned forward earnestly—"you must not forget that this inn is a public place. How can I tell which one of the guests on Tuesday evening that unfortunate man was searching for? Which one later found him—and killed him? For instance, there was the man who dined alone, the one I thought was the second victim. Who was he? What have you found out about him? I'm not minding my own business when I say it, but if I were you I'd think it terribly necessary to find that man."

He nodded gravely, opened his mouth to say something, and then pursed his lips in a silent whistle.

I pushed the microscopic advantage I had gained. "There's no reason at all that he couldn't have been the second man in the yellow car. That second man, Mr. Ellender, where is he?"

"Miss Fergus, I believe him to be the man whose body Pryde will be shipping east for burial as soon as the proper authorities release it. I'm not sure—I'm not sure."

"Laurence Gregory!" I exclaimed. But after all, why not? "You found his fingerprints on the car? In the cabin?"

He gave a curt yes.

I twisted my mother's emerald ring nearly off my finger. "But someone killed Mr. Gregory, and it couldn't have been Smith. You still need my man, the one who ate dinner here alone on Tuesday night."

"I need him all right, but I'm beginning to think it's going to take a bunch of money to get him."

"A king's ransom." I spoke the words idly to hide the rush of elation that filled me. I believed I had got his mind off Mary McCann's fingerprints on the glass and plate.

"That's at the bottom of it—" And he sighed.

I had to think back. Ransom—that's what I had said. But I gave no sign that I had made the obvious connection.

He glanced at the watch on his wrist. "I must be moving. You're not a lot of help, Miss Fergus. You'll be seeing me again, however. Obstructing justice is another label that could be used . . . There's only one thing I know about you for sure, and that is—you did not murder Laurence Gregory."

Chapter Thirteen
I Entertain Suspicion

It was not until Ellender had left that I began to think how queer it was that he had made no allusion to my experience the afternoon before at the Newagen house. Maybe the whole adventure was fishy and Steve was kindly saving my face, but the chalk marks were real . . . On the other hand, if I was asked no questions about those childish hieroglyphics, it might be that to the detective they were no puzzle.

Also, what had become of William Pryde? I asked Lola if he had been in for lunch.

No, the bald-headed fella that had gone out the day before without paying hadn't been in. Positively not.

Just as I was reassuring her that the bill had been properly taken care of, the door opened and Mr. Pryde himself stepped inside the hall. He slipped out of his raincoat and advanced toward me as if he were really glad to see me.

"Am I too early? I felt that I could not leave without seeing you again. If I could have my dinner and talk to you at the same time—?"

"You are leaving?" I echoed blankly.

"They tell me I can catch the night plane from Columbus. One of Sheriff Harvey's men is driving me that far. It has become necessary to consult Mr. Gregory's files, and I am the one to do that."

I led the way to a corner table, usually not desirable, and tipped Lola off not to seat anyone near us if she could manage. I seated myself opposite to hear what he had to say.

"Something has happened today that makes your trip necessary." I stated the words as a fact.

"Yes. Ellender and Roscoe Neill met again this afternoon. I was included in the conference, from which you can safely conclude that the matter under discussion pertained to Gregory's services for Mr. Neill. Mr. Neill's statement completely amazed me."

William Pryde's amazement apparently was to be my mystery, for he relapsed into silence that ate into the narrow margin of time he had warned me about. The succulence of the T-bone steak that Lola had just slid before him might have been a contributing factor.

"Mr. Neill stated," he at last resumed, "that Gregory had assured him that the claims being put forward about the child were absolutely false."

"And that's supposed to be the reason you're rushing back to see what your files say!"

My precipitate abridgment did not greatly please William Pryde. He went on exactly as if I had not spoken. "All that I could offer at that juncture was the discreet comment that I was unaware that Mr. Neill had consulted Mr. Gregory in person."

"By correspondence? Oh, I see—"

He gave me a sharp look, but did not ask what I saw. "It was not until we had left Neill's hotel that Ellender suggested this hurried trip of mine."

He waited expectantly, but if I was supposed to see something else I failed him. "Is that all your huddle with Roscoe Neill amounted to?" I asked, feeling slightly confused. "Hasn't Steve found out yet where Margot Neill is?"

"During the conference this afternoon—no. I happen to know, however, that Ellender is in process of getting in contact with Neill's lawyer, from which I should conclude that Neill must have made the same statement to Ellender yesterday that he made to Mrs. Paxton."

Perhaps I was rash. I said, "What do you want to bet that she and I find out first?"

"You do not offer me a sporting chance."

I should have rated that reply high for ambiguity except for a curious warmth in his voice that set me to twisting my emerald ring and feeling conscious of my emotions. I cast about for something to say quickly. "What I'd like to know is just what Mr. Neill makes of the whole affair."

"I can tell you that. Indeed, we got the gist of it yesterday from the enterprising Mrs. Paxton. Neill is convinced that his child is dead. He turned over to Ellender all the data in his possession, by which Ellender may test his conclusion for himself if he chooses—"

"You mean the results of Laurence Gregory's investigations?"

William Pryde lifted his eyebrows. "So I understood from Ellender. That was not dwelt upon this afternoon. Nor was his personal knowledge of the accident and his investigations at that time."

With a flourish he consulted his watch. "The sheriff's charioteer is due at any moment. To return to your query, briefly. Neill's theory is that the criminals had already had a rendezvous with Mrs. Neill or her representative and that the murders followed as a result of a quarrel over the money. The surviving member of the gang made off with the money."

I gasped, strangely relieved about one point. Until I heard William Pryde's next words.

He leaned across the table and for an instant his hand brushed mine. "Let me make you my confidante about one matter, Miss Sara. In my opinion, Mr. Neill thinks his former wife herself was on the scene that night."

A raucous tooting from Pete's asthmatic horn at that moment announced his arrival and William Pryde rose obediently. My swift dismay went unheeded. If Mary Mc-Cann were a half-crazy divorcee— But I had seen Margot Neill's picture. Roscoe Neill was wrong.

I followed Pryde to the door, my head still swimming. He turned and began shaking both my hands at once. "Wish me a safe journey, Miss Sara. I'm not wholly air-minded yet, I must confess."

"But think how much sooner you'll be able to return," I babbled.

He squeezed my hands shyly and stepped out into the darkness.

Just as Pete put his car into gear William Pryde came plunging back through the drizzle. "I almost forgot, Miss Sara—my apologies! Mrs. Paxton sent you a message. I met her in town as I was leaving. The nurse-companion you were inquiring about for your friend Miss Brookfield—I believe I have the correct name—was in Detroit the last she heard from her. And now, I am off!"

I must have been completely flabbergasted by that significant news. It's the only explanation I can offer for calling after him, "Call me Sally, for goodness' sake! I don't like the way you say Say-ra."

I had to resume management of the Dark Lantern. It was some time before I was free to ensconce myself at the cashier's desk and let my mind wrestle with what I had just heard—and seen.

Mostly I thought about Mabel Turvene. According to Georgia's disguised message, she had last been seen in Detroit. Well, there were a number of sanitariums situated in that district. I tried to think of the names of some well-known places. St. Ignace came to my mind first, but that was too far up on the peninsula. Then there was Mt. Arbor—or was it Ann Arbor I was thinking of? Mount something-or-other, I was sure. I spread open the automobile map we kept ready for travelers, and made a nervous search for what I wanted to find.

And there it was! Let Steve fumble about waiting for a legal mind somewhere in Philadelphia to decide whether or not to divulge the address of his client's former wife, he'd still have to wait for Margot Neill's forwarding address. In the meantime there would be nothing to lose and perhaps everything to gain by taking a chance on my brilliant hunch about Mt. Clemens. As usual, I'd been a bit wrong about the name, but the map backed me up now. Mt. Clemens.

Yet what could I accomplish as a private citizen? I needed the moral support of somebody, for choice Georgia Paxton. Since she had traced Mabel to Detroit, perhaps she had ideas of her own, yet I was hopeful that she would be mightily impressed with my Mt. Clemens theory.

My mind cleared of Mabel for the time, I had to face an item that set me jittering. William Pryde's cigarette case . . . For when he had flicked it open so airily just as he finished his dinner, I had seen, briefly but with horrifying distinctness, gold-tipped cigarettes.

I tried to keep my head, but waves of suspicion washed me darkly. I rallied every fact in his favor, but uncertainty and doubt mounted steadily. It would take more than a gold-tipped cigarette to convince me that this prissy William Pryde was the mysterious man who had eaten a solitary dinner at the Dark Lantern on Tuesday night. And anyway, he had been far up in northern New York on that night. He had told Georgia and me all about the fishing trip. Alibi—hateful word. And he had identified the man Smith. Yet he had insisted that he knew nothing about Gregory's commission for Roscoe Neill, beyond the bare fact that such a commission had been undertaken. If William Pryde were Gregory's confidential secretary, such ignorance of his employer's important cases was certainly not usual. It struck me all of a sudden that there was no one—no one since Laurence Gregory had been stabbed in the back—who could verify one single solitary word that William Pryde might say.

The last group of diners paid their checks and drifted in and out of the lounge preliminary to departure. Once more I thought of Georgia and wondered whether I would be wise to begin a telephonic search of my own for Mabel Turvene. The door swung open and a late-comer hurried in. No customer demanding dinner; I caught the glint of a badge.

"You Miss Fergus?" The man fumbled in a pocket—for a warrant, I was sure. I was being arrested at last.

"Steve Ellender wants you to come over to Attica to the county jail right away. He sent me to bring you back."

He drew forth a large blue handkerchief and blew his nose nobly. I squeaked with relief.

Chapter Fourteen
I Listen to Steve

Ellender ushered us across the hall into a room and indicated where he wanted each of us to sit.

Ellender swung upon Delphine and stiffened to business. "Once more, what is your real name?"

"I am called Delphine Thibault."

"Sure, they call you that, but what's your name?"— Not one up for Steve. I almost could hear her saying, *"Je m'appelle* Delphine Thibault—"

"But it is my name." Her voice showed no emotion, only patience.

"Then why is it that we cannot identify you?"

She shrugged faintly. His problem did not trouble her.

"Neither can I identify your alleged employer, Alicia Longwell, nor find the slightest trace of her. But then, red herrings don't interest me much. Perhaps if you'd name a *bona fide* employer I might have better luck."

He waited a moment, but she made no response.

"You stated that you were not a registered nurse but that you were qualified to serve as an invalid's companion, yet you have produced no credentials or references of any kind. Furthermore, the New York address you gave as your permanent one does not exist. I'm not exactly convinced by you."

Again a slight shrug, and then she spoke. "It might be that I have been missed at every census. I have traveled with many patients."

"Abroad?" The way Steve snapped at that I knew he was thinking of passports.

She gave a Mona Lisa smile.

"Where were you last winter?"

She turned her head slightly toward me and said, "In Miami."

"With a patient? Who? Name him—or her."

And the irrepressible Georgia broke in with, "I dare you! Name three!"

I deflected Steve Ellender's wrath from Georgia upon myself. "Were you ever employed by Mrs. Neill?"

Another cryptic smile from Delphine, but no answer. Georgia looked as if she were giving me three rousing cheers, but Steve—well, without saying a word he put me in my place.

There was an awkward moment before he spoke again. "Your friend in Indianapolis with whom you spent Wednesday night seemingly knows little of you beyond your name. I found that fact interesting."

In spite of having been made to feel as though I had spilled the beans, I had rebounded sufficiently to detect an added wariness about Delphine the instant the friend in Indianapolis was mentioned.

Steve went on chattily, "Your friend Nora Beech lives in an apartment, one not strongly entrenched in privacy, and yet no one else in and about the place seems able to recall that Miss Beech had a guest from Wednesday afternoon till Thursday morning. Rather strange, isn't it?"

I could not tell from that whether Ellender had broken down this Nora Beech's statements or whether he had not been able to substantiate them. Moreover, I believed that Delphine herself was equally uncertain. Perhaps that was exactly what Steve meant to accomplish.

He rose at this point and moved around the desk to stand directly over here. "Look here, Delphine Thibault, all this sounds as if we were getting nowhere at all. Don't deceive yourself. Events are moving, and not too favorably for you. You've been a little too dramatic. I don't have to tell you a thing, but I'm going to . . . I'm going to tell you two things, just so you'll have something to think about overnight.

"The first is this: There is no Miss Alicia Longwell, great lady in retreat. No such person has been living at the Newagen farm. The straw you seized upon as an anchor for your story was delightfully false, and if you don't believe me, Mrs. Paxton here will gladly establish herself as the author of it. And Delphine Thibault, wouldn't you like to know *the real reason that took Mrs. Paxton to the farm?*"

Delphine's face was enigmatic, sphinx-like, yet somehow I could sense a deepening of the weariness that I had already noted.

Ellender had not paused, "A second thing is this: We have got in touch with the owner of the Newagen property, Byron Leslie. He has authorized no one to enter or occupy his house. That fact in itself prefers a charge against you. I can think of a very compelling reason that brought you to the farm, Delphine Thibault, but I'm not sharing that with you tonight, unless you choose to discuss the matter yourself."

She sat silent and motionless.

"I know, too, that you weren't always alone at the farm. For instance, Tuesday night. You had callers on Tuesday night . . . By the way, what did you think of the bicycle?"

Delphine's eyes flashed in startled question, quickly veiled by dropped lids. Steve gave a satisfied little laugh. I could have sworn the bicycle was news to Delphine.

"Nor did you always remain at the farm. Nice little car you picked up—a real bargain, I'd say. Lots of mileage you put on it, too, the dealer tells us. A night driver, I take it. Well, cars are always seen and heard by somebody."

The young man's lazy comments were interrupted by an official tread without. "Sorry, the sheriff is waiting. We'll go on with this discussion tomorrow, Miss Thibault."

Sheriff Harvey appeared at the door. When he had departed with Delphine, I considered that our cue for good night had likewise come, but Georgia gave me a significant nudge and drew her chair closer to the desk where Steve had again seated himself.

"Now then, where are we?" she demanded, quite as though she knew the answer.

"Just about where I was," replied Steve. "We learned that she's white, but that's all."

"Were you bluffing?" I asked timorously. "Have you got more than two things against her?"

"Sounded dangerous, didn't I?" And he laughed. "At that, what I hold in reserve isn't much, but I hope it worries her plenty. The devil of it is that I can't identify her. The woman in Indianapolis says she's known her for about three years— met her in New York at an Automat, of all places. She seems to know no facts about her, where she lived, what she did, where she worked—nothing hard and fast like that. Nora Beech herself is a social worker of sorts, employed in Indianapolis for the past eight or nine months. This spring she had a line from her old pal Delphine telling her she was on a case in the country near Dayfield and would love to see her some time. Nora writes back and then last week Delphine replies that she'll be dropping in for a day soon—"

"Did she say exactly when?" Georgia asked.

"Had they kept in touch? How did Delphine know Nora Beech's address?" Those were my questions.

"No to the first two, and Miss Fergus has put her finger right on the queer spot in the Beech woman's story. She admitted it was queer herself. She hadn't seen anything of Delphine for a blue moon and she hadn't the slightest idea of what had become of her, and yet Delphine wrote her out of a clear sky, correct Indianapolis address and all."

"If Nora Beech is on a public payroll it wouldn't be utterly impossible for anyone to ferret out her address. Her name might have been in a newspaper or report of some kind. . . ." Georgia appeared to be thinking aloud.

"I couldn't crack her story about Delphine's visit, but I couldn't find anyone about the place that had seen Miss Beech's guest, though there were those who had been told by Miss Beech that an old friend had driven over to see her. I don't feel satisfied about the set-up, and that's flat." Steve twisted unhappily in his chair.

"Did you search her car?" demanded Georgia.

"Sure. Nothing in it but her overnight bag. And no fingerprints that have shown up on anything else except at the Newagen house. I suppose I don't have to feel so edgy about what she was doing Wednesday night. Once in a while they tell the truth. Oh, but damn it all—I'm sure she knows all the answers."

"I think she was telling the truth about one thing," I offered. "Her name. And maybe she was right about always being missed when directories were made."

"If the New York police have anything, I'm due to get it soon. Her fingerprints, I mean, no matter what name she may have called herself. There'll be a report from Washington, too." Steve lapsed into morose thought.

"Was there much in her overnight bag?" I inquired quite as though I hadn't been following Steve's pessimistic observations.

"Nothing but a nightgown and a little toilet kit." He tossed the words to me absently, but my next question brought him up standing.

"Then there would have been plenty of room in it for something else, wouldn't there? Maybe she carried away a bundle of money."

Georgia bubbled into exclamations, but Steve Ellender said nothing. His eyes bored into mine until I wished I had kept my bright idea to myself. He wasn't sure about me.

I had merely added to the question marks after my name. Then in a minute be said, rather quietly, "Not bad, Miss Fergus . . ."

"A swell thought, Steve, and you know it. Sally's got a good mind. You yourself said Delphine had company on Tuesday night. Now go on from there."

"It's like this—the Newagen place is in a backwater. It's the only house on the stretch they call the Barton road, but the people living at either entrance to the road know when cars turn in there. At least they do in daylight, and according to their data they've noticed Delphine's car only once or twice, which is why I threw night driving at her. But that's not what I'm telling you right now. We picked out some strange tire tracks in the drive at Newagen. Not Delphine's car, see. Furthermore, we've established that they are the marks of the Packard roadster."

Exclamations from the ladies, which Steve indicated were premature.

"Wait—your thrill's coming. These people at the end of Barton road say that no car passed on Tuesday or Wednesday except the one that Delphine drove away. But—the folks who live at the lower end of the road report two highly significant bits. A man on a bicycle was seen pedaling up the road; that would be toward the Newagen house. And the yellow car was seen. Not on the Barton road, however. Both of these observations were made on Tuesday evening before dark. Now the Newagen place was under guard after the discovery of the murder on Wednesday. The Packard was positively not moved after it was parked by cabin eight on Tuesday. It arrived, as we know, coming from the east on US40 just as darkness fell. So I say that early on Tuesday evening the yellow roadster made a short call at the Newagen farm."

"Very neat, Steve, very neat indeed," Georgia applauded. "Now what about the bicycle?"

"You tell me. A man on a bicycle going up the Barton road toward the farmhouse. A bicycle discovered the next afternoon parked in a shed. Said bicycle painfully shiny and new. No license tag on it; therefore not intended to be ridden in towns where licenses are required by law. Dealers in all the towns 'round about being canvassed as to sales. No definite report yet. Yes, Mrs. Paxton, you tell me about the bicycle."

"A nice tie-up between the two murders, my boy. The question boils down to this: whom is Delphine protecting?"

He glanced at his watch and stretched himself to his feet. "Sorry to hand you your hats and all that, but I've got to put in a New York call about now. You have your car here, Mrs. Paxton? You two Amazons don't mind a night run?"

"I think I'd like to have Mrs. Paxton stay with me," I put in as timorously as I could. "I'm really not nervous, but— If she has work to do, the inn typewriter and telephone are hers."

Clumsy, no doubt, but I wanted telephonic activity to sound natural and unsuspicious. However, Georgia didn't play ball.

"Glad to stay, old dear, but it's a day at the paper and I can look your toy typewriter in the face without flinching. On our way!"

We climbed into Georgia's coupé and then she called back to Steve, who had turned away. "Hey, wait a minute. You rate a minor break. Maybe you'd like to know that Margot Neill maintains a residence at 1066 Cottonwood Drive, Shaker Heights."

Georgia stepped on the gas. "And that's all I'm telling him—now."

Chapter Fifteen
I Confront Mabel

By the time I had explained to Georgia in words of one syllable that I was no more afraid than she was but that I'd been forced to make an opportunity to enlighten her about my hunch that Margot Neill and her nurse might be found in Mt. Clemens, we were well on our way to the Dark Lantern. She agreed with me that a series of telephone calls would be our best procedure.

I produced an automobile blue book and found the names of the leading hostelries in Mt. Clemens and put in a call for the first one on the list. During the two or three minute pause that followed, I could see determination growing on Georgia's face.

"Here," she said, "let me. It's your idea, but I believe I can save us time and money." She took the receiver from me in time to inquire briskly, "Night clerk? This is the Midwest Press Service. We're trying to locate a Miss Mabel Turvene, a nurse engaged by a Mrs. Neill who may be registered with you . . . Not there? I say, would you mind tipping me off on the most exclusive private sanitarium? It's likely . . . Will you please repeat that? Dr. Maddox . . . I see. Thank you very much."

Without pause or explanation she asked for another connection and then while she was waiting she said, "It's taking another call, after all, but somehow I've a hunch . . ."

Indeed Georgia did have a hunch. But to my furious amazement, all she did when the night porter at Dr. Maddox's exclusive establishment for hypochondriacs responded to the call was to repeat her inquiry about Mabel Turvene. "She is? Okay . . . Staying long? No, no message."

As she swung around from the telephone my state of mind was undisguised. "Keep your shirt on, Sally, my pet. We've spotted her, thanks to you, and I'm going up there this minute. I'll be there in plenty of time for breakfast. About the time that Steve Ellender discovers that there's no one at home on Cottonwood Drive, I'll be back with the whole thing in the bag. Don't you love it?"

I had to find out about Margot Neill's cousin . . . "Georgia Paxton, I'll pay for everything—but I'm going with you. And may Ella Brookfield forgive me!"

Georgia stared at me and then laughed. "The cousin has a strange fascination for you. Well, have it your own way. I'll just dash upstairs a minute and then make us more coffee, and off we go!"

We reached Mt. Clemens in plenty of time for an early breakfast. Georgia looked at me and I looked at Georgia and we were unanimous in agreeing not to invade the Sabbath calm of Dr. Maddox's elegant establishment until we could look a little less like two wild women who had been up all night. After toilet repairs and a pot of coffee apiece, we were ready to advance upon Mabel Turvene.

We found her slick enough. An obliging information clerk in the hotel-like lobby pointed her out as she emerged from a dining-room. Before she could press the elevator button we had nabbed her. In spite of my frantic hope about Mary McCann, I weakly allowed Georgia to take the lead.

We were from Dayfield, Georgia announced, and it was of the greatest importance for us to have a few minutes' talk about her patient, Mrs. Neill.

Mabel Turvene was a made-to-order trained nurse, well turned out, very capable-looking, but with a steady eye and a very firm manner. At that, she bore a slight resemblance to the fatuous Mrs. Rockey. The minute Georgia mentioned Dayfield there was a satisfying gleam in her eye. She knew at once what there was to talk about and, I was willing to bet, she wanted to know more.

It was out of the question for anyone to see Mrs. Neill, she told us very pleasantly.

Not at all necessary, if we could have a few words with her.

With that Nurse Turvene ushered us into the waiting elevator and led the way to a private suite. She left us in a sitting room and vanished, but only long enough for us to note that Margot Neill was doing herself very well at Dr. Maddox's. Then she reappeared, closing doors behind her very carefully.

"My patient is still sleeping. I can give you a few minutes."

"The two of you are alone here?" I asked. I couldn't help it. I could scarcely stand not knowing for sure about the cousin.

"At the present, yes," and she gave me a coolly appraising look.

Georgia took over at once. She produced a police card, which surprised me as much as it alarmed Mabel. I still think we would have got more out of Mabel if we had posed as old friends of Mrs. Neill's, but that's all water under the bridge now. For, alas, we did not get much out of Mabel . . .

Mrs. Neill was greatly worried about something, a matter that was very intimate and personal, Georgia announced. It was doubtless having a grave effect upon her condition—no need to point that out to her nurse. If she could be induced to talk freely to properly authorized persons—here Georgia waved her card; she admitted afterwards it was only a courtesy thingummy for fire lines, the nerve of the woman!

But it froze Mabel. Slowly we pried out of her that yes, she knew something was up, but no, she herself had no idea of the straight of it. Yes, she was pretty sure that Mrs. Neill's cousin knew. She's been making so many trips lately . . .

I gasped and tried to ask my fateful question, but before I could say, "What's the cousin's name?" we had a real heaven-sent break. I call it that now, but I had reason to feel discriminated against when it happened.

A door behind us burst open. A shrill voice called, "What's this about Mary? Come in here and tell me!"

It was Margot Neill. Mabel fled to her protectively, Georgia at her heels. I had only a glimpse of a set, white face and unhappy dark eyes, and the door was shut in my face.

Georgia Paxton was in there with Margot Neill, and I was out of the picture . . .

An instant later the door opened and Mabel emerged, looking angry and, I swiftly concluded, of two minds about something. She marched to a telephone, the picture of one about to call for help. Being the kind, generous creature that I am, I rallied around Georgia. She'd get somewhere with Margot Neill, if only there were no interference.

"Please, Miss Turvene, don't . . . It's all right, really. You can believe me, we're all working hard in Mrs. Neill's interests."

Her second mind prevailed. Her hand dropped from the telephone.

I pled, "If I could only get in touch with Mrs. Neill's young cousin, it would help so much . . . Can you tell me where I may reach her at once?"

Once more she took my measure, and then to my ineffable delight she replied, "I suppose you mean Miss McCann. I'm sorry, but I don't know where she is."

"Has she been with you here?"

"Yes, two or three days ago. She left on Thursday."

"Where was she going?"

"That's just what I said—I don't know. And I know Mrs. Neill doesn't know either, because only last night she was fretting about her and said if she only knew where Mary was—"

"Was Miss McCann with you on Tuesday evening?" That was vital.

I may have imagined it, but I thought there was a distinctly different note in the nurse's voice. "No-o, she wasn't here Tuesday. She came in on Wednesday afternoon, rather late."

"And left again on Thursday and you haven't seen her since?"

"Yes, on Thursday—and I haven't seen her since."

I was sure this time. Mabel had emphasized her first-person pronoun quite noticeably, but before I could pounce on that fact for my own ends, we heard Georgia calling. Mrs. Neill needed her nurse for a moment.

Georgia brazenly remained in the bedroom, but I was simply too inhibited to charge in behind Mabel. Instead I made a tour of the luxurious little suite, hoping to solve the case by coming on plainly labeled photographs of all the mysterious unknown involved in the affair, but of course nothing so stereotyped occurred. Georgia's voice drew me back to the living-room. She and Mabel were right at it.

"And what do you know about the Newagen farm, Miss Turvene? I'd not stall around, if I were you, but keep on the side of the law and the angels—meaning me."

Mabel blinked and tried to look stubborn and then broke right down. "All in the world I know about anything or any place called Newagen was in a letter from a friend of mine. She's a case worker in Indianapolis—"

Right on our chins!

"Go on," breathed Georgia, waving at me not to interrupt.

"—and all Nora said in her letter was that she's just located an old pal of hers. She hadn't seen her since her

New York days, but now she was on a case at country place named Newagen."

"Beautiful, beautiful," Georgia sighed. "And the dear old sidekick in Indianapolis is named—?"

"Nora Beech."

Georgia rushed on. "Another thing, Miss Turvene. What can you tell us about the man who came to Shaker Heights, the one in the yellow car?"

Not much, it developed. All she saw was just a man leaving the house and driving off in a yellow car. Mrs. Neill was in such a state that she had no time to trail strange men in sports cars.

"When did it happen?" Georgia demanded.

Mabel pondered. "Let me see now—just before I decided we'd have to come up here. The last week of May—that's when. On a Thursday."

"And on Thursday evening of this week you called your sister in Dayfield, Mrs. Rockey. What for?" Georgia persisted.

Mabel gulped miserably. She looked like a stout character, but Georgia Paxton was plainly the better man. "I—I was at my wit's end and Mrs. Neill's cousin had rushed off again without saying a word to me. I'd picked up a good deal from Mrs. Neill, naturally, only with her, I just couldn't be real sure of the straight of it. Mysterious phone calls and the woman who brought the little boy's identification tag—Mrs. Neill had shown me that. I was dreadfully alarmed about my patient. She was cracking right up—"

Both Georgia and I realized that Mabel was verifying everything we had dragged out of Mrs. Hockey. Georgia beamed at her. "So when the hoo-rah broke out in the papers this past week, you began to have ideas of your own," she summed up.

Mabel nodded. "I just had to talk to somebody, and I'm here to tell you that my own sister had gone and found little Tommy's name-tag. It sure is a small world! I was real relieved when she told me she'd already turned it over to the police."

A faint sound within Mrs. Neill's room jerked the nurse back to duty. "She's got to be watched, ladies. You two have got to go. And if I get fired, it's your fault."

To my surprise Georgia marched obediently toward the door. "Thanks a million, Miss Turvene, and don't worry about your job. My girl-friend here will take you on. I can see she's headed toward a breakdown."

She dragged me after her, but I got one word in myself. "Please, Miss Turvene, when Miss McCann returns, tell her she must call me at the Dark Lantern at once."

Georgia said nothing but led the way resolutely to her car, parked without Dr. Maddox's sanatorium. She climbed in and started the engine. "Step on it if you're going back with me," she ordered. "I'm off!"

Once out of the town and on the road toward Detroit, Georgia challenged me. "And why must Cousin Mary call you so hotly?"

"Silly! Don't you see—how are we to know when she can be reached? I think she rates an interview, don't you?"

"Hm-m. Well, if you won't, you won't, but don't think you're fooling me."

"Aren't I even to be told what Margot Neill said? If you only knew how I kept Mabel off your neck when you first barged into the bedroom—"

"That was swell, Sally. The gal plunged out, yodeling fire alarms and riot calls, and then nothing happened but my nice unbroken chat with Margot. I might have known it was your winning ways. When our paths next crossed, there we were, just like that—" And Georgia imperiled our necks in the midst of heavy traffic to hold up the usual two fingers.

"That was when you threw Newagen at her. But begin at the beginning, please."

"Feature me and Margot in a close-up. No foolin', Sally, she clutched at me and demanded to know where Mary was. Had she found Tommy yet? Where was he? Friend Mabel tried to shut her up and Margot ordered her out. She went, but I was afraid from the look in her eye that she'd be back with reinforcements, so I lost no time. Since Margot thought I'd brought news of some sort, it was no trick at all to get out of her who Mary was and what they were trying to do, and then the poor soul would cry and laugh at the same time and babble, 'My little boy isn't dead . . . She's going to bring him back to me. Tommy isn't dead.'

"It got under my skin, I'm telling you, but I plunged right in about something else—my own private mystery. I told Mrs. Neill that I had received a mysterious tip to the same effect—that the little boy was not dead, but that I hadn't been able to run it down. Had she, I asked, told anyone at all about her hopes? No one but Mary, she replied quite lucidly. And Mary had made her promise not to talk about it to Mabel, though that was really Mabel's job, to listen to her troubles. She had no friends to talk to—she'd been ill ever since she'd taken the Cleveland house. It had been months since she'd seen anyone from Dayfield—

"I hope you're getting the idea that she rambled along. It was pretty hard to break in, but she had given me a thought. Only Dayfield people, I said, would be truly interested in Tommy. She bit beautifully. Yes, she said, that was why it was such a comfort meeting Ursula Twain in Halle's one day. It was soon after she'd first dared to hope about Tommy and she'd been so excited she'd—well, maybe she had said more than she should, but it had done her a world of good talking to dear old Miss Twain.

"My dear," Georgia broke off, "that told me plenty. You'll have to have Ursula Twain explained to you. She's a local character, fonder of raisin' hell than anything else but. Ursula had come home, scattered the story in her own finished fashion, which means that whoever she told it to would end with the idea that he had passed Ursy the juicy bit himself, and then she'd left town. Gone to Hawaii or China or some such jumping-off place. No wonder I couldn't run the thing down. If that old girl had been home minding her knitting, she'd be right here helping me solve the cr-rime. Umph! She'd have it tagged and on the shelf, if I know Ursy."

Chapter Sixteen
Ultimatum

The Dark Lantern, as Georgia had so caustically remarked, was still standing. It had been the kind of June day that justifies the poems and the inn had broken all records. Lola confessed they had been forced to open cans and make emergency salads with pineapple and cheese. They had even dispensed commercial ice cream without a qualm. The patrons were more interested in murder and mystery than in honest-to-goodness home cooking, and no doubt Ella Brookfield's reputation came through the day unscathed in spite of my dereliction.

Viney and Lola were now picking up the pieces after the day's rush. All I wanted was a hot bath and my bed—I could scarcely remember when I had last had a decent sleep. Nothing about the murders made sense and I resolved to blot all their problems from my mind.

Swaying with weariness I made my way to bed, and the next thing I knew it was bright and early Monday morning. At precisely twenty-five minutes after ten the next event occurred. A taxicab from Dayfield rolled into the drive and a tense-looking gentleman sprang out and dismissed the driver. At the same instant a shabby car chugged along US40. Its driver craned his head toward the inn. I could have sworn it was Pete the deputy.

Two frantic strides and the gentleman from the taxi had entered. It was William Pryde. "For God's sake, where is Ellender?"

I tried to explain that I didn't know the answer to that
one. Had anything special turned up?

"I don't like night flying. My stomach—Could I have
some strong black coffee? And while I drink it, I should
like to put the whole thing to you. I respect your judgment,
Sayra. I fear I have made a grave mistake—it's not as if I
hadn't tried to reach Ellender. Why isn't the young whippersnapper here attending to business?"

"Never mind. We can't have lost him for good. Here's
your coffee. Now tell me—" Surely this grim, worn man
wasn't merely pretending to have made a plane trip to New
York and back. Yet whatever he had been up to, he had
been supervised by Steve Ellender's department, according to Georgia. And she was certainly right about another
thing—William Pryde's connection with the late Laurence
Gregory rested, so far as I knew, upon his own statements.

But before he could tell me anything, I had another
blow. Lola called me to the telephone. Someone purporting
to speak for Ellender gave me a string of directions that
made me gasp. Pryde had just been trailed to the Dark Lantern. I was to keep him there if I had to tie him. Anyway,
tell him to hang around till Steve could catch up with him.
Let him talk. Kid him along. Agree with anything he might
say, but don't let him get wise. And don't, for gosh sakes,
let him get away . . .

Quite understandably I returned to William Pryde like
an actress about to go up in her lines.

"You were saying—Mr. Gregory's files?"

"I believe I can now explain the man Smith—that is, in
a sense. I came upon an entry—er—in the private records,
which of course I was now quite justified in examining;
Smith, as Gustav Dorpf, was one of Gregory's authorized
agents."

"As Gustav Dorpf—"

"He used the name to acquire the Packard, evidently
with Gregory's full knowledge. I came upon the proper foil

in Gregory's checkbook. Also, the record showed that he had operated in Mexico and in Cleveland. The last item was dated June 16 and merely said, "Ohio via US40.'"

How easy, I was thinking, for a smart and desperate man to forge such a record. But I had to keep him talking. Something Mabel had said—"When was he last in Cleveland?"

"The latter part of May, if I recall correctly, Sayra. Just before Memorial Day. I should add that there was a sweeping cross in red ink that indicates to me that Gregory had abolished Smith's record.

"This is what puzzles me, Sayra. Let us say that Gregory sent Smith out here. What brought Gregory himself here? Had he followed Smith or had he accompanied him? He was very insistent about my vacation. Otherwise I could be sure of what happened. Though of course I couldn't have stopped him, for how could I have known that he was going west to be murdered?"

Maybe I was talking to the man who knew that very thing— "Since the memo about Smith was red-inked, maybe Mr. Gregory did know that he might be—murdered."

"Sayra, you have an uncanny way of guessing the right answer. Let us say, at least, that he anticipated serious trouble. But I am getting ahead of my story."

I smiled at this reminder of William Pryde's unfaltering devotion to chronological narrative. "Do you suppose that Mr. Gregory wanted you out of the way? You've said several times that he insisted on your taking a breather. Can you tell for sure whether he was in town on the sixteenth?"

"When I searched the office yesterday morning I found some routine dated memoranda that indicated that he had been working as usual on that date." He pushed back his cup and produced a packet of cigarettes. Nothing in the world but Camels. Where was the case filled with gold-tipped ones that had so startled me when I last talked to him in this dining-room?

He balanced his cigarette on the edge of a tray and looked across at me, oddly, I thought . . . "I approach my climax, Sayra. Yesterday I took the opportunity of looking in at my rooms. I'd been gone for two weeks and a miscellany of mail had accumulated. At the first shuffle I saw it—and, you must believe me, Sayra, it was a shock, a distinct shock. A letter from Laurence Gregory, mailed from Dayfield and postmarked 4:30 p. m., June 20."

With the words he drew from his pocket a letter and extended it so that I could see for myself the cancellation marks on the envelope. The address was not typed but written in ink that had the same metallic glint we had come across before. And there had been an inkstain upon Laurence Gregory's middle finger . . .

Let him tell you anything, Pete had said.

Pryde did not remove the letter from its envelope. Nor did he offer it to me.

He picked up his cigarette and blew smoke carefully. "This letter is—er—quite incomprehensible to me, though it is plain that it bears directly upon Gregory's death. The first step I took was to put through a call to Ellender, but I failed to get him. God, the boy's job is too big for him! I left word that I'd be in this morning, but did he meet me? He did not! I must ring him again—" He looked toward the telephone.

Should I tell him that Steve was headed this way?

"You intend to turn the letter over to Ellender?" I asked.

"If you so advise, my dear Sayra. But there is something I should like to tell you first—to explain to you. You will be kind, Sayra—"

Steve's car rattling into the drive and Steve bearing down upon us!

"Good man, here you are! Miss Fergus, can you turn over a quiet spot to us where we won't be interrupted?" As he turned to me with his request, he let one eyelid droop. Evidently I had carried out Pete's instructions.

The office door was firmly shut in my face, but I had no time to brood about it. Circumstances forced me to return quite strenuously to my job as manager of the Dark Lantern. When at last I received my summons, Ellender was returning a letter to its envelope. Gregory's last letter—

Steve was glaring at me rather nastily. There was no doubt— I was in for it.

"Miss Fergus, your relation to this case steadily increases in seriousness. I am giving you"—and he spaced the words so as to make them sound like a menace—"one—more—chance—to—talk. I have here a number of documents that may act as an urge. This letter, which Mr. Pryde has so opportunely received, mentions a girl. You well know that I have evidence that someone besides yourself was here on Tuesday night. In spite of that evidence, you have persisted in denial. But I have something else here—" He pulled a heavy envelope from his pocket. "It is going to speak for you if you will not speak for yourself. And I have also a properly executed warrant. Unless you come across completely, Miss Fergus, it becomes my duty to hold you as a material witness."

The words were serious enough, and the young man who spoke them was talking turkey to me, and I knew it. William Pryde was looking unhappy and his eyes swung away from mine. My only thought was, "You're holding Delphine, too, but that's not making her talk either . . ."

In another second I should have been wretchedly curious about the "something else" that he had mentioned, but he did not wait for me to feel the appropriate emotion. He drew out a letter from the heavy envelope and began to read aloud. It sounded familiar. No wonder; it was the amazing epistle I had addressed to Mary McCann at Perry. I declare that William Pryde's jaw dropped as he listened.

My own interest centered more upon the appearance of the letter than upon its content. Steve had quite come to the end before I understood that the letter looked like a

neatly solved jig-saw puzzle because it had obviously been
torn to bits, reassembled, pasted upon a heavier sheet of
paper, and the whole covered with a transparent sheet of
something, probably cellophane. Evidently the girl from
Perry had at least made an attempt to destroy the letter.

"You wrote this," Steve Ellender was saying. It sounded
like a statement and so I did not reply. "You mailed it in
Clear Portage on Friday morning. On Saturday morning
you received a long-distance call from Perry. Within a couple of hours a call went out from Dayfield to Perry. You
were in Dayfield at that time. I say you made that call, Miss
Fergus. A little trip to Perry was indicated. The business
did not prove difficult . . . Miss Mary McCann of Perry,
Michigan, is a mighty nice kid and she hated like all get-
out to let you down, if that's any comfort to you, but the
majesty of the law did the trick. She broke down and told
me all about it. She was even dreadfully sorry that she had
torn up the letter, but it wasn't cleaning day and I had luck
with the scrap basket.

"So now, Miss Fergus, how about it? Upon your own
admission a girl named Mary McCann was here with you on
Tuesday night. You have been making frantic and persistent
efforts to get in touch with her again. You made an unexplained trip yesterday . . . I am waiting to hear from you
about Mary McCann's stay here in this house on Tuesday
night last."

I had one last play for time. "Why didn't you ask her
yourself? Upon your own admission you have been talking
to her."

"You know the answer to that one. I am as satisfied as
you were that the young lady in Perry is not at all involved
in what went on here, except as your letter and telephone
calls involve her. Not that I wasn't professional about it.
She can establish an unimpeachable alibi, and her fingerprints match none of the interesting sets noted in this case.
So that's out."

I could feel myself braced against the office door, quite the proper pose for one at bay. I looked at William Pryde and wondered why the spotlight had suddenly been turned from him to me. I looked at Steve and wondered if he had got my message about Mrs. Carson Bray. I looked down at my mother's emerald ring on a hand that was nervously grasping another hand, surely not my own, and wondered whether by some miraculous chance Steve Ellender did not yet know that a girl named Mary McCann was closely associated with the mother of the Neill child. If he had not heard from Georgia—could I risk another sidestepping?

All this in a mere flash of time, though to me it seemed like a moment gone tangenting into eternity. Behind my back I could hear the bustle of arriving people. I could hear Georgia Paxton's hearty inquiry. "Where's Miss Fergus, Lola?" I could hear Lola's complacent murmur. I could hear Georgia again. "Why not go right in?" I could feel the handle of the door turn against my back.

And Steve Ellender stood there before me, frowning and saying, "So what, Miss Fergus?"

I shook my head, not at all sure of what I was about to deny. Someone pushed on the door behind me, shoved me steadily aside. I heard a young and lovely voice.

"Miss Fergus? Oh— Is it Mr. Ellender? I think you ought to talk to me. My name is Mary McCann."

Chapter Seventeen
I Listen

All I heard was her voice, for the opening of the door had thrust me back into the acute angle between door and wall, but it was enough. It was the voice of the girl who had so frantically begged me for shelter on the Tuesday night that the affair began, only now there was no terror in her tone. Yet there was something almost as urgent, though cool and controlled, that told me the end was not yet.

There we were, five of us, for Georgia had followed Mary McCann in, all crowded into the ridiculous space of Ella's office.

"Why ought I talk to you?" Steve snapped, his glance swinging from Mary to me. My giveaway expression made his question purely rhetorical.

"Because Laurence Gregory told me that I shouldn't hesitate to go to the police when or if I felt the time had come."

At these words a queer thing happened. In the cramped space of the office William Pryde and I were standing shoulder to shoulder. William Pryde was trembling!

But Ellender was firing a question at me. "Miss Fergus, have you ever seen this young woman before?"

I was once more tempted to maintain my stubborn silence, but Mary McCann smiled at me and gave me a brief nod.

So I plunged in. "Yes, Mr. Ellender, I have seen her."

"When and where?"

"Here, on the night of the nineteenth."

"Why don't you talk to me?" repeated Mary McCann. "I think I have important things to say."

With a gesture Steve accepted her advice. "Miss McCann, have you ever seen this man?" He pointed at Pryde.

I couldn't watch both faces at once; I chose Mary's because I was afraid to look at William.

Her candid eyes were resting upon him doubtfully. "I—I don't think so. Oh, I don't know . . ."

Steve made a sound deep in his throat that seemed to indicate pleased satisfaction. "Well, then, what brought you here last Tuesday night?"

"I was seeing about Tommy—my cousin's little boy. And Mr. Gregory told me—"

The way Ellender looked at me labeled me once more a highly suspicious character. William Pryde had the nerve to squeeze my hand again, and Georgia said:

"Start nearer the beginning, Mary. There's a lot Mr. Ellender doesn't know."

"When Margot first began to get the messages about Tommy, she had no one to talk to, and that made her worse. She's sick and dreadfully unhappy and terribly alone except for me. Then she told me, and it worried me a lot, for I thought it sounded pretty screwy. I couldn't tell Margot that, though, for she was nearly wild. So I decided to talk to Tommy's father about it. He told me not to let her be victimized, that there couldn't be a thing to it. Naturally he had already done all he could to convince Margot that poor little Tommy was really dead."

"Just a minute, Miss McCann." Steve halted the girl's red and I was grateful. I hoped he'd asked the questions that were lashing me. "Please be more exact about the messages."

"I only know what Margot has told me. Most of them came by telephone, but once there was a man and a few other times a woman. Mabel—that's my cousin's nurse—

backs her up about the man. No one but Margot ever saw the woman."

At this point Georgia gave me a sort of triumphant signal.

Mary McCann continued, "These people told Margot that they knew that Tommy had not been drowned and that she could get him back, but that it would cost a lot of money. They even gave her the little identification disk that Tommy had always worn on his ankle, and—well, that was just too much for poor Margot to stand. She was in such a state that she couldn't accept the only rational explanation of that."

"That the child's body had been recovered, not that he was alive. I see—" Ellender nodded.

"Yes. Tommy was wearing the tag when it—when the accident happened. As I have said, I went to Roscoe Neill and he said he'd consult an expert and let me know what his advice was. In the meantime I was to try to keep Margot from doing anything rash. But she was sure Tommy was alive, and what was money to her if she could get her little boy back again?

"So I waited and did the best I could with Margot, and there was another message—I just missed seeing the woman myself by about ten minutes, and did that burn me up! She'd told Margot that Tommy was sick, not eating and losing weight and crying all the time, and Margot was frantic."

At that point William Pryde offered a cool criticism. "You should have gone directly to the police."

"Oh, don't you understand? Margot wanted Tommy all for herself. If the police find him, they'll have to give him back to his father, and that will be the end of Margot. She'll go over the edge completely. That's the reason I didn't dare tell her that I'd talked to Roscoe Neill."

"I don't see," I burst out, "what earthly difference there was in not going to the police and in telling Mr. Neill the whole story. He'd know that you had recovered the child, which is just what you've said kept you from the police."

"It does sound cockeyed, I admit. But what will have to happen officially, according to the terms of the divorce, and what can be arranged privately might be—different. It was a big load off me when Roscoe Neill said he was going to consult Laurence Gregory. In due time I heard the report. Mr. Gregory's opinion was that the smart thing to do was to play up to these awful people, let them think that Margot would pay the money, and then catch them and get Tommy back, too, since it wasn't absolutely impossible that he might be alive, though it was about a million-to-one chance. I was just to follow directions, and Roscoe Neill and Mr. Gregory would see to everything else.

"The very next day Margot got a telephone call, a kind of ultimatum. She took it herself, for neither Mabel nor I was in. It was the woman. She said that if anything was going to be done about Tommy it would have to be done at once. She told Margot to listen and she'd know why, and Margot swears she heard a child crying, *a sick child crying* . . . There was no reasoning with Margot after that. The woman said to send someone she could trust to Dayfield to arrive June 19th and to be waiting in the lobby of the Chisholm Hotel no later than three o'clock in the afternoon for further directions. The child's tag should be used to identify the trustee."

"This message came—when?"

"Early on Sunday evening. Margot was in a state of collapse by that time and Mabel rushed her off to a sanitarium. I stayed on by myself, in case there should be more messages, until late Monday night, when I took a train down to Dayfield and registered at the Chisholm. I stayed pretty closely in my room, trying not to feel nervous—and it seemed a long time till three o'clock.

"But something nice happened that I didn't expect." The girl broke off self-consciously. "Is it all right for me to tell it this way, or would you rather I just hit the high points?"

"Go ahead," Steve growled. "Don't leave anything out."

"Laurence Gregory came."

At that I was sure that William Pryde stirred uneasily. To be fair, all of Mary McCann's listeners, crowded together in that oven of an office, felt that they were about to catch a glimpse of the way out of the labyrinth of mystery.

"He slipped into my room without being announced, but I wasn't scared. I just knew he was who he said he was . . . First, he asked me how I happened to be there and I told him that I was doing as he had advised—following directions. And I told him about the last message and that I was to wait in the lobby at three. And then I asked him—well, I thought it was queer—"

"I understand, Miss McCann," Ellender said. "Quite naturally you wondered how Gregory knew you were at the hotel. Did he tell you?" I noted that Steve's eyes rested upon William Pryde.

"Yes. He said that Roscoe Neill had turned everything over to him and that when I had sent Roscoe word that I was 'following directions,' he had got in touch with him, and so he—Mr. Gregory—was on the scene waiting for my arrival at the Chisholm."

"So you had sent Neill word of what you were going to do?" Steve mopped perspiration and looked worried.

"Yes, after Margot left for the san. I couldn't let her know that I was working with him."

"Did you tell Mr. Neill where Mrs. Neill had gone?" I knew exactly why Georgia asked that question.

"It wasn't necessary," Mary replied. "Nor was Roscoe Neill interested." For the first time I detected a note of partisanship in the girl's reference to the man and woman whose lives would not remain separate.

"Okay. Go on," Steve commanded.

"Then Mr. Gregory told me that we were dealing with a horrible plot to get a lot of money from Margot. He said he had an idea about it and that if I would do as he told me I might help him to catch the ones who were doing it. And I said I would . . .”

We were all spilling with questions, but Mary McCann went on, “No, he didn't tell me anything more than that, and I didn't have the nerve to ask him—what his idea was and who he thought it was.”

Here William Pryde released his breath. I could feel him relax, but I couldn't look at him.

“I kept thinking maybe he'd explain more, but he didn't . . . He asked a lot of questions, though. All about Margot's side of it—the divorce and about Tommy, and about the messages. Only all I knew about them was what Margot had told me, and she—well, you know she's really ill, poor darling.

“Then he told me not to worry about anything, but to go ahead and keep the three o'clock appointment, and he'd find a way of getting in touch with me afterwards.

“It was a long time before it was three o'clock . . . I stayed in my room and gave myself a manicure and read the Gideon Bible. At last, at five minutes of three, I went down and sat in the lobby. I was shaking so, I couldn't have stood. And at exactly three I heard myself paged.

“The boy took me to a telephone booth. It was a woman—I suppose we could guess that it was the same one that had been calling Margot. She told me to take a seven o'clock bus that very evening going to a place called Clear Portage, but only to ride as far as stop five. There I should start walking along the road in the same direction until I should be picked up by a yellow Packard. I should get in— I'd be perfectly safe, she kept telling me—and I'd be driven to a place where the final directions could be given. If I didn't agree, she said, I'd receive ugly evidence the next day that would make me wish I had . . . That was all. I heard the telephone click.

"I went back to my room and tried to pull myself together. I was frightened and was I glad when in less than half an hour Mr. Gregory appeared!

"He already knew I'd had a phone call, but he'd had no luck tracing it. I told him everything the woman had said, and at the part about the yellow Packard he burst out with, 'I'm right! God, I'm right.' And then he said, 'Let me think, let me think . . .'"

I looked at William Pryde then. His face was a queer gray. Yet the creature was pawing at my hand again.

"'Are you willing to go on with it?' he asked me again, and I said I was, scared pink as I was. He said for me to do just what the woman had said and not to worry, for he'd be hovering around. He was going to find out who was in the yellow car and where I'd be taken. And I was to agree to whatever should be proposed. They'd undoubtedly talk money to me and see to it that I was returned where I could get in touch with my cousin again, for I was the go-between. Then he went away, saying there were things he'd have to take care of before my seven o'clock adventure began."

"Do you mind," I interrupted, "if I sent out for cool drinks? This hole of Calcutta can be relieved." We were all streaming and Georgia's face was the color of a tomato.

By the time the frosted glasses were being tipped upward, Mary McCann was saying, "—And I got off the bus at stop five and walked along the road. I walked and walked. Cars kept passing, but no yellow ones, and no one paid any attention to me, only a man on a bicycle who went wheeling by and said something like, 'Cheerio, Mary, my dear.' I knew that must be Mr. Gregory, but he was dressed differently. He disappeared around a bend in the road, but it set me up a lot—"

"And also clears up the bicycle." Georgia set down her empty glass.

"A report came in this morning about the sale of one on Tuesday, late in the afternoon." Steve Ellender sounded pleased. "But go on, Miss McCann."

"Well, when I heard a car behind me put on its brakes, I felt ready for anything. It was the yellow Packard! There was just one man in it, not a very grand-looking man, but nothing about him that made me too jittery.

"'Jump in, Mary McCann,' he ordered. 'Don't worry, sister, It's all on the up and up.'"

To me that sounded like the man Smith.

"So I got in and he turned off the main road almost at once to our right into a narrow little dirt road more like a lane. But I wasn't allowed to see much more, for suddenly the man threw something over my head and bandaged my eyes. I tried to scream—I wanted Mr. Gregory to rescue me then and there, but it was like a scream in a nightmare, a lot of effort and very little sound. The man told me, not at all roughly, that there wasn't a soul around to hear me. He got me fastened up and drove on. I'm sure we turned at least twice after that, and the road was bad, but it didn't sound like gravel. At last the car stopped and the man helped me out and led me into a house, and then he took the blindfold off."

"Describe the room—and who was there," Steve ordered.

"It was a plain, bare room, a kitchen—there was a coal range, but very little furniture. There was a calendar hanging behind the stove."

"Did you notice the calendar particularly?" Georgia could not, understandably, resist that question.

"I don't think so." The girl's reply came uncertainly, but I, for one, was quite convinced that she was describing the Newagen kitchen.

"A woman came into the kitchen from somewhere behind me, and as she closed the door through which she entered I—I thought I heard a child's voice. The woman did the talking. She was tall and slender and dressed like a nurse. Against her white uniform her face looked awfully brown—tanned, you know, like people who have lived on a beach all summer. She was young, I suppose, but older than I. Her voice was pleasant, but her eyes—they were hard and expressionless."

We were all nodding our heads in beautiful unison, ready to burst out into "Delphine—Delphine!" But Steve checked us with, "What did she say?"

"I had to show her Tommy's tag first. I had it fastened on my arm like a bracelet. Then she said, 'I have been placed in charge of the child and you can take my word for it when I say that it is my professional opinion that he needs expert medical attention. If Mrs. Neill will agree to the procedure I am to suggest to her, the child can soon come under that care. If not—' And she shrugged her shoulders in a horribly cold-blooded way.

"I mustn't forget to say that after she began to talk, the man sort of drifted around the room and disappeared. I couldn't see where, because he was behind me, but afterwards I heard—and I knew I'd heard it this time—a child's sounds. Not any words nor crying exactly, but they were the human sounds that are not grownup but childish. Maybe it was stage-managed; it was terrifically effective on my nerves."

"My God!" breathed Georgia.

"Then the nurse said, 'Go back to Mrs. Neill and tell her that you *know* her child is here. You can take some of his clothes back if you want to, though I daresay she'll believe what you yourself have heard. Come back on Friday—that will be—'"

Mary McCann swung abruptly to face Georgia. "I remember this about the calendar. The nurse stepped across to verify the date and drew a ring around the day. 'That will be the 22nd,' she said. 'Wait at the hotel as you did today and you will hear what to do. Bring with you sixty thousand dollars. Half of it can be in treasury bonds; Mrs. Neill

has some that are not registered. The rest in old money,
fifties and hundreds.' She repeated her instructions. 'Make
it clear to Mrs. Neill. It will save her a lot of trouble to use
her bonds. After the money has changed hands, if you don't
find yourself in almost immediate possession of the child,
you are at liberty to report the matter to the police and
publish far and wide the numbers of the bills. That's all.'

"When she said that, the man slipped into sight again
and handed the nurse a little bundle. She gave it to me,
saying it was some of Tommy's clothes his mother would
probably be interested in. They bound my eyes again and
the man led me out to the car. We started off.

"The way was as bumpy as ever, so I suppose we were on
the same road as before. We had made a right-hand turn—
I'm sure I'm right about that—when suddenly I heard Mr.
Gregory's voice. It came from right behind my ear. He must
have been standing up in the rumble. I felt him working at
the blindfold and when it fell I could see he was sticking a
pistol into the man's neck. He had made him stop the car.
Then he told me to jump out and climb in the back. He
gave me the pistol and said I was to keep on holding it the
way he had it. Mr. Gregory got out then and made the man
move over. He took the driver's place, but he didn't start
the car right away. He said to the man:

"'I've thought as much, Smith, for some time, and I'm
sorry—sorry as hell. You've nothing to gain from this now,
whatever your idea may have been. You might pull yourself
out if you'll come across with me. What do you say?'

"But Smith wouldn't say one word.

"'I see,' Mr. Gregory said. 'You're betting that I don't
know enough to hurt you. I know this much—the child
hidden in that farmhouse is a girl, not a boy.'"

And at that Georgia Paxton gave a squeal of triumph,
promptly smothered.

"'And I know where the house is, which will bear thinking over.'

"Not a word from Smith. Mr. Gregory turned on the engine but didn't start the car. 'You realize that I could still cover you by saying that you were still—what you are not—my *bona fide* agent, working with me to uncover this devilish plot. That might let you out as far as the law goes. With me—you're washed up!'

"Smith mumbled something, but it was so thick I couldn't understand. Mr. Gregory started the car. 'Have it your own way,' he said.

"Smith spoke up then. His teeth were chattering, but I heard him distinctly. 'She's doing it for a guy—who the hell he is I don't know, and that's the God's truth. She'll get me if you don't, so what the hell.'

"But he wouldn't tell Mr. Gregory who the woman was—"

Steve broke in abruptly. "Don't worry. We know the woman."

"That's what Mr. Gregory said, or rather, he said it would not take much for him to clear that up. And Smith said:

"'But she won't tell you who's in it with her—don't fool yourself. She'll fry in hell first.' And Mr. Gregory"—here Mary McCann's eyes almost twinkled—"He hummed that bit about making the punishment fit the crime. By that time we were coming back to the main road. He told me not to let up with the gun as we got into traffic, but to stand up and act as if I were having a lot of fun with my two best boy-friends. He talked fast, dropping into French when it was something Smith couldn't be allowed to hear. That was pretty terrible for me—I never got much beyond Fraser and Squair.

"He said he'd heard everything the nurse had said to me. There were two things that could be done, one wise and safe, the other wise and pretty dangerous. He hoped I'd be willing to choose the dangerous one. I could go back to Margot with proof, proof that he'd turn over to me, that

her little boy was really dead. That would wreck the plot
to get her money. Only the people in it wouldn't be caught
and punished if I choose that way. Or I could go on and
do just what the nurse had stipulated and he'd guarantee
that he could catch the terrible person who was behind it
all. He advised me, if I felt uncertain, to see Roscoe Neill
again, who had engaged him to solve the case. And there
was still that piece of evidence that absolutely clinched the
whole matter.

"We were now driving on a highway marked US40, only
we were driving away from Dayfield. It was almost dark and
getting hard to see people on the road, pedestrians. But I
noticed a man walking toward us on our side of the road,
and I suppose the men did too. Smith gave a queer convulsive shudder and shouted something, and Mr. Gregory
almost crooned, 'So that's it—so-o that's it!' and he stepped
on the gas so that I was almost jerked off my feet.

"'Did you see that man?' he called back to me. 'Did you
know him?' I—I didn't think I did; it was so dark." Here
Mary McCann broke off short. Her eyes were wide. She was
looking at William Pryde.

"Go on, Miss McCann. All this is very enlightening."
William was calm.

"Mr. Gregory was telling me that I was to jump out when
he pulled up at the crossroads we were coming to and—and
vanish. He said, 'Stay in the vicinity all night—there'll be
tourists' places—and I'll find a way to get to you, if necessary. If I don't, don't worry, but get on the first thing in
the morning to Mrs. Neill and carry on as we've agreed. We
have agreed, haven't we, that you're seeing it through the
hard way?'

"I wasn't thinking of right and wrong and justice and
crime, but I said yes . . .

"'Mary is a grand old name,' he said, and it made a thrill
run over me. 'The vital thing is to hang on to the evidence
we've got. The little bracelet you're wearing and the bundle

she gave you, though I'm pretty sure that's faked, and above all, this—' And he handed me an envelope over his shoulder. 'That is the last unanswerable word, only they must not know we have it until we've caught 'em. Hold on to it, Mary m'dear. It's worth sixty thousand, but the poor kid's mother won't think so . . . Sit back now and act like a joyride. We're coming to the bright lights.'

"I tried to do as he told me, but like a clumsy idiot I let the most terrible thing happen. The little bundle I'd been gripping like life and death under my arm suddenly slid out and fell out of the car. And the next minute the car went round a curve on two wheels and stopped at a filling station."

I drew a long quivering breath and Steve looked as if he could gladly choke me. I knew why . . . But William Pryde gave my hand another comforting squeeze.

Mary quavered on. "I climbed out and ran into the restroom. I meant to take the pistol, but it slipped to the floor of the rumble. I wanted to do just what Mr. Gregory had told me to, but the trouble was I hadn't any money, just a little change in my compact, enough for bus fare to stop five and back. I'd left everything in the safe at the Chrisholm. And besides, there was the little bundle; I had to find it again. I'd noticed a sign and someone standing by a gate just as the darned thing went overboard, and so since Mr. Gregory had suggested that I stay at a tourist place, I slipped off in that direction.

"I don't know what happened at the gas station, but my guess is that Smith got away. I heard his voice, roaring and angry, and it frightened me . . . I began to run. I had a terrible feeling that he would try to get that envelope away from me. But I found the house where I'd seen the woman—this house, and—"

Steve Ellender held up his hand. "If you don't mind, Miss McCann, you'd better rest a little. This has been a big strain. Miss Fergus will go on from that point."

And Miss Fergus did—gladly . . .

Chapter Eighteen
I Make Honest Confession

I began to talk . . . I offered my listeners a painstakingly accurate recital, omitting neither my lace nightgown nor the glass of milk and plate of sandwiches. My first minor climax came with the bit about seeing her slip something under the hall rug and a major one when I reached the point of seeing her return to the house at ten minutes after three.

"And that's all I know—all I know, Mr. Steve Ellender, about Mary McCann's being here on the nineteenth."

Steve gave me the kind of look that's described as dirty. "You've rather put it up to Miss McCann again," he grunted.

Mary was eager. "It's all just as Miss Fergus says. But first, I do want to tell her that a boy I know told me all about a girl with the same name as mine who goes to Greenwater."

Georgia laughed at that, but Steve still glowered.

Mary was saying, "—I don't know what time it was when I roused, but I got to worrying about the little bundle. The floor was feeling pretty hard and I thought, why not slip outside and hunt for the bundle? Anyway, I brought some of the blankets down to the davenport, but I couldn't get to sleep again and so I prowled out into the kitchen. I could see it would be no trick to open the back door. I was worried . . . I'd been so stupid letting the bundle fall out of the car. The lace nightgown was a bit airish, so I took a long dark coat that was hanging there before my eyes. And— you'd laugh at me for this if it hadn't turned out so ghastly! I carried along a knife, a common kitchen knife. I'm just a natural born coward.

"I slipped around the house and began looking along the road, but I couldn't find the bundle." She gave me a nod, as if she, at least, approved of what I had done. "And then what do you think happened? I heard someone calling my name! I wasn't scared, though, because I knew at once it was Mr. Gregory. He kind of popped up from behind your hedge." She pointed vaguely, quite confused about directions, but no matter.

"He wanted to know what I was doing and I told him, and he said it might be worse because he was sure that the real Tommy had never worn those clothes. He said he was almost sure now who was behind it all, but that the only possible way for me to help him see it through was not to know—just to carry out the woman's directions. He said not to worry about Smith, that he had Smith where he wanted him. Then he asked me if I would mind walking back to the tourist camp with him, that there was a written statement he'd better entrust to me in case anything happened to him—that's exactly what he said."

The poor girl shivered with nerves in spite of the unholy heat of our star chamber, and Steve asked hoarsely:

"What time was it? If you'll only know what time it was—"

"But I don't," she wailed. "Miss Fergus knows when I came back, but I hadn't even gone yet . . ."

Incoherent, but we understood her.

"We walked along a path that Mr. Gregory found as if he already knew it was there, and came to the camp. We were quiet and there wasn't a sound anywhere and no cars on the road. He told me he'd let Smith get away, but he'd followed him and he'd gone back to the house where the woman was, which wasn't very far away, it turned out, from this camp.

He was sure, he said, that the principal in the case would show up at this place too and he, Mr. Gregory, meant to be there also. That's why he wanted to give me this statement, in case something should happen.

"So we got to the little cabin and he asked me if I minded sitting in the dark, or practically in the dark, while he wrote what he wanted to give me by the light of his flash. But he'd hardly started when he heard something—I don't know what.

"'We'll both have to vanish,' he whispered. 'Quick, out that way and get back to the inn,' and he gave me a push through a door we hadn't come in by.

"I was outside in the dark with no idea what had happened or where Mr. Gregory was. Suddenly a light flashed on in the cabin, but I was against a blank wall—I couldn't see in. I heard vague sounds from inside, but not voices. The light went out and someone ran away from the cabin, long silent leaps. I began sneaking around the cabins toward the road. I was doing pretty well, too, when all of a sudden I realized I didn't have my knife. I'd left it on the bed where I'd been sitting during those few minutes that Mr. Gregory had tried to write something.

"Having the knife in my hand had helped a lot, and the minute I knew that I didn't have it, a cold sweat broke out all over me and I started to run, like a little fool, for my feet crunched in the gravel, and someone began to chase me. I had crossed a road by that time and by a miracle struck the path that led back to this place. Someone was pounding after me, and then something hit me on the shoulder. I stumbled and almost fell but kept on going. I heard a voice say, a voice I know I've heard somewhere, 'You damn fool, come back!' But it wasn't the man who was chasing me, because he just grunted.

"I kept on going and after a million years I got back to the kitchen door—"

"At ten minutes after three," I repeated. "But I swear I heard you go comfortably back to bed."

"Comfortably is not the word." Mary grimaced wanly. "I remember shaking off the long coat I had borrowed, and then I collapsed on the davenport. Maybe I fainted—I don't know. When I opened my eyes and my head cleared, it was beginning to get light. My shoulder felt funny. It was terribly stiff and stung a little. I got up and went out to the kitchen, where the light was better, and took a good look at the coat. There was a queer sort of cut in it. I squirmed around trying to see what had happened to my shoulder and managed to make out that the gown was bloody and sticking to me. I wet a towel and soaked myself loose and decided whatever it was hadn't gone in very deep. The scratch wasn't bleeding any longer.

"While I was cleaning myself up and rinsing out the towels I had to use I was thinking what I ought to do. I slipped upstairs and got the envelope. It was just where I had put it; I didn't dream that anyone had looked at it, or I shouldn't have done the rather silly thing I did next, after I saw what was in the envelope. Miss Fergus is right; it was a death certificate—Tommy's.

"I hid it down inside my clothes, but I thought it might be smart for me not to carry all the evidence around, since the gang would be after me, or so I flattered myself after being slashed at by one of them. The bundle was gone, though I meant to look for it again. But there was the name-tag. I slipped it off my arm and looked around the room where the davenport was, and my wild idea was to hide it in the pencil sharpener. After I should get safely away I meant to call Miss Fergus by telephone and tell her to keep it for me."

Mary McCann smiled shyly at me. "You see, I trusted you, too, and you weren't even wearing a pin . . . Then I left by the back door and looked up and down the road again. But I couldn't find the bundle. I was sure someone in the tourist cabin had picked it up and so I went back along the path and across the road to the camp."

She paused and looked about at the circle of tense faces bent upon her. Her eyes filled with a dreadful picture.

"I looked through the cabin window. You know—oh, you know—what I saw. A man lying there with a knife in his back. It was Smith, and he was dead! He had to be dead, the terrible way he was lying there.

"I didn't go in. I didn't stay a second. I ran . . . I ran back to the road and kept on running as fast as I could. After a while I made myself stop and then I realized that I hadn't passed the filling station. The sun was coming up and I knew I was going north. I kept on walking until I felt I was in complete control of myself, and then I accepted the first offer of a lift that I got. It was a nice young couple going up to Michigan to fish. When I left them I wasn't very far from Mt. Clemens. By the end of the afternoon I was with Margot."

She sighed and stopped as though she had no more to tell. Steve cleared his throat, but Mary spoke again.

"It was the only thing I could do—to do just what Mr. Gregory had said. If whatever had happened—back there in the tourist camp—changed our problem, he'd let me know; I felt sure of that."

"What did you tell Mrs. Neill?" Steve asked.

"Nothing, except about the money. But by the time Friday came I had to account to her for the delay. Mabel helped by keeping the papers away from her."

"What do you mean—delay?"

That was Georgia's question, but Steve intervened. "Just a minute, please. I want to take a sort of poll." He looked at each one of us. "It was a mistake not to have Neill here."

Georgia's hand advanced toward the telephone, but Steve shook his head. "No, I'll be getting in touch with him directly. Miss McCann, have you any idea who is the principal in this plot? Just a yes or no, that's all I want."

"No—oh, no!"

"You, Miss Fergus?"

"Not the slightest idea. It wasn't Mary. You know that for yourself now, and that's all that worried me."

"Never mind that. Anything to say, Pryde?"

"No."

"Mrs. Paxton?"

"Yes—a wild glimmer of an idea. Haven't you?"

The two eyed one another, poker-faced.

Steve answered her. "More than a glimmer, and it's not so wild. But I've got to catch my bird to prove anything. Now then—I'm going to ask questions. Miss McCann, while you were waiting in Mt. Clemens, as Gregory had directed, I suppose you followed his advice in another particular?"

She looked puzzled for only an instant, then nodded her head. "You mean about Roscoe Neill? Yes, I tried to get in touch with him at once. He wasn't at his Philadelphia place—I used long distance pretty freely. He'd just left for Cleveland. Evidently he intended standing by Margot, if she'd let him. But he was driving, they told me, and it was a couple of days before I caught up with him. I went back to Cleveland myself."

"Miss McCann, why didn't you report to the authorities at once what you knew?"

"You won't believe me, I suppose—but I tried to. The connection was delayed for some reason, and then I got a message from Roscoe Neill."

"I thought you said it was several days before you caught up with him."

"It was. This was a wire forwarded to me from Cleveland. He was on his way to Dayfield and I was to do nothing until he saw me there. He didn't say when, but I left Detroit that afternoon."

"That would have been Thursday," Steve checked. "What about the money?"

"Nothing. Roscoe had said to do nothing until I saw him. The bonds were in safety deposit in a Cleveland bank and Margot was arranging for me to get them—and the money too, but I managed to explain to her about the time being postponed because it was just impossible to get sixty thousand together by Friday. I felt too shaky to drive and it never occurred to me to fly down, but I got a good train by just fool luck. The people at the hotel were just beginning to wonder what had become of me."

Stupid of us never to think of the Dayfield hotels.

"And then what?" demanded Steve.

"The first thing the next morning there was another message.

"It was a hoarse, thick whisper over the telephone. 'Hold everything until excitement dies down. Child perfectly safe. We'll reach you later.'"

"If the telephone company could only play ball—" Steve groaned. "Did you hear from Neill in the course of the morning?"

"Yes. I'd just finished breakfast when he called from the desk and came up. He was terribly distressed about Mr. Gregory. I told him everything—I don't think I could have stood it much longer without talking to someone."

"What did he say about the death certificate?" Georgia asked, looking a little as though Roscoe Neill had taken her for a ride.

"He said of course there were death certificates and he was glad that Gregory had procured a copy independently— that's what he'd engaged him to do. But he wasn't shocked, because he knew—I mean, he'd accepted the fact of the little boy's death. He said that if nothing more developed within the next few days, I'd better put the certificate in safety deposit."

"What did he himself propose to do?" That was the first sound out of William Pryde.

"He went over everything with me and decided that the only sane thing was to consult the authorities, although his real wish was to follow Gregory's advice. To do that, now that Mr. Gregory had been wiped out, required aid from the police. When he left me he was on his way to get things started."

"And what were you to do?"

"Go back to Margot and get the money ready."

"Get the money ready!"

"It was my idea," she defended. "In case I was to go through with it up to the very minute that Roscoe and the police would do the nabbing, there would have to be something that looked like money, wouldn't there? From the little way that Margot and I had got with it, I'd learned that it wasn't something you could do in a spare fifteen minutes.

"So that afternoon I left Dayfield for Mt. Clemens. Mabel was having her hours off duty and I went back to Detroit for the night, which was all to the good because I was afraid that Mabel was getting too curious about everything. I told Margot I'd been ordered to get the money ready. However it ended, I knew there was only the death certificate for poor Margot, and how I'd ever manage that— The next morning I flew from Detroit to Cleveland. Roscoe Neill had reminded me of the advance of aviation and I got in just under the wire to do my banking. It was Saturday. I took an afternoon train down to Dayfield."

"You've been right here since Saturday evening?" I murmured fatuously.

"I was waiting. It wasn't easy."

"My God, girl, did you get another message?"

"Where's the money now?"

"But today you came *here,* with Georgia. How did that happen?"

Sort out the askers of these questions to suit yourself. We were all shouting at once.

"She found me and made me come. We left the money in the hotel safe. There's to be another message this afternoon—at five o'clock." And then Mary McCann began to cry, not hysterically, but with a tired, little-girl whimper.

Steve Ellender stood up. "Poor kid! Let her cry a little. Then we'll fix her up with something. She's got to see this through now. But first I'll have to try her out on Delphine. That may be all that's necessary. And I must get hold of Neill—" He interrupted himself and picked up the telephone.

When he had talked briefly with someone at the sheriff's office, he disposed of the rest of us. "Pryde, suppose you come with us, and Mrs. Paxton, too. If you don't, I can't keep my eye on you—and this is no time for the wrong newspaper story to break. Can you make it now, Miss McCann?"

Georgia was at the door. "I'm staying right here, thank you, Steve. Lunching with Sally and having a good old heart-to-heart. And don't worry about the story for the paper. You see, I know *why Mary McCann has been here talking to you* instead of waiting in that god-awful hotel room."

And Georgia Paxton slid neatly out of the office and vanished into the woman's room across the hall.

After Steve Ellender, William Pryde and Mary had left, headed for Delphine's cell, Georgia and I sat down to a lunch of chicken aspic and tomato sandwiches. Georgia could see that I was angry with her, and so she calmed me by telling me the things I didn't know.

When Lola had seen her that morning, she had been on her way to Indianapolis and Nora Beech. Delphine had some sort of a hold on the woman, but eventually she'd tired of Delphine's high-handed threats, and by the time Georgia reached her she was ready to talk.

She said that she had furnished Delphine with a little girl from the day-nursery to which she was attached. The child was to stay with Aunt Delly for a week and have lots of milk—or that is the way it was explained. But Laurence Gregory saw the child there Tuesday evening, and so the brat had to be returned—via Delphine's rumble seat.

I interrupted then to ask whether the child couldn't testify to that in court. But Georgia shook her head and told me that the little girl was a low-grade moron who talked an unintelligible gibberish.

So that was that.

The business of the Dark Lantern called me off. When I came back to the dining-room Georgia had disappeared. "She went up to lie down," volunteered one of the girls.

I trailed her at once, only to find her stretched out on my bed, sound asleep. And I, being an old softie at heart, let her sleep. According to her own story she'd had four hours in the last three days.

Between five-thirty and six, as I was bidding godspeed to a cheerfully procrastinating set of tea-drinkers and pointing out the washrooms to the first diners, tourists from Peoria, a car turned madly into the drive and grated to a stop. Out leaped Steve Ellender, followed by a perspiring and almost disheveled William Pryde.

"Mrs. Paxton here?" barked Steve.

"Yes. I'm here. I'll be right down," Georgia's voice caroled from an upper window.

"Stay where you are, I'll be up. You and I have to go into a huddle and this damned tea room's not exactly the place I'd choose." He vanished, three steps at a time, to the vast entertainment of the party from Peoria.

William Pryde shook out a beautifully laundered handkerchief and patted his bald head. "The young man thinks he sees the finish," he murmured calmly, "I daresay he's correct. I must see about parking this car."

I watched him return to the car, which I saw now was not Ellender's. He backed it slowly and returned to US40. Well, I thought, if he escapes, he escapes . . .

Chapter Nineteen
I Do My Bit

Where he parked his precious car and when he came back, I do not know, but there he was at the little corner table for two, politely trying to catch my eye. The Dark Lantern was having a big night and I was rushing madly about.

"This jellied soup is quite delicious, my dear Sayra. After all the excitement of this afternoon I really fear my digestion would not be able to cope with anything heavier."

"More excitement and less digestion, please," and I settled myself for an instant across from him. "Carry on from Mary waiting in the hotel lobby at five. I can follow you."

I had reckoned without the man's weakness for telling a story at his own pace. "Upon our return from the interview with Delphine, who was positively identified by Miss McCann, by the way, we went at once into a conference with Mr. Neill. He was much relieved at Miss McCann's reappearance with us. Ellender explained that it was only a matter of routine before he became aware that a person playing Miss McCann's role was one of the principals in the mase and that it was inevitable that he should catch up with her, as he had just that afternoon. In that way, you see, Mrs. Paxton's part in the discovery of Miss Mary, to say nothing of your own extraordinary associations with her on last Tuesday night, were not called to Mr. Neill's attention, a point upon which Miss Mary seemed strangely insistent.

Something about a promise to Mrs. Paxton— In that Ellender was quite happy to concur."

If William Pryde could dodder along like that his poise was admirable.

"Next, plans were made for Neill and Ellender both to be in the lobby at the appointed time," Pryde continued after complimenting the Dark Lantern on the quality of its vegetables. "I was stationed there myself at ten minutes of five. Yet at the hour nothing spectacular occurred. Miss Mary was already seated and apparently absorbed in a book. A page from the desk approached her and handed her a note. She tore it open, read its contents, and then went up to her room.

"Within a few minutes the three of us had joined her. The message was typed on a sheet of white copy paper, the typewriter ribbon very fresh and black. I think, Sayra, that I can quote correctly . . . 'Take last bus tonight. Get off at filling station—you know where. Have money with you, as prescribed. Wait back of filling station until one a. m. Walk from there across to tourist camp. Go around the house and enter camp from rear. Walk through to main entrance. On the way transfer will be made. If we double-cross you, you can get us and we know it, so we are playing square. You do the same.'"

* * * * *

Somehow the hours of that evening of the twenty-fifth of June went by. William Pryde made no offer to leave the Dark Lantern. When the departing dinner guests at last cleared the inn, he and I established ourselves on the veranda, as if to enjoy to the last moment the lingering June twilight. Yet fireflies and garden scents and the faint eerie call of a whippoorwill hidden in the dusky trees of the Old Cut behind the inn could not have swayed me from the obligation that rested so heavily upon me. I must play

pretty dumb to keep William Pryde from suspecting what
I suspected.

In a way, William co-operated. I shall put it plainly. The
man made love to me. What a pity it couldn't have been
someone else: the experience has not been frequent in the
last decade.

This dreadful play-acting of ours came to an abrupt end
not long after ten o'clock, when the familiar rattle of Steve
Ellender's car approached. As soon as he made the drive I
could see that there were four persons in the car. The woman
was Georgia, but two of the men I did not know. The car
stopped and Steve and Georgia alighted.

"Is Pryde still here?" Steve called. "Okay—climb in and
we'll get going. Carry on, Mrs. Paxton."

The car backed and turned noisily and the party was off.
I watched to see that Steve turned right and disappeared
around the bend in the direction of the filling station.

I sniffed and Georgia said, "The young man thinks that
woman's place is in the home."

"He hasn't kept you there that I've noticed," and I daresay I sounded peeved. I knew that Georgia's remark had
been tinged with the same emotion.

"Furthermore," she continued, "we're to darken this
place and pretend that we've gone to bed. I'll admit he said
pretend. I think his idea is to drop in for food after all the
shootin's over."

"The lights," I pointed out, "are already out, and there's
no reason why two ladies can't sit on their front veranda
and chat idly of the happenings of the day. If there isn't
some chatting done—well, Mrs. Porter can provide hamburgers for the mounties."

"Don't cut off my nose to spite your face, Sally pet. I have
official instructions to tell you what's going to happen."

"Says who—what's going to happen?" But I smoothed
my feathers and let Georgia talk. It's never difficult.

"I don't need to smother you with all the little cut and
dried routine that Steve and his men have checked up on.
The lad's thought of everything, even some hocus-pocus
about the bag with the sixty thousand in it. It was still
in the hotel safe when he let me see it, but he's planned
something—

"Steve sent me off at that point to hold Mary's hand.
In a little while Roscoe Neill came up and we played
three-handed bridge to keep our minds off things. However,
it wasn't much after nine when Steve came breezing in.
Everything was all set. Mary was to wait until time to catch
the last bus out this way. That will be 11:35. She gets off at
the junction and is to follow her instructions absolutely."

"Not alone?"

"Yes, alone—except for a dozen or more hidden scouts.
Steve's got a good plan, if it works. Roscoe Neill took some
persuading. He was determined to ride out on the bus with
Mary, but Steve told him he'd have a good man on the
bus. Mary won't know which one it is unless it happens
they're the only two passengers. He won't get off with her,
of course, but there will be plenty of help around and about
the gas station and the camp. In fact, he seemed to have a
job for everyone, except you and me."

"You don't like it any better than I do. He's ditched you
too. What's Mr. Neill to do?"

"That was Roscoe Neill in the car I came out in. He ob-
jected to leaving Mary even for this last hour or two, but
Steve had to get his men posted long enough ahead not to
queer the big scene."

"He seems pretty sure of himself. What if it foozles into
a snipe hunt?"

"He's sure . . . The other man in the car was Steve's most
reliable understudy."

"I feel put upon. I don't know any of the answers. Of
course I know why I'm in bad with him," I sighed.

"I hope you don't give two hoots. I loved the way you went dear-old-Siwash!"

"Georgia, this is pretty tame, sitting here. He even asked William Pryde to come along."

"You're priceless, Sally. I saw the hasty way William jerked himself into the other end of this swing as the car turned into the drive. But Sally—!"

"Well?"

"Do you still think it might be William Pryde?"

"Yes, I'm afraid I do . . ." In the darkness of the veranda I found it easier to tell her everything, all the odds and ends of suspicions that I had accumulated. "And don't forget about the gold-tipped cigarettes in his case, and then just this evening, he acted so oddly about his car. If you ask me, Georgia, I think he's hidden it somewhere for his getaway."

"That's something Steve ought to know." Georgia's voice sounded strained; she hadn't burst into her usual exclamations.

"Steve's had me watching him all day. I'm not so slow that I haven't caught on to that."

"Yes, you've played your part like a captain," and she patted my arm.

"And besides, Georgia, we positively know that Delphine is protecting a man."

Georgia shouted with laughter. "Not that, Sally Fergus, not that! A tie-up between William Pryde and Delphine— you're just jealous."

I drew away, very straight and offended, and time dragged on. Then Georgia rose abruptly to her feet, snapped on her lighter, and looked at her watch. "Whether we like it or not, we'd better mind Steve. Let's get inside and close up the lower part of the house. If you hanker to see the bus roll by, perhaps we can watch for it from upstairs."

The night was very still, and dark except for the stars. We waited, without a light, at Ella's bedroom window. The bus was a little behind schedule. It must have been a quarter past twelve before we heard it pound by. We could distinguish nothing but its lights.

Georgia was restless. She prowled about from window to window. She checked Mary's planned movements until I felt that I was being subjected to deliberate, fiendish torture.

"She's got off now. I could hear the gears of the bus. The gas station's closed; whoever's the guilty party knew all about their hours . . . She was to scuttle down behind the station. There's a kind of washed-out gully there, Steve says. The girl's a star—and why he assumes that we're a couple of grannies that can't stand night air—"

I was blithering—no less, and I should have realized that Georgia was the same. When she had paced the nap off the hall carpet she brought herself up standing.

"Come on, Sally. This is a free country and we no longer tell our right ages. Let's go!"

She led the way downstairs and out the kitchen door, but when she came to the spot where the paths diverged she paused, inviting me to take the lead. "All I know is that this is the short cut across to the camp, but I'm not sure enough of it to sneak. I'll follow you."

"Back to the kitchen, then, unless you don't mind telling me right out where it is you want to go."

"Where we can see what happens, silly. Why should we miss the big scene?"

"Scouts hidden everywhere—you said so yourself. We'll run smack into a sentry first thing."

As William Pryde would have put it, Georgia was advised. I led her perhaps a quarter of a mile at an angle toward the State Line Pike before we undertook to cross it, and then we circled back towards the Porter camp. At the time we considered ourselves marvelously adroit to have avoided Ellender's men. Later we understood the reason that no one stopped us. The car hidden under the elderberry tangle gave me my first thrill.

Being the unobservant person I usually am, I could not be at all sure about the car. It was a fairly new, expensive coupé, thickly coated with dust, and it was drawn up to one side of the faintly marked lane which formed the northern boundary of the tourist enclosure. A thick mat of elderberry and scrubby second growth screened the cabins completely from view and helped to conceal the car. We were advancing without benefit of flashlight, and I think I should have stumbled over the front fender if the chromium trimming had not caught a ray of pale starlight.

"Um-mph," sniffed Georgia. "Guess you were right about his hiding his car." She peered at a license plate and then scrubbed at it with her handkerchief. "Not an Ohio car, right enough. Now I wonder—" She felt her way along the left side of the car. "It's been standing here some time. There's not a particle of heat about the hood." By that time she had reached the door by the wheel, "And it's not locked, either," she reported and swung open the door. Below the level of the seat she ventured to use her faithful lighter. "Nothing doing," she announced within ten seconds or so, and stepped back to where I stood poised in the center of the lane in desperate expectation of a peremptory challenge.

"Where does this lane come out?" she asked. "I mean the other end. We got it as the State Line road."

"It comes into US40 about a half mile beyond the gas station. I think it's the way Viney comes to work."

"Um-mph, all set for a quick getaway, your own word, Sally. Now, let's make for the back of that cabin over there."

Breathing hard with excitement, we reached the lee of the last cabin in the northern row. There was not a sound, nor a glimmer of light. "I don't see a car parked here," I whispered. "Evidently this cabin's not occupied tonight."

"We haven't started a riot yet, and that's a still better sign. Come on. I'm going to take a squint at the other side. She's supposed to come around from the shack opposite and then run the gauntlet."

At this casual reference to Mary's ordeal my spine
chilled. Nevertheless I stumbled silently in Georgia's wake.
At the front corner of the flimsy cabin we stopped in the
quite inadequate shelter of a clump of hollyhocks not much
higher than our waists.

"Stop me if I'm wishfully thinking, Sally, but I'm inclined to believe that the opposite cabin is likewise not
rented on this festive occasion. That would be a break for
the kid. She ought to be hiding behind it this minute. Maybe Steve wangled that . . ." She fumbled in the pocket of
her jacket and I suspected the lighter.

"Don't, Georgia—" I pinched her arm. "Don't try to
look at your watch. Listen! I think I hear something."

Faint cautious footsteps. Then we both saw something.
A slight blurred shadow detached itself from the side of
the opposite cabin and stepped timorously into the central
drive that separated the two rows of shacks. A slim, girlish
shadow carrying a bag.

She moved silently along, away from us. I gripped Georgia and she grabbed me, though why Georgia should have
thought that I would be the one to break cover and betray
our presence! Breathlessly we leaned over the hollyhock
spires. Before Mary had gone fifteen paces it happened.

Georgia swears now that she saw him come out of the
door of the second cabin opposite. Maybe she knew all
along just where to look. She knew so much that she hadn't
told me! All I know is that with my own eyes I saw a man's
figure sweep out into the drive as if to stop Mary McCann.
And I heard the words:

"Under the milk-can on the Porter back porch you'll
find the kid's address. I'm taking the bag—now!"

Swift running feet pounded by, swerved into our hollyhock clump. I insist that I felt the bag knock against my
hip. Georgia leaped one way, I another; and my way was
in pursuit of that sinister fleeing figure making off with

the sixty-thousand-dollar bag. There were calls and shouts behind me, and the flashing of lights and a woman's high hysterical shriek. That, I remember thinking, is the first set of tourists to be heard from.

I was in the grassy lane down which Georgia and I had so recently felt our way. The car! We were right. He was going to escape in the hidden car. Indeed, I heard the faint creak as if someone had leaped on the running board. But I failed to hear the burr of a starting motor. I heard an unmistakable thump as though a weight had been dropped or thrown.

And then I had to be awkward enough to stumble and fall. In fact, I almost knocked myself out. When I had pulled myself up, swaying and dizzy, in the darkness ahead I heard a breathless, hearty voice call out, "Good man, Steve! He's just ahead along this lane, making for the north road."

"He'll be blocked there, Neill." That was Steve Ellender.

Maybe it was sheer relief at hearing Steve; maybe it was the hard tumble I had taken; at any rate the next thing I knew was that I had dragged myself to the hidden car still waiting silent and unmolested. I pillowed my head cozily on the running board and did not lift it until I heard returning steps and voices.

"Slick devil, Ellender. He's got away. Climb in a car and step on it. You parked in Porter's private drive, didn't you?"

"Some of the boys are already on the road, Neill." Steve talked as though he were still out of breath. He and Roscoe Neill were loping back toward the camp. "The thing to do is to telephone ahead. He can't get far now."

I piped up from under the fenders, fuzzily impressed with the chance to be helpful. "Here's a car, Steve, headed in the same direction the man with the bag ran. I saw him."

There was a snarl, a lurch, a leap. Someone rolled me out of the way. I heard the grunt and strain of a struggle, then the imperious but impotent whirr of a starter.

"No, you don't . . . I've got you covered!" That was Steve's voice and it was followed by the shrill summons of his whistle.

The man in the car became perfectly quiet. Taking poison, I thought, they always do . . . But Tommy's own father— Maybe the bump on my head brought the right answer.

Chapter Twenty
I Insist on a Neat Finish

All that within a flash, for Steve's police whistle brought allies at once.

"Here he is—put the bracelets on him! A pretended kidnaping, an attempt at sixty grand, and two accomplished murders. His accomplice already jailed and everything in the bag that Downing needs against this bird. Pretty slick!"

Steve Ellender had a right to feel satisfied, but he was even jaunty. There was no sound out of the captured man being led along the lane toward the now brightly lighted camp. I was quite wrong about his having swallowed a white pellet with a mocking ha ha. By the time his case came to trial he had gained ten pounds, so I heard.

"Where's the bag, Steve?" an underling queried. "Start a search right now, what say?"

"The bag with the bonds and the thirty thousand in honest-to-Gawd money is just where it belongs—down in the hotel safe."

"But I saw it," I protested. My voice must have sounded wraithlike coming from under the elderberries where Steve himself, he explained later, had pulled me in case the car should actually get under way. Both he and Georgia had done a little mechanical tampering as an extra precaution.

"I heard it!" I insisted. "He threw the bag in the car when he ran down the lane the first time."

That was a flash of inspiration on my part, but I was right! There was the bag on the floor of the car. Not that it mattered at all, for the bag that Mary carried to the rendezvous was a faked one, though even she did not know it. The substitution was a part of Steve's plan and he had accomplished it under the very eyes of Mary and the hovering Neill.

"—in case something in my set-up should slip," he explained, "and that devil actually succeeded in getting away with the bag. I had enough pinned on him, but what a case for Downing if I could catch him red-handed!"

But all that sort of talk came considerably later. I found myself the center of interest to at least one person, William Pryde. He got me to my feet and fluttered about trying to feel my pulse. I insisted that I was quite able to walk back to the camp, for I wanted to keep up with the excitement. So under his tender watch-care I reached the Porters' kitchen porch where Mary McCann and Georgia were now holding the center of the stage. And was I ever glad that William could not see how red my face had been—

There had been nothing at all under the milk-can, which was no surprise to any of us. Mary had caught one glimpse of the handcuffed figure being marched to an official car and had gone off into hysterics. By the time Georgia and Mrs. Porter, assisted by a nice grandma from one of the cabins, had calmed her, William and I appeared. One look at me and she nearly went off again; the bump on my forehead was already beginning to swell, my face was streaked with black grease, and I had one rather nasty scratch.

William insisted that I be taken home at once and I believe he was asking Mrs. Porter about nurses when I put my foot down. "When I wash my face, most of what you're worrying about will come right off," I scolded. "Gather up Georgia and Mary and come along. We must let the Porter outfit settle down or they'll never get another customer."

A half hour later, in Viney's kitchen over pots and pots of coffee and mammoth sandwiches, we began to tie up all the ends as neatly as we could.

"If only Steve were here," I mourned. "There are still so many things I want to know."

"Don't worry. The lad has to come back this way from Attica, where they took Neill to join Delphine." Georgia poured herself another cup of coffee. "You've found one thing wasn't so, haven't you, my angel?" and she winked at William Pryde.

"You deliberately let me think—and here it was the child's own father—" I broke off self-consciously and looked at Mary.

"I didn't know, Miss Fergus," she replied gravely. "I never suspected. But Margot always said he was a perfect rotter. She should have suspected about the unregistered bonds—but of course, she isn't herself. He was the only person who knew she had them."

"You were the go-between, Mary child, and the less you knew the safer you were. The instant that Steve began to work things out it became highly essential that you, of all people, should have no idea where the guilt lay. It even helped to have you talk everything over with your ex-cousin-in-law."

"I don't see that, Mrs. Paxton," Mary said.

"It lulled him, for one thing, and then as the so-called unknown always proceeded to act accordingly, it made Steve surer than ever that he was on the right track." Georgia was enjoying herself.

"How did he and all of you get started on the right track?" I demanded again. "I seem to be still waiting on a siding."

"Misrouted entirely, if you ask me," Georgia murmured. I realized then that sooner or later she'd tell William all. But this time he saved me.

"I believe I am correct in saying that my first intimation of the truth came when Mrs. Paxton reported that during her first interview with Neill he announced his determination to put the matter in the hands of the police at once. Without hesitation he asked for long distance and called Ellender. According to his story, he had just arrived in town and knew nothing of what had been happening. If he were as uninformed as that, he would have rung the local police."

"Not bad," commended Georgia. "But why do you suppose Neill came here that night? Why wouldn't he have kept under cover with Delphine?"

"Unless they themselves confess their every move and motive, those are probably questions about which we can only speculate. If I might be permitted to theorize a bit—" William was off again.

"Knowing Gregory and his methods of work as I do, it is my considered opinion that he must have suspected Neill's problem from the first. When I inquired of Neill the other day, he told me that he had put the case to Gregory in Philadelphia. That accounts for the lack of records in our office and my not having seen Neill there.

"Let us grant that Gregory had his doubts about the affair from the first. He set Smith to work and perhaps Smith served in good faith for a time. Perhaps Gregory was testing his man Smith. At any rate, something went wrong and Gregory struck Smith off his records. He probably retraced every step of the investigation himself; that would be like him. We know that he procured a death certificate. It may be that all along such a paper was procurable. Undoubtedly Neill told Gregory what he had caused to be reported to the child's mother—that the boy's body had not been recovered and hence no certificate could be issued."

"Yes," breathed Mary. "That's what Margot was told."

William Pryde lighted one of his own plebeian cigarettes and talked steadily on. "I confess myself at a complete loss with the Thibault woman. Knowing Neill's type, it is not hard to imagine the relation that might exist between the two. So far, she has protected him completely. There is also a connection between them and Smith that is not clear. It is quite possible that Smith betrayed himself to Neill, and Neill bought him over—"

"Then that would be the reason that Neill got Smith out of the way. He knew too much," I contributed.

"I'd like to hear Delphine on the subject of Smith. She ought to be good," Georgia mused.

"None of this twiddle-twaddle is answering my original question: why did Neill come here last Tuesday night? He's certainly not the tea room type."

"Maybe he didn't like Delphine's diet." Georgia's nose expressed her own opinion of custards and creamed spinach. "I'll bet he ordered a steak and French frieds!"

"I believe he did," I faltered.

"And another thing, I've got a hunch that all that baby food went for no one but Delphine herself. You can tell by looking at her that she's dyspeptic. The sheriff's wife says she can't get her to eat a thing she cooks." Georgia gave a prodigious yawn.

Loyal to Ella Brookfield as I am I murmured, "A road-side tea shop would seem the safest place in the world for a villain to dive into for a breather."

Georgia frowned and leaned forward. "There's another point that's not been taken care of yet. Maybe Steve told you, Mr. Pryde. The mysterious man at the table was Roscoe Neill, but one of Mrs. Bray's party babbled something about Gregory, which was what set Sally off. He had seen Gregory somewhere, but not at the inn that evening. Since Mary has told her tale we know that Gregory was hovering about through the whole of Tuesday night. Here we are—assuming that Neill chased Mary back here to the inn after doing a knife-throwing act, stabbed Smith, and the next afternoon killed Gregory. If Neill won't talk—"

"Not assuming much at all. Only some of your guesses are wrong." The voice came booming in through the kitchen window and we all jumped. It was Steve Ellender, on his way back from Attica.

He stalked into the kitchen and grabbed the last sandwich. "My star witnesses should be put to bed. You're all going to see plenty of limelight before the trial's over, and here you are, reveling. But let me set you right . . . Neill did not chase Mary. That gallant act was Smith's. Smith beat it to the Newagen place after Gregory let him get away Tuesday night, and when he had spilled the beans to Delphine and Neill, the two men came back to the camp to lay for Gregory. They almost caught him too, but, as Mary has told us, Gregory heard a suspicious sound in time. Then as Mary tried to slip away to the inn, Smith followed her, no doubt thinking at first that he was trailing Gregory. Neill managed to stop him and Mary got away. Smith's number was then up and whatever followed between the two men ended in the murder of Smith."

Georgia pounded the table. "How do you know all this? Has Neill confessed?"

"No such luck yet—but I'm hoping. Something better has happened. Delphine's going to break! When we got to Attica tonight we staged a little show. It was good if I do say it. When Delphine saw Neill paraded up and down in handcuffs she let out a screech and went into a faint. She came to babbling, 'I didn't kill them . . . I didn't! If that devil Roscoe says I did—' And then she shut up like a clam again because her head had cleared enough for her to realize we were watching and listening. So, says I, Delphine will come across. That's definitely slated."

He stretched luxuriously and grinned at us all. "Any other little thing?"

"I'll bite," I answered sweetly. "I'm quite beyond my depth with all you smarties. When did you get the right answer? The day before it happened?"

"Now, Sayra," murmured William Pryde. "She's completely exhausted," he apologized to Steve.

"You didn't make things any easier for me, did you? Serves you right, too, that you were my prize suspect at first. After I crossed you off, I had the fun of letting you and Pryde worry about each other. Kept you both out of my way, for one thing. Pryde, every time you looked at Neill today I held my breath. I thought I could trust you with Miss Fergus, but—I don't know." He and Georgia exchanged grins.

"About Neill, I've been pretty sure since Saturday, though the first click that clicked was the name-tag Mrs. Rockey found. But the fingerprint mess got me down. My idea is that Neill worked in gloves throughout. I got his prints as soon as he appeared on Friday, but we couldn't spot 'em on a thing.

"Then he wanted to see the Newagen house. I suspect he wanted to look it over for himself in case something had been left. Miss Fergus knows what happened there. The incident gave me a hunch. I looked the gentleman up, found that the crash had cleaned him out, and that he spent most of last winter in Miami, if that matters."

Georgia and I could fit it in, recalling the label in Delphine's hat.

"But you couldn't give up tonight's fireworks," Georgia chided. "Just what evidence have you now that Neill killed Gregory?"

"By elimination, he is the only possible actor left to commit the deed." William spoke up promptly. "If he fails to confess and if Delphine maintains her—er—loyal silence, I have no doubt that Ellender can enmesh Neill when he demands an alibi. The man has said that he was in transit most of last week, but both Mrs. Paxton and Miss Mary can testify how impossible it was to reach him at any place he was said to be. And, as Ellender has just said, his car seems to have had its headquarters here."

"But your car, William—" I had to hit the last nail on the head. "The car you hid to make your escape in—"

He looked at me as though his worse fears of my condition were justified.

"That was Neill's car in the lane, Sally. I knew it all the time. Frankly, my angel, I was pulling your leg. What's worrying her, Willie, is the car you and Steve came out in last evening. She was sure you parked it secretly and she marked it down as a sinister gesture."

William checked Steve's and Georgia's laughter. "That, my dear Sayra, was Gregory's car. He had evidently driven on in pursuit of Smith. One of Ellender's men found it in a parking lot and it was turned over to me. It's still at the filling station, I daresay. I left it there for an oil change." Georgia drew a deep breath.

"It's Tuesday morning now—why bother about going to bed? It's going to be a big day at the *Record* for me and I'm starting at once. I was all wrong about my bright, particular talents—as a detective I'm still a darned good sob sister. My pet ideas were all wet, even my precious calendar. Didn't Mary with her own eyes see Delphine draw rings around the fatal dates! Gregory's fountain pen ink was no private mixture—I'll bet they sell it at the five and dime." Again she yawned enormously. "I must get going. I'll give you a ring, Sally."

She slammed the door behind her and left me to cope with William. Even Mary deserted me. She repeated reminiscently.

"I can sleep on the floor. You'll never know how heavenly good you were . . ."

About the Author

Helen Joan Hultman (1891-1985) was a Dayton, Ohio, native who graduated from Denison University with a Bachelor of Philosophy (PhB) and went on to teach English at Stivers High School in Dayton for thirty-five years. Her first mystery, *Find the Woman,* received the Doubleday-Doran prize for best mystery story sent in during the summer of 1928, and it was published in 1929 (later reprinted as *Murder in Odd Sizes*). She wrote it while teaching full-time, and noted that when it was published, "They were loosening up old Victorian standards." She wrote five more mysteries by the early 1950s.

"How do I get my ideas? The backwash of all sorts of trifles goes into it but they're almost unrecognizable when they get into a story. . . . Settings often get me started."

Several of her mysteries were set in southwestern Ohio locations: Dayfield in *Murder Rings Twice* (originally *Murder on Route 40*) stands in for Dayton. Two of the novels in this volume have West Virginia settings. It shouldn't surprise that Hultman briefly taught at Tyler County High School, West Virginia, early in her teaching career.

Death at
Windward Hill

Murder in the
French Room

HELEN JOAN HULTMAN

Also Available

CoachwhipBooks.com (print)
Coachwhip.com (epub)

A strange clan—a grotesque dinner party—and
violent death in a little Pennsylvania town!

MURDER
BY JURY

MURDER
ON THE
APHRODITE

RUTH BURR SANBORN

LADY IN LILAC

SUSANNAH SHANE

www.ingramcontent.com/pod-product-compliance
Lightning Source LLC
Chambersburg PA
CBHW030740030726
47497CB00001B/69